Christy & Todd
The COLLEGE YEARS

From Robin Jones Gunn

CHRISTY MILLER COLLECTION
Volumes 1–4

CHRISTY & TODD: THE COLLEGE YEARS
1. *Until Tomorrow*
2. *As You Wish*
3. *I Promise*

SIERRA JENSEN COLLECTION
Volumes 1–4

KATIE WELDON SERIES
1. *Peculiar Treasure*
2. *On a Whim*
3. *Coming Attractions*

Christy & Todd

The COLLEGE YEARS

ROBIN

JONES

GUNN

BETHANYHOUSE

MINNEAPOLIS, MINNESOTA

Christy and Todd: The College Years
Copyright, 2000, 2001
Robin Jones Gunn

Previously published in three separate volumes:
  Until Tomorrow Copyright © 2000
  As You Wish Copyright © 2000
  I Promise Copyright © 2001

Cover illustration and design by Bethany Hway / Koechel Peterson & Associates, Inc.

This story is a work of fiction. All characters and events are the product of the author's imagination. Any resemblance to any person, living or dead, is coincidental.

Published by Bethany House Publishers
11400 Hampshire Avenue South
Minneapolis, Minnesota 55438

Bethany House Publishers is a division of
Baker Publishing Group, Grand Rapids, Michigan.

Printed in the United States of America

Library of Congress Cataloging-in-Publication Data is available for this title.

ISBN 978-0-7642-0592-7

ROBIN JONES GUNN loves to tell stories. Evidence of this appeared early when her first-grade teacher wrote in Robin's report card, "Robin has not yet grasped her basic math skills, but she has kept the entire class captivated at rug time with her entertaining stories."

When Robin's first series of books for toddlers was published in 1984, she never dreamed she'd go on to write novels. However, one project led to another, and *Until Tomorrow* was Robin's forty-ninth published book. Other series include THE CHRISTY MILLER SERIES, THE SIERRA JENSEN SERIES, and THE GLENBROOKE SERIES. Combined sales of her books are over two million, with worldwide distribution. Many of the titles have been translated into other languages.

Robin and her husband, Ross, have been involved in youth work for over twenty-five years. They have lived in many places, including California and Hawaii. Currently they live near Portland, Oregon, with their teenage son and daughter and their golden retriever, Hula.

Visit Robin's Web site at *www.RobinGunn.com*

Until Tomorrow

For Luanne, who said in the spring of our twenty-first year, "Why don't we go to Europe this summer!" And so we did. (I still have the wild flowers we picked in Adelboden, Lulu.)

For Laurie, who shared her rationed cotton balls and 1006 lotion that sweltering night in the Paris youth hostel.

For Carol, who led us laughing all the way on our journey to find the statue of the *Little Mermaid* in Copenhagen.

For Laraine, who kept us searching until we found the best gelato in all of Florence. Remember, Lola? You said the Amaretto at Vivolli's was "exquiz.")

And for Chuck, who told me to close my eyes right before we entered the Blue Grotto. Thanks for paying for the pizza that night at the train station in Roma. I think I still owe you.

"Old friends are as close as a memory when the heart is always young."

— *Robin Jones Gunn*

CHAPTER 1

The morning light had not yet tinted the June sky with the promise of a new day as Christy Miller hurried down the cobblestone street of Basel, Switzerland. With long-legged strides, she turned the corner and realized that her heart was racing toward the train station faster than her legs.

This time I'm not going to cry when I see him.

Christy remembered how weak and awkward her endless stream of tears had made her feel last Christmas when she had gone home to California. Todd had just stood there as if he didn't know what to do with her.

I'm a stronger person than I was at Christmas. I won't cry.

At the end of the street she turned left. Only six more blocks to the station.

And I won't let Katie talk me into anything I don't want to do, either. If Katie, Todd, and I are going to get along while we travel around Europe for the next three weeks, then everything needs to be a group decision.

Christy grasped her long, nutmeg brown hair to check how wet it was after her hasty early morning shower. She reminded herself that in a month she would celebrate her twentieth birthday. Certainly at twenty she should be facing life as a strong, independent woman, right?

It's time I take a stand for myself. Katie will not rule my choices. I won't let her.

Decision-making had never been Christy's strength, which was why she felt determined to make a fresh start with her closest friends. She would show them how much she had changed and how strong she had become during her school year in Switzerland.

The fragrant aroma of freshly baked bread floated her way from her favorite bakery, or *Konditorei*, at the end of the street. Every Saturday morning Christy would make a trek to this special pastry shop. It had become her way of treating herself for making it through another difficult week of classes and volunteer work at the orphanage.

A much better "treat" will be arriving on the 6:15 train from the Zürich airport, she thought with a smile. *The first thing Todd and Katie and I will do is come back here to my Konditorei, and I'll treat them to some Swiss pastries.*

Christy tilted back her head and drew in a deep breath of the delicious aroma. She stood still a moment, quickly folding her hair into a loose braid and fastening it with a clip she had stuck in her jeans pocket. The sky had just begun to lighten with soft shades of lavender and gray. Glad-hearted songbirds twittered in the trees.

Christy hurried the final stretch to the station with light steps. Smiling at the two large stone lion statues that guarded the entrance to the Basel *Bahnhof*, Christy entered and checked the schedule. Todd and Katie's train was to arrive in seven minutes on track four. She rushed to the platform so she could be there the moment they stepped off the train.

Christy was surprised at how noisy and crowded the station was compared to the quiet streets she had just walked. She arrived on the platform facing track number four only moments before the train pulled in. Carefully positioning herself in the middle so she could see Katie and Todd no matter which part of the train they exited from, Christy waited for her two best friends.

Throngs of early morning businessmen and businesswomen exited the train. Christy thought she heard a familiar squeal over the roar of rushing footsteps. She looked right and left, expecting at any moment to catch a glimpse of Katie's swishy red hair. But Christy didn't see her in the crowd.

Turning her head to check the other end of the train, Christy felt everything around her slip into slow motion. She didn't know if she was experiencing a dip in the adrenaline she had felt pumping through her veins on her walk to the station or if the crush of people rushing past her made her feel dizzy. One thing she was sure of—the screaming silver-blue eyes she had spotted could only belong to one person.

"Todd!" Her lips formed the name she had held in her heart for half a decade. Pushing her way through the crowd, Christy rushed to her favorite blond-haired surfer boy.

Todd quickly unclasped his backpack and grabbed Christy's arm, pulling her close. In an instant his arms were around her, his eyes locked on hers, and his lips were only inches away.

"Kilikina," he murmured right before his lips met hers.

Christy melted whenever Todd called her by her Hawaiian name. Absolutely melted. Add to that the sweetness of his kiss, and she couldn't take it all in. Uninvited tears coursed down her cheeks.

Todd pulled away from their reunion kiss, his expression hesitant.

"Hi," Christy said, quickly wiping her damp cheeks.

"Hi," Todd returned. His smile widened, showing his dimples. His solid jawline was rough with stubble, and she smelled chocolate on his breath.

Christy playfully brushed the back of her fingers along his jaw. "Hard day's night?"

Todd ran his thumb under her left eye, catching the last tear. He seemed to be studying her, trying to read what she held behind her clear, distinct blue-green eyes. His eyebrows raised as he said, "You all right?"

Christy nodded and smiled warmly. "I told myself I wasn't going to cry."

"And I told myself I wasn't going to kiss you," he said with a teasing grin.

His eyes were locked on hers. Christy felt as if Todd could see right through her, all the way to the secret place deep in her heart.

A settled peace came over her in the noisy station. The peace seemed to cover the two of them like an invisible canopy. They stood completely still, holding hands, basking in each other's presence. Christy wondered if she would spend the rest of her life gazing into those silver-blue eyes that now seemed to be searching her soul.

"Sorry, Todd, to interrupt," a male voice with an Italian accent said, breaking in between Todd and Christy, "but I am parked for only a short time."

Christy pulled herself away from Todd and was stunned to see Antonio, an Italian friend of theirs who had been an exchange student in California.

"Christiana," Antonio said, reaching for her shoulders and planting a kiss on each cheek. "So good to see you. You are surprised?"

Christy felt off-balance. "What . . . how . . . ?" Before she could form her question, she heard a squeal that could only come from Katie. Christy's ever-exuberant best friend pushed her way past Antonio and threw her arms around Christy. As Katie did, the frame of her backpack hit Christy's forehead.

"Ouch!"

"Ouch? You haven't seen me in months, and all you can say is ouch?"

"Ouch and hi!" Christy said, giving Katie another, less aggressive hug. "You look great."

"So do you," Katie said.

"Did you know Antonio was coming?" Christy asked.

Katie's green eyes flashed. "Yes. We just figured it all out two days ago."

Christy turned to Todd. His grin grew wide. "Tonio set it up for us to go camping in Italy with him."

"Camping?" Christy echoed.

"We can talk as we go," Antonio said, taking Katie's pack and carrying it for her. "My car . . ." He indicated the door he wanted them to move toward.

Todd strapped his backpack on his broad shoulders and grabbed Christy's hand, pulling her with him out of the station. Katie latched on to Antonio's arm as if she never meant to give it back, and the two of them led the way out of the station at a fast clip.

"So we're going camping?" Christy asked.

"Yep. Tonio has the equipment. It's all set up."

"What about Scandinavia?"

"What about Scandinavia?" Todd asked.

"I thought we were going there first."

Todd stopped walking. "Did you tell me that? Because I didn't think we had a plan yet. That's why I set this up with Antonio. If you told me and I didn't catch that email, I apologize."

"No, you're right." She knew she didn't want to be the one to start an argument. Not here. Not now. "We don't have a plan yet. This is fine."

Christy was having a hard time thinking straight. She thought Todd had mentioned starting their journey in Norway and working their way down to Italy. But now she wasn't sure. Maybe Katie had suggested that itinerary.

Tonio led them to his small white minivan illegally parked across from the Bahnhof. He opened the side door, and Christy noticed a large dent on the front bumper.

Tugging a gray canvas bag out of the open area in the center of the van, Antonio said, "Give me some help. This must go on the roof."

The four of them moved all of Antonio's camping gear out of the van and onto the roof, securing it with ropes under a tarp.

"How did you two plan all this?" Christy asked Todd, trying to sound calm.

"Through email." Todd shoved his and Katie's travel packs into the van's belly and climbed in. A bench seat ran the back width of the van, and along the van's sides were built-in cupboards. The van's center was empty except for their packs.

Katie gave Christy another excited hug before climbing into the back-seat next to Todd. "Are we going to have the adventure of our lives or what?"

Christy nodded numbly. She settled into the front seat and fastened her seat belt, but not a moment too soon. With only a quick glance over his shoulder, Antonio hit the gas pedal and pulled out into the traffic with a roar. Christy clutched the edge of her seat and sat as still as she could as Antonio yelled at the other drivers in Italian and darted his way down the street.

From the back of the minivan, Katie laughed hysterically because, as the car lurched, she had crashed into Todd.

"Tonio," Katie cried out, "we're not in Italy yet! Do us a favor and let us live long enough to get there."

Tonio glanced at Katie in the rearview mirror with a grin. He slowed down and put on his turn signal for the first time. He was pulling onto the main highway that led out of town, the opposite direction from Christy's dorm.

"We need to go the other way, Antonio," Christy said. "The university is that way."

"No, I have been to Basel before. This is the road we take back to Italy."

"No!" Christy practically yelled as panic took over. "We can't go to Italy now!"

"Why not?"

"I don't have any of my things!"

Antonio said something in Italian that sounded like an apology, jerked the car onto a side street, and then stopped. He looked at Christy with a friendly expression and said simply, "Which way?"

With Antonio at the wheel, they reached Christy's dorm in a few minutes. During the drive, she calmed down and tried to think straight.

"We'll wait here," Antonio said, stopping the car in another illegal parking place.

"I'm not exactly ready," Christy said, looking at Todd and Katie for support. "I didn't know anything about this. I mean, I'm mostly packed, but it will take me a few minutes to finish getting all my things together."

"I want to see your room," Katie said, crawling out of the back of the van. "Come on, you guys, let's all go in."

"They're really strict about parking around here," Christy told Antonio.

"We'll wait here," Todd suggested. "In case we have to drive around the block a few times."

"And we'll hurry," Katie called over her shoulder as she followed Christy into the brick building.

Christy scurried to her room and opened the door.

"Wow! This room is a lot smaller than I thought it would be," Katie said, looking around. "Wait until this September when we're at Rancho Corona University. The rooms are twice this size and for just two people, not three. It's way better than here."

"Hey, it's great here, too," Christy said defensively.

Katie looked startled. She quickly reached over and gave Christy's arm a squeeze. "Oh, I'm sure it is. Don't get upset. I was just saying how it's only going to get better in the fall when we're all together at the same school. Don't you agree?"

Christy nodded slowly. Nothing was going the way she had imagined it would. They were supposed to be sitting in the bakery right now, calmly discussing their plans over coffee and pastry. Instead, they were bolting out of town in Antonio's rocket-mobile.

"So," Katie said, clapping her hands together, "what do you need to pack? I can help."

"That bag is ready to go," Christy said, pointing to the backpack in the corner. "I need to grab a few more things for my day pack, though."

Katie suddenly threw her arms around Christy in a breathless hug. "Can you believe we're standing here, in your dorm room, casually talking as if we do this every day? Christy, we're in Switzerland!"

"Yes, we are, aren't we?"

Katie pulled back and put her hands on her hips. "Okay, what's with you? What's wrong?"

"I'm just trying to think of what I need." Christy reached for her day pack and began to fill it with items from the desk.

"You would tell me if you were upset about anything, wouldn't you?"

"Of course."

Katie picked up one of the travel books from the desk and said, "You're not planning to take any of these, are you?"

"A few of them. At least one."

"They're too big," Katie said. "We don't need tour books. We're on an adventure! Why would you want to haul them all over the place and look like tourists?"

Christy ignored Katie's comment. She grabbed the book on top of the stack and stuffed it into her pack. "I'm ready. Let's go."

Katie carried Christy's pack out for her and commented on how much lighter it was than hers.

"I hope I'm not traveling too light. I can't think of what else I need." Christy pursed her lips together, trying hard to come up with anything she might have forgotten.

The guys were waiting in the van with the engine running. Todd had moved up to the front seat.

Christy climbed into the back of the van and said, "I was thinking maybe we could stop at the Konditorei before we leave. It's the best bakery in Basel, and it's only a few blocks away. It would give us a chance to talk through our plans."

"I'm not hungry at all," Katie said, clambering into the van. "Are you guys?"

Todd shrugged.

"Then we will hit the street," Antonio decided.

Katie laughed and playfully tagged him on the shoulder. "You mean hit the road, Tonio."

"Yes, hit the road. Here we go."

The van lurched forward as Christy grabbed for her seat belt and fastened it tightly. She stared out the window as Tonio roared past the bakery and headed toward A-2, which would take them south to Italy. For weeks she had dreamed about going to her special Konditorei with Todd. When they were in London together a year and a half ago, the two of them had walked hand in hand down the streets until they found a small bakery. They sat in a booth in the back corner of the tea shop and opened their hearts to each other. During that conversation, they decided they weren't ready to commit to a more serious relationship.

But that was a year and a half ago.

In her dreams and in her waking hours of sitting alone in the Basel Konditorei, Christy had imagined the conversation she and Todd would share over tea and scones. Now she drew in a deep breath and exhaled slowly. She felt ready to move on and to define their relationship more solidly than ever before.

What if Todd isn't ready to move on? What if I'm ready to make a stronger commitment and he's not? At least I think I am. At the moment, Christy was so frazzled she didn't know if she should trust any of her thoughts or feelings. The only thing she was sure of was that her seat belt was buckled as tightly as it would go, and they were on their way to Italy.

CHAPTER 2

Katie wiggled into a comfortable nest she had made with their packs in the middle of the van. She jabbered a mile a minute about how incredible all this was.

Christy smiled at Katie and nodded every now and then. But her gaze kept going to the back of Todd's head. All her thoughts were about what was going on inside that head, under the short, sun-kissed blond hair. Or more important, what was going on inside his heart?

How do you really feel about me, Todd? Are you in love with me? Really in love?

Christy realized again, with sadness, that their chance to bend their heads close together in quiet conversation at her favorite thinking spot had been snatched from her. They were part of the group now. The gang. And if Todd was true to form, he would be a team player the rest of the trip. That meant he would give equal attention to everyone. He was like a mellow golden retriever—always loyal, ready to go along with the others on a moment's notice, and generally content with life no matter what the circumstances.

Christy knew she didn't want to become the hyper schnauzer of the group, *yip-yip*ping the whole time.

"Hey, Tonio," Katie said, "where exactly are we going?"

"Italia. Mi Italia," Tonio said dramatically. "I am taking you to my favorite camping ground. You will love it. At night, hundreds of baboons

come from the forest and eat everything they find in the camp. This is why you must close up your tent."

"You must mean raccoons," Katie said. "I doubt any baboons are in Italy."

"Ah yes," Antonio said, looking at Katie in the rearview mirror. "Raccoons. Once again you are right. Where would I be without your helpful lessons in English?"

"Admit it, Tonio. You've missed me."

"I've missed you, Katie," Tonio stated loudly.

"Go ahead, tell me you can't live without me," Katie continued.

"I can't live without you."

This was typical banter for Tonio and Katie. They used to tease each other back in California all the time. And a tinge of romance had existed between the two of them. At least Katie had thought so—or was Antonio just being a romantic Italian? Christy wished she and Todd could express themselves boldly like Antonio and Katie—only not as a joke, but sincerely.

Will I ever hear Todd say, "I can't live without you"?

"He's crazy about me," Katie said, turning her attention back to Christy and smiling broadly. "Hey!" She leaned closer to Christy. "If Tonio and I decide to get married this week, you will be my maid of honor, won't you?"

"Of course." Christy's voice came out small and thin. These topics weren't laughing matters for her. The day she would ask Katie to be her maid of honor, Christy knew she would be asking seriously.

Katie laughed. "This all feels like a dream, doesn't it? I don't care if it is a dream. If it is, don't wake me. I've never been happier in my life. Deliriously happy!"

For the next few hours, as they roared down the highway through Switzerland and into Italy, Antonio and Todd kept a tight conversation going between themselves. Christy couldn't hear what they were saying since the windows were open and the van was noisy. Katie scooted her nest closer to Christy and filled her in on all the details of what had been going on with their friends back home.

As Christy listened to Katie, she found herself settling in. Their journey might not have started off the way Christy had thought it would, but they were on their way. She was determined to be a team player and not give in to moody contemplation.

They stopped only once for gas, or "petrol," as Antonio called it, before arriving at the campground. Their spot had a large open space for tents under a circle of tall trees. Christy had no idea where they were, but she was surprised that the terrain was so similar to what she had become used to in the hills around her school. It seemed odd to think of Italy as having the Alps, too.

The fresh air invigorated the four travelers as they unloaded the van and set up their two tents. Katie playfully drew a line in the dirt with her heel and said, "Girls on this side, boys on that side."

"Only one problem, Katie," Christy said. "The kitchen is on the boys' side."

Katie carefully walked around the end of her dirt line and said, "This is the path to the kitchen. All starving campers may pass this way." She went over to the wooden box Antonio had brought and opened it up. "Okay, I see some mugs in here, a coffeepot, and a frying pan. Where are you hiding the food?"

"Over there," Antonio said with a nod of his head as he hammered the last tent stake into the ground.

"I don't see anything but trees," Katie said.

"Beyond the trees is the refrigerator," Tonio said. "Come. I'll show you." He put his arm around Katie's shoulder and led her down a narrow trail through the woods.

"Listen to that," Todd said. He had been stringing up a hammock between two trees when he stopped and looked up, listening closely.

Christy knew what he was referring to. She closed her eyes and listened to the sound of the wind rushing through the treetops. All kinds of memories came riding in on that breeze. Her strongest memory was of the wind in the palm trees at a certain train station in Spain. That's where Todd had placed a gold ID bracelet on Christy's wrist a year and a half ago. The word "Forever" was engraved on the bracelet. Christy ran her finger over the bracelet now, her eyes still closed, her face toward the sky. A smile graced her lips as she said, "They're clapping, Todd."

"Bravo," Todd said in a voice that sounded faint.

Christy opened her eyes and saw that Todd had climbed into the hammock and now swayed contentedly with his hands folded behind his head.

"Hey, you got it strung up," Christy said, walking over to the hammock. "Good for you."

"Did you have any doubts about my ability?"

"Not you, nature boy. I believe you could be the world's premier expert in hammocks." Christy grabbed the side and pulled the hammock toward her. She let go and the hammock swung wide, making a creaking sound where the ropes looped around the tree. Suddenly a rope snapped and down came the hammock, dumping Todd on the ground with a thud.

Christy felt like bursting out laughing, but she held back and quickly checked to make sure Todd was all right. He looked startled but not hurt.

"I'm so sorry!" Christy giggled. "Are you okay?"

Before Todd could answer, Katie came tromping through the woods with Tonio right behind her. "There's no food over there. Tonio's 'refrigerator' happens to be a lake! We're supposed to catch our own dinner."

"Cool," Todd said, getting up and dusting off his backside. "Did you bring poles?"

"Poles, hooks, everything," Tonio said.

"What are we supposed to eat in the meantime?" Katie asked.

"Jerky," Todd suggested.

"What did you call me?" Katie spun around to face Todd.

Christy felt like laughing again, but Katie's red face told her she had better bite her tongue.

"I didn't call you anything. I was just saying I brought some beef jerky. It's in my pack in the van. Help yourself."

Todd and Tonio were bent over the box of camping gear, twisting together a collapsible fishing pole. Todd rummaged through a plastic box of lures and hooks.

"What you need is an afternoon cappuccino," Antonio said to Katie as she paced in front of them like a cougar.

"I didn't happen to see any coffee shops on the way in," Katie said sarcastically.

"I have coffee right here," Antonio said, lifting a small box from the middle of the camping supplies.

"Do you have any food in there?" Katie asked.

"No, only coffee. Hey, Christy, you start a fire, will you? Todd and I will get some fish."

The guys took off, and Christy gathered kindling.

"I don't want coffee," Katie said with a slight whine in her voice. "Do you?"

"No. I'm hungry, though. If they don't catch some fish right away, let's break into Todd's jerky supply."

"What happened to the hammock?" Katie asked, examining the end of the hammock rope.

"I pushed Todd a little too hard and it broke."

"It didn't break. The rope is fine. The knot must have come out. I doubt that Todd knows as much about knots as I do. This rope needs a Katie special knot."

Katie went to work on the hammock as Christy dropped twigs onto her stack of kindling and returned to the surrounding woods for more. She managed to haul a good-sized log over to the fire pit and then opened the wooden chest to see what she could use for a grill over the top. Everything she needed was in the chest. She hummed as she set up their camp kitchen. All she would have to do was light a match when the guys returned.

"You know what this reminds me of, Katie?"

"What?" Katie had settled herself into the hammock and answered Christy without opening her eyes.

"Remember that time I cooked Christmas breakfast on the beach for Todd, and the sea gulls came and ate the bacon and eggs?"

Katie didn't answer.

Christy went over to the hammock. It was wide enough for two people. The ropes and knots looked strong enough. Golden rays from the afternoon sun slipped through the trees, and Katie had turned to catch their full warmth on her face. Christy pushed Katie's legs over gently and said, "Make room. I'm coming aboard."

"I couldn't move if I wanted to," Katie said, her eyes still closed and her hands folded across her middle.

Christy tried to hold the hammock steady as she climbed in with her head at the opposite end from Katie's. "This is pretty comfortable."

"Just don't kick me in the face, and everything will be fine," Katie said, her voice fading.

That was the last thing Christy remembered hearing until the sound of Todd's voice called to her from a few feet away. "Anybody hungry?"

Christy forced her heavy eyelids open. The brightness of the afternoon had faded. In the early evening shadows she made out Todd's form standing there, holding up a fish about a foot long. She could smell smoke from the fire pit and turned to see Antonio starting the fire.

Christy patted her friend's legs. "Katie, they're back. Wake up."

Christy noticed how stiff she was. Stiff and cold. She carefully tumbled from the hammock and shuffled to the fire, where she warmed her hands over the low yellow flames.

"Some campgrounds in Europe won't let you make an open fire," Antonio said. "But here it is allowed. This fire is just the right size, Christy. *Grazie.*"

"No problem."

"How long did we sleep?" Katie asked, joining the four of them with a yawn.

"A couple of hours at least." Christy yawned, as well. "I'm glad you guys caught something. Was it hard?"

"Just took a little time," Todd said, cleaning his fish with a pocketknife.

What also took a little time was cooking the fish. The stars had all come out to watch them before they had finished eating. As they gathered their plates, Antonio started some coffee in his charred camp coffeepot.

Christy smiled. It officially felt like summer now.

Every summer since she was fourteen Christy had gathered with her friends around a campfire on the beach in Southern California. There, under these same stars, they sang to the Lord, roasted marshmallows, and opened their hearts to each other.

Being here, beneath the cloudless heavens with her closest friends, made Christy feel something she hadn't felt in a long time. She had several friends at the university that she would go out with. They would sit around talking and drinking coffee on Saturday nights. But it wasn't the same as being with Todd, Katie, and Antonio. What Christy had with these friends was deeper, sweeter, and different from what she experienced in other friend-ships. At this moment, she felt as if she could close her eyes, take one step toward the star-filled heavens, and be swallowed up in eternity.

"Come here," Todd said, inviting Christy to scoot closer.

She leaned her head on Todd's shoulder and felt herself warming all over. She remembered a phrase she had heard long ago, something about how *"God is in His heaven and all is right with the world."* That's how she felt. All was right between her and Todd. Just right. And God was near.

Christy hummed softly. Todd picked up the tune, and the four of them began to sing. The woods around them resonated with the sound of their praises for the One whose breath rustled in the treetops and whose whispers hummed low through the earth on which they were seated.

As the night around them grew darker, Christy began to shiver. Todd put his arm around her and drew her close. Together they sang softly and poked the embers of their dying fire with long sticks.

"I'm going to get my jacket," Christy said, finally pulling away from Todd. "Anyone want anything from the van?" Then she remembered. Her jacket was still hanging on the back of her door in the dorm room.

"Oh no," Christy said. "Did anyone, by any chance, bring an extra jacket?"

"You didn't bring a jacket? What kind of an expert happy camper are you?" Katie said with a snap in her voice.

The comment rubbed Christy the wrong way, and suddenly the special tone of the evening evaporated. "I packed in a hurry, if you remember. I didn't exactly have a lot of time to plan out what I needed for camping."

"Sorry," Katie said, but Christy didn't think Katie sounded apologetic.

"Hey, I have a sweater," Antonio said, going to the van. He grabbed a hand-knit wool sweater that had been wadded up on the floor.

"You don't need it?" Christy asked as Tonio tossed it to her. She took one whiff of the sweater and regretted asking for it. It smelled as if it had lined the bottom of a birdcage, then been used to wrap up fish, and finally to wipe off the bottom of a farmer's boots.

"And here is your blanket," Antonio said, tossing another smelly, woolen object at her.

"No sleeping bags?" Christy asked. As soon as she said it, she regretted it. She couldn't stand it when she sounded like a spoiled American who couldn't cope with Europeans' simpler approach to life.

Katie echoed Christy's surprise at their rationed one-blanket-per-camper. "Are you serious? This is all we get? No air mattresses? What about pillows?"

"Use a sweater," Todd suggested.

Christy knew she wasn't going to rest her face on Antonio's fish-gut sweater.

Todd rose to his feet, and what remained of the closeness of their evening together immediately dissipated. Stretching and yawning, he made his way to the guys' tent. "I'll take one of those blankets, if you have another, Tonio. Good night, Christy. Night, Katie."

"Good night," they echoed in unison.

Christy crawled into their tent and tried to make the best of the smelly sweater and wool blanket. She stretched out the sweater underneath her to use as padding. She then tucked the wool blanket all around her and used a pair of clean shorts and a folded-up T-shirt as her pillow. It didn't work. She was too cold to fall asleep.

Katie managed to doze right off. That irritated Christy since she had wanted to ask Katie how she felt about Antonio and if more than teasing was going on between them. Now Christy would have to wait until tomorrow.

From the boys' tent across the line in the dirt came the steady sound of Antonio's snoring. At least Christy thought it was Antonio's.

What if it's Todd's? What would it be like to be married to a guy who snored like that? I'd never get any sleep.

26

Christy heard a twig snap right outside their tent. She froze. *Robbers? Are they coming into our camp to take our gear? What if they hot-wire the van and leave us here? Should I scream?*

Another twig snapped. Christy grabbed Katie's arm and shook her. "Wake up, Katie! Did you hear that?"

"What?"

"Listen," Christy whispered.

"That's just the guys' snoring. Go back to sleep, will you?"

"No, it's not snoring. Something's out there. Listen."

Katie turned on her flashlight, and Christy immediately grabbed it and turned it off. "Don't turn it on!"

"Come on, Christy, cut it out!" Katie reached over in the darkness and felt around until she found the flashlight in Christy's hand. "The idea is to scare them away."

Katie unzipped the tent and poked her head outside, shining the light around. Suddenly she pulled back and caught her breath. "Christy, you aren't going to believe this."

CHAPTER 3

"What is it?" Christy's heart raced.

"You have to see this. Come here." Katie leaned to the side. Christy joined her and peered into the darkness. The flashlight caught on something by the fire pit that shone back at them like a dozen tiny, round reflectors.

"Tonio's baboons," Katie said.

"Man, Tonio wasn't kidding. Look at all those raccoons. What are they eating?"

"Fish guts."

"Gross."

"I wonder if Tonio left them out on purpose?" Katie twirled her small light around. The eight or nine scrawny raccoons continued to devour their treat, unmoved by Katie's attempt to scare them away. "That is one gang of mean-looking raccoons."

"Maybe you shouldn't get them all nervous with your light," Christy suggested.

Katie laughed. "Why? You afraid they're going to turn on us after the fish guts and come pouncing over here, clawing their way into our tent?"

"I'd feel better if they went away. Can we zip the tent back up? It's freezing."

Katie pulled herself back in the tent and zipped it up. "Do me a favor and don't wake me again unless it's something over six feet tall." She burrowed back under her blanket and added, "With dark hair and brown eyes and lots of money."

Christy had to smile. No matter how upset Katie got, she never lost her sense of humor. "So is that your latest criteria for the man of your dreams? Tonio could almost fill that, you know. Except for the height."

"And the money," Katie added.

"What? You don't think his family has money?"

"Call me crazy, but I'm thinking only really poor people go camping without sleeping bags. Or food."

"I guess that makes us really poor people, doesn't it?" Christy curled up into as tight a ball as she could on top of the wool sweater and tucked the blanket all around her in hopes that the cocoon method would make her feel warmer. "So how are things going between you and Tonio?"

"Fine."

Christy waited for more details. When Katie didn't offer any, Christy prodded. "Do you think you guys might have some feelings for each other like you had last summer?"

"It's all just a game, Christy," Katie said in a low voice. "You know that. I'm nothing special to him. It's no big deal."

"But how does that make you feel?"

"It's my life, Chris. I'm everybody's buddy and nobody's honey." Katie adjusted her position and added, "I don't want to talk about guys right now. I'm really, really tired. Can we get some sleep?"

"Sure," Christy said, wishing she felt warm enough to sleep. She tried rubbing her legs together and pulling the blanket over her head.

Katie's rhythmic breathing soon indicated she had fallen asleep. Christy lay awake for hours, shivering. None of her thoughts could be trusted, but she allowed all of them to parade before her. Thoughts of Todd. Thoughts of what would come next for them in their relationship. Thoughts of getting married. Thoughts of what precise words she would use when they finally had their heart-to-heart talk.

When dawn came, Christy felt exhausted. She wanted to drop off into a deep, dreamless sleep. But the others were up with the birds, coaxing Christy to join them for some of Antonio's specialty coffee.

She gave in, thinking the coffee would at least wake her up. Crawling out of the tent with the blanket around her shoulders, Christy couldn't believe how grungy she felt. Her face and teeth felt sticky, her hair was a tangled mess, and she knew she now carried with her the disagreeable odor of the knit sweater she had slept on all night.

Todd, however, looked fresh and friendly. He bent down and reached for the coffeepot on the grill. "Hey, how's it going?" he asked, holding out a coffee mug to Christy.

She replied with a groan before sipping the strong coffee, trying hard not to make a face. Tonio's special morning brew had to be the thickest, strongest coffee she had ever tasted. If she had a spoon, she could have eaten it like hot pudding. He had added lots of sugar, which made it seem even more like a dessert than a beverage.

"This should wake me up," she said, noticing that Todd's hair was wet. So was Antonio's. "You guys didn't tell us they had showers here. Which way?"

Antonio's face lit up with a mischievous grin. "Right through there." He pointed to the trail through the trees. "Same place where we get our food."

"Very funny," Katie said. The morning sunlight poured through the trees like golden syrup, spilling all over Katie, who sat on a log, sipping her coffee.

"How cold is the water?" Christy asked.

Todd and Antonio looked at each other. "It's refreshing," Todd said.

Christy knew all about Todd's idea of "refreshing" water. "Would it be okay if I use this pot to heat some water?" Christy bent down to pick up a well-used cooking pot and noticed part of a fish head in the dirt. "Did you guys leave the fish guts out on purpose for the raccoons last night? Those were mean-looking critters."

"I heard you and Katie talking to them in the middle of the night," Todd said.

"We were not talking to them," Katie stated. "We were talking about them. There's a big difference."

Christy took another sip of coffee and deduced that if Todd was awake, listening to them talk about the intruders, that meant Antonio was the one doing all the snoring. Somehow that little bit of information brought great comfort to her.

"What's on the schedule for today?" Christy asked. What she really wanted to ask was, "When do we pack up and get out of here?"

"Antonio and I were just leaving to get breakfast," Todd said. "Do you two want to come with us?"

"Sure. Are you driving into town?" Christy thought the idea of breakfast at a quaint roadside café sounded wonderful, but she was far too grubby to go as she was. She hoped they wouldn't mind waiting for her while she cleaned up.

Tonio laughed.

"They're going back to the refrigerator for breakfast," Katie said. "Doesn't some fresh fish sound good to you right about now?"

"Oh. In that case, I think I'll stay here and warm up by the fire. I was freezing all night."

"Doesn't look like you got much sleep," Antonio said.

"I didn't."

Katie decided to go with the guys, and as soon as they left, Christy slipped into the tent to snatch Katie's blanket. She headed for the hammock, which was bathed in a stream of sunlight. Within minutes she was wrapped up in the scratchy wool and rocking herself into a deep sleep.

When the others returned with the fish, Christy could hear them discussing whether they should wake her. She was too groggy to respond. Even when the scent of fried fish floated her way, Christy kept snoozing.

She didn't wake until hours later when the sound of a rattling metal pot roused her from her stupor. Through bleary eyes Christy saw a mangy cat prowling for treats among their cooking gear.

"Get out of there," Christy shouted. She untwisted herself from the blankets and tumbled out of the hammock. The day around her had turned warm, and even though the sun had shifted and the hammock was in the shade, she had been sweating inside her tightly wrapped nest.

"Katie? Todd? Antonio?"

No answer.

Christy noticed a piece of a cardboard box propped up in front of her tent. It looked as if her friends had left a note written with the end of a burned twig. All it said was "Went hiking."

"That's great, you guys," Christy muttered. "Leave me all alone in the wilderness with a gang of wild animals on the prowl for fish guts."

Christy's feelings of abandonment lasted only a few moments. She was determined to get cleaned up. Unzipping the tent, she was assaulted by the horrible smell of the pungent wool sweater. She pulled out the sweater and hung it over a low tree branch to air it out. Then she returned to the tent, changed into her bathing suit, and collected everything she needed for a refreshing wash. She headed down the trail to the "refrigerator."

To her surprise, the lake was close. The trees were so thick that they blocked the view from the campsite. She noticed two boats on the shimmering blue water. One was an old, wooden rowboat manned by two boys who appeared to be fishing. The other was an aluminum fishing boat with a small outboard motor, making all kinds of noise as it skimmed across the water. To the right of Christy stood a small bridge.

Tightening her towel around her waist, she strode over to the bridge and discovered a narrow stream that fed into the lake. Two children floated on an inner tube as the stream carried them on a leisurely journey to the lake. *"Ciao!"* one of them called to her. She waved back and smiled.

Christy walked along the stream's shore until she came to a sun-baked gravel cove where the shallow water felt warm to her touch. With careful steps and a deep breath, she waded in and lowered herself into the water. The cool, refreshing sensation shocked her and delighted her at the same moment. Turning on her back, she floated with her face to the sun.

I feel like such a nature child! This is exactly what Todd said it was: refreshing.

Christy undid her long braid and reached for her soap and shampoo. Luxuriating in the shallow water, she hummed as she lathered up. A small brown bird perched on a low branch a few feet away and cocked its head at Christy as if trying to figure out what she was doing. With slow movements, Christy leaned back and dipped her hair into the water to rinse it. The current from the middle of the stream pulled her tresses away from her head.

I feel like I'm in that old oil painting in the university library. The one with all the women swathed in sheer ivory fabric as they bathe at some primeval cove with fat cupids fluttering around the waterfall.

Christy didn't see a single flying cupid as she emerged from the stream and dried off. But the exhilarating sensation of being refreshed fluttered about her as she made her way back to camp.

The others still weren't back yet, so after she changed, she took extra time brushing her hair and letting it air dry in the glorious sunshine. From a campsite not far away came the sound of children's laughing. It made her think of the children at the orphanage where she worked in Basel.

For a long while Christy rocked herself gently in the hammock and did something she hadn't had the luxury of this past school year. She thought about her life, her future, her hopes, and her dreams. She evaluated her school experience in Basel and thought about how much the work at the orphanage drained her emotionally.

What am I doing wrong, God? I want to serve you, and I thought I was by helping at the orphanage. But it has worn me out. Is that the way it's supposed to be?

The only answer to her questions was the sound of the wind in the branches above her.

And what about Todd? What's next for the two of us? Does he still want to live on some remote island and serve you by being a Bible translator to an unreached tribe? Am I the only one who's thinking about us getting married someday?

She knew God was listening to her heart. It had never been difficult for Christy to believe that God heard and saw and knew. Gazing up into the pale blue sky that was now streaked with feathery, thin white clouds, Christy whispered, "But really, Lord, could you see me living on a tropical island? I mean, bathing in the stream is about as close to roughing it as I've ever come. You wouldn't really have that in mind for the rest of my life, would you?"

Christy tried to convince herself that river bathing wasn't that terrible. It was actually sort of exotic. She pictured herself sleeping every night in a hammock like the one she swayed in now. She thought about eating fish every day. Fish and mangoes. Todd liked mangoes.

Cooking outside is fun. I do love seeing the stars at night. But I can't stand the way everything gets dirty so fast. Dirty and smelly. And being hungry, like I am right now.

Christy found the remainder of Todd's beef jerky in the van and ate it. She glanced around their remote campsite and began to feel less exhilarated about her solo afternoon. The surrounding woods, with their curious birds and slumbering, nocturnal wild raccoons, no longer felt enchanting. For months she had been on a rigid schedule and constantly around other people at school and at the orphanage. Many times she had wished for an afternoon exactly like this one, in which she could be all alone to think and daydream. But now she was ready for her friends to return. It was too quiet.

To busy herself, Christy collected lots of wood and cleaned up the campsite. She lit a fire and hiked down to the stream, where she filled the large pot with water and hauled it back to camp.

Maybe I could learn to be an organic, wilderness-type woman after all. This isn't so bad.

After heating the water, she washed the frying pan, their four coffee mugs, and four forks. Every time she heard the slightest noise, she looked around, expecting to see her friends returning from their hike. When the late afternoon shadows stretched across the campsite, Christy started to feel irritated as well as frightened.

Why did they leave me alone like this for so long? We should have a few rules on this trip, such as never leave anyone alone for an entire day.

Just then she heard footsteps coming through the woods, and she got ready to deliver the lecture of her life to her so-called friends for putting her through this agony. However, the footsteps didn't belong to Todd, Antonio, or Katie. They belonged to a man wearing a plaid cap and a thick knit sweater like the one Christy had left on the branch to air out. He carried a string of medium-sized fish and greeted Christy in Italian.

"Ciao," she replied without much expression. She hoped if she acted as if she meant to be here all alone and as if she knew what she was doing, the man would keep on walking past her campsite.

But he entered. And he spoke to her again in Italian.

Christy thought fast. During her time at school, she had learned the best response was to answer in German.

"Ich verstehe nicht," she said, which meant, "I don't understand."

The man moved closer to where Christy sat by the fire pit and spoke to her again, with longer sentences and more hand gestures.

"Ich verstehe nicht," Christy said quickly.

Undaunted, the man continued to speak. He removed two of the fish from his line, then pulled at his sweater and laid the fish in the clean frying pan.

"I don't understand you," Christy said.

With more hand gestures, the man removed another fish, laid it in the pan, and patted his chest. He looked at her as if waiting for an answer.

"Danke" was all Christy could think to say, assuming, hopefully, that he was just being a kind person and sharing his daily catch with her since it was obvious she had no dinner cooking in her pot. Then, because she remembered how to say thank-you in Italian, she added, "Grazie."

"Prego," the man said with a nod of his head. He said something else, patted the sweater again, and was on his way.

Christy sat frozen. Only her eyes moved from the man's retreating back to the fish in the pan. The distinct odor of fish guts hovered over her. It was more than fish guts, though. It was the strong scent of fish guts mixed with lining from the bottom of a bird cage and the bottom of a farmer's boot.

Oh no! Christy jumped up and dashed around to the back of the tent by the trail's opening. She looked around where she had hung Tonio's smelly sweater. It was gone.

CHAPTER 4

Before Christy could run after the fisherman and demand that he return Antonio's stinky sweater, Todd's voice called to her from the woods, "Hey, Christy! You awake yet?"

She ran down the trail, met him halfway, and flew into his arms. But her hug lasted less than two seconds. With a frustrated push against his chest, she said, "Where were you guys? You left me here alone! Some guy came and traded me fish for Antonio's sweater, and I didn't know what was going on!"

Todd seemed to be looking at her hair, which hung straight down over her shoulders and was tousled wildly from her running about. "You smell good," he said.

"Did you hear anything I said?"

"Yes. He left you with three fish. Have you started to clean them yet?"

Christy looked at Todd incredulously. "No."

"Come on, I'll help you. Tonio and Katie are going to be here in a few minutes."

"Where were you guys?"

Todd grinned. "We got turned around on our hike."

"You were lost?"

"A little."

"How can you be a little lost, Todd? Either you're lost or you're not."

Todd slipped his arm around Christy's shoulder. He seemed amused by her raving comments and acted as if nothing were wrong.

Christy became acutely aware of how good she smelled in contrast to how Todd smelled. And when the other two arrived and gathered around the fire pit while Todd cleaned the fish, Christy realized how pointless and rather agonizing it was to be the only clean, sweet-smelling person in a group.

She apologetically told Antonio what had happened with the fish and the sweater.

He laughed. "You should have held out for five fish, minimum. My grandmother made that sweater. Next time, hold up your fingers like this and say, '*Cinque.*' "

"Your grandmother made it? Antonio, I feel so bad."

"No, don't. It was an old sweater. She makes me one every Christmas."

"It's actually a God-thing, Christy," Katie said. "Can you imagine how long it would take us to catch some fish for dinner? This is perfect. We get back, and dinner is waiting. Well, almost waiting. Provided, at least."

Katie continued to talk, bubbling over with stories of their beautiful hike, how she was certain they must have walked at least thirty miles, and that she would never agree to go anywhere with those two again.

"Believe me, Christy, you made the right choice to stay here and sleep all day. I'm exhausted. And starving. This living off the bounty of the land takes time, doesn't it? Is there any beef jerky left?"

"No, I ate it."

"How long before the fish is ready?" Katie asked.

"Not long," Tonio said, fanning the fire and feeding it more of the twigs Christy had collected.

"You know, you guys, we could just find something to eat along the way," Christy suggested. "The raccoons would be happy if we left the fish for them."

"Along the way where?" Katie asked.

"Along the way to wherever we're going to stay tonight."

Christy's three friends stopped what they were doing and looked at her. She scanned their expressions and said, "Or were you guys thinking we would stay here another night?"

"Of course," Antonio said decidedly. "I don't have to be to work until Saturday. We will stay here four more nights."

When neither Katie nor Todd balked at the possibility of spending the rest of the week here, Christy kept her mouth shut, more from shock than anything else. She remained quiet the whole time they ate their fish. Todd let her borrow his navy blue hooded sweat shirt. She sat huddled next to him by the fire with the hood up, hiding her face from him and only halfheartedly joining in the singing with the others. She couldn't imagine spending five more days of their three-week vacation here with the masked midnight prowlers dining on fish guts while she tossed and turned on the hard ground, shivering like crazy.

Christy went to bed wearing Todd's sweat shirt pulled over her head, which at least helped to keep some of her body heat in. But without the smelly knit sweater, the hard ground poked her and chilled her more miserably than the night before.

Christy listened to Katie's steady breathing. Then a band of scavenging cats got into a fight with the raccoons over their midnight helping of fish guts. Christy cried tiny, silent tears. This wasn't the vacation she had dreamed of with her friends. How could she say anything to them, when obviously she was the only one who thought continuing to camp was a bad idea?

Christy shifted uncomfortably on the tent's floor and rubbed her stockinged feet together. *I'm not much of a nature woman after all, am I?*

A wind picked up, and the canvas tent's sides began to billow. With the wind came a sudden downpour of rain. A leak in the tent's corner next to Christy's head caused the rain to come flying in with the wild wind. Within a few minutes, the sweat shirt's hood was soaked.

"That does it!" Christy shouted, jumping up and vigorously unzipping the tent.

"What's going on?" Katie mumbled. "Can't you just ignore the raccoons tonight?"

"Katie, it's pouring rain! I'm soaked. I'm sleeping in the van."

Running through the downpour, Christy yanked open the side door of the minivan and climbed in. She pulled the door shut and settled herself onto the back bench seat. *Why didn't I think of this last night? It's much warmer in here.*

The rain pelted the van's roof, but Christy was safe, dry, and almost warm. She pulled her scratchy blanket up to her chin and thought she might actually get some sleep now.

Just then the van's door slid open. "Make room, I'm coming in! Our tent is flooding." Katie sprang inside, accidentally smashing Christy's index finger against the seat's underside metal frame.

"Ouch!" Christy yelled.

"What happened?"

Before Christy could answer, the van's side door opened again, and Todd hopped in. "Guess you two had the same idea."

Antonio stood right behind him in the pouring rain and shouted, "Hey, come on! Make some room!"

"You guys are all wet," Katie said.

Todd held a flashlight and turned it toward Christy. Tears streamed down her cheeks as she pressed her lips together and held her smashed finger tightly.

"You okay?" he asked.

Christy shook her head but couldn't speak. Todd motioned with a chin-up gesture and said, "Did you hurt your hand?"

She nodded, and he reached for her hand, shining the flashlight on it. Antonio moved in, and all four of them peered at Christy's finger. It throbbed like crazy, but there was nothing to see. It wasn't swollen, cut, or black-and-blue. It just hurt like everything. The way her three friends looked up at her made Christy feel again like a failed nature woman.

"It'll be all right," Christy said quietly, pulling her hand out of the light.

"Well, then, since we are all together," Antonio said, "what should we do?"

Christy leaned back on the bench seat and tried hard to keep from crying over her throbbing finger. Todd made himself comfortable on the van's floor, leaning against her legs. At that moment she didn't want anyone to touch her or to press against her. Not even Todd. The tight quarters were beginning to smell like wet wool socks and mildewed boots. She knew if she popped open one of the windows, the wind would bring in the rain.

"We could tell detective stories," Katie said. "Or play chess. Have you ever played chess in teams? Guys against the girls. What do you think, Christy?"

Christy didn't feel like playing any kind of game. She didn't view this as the impromptu slumber party everyone else seemed to think it was.

"I have another flashlight somewhere," Antonio said, fumbling through the cupboards.

Todd turned around and said to Christy, "Listen to the sound of that rain. Isn't it amazing? What does it remind you of?"

When Christy didn't answer, Todd added, "I'll give you a hint. Think of an open jeep and a sudden downpour."

Antonio turned on a large flashlight, illuminating the enclosed area. Todd appeared surprised when he saw the expression on Christy's face in the light. "What? Did I say something wrong?"

"No," Christy said, trying to change her aggravated expression.

"Then, what's wrong?" Todd looped his arm across her knees and looked at her with concern.

"It's nothing."

"Oh, come on, Christy, it's obviously something," Katie said. "We all know you too well for you to try to hide whatever it is. Just tell us."

Christy hesitated. She hated the way she felt right now. Holding her still-screaming finger, she spouted, "I'm not particularly enjoying this downpour the way you guys are, and to be honest with you . . . I don't know if I can do this."

"Do what?" Katie prodded.

"This!"

"Camping?" Antonio ventured.

"Yes, camping and all this. I mean, you guys love the adventure of roughing it, but this is the first time in my life I've ever been tent camping, and I hate to be the big baby of this group, but this is hard! I'm cold, wet, and hungry, but you guys all think this is great and want to live this way for the rest of the week. Or for the rest of your lives, for all I know!"

They all stared at her.

"I'm sorry, but this isn't what I had in mind when we said we were going to travel around Europe."

Looking at Todd again, she decided she had better keep going while she was at full speed. "You guys, we only have three weeks to see everything in Europe. Three weeks! And if you want to spend the first week sitting here in the rain, eating fish, I guess that's okay, but I have to tell you, it's not as easy for me as it is for you."

Christy felt hot tears coming to her eyes. She forced them to back off. "I'm sorry I'm being like this, but I feel as if the three of you would have a much better time without me. I mean, you took off and went hiking without me. You could have just done this whole Italy camping thing without me, and I could have caught up with you on your way to Norway or something."

"Is that what you want?" Katie asked. "You want to go to Norway?"

"I don't care about Norway. I thought *you* wanted to go to Norway." Christy raised her voice. "Weren't you the one who sent the email about seeing a fjord and the country your great-grandmother came from?"

"Sure, I want to get to Norway eventually," Katie said. "No rush."

"But that's what you don't understand. You don't just say, 'Oh, let's go to Norway today' and arrive in time for lunch. You have to find out when the trains are scheduled. Some trains require reservations. And what if we want to stop and see something else along the way? We need to have a plan. Why can't we have a plan?"

"We can," Todd said. "We can make a plan."

"Three weeks isn't as long as you guys think," Christy said, calming down.

"So what's your plan?" Katie asked. "Give us a plan."

"I don't have a plan."

"Neither do we," Katie said defensively. "That's why we were just letting things happen as they came along. This camping trip with Antonio is a once-in-a-lifetime opportunity."

"No." Antonio held up his hand and shook his head. "Christy is right. The once-in-a-lifetime opportunity is more than this camp, this lake, these trees. You must see the Sistine Chapel and the Eiffel Tower. Europe has much to offer you. More than what you are seeing here. Five days is too long in one place when there is so much to see. We will go in the morning, okay?"

"Antonio," Christy said quickly, "I didn't mean we had to leave right away. I was just trying to say we need a plan. That's all. We need to work together as a team."

All four of them were quiet for a moment. The sound of the pounding rain on the van's roof made Christy realize how loud her voice had been as she had tried to make her point.

"Where would you like to go next?" Todd asked Christy.

"I don't really care."

"Oh, come on, Christy," Katie said. "You can't give us a big pep talk like that and not have something in mind."

"Well, okay. If it were up to me, I'd like to see other parts of Italy," she said cautiously.

"So would I," Todd said.

"It's settled." Antonio clapped his hands. "As soon as the rain stops, we take down our tents, and you go see more of Italy. Mi Italia. You will love it all."

The others seemed to agree with Antonio, which made Christy feel better.

However, the rain didn't stop when the morning came. In a miserable group effort, the four tired and hungry campers took down their soaked tents in the rain, tied them to the van's roof, and lugged the wooden box of camping gear to the back of the van, where they tied it to the bumper. Christy was certain she was soaked all the way to her skin. None of them had anything waterproof to use as a cover-up. Not even a plastic bag. They took turns changing clothes in the van and chugged their way across the muddy gravel road that led to the highway.

"Let's stop at the first place we come to that has food," Katie pleaded. "I don't care what kind of food it is."

Antonio drove faster when he reached the paved highway. "At my house, my mama will be happy to feed all of us. You will love her."

"No doubt, Tonio," Katie said, "but how far is it to your Mama Mia's Pizzeria?"

"That is very good, Katie. Mama Mia's Pizzeria. That is funny. It is not a long drive. We will be there within the hour."

Christy felt the hour was awfully long as they drove past green, rolling hills and huge fields of sunflowers. The rain had settled into a fine mist with a few sun breaks once they left the foothills. She stared out of a corner of a side window, watching the sun pierce through the clouds and send golden spears of light down on the grape fields. The light turned the leaves a vibrant lime green. Somehow, she found comfort in the beauty of the pastoral scene, which helped because she was still feeling twinges of guilt over being so upset and making everyone pack up and leave because of her.

She glanced at her smashed finger and noticed it had turned a deep shade of purple. Her spirit felt bruised to a deep purple, as well.

Todd slept stretched out on the backseat, and Katie slept on the floor. Christy envied their ability to sleep anywhere in any position. She couldn't sleep, no matter how hard she tried. She noticed that Todd's arm hung over the side and rested on Katie's shoulder since she had backed herself up against the bench. They, of course, didn't mean to be touching in such a cozy manner, but they were. Christy didn't like seeing Todd and her best friend casually flopped over each other that way. She kept glancing back at them.

When Antonio pulled off the main road and headed into town, Christy asked, "Is this it? Is this where you live?"

"Not far," he answered. "This is Cremona."

"It looks so old," Christy said, gazing at a tall tower that rose above the rooftops.

Antonio pointed to the tower. "That is the Torrazzo. The 'big tower.' Built in the thirteenth century."

"It's beautiful," Christy remarked.

"My family is related to the Amatis of Cremona." He made the statement with great pride, as if it should mean something. When Christy didn't respond, he added, "You *Americanos*. You do not know Amati, do you?"

"No, sorry," Christy said.

"Perhaps you know the apprentice of Amati—Stradivari. He is the one I am named after. Antonio Stradivari."

"Is he the one who invented violins?" Christy asked. "Stradivarius violins?"

"*Si!* You have heard of him. But it was my relative, Andrea Amati, who created the violin. Stradivari only perfected it. This is the town where they both lived. Stradivari made violins here more than three hundred years ago. They still make violins in Cremona. Musicians from all over the world come here to buy them."

For the first time, Christy began to feel excited about being in Italy. This was the kind of intriguing blend of history with the present that she had hoped they would discover and explore.

"You see that street there?" Antonio continued. "I work down there at a restaurant near the cathedral. I tell all the tourists that Antonio Stradivari made by hand twelve hundred instruments, and I am named for him. No one believes me."

"They don't believe you about the twelve hundred instruments or that you're named for him?"

"Both. They think I am making it all up."

"Well, I believe you, Tonio. And I think it's amazing." She stretched to catch a final glimpse of the cathedral.

With a few more turns on the narrow road, they came to a wide bridge and crossed a large river before Antonio headed down a poorly maintained road. It led them to a modest whitewashed farmhouse with a red tile roof. The place reminded Christy of the Wisconsin farmlands where she grew up.

Antonio honked the minivan's horn. Katie and Todd stirred from their slumber, and Christy smiled at the woman coming out the side door of the humble house, who was waving and blowing kisses to them.

With a round of warm introductions to Antonio's "mama," the filthy, starving campers were welcomed into the small kitchen. Mouth-watering aromas met them as they entered. Tonio and his mother spoke to each other in rapid Italian as she kept motioning for Christy, Todd, and Katie to sit at the table.

Christy liked the woman at once. And she liked the kitchen. The chairs they pulled from under the table had woven straw seats, and the wood was painted a royal blue. On the wall in front of Christy was an ornate wooden plate rack painted the same blue. It held bright white, yellow, and blue pottery dishes with a matching water pitcher.

Antonio continued to speak with his mother in Italian while she scurried around the kitchen gathering ingredients and talking at the same time Tonio was.

Christy felt like laughing. So much commotion for this obviously beloved son and his three weary friends.

"She says you can take a bath if you want while she makes some pasta." Antonio looked at Christy. "You want me to bring your bag in?"

"Sure. I'd love to take a bath. Are you sure she doesn't mind?" Christy could tell his mother didn't mind. If anything, she probably didn't appreciate these filthy people in her nice, clean kitchen.

"I'll go first, okay?" Christy said, glancing at Todd and Katie. She knew if she looked anything like the two of them, a bath would be a vast improvement.

Tonio showed Christy to the small bathroom with a tile floor and a strange-looking tub. It was short and deep and had a hose sort of fixture attached, which Christy figured must be the shower. It took her a few minutes to figure out how to work everything, but once she did, the warm water pouring over her head felt like a dream. She scrubbed up quickly and dressed in one of her last two clean outfits.

Katie was waiting as soon as Christy exited the bathroom. "Todd and I just washed some clothes, and guess where you do it. Outside in a big tub with one of those old-fashioned washboards. Then you hang it on a line strung between two trees. Is this bizarre or what?"

Christy noticed that Katie was all wet.

"Oh, we had a water fight. Todd and me. I won. You should see him. He barely needs a bath anymore."

Christy left cheery Katie to her bath and went out back to scrub up her clothes. Todd was in the sun, drying off. He and Antonio sat in straight-backed chairs, talking like two old men. Antonio leaned back and commented on how warm and clear it was here compared to the hills where they had camped. Todd acted as if he was completely at home, adding his own comments about the weather.

When Katie's around, he has water fights. When I come out, he barely notices me and sits there, talking about the weather. I feel like the big, bad meanie. We left the campgrounds because of me. It's probably nice and sunny there now, too, and we could be washing our clothes in the stream. Have I ruined everything?

Within an hour and a half, they were all cleaned up and seated around the kitchen table, eating a banquet of delicious food. Todd raved about the pasta. Katie kept taking more of the sausage, and Christy especially liked the ravioli. Antonio relayed messages to his mama about how much everyone was enjoying the food. She smiled and motioned for them to eat more, more, more!

Christy was sure she didn't have room for another bite, and yet loads of food was left over. "Would you please ask your mom if we can help clean up?"

Antonio asked. His mother motioned with hand gestures that they should shoo and leave her alone in her kitchen.

"We can at least do the dishes," Katie suggested.

That was agreed to, and the four of them set up an assembly line to wash and dry the blue-and-yellow ceramic plates as well as all the pots and pans. It didn't take much time with all of them crowding around the sink and laughing. Christy had a feeling Antonio's mom was glad to have them leave her small kitchen in peace.

They all set to work unloading and cleaning up the camping gear with the assistance of one water hose and one rough scrub brush. It took all afternoon to clean everything, dry it in the warm afternoon breeze, and repack. Christy noticed that Todd and Katie were working almost side by side. After they finished, Todd challenged Katie to a game of chess, and they sat under the shade trees, heads bent close in serious contemplation of the board.

"Can I help your mom get dinner ready?" Christy finally asked Tonio after she got tired of watching Todd and Katie.

"No. She is not so comfortable with someone else in her kitchen."

A few minutes later Antonio's father came in from working the fields. It was nearly sunset. Christy thought Antonio's father seemed stern, or maybe he was tired. He was shorter than Antonio and more muscular. He welcomed them to his table warmly and had Antonio ask them questions while they ate. One of the questions he directed to Christy was "Where did you get your beautiful eyes? From your father or your mother?"

"I don't know. Maybe from both of them," Christy said, feeling her cheeks warm.

"My father says they are the most beautiful eyes he has ever seen." Antonio smiled. "And he is right."

Christy lowered her head and concentrated on her pasta. She felt as if everyone was watching her. Tilting her head and glancing up at Antonio's father shyly, she said, *"Molte grazie, signore."*

"Ahh!" Antonio's father exclaimed with surprise at the way she thanked him so politely in Italian. He rattled off more quick words and play-fully swatted Antonio on the arm, pointing at Christy and swatting him again.

"What did he say?" Christy asked cautiously.

Tonio looked embarrassed. He answered his father in Italian, and suddenly Tonio's parents both turned to Todd with surprised expressions.

Todd gave Tonio a half grin and said, "What did you say? What am I missing here?"

Looking at his plate, Antonio used his hands along with his English as he interpreted for his American friends. "My father asked why I have not proposed to Christy already. I told him she was your girlfriend."

Christy looked at Todd. *This is it, Todd. Go ahead. Tell them you're crazy about me. Tell them you can't live without me. Let me hear you say it.*

Todd hesitated. Christy knew Todd was open-ended about much of life, and several times he had let her know she was free to come and go from their relationship as she pleased. And she had done that. And so had Todd. But was he ready now to publicly close at least one of those open ends? All he had to do was declare that Christy was his girlfriend.

As everyone looked at Todd, Christy pressed her lips together and waited.

With a trademark chin-up gesture Todd said, "Please tell your father I'm flattered by his question."

What is that supposed to mean?

At first Antonio's father looked surprised at Todd's vague response. Then a smile grew, and he nodded his head. With a deep chuckle, he shook his finger at Todd and merrily rattled off a string of Italian words.

Christy wasn't sure she wanted to hear the interpretation from Antonio.

"My father says you have learned early in life the secret, which is to always keep a woman guessing."

Oh yeah, that's Todd's specialty. Always keep a woman guessing. And where does that put our relationship? Obviously not as far along as I thought it was.

Something inside Christy squeezed shut. The hurt in her heart pounded on that invisible shut door. It was an old, familiar hurt.

Don't do this, Christy. Don't sink into this depression. He's not rejecting you. He's just being his usual, noncommittal self. You and Todd have been through five years of a very special kind of friendship. A forever friendship. For now, that should be enough for you.

But deep inside, Christy wanted so much more.

CHAPTER 5

Christy woke the next morning to the sound of a car horn in front of Antonio's farmhouse. She slipped out of bed while Katie slept and padded across the rug to the halfway open window. Pulling back the white lace curtains, she peered out at the taxi that had pulled into the driveway.

A tall, slender Italian about Antonio's age was paying the driver. The passenger wore dark, straight jeans and a white dress shirt with the sleeves rolled up. Christy stared at the handsome, dark-haired stranger.

"Ciao!" he called out as he turned and apparently spotted Christy at the window. Then he waved with one hand, lifted his suitcase with the other, and headed toward her. She quickly pulled back, letting the curtains shade her from his view.

"Katie!" Christy whispered, hopping over to the bed and shaking her sleeping friend. "Katie, wake up."

"What?" Katie sounded grouchy, as she usually did first thing in the morning.

"Katie, you have to see this guy. I think your order for tall, dark, and handsome just arrived!"

"What are you talking about?"

"Come here. Get up." Christy pulled on Katie's arm. "Quick, before he comes in the house."

Katie groaned, "Why can't you ever leave me alone when I'm sleeping?"

A voice behind Christy made her jump and turn away from Katie. "Ciao." The visitor was standing at their bedroom window. Since there was no screen, he simply had raised the window the rest of the way and pushed back the curtains with his hand.

Katie screamed, but he laughed and spoke to them in Italian.

Christy self-consciously wrapped her arms around her baggy nightshirt and quickly reverted to her emergency response, "Ich verstehe nicht."

The visitor spoke to her in German.

Katie grabbed Christy's arm and said, "Who is this guy, and what in the world is he saying?"

He laughed again and said in English, "I know who you are now. You are Antonio's American friends, aren't you? I have heard about you. Are you Christiana?"

Christy nodded.

"And you are Katie. Ciao, Katie."

"Yeah, hi," she said, pulling the bed sheets up to her neck.

A knock on their bedroom door interrupted the awkward introductions, and Antonio entered, speaking Italian with their visitor and using lots of hand gestures.

"You have met my cousin Marcos?" Antonio asked Katie and Christy.

"Sort of," Katie said.

"He's on his way to Rome. You want to go with him?"

Ten minutes later Christy was seated in the kitchen, sipping strong coffee and eating round rolls that were soft inside and crusty on the outside. Around her swirled a lively conversation, partly in English and partly in Italian. Spontaneous plans for the next part of the journey came together effortlessly.

Marcos had arrived by way of an early morning train that enabled him to stop in for a quick visit with his relatives. Since he was on his way to Rome, the three "Americanos" could join him. Marcos would show them the sights after he made a delivery to one of his father's clients.

"We better pack," Katie said when she found out the train to Rome left in an hour. "I still have clothes out on the line."

Christy glanced at good-looking Marcos and found his gaze was fixed on her. She looked away quickly, feeling her cheeks warm with embarrassment. It was the fourth time during breakfast that she had glanced at him, and each time he was gazing at her.

"Care to join me?" Katie said, rising from the kitchen table and tugging on Christy's arm.

"Sure." She rose and carried her dishes to the sink despite Antonio's mother's protests. "Grazie," Christy told her and comfortably received the woman's kiss on her cheek. Christy had gotten used to a lot of cheek kissing during her time in Europe, and she gracefully kissed Antonio's mom back, thanking her again in Italian.

Katie hung back, offering a stiff nod and saying, "Thanks for the chow."

The two of them turned to exit the kitchen, and Christy glanced at Todd. He was looking at her. She quickly swept her gaze past Marcos. Marcos was more than looking at her. He was watching her every move.

As soon as Christy and Katie were out the back door and away from the open kitchen window, Katie grabbed Christy by the elbow and yanked her around the side of the house by the clothesline. "What in the world are you doing?"

Christy couldn't believe how red Katie's face was. "What do you mean? I'm not doing anything."

"Oh yes, you are! You're flirting with Marcos right in front of Todd! What are you thinking? I've never seen you like this, Christy."

"What are you talking about?"

"What am I talking about?" Katie lifted her hands in a gesture of disbelief. "We're all sitting around the table talking, and all you're doing is taking tiny little bites of bread, and after each bite, you look at Marcos."

"I wasn't doing that."

"Trust me, that's exactly what you were doing. And then you would sip your coffee and pretend he wasn't staring at you. Did you even notice Todd sitting there, watching you flirt?"

"Katie, I was not flirting!" Christy lowered her voice and looked right and left to make sure they were still alone. "I don't know what you thought you saw in there or what you're thinking now, but I wasn't doing anything."

Katie shook her head. "Then that had to be the most intense case of subconscious flirting I've ever seen. I mean, I'm the first to admit that the guy is absolutely gorgeous, but come on, I could feel the heat passing between the two of you."

Christy felt baffled by Katie's statements. "I didn't feel any heat."

"You are so naïve."

"I am not."

"Just do me a favor," Katie said, going over to the line and yanking off her stiff, dried clothes. "Don't do it."

"Don't do what?" Christy felt her anger rising.

"Don't pull a Rick Doyle on us. Not now. You're smarter than that." With a swish of her red hair, Katie turned and marched off, her arms full of clothes.

Christy stood frozen in place, her mouth open in disbelief. *What was that all about? She knows Rick was a big-mistake crush . . . how many years ago? Four? And what's more, Katie made the same mistake herself when she fell for Rick!*

Christy aggressively pulled her clothes off the line and marched back into the house through the front door to avoid seeing anyone in the kitchen. She made a beeline for the guest bedroom and closed the door soundly behind her. Katie stood five feet away, jamming her clothes into her travel bag.

"That was completely unfair and mean," Christy growled at Katie. "Why are you mad at me? You wouldn't be acting mean unless you were mad at me."

"I'm not mad," Katie said without stopping her quick packing job. "Can we just forget it? They're going to be ready to go, and I don't want them waiting for us because we're sitting here having a fight."

Christy was so mad now she could hardly think straight. *I can't believe this is happening! Why is Katie being like this?*

Katie zipped up her bag and, without looking at Christy, lugged it to the door. "I'll be out front with the others."

Slumping down on the edge of the bed, Christy stared at the stiff pair of jeans she held in her lap and tried to calm down. She knew Katie well enough to realize pressing her to talk when she wasn't ready would be a mistake.

Why would she say all that? Was I unconsciously flirting? Was Marcos really staring at me like Katie said? Did Todd think I was flirting with Marcos?

Of course Christy had been aware of Marcos's steady gaze at the breakfast table. But that didn't mean she was flirting with him, did it?

I sure don't get stares like that from Todd. Am I feeling sorry for myself because Todd didn't take a stand about our relationship last night? The way Marcos looked at me this morning is the way I've always wanted Todd to look at me.

A knock on the door pulled Christy away from her evaluating. "Yes?"

The door opened, and to her surprise, Marcos stepped into the room with a grin on his face. His deep brown eyes met Christy's. "Do you need some help?"

Christy felt her heart pounding. "No. Thanks. I'm fine. I can get it. I'll be out in a minute."

"It's no problem. I will wait and carry your luggage for you."

Christy pushed her clothes into her bag and nervously tugged at the zipper.

"Here, let me get that for you." Marcos stepped over to her side and reached for the stuck zipper.

Christy pulled away. She felt self-conscious and nervous about this guy, who was acting as if he had free access into her private space. "Thanks," she said, grabbing her day pack and making sure she hadn't left anything on the dresser. "I'll go on out with the others." With that, Christy left Marcos to wrestle her bigger bag out of the house.

She found Todd and Katie loading their luggage into the back of Antonio's clean minivan. Christy said good-bye to Antonio's mom with another kiss on the cheek and then claimed the front passenger seat. She certainly didn't want to be in the back of the bus with Marcos and Katie while Todd sat in the front seat.

As Antonio steered his van down the bumpy road, Christy kept looking straight ahead. *This is all my fault for making such a scene about leaving the campground. If we were still there, we wouldn't be on our way to Rome with a guy who makes me incredibly nervous. Katie wouldn't be mad at me. Todd wouldn't be ignoring me. At least Antonio is still speaking to me.*

"Do you like Rome?" Christy asked Antonio, trying to start a conversation.

"Yes, very much. But I'm not going with you."

"You're not?"

"No," Antonio said, "I do not have money for travel."

Christy realized then that the camping hadn't cost anything. Even the fish were free. "What if we all pitched in and gave you some money?"

Antonio took his eyes off the road and smiled at Christy. "You sound sad because I am not going with you. That's nice, Christiana."

"I am sorry," she said, turning her attention back on the road and hoping Antonio would do the same. She couldn't figure out why Antonio could be sweet and flirty with her yet she never felt uncomfortable. He had been that way with all the girls when he was in California, and they all had loved it and called him the "romantic Italian." It felt different with Marcos.

Why? Because he's exceptionally good-looking? He must know how handsome he is. Does Marcos just expect all women to swoon over him? Or is it me? Am I somehow looking for more attention? What's going on?

Antonio pulled the minivan into an illegal parking place near the train station and left the motor running as he worked to unload their luggage. Christy felt sorry that they didn't get to stay and explore Cremona.

"Christiana," Antonio said, motioning for her to come around to the other side of the van, away from the others. In a low voice he said, "I told this to Todd and Katie while you were in the house. When I came home from California, I told Marcos about the decision I made in America to dedicate my life to Christ. Marcos said he is not ready to make the same choice. I think your going to *Roma* with him is what Katie calls a God-thing. This is the reason we left the camp. You can show Marcos God's love the way you showed me, and I am sure he will decide soon."

Christy felt her stomach tightening. "I wish you were going with us."

Antonio kissed her soundly on both cheeks. "Maybe you will come see me again before you leave Europe. You are welcome any time."

"Thank you so much, Tonio." Christy felt the tears welling up in her eyes. "Grazie."

"Prego," he said. "I will be praying."

"And I'll pray for you, my friend. Ciao!"

"Arrivederci," Tonio said, handing Christy her luggage. He then hurried over to say good-bye to the others.

Christy suddenly realized how selfless Tonio was being. She knew he had gone to school in California at the expense of a generous uncle. Marcos's father, perhaps? Antonio's family obviously lived very modestly. The camping trip had been Antonio's vacation. A very inexpensive vacation. When Christy had complained and they had left the campground, that meant the end of Antonio's vacation, even though he didn't give any hint of it at the time. Christy wished again that she hadn't complained.

She followed the others into the train station and watched as Marcos arranged for them to pay extra on their Eurail train passes so they could ride with him in first class. Marcos offered to pay for all of them, but Todd told Marcos they would rather pay. Christy chimed in with Todd and insisted on paying. Marcos held up his hands in surrender, and the three of them each paid for their first-class passes.

"Well," Katie said under her breath to Christy as they hurried to the train track. "He sure gave in when you told him how you wanted things to be."

Christy pressed her lips together and tried not to let herself become angry with Katie all over again. "Can we not do this, Katie?"

"What?"

"Pick at each other. I don't want to fight with you."

Katie looked down. Todd called for them to come on. "Okay," Katie said and took off for the train.

As they boarded, Christy tried to let go of her frustration with Katie and everything else. She felt little bubbles of excitement building up inside her. She loved traveling on the trains in Europe and had been looking forward to this part of the adventure.

Christy made sure she was seated next to Todd on the nicely upholstered train seat. Katie and Marcos sat on a matching seat directly across from them. Their luggage was stowed on shelves over their heads, and the four of them had the small, first-class compartment to themselves.

"How long will it take to get to Rome?" Katie asked.

"About five hours," Marcos said.

"That long?" Katie said.

"We could stop in Florence, if you like. I do not have to meet with my father's client until tomorrow morning."

"I have a tour book," Christy said, reaching for her day pack. "I could read about some of the things to see in Florence, and then we could decide if we want to stop there."

"We don't need a tour book," Katie said. "I'm sure Marcos can tell us what to see."

"I'd like to see the tour book," Todd said.

Christy felt relieved. Todd was on her side. The two of them could sit close and read about all the great sights awaiting them in these fabulous cities. At least that way they would know some of the history behind the things they saw.

With her sweetest smile, Christy handed Todd the tour book and hoped he was in the mood to snuggle with her while they read. That, more than anything else, would convince Katie and Marcos that Christy and Todd really were a close couple and that Christy wasn't flirting with Marcos—subconsciously or any other way.

Todd took the thick, soft-covered book from Christy, thanked her, and placed it between his head and the glass window of their train compartment. "Perfect," he murmured, closing his eyes. "Wake me when we get there."

CHAPTER 6

"So it is up to you," Marcos said, staring at Christy. "Would you like to go to *Firenze* first? Or directly to Roma?"

"What do you think, Katie?" Christy was eager to get Marcos to stop looking at her.

"Rome, I guess. Doesn't matter."

"There's a lot of art to see in Florence," Christy said. "Like Michelangelo's statue of David."

"Are you saying you want to stop in Florence so you can see a statue of a naked guy?" Katie asked.

Marcos laughed.

"Of course not!" Christy snapped. "You're missing my point, Katie."

"And what was your point?"

"We might be sorry later if we don't stop to see Florence while we have the chance."

"Fine. I don't care. I think it's all great. The only thing I really want to see is Venice. That is the place where they have the gondolas, right?"

"Right," Marcos said. "That is where I live. *Venezia.*"

"You live in Venice?" Katie said.

Marcos nodded.

"Do you have water right outside your front door and ride around in gondolas?" Katie asked.

"Of course. Venezia is built on more than a hundred islands. Nearly everyone has water outside the front door. My father owns a jewelry store near the Piazza San Marcos. Carlo Savini Jewelers. If you go to Venezia, you must go to his store. Carlo Savini. Don't forget."

"That is so cool. Let's definitely go to Venice," Katie said.

"After Rome," Christy suggested.

"Sure. After Rome and whatever that other 'frenzy' city was."

"Florence," Christy said, using the English pronunciation of the city.

"Firenze," Marcos corrected her.

"There is one place I'd like to see in Italy," Christy said. "I don't know where it is. It might be in Venice."

"If it is, I would know it," Marcos said. "What is the place?"

"The Blue Grotto. Have you ever heard of it?"

"Of course. It is on the Isle of Capri. Not in Venezia."

"Where's Capri?"

"South. The way we are going. You take a hydrofoil over from *Sorrento* or *Napoli*. It's only a few hours from Roma. It is best to see it in the morning. By afternoon there are too many people, and it's not worth the trip."

"That's good to know," Christy said. "Thanks."

"You could go there tonight," Marcos suggested. "Capri has some of the most expensive hotels in all of Italy, but I know a place you can stay. You would then take the first morning tour boat to the *Grotta Azzurra*. Then you go to Roma, and I can meet you in the afternoon."

"That sounds like a good idea." *Katie can't think I'm flirting with Marcos if I'm planning how to get away from him.*

"What's the Blue Grotto?" Katie asked. "And why do you want to go there?"

"It's a cavern I've heard about," Christy explained. "You take a boat in, and the refracted sunlight makes the water a unique shade of blue."

"I remember hearing about that place," Katie said. "Didn't we know someone who went there and was always talking about it?"

"Rick Doyle," Todd said without opening his eyes or giving any other indication he was awake.

"That's right!" Katie's green eyes sparkled at Christy. She reached over and slapped Christy on the leg. "Rick called you from Italy on your birthday. I remember you telling me. That's why he took you out to an Italian restaurant for your big date—because he was in Italy the day you turned sixteen."

Sometimes Christy wished Katie suffered from memory lapse. Unfortunately, Katie remembered every word Christy had told her so many years ago. And Katie seemed to feel compelled to recount every detail now in front of Todd and Marcos.

"And Rick went to the Blue Grotto that morning, on your birthday. You were in Maui, and he called you there and told you the water was the same color as your eyes. That's where I've heard of the Blue Grotto."

Todd opened one eye and turned his head toward Christy. She looked at him, knowing she had nothing to hide yet still feeling put on the spot.

"Rick was here in Italy when he called you?"

Christy nodded. Then she noticed Marcos was staring at her again.

"I think he is right," Marcos said. "Your eyes are the color of the water in the Grotta Azzurra."

What is it with Italian men and my eyes?

"Well, then," Todd said, adjusting his position and handing the tour book back to Christy, "guess we better go to this famous Blue Grotto and compare the two for ourselves."

Christy couldn't tell if he was upset or teasing her.

"I'm going to find the dining car and get something to drink," Todd said, standing. "Anyone else want anything?"

"I'll come," Christy said. She was glad for the chance to have a few minutes alone with Todd.

"Wait for me," Katie said, joining them.

Christy gritted her teeth. *Can't you tell I want to be alone with him, Katie? We haven't had a chance to talk privately this whole trip.*

Leading the way down the narrow hall, Christy didn't turn around to look at Katie and Todd until they were in the dining car. Rather than a simple snack bar with a few booths, like the snack car where she and Katie had eaten on a train in England, this dining car had cloth-covered tables and uniformed waiters who seated them and brought the food to them. She had been in a dining car like this last summer with her friend Sierra when the two of them had visited the school in Basel.

Christy sat first, and Todd slid in across from her. Katie slid in next to Todd instead of sitting next to Christy. He leaned across the table and said, "So you're the Blue Grotto girl, huh?"

Christy wasn't sure what to say. She reached over and brushed her fingers along Todd's unshaven chin and said, "And are you the mountain man?"

"I thought I'd let it grow. What do you think?" He leaned back and turned his chin to the right and then the left to allow Christy a thorough evaluation.

"I guess it might take a little while," she said cautiously. Todd's hair was so blond it barely showed unless the light hit it just right. Most of the time, she had noticed, it looked like a faint shadow or as if he hadn't washed his face. "Ask me again after it's been growing for a week."

Todd laughed. "I haven't shaved for a month."

Christy laughed with him. "Oops! Sorry."

Todd rubbed his chin with his thumb and forefinger. "I guess growing facial hair isn't one of my talents."

"Try a goatee," Katie suggested, reaching over and touching Todd's chin.

"You think?" he asked.

"Sure," Christy agreed. "Try shaving all of it but this part." She reached across the table and rubbed the soft fuzz across his chin. "It's actually a little darker there."

"Really?" Todd held up the back of a spoon and tried to catch his reflection. Then, without looking up, Todd asked, "Do both of you want to go to Capri?"

"I do," Christy said.

"Sure," Katie agreed. "Does this mean we have a plan?"

"I guess so," Todd said, putting down the spoon and ordering a mineral water from the waiter who now stood before them. Christy ordered the same.

Katie shrugged and said, "Okay. Another one of those."

The waiter looked unclear as to what she was telling him.

"Tre aqua minerale," Todd ordered for them.

Christy was impressed and gave Todd a look of admiration.

"It's so close to Spanish," he said. "When I was in Spain last year I picked up a few key phrases."

"Good," Katie said. "Teach me how to ask, 'Where is the bathroom?' "

"Out that door and to the left," Todd said. "We passed it on the way in."

"That doesn't do me any good," Katie said. "I'm serious. Teach me whatever phrases you know. I get nervous when I can't communicate."

"And I get nervous when you do communicate," Christy said under her breath.

"What was that?" Katie leaned forward, her arms resting on the white tablecloth.

Christy hesitated before deciding honesty was the way to go with her friends. "I've been having a hard time not getting upset at you all day, Katie."

"Why? What did I do?"

"First, this morning you had all those accusations outside Antonio's house after breakfast. I think you'll notice from the way things are going that those assumptions weren't completely accurate."

Katie tilted her head back and forth as if weighing Christy's words. "I still see some potential, but you're right. It doesn't appear to be what I thought it was earlier."

"I can assure you, from my perspective, it is not." Christy glanced at Todd.

"Am I supposed to know what you guys are talking about?" he asked.

"No," Christy said quickly. She went right on to her next point. "And the whole thing about Rick was more than needed to be said, Katie."

"Why? What did I say wrong? Todd didn't mind. Did you, Todd?"

Todd shook his head. "We all go through different stages in life. Some relationships last and others don't. That's reality."

Christy thought his evaluation was a little too down-to-earth, even for Todd. It sounded as if he could be referring to another relationship, a larger one than the brief handful of dates Christy had with Rick.

Maybe he's talking about his relationship with Rick. The two of them shared an apartment in college with some other guys, but now Todd and Rick never see each other.

"Can you let me out, Katie?" Todd asked. "I'll be right back."

"Nope. Not until you say it in Italian."

"I don't know how to say it in Italian," Todd said.

"Then too bad. You're stuck."

As Christy watched, a little-boy grin appeared on Todd's face. It was the same look he and his buddy Doug used to get at the beach when they were about to pick up one of the girls and throw her into the ocean. Todd reached under the table, and Katie immediately gave in.

"Stop squeezing my knee," she said with a giggle as she swatted at Todd.

How did Todd know her knee was so sensitive? I didn't know that.

He exited as the train swayed back and forth. "Katie, I mean it about the flirting stuff you said this morning," Christy continued. She didn't feel she had been able to say everything she wanted to earlier, since they had been talking in code in front of Todd. "That really upset me, and I don't want us to communicate like that on this trip."

"Fine," Katie said. "What else do you want to say to me before Todd comes back? Because if you don't have anything else to yell at me about, I have something I think I should mention to you."

"I'm not yelling at you, Katie."

"Okay, is there anything else you want not to yell at me about?"

"No."

The waiter arrived with their bottles of mineral water and the bill on a small tray.

"I've got it," Christy said, pulling some money from her pocket and placing it on the tray. He gave her some change, and she thanked him in Italian.

"I'll pay for something next time," Katie said. "Now, do you want to hear my observation?"

"Yes." Christy meant it. She really did appreciate Katie's insights. She always had. But she didn't always like them when she first heard them.

Katie leaned forward. "Okay. First, I should tell you that Todd and I got into a big discussion on the plane. We talked about how he and I are more the outdoorsy type. We were talking about camping, and he said he wasn't sure you would want to do much roughing it on this trip. I told him he didn't have to worry, that you could handle anything we threw at you."

"Guess I proved you both wrong, didn't I?"

"Don't worry about it," Katie said. "Todd and I talked about it yesterday while we were washing our clothes and you were in the bathtub."

"You and Todd talked about me again?"

Katie swished the air in front of Christy with her hand as if to brush away any misunderstandings Christy might be formulating. "I told him we should be sensitive to you and try not to do anything that would push you over the edge. He said you were probably still stressed from school and working at the orphanage and everything. We both know it's been a difficult term for you."

"Well, you know what? I don't know if I appreciate your analyzing me whenever I'm not around."

"It was no big deal, Christy. I think you should be glad that Todd feels comfortable enough to talk with me about you."

Christy wasn't sure she agreed with that. She sipped her bubbly water and reluctantly listened as Katie continued.

"Can I just say that I think you have way too many expectations of yourself, of me, and of Todd for this trip? Either that, or you're living too much in the past."

"And what is that supposed to mean?"

"If you think about it, Christy, you could be having some kind of weird flashbacks to our trip to England, but this is nothing like that trip."

"You're right. It isn't." Christy felt certain this trip couldn't be compared in any way to that one. In England they were with a group on a short-term missions project. At the beginning of the trip, Christy had been dating Todd's best friend, Doug, because Todd was long gone from her life. Or so she thought at the time. Christy had ended up seeing that she and Doug were incompatible but how perfect her friend Tracy was for him. Christy broke up with Doug during the first week of the trip, and now, a year and a half later, Doug and Tracy were married.

"I don't see how the two trips compare at all," Christy said.

"That's my point exactly," Katie said. "This is a completely different trip, and all the circumstances are new. You shouldn't allow yourself subconsciously to make any comparisons to the challenging stuff that happened to you on that trip and think it's all going to happen to you again just because you're in Europe with your friends."

Christy didn't follow Katie's thinking until she delivered her last line, which was a zinger. "I mean, it's not like you and Todd are going to break up on this trip or anything."

The dining car door slid open, and Todd entered with Marcos behind him. "I went back to get the tour book, and I talked Marcos into joining us so we could a make a plan for the next few days."

Marcos slid into the booth next to Christy. Katie scooted over, and Todd sat next to her.

Christy felt her heart pounding so hard it throbbed in her ears. Katie's words bounced off the inside of her head with each pound of her heart. *"It's not like you and Todd are going to break up on this trip or anything."*

All the odd little pieces began to fit together. Todd had been happy to see Christy at the train station and had given her a sweet hello kiss, but since then he had barely touched her. Except for when they sat close by the campfire.

Todd didn't agree that I was his girlfriend in front of Antonio's father. Why? Has he realized we're an uncomplimentary match? He loves roughing it, and I fall apart when it starts to rain.

Christy remembered how, during the England trip, she had seen clearly that she realized she and Doug weren't a good match. She wondered if Todd had made that same discovery about her.

Is he just waiting for the right time to tell me? Knowing Todd, he wouldn't break up with me for good unless he was convinced God was telling him to. . . . Christy's mind raced through a number of facts. Todd was nearly finished with college. He had only a few more credits to go, and they both were planning to attend Rancho Corona in the fall. A year from now, Todd would be graduated and twenty-four years old. That was old enough by anyone's standards to be married.

But where is it written that he has to marry me? I was the girlfriend of his teen years. He's a man now. Definitely. Facial hair and everything. He can have any woman he wants. Why wouldn't he marry someone more outdoorsy and easygoing like he is? Someone who is fun to be around and a good friend. Someone like . . .

Christy's heart pounded wildly, deafening all her senses as she stared across the table at her red-haired best friend.

Someone like . . . Katie.

CHAPTER 7

Christy felt numb all the way to Rome. As the others in the dining car talked and planned, she barely responded. When the group discussed going straight to Naples and skipping Florence, Christy merely nodded in agreement.

Everything inside her felt shaken by the thought that Katie could be a better match for Todd than Christy was, just as Tracy was a better match for Doug than Christy. When the earthquake inside her stopped, all the pieces were in places they didn't belong. She scrambled emotionally to pick up whatever wasn't shattered and to find a safe place to store her feelings in her heart.

Why would Todd have kissed me at the train station in Basel if he's been thinking about our breaking up?

Then she remembered his words after she said she didn't want to cry. *"And I told myself I wouldn't kiss you." That's what Todd said. He didn't want to kiss me. He's probably waiting until the end of this trip before he tells me it's over between us.*

In her numbed state, Christy thought of the water fight between Todd and Katie. The way they had bent their heads close together over the chessboard. The way he knew where to squeeze her knee. Was it possible something was going on between them right under her nose, but she hadn't read the signs?

The four of them ate lunch. Christy didn't taste a bite. They returned to their first-class compartment, and she sat like a blob while the rest of them discussed the sights they should see, which included some of the museums and churches Christy had marked in the tour book. It was what Christy had wanted all along; they were making a plan, and they were working together as a team. Yet Christy was with them in body only. She kept watching Todd and Katie for any further signs of special interest in each other.

At the train station in Rome, Marcos directed them to the track for their next train. Katie tugged on his arm and said, "Marcos, I want you to come to Naples with us." She tilted her head and gave him a smile. "It won't be the same without you."

"Okay, why not?" Marcos said. "I'll ride the train with you to Naples, and when you go on to Capri, I will take a train back to Rome."

Christy thought Marcos might change his mind when they found out the first-class section on that train was booked. But he didn't. Instead, the four of them ended up in second class, which was radically different. They stood part of the way until Marcos found two seats in a different compartment.

The seats turned out to be more like twelve inches of open space. At Marcos's insistence, Christy and Katie wedged their way into the space while the guys stood in the walkway. The woman next to Christy held in her lap a large straw basket that smelled of garlic. The basket slumped onto Christy's lap as the woman slept. As the close smell of perspiration and garlic grew in intensity, Christy drew in little breaths with her hand over her nose. No one else in the compartment suggested opening the window. Everyone seemed content. Finally, Christy couldn't take it any longer. She rose and told Katie she needed to get some fresh air.

"I'm right behind you," Katie said.

The guys followed them to an open window in the wobbly train's hallway. Katie was the first to burst out laughing. "Whoa! What were you trying to do, Marcos, cure us of ever wanting to travel on a train again?"

"This is why it is better to pay more for first class," Marcos said.

"How much farther is it?" Todd asked. "I don't mind standing here if you guys don't."

"The conductor may tell us to move, but until he does, we can stay," Marcos said. He checked his watch. "I would say we should be in Napoli in less than an hour. This is a direct train. That means two hours exactly from Roma to Napoli."

Christy stood next to her luggage with her arms folded on top of the open window frame. The rush of warm afternoon air helped to clear her thoughts. Todd was standing right beside her. If he wanted to, he could easily put his arm around her. Or lean his head next to hers and whisper something sweet.

But he didn't. He stood back just slightly so they weren't touching. His attention was on Katie. She was busy plying Marcos for useful Italian phrases, and Todd was repeating them along with her. Marcos seemed to enjoy the role of tutor in their tight quarters. He also seemed to enjoy Katie.

Christy thought back on how Marcos had pretty much ignored Katie that morning. Now Katie had two ardent admirers, and Christy felt heartsick.

Relationships have to be two ways. Todd wouldn't be interested in Katie unless she let him know she was interested in him. And she is, isn't she? Maybe that's why she's being so cute with Marcos now. Maybe she's trying to make Todd realize how wonderful she is.

Christy watched. At that moment, with her tumbled spirit in agony, she found it easy to imagine anything.

It was one thing for you to go out with Rick after I did, Katie, but at least you waited until after I'd broken up with him.

She ran her thumb across her gold Forever bracelet. When Todd had given it to her on New Year's Eve almost five years ago, he had said it meant that whatever happened in the future, they would be friends forever.

Is this about to become part of the "whatever"? Are we going to finally tell each other we're just friends? A year and a half from now will Katie and Todd be married like Doug and Tracy are?

Christy would never have expected herself to feel so overwhelmed. Katie was right about one thing she had said in the dining car: It had been a difficult school term for Christy. Her notes home had been cheerful, and almost all her diary entries had been positive. But that was because she only wrote when she felt good.

During most of the past ten months she had gone to classes, given all she had emotionally to the needy children at the orphanage, and returned to her dorm room, where she fell asleep while doing classwork.

That's one of the reasons her Saturday morning trek to the Konditorei had become so important to her. It was her way of treating herself for making it through another week without collapsing.

Christy wondered if part of what she had been feeling the past few days was the result of so many stressful months and such a rigid schedule. She didn't remember how to relax and have fun. She didn't know how to be anybody's girlfriend. Maybe Katie was right, that Christy's expectations of herself and her friends were too high. Maybe she had only imagined the invisible canopy of peace when Todd arrived. Maybe this relationship was never meant to be anything more than what it was right now. If that was true, Christy had to know now, not at the end of the trip.

"Todd," Christy heard herself say, touching him lightly on the shoulder. He turned, and she said, "Could I talk to you for a few minutes?"

"Sure." He leaned against the windowsill with his back toward Katie and Marcos.

Christy felt awkward. She hadn't thought this through. "I guess what I meant was, could you and I go to another part of the train to talk for a few minutes?"

"Sure." Todd picked up his pack and slung it over his shoulder. "Hey, Marcos, Katie, we're going to the next train car for a while. Where should we meet in case we get separated when the train stops?"

Marcos gave Todd instructions, saying that they needed to go right to the bus that would take them to the harbor. At the harbor they would purchase their tickets for the hydrofoil, not the boat, to Capri because the hydrofoil was twice as fast. He emphasized to all of them that Naples wasn't the best city for tourists and that they should watch their belongings carefully.

"Got it," Todd said. "When we get off the train we wait for each other."

Marcos added one more bit of instruction. "When you get to Capri, go to the Villa Paradiso. A friend of my father owns it. Be sure to tell him you know the son of Carlo Savini. He will give you a good price."

"Thanks," Todd said. He and Christy made their way through the train with their bulky travel bags. It seemed they wouldn't be able to find any open corners anywhere. They were about to give up and go back to where they had left Katie and Marcos, but then, in the very last train car, they found a corner in the passageway.

Christy dropped her pack and jiggled the window until it opened to let in a welcome rush of air. The train was rolling past a grove of old olive trees. Some of them had gnarled trunks that were at least three feet wide. A small village appeared on the hillside as the train curved to the left. Noting the charming whitewashed houses with their red-tiled roofs in the distance, Christy thought about how they were probably much older and much more humble up close than they looked from a distance. At least that had been true of Antonio's home.

Christy turned her face to the open window and let the rushing air dry the perspiration on her face.

"How are you doing?" Todd asked.

Turning to face him, she said, "Todd, I need to ask you something."

"Sure."

"I know you'll be honest with me." She looked into his strong, steady face and hesitated before going on.

"I'm always honest with you," Todd said. His short, sun-bleached blond hair stood straight up as the wind blew over him through the open window.

"I know you are. And I really want to always be honest with you."

"So what's going on?" Todd asked, turning to give her his full attention.

Christy pulled her eyes away from his piercing gaze. She didn't know what to say. It seemed that for years she had been the one to ask the are-we-more-than-just-friends question. She was the one who always wanted to know where their relationship stood and what was expected of her. Todd didn't seem to need to know. While she needed a plan, he seemed content with the adventure of it all.

Christy said the first thing that came to her mind. "Katie said she thinks my expectations are too high for myself and for the two of you. Do you think that, too?"

"Maybe," Todd said.

"What do you mean?"

"I guess I'd have to know what your expectations are, exactly, to know if they are too high or not."

"Okay, forget I asked that. This is what I really want to know. Do you think we've changed?"

Todd paused and then nodded slowly.

"I mean, have we changed a lot? Maybe changed too much? Or maybe we haven't exactly changed but become more of who we really are. And is it possible that the true people we are now aren't the same people we were five years ago? Or the people we will be five years from now."

Todd ran his hand across the stubble along his jawline. "Can you give that to me again?"

Christy looked down at her hands. Her fingernails were all broken off from the camping trip. Her injured index finger had gone from deep purple to black-and-blue. Inside, she felt as rough and bruised as her hands looked.

"Todd, do you want to break up?" She spoke the words in a thin voice without looking at him.

Todd didn't answer. Since he didn't immediately protest and say, "No, of course not," Christy took it to mean only one thing. Her throat tightened. All her hope drained out of the soles of her feet. Slowly raising her head, Christy glanced up at Todd. His face was turned to the open window, and she could see him swallowing several times.

"You know," Todd said after a full minute of only the consistent sound of the railroad tracks thundering in their ears. "I think I'd like to talk about this later, if that's okay with you."

Christy couldn't stop the tears that sprang to her eyes. "Okay," she managed to say.

Several people were coming down the passageway, forcing Todd and Christy to move out of the narrow aisle.

"Maybe we should go back to where Katie and Marcos are," Christy suggested, lifting her bag.

"Okay," Todd said.

Each step Christy took through the train became heavier than the last. Her mind raced through her options. Once they reached Naples, she could take a night train back to Basel and be there by morning. Back to her safe dorm room. Back to her routine and everything that was familiar. She could pour herself into the children at the orphanage. They needed her and wanted her. Why stay with Todd and Katie if they neither wanted her nor needed her?

Her stomach twisted in a huge knot. *All these years for what, God? Was this whole relationship with Todd a big joke on me? A testing of my emotions? Well, I failed, didn't I? I seem to be doing that a lot lately.*

As the train slowed, more passengers and their luggage crowded into the narrow aisles. They soon became so clogged it was impossible to move. That's how Christy felt inside, too. Stuck. Uncomfortably waiting for the inevitable.

When the train came to a stop and the doors opened, the crush of people pushed Christy out onto the platform. She stepped away from the stream of noisy travelers. Todd was right beside her. Neither of them spoke as they watched for Marcos and Katie. The mass of people moved past them, and the two of them waited, still not seeing their friends.

"Do you think they got off before us and went straight out to the bus?" Christy asked.

"We can go see." Todd headed for the exit. His voice sounded flat and low.

Is he hurting over this as much as I am? We have to talk! This is too painful.

Todd found the bus to the harbor, and they looked all around for Katie. The driver indicated that if they wanted to go, they had to board the bus now or wait for the next one.

"I wonder if she got on an earlier bus?" Christy said. "What should we do?"

"She might have thought we went on to the harbor," Todd said. "Let's take this bus."

They rode to the harbor standing on the crowded vehicle, neither of them looking at the other or talking. Christy kept looking out the windows, expecting to see Katie running after the bus, waving and yelling.

But at the harbor there still was no Katie or Marcos.

"Should we go back to the train station?" Christy asked.

"We could end up passing each other on the way," Todd said. "I think we better stay here and wait. She's with Marcos. He'll make sure she's okay. It's possible he sent her on to Capri. She might be on her way to the hotel already. I'm going to get something to eat. Are you hungry?"

Christy couldn't imagine how Todd could be hungry in the midst of all this emotional tension. Her stomach was aching, but she guessed it was from emotions, not lack of food.

They waited in line at a pizzeria while the city's deafening noises roared all around them. From the street came the continual honking of car horns, the squealing of old brakes on city buses, and noisy hordes of people walking along, many of them using their hands as they talked.

Christy kept watching for Katie. When Christy got up to the window, she felt like her stomach was in too many knots to eat. But she was learning on this trip that it was best to take food whenever it was available.

Their pizza slices came wrapped in newspaper, and the extra gooey mozzarella cheese stuck to the cheap paper. They found a corner of cement that was in view of the bus stop yet away from the main flow of pedestrian traffic. Taking off their packs and using them as seats, Todd and Christy quietly ate their pizza and watched for Katie.

"Did you hear Marcos talking about this cheese on the train?" Todd asked.

Christy shook her head. She didn't remember any such discussion. Her thoughts had been and still were absorbed in what she was feeling.

"Marcos said the food in southern Italy is best, and the cheese here comes from buffalo milk."

"Was he serious?" Christy asked, quite certain she didn't feel hungry now.

Todd nodded and chomped into his second slice. "It's good, isn't it?" He didn't sound enthusiastic when he said it, but as if he was trying to come up with small talk to keep them from having the conversation they really needed to have.

"What should we do if we don't find Katie?" Christy asked, making her own contribution to changing the subject from the obvious one that hung over them.

"I'll go check at the booth over there where we're supposed to buy the tickets for the hydrofoil. Maybe they'll remember seeing a redhead going through the line." Todd stood up. "Will you be okay here?"

"Sure."

Christy didn't feel okay. She didn't want Todd to leave her. Ever. Watching him walk away from her made her ache in a symbolic way. When she had watched Doug walk away after their breakup talk in England, she had felt strangely content. She remembered feeling confident that she had done the right thing. She didn't feel that way at all about letting Todd go.

But then, we haven't exactly had our breakup conversation yet, have we? It's not really over yet.

As Christy watched the mobs of people move past her, she noticed a man in tattered clothes approaching, mumbling something in Italian.

She was not in the mood to deal with beggars and got up, determined to walk away, even though it meant carrying her pack and Todd's, which he had left with her.

"Hey!" Todd called to her as she was hoisting his heavier pack onto her back. "Christy, let's go!" He ran toward her and grabbed her bag. "The last hydrofoil for Capri already left. We missed it. We have to run to catch the boat that's leaving right now. Come on!"

CHAPTER 8

"What about Katie?" Christy yelled at Todd as they dashed to the boat.

Todd jogged ahead of her and let out a shrill whistle to keep the gang-plank from being pulled away from the large passenger ferry. The uniformed employee looked irritated as Todd waved their tickets at him and ran onto the boat with Christy right behind him.

"That was close," Todd said, entering the enclosed passenger seating area.

Christy, who was right behind him, caught her breath. "Do you think Katie might be on board this boat?"

"She might. I'm guessing we missed her in the crowds, and she caught the hydrofoil. Maybe Marcos went on to the hotel with her."

Christy thought about how Katie, Todd, and Antonio had gotten "a little lost" on their hike a few days earlier, and she felt less than confident that Katie would be waiting for them at the hotel.

"I'll walk around the deck to see if I can find her," Christy said.

"Okay, I'll stay here and watch our stuff. It looks like a seat is back there by the window."

Christy didn't expect Todd to walk around the large ferry with her, especially since it meant they would have to lug their packs if they both went. But it still made her feel alone when he sat down in the very last row, with their bags taking up the narrow space next to him.

Christy physically ached as she stepped out onto the deck in search of Katie. The longer she and Todd avoided having their big conversation about breaking up, the larger her ache grew.

Katie was nowhere to be found.

Instead of going back inside to tell Todd, Christy found a bench that was blocked from the wind. She sat with her arms wrapped around herself, as much for comfort as for warmth.

The lights of Naples were coming on all along the large bay they had just left. Tall cliffs, studded with villas and ancient monasteries, rose from behind Naples. The demanding form of Mount Vesuvius towered to the south. Even in her numbed state, Christy remembered Marcos talking about Vesuvius and saying they should visit Pompeii, the ancient Roman city that was destroyed by the now-sleeping volcano.

From this distance, Christy thought the volcano looked harmless. The crescent-shaped bay of Naples appeared to be a magical fairyland, twinkling in the fading light of the late spring evening. None of the traffic, drunken beggars, or street confusion could be viewed from this distance.

A clear, intense memory came to Christy. On her sixteenth birthday, Rick had called from somewhere in Italy. Right here in Naples, perhaps? Or from Capri? Christy and her family had gone to a luau, she had opened her presents, and then she and Todd had sat alone on the balcony lanai of her uncle's Hawaiian condo, watching the moon shimmering on the Pacific Ocean. Christy remembered the way Todd had sat beside her that night, holding her hand, rubbing his thumb over the Forever bracelet. He had told her to look out at the island of Molokai.

Instead of thousands of lights, like the ones she was now watching come alive in Naples, two lights from Molokai twinkled at them like stars, right next to each other on the shoreline. Todd had given Christy one of his famous object lessons that night. He said that just by looking at the lights from a distance, you couldn't tell which one you wanted to go to. You had to get closer and closer until you could see clearly what was there. Then you could decide if what you saw was what you really wanted.

An overwhelming sense of grief came over Christy. *All this time Todd has been getting closer and closer to me, and now that he's close enough to see what I'm really like, he knows I'm not what he wants.*

She couldn't sit there another moment with the lights of Naples wink-ing at her, mocking her for being such a dreamer and for believing that she and Todd would go on forever. She rose and made another round of the deck with deliberate, long-legged strides until she came to a portion of the railing where no other people were around.

A taunting voice in her head dared her to rip off her gold bracelet and heave it into the sea. Better for her to do it now than for Todd's fingers to unfasten it later. Numbly unclasping the bracelet's catch, Christy held it in her fist and stared at the dark water.

She knew that the "Forever" on the bracelet meant far more to her than being Todd's friend forever. The "Forever" also represented her com-mitment to God. When Christy gave her heart to the Lord five years ago, she had told God that her promise wasn't just for the summer, but that it would last. It was a forever promise. A promise that she would trust God always and love Him more than anyone or anything.

Tears fell on Christy's closed fist as the wind whipped her hair, pull-ing long strands out from her loose braid. She shivered in the strong sea wind.

I've failed again, haven't I, Father? I'm not trusting you with all my heart. I'm not loving you more than anything or anyone. I'm all wrapped up in myself, my feelings, my needs, my wants. I'm sorry. Change my heart. I surrender everything to you, God.

Christy suddenly felt a warm breeze, as if the boat had hit a warm pocket of air. But it didn't come up from the Mediterranean Sea. It felt as if it came from behind her. Christy turned. No one was there. No giant heater pointed in her direction, yet the warm air still poured over her, calming her.

She was about to turn her attention back to the sea and finish her prayer when she noticed Todd. He was seated inside the ferry, next to the window, not more than ten feet away. She hadn't realized when she walked around the deck that she had ended up in his view.

But Todd wasn't looking at her. As she studied him more closely, Christy could see that his eyes were squeezed shut, his chin was tilted heavenward, and his lips were moving rapidly.

He's praying, too.

Christy watched Todd for a few moments, still caught in the soothing pocket of warm air. She opened her hand and peered at the gold ID bracelet that lay in her fist.

I meant it, Lord. My promise to you is forever. I want what you want for my life. If you want Todd and me to be together, I'll be grateful. If you want us to go our separate ways, I'll still be grateful. And I mean that. I trust you, Lord. I love you first, above all else. The future is in your hands, not mine.

The aching in the pit of her stomach seemed to ease up. She found she was breathing more deeply, and she noticed her jaw hurt from clenching her teeth for so long.

Here we are, just two tiny people lost in all our complex emotions, and yet you see us. You care. You're here. I know you're here. I feel you're so close right now, God. It's almost as if I can feel you breathing on me. Keep breathing on me, God.

Just then the boat rolled forward, as if it had gone over a speed bump in the water. Christy lost her balance and started to fall. Then her gold ID bracelet flew out of her open hand.

"No!" Christy screamed, lunging forward. She came down on the deck on both knees, her head down. As the bracelet slid toward the edge of the deck, the wind whipped Christy's hair madly, and for a moment she couldn't see. Pushing her hair away from her eyes, she frantically scanned the deck.

It was too late. Her bracelet was gone.

"Christy!" Todd's voice called to her. She turned and saw him coming toward her, lugging their gear. Todd dropped it all and knelt beside her. "Are you okay?"

Christy couldn't speak. She couldn't cry. She couldn't utter a sound. Todd waited, staring at her.

"I lost it," she finally managed to squeeze out of her tightened throat.

"Lost what?"

Christy pulled herself up from her precarious kneeling position and moved over to a bench seat along the back of the ferry. Several people had been watching her, but she didn't care. Todd didn't seem to care, either, because he pulled their gear over to the bench and sat down next to her, patiently waiting for her explanation.

"This is a very bad way for us to end." Christy's voice was shaking. "No matter what, I should have been more careful. I shouldn't have taken it off. I'm so sorry, Todd."

"What are you sorry for? I don't understand."

Christy turned and looked into Todd's eyes. They looked red, as if he had been crying, too.

"Todd," she began, trying to draw in a deep breath but finding it difficult. "Todd, I don't blame you for wanting to break up with me, but I should have been more careful with—"

"Wait!" Todd grasped her elbow. "What do you mean I want to break up with you? I don't want to break up with you."

"You don't?"

"No, of course not! I thought you were saying on the train that you wanted to break up with me! That's why I couldn't answer you right then. I didn't see it coming."

"No, Todd! No! I don't want us to break up. I thought—"

"You honestly don't?"

"No! I thought—"

Christy wasn't able to finish her sentence because Todd suddenly reached his arm around her shoulders, pulled her close, and silenced her with a kiss. When he slowly drew his scruffy chin away, Christy could barely breathe.

Todd looked at her. Then he laughed aloud and wrapped both his arms around her in a tight hug. As he let go, his hand smoothed her hair, stopping halfway down her back.

"Todd, you don't understand," Christy said. "I lost our Forever bracelet."

"No, you didn't."

"Yes, I did. It was really dumb. I was all emotional and I took it off, and I was going to throw it in the sea because I thought you wanted our relationship to end. But then I realized that the 'Forever' on the bracelet meant my relationship with the Lord as much as anything, and that part of my life will never end. No matter what. I started to pray, and then I saw you praying, and then the boat tipped and—"

Todd gave the end of her matted hair a little yank.

Christy interrupted her speech with a small "ouch" before finishing with "And I honestly wasn't going to throw the bracelet overboard in the end, but it slid off the deck, and I'm so sorry, Todd."

Todd just grinned at her.

"What? You think I'm a nut case, don't you?"

"No."

"Then why are you smiling?"

"Give me your hand."

Christy held out her right hand. Todd moved his arm that had been around her shoulder. With a wide grin he produced the gold ID bracelet in his hand and clasped it around Christy's wrist.

"Where was it?"

"Caught in your hair."

"You're kidding! I can't believe it."

"Believe it," Todd said. Then, taking both her hands in his, he leaned close. Looking into her eyes he said, "Also believe something else, Christy. Believe that I want our relationship to continue. I want us to grow closer to each other and closer to the Lord."

Christy silently nodded.

"Do you believe that, really?" Todd asked.

"I believe you," Christy said. "And do you believe that I want the same thing?"

"I do now," Todd said, drawing in a deep breath and letting go of Christy's hands. He put his arm across the back of the bench and drew her close to his side. "That's not what I was thinking the past few hours."

"I know," Christy said. "Me either. I've been bombarded with doubts all day long. I started thinking about how I'm not a very good camper, like Katie. And how this could be like the whole thing with Doug and Tracy, and I wondered why you would want to be stuck with wimpy me when someone more perfect for you was out there, like Katie."

"Katie?" Todd said, raising his eyebrows. He looked at Christy as if the thought of being interested in Katie had never entered his mind.

"Katie or someone else. I figured as you got to know me better and saw me so close up, you were realizing I wasn't a good match for you. It's like those lights on Molokai, when you said you have to wait until you get close enough to see them for what they are to know whether you want to go there or not."

Todd gave her a look that showed he was even more confused now. "Molokai?"

"Never mind. It's just that when Antonio's father asked about us at dinner, you didn't really answer him."

"And that's what got all your doubts started?"

"That and at the Basel train station, your saying you hadn't planned to kiss me."

Todd grinned. "Oh, I planned to kiss you, all right. I'd been planning that one for a long time. I thought you knew I was being sarcastic when I said that."

Christy looked at her hands, feeling ashamed for her reactions to everything.

"As for Antonio's house," Todd continued, "I thought that whole conversation might be making Katie feel bad."

"Katie? Why?" Christy looked up at Todd.

"Think about it. You know how she was interested in Antonio last year. And here we were, sitting in front of his parents, and they were telling Tonio he should propose to you. I thought all the attention on you might make Katie feel bad, so I tried to get them off the topic."

Christy leaned back and shook her head. "I didn't even think of that. You are so right, Todd. Man, when my eyes are turned on myself and all my feelings, I sure miss out on what's going on around me."

"Don't be too hard on yourself," Todd said. "You're not supposed to know everyone's thoughts and feelings every moment. Only God can do that. That's why His mercies are new every morning."

Christy smiled.

"As I see it, we all need a little fresh mercy every morning."

They felt the boat slowing as they entered the harbor at Anacapri. The sun had set while they had motored to the island, and now the world before them looked like Naples had from a distance, a fairyland of lights.

"Everything okay now?" Todd asked, gently smoothing back her hair with his hand.

Christy nodded and gave Todd a tender smile.

They rose and slung their packs over their shoulders. A shimmer of light from the harbor caught on her bracelet, and Christy, in her glowing mood, smiled and winked back at her bracelet.

You amazing little Forever bracelet, you. You have more lives than a cat!

"Do you remember the name of the hotel Marcos told us to go to?" Todd asked as they exited the boat side by side.

"It was Villa something," Christy said.

"We can ask at the harbor. They probably have some sort of information kiosk."

Christy and Todd moved with the rest of the crowd down the gangplank. A long line of taxi drivers stood outside their cars, reaching in to honk the horns and yelling at the new arrivals in several languages.

"Let's take a taxi," Todd suggested. "It'll save time."

They stopped at the first cab in the line only to realize there didn't seem to be any system to the taxi service. Several cabs already were pulling out of the line and taking off with customers.

"Can you take us to the Villa Hotel?" Todd asked once they were in the backseat with their luggage.

"Villa Nova, Villa Rialto, Villa Paradiso?" the driver asked with a thick accent.

"I think it was Paradiso," Christy said.

"Villa Paradiso?" he asked.

"Yes," Christy said. *"Sì."*

With a roar, their taxi pulled onto the narrow street. The driver yelled out the window at another cab driver, using aggressive hand gestures with his left hand and turning up the radio with his right hand. He appeared to be steering only with his knee.

Christy reached for Todd's hand, held it tight, and squeezed her eyes shut.

"Come on," Todd teased her, leaning over and whispering in her ear. "Didn't Tonio's driving prepare you for this?"

"If you want to live, don't bother me," Christy muttered. "I'm praying my little heart out for us both at the moment."

When the cab came to a screeching halt in front of a small café, Christy opened her eyes. "This looks like a restaurant. Where's the hotel?"

The driver took the money Todd paid him and, with lots of fast Italian words and pointing, seemed to communicate that the hotel was behind the café.

"Grazie," Christy said, sliding out of the backseat.

She and Todd ventured down a wide alleyway next to the small café. It was well lit and was marked by a tile sign with an arrow that read *Villa Paradiso*.

"Hey, cool!" Todd said when they reached the end of the alley. Before them rose an ornate garden with a large pool in the center. Violin music floated toward them from a white gazebo, where guests were seated at small tables. The guests were wearing evening clothes.

"I think the cab driver brought us to the back entrance," Christy said. "He probably took one look at us and knew we weren't the usual Villa Paradiso clientele. Do you think we should leave?"

"No," Todd said. "This is the only place Katie knows to meet us. Let's go around the block and enter the front of the hotel. Katie might be there already. Then we can find some place we can afford to stay in."

"I sure hope she's there," Christy said as they walked down the alley past the café. She drew in a wonderful aroma and realized she was very hungry. "What would you think of coming back here to eat after we find Katie?"

"Sure. Smells good, doesn't it?"

"Really good," Christy said.

They strolled uphill past small houses pressed right next to each other along the narrow street. A crazy chorus of night sounds spilled out of the open windows above them. Babies cried, televisions blared, mamas called out for their children to come inside. A cacophony of smells came to them, as well: garlic, hot olive oil, strong wine, and a hint of sweet almond.

Something profoundly clear seemed to be settling inside of Christy. She felt ready to let go of the doubts she had carried for so many years and calmly walk beside Todd, taking each step to whatever came next in their relationship. Along life's road, she decided, she wanted to be a good traveling companion, no matter how long or short the journey would be with Todd. She wanted to make each day, each moment, count.

Todd reached for her hand. He gave it a squeeze and said, "This is what I thought our trip would be like."

Christy smiled. "Me too. You and me, lugging our bulky backpacks up cobblestone streets, holding hands, and just being together."

"This feels right, doesn't it?" he said. "This fits. You. Me. Not trying to figure out tomorrow. Just experiencing the mercies God put into this day."

She suddenly felt it again, the canopy of peace. She and Todd were under that invisible canopy, and she knew she had been the one who had stepped out from under it.

"Let's not do that should-we-break-up stuff again, okay?" Todd said. "I don't think my heart can take it."

Christy gave his hand a squeeze. "Neither can mine."

Todd stopped walking. In the amber glow of the evening light, he turned to Christy and gazed deep into her eyes. "Promise?"

Christy smiled. "I promise."

They stood on the narrow, uneven street, holding hands and looking at each other as if they were both trying to memorize every detail. A balmy island breeze wrapped them in a private circle of quiet. All doubts flew from Christy's heart. She knew in that moment that she had changed. She was no longer a teenager, caught on an endless emotional roller coaster. She was a woman. And as a woman, somehow she knew that no matter what the future held, she would forever be in love with the man who now stood before her.

CHAPTER 9

Christy and Todd lingered only a few seconds in their private world before two women came around the corner and bustled past them. With their hands firmly clasped together, Todd said to Christy, "Come on, let's keep going."

Christy thought his words reflected their relationship as much as the private moment they had just shared under their invisible canopy. She felt ready to go on. Todd hadn't indicated that he viewed her or their relationship any differently than he had before the breakup question had driven a wedge between them. All she knew was that she was different. She loved Todd. Maybe he felt the same way about her. Maybe he didn't. Maybe he would have the same internal revelation soon—but maybe he never would.

Somehow none of that bothered Christy. It was enough to know that she loved Todd and, more important, that she fully trusted God with what would happen next in their relationship.

As they walked uphill hand in hand, Christy said, "I think I'm beginning to figure out a few things about myself."

"Oh?"

"I think I need to trust God more."

"Don't we all," Todd said.

They turned the corner and found themselves at the front of the large, salmon-pink hotel. The entrance wasn't especially huge or dramatic, but the intricate designs on the building's front made it look old, grand, and very expensive.

Christy scanned the front of the hotel for any sign of Katie. She wasn't there. They entered the lobby and treaded lightly across the rich burgundy- and gold-patterned carpet. Christy hoped Katie was sitting on one of the thick, upholstered chairs or couches, but she wasn't.

"Let's ask at the desk," Christy suggested. "Maybe she left a message."

"Or maybe she got here before us and got kicked out," Todd muttered. "Marcos didn't tell us this was a five-star hotel."

The uniformed desk clerk looked up at Todd and Christy with a smile that noticeably diminished when he took in their backpacks and casual clothes.

"Sorry. We have no vacancy."

How did he know we speak English? Do we look that much like typical Americans?

"That's okay," Todd said. "We don't want a room. We just wanted to check if any messages had been left for us."

The clerk looked at them impatiently. "If you do not have a room, we would not have kept a message for you."

Christy stepped in and tried to explain, giving him her best smile and making sure he noticed her eyes. That feature seemed to have helped her with other Italian men, and she figured it couldn't hurt this time. "We were supposed to meet our friend here. Katie Weldon. By any chance did she leave a message for Christy Miller?"

"No," he said with a flat expression, without even checking. Apparently Christy's eye color wasn't a novelty with this Italian.

"Grazie," Christy said, reverting to her limited Italian. "Molte grazie." Speaking Italian had scored points with Antonio's father but had no effect on the desk clerk. She smiled her best eye-sparkling smile at him one more time, then turned to leave. She figured they could go back out on the street to decide what to do next.

"One more question," Christy heard Todd say to the clerk. She turned around and noticed that a distinguished gentleman in a black tuxedo had joined the clerk behind the desk. She was afraid that it wouldn't matter what Todd said. By the looks on the two men's faces, Christy guessed she and Todd were about to be thrown out of the hotel.

Todd stood his ground and said, "Do you happen to know a guy named Marcos? We're here only because Marcos told us to come and to tell you that we know him. His father is Carlo Savini."

Both of the gentlemen froze.

Christy had a terrible feeling that she and Todd should start running for their lives.

The man in the tuxedo exclaimed, "Carlo? You know Marcos and Carlo Savini? Why did you not tell me you were friends of Carlo Savini?" He rushed around to the front of the hotel registration desk and kissed Christy on both cheeks. Then he grabbed Todd and kissed him on both cheeks, too. If Christy hadn't been so stunned, she would have burst out laughing at the expression on Todd's face.

"I am the manager of Villa Paradiso, Emilio Mondovo. How do you know Marcos?"

Todd explained the connection through Antonio, and Mr. Mondovo patted Todd on the back enthusiastically. "You are welcome here. You will be my personal guests." He turned to the desk clerk and said, "Put our guests in the Galleria Suite."

"We really didn't plan to stay here," Christy said.

"That's right," Todd agreed. "We thought a friend of ours might be here waiting for us."

The manager rattled off something in Italian and swatted the air in front of Todd's face. "You are my guests," he repeated aggressively in English. "You and your friend you are meeting here. You are all my personal guests. *Per favore.* Please. Stay."

Christy had the feeling this man would be offended if they didn't accept his offer. She also realized that the money she would spend at this hotel for one night would gobble up the entire amount she had budgeted for three weeks' worth of youth hostels. She gave Todd a desperate look, hoping he would know what to say next.

"We would be honored to stay in your hotel, sir," Todd said.

Christy felt like slugging him. *What are you thinking, Todd? We can't afford this place!*

"Giovanni here will check you in and call for assistance for your bags. Please call on me if you have any problems at all. You are my guests." The dramatic Mr. Mondovo stepped away from them to greet another guest who had just exited the elevator.

"Your key, sir," the clerk said. It was the same businesslike tone he had used with them a few minutes earlier when he said he had no vacancies.

"Thanks," Todd said, taking the key. "And for Christy?"

The clerk handed Christy a second key. It didn't have a room number on it. "What room am I in?"

"The Galleria Suite, miss."

"I thought you said Todd is in the Galleria."

"He is."

"Well, I need a separate room."

"That's right," Todd said. "I thought you understood that."

The desk clerk looked at them with a cold glare.

"And if you would be so kind," Christy said, leaning closer and lowering her voice, "could you give me one of your lower-priced rooms? I don't know how expensive the Galleria Suite is, but I'm on a limited budget."

"The Galleria Suite is the nicest room in the hotel."

Todd immediately put his key back on the counter. "Oh, well, then could you please give me one of your lower-priced rooms, as well? I'm on a tight budget, too."

The clerk appeared put out with Todd and Christy. He pushed the same keys back at them and stated with staccato words, "You are Signore Mondovo's personal guests. The room is *gratis*."

Christy and Todd looked at each other, still not understanding.

"Gratis," the clerk repeated. "No charge. Free. You are Signore's personal guests. Anything you wish in the hotel is yours."

Christy was so stunned her mouth dropped open.

"Cool" was all Todd said.

"Your keys," the clerk repeated, pointing to them. He rang a bell on the counter twice, and a young man in a burgundy uniform with gold braid around the arms immediately appeared and picked up Christy's pack. He offered to take Todd's bag, but Todd said he could take it himself.

The clerk then walked away from the desk as if dismissing Todd and Christy.

Todd picked up both keys and said to Christy, "Let's check it out. Then we can find Mr. Mondovo and explain that we need two rooms. I'm sure Katie will be here by the time we figure all this out."

Christy followed the bellhop to the elevator. He pushed a button, and they rode to the top floor. He then ushered them down a long, carpeted hallway to the door at the very end marked *Galleria Suite.*

Todd unlocked the door. Christy followed him in, and once again, her mouth dropped open as she took in the huge living room area with a brilliant golden chandelier hanging in the center. Straight ahead was a fireplace with an elaborate golden mantel. To the left were large windows covered with elegant gold brocade drapes. To the right were a huge entertainment center and a round dining room table.

The bellhop walked over to the curtains and opened them, displaying a view of the enchanting lights of the town below. A sliding-glass door opened to a balcony trimmed in salmon-pink wrought iron. He went to the door on the far left, opened it, and motioned for Christy to enter.

As she strolled through the door, she saw a huge bedroom with two large beds, a table, a couch, a television, and an adjoining bathroom with a sunken bathtub. She had never seen anything like this!

She returned to the living room area to find that the bellhop had opened another door on the far right side, past the bar. Todd was examining a separate bedroom as extravagant as the one Christy had just seen.

"Here you go," Todd said, pulling some money from his pocket to tip the bellhop. He refused to take Todd's money. "Enjoy," he said with a smile and then left.

For a full minute and a half, Christy and Todd stood in the opulent living room, staring at each other without saying a word.

Todd spoke first. With an overly calm, chin-up gesture, he said, "Cool."

Christy burst out laughing. "Cool? That's all you can say? Cool? Todd, this is unbelievable!" She did a little free-spirited gypsy dance and said, "Look at this place! Two separate rooms and everything! Katie is going to freak out when she gets here. Did you see the bathtub in my room?"

"And just who says that's your room?"

"Oh, you want to race me for it?"

Without answering, Todd took off sprinting across the room.

"No fair!" Christy squealed, dashing after him.

Todd arrived at the sunken tub first and said, "Cool!"

"You can't have it. This is my bathroom and my room. Did you even check out what kind of bathtub you have?"

Todd grinned again and said, "Race you!"

He took off first, but Christy was ready this time, and she almost tied with him.

"I only get a shower," Todd said, catching his breath.

"Look at this thing," Christy said, opening the double doors. The shower offered eight separate shower heads coming out of the tile at different heights.

"It looks like a compact car wash," Todd said. He reached in and turned the knob. They both laughed as the water squirted out in all directions.

"We better go find Katie," Christy said after Todd had turned off the shower and they had returned to the living room. "Do you think she got mixed up and ended up at one of those other 'villa' hotels the cab driver mentioned?"

"Good deduction work, Sherlock. Now tell me how we missed her."

"Did we take the last boat out of Naples?" Christy asked.

"No, we missed the last hydrofoil, but a couple more boats were scheduled for tonight. Or at least one."

Christy didn't feel very confident of Todd's calculations. "What should we do if she doesn't show up?"

"Eat," Todd suggested.

Christy had to laugh. "I should have guessed that would be a priority for you. Then what do we do?"

Todd headed for the door and opened it for Christy. "If Katie doesn't show up, I think we should figure out other arrangements for where we stay. It wouldn't be right for us to be in this suite, just the two of us."

Christy knew Todd was being wise and using good discernment, but she couldn't help feeling a twinge of disappointment. The suite was incredible. Staying there would be a treat. But Christy knew that being alone in such a place could easily awaken dreams that needed to stay asleep in innocent bliss. This would not be the right time to give those dreams a place to unfold.

"You're right," Christy said. "That's what we should do."

They exited the room and headed for the elevator.

"Do you have the room key?" Christy asked.

"Right here," Todd said, patting his pocket. "I hope they have fish at that café. Doesn't fish sound great right now?"

"I take it you didn't get enough while we were camping."

"I can never get enough fresh fish," Todd said as they reached the elevator and pushed the button.

"Or mangoes," Christy added.

Todd gave her a surprised look. "How did you know I like mangoes?"

"I take notes."

"You know," Todd said after they had stepped into the elevator and began going down, "that's what amazes me about you. You know me, Christy. You probably know me better than anyone else. Even better than my mom and dad. You know me, and yet you still want to be around me. That amazes me."

"I feel that way about you, too, Todd. That's what I was trying to say about the lights and Molokai. I keep thinking that the closer you get to me and the more you get to know me, you'll see what I'm really like. When that happens, I'm afraid you won't want to be around me anymore."

"No." Todd shook his head for emphasis. "It's not like that at all. The closer I get to you, the more you amaze me."

"But we're so different."

"Haven't you ever heard of opposites attracting? Besides, I don't think we're completely different. We're alike in a lot of ways. You're good for me, Christy. And I think I'm good for you."

As the elevator reached the lobby level, Christy did something she had thought of many times before but never had allowed herself to do. She leaned over and kissed Todd tenderly on his stubble-covered cheek.

Just then the elevator door opened, and before them stood Katie. Frazzled, red-in-the-face Katie.

"Oh well!" Katie exclaimed, holding up a hand for dramatic emphasis. "Don't let me interrupt anything between you two. I'll just go back to being lost for a few more hours."

CHAPTER 10

"Katie! What happened?" Christy exclaimed as she and Todd both rushed to hug their friend.

"Don't ask. You won't believe me when I tell you. Have you guys eaten yet? I'm starving."

"We were just on our way to a café we saw earlier," Christy said. "I'm so glad you're here. Are you okay?"

Katie nodded as Todd pulled her pack off her back.

"I'll take this up to our room for you, and then we can go get some food," he said.

Christy led Katie to a couch in the elegant lobby. Katie motioned toward the desk clerk and muttered, "That guy sure isn't going to win any awards for his love for Americanos. Even though I dragged it out of him that you two were registered here, he wasn't real thrilled about letting me join you. Didn't you tell him I was coming?"

"Yes, he knew. Don't worry. It's all fine. Thanks to Marcos and his dad, all three of us are the honored guests of the hotel manager. We get to stay here for free."

"Free?" Katie spouted way too loudly.

Christy nodded, hoping Katie would lower her voice.

"Awesome! What a God-thing! Good ol' Marcos!"

"I know," Christy said. "Good ol' Marcos."

"Hey, I'm sorry I said all those things this morning about your flirting with him. By the way, what was going on with you and Todd?"

"What do you mean?"

"I saw you two snuggling and kissing in the elevator. That's a little more, shall I say, 'expressive' than you two usually are. What did I miss?"

Christy nodded, feeling shy about divulging any of the details. "We had a couple of good talks. I had misunderstood a few things."

"Oh, like that has never happened with you before," Katie said. "What was it this time?"

In years past Christy had told Katie almost everything. But Christy didn't want to share all the details from her latest roller-coaster ride over Todd. She wanted her exchange with him to be between just the two of them, especially since part of Christy's inaccurate imaginings had involved Todd's being interested in Katie.

"It was nothing, really. I realized I need to stop trying to have everything in life figured out. I need to trust God more and not always be worried about having a plan."

"Yeah, well, I've certainly changed my opinion about having a plan on this trip," Katie said, stretching out her legs. "Plans are our friends. I'm telling you, I am a reformed traveler, Christy. If we hadn't had a plan to meet up here, I don't know where I'd be right now."

"What happened? How did we miss you at the train station?"

Todd arrived in the lobby just then, so Katie waited until the three of them were seated at the café and had ordered before jumping into her crazy story. She described, with great detail, how she had decided to use the rest room on the train right before they pulled into the Naples station. She had leaned her large backpack outside the door of the bathroom stall, and when the train came to a stop, her backpack fell against the door, locking Katie in the stall.

Christy tried not to laugh too hard. "What did you do?"

"I yelled and pounded until poor Marcos had to come into the women's rest room to let me out."

"We thought you got off the train before we did and that you went straight to the first bus and took off," Christy said.

"Hardly! Marcos and I barely jumped off the train before it pulled out of the station. He took me to the bus stop and waited with me for the next bus. Then a huge car accident happened about a block away. It was awful!

You could hear the metal as it crunched. Marcos went down there, and when he came back he said no one was hurt. But it took forever to clear the road so the bus could get through. I think I caught the last boat out of Naples. Marcos wrote down the name of the hotel and gave me his home phone number, too. He was really great about watching out for me."

"I'm glad you got here okay," Christy said.

"Well, I hate to admit it, but you were right, Christy. We did need a plan. I'm glad we did, otherwise I don't know what would have happened. Marcos is going to meet us tomorrow in Rome. He wrote down all the information. Like I told you, I'm a reformed traveler. From now on, we stick together, and we always have a plan."

Christy smiled at her friend, but her smile wasn't prompted just by Katie's admission that Christy was right. She was smiling because Todd had reached his arm around the back of her chair and was fingering the end of her hair. She was thinking of how far their relationship had come in this one very long day.

She was still thinking about it after Katie had fallen asleep in their luxurious bedroom. Katie had gone crazy over the free, first-class accommodations. She treated herself to a bath and crawled into bed still commenting on every gorgeous detail of their room. Sleep found Katie when she was in mid-sentence and took her away someplace very quiet.

Christy lay in the silence, smiling. She tiptoed over to the window for one last glimpse at the sky on this enchanted evening. Curling up in the chair next to the large picture window, Christy tucked her bare feet under her and wished she had a new diary so she could record all her feelings about being a woman and knowing she was in love with Todd. She leaned back and gazed into the heavens.

What an amazing night, Father! All those stars! It looks like you embroidered a thousand twinkling diamonds to the velvet train of midnight's sweeping cape.

She thought of when she was on the boat and God had felt so close that she could feel His breath. *Sweep over me, God. Breathe on me. I always want to feel as close to you as I do right now. And I always want to trust you completely.*

Christy closed her eyes and fell asleep in the chair. She woke sometime later with a stiff neck and cold feet. Padding back to bed, she slept and dreamed deep, luxurious dreams.

The next morning, Katie woke early. Christy could hear her on the phone trying to order eggs and Italian sausage for breakfast. When Katie noticed that Christy had her eyes open, she said, "Do you want the same thing?"

"Sure. Tell them to bring three orders. I'm sure Todd will want to eat, too."

They rose and dressed, still in awe of their glorious surroundings. Todd was the one who answered the knock on the door when room service arrived. He was dressed, packed, and ready to embrace the new day.

Christy ate the huge breakfast too fast and felt her stomach doing flip-flops as they arrived at the Marina Grande and boarded a motorboat that took them to the entrance of the Blue Grotto. They were instructed to transfer two at a time into small, narrow rowboats that would enter the cavern. A guide wearing a blue-and-white-striped shirt manned each boat. The men also wore straw hats with blue ribbons hanging down the back.

Christy could tell this was all daily tourist business for them. But as she stepped into the boat and settled herself in front of Todd, she felt as if she was about to experience a dream come true. For some reason, the Blue Grotto represented the end of the world to Christy. She thought of it as the ultimate I've-been-someplace-rare-and-exotic-and-now-I-measure-my-life-with-a-different-ruler experience. She didn't know exactly why this remote corner of the world had come to represent so much to her, but she was ready to have her horizons expanded. Leaning back against Todd's chest and ducking as the guide paddled their boat through a small opening in the rock, Christy felt tingles on the back of her neck.

After a moment, her eyes adjusted from the brightness of the morning they had just exited to the muted light of the grotto. The guide paddled them to the center, giving them the dimensions in English, German, and Italian. Christy caught that the cavern was almost one hundred feet high and about fifty feet wide. But she didn't care for any more details after that. All she wanted to see was the water, the clear blue-green water that caught its light from refracted sunshine as it poured itself on the ocean and slipped under the rocky overhang.

Christy squinted at the wonder around her. The light really did seem to rise up from underneath them, from the water itself, illuminating this cave that otherwise would have been deathly dark.

"It's like my life," Christy whispered to Todd.

"Like your eyes? Yeah, that's what I've heard."

"No, like my life. It's like the way God's light shines in the dark places of my life, and He makes it come alive."

Todd wrapped his arms around her and put his lips right beside her ear. "And that's what I see in your eyes. I see His light shining through you."

Christy's heart soared.

Their guide tilted his chin to the roof of the grotto, and in a rich, reverberating voice he sang, *"O Solo Mio."*

They spent less than five minutes inside the Blue Grotto. By 10:30 the three of them were on the modern hydrofoil jetting their way back to Naples, where they would catch a train at noon so they could meet Marcos in Rome at two.

Katie remarked again about how unmonumental the Blue Grotto was in her opinion. "I still can't believe we came all this way just to duck into some little cave and listen to a fat guy in a straw hat sing to us. We should have stayed in Rome with Marcos."

Christy didn't respond. She was still smiling. And still feeling euphoric over her experience in the Grotta Azzurra. Not even Katie's sarcasm could spoil the event.

In every part of her being, Christy felt as if she had connected with God in a deeper way during the past twenty-four hours. She felt as if she had stepped into womanhood with both feet. God held the "tour book plan" for her future, and she was ready and eager for whatever happened next.

What happened next was Rome.

After an uneventful forty-minute ride on the hydrofoil and a smooth train ride from Naples to Rome in first class, Christy, Todd, and Katie made their way through the gigantic, ornate train station in Rome and caught a taxi to the hotel where Marcos told them to meet him. Even though the front of the hotel was unassuming, Christy suspected it offered five-star lodging like the Villa Paradiso.

"Is it just me," Katie asked as they entered the lobby, "or is anyone else beginning to guess that Marcos's family has a little more money than Antonio's?"

"I hope Marcos and his dad are buddies with the manager of this hotel, or we're going to spend a whole lot of money tonight," Christy said.

"We don't have to stay here," Todd said. "We can find the youth hostel and stay there."

Christy was thinking about how nice it would be to stay in a fancy hotel again. They could stay on cots in a youth hostel anytime. Before they could discuss their options, Marcos came toward them, looking dashing in a dark business suit with his hair combed straight back.

"Boy, do I feel like a bunch of fish guts the 'baboons' dragged in," Katie said under her breath.

"Ciao!" Marcos greeted them, kissing the girls on the cheek and shaking hands with Todd. "You are here! This is good. I have finished my lunch meeting. Your timing is *perfecto*. I have one small problem, though."

"You're embarrassed to be seen in public with us," Katie quipped.

Marcos looked surprised at her comment. "No, of course not. My problem is that I must return to Venezia tonight. I can only show you around Roma for a few hours."

"That's okay," Katie said. "We'll take what we can get. Where do we go first?"

"Would you like to leave your luggage at the hotel?"

"We haven't checked in anywhere yet," Todd said.

"And I can tell you this place is a little over our budget," Katie added.

"Then at least leave your luggage here with mine," Marcos said, motioning to the bellhop.

Christy knew then that no more soaks in sunken bathtubs were in her near future. Their luggage could stay at the hotel for free, but they couldn't.

Back in a taxi they went. Marcos directed the driver, and they darted about like a drunken hornet through unbelievable traffic. Hundreds of noisy motor scooters zipped in and out around the cars as if they were in a race with death through a gauntlet of motor vehicles. The noise was deafening.

Christy closed her eyes. She didn't want to see how they were getting across town. All she cared about was arriving in one piece—preferably still breathing. Marcos pointed out fountains and statues, and Christy only opened her eyes long enough to catch a glimpse of each before squeezing her eyes shut again.

The taxi came to an abrupt stop, and they climbed out while Marcos paid. "Follow me." Marcos briskly led them past several small shops and cafés and up a wide set of stairs. At the top they saw a long line of people wrapped around one of the many gray stone buildings in the area.

"This way," Marcos said. He directed them past the long line of tourists at the building's front and took them around to the side. A guard, dressed in a purple-and-gold-striped uniform that was so colorful it looked like a Mardi Gras costume, stood at the side door. The guard recognized Marcos immediately. The two men greeted each other and spoke in rapid Italian.

"Where do you suppose we are?" Christy asked Katie.

"Like I would have any clue," Katie said. "Does any of this resemble pictures in your tour books?"

The guard motioned for them to come closer. He opened the side door with a key and greeted each of them heartily as they walked past him and into the ancient building.

"Welcome to the *Cappella Sistina*," Marcos said. "Come, I will take you to the room with the most famous painting."

"This is the Sistine Chapel?" Katie asked.

"Yes, Cappella Sistina."

They entered a main hallway, where a thick line of tourists shuffled forward. Most of them wore headsets and held brochures as they glanced at the paintings and statues on the walls. Christy noticed the spectacular tapestries that hung from the floor to the ceiling. She fell behind her friends when she stopped to admire a particularly striking wall hanging.

Katie turned and motioned for Christy to catch up. She hurried, and as soon as she reached Todd, she linked her fingers with his. "I can't believe we just got in here the way we did," she whispered to him. "This is the Sistine Chapel."

"I know. Cool."

Marcos stopped walking and motioned for them to look up. Above them on the ceiling was the famous Michelangelo painting of God's outstretched hand giving Adam the spark of life as their fingers touched. Seeing the actual ceiling of the Sistine Chapel didn't amaze Christy the way she thought it would. As a matter of fact, her neck got sore staring up at it while so many other tired, perspiring tourists bumped into her in the crowded area.

Christy heard a tourist with a British accent say to her companion, who apparently was her husband, "It says here Michelangelo started in 1508, and it took him only four years to paint this ten-thousand-square-foot ceiling. How long do you suppose it will take you to finish painting the kitchen?"

"Look, Christy," Todd said, pointing to another section of the large ceiling. "It's the story of the whole Bible."

Katie pulled out her camera and was about to snap a photo when a guard reached over to block her view with his hand. He spoke to her in French and then repeated his demand in English. "No flash photography."

"Sorry," Katie said, slipping her camera back into her day pack.

"Come," Marcos said. "If you want to take pictures I will take you to the top of the *Basilica di San Pietro*. I will show you the seven hills Roma is built on. Come. It is not far."

Christy had read a lot about this gigantic cathedral in Vatican City. Saint Peter's Basilica was one of the largest churches in the world and could hold one hundred thousand people.

They entered through the massive main entrance. Christy felt overwhelmed by the basilica's size and its ornate decor. Marcos took them first to the famous sculpture, the "Pieta." He told them that Michelangelo was only twenty-two years old when he sculpted this statue of Mary holding Christ after the Crucifixion. That bit of information seemed to stick with Todd.

Marcos walked them past the breathtaking altar and past a huge statue of Peter seated, holding the keys to the kingdom. Peter's left foot was positioned forward from his right foot on the five-foot-high, thick base. Marcos told them to stand back and watch.

Soon a short woman with a dark scarf on her head approached the statue. She rose on her tiptoes and kissed Peter's marble foot. That's when

Christy noticed that Peter didn't have any toes on his left foot. She looked at Marcos with a surprised expression, indicating that now she knew why he had them stop to watch.

"For centuries people have kissed his foot," Marcos said. "And now it is rubbed smooth."

Katie wanted to see who else came up to kiss Peter's foot, but Marcos persuaded her to go on to the elevator that would take them part of the way to the top of the basilica's dome.

"He was only twenty-two," Todd mentioned again after they got off the stuffy elevator and climbed the endless winding stairs on their way to the top of the dome. "Can you imagine being able to direct all your talent and passion into something like that when you're our age?"

Christy only said, "Amazing, huh?" in response because she was beginning to feel light-headed. They had to tilt to the side as they climbed the rounded dome. The heat rose along with them. Even though the view of Rome was spectacular from the top, and all of them took as many photos as they wanted, Christy felt as if she couldn't appreciate it fully because all she could think about was finding something to drink.

The refreshment she was hoping for came after they took the subway to the Colosseum. Marcos directed them to a *gelato* cart across the street. Christy soon discovered that gelato was the best ice cream she had ever tasted. It came in cups, filled by a metal spatula instead of a scoop. Her two flavors of choice were strawberry and chocolate, which tasted especially good together.

"We will take a quick tour of the Colosseum, and then I will go to the station," Marcos said.

Todd had been studying a small sign near where they were standing. "Hey, check it out. This was a prison. The Mamertine Prison. It says Paul was held prisoner here."

The prison was almost level with the sidewalk and appeared to be a maze of subterranean prison cells.

"Do you suppose Paul wrote his prison letters from this cell?" Todd asked.

Marcos shrugged. "It is possible."

Christy noticed that Todd's eyes had lit up with wonder over what appeared to her to be an insignificant discovery. He looked at her and said, "Can you imagine? Paul could have written his letters to the Philippians while looking out this very window."

Todd and Christy had a special verse from that book of the Bible. He had written Philippians 1:7 on a coconut years ago and mailed it to her from Hawaii. She still had the coconut in a box at home. The verse simply said, "I hold you in my heart."

Christy stood next to Todd and stared at the gray rock structure with the narrow slit for a window. "Do you think Paul was actually sitting in there when he wrote, 'I hold you in my heart'?" Christy asked.

"Possibly," Todd said.

Christy felt the hair stand up on her arms. She shivered at the thought of Paul's writing such beautiful words while in such a dismal place. "That astounds me," she told Todd. "I mean, it isn't as if I had pictured Paul writing all those letters in a hammock while sipping pineapple juice, but here? Right here?"

Todd held her gaze, equally amazed. "I know. It gives new meaning to Paul's New Testament letters, doesn't it? Paul knew what it meant to suffer for what he believed."

Christy couldn't shake the feeling that came over her as she looked into the dilapidated cell window with Todd. The taste of sweet strawberry and chocolate gelato lingered in her mouth, making a sharp contrast to the realization that many who walked these same streets centuries before had been persecuted for their Christian faith. Many had even been martyred.

They moved on to the Colosseum, which was massive, overwhelming, and fascinating. Yet Christy felt as if she couldn't take in any more sights or information. She stared down into the remains of the underground compartments beneath the Colosseum, taking pictures and listening to Marcos describe how the first-century Romans had kept the lions in those cells. She could see the ramps used to bring up the lions to face the gladiators.

"Weren't the lions set loose on the Christians, as well?" Todd asked. "I know I've heard about Christians being fed to the lions while Emperor Nero watched. Was that here?"

"It is possible," Marcos said. "They burned Christians alive on poles to light the garden parties for Nero."

"You're kidding!" Katie exclaimed. "That's awful! I can't believe civilized people would torture and kill other humans over their faith in God. It's barbaric."

"It still happens today," Todd said. He leaned against one of the stone pillars.

"Where?" Katie asked.

"All over the world. We just don't hear much about it. People are martyred all the time for putting their trust in Christ. There may come a point when we'll be challenged to take a stand. If that day comes, I want to know that my relationship with Christ is so solid I'd be willing to die for Him," Todd said.

Christy felt like sitting down. This was all too much for her. She had never seriously considered the possibility that one day she might have to make such a choice. Her eyes swept across the Colosseum's vast ruins.

What she saw with her mind's eye wasn't the Hollywood glamour of a Ben Hur-style chariot race. As deeply as the light of the Blue Grotto had pierced her soul that morning, an image came alive inside her mind under the pounding afternoon sun. She saw the rows and rows of Colosseum seats that now circled her filled with a wild, cheering crowd. Starving lions were about to be let loose. All she had to do was denounce Christ and she could go free. If she remained steadfast in her commitment to the Lord, the lions would maul her.

Oh, Father God, with all my heart I hope I would be true to you in such a situation!

CHAPTER 11

In the cab on their way back to the hotel, Todd and Marcos discussed what they believed about Christianity. Christy had her eyes closed again to avoid seeing all the near-accidents their driver barely skirted around. She also was glad to avoid the heavy discussion. Her head and heart felt overwhelmed with all that she had seen that day.

"But that's not enough." Christy listened to Katie as she jumped into the discussion with Marcos. "You can't just be a good person and try to live a good life and think God will let you into heaven. Have you ever heard that verse in Romans 10:9? That if you confess with your mouth Jesus is Lord, and believe in your heart that God raised him from the dead, you will be saved."

"Romans?" Marcos questioned.

"Oh yeah, Romans! Hey, cool!" Katie said. "I didn't realize it until this minute. The book of Romans was written to the people that lived in this very city! That is so amazing!"

"This is in the Holy Bible?" Marcos asked.

"Yeah," Katie said. "There's a whole book written just for the Italians."

Christy smiled. The coincidence of Katie's choosing to quote Romans while they were in Rome was definitely a God-thing.

"No one can get to heaven on their own efforts," Katie continued. "It says that in the book of Romans, too. 'All have sinned and fall short of the glory of God.' And what's that other verse in Romans about the gift of God?"

"Romans 6:23," Todd said. " 'For the wages of sin is death, but the gift of God is eternal life in Christ Jesus our Lord.' "

"See?" Katie said. "We can't earn eternal life. It's a free gift from God. But we have to accept it. We can't earn it."

Christy wondered if Marcos thought Katie was coming on too strong. But Christy also understood how impossible it was to have been confronted with everything they had seen in the last few hours and not be passionate about one's faith.

"Doesn't God love everyone?" Marcos asked.

"Yes," Todd answered.

"Then good people have nothing to worry about. God will let them into His heaven," Marcos concluded.

"It doesn't work that way," Todd said. "You know what it's like? It's like when we went to the Villa Paradiso. On our own, they would never have let us in just because we were good people. But when we mentioned your name and your father's name, we were welcomed with open arms. All the riches of the hotel were ours for free."

Christy opened her eyes, stunned at the perfect example Todd had just given. Surely that made sense to Marcos.

Marcos was sitting in the cab's front seat and had turned around to talk with Todd. "It helps to know the right people in high places," Marcos said with a grin.

"Exactly. It's the same way with eternity," Todd responded. "It's not what we do, it's who we know. We knew you and that opened the door to the Villa Paradiso. Knowing Christ opens the door to the eternal paradise."

"Antonio has tried to convince me of this, as well," Marcos said. "He told me I must have a relationship with Christ. It is different from how I was taught all my life. I must tell you, though, I see something more in Antonio's life since he has come back from California."

"That 'something' is really 'Someone,' " Katie said.

Just then the taxi stopped in front of the hotel, and the four of them got out. This time Todd insisted on paying for their ride. "It's a free gift from me," Todd said, giving Marcos a friendly, chin-up gesture. "Just accept it, man."

Christy knew Todd's words had a double meaning and wondered if Marcos caught it, as well. They went into the fancy hotel, retrieved their luggage, and walked back out to the street to say their good-byes.

Christy felt sad as she received Marcos's parting kiss on her cheek. With Antonio she could say good-bye more easily, knowing she would see him again in heaven, if not before. With Marcos, this might be the last time she ever saw him, in this life or in eternity.

Christy looked into his handsome face. She remembered how Katie had persuaded Marcos to go to Naples with them, and with a charming grin equal to Katie's, she said, "Marcos, I want you to come to heaven with us. It won't be the same without you. Please surrender your life to Christ."

He looked surprised at her oddly worded farewell. "You have me thinking. Antonio gave me a Holy Bible. Maybe I will read this part for the Italians."

Christy stood on her tiptoes and kissed him lightly on the cheek. *"Buona,"* she said because she was pretty sure that meant "good" in Italian.

Marcos smiled. He stepped into a cab and waved as it lurched into the traffic, heading for the train station.

"And now are you going to tell me that was supposed to be a 'holy kiss,' Miss 'Christiana'?" Katie teased.

"Yes, it was." Christy thought for only a moment how different it was to kiss Marcos's smooth-shaven cheek compared to Todd's prickly face. But the comparison went nowhere else in her imagination. In every way, to Christy the kiss was pure and holy.

Then, because she couldn't resist, she said, "When in Rome, do as the Romans do."

Todd laughed. Katie only shook her head. "Can I just say that I've noticed you've certainly become the little kissing bug since you've moved to Europe?"

"You don't see me complaining," Todd said with a grin still on his face.

"Okay, let's drop the kissing talk," Katie said. "I'm getting depressed being around you two happy hearts. Let's find a place to dump this luggage."

"Where's your tour book, Christy?" Todd asked. "Does it list places to stay?"

Christy reached inside her day pack and said, "Shouldn't we at least go down the block a little? I feel kind of tacky standing in front of a hotel looking for a cheap place to stay."

"Nobody knows that's what we're doing," Katie said. "I feel safer standing here than in the middle of the street with our backpacks announcing to the whole world that we're tourists."

"Here," Christy said, handing the book to Todd. "You look it up. My brain is fried."

Todd suggested a *pensione* he saw listed in the book. He said it was a house that rented out rooms, like an American bed-and-breakfast. The best feature was the low price and the closeness to where they stood at the moment.

Walking six blocks in the early evening heat, they found the pensione, only to be told no rooms were available. Undaunted, Todd consulted the tour book again as they stood against the side of a shop that sold leather jackets. The shop was closed, its windows barred shut.

"A youth hostel is listed here, but if I'm reading the map correctly, it's on the other side of town. We could take a cab."

Christy felt her teeth clenching at the thought of trusting her life to another Italian cab driver. "Isn't there anything else?" She took the book from Todd when he offered it and scanned the lodgings page. "I had another little book I should have brought because it was only about Italy, and it listed dozens of places to stay in each of the big cities." She tried hard not to place her frustration on Katie, who had said they didn't need tour books because they were on an "adventure."

"We could jump on a train and go to that 'frantic' city," Katie suggested.

Christy gave her a pained expression. "Do you mean Firenze? Florence?"

"Yeah. The frenzy place. I mean, tell me, what is there left to see here?"

"Lots," Christy said.

"Like what?"

Christy took off her backpack with exaggerated motions, as if she knew this would be a long discussion. "There is a lot of art, fountains, statues, and churches."

"That's what Marcos showed us all day. What's to see in Florence?"

"Fountains, statues, and churches," Todd said.

"Fountains and statues and churches, oh my!" Katie quipped, smiling at her joke as she took off her pack. "I don't think we're in Kansas anymore, Toto!"

Christy didn't laugh. She wanted to tell them again that this was why they needed to have a plan. How could they make decisions like this when they were all tired and hungry?

"Let's find a place to eat," Todd suggested. "We need to sit down and discuss all our options."

Fortunately, a pizzeria was only half a block away. The food was fast and delicious. The only drawback was they had to stand and eat at small, round tables with high legs. They were discovering it was popular in Italy to grab a quick plate of pasta or a slice of pizza and eat it standing up around tables that came up to Christy's elbows. The food helped, but the standing didn't make for a relaxed discussion.

"I think we should go on to Florence," Katie said. "Or Venice, or what about that leaning tower? Where did you say that was?"

"Pisa."

"Oh yeah. The Leaning Tower of Pisa. How could I forget? Where's Pisa?"

"North," Christy said flatly.

"North near Venice?"

"No, north but the opposite direction. It's actually closer to where we went camping."

"We should have gone to see it then."

Christy couldn't control her tongue another minute. With spicy breath from the pizza sauce, she said, "That's why I said we should have a plan.

If we just jump on a train and take off for Venice or Florence, we might miss something we really wanted to see."

"So what do you really want to see?" Katie asked.

Christy couldn't come up with a specific answer. She wanted to see everything.

"I'd like to see Pompeii," Todd said.

"Marcos was telling me about that place," Katie said. "How the whole city has been excavated, and you can walk around and see what happened after the volcano erupted and destroyed it. He said the volcanic ash actually preserved some of the people who were running to get away."

Christy had read about Pompeii in her other Italian tour book. It didn't sound appealing to her then, and it sounded even more depressing now. She didn't find herself fascinated with the same things that intrigued Todd and Katie.

"I'd like to go there, too," Katie said. "I know it's south, not far from Naples, because Marcos showed me Mount Vesuvius while we were waiting for a bus."

Christy remembered seeing Mount Vesuvius from the boat deck on their way to Capri. "That means we go back to where we were this morning. That would take two hours or more to get there, and then what? Find a place to stay in Naples or Pompeii?"

"I wouldn't want to stay in Naples," Katie said. "Marcos told me some stuff about that city. It's not the safest place for tourists."

"So we would stay in Pompeii?" Christy flipped through the tour book. It listed a whole page of interesting facts about Pompeii and how to get there, but it didn't list any lodgings.

"We could stay here and take a morning train," Todd suggested.

"But where? The youth hostel?"

They stood in the pizzeria for almost an hour, discussing all the possibilities. Their final decision was a surprise to Christy, and she couldn't figure out quite how they ended up agreeing on it. They would go to Oslo, Norway.

Instead of staying in Rome, they decided to catch a night train north. The logic that emerged from their lengthy discussion was that they would shoot straight up to Norway and spend the rest of their trip working their way down until they ended up back in Basel, Switzerland, by 8:00 Monday morning, June 27. That's when Christy's summer classes began. Todd and Katie's flight back to California left that afternoon from Zürich.

The part of their plan Christy liked the most was that the long train ride would give them plenty of time to talk and plan so that the remaining sixteen days of their journey would be thought out. She hated to admit it, but she was exhausted. Her stamina hadn't exactly been at a high point when they had started this trip, and their fast pace had worn her out. With a bittersweet twist, Christy wished they were still camping so she could curl up in the hammock or bathe in the stream and feel her senses come alive again. If they had stuck with Antonio's plan, this would have been their last night camping.

As they strapped on their packs and walked the sixteen blocks to the train station, Christy decided she was glad they hadn't stayed at the campground after all. She wouldn't have wanted to miss Capri or Rome for anything.

They stopped at a small shop that carried mostly magazines and cigarettes just inside the train station. Katie wanted to buy some candy bars, and Christy was curious to see if they sold any tour books in English.

She didn't find a tour book, but she did find a blank journal with a brown leather cover. Years ago her uncle Bob had given her a diary, and he had told her to write out all her thoughts and feelings on the diary's pages, trusting that it would become a good friend. His words had come true.

The night before Christy left for this adventure with Todd and Katie, she had written on the final page of her diary and had felt a strong sense of loss. For the first time in almost five years she didn't have a special place to record her heart's secrets. That diary had become a close friend.

She paid for the leather-bound journal, having no idea if the price was fair. *It sure would be helpful to have Tonio or Marcos around now.*

Christy studied the change the salesperson had placed in her hand. So many coins. To her surprise, the salesperson muttered something in Italian and placed three more coins in her hand.

Does he think I just figured out he shortchanged me? How funny! I don't have a clue how much I paid or how much I now hold in my hand.

She continued to hold the coins in her hand without turning away. For fun, Christy glanced up at the man and gave him an expression that said, "Shame on you for trying to cheat me."

This time he didn't mutter anything in Italian. He simply leaned over and handed her three more coins and two paper bills.

Still uncertain as to just how badly she had been treated, Christy decided to get while the going was good. She stuffed the money in her pocket and exited the small shop while trying to keep from bursting out laughing. Todd and Katie were waiting for her out front, and after Christy recounted the story to them, Katie said, "Hey, I think I'll go back in there, hold out my hand, and give him the evil eye. He probably overcharged me for these two candy bars."

"I don't know if it would work after you've already left the store," Todd pointed out.

"Let's go to that shop over there," Katie suggested, indicating another small store inside the train station. "It looks as if they sell food. I think we should pack ourselves a picnic."

"I'm all for that," Todd said. He was the first one in the shop.

As Christy watched, he selected several hard, round rolls; some small, oval-shaped tomatoes; and a triangle of white cheese. Christy was more interested in buying something to drink for the train. She found liter-sized bottles of water and bought three of them.

Katie purchased two more candy bars and stood at the register, examining with a critical eye the change she had been handed. The woman behind the counter appeared irritated at Katie and rattled off something in Italian, motioning for Katie to move so the next customer could pay.

"Guess I'll never know if she ripped me off or not," Katie said as they entered the main terminal. "You just have the right look, Christy."

"Okay, now we're getting organized." Todd walked over to the computerized schedule board and read the departure times. "This is the one we want. Roma to Venezia departing at 20:35 at platform . . ." He glanced at his watch. "Come on! We're going to have to run to catch it!"

Todd took off at a sprint, and Christy fell in line behind him. She glanced over her shoulder to make sure Katie was with them. As they jogged through the crowds, Christy felt her pack dig into her shoulders and hit her repeatedly on her hip. The spicy pizza in her stomach threatened to come up for another visit.

Despite all the discomfort, they made it to the train. And, thanks to Todd's quick thinking, they arrived in time to upgrade to first class at the ticket window. First class was packed. It seemed everyone was leaving Rome on this Friday night. Christy figured second class was even worse. They found two seats at the end of an aisle, which Katie and Christy took while Todd stood, studying the tour book.

The train rumbled out of the station, and Christy closed her eyes and tried to find a comfortable position. They were definitely on an adventure now, and they were also coming up with a plan. It seemed to her that both wishes were being fulfilled. She hoped that meant the next two weeks would be less stressful.

During the five-hour trip to Venice, Christy slept some, walked around some, and visited the rest room with Katie so Katie could demonstrate exactly how she managed to lock herself into the stall in Naples. Christy laughed at her crazy friend and thought how glad she was that they were getting along this well. Much of the earlier tension they both seemed to have struggled with had dissipated. Now Christy felt that the wide gap that had spread between them while she was in Switzerland was closing, and they were getting back to being the close buddies they had been for so many years.

About an hour before they arrived in Venice, Todd and Christy left Katie so they could sit across from each other in the dining car, sipping cappuccino and discussing plans. Todd had done some serious reading during the past few hours, and he now was a huge fan of Christy's travel guide. His eyes glimmered as he told Christy about the sights that lay before them in Scandinavia.

"And this Fredericksborg Castle in Denmark sounds pretty interesting," he said. "I know you like castles. It's only about half an hour from Copenhagen, so when we go through there, I thought that might be a place you would like to stop."

Christy smiled at Todd. "You remembered that I like castles."

"Hey, you remembered that I like mangoes. Maybe we've both been taking notes on each other for a long time without realizing it."

"I'd love to see at least one castle on this trip. More, if we can fit them into the schedule. What about you? What do you want to see? I doubt many mango trees will be along the way."

"There's this museum in Oslo." Todd pointed to a short paragraph in the tour book. "It says they have the original *Kon-Tiki* on display there."

Christy waited for an explanation. *"Kon-Tiki"* sounded Polynesian, which would explain why Todd, who had lived in Hawaii when he was young, would be interested. She just didn't know why a museum in Norway would have something Polynesian.

"It's Thor Heyerdahl's raft. He sailed it from Peru to the Easter Islands to prove that early civilization from South America could have found its way to the islands of the Pacific."

"Oh," Christy said. "And Thor was Norwegian, I take it."

Todd nodded. "I think Katie is going to want to see this." He pointed to the words *Lille Havfrue* in the tour book.

"What's that?"

"It's a statue of the *Little Mermaid* from the Hans Christian Andersen fairy tale."

"We'll definitely have to see that," Christy agreed. "This is going to be fun."

"It's already been fun." Todd reached across the table and gave a playful little tug on a strand of Christy's hair that hung over her shoulder. "It'll only get better."

With a smile at Todd that reflected all the delightful anticipation she held in her heart, Christy said, "I can't wait until tomorrow."

CHAPTER 12

At two in the morning, their train pulled into the Venice station. They grabbed their packs and headed through the ornate terminal, trying to find their connecting train north to Salzburg, Austria.

In the middle of the platform, Katie stopped and said, "You guys, we have to talk."

"We can talk on the next train," Christy said. "We have to make that connection to Salzburg."

"No, we need to talk now. I have to be honest with both of you about something."

Christy thought Katie was going to say she had felt left out during the past hour when Todd and Christy had gone to the dining car to sip their cappuccinos. Christy already was preparing her apology for excluding Katie and planning their transition to the next train, which left for Salzburg in forty minutes. If they were among the first on the train, Christy hoped they would be able to find better seats than they had had to settle for on the ride from Rome.

"I want to stay here," Katie said.

"Stay where?" Christy asked, looking around the platform.

"In Venice. The one thing I wanted to see was a gondola. Marcos lives here. He told me a lot about Venice. Remember? His dad has the jewelry store. I'd like to stay here for a day or two and then go on to Norway."

"Okay," Todd said. "We can do that."

Christy felt reluctant to agree. She wanted to see a gondola, too, but for the past hour, Todd had been telling her about Scandinavia, and now she had visions of castles and mermaids floating in her head.

"I know I should have said something sooner," Katie said. "I kept going back and forth in my mind, trying to decide if I was being a team player by bringing this up. I guess it just hit me when we stepped into the station. This might be the closest I'll ever be to a real gondola. I want to see one. I don't have to ride in one; I just want to see one."

"We'll need to find a place to stay," Todd said, turning and heading for the exit instead of for the track to board the train for Salzburg. "Let's ask at information. It's the middle of the night, so we'll have to take what we can get. Are you guys okay with that? It might be pretty expensive."

"I think it would be worth it for one night," Katie said. "Besides, we haven't had to pay for a single hotel yet. We have money to burn."

"I wouldn't go that far," Christy said.

"Or you know what?" Katie said. "We could call Marcos and see if we could stay with him for free."

"Doesn't that seem a little pushy?" Christy asked. "It's like we're following him. He left Rome on the six-o'clock train, and we followed him here on the eight-thirty train. That feels odd to me."

"Okay, we don't have to call him," Katie said. "We can find a place for tonight and then stop by his dad's jewelry store tomorrow. I'd like to see Marcos again."

Christy tried to evaluate what was going on. Was Katie's real passion for the elusive gondolas? Or was she attracted to Marcos the way she had been attracted to Antonio last summer? Their train ride to Venice was the first time only the three of them had been traveling, except when they went from Capri to Rome. Christy wondered if Katie had felt the loss of a counterpart when Todd and Christy went to the dining car. Maybe Katie didn't like the idea of being number three when Christy and Todd were a couple, and she was trying to delay the odd numbering by touring around with Marcos a few more days.

Todd took the adjustment to their plans in his easygoing stride. He suggested Katie and Christy wait with the luggage on a long, polished wooden bench in the center of the station while he did some research.

Christy tried to think of a delicate way to ask Katie about Marcos and if she was feeling brushed aside by Christy and Todd. But her mind grew foggier and foggier as she sat with the noises echoing off the high ceiling and reverberating inside her head. The cappuccino's caffeine seemed to wear off in a single, crashing moment, and Christy could barely keep her eyes open, let alone discuss Katie's psyche with her.

Christy was glad to see Todd returning. Once they were settled in a hotel, had slept a bit, and then ate a good breakfast, Christy thought she would feel a lot more optimistic about their sudden change of plans.

"I found a place we can stay," Todd said. "And it was no small task since it's the middle of the night. But they only accept cash. How much do both of you have?"

Katie, Christy, and Todd pooled their money and found that between the three of them they didn't have half the cash needed since the hotel was pretty expensive.

"Why won't they take traveler's checks?" Christy asked.

"Don't know. It's their hotel. They answered the phone. They get to set the rules, I guess."

"Isn't there a place here in the station where we can change our money?" Katie asked.

"I already tried that. They don't open until six in the morning. If we had a credit card or an ATM card, we could use the machine. Guess none of us thought of that ahead of time."

"So what you're saying is that we have to wait here until six, change some money, get ourselves into Venice by water taxi or whatever, and by around seven o'clock we can check into the hotel," Christy summarized.

"You got it," Todd said. "And check-out time is noon."

"I don't want to pay all that just for a place to sleep for five hours," Katie said.

"We could sleep on these benches," Christy suggested.

"Or take a train to Salzburg," Katie said in a low voice. "I'm so sorry, you guys. I messed everything up."

"No, you didn't."

"Yes, I did. We had a plan, and now we've missed the train, and we didn't make arrangements ahead of time for here so we can't do anything. We're stuck."

"I checked a couple of the train schedules," Todd said. "A train leaves at 8:02 for Salzburg. It has only one stop in Villach at noon and has a three-hour layover before it leaves for Salzburg. We would be in Salzburg by seven o'clock tomorrow night."

"That's all day on the train," Katie said. "Wasn't the night train we were going to take direct, without any stops?"

Todd nodded. "Yes, but we can't look back. We're here now. What do you guys want to do?"

"What time is it?" Christy wished she had a watch. Her old one had broken months ago, but she never had replaced it.

"It's 3:10."

"No wonder I feel as if I've been run over by a truck," Katie said. "I say let's get out of here."

"And go where?" Christy asked. "Roam the streets of Venice?"

"They don't have streets. They have canals, remember?" Katie said. "No, let's just get on the next train and take it wherever it goes."

"What about seeing a gondola?" Christy asked.

"Right now, I don't care. I made a bad decision when I insisted we stop and get off track after we had set up a schedule and everything. Let's go back to the schedule as much as we can. Only, can't we get to *Sound of Music* land without it taking all day?"

Todd consulted a small pamphlet of train schedules as Katie talked. "Because I'd kind of like to stop and see some of Salzburg. It's the only Austrian city I know anything about."

Christy added, "That's because you've seen *The Sound of Music* a hundred times." She thought of lyrics from one of that movie's songs, "How do you solve a problem like Maria?" and felt ready to sing her own version, "How do you solve a problem like Katie?"

"Looks like a ten-thirty train out of Innsbruck gets into Salzburg at two-thirty," Todd said. "We could find a place to stay and then look around Salzburg that afternoon."

"Does that mean we sleep here for the next two hours?" Christy asked.

Todd examined the four long benches placed back to back. "You know, I always wondered what a homeless person felt like. Now I'll get to find out."

Christy had never wondered such a thing. *Only you, Todd.*

Todd and Katie had no trouble catching some *Z*'s on the hard benches. Christy, on the other hand, couldn't fall asleep. She felt nervous about people walking by, seeing them asleep, and taking their gear, even though they had fastened their packs all together and anchored them to the benches. The train station wasn't full of people, but enough travelers were coming and going to make Christy nervous.

The more she thought about it, the more frustrated she became with Katie for the way she had thrown their plan off course. Christy tried to be understanding and forgiving. She reminded herself how everyone had been kind to her when she had melted down in the minivan on the camping trip. They all had agreed to alter their plans to accommodate her. She knew she wasn't being fair to begrudge Katie the same courtesy everyone had shown Christy.

Since she didn't want to get any more upset with Katie, Christy turned her thoughts toward Todd. Her scruffy-faced sweetheart lay curled up on the wooden bench across from hers, with the hood of his navy sweat shirt pulled over his head. Christy was amazed that he could clock out whenever he wanted to, although she knew she shouldn't be surprised. Over the years, Todd had managed to clock out emotionally at times when she was wide awake, so to speak, in her feelings for him. Or at least that's how it had seemed to her.

So what have we decided, Todd? We're not going to have any more should-we-break-up conversations, but where does that put us? Where we've always been? Friends? Close friends? Friends-forever kind of friends for another five years until your internal alarm clock goes off and you wake up to me? I'm here. I'm wide awake. I know I'm in love with you, and I always will be. I'm ready for more. Are you?

Christy closed her eyes and turned over on her side. She tried with all her might to force herself to go to sleep, physically and emotionally. Her efforts didn't meet with success. Instead, her thoughts wandered off to her family. She knew her parents had grown used to her calling home only about once a month and emailing a note every few weeks. As a matter of fact, she had talked to her mom for about twenty minutes the day before Todd and Katie had arrived, and her mom had told Christy again how she hoped Christy would have a great time on this trip. Maybe Christy should call her parents now. What time was it at home? Her mind was too tired to do the calculations.

And what exactly would she tell them? "Hi. We're sleeping on benches in the Venice train station, and we haven't exactly been eating balanced meals or managing to stay together all the time, but don't worry about anything. The trip is going great so far. The three of us are getting along just peachy"?

Christy knew she couldn't call them. Not now. Not when she didn't have a positive report. It wouldn't help to let them know details at this point, she decided. It would be better to call them at the end of the trip, after she was back in her dorm room and life was normal again.

Things will get better in Austria. They have to. Then I can send a postcard home, and nothing in my news will be false or strained.

The train ride to Innsbruck and then on to Salzburg turned out to be comfortable. Their compartment had pullout beds called *couchettes,* and Christy stretched out and slept deeply for the first four hours. When she woke, Todd said he had breakfast for her. It turned out to be one of his oval tomatoes, some cheese, and a hard roll. Christy ate it gratefully and shared her water with Todd and Katie.

They barely made it to the train that took them to Salzburg. But, once settled in, they found their window seats provided a fantastic view of some of the most spectacular scenery Christy had seen since she had been in Europe. It was much better than the view out of Tonio's van. This was the kind of experience she had hoped to have with Todd, and she scooted closer to him as they gazed out the window so they could comment on the dramatic mountain ranges that seemed to go on forever.

Katie was noticeably quiet by the time they arrived in Salzburg. They found a *Gasthof* that was recommended in the tour book and checked into two rooms. The friendly owner of the Austrian-style bed-and-breakfast told them that *Jause* would be served between 4:00 and 5:00. She explained that was a traditional coffee time. However, they were too hungry to wait and politely excused themselves to go find a full meal.

They left their heavy luggage, exchanged their money, and went off to see the sights. Christy wished they had taken time to shower and change before hitting the streets. She promised herself that a shower would feel even better that night when they returned.

Deciding on a restaurant they could all agree on turned out to be easy. Two blocks from the Gasthof they came to a large, open-air restaurant. It offered plenty of outside tables under umbrellas, allowing them to sit below an austere fortress on the top of a hill and watch the horse-drawn carriages promenade by on the cobblestone streets.

After they had eaten *Schnitzel* and discussed what to do next, Katie said, "We need to find the fountain where all the Von Trapp children danced and sang. I think it had statues of horses in it."

Todd consulted the tour book while Christy savored her cherry strudel dessert. She didn't feel the need to run and see and go and do. Salzburg seemed willing to strut by and show Christy plenty of her charms. A young couple strolled past the outdoor café walking a small, fluffy dog. The woman laughed a light, airy titter at something the man said, and Christy saw him wink at her.

Someday. Someday you and I will stroll side by side, Todd. And someday you'll wink at me like that.

Christy turned her attention to two women at a table next to them. As the women carried on an afternoon chat, she thought about how different the Austrian people were from the Italians. Here the local language around her flowed like a broad river with earthy, rolling sounds. In Italy she had felt as if the entire population was eager to get its point across with whatever amount of drama required. At one point, when they were at the top of Saint Peter's Basilica in already close quarters, Christy remembered thinking that about Marcos's style of communicating. She felt as if he were trying to lick her nose at the top of his voice.

"Hey, this sounds like something Christy would want to see," Todd said, reading an entry from the tour book. "It's a castle called *Schloss Hellbrunn*. We should go there first, in case they close in the evening."

Christy felt warmed inside knowing that Todd had been taking notes again and that he remembered her saying she wanted to go to as many castles as they could find. She let Todd figure out how to get to the Schloss Hellbrunn, and once there, she continued to feel charmed by Salzburg's unique beauty as they toured the castle. The guide told them to pay attention to the outside dining table. It looked as if it was made of cement with individual cement seats. Suddenly jets of water shot straight up from the seats and from the middle of the table, spraying the tour group with a light mist.

After the laughter subsided, their guide said, "Yes, Marcus Sitticus, the host of Schloss Hellbrunn, had a grand sense of humor. He enjoyed surprising his guests this way at summer picnics. To appreciate such innovation, remember, this was all built in the early 1600s."

The tour guide directed them to the garden exit. On both sides a line of spraying water shot into the air and formed an arch for the visitors to run beneath. Todd and Christy went first, holding hands and moving quickly under the refreshing mist. Katie was right behind them, but when she jogged through, the direction of the water changed, and she was doused with a jet of wet stuff that came at her from all sides.

Dripping and laughing, Katie said, "Now I know why the ladies from that era wore those long dresses. It was protection from crazy dinner hosts like this guy. I wonder if his guests ever came back a second time?"

When Christy snuggled under her down comforter at the Gasthof late that night, she thought about how she wanted to come back to Salzburg a second time, if ever the invitation was given.

She wrote that in her new diary the next day on their train ride through Germany. Part of her entry read,

The charm of that happy city will never leave me. When we walked past Mozart's birthplace this morning, I thought of how his music still resonates here in a timeless, majestic way. The tour book said that people lived in Salzburg five hundred years before Christ was born, because of the salt deposits found here. That astounds me. All Katie seemed to be impressed with was the number of fountains we found as we walked around yesterday evening. At every fountain that had a horse statue in it, she made us stop and listen to her sing, "Doe, a deer, a female deer, ray . . ." etc.

Poor Katie tried so hard to get Todd and me to stand on the edge of the fountains and sing with her, but we let her do a solo every time.

Their train rolled to a stop at the Munich station in Germany a fast two hours after they left Salzburg. Christy threw her diary into her pack and followed Todd and Katie off the train. It took them a while to figure out which train they wanted to take next. With the help of an attendant at the ticket window, they made reservations on one of the newer direct trains. The attendant told them the train would shoot them to Hamburg in the northern part of Germany at 165 miles per hour. They had to pay an extra amount, but they had become used to that in Italy.

Instead of compartments, the train to Hamburg had comfortable seats similar to first class in an airplane. Each seat came equipped with earphones and a dial so all the passengers could select their own favorite music.

"This is a big change from the Italian trains," Katie said. "How long are we going to be on this one?"

"I think she said it was six hours to Hamburg." Todd settled into his seat next to Christy and said, "Not bad, huh?"

"We'll have to stop in Hamburg to buy hamburgers," Katie said. Her seat was directly across from Todd's and Christy's. They all stacked their day packs in the empty seat next to Katie.

"Do you suppose Hamburg is where hamburgers were invented?" Christy asked.

"Your handy tour book might help us." Todd unzipped his pack and pulled out the book.

"Didn't some cook invent hamburgers for an earl of something?" Christy said.

"You're thinking of sandwiches," Todd said. "I've heard that before, too. The Earl of Sandwich. His chef invented sandwiches for him. I don't think any Earls of Hamburg existed. Although it says here that Hamburg dates back to the medieval times. But the city was almost destroyed in World War II. That's awful."

"Can I just say," Katie said, leaning forward, "that you have your face in that tour book just a little too much to make me believe we're really on an adventure, Todd."

"It's a great book," he said, looking up. "But it doesn't say anything about hamburgers in Hamburg."

"It might have said something about Hamburg in one of the other books I left back at my dorm," Christy said.

"You had more books?" Todd asked.

"Seven. One of them was just about Italy and another one was about Scandinavia."

"You should have brought them. I'm really getting into finding out some of the history of these places," Todd said.

Christy glanced at Katie and gave her friend a sassy little see-I-told-you-so expression.

"I didn't stop you from bringing your books," Katie flared at Christy. "All I said was that they would take up a lot of space, and they would. Don't blame me, Christy. You could have brought them if you really wanted to."

Christy hadn't expected such a reaction. "Katie, it's not that big a deal. I think the book I brought is the best one. It's helped us out a lot."

Katie turned away, fiddled with her earphones, and then curled up in her chair with a sweat shirt over the front of her like a blanket. The air-conditioning was blowing right on them, and Christy felt chilled, too. She slipped her arm through Todd's and cuddled up close to him to get warm.

"What are you reading about now?"

Before Todd could answer, Katie stood and, pulling off her earphones, said, "Six hours is a long time. I'm going to walk around and see if I can meet some people."

Christy felt the words "Just don't lock yourself in the bathroom this time" burning on the tip of her tongue. But she made herself keep quiet.

Then, as if Katie could smell the smoke from Christy's burning words, she said, "Don't worry. I'll be back before we reach Hamburg."

With that, she brushed past Todd and Christy and took off down the long aisle.

CHAPTER 13

As soon as Katie walked away from Todd and Christy, Christy thought, *Good. Now Todd and I can snuggle and talk quietly, just the two of us.* But then another thought marched into her mind. *Katie looked really upset. I better go after her and find out what's wrong.*

"Do you think she's okay?" Todd asked.

Christy continued to struggle. She wanted to hold tighter to Todd's arm and brush off Katie's mood as normal Katie behavior. With a sigh, Christy said, "I don't know. She's upset about something."

"I'll go check on her," Todd said.

"No, that's okay. I'll go."

"Actually, Christy, I think I should go. What if she's mad at you?"

Christy felt her defenses rise. "Mad at me? What for? What did I do?"

"I don't know," Todd said calmly. "That's what I might be able to find out."

Christy reluctantly pulled her arm out of Todd's and took the tour book as he handed it to her. He didn't even look back but strode down the aisle in the direction Katie had gone.

This is just great! Since when did Todd become everyone's counselor? That used to be Doug's job. Todd should be here, with me.

Christy watched Todd until he passed through the sliding door to the next compartment. She wondered if she should write out her frustrations in her new diary. She didn't feel like writing the way she had from Salzburg to Munich. Instead, she pulled Todd's navy blue sweat shirt from his pack and draped it over her to protect her bare arms from the air-conditioning, and to feel close to him. If his real arms couldn't be around her, then she would settle for the arms of his sweat shirt.

With her eyes on the door, Christy waited, watching for Todd and Katie to return. She considered going to find them, but then she would have to carry all their packs.

The earphones came in handy as she waited. The scenery outside the window resembled what they had seen in Austria—green hills, small towns, tunnels, and an occasional small train station. The main difference was that all these things were going by so fast everything was a blur of color. Inside the air-conditioned train that was traveling at such great speed, Christy had a hard time absorbing that they were in Germany now rather than Austria. On the second-class train in Italy, when she had to hang her head out the window to breathe because all she could smell was garlic, she had known she was in Italy.

Selecting classical music on her radio dial, Christy let the sounds of a cello be her companion and comfort. She tried not to make a big deal out of Katie's exit and Todd's going after her.

To distract herself, Christy looked through the tour book. What caught her eye in the section on Germany was a picture of a light blue castle with several pointed turrets rising into the sky. The castle was set on a high place overlooking a brilliant blue lake and vast, rolling green hills. The forest, like a velvet green skirt, hugged the base of the huge castle grounds. The words *Famous Neuschwanstein Castle* appeared underneath the photo.

Christy pulled out a pen and marked the places she really wanted to see. She had just drawn a circle around a Rhine River castle boat tour when Todd returned and sat next to her.

"How's Katie?" Christy asked.

"Good. She just needed some space."

"Is she mad at me?"

"It wouldn't hurt for the two of you to talk everything through."

"What do you mean by 'everything'?"

"You would have to ask her that."

Christy's irritation built toward Todd as much as toward Katie. He made it sound as if some big, unsettled issue lay between Christy and Katie.

"Should I go talk with her? Where is she?"

"She's sitting by herself in the next car."

"I'll go talk with her." Christy really didn't want to. She wished Katie would come back so the three of them could all talk openly. Slipping past Todd, Christy put his sweat shirt back on the seat and said, "Sure you don't want to come with me?"

"You want me to come?" He sounded surprised.

"Yes. I think it would be better if we could all discuss whatever this is about. We're on this journey together, you know."

"I think you're right," Todd said, looking past Christy. "But you can sit down. Katie's coming back."

Christy returned to her seat. Katie plopped into the seat across from her. "Okay," Katie began. Her face was red. "I just decided I don't want to be alone and have my own space anymore. As soon as Todd left, this really creepy guy sat next to me and asked if he could buy me a beer."

"What did you do?" Christy asked.

"I told him to get lost, but when he didn't move, I came crawling back to you guys. I'm sorry I took off like that."

"It's okay," Christy said.

"No, it's not. I need to tell you something, Christy. I told Todd, but I told him not to tell you because I wanted to."

Christy braced herself.

"I met this guy," Katie said after a long pause. "I met him the last week of school. Great timing, huh? I didn't tell you about him, Christy, because there wasn't much to tell. He plays baseball on the team at Rancho Corona, and I happened to go to the last game. His name is Matt. Number 14. That's all I know. We talked after the game for a while. We hit it off great. The problem is, I've been thinking about him day and night for the last two weeks."

Christy didn't think that was too unusual for Katie. When she got going on a project—any project, including relationships—she jumped in with both feet. That's how she was with Michael, the guy she had dated her senior year of high school.

"Will you see him again?" Christy asked.

"I'm pretty sure he's coming back to Rancho in the fall. But that's not my problem. My problem is that I'm being eaten alive with jealousy. I'm so envious of you and Todd that I can't stand it. I know this is really bad to tell you, but Todd said it was better to get things out in the open than to let them burn holes inside of me."

"I agree," Christy said. "So what should I do to make things more comfortable for you?"

"Nothing. That's just it; you're not doing anything to make me feel this way. If anything, I think both of you are holding back and not being as close to each other as you would like because you don't want me to feel left out."

Christy glanced at Todd. He had a calm, steady expression on his face and was concentrating on Katie. Christy could tell from the way Katie was talking that this was difficult for her to discuss.

"I really, really wish a guy were in my life," Katie said. "I want what you two have. Is that wrong to wish for?"

Just then an older guy who was walking down the aisle stopped and looked over at Katie. He looked as if he hadn't bathed for a month. When he saw Katie he said, "There you are."

Christy could tell from the paralyzed expression on Katie's face that this was the same guy who had offered to buy her a beer in the other train car.

"That seat isn't available," Todd said without moving any of their day packs.

"I don't see anyone sitting there," the guy said. He talked like an American, and from the way he slurred his words, Christy guessed he was either on drugs or drunk. "Unless you paid money for that seat and can prove it, that seat is open." He picked up the first pack and dropped it on the floor by Todd's feet.

Christy's heart pounded. She had never seen Todd confronted like this. Would he stand up and punch the guy in the nose?

"We were just leaving." Todd spoke in a calm, even tone. He picked up Christy's pack and handed it to her, motioning with his head that she should stand up. She stood. Todd handed Katie her pack with the same gesture to stand.

"There you go. The seat is all yours," Todd said to the guy. Then Todd stepped into the aisle with Katie and Christy right behind him. Without a word, he led them to the dining car.

"Is he following us?" Katie muttered over her shoulder to Christy. "I don't want to turn around to find out."

Christy cautiously glanced back. "Nope. He's going to the car behind ours."

"Do you want to go back to our seats, Todd?" Katie asked. "I think he took your hint."

"No, I'm not very good at trying to talk to drunk guys. We might as well eat since we're halfway to the dining car."

It turned out they were a full eight cars from the dining car, and when they arrived, a line of people was waiting to be seated. Christy knew it wasn't unusual for Europeans to eat their main meal at two in the afternoon. That's what they did at the orphanage where she worked in Basel. Since this was Sunday afternoon, people were more likely to linger a long time over their meal.

"We could be here awhile, you guys," Christy warned them.

"It's too far to go through all eight cars again, turn around, and come back here in half an hour," Katie said. "I don't mind waiting, if you don't."

"No, that's fine." Actually, it was pretty squishy. Christy wouldn't have minded being this close to Todd if it hadn't been for the way they had left Katie in midconfession over her struggling as she watched Todd and Christy together. Christy knew this wasn't the time to wrap her arms around Todd and lean on him in an effort to condense space.

They didn't talk. It was too noisy with all the conversations going on around them. The four people in front of them spoke in a deep, loud German dialect and laughed even louder.

By the time the three of them finally were seated, they were eager for a huge meal. The dining car chef on this deluxe supertrain didn't disappoint. They all had roast beef with potatoes, carrots, turnips, a creamy broccoli cheese soup, and dinner rolls. Christy ordered hot tea to drink with her dessert of apple cake, and the tea came in a white ceramic pot with a matching creamer.

"Katie, when we move into the dorms this fall, let's find some little teapots like this and buy two of them. Then, on long nights, when we need to keep ourselves awake, we can brew up our own little pots of tea and have a midnight tea party."

Katie smiled at Christy's suggestion. The excellent food had done wonders for all of them, and just like the "locals" seated around them, they took their time over dessert.

Katie commented on how dark and rich her coffee was and asked Todd about his cappuccino.

"Not as good as I had in Italy. But not bad."

"Katie," Christy said, holding her teacup in her hands to warm them from the chill of the air-conditioning. "Do you want to talk some more about what you were saying before that guy came and interrupted us?"

"I don't know. Sometimes I make too big of a thing out of nothing. We can drop it. It doesn't matter."

"I think it matters because it's been bothering you, and if you stuff it away, it might come back and bother you again before the trip is over. I'd like to talk it through now, if we could."

"It's dumb. I know it is. I get my eyes off the Lord and my perspective goes crazy. I told you guys I was jealous, and I am. But I know that's wrong. I know God says we're not supposed to envy what someone else has. The thing is, I don't know what to do with my feelings. I try to ignore them, but then they overwhelm me."

"Pray," Todd suggested immediately.

Katie sighed and looked down at her half-empty cup of coffee. "Yeah, pray. That's what I should do. I don't know why I don't. I get tired of confessing the same thing over and over. But whenever I do talk it through with God, I always feel better."

"And He always forgives us no matter how many times we come to Him," Todd said. "I think it helps to find out what triggers those weak areas and recognize the warning signs before you get blindsided."

"What do you mean?"

"Well, what triggers the jealousy?"

Katie paused a moment before saying, "I see somebody with something I wish I had, and I start to compare myself. Then I get jealous."

"We all do that," Christy said.

"That doesn't make it right," Katie said.

"I know," Christy agreed.

"One thing that helps me is when I see the cycle beginning. I can almost stop the sin in midair before it hits me," Todd said. "Like the comparing part. I memorized a couple of verses that relate. Whenever I start to compare myself with somebody else, I repeat those verses and get my heart back on track with God."

"Then you better teach me those verses, quick!" Katie said, "Because I have a horrible problem of comparing myself with other people."

"One is real short. It's in Isaiah 45:9. It just says, 'Does the clay say to the potter, "What are you making?" ' The other verses are in the same book, Isaiah, in chapter 64, verses 6 and 8. The first time I read this it put me in my place, if you know what I mean."

"Yes, I think I probably know what you mean," Katie said. "What are the verses?"

" 'All of us have become like one who is unclean, and all our righteous acts are like filthy rags; we all shrivel up like a leaf, and like the wind our sins sweep us away. Yet, O Lord, you are our Father. We are the clay, you are the potter; we are all the work of your hand.' "

"Let me see if I caught the same meaning here that you did," Katie said. "When you start to compare yourself with someone else, you think of those verses and how all of us are basically the same before God. Like the clay."

Christy jumped in and said, "And God is the artist. The craftsman. He's making something out of us, the clay. We're not supposed to say to Him, 'Why did you make me like this?' or 'Why can't you make me like her?' "

Todd nodded. "Exactly. Each person's life is a different work of art. God's design for me is different than what He has planned for you."

"Does that really work for you?" Katie asked.

He nodded again. "I find it hard to be jealous when I realize God is the one in control, not me. If He chooses to bless someone more than me, who am I to tell Him what He's doing isn't fair? Do I ever say it's not fair when someone is going through a tough time? Do I tell God it's not fair because He hasn't given me as many difficulties as the other person?"

"You better write those verses down for me, Todd. This is a huge area in my life. I think I have it figured out, and then it comes back stronger." Katie downed her last sip of coffee. "You guys ready to go back to our seats and see if my guardian hobo is still waiting for me?"

He wasn't there when they returned. Instead of sitting beside Todd, Christy sat down next to Katie. She had a lot of questions for her friend and started by saying, "Thanks for being so open, Katie. I'm glad you let both of us in on what you're feeling."

"I wasn't going to. I was going to try to figure it out myself. But Todd was right when he said it's better when we get everything out in the open."

"Then I want you to explain something to me," Christy said. "I don't quite understand how the guy from Rancho made you feel as if you wanted a boyfriend. I mean, why him? Didn't you feel that way around Antonio or Marcos?"

"No. I can't explain it, Christy, but when I met Matt, I thought he was awesome. The only other guy I've ever felt that way about was Michael." Katie turned to Todd and included him in their conversation. "Do you think love at first sight is a big lie?"

Todd rubbed his hand across his jaw. It looked as if he was trying to hide a smile.

"What's so funny?" Christy asked.

Todd looked at Katie and said, "All I can tell you is that the first time I saw Christy I knew." He glanced at Christy.

"Knew what?" Katie asked.

Todd's voice lowered and became deep and dramatic. "I knew that she was God's gift to me and I would never consider anyone else."

For a moment Christy felt overwhelmed by Todd's romantic words. Words he had never before expressed to her. Then she doubted his words and thought he must be teasing or even mocking her.

"You did not!" Christy said, reaching over and whacking Todd on the leg. "The first time you saw me I had just been tumbled by a huge wave and was spit up on the shore covered with seaweed."

"My little mermaid," Todd said, his grin returning. "God's gift to me from out of the sea."

"That reminds me." Christy turned to Katie, eager to change the subject before Todd had a chance to tease her any more. "Todd found out from the tour book that in Copenhagen they have a statue of the *Little Mermaid*. We definitely will have to go see it."

"Okay," Katie agreed.

"Anyone for a game of chess?" Todd asked.

"Are you interested, Katie?" Christy said. "Because I'd like to go back to reading the tour book."

"Oh, I wouldn't want to keep you from your precious tour book," Katie teased.

Todd unpacked the chessboard and set it up. Christy had just turned to the Denmark section of the tour book when Katie leaned over and quietly said, "Thanks, Chris."

"For what?"

"If the Big Artist upstairs isn't ready to paint a boyfriend into my life, thanks for letting me share yours."

CHAPTER 14

Their train rolled into the Oslo station at ten o'clock Monday morning. They had been riding trains for more than twenty-four hours. And Christy had decided that Katie's idea of "sharing" Todd no longer felt like a comfortable, friendly arrangement.

The reality was that Katie hadn't shared Todd at all. She hogged him. When they changed trains in Hamburg and rode through the night in a sleeper car, Christy had stretched out on one of the bunks and managed to fall asleep.

She woke up sometime around six in the morning and found herself alone. Todd and Katie showed up an hour later, laughing and carrying on about what a great time they had had staying up all night drinking coffee and talking. Todd had helped Katie memorize the verses in Isaiah he had told her about. In every way, the two of them seemed to have shared a wonderful time together while Christy slept.

The worst part was that now Christy was the one who found angry bats, poisoned with jealousy, flapping around in her belfry. "Get outa here," Christy muttered to the evil bats.

"What did you say?" Katie asked as they exited the station. "Which way is it out of here?"

"This way." Todd led them into the brilliant light of the new day. "We should find a place to stay first, then do some exploring. What do you think?"

"Do you have a place picked out, Christy?" Katie asked. "You were the one who studied that tour book."

"I marked a couple of places." Christy pulled out the book. "This one sounded the best to me, but if you guys want to go someplace else, that's fine, too." She was surprised at how calm she felt now. Maybe Todd's theory of stopping a sin in midair really worked. "This place is a guesthouse like the one we stayed at in Salzburg. It says it's near the train station."

"Sounds perfect," Katie said. "Which way?"

Christy read the map and led them to the *pensjonater*, as their hotel was called. A three-story square building, it was adorned with a gorgeous stained-glass window above the front door. Christy liked the winding staircase that led them to their third-floor rooms. The first thing she did was open the window's shutters, which unlatched in the middle. Both sides opened outward, letting the sunlight stream into their room. Bright red geraniums spilled over the edge of the window's flower box. Christy drew in a deep breath. Clean air filled her lungs and made her feel invigorated and ready to see the sights.

Katie flopped on the poofy bed and said, "The power of a real bed should never be underestimated."

"You're not thinking of going to sleep now, are you? We're in Oslo! Finally! Fjords are waiting to be visited and folk museums to be explored."

"You and your folks can visit all the museums you want. I'll be here. You can come back and tell me all about it."

Christy pulled on her friend's foot. "We're in Norway. This is the home of your ancestors and all that. Aren't you even a little bit excited about exploring? What happened to your 'We're on an adventure' motto?"

"I've traded in that motto for a new one, 'Sleep is sweet.' "

Christy gave up. She knew in a few minutes Katie would sink into slumberland, so Christy quietly unpacked and made herself at home in the quaint room with the painted wooden furniture. The small desk in the corner was white with tiny red and blue flowers painted along the edge. The matching chair had a high back with a woven straw seat. The wooden bedposts were also painted white with red and blue flowers. A small vase of blue glass held a handful of yellow, white, and blue wild flowers.

After pulling out all her dirty clothes from her backpack, Christy decided to go down the hall to the shared bathroom and wash what she could in the sink. With the sunshine and fresh air pouring through the window, her clothes would dry quickly.

On her way to the bathroom, she knocked on the door to Todd's room. She wondered if he had discovered his bed the way Katie had and had also taken on her "sleep is sweet" motto. Christy hoped he was still awake. She felt ready to explore with him for a few hours. They could let the sleeping redhead get her beauty rest.

Todd didn't answer. But the door to the shared bathroom opened, and he emerged, freshly showered and shaven, wearing a crumpled but clean T-shirt and shorts.

"You shaved!" Christy said.

"Too itchy."

"You look good."

"Hope I didn't keep you guys waiting. A shower sounded too wonderful to pass up."

"A nap sounded too wonderful for Katie to pass up. She'll be out for at least a couple of hours. Do you want to go exploring and then come back and get her?"

"Sure. As long as food is included in that exploring." Todd glanced at the mound of clothes Christy held. "Were you going to wash those?"

"Yes, I thought they would dry in the fresh air that's coming through our window."

"That's a good idea. Why don't we plan to leave in about ten or fifteen minutes? I'll take my stuff to the bathroom on the second floor."

Christy decided to wash more than her clothes. In twelve minutes flat she showered, shaved, washed her hair, changed, and washed her clothes and hung them on a collapsible rack in her bedroom's sunshine. She was just finishing her note to Katie when Todd appeared at her open door. He smiled when he saw Katie asleep with her shoes on.

"Do you think she'll be okay?" he whispered.

"I think so. I'm leaving her a note."

As they walked out, quietly closing the door behind them, Todd slipped his arm around Christy's shoulders and pulled her close. He planted a tender kiss on her temple, halfway on her still-wet hair and halfway on her skin.

Christy was surprised and about to ask, "What was that for?" But when she turned and looked into Todd's clear blue eyes, she knew the answer. He was happy. Happy to be with her, happy to be in Norway, happy to be alive. She decided it was a kiss of contentment and would only retain its magical happiness if she didn't ask to have it explained.

Reaching her arm around his waist, Christy leaned close as they tried to walk down the narrow, winding stairs side by side. She giggled when the curve made them bump into the railing. The owner of the pensjonater met them at the bottom of the stairs and smiled.

"Can you tell us a good place to eat?" Todd asked the cheerful woman. She gave them directions to a place nearby that served what she said was the best *koldtbord* on this side of town.

The restaurant offered outdoor seating. That made Christy happy. She was eager to soak up all the pure air and sunshine. The day felt so fresh to her. The koldtbord turned out to be an abundant buffet. Todd went back twice and ate more salmon than Christy could imagine eating in a lifetime. She tried a stew that the waiter later told her was made from lamb and cabbage. She never would have ordered it if she had known what it was, but she found she liked it.

Lunch wasn't cheap, but Christy felt they had gotten their money's worth. She had eaten so much she felt uncomfortable as they walked hand in hand to the bus stop. The waiter had told them this bus would take them to the *Kon-Tiki* Museum, which Todd was so eager to visit.

They sat close on the bus, holding hands and talking about what they would see after the museum. Christy pulled her tour book from her day pack and noticed how worn it was beginning to look. Todd pointed out a couple of places of interest. The one that intrigued him the most was the *Norske Folke Museet* because on the map it appeared that the *Kon-Tiki* Museum was part of it.

"You know," Todd said, "I was going to tell you, Katie and I looked up a bunch of stuff in our Bibles last night when we were talking, and I found out that Paul didn't write the letter to the Philippians from the Mamertine Prison. He was in Rome when he wrote it, but under house arrest. Apparently he could come and go from the house, and people could visit him."

"So he didn't write anything while in that dungeon?"

"Yes, he wrote his second letter to Timothy. Nero was the emperor at the time."

"Didn't Marcos say Nero was the ruler who used Christians as human torches to light his garden parties?"

Todd nodded.

"That overwhelms me," Christy said. "I mean, to be tortured and killed like that because of what you believe."

"I know," Todd said. "I read the whole book of Second Timothy last night and tried to picture Paul in that dismal cell, within view and earshot of the Colosseum, where other Christians were being fed to the lions. And there he was, in chains, writing stuff like, 'For God did not give us a spirit of timidity, but of power, of love, and of self-discipline.' "

Christy felt like crying.

"At the end of the last chapter," Todd added, "Paul even said, 'But the Lord stood at my side and gave me strength.' And he wrote about how he was delivered out of the mouth of the lion."

"When we were at the Colosseum, the whole idea of persecution really hit me," Christy said. "I stood there and felt as if I could see that arena come alive with spectators watching as the lions were let loose on the Christians."

Todd looked at her intensely. "I felt that way, too."

"I prayed that if I ever was in that situation, I would be able to stand firm in my commitment to the Lord."

A gentle smile came across Todd's lips. "You know what I want? I want to be confident like Paul so that no matter what the circumstances, I'm willing to give my life for Christ. Because the truth is, we all die. And once we've stepped into eternity, all that will matter is if we remained faithful to the Lord through this short life on earth."

Christy felt a tear roll down her cheek. "I agree," she said in a whisper.

"Do you know what, Kilikina?" Todd caught her tear with his finger and then pressed his finger to his chest, directly over his heart. "This is where I save all your tears. Right here, where I hold you in my heart."

The bus pulled up at their stop for the folk museum. Christy pulled herself together, blinking quickly as she followed Todd out onto the street. She felt as if she had been conversing with him in a different realm, another world beyond the stars. Yet here they stood, with both feet on solid earth, and the blue sky spread above them like a sealed dome, locking out that other realm's secrets.

Holding hands and not speaking much, Todd and Christy toured the Norwegian Folk Museum. More than one hundred antique Norwegian buildings were reconstructed and set up like a village under a grove of large trees. A dirt path linked the houses. Some of the houses had sod roofs and faded, stencil-like paintings over the fireplaces and doorframes. One of the houses seemed especially small, and Todd joked about the Vikings actually being a race of short people who wore really tall hats with pointed horns to make them look ferocious.

Christy liked the simple, reconstructed church that originally was built almost eight hundred years ago. "Just a little different from Saint Peter's Basilica in Rome, don't you think?" It intrigued her to see how people through the ages built special places to worship God. The inborn longing to make a meeting place where humans could connect with the eternal God carried on from generation to generation. She was even more amazed to see something this humble stand after eight hundred years.

Todd wasn't overly impressed with the ancient church, but he came alive when they toured the *Kon-Tiki* Museum. They stood side by side, staring at a very small raft constructed of logs that had been intricately roped together.

"Can you believe six men spent one hundred and one days floating on this raft in the Pacific?" Todd studied the raft from every angle. "That's unbelievable. Don't you think that's incredible?"

"Yes," Christy agreed.

"They must have driven each other crazy. There's barely enough room for six people to sit on that raft, let alone sleep and carry supplies. But, man, what an adventure!"

Christy didn't want to admit it to Todd, but she knew if she were sent to sea on such a small raft with Todd and Katie for one hundred days, she would go crazy. She was challenged enough to be with them twenty-four-seven for just three weeks. This little break alone with Todd was refreshing to her.

They also viewed the *Ra II,* which was the second craft Thor Heyerdahl built. This one he constructed in Egypt out of reeds to test the theory that such a boat could have reached the Americas before Columbus did. For whatever reason, the *Ra II* didn't astound Todd as much as the *Kon-Tiki.*

"You know, I've been thinking about getting a new surfboard," Todd said.

"What happened to old Naranja?" Christy asked. Todd's orange surfboard had been a part of his life long before Christy had entered it. She couldn't imagine him giving up Naranja.

"I'll keep Naranja around, but I've been looking at this really sweet board that was made by a guy I know in San Clemente. If I buy this new board, I'm going to name it *Kon-Tiki*."

Christy smiled as they strolled back to the bus stop. The afternoon seemed to grow only more beautiful under the clear skies. She knew that at this time of year, in this land of the midnight sun, they could expect more than eighteen hours of daylight. The light felt different to her, even at two in the afternoon, because the sun came at them from a different angle than she had ever experienced. Norway felt like a crisp, clear, completely different world than the one she had spent her life in.

Christy tried to express those thoughts to Todd as they took the bus back to their lodgings. The more she tried to describe it, the more Todd nodded, and the wider his grin became.

"Do you realize how close we are to the Arctic Circle?" he asked.

"How close?"

"We could take a train out of here tomorrow morning at eight and cross the Arctic Circle at four that afternoon."

"Wouldn't it be all frozen?" Christy hadn't missed her jacket since their camping trip. A visit to the Arctic Circle didn't seem like a good idea unless a person had at least a jacket for the journey.

"It's not the North Pole," Todd said. "The Arctic Circle is basically the line where the Atlantic Ocean stops and the Arctic Ocean begins. A dozen or more Norwegian towns are above the Arctic Circle."

"It sounds like the end of the world."

"I know." Todd's expression lit up. "So how about it, Kilikina, do you want to go to the ends of the earth with me?"

CHAPTER 15

As adventuresome and appealing as Todd's invitation sounded to Christy, they had only one problem with going together to the ends of the earth: Katie.

"I can't explain it," Katie said during dinner that night in downtown Oslo. Even at eight o' clock the city was as bright and warm as it had been at three that afternoon. "I just don't want to go to the ends of the earth with you guys."

"We can't go without you," Christy said, remembering her parents' restriction that she and Todd should never travel alone.

Katie looked at Todd and then back at Christy. "It sounds boring to spend all that time on a train just to see some marker in the ground and herds of reindeer. Sorry."

They had been discussing their options for more than an hour, and clearly Katie wasn't about to budge. As much as Christy hated it, she knew what she needed to say. "Todd, why don't you go by yourself? You really wanted to go to Pompeii, and we didn't make it there. I think you should go to the Arctic Circle. Katie and I can take a boat ride around the fjords tomorrow. If you decide to fly back, like you were saying earlier, then maybe you could fly into Copenhagen instead of here. Katie and I would take the train to meet you there."

Todd studied Christy's expression. "Are you sure?"

In truth, Christy liked the idea of traveling north to the ends of the earth with Todd, but she still was bothered about not having a jacket. And it did sound a little boring. With their limited travel time, she wanted to see Copenhagen more than she wanted to see an Arctic Circle marker and herds of reindeer.

"I'm sure," she said.

"Oh, now I feel like the toad of the week," Katie said.

"Don't," Christy said. "I think this will work out fine. We'll stay here tomorrow night and then take the train down to Copenhagen to meet Todd. You said there were openings on the flight out of Narvik, right?"

"Right. That would work out perfectly," Todd said.

Christy couldn't tell if he was sounding calm because he was disappointed she wasn't going with him or if he was just being his easygoing self.

The next morning, when Christy and Katie walked Todd to the train station and sent him off for what Katie called his "male bonding with the polar bears," Todd appeared much more enthusiastic about his solo journey. Just before he boarded the train, he reviewed the details of where and when they were to meet in Copenhagen.

"We'll be there," Christy said. "Have a great time."

"Say hi to Santa Claus for us," Katie said.

The conductor called out something, which Christy guessed meant "All aboard" in Norwegian. Todd grabbed her, wrapped his arms around her, and kissed her soundly. Then he leaped onto the train and waved good-bye as if he were a soldier going off to war.

"Well!" Katie said. "Good thing I'm along on this excursion to chaperone you two. When did Mr. Casual turn into Captain Passion?"

Christy smiled. Her lips still tingled from Todd's kiss. She remembered when he had kissed her that way once before. They were in Maui, and he was about to jump off a high bridge. Her heart had cried out with fear that he might not surface from the water below. But he had. Now she had confidence he would return from this "leap," as well.

"Do you want to find a little Konditorei and have a morning pastry with me?" Christy asked, changing the subject as they left the train station.

"You're going to put food past those lips while they're still sizzling?" Katie teased. "Man, if I were you, I wouldn't be able to use my lips for a week."

"Katie, come on. It wasn't that wild."

"You should have had the view I did. It was wild. In all the years I've been around you guys, that was about the most intense outward flash of emotion I've seen from Mr. Cool. Or does he kiss you like that all the time, and I just never see it?"

"No, he doesn't kiss me like that all the time. He doesn't kiss me very often, actually."

"That must be hard."

"No, I think it's just right. It would be hard if we were more expressive." They entered a café, and Christy tried to change the subject. "Do you want to sit here, or should we buy something to take with us and go on down to the harbor? I think the next tour boat of the fjords leaves in an hour."

"Let's take it with us," Katie said. "I don't want to miss the boat."

They bought several delicious-looking pastries and decided to take a cab to the harbor. Katie found it humorous that the taxicab they rode in was a Mercedes. "Only a slightly different experience from our taxi rides in Rome, wouldn't you say?"

About two hours into their relaxing boat tour, Katie brought up the subject of Todd again. "How do you guys keep your kisses to a minimum?"

"What?"

"I want to know how you and Todd have stayed so pure and controlled for five years. I think it's hard. It was hard for me when I was going with Michael. I mean, you want to be close; yet the closer you become, the more you want to be even closer. Do you know what I mean?"

Christy nodded. She knew exactly what Katie meant.

"So what's your limit? Where do you guys draw the line?"

Christy had to think a moment. "Light kisses, I guess."

"And you're going to tell me what I witnessed at the train station was a 'light' kiss? I don't think so, honey."

"He doesn't usually kiss me like that," Christy said quickly, although she did remember that his kiss when he arrived at the train station in Basel had pretty much taken her breath away. And then the kiss on the boat to Capri hadn't been light.

"Have you guys ever talked about it?" Katie asked.

"Not exactly. It hasn't been a problem."

"I'm sure it's helped that you haven't been on the same side of the globe for half of your relationship, whether Todd was leaving or you were." Katie leaned back in her seat on the deck of the tour boat. She closed her eyes and took the sun's full force on her face. "I'm going to have so many new freckles by tonight, but doesn't this feel incredible?"

"I love it." Christy looked over at an inlet their boat was about to enter. Dramatic, sharp cliffs shot straight up from the water and towered above them like a great stone ogre with a gnarled face. "Look, we're entering another fjord."

Katie only opened one eye and glanced, unimpressed, at the magnificent sight. "Yeah, it's gorgeous. Just like the last twenty-five fjords we've visited. You see one fjord, you've seen 'em all."

Christy thought it was funny that there they were, finally in Norway, Katie's destination of choice, and they were on a tour of the one thing she wanted to see, fjords, but she was about to take a nap.

The silent time Christy now had to herself was a precious gift. She basked in the sun's warmth and felt comforted by the boat's peaceful motion as it motored through crystal water. The quietness gave her a chance to reflect on what Katie had said about kissing.

Christy wondered if she should draw up some guidelines and standards for herself. She never had to consider that before because over the years Todd had been so slow and sparing in expressing his feelings for her. She had broken up with Rick before kissing had become a problem. It never had been an issue when she went out with Doug because he had made a personal vow never to kiss a girl until his wedding day, and he had succeeded. A special sense of celebration had filled the air at Doug and Tracy's wedding because of their intense purity.

I'm glad Todd has given me his kisses over the years. Each one has meant something different. If Todd saves my tears in his heart, I save his kisses. And I'm saving thousands of kisses to give back to him if we get married.

Christy allowed herself a few moments to consider the possibility that she and Todd wouldn't get married. She had no regrets about the kisses and tears she had bestowed on him over the years. But she also knew that she didn't want to give him a whole lot more, just in case it would be too hard to stop. The full expression of her dreams of passion was wrapped in innocence, and she wanted that delicate wrapping to stay on those dreams until her wedding night.

Pulling her new diary from her day pack, Christy wrote her thoughts out as quickly as they came to her. Part of what she wrote was,

I have so much saved up inside my soul that I'm sure it will take me a lifetime to fully express physically my love to my husband. I want to save all of that until we enter into "holy matrimony." I think that's part of what makes it holy. I think God honors virginity in a special way. When He chose to send His Son to earth, He did it through the body of a virgin. I want my marriage to be holy before God. For the first time I've begun to think that maybe I need a plan instead of just assuming that's how everything will go. At this point in my life, I assume I'll marry Todd. But I don't know that for sure. It's as if I need to save myself from him to save myself for him.

The concluding thought on the topic came to Christy that night as she and Katie walked through Oslo's streets at nine-thirty in what felt like broad daylight. The sky carried only a tinge of tangerine-shaded dusk as they strolled past a row of shops. Dozens of people were out, walking or sitting in open-air cafés, talking as if it were lunchtime.

"I can't believe we waited this late to eat dinner," Katie said. "Although it hasn't exactly felt late. But I am starving."

Christy saw a vendor across the street and said, "Do you want a pretzel or whatever he's selling?"

"No, I don't want to waste hunger like this on a pretzel. I'd rather save it until I can have a real, full, long-anticipated dinner. Are we almost to that restaurant you and Todd liked so much?"

"One more block this way," Christy said. Her mind was spinning with Katie's words. She wanted to remember them and write them in her diary. It made so much sense. She did have a hunger in her life for passion. So did Todd. It was a natural, wonderful gift from God to feel that way about someone you loved.

What was it Katie just said about not wasting such hunger on a pretzel? She wanted to save her hunger for the real, full meal. That's exactly what I want. I don't want to waste my physical longing on some incomplete expression of affection

that could never be satisfying. I want to wait for the real, full expression that can only come in marriage.

As they loaded up their plates at the koldtbord, Christy kept formulating her purity plan. Her parents had never talked about this with her, and they had never given her a purity ring, like her friend Sierra had received from her parents. It was up to Christy to make a plan, and Christy liked plans. She always felt more secure when she had a plan.

I'm going to save my really big kisses for Todd and tuck them away, safe and warm, in the secret place in my heart. When we're together and I feel like kissing him, I'll just tell myself to save that kiss. It will be like saving pennies in a piggy bank. One day I'll give that piggy bank to my future husband, whoever he is. And I'm quite sure that piggy bank will be full! Christy smiled.

The huge dinner and the short but good sleep they had that night prepared Christy and Katie for the ten-and-a-half-hour train ride to Copenhagen. They left on the seven-thirty morning train, which arrived in Copenhagen at five-thirty that evening. The scenery of endless green forests and of lakes with huge floating lily pads was beautiful and refreshing. Katie and Christy rode comfortably in the modern train. They wondered aloud about Todd and how he was enjoying being on top of the world.

Then, about four hours into their journey, Katie surprised Christy. She asked if she could see Christy's tour book.

"I don't know . . ." Christy said.

"Why not?"

"I'm afraid you're going to throw it out the window or something."

"No, I just want to see it."

For the next several hours, Katie became an even bigger tour book maniac than Todd. She read everything about Denmark aloud to Christy and even made Christy repeat Danish phrases back to her.

"Okay, now, this is how you say, 'Where is the bathroom?' *'Hvor er toilettet?'* Try it, Christy."

"Hvor er toilettet," Christy repeated. "You do know, don't you, that we have no idea where the accent should be, so we could be saying these phrases completely wrong."

"At least we're trying to say them. Now say, *'Tager de kreditkort?'* "

"What does that mean?"

"Do you take credit cards?"

Christy laughed. "We don't have any credit cards."

"Okay, fine, if you're going to be that picky, try this: *'Er der nogen her der taler engelsk?'* "

Christy felt reasonably certain that Katie had slaughtered the pronunciation of that sentence. "And what was that supposed to mean?"

"That means, 'Does anyone here speak English?' "

Christy burst out laughing.

"What? That's a useful expression."

"But, Katie, if anyone speaks English, couldn't you just ask in English and that person would understand you?"

"Oh." Katie buried her nose in the book and muttered, "Never mind."

"Let's decide where we're going to go after we drop off our luggage. I'm glad Todd had us call the hostel and make reservations before he left. This is the first time we've actually known where we were going to stay before we arrived in a city."

"The *Little Mermaid* statue is a must-see, in my opinion," Katie said. "And this Tivoli Gardens sounds fun. They have rides, free concerts, puppet shows, fireworks, and get this—they even have ballet performances. Oh, and I definitely would like to go to this one palace or whatever it is that holds the Danish crown jewels. I love that kind of thing. Remember when we saw the British crown jewels at the Tower of London?"

Christy remembered the cold, old tower and that they had climbed lots of stairs. She didn't remember much about the jewels. But she said, "Crown jewels would be fun to see. Where should we go first?"

"Either to see the *Little Mermaid* or Tivoli Gardens."

"Let's check out the mermaid," Christy suggested. "I think Todd will want to see Tivoli Gardens when he gets here, but I don't think the mermaid is at the top of his list."

Christy was feeling pretty confident as the two of them set out from their youth hostel in search of the *Little Mermaid*. She had worried a bit earlier that the two of them traveling together might attract a few drunken hobos like the one Christy had seen in Naples or the guy on the train who had bothered Katie a few days earlier.

But traveling, just the two of them, had been fantastic so far. They were getting along wonderfully. No one had tried to harass them. The youth hostel was easy to find, and they hadn't gotten lost yet.

Katie led them down the clean, darkly paved streets of Copenhagen, reading the tour book aloud as she walked. "It says the statue of the *Little Mermaid*, or the *Lille Havfrue*, as they call it, is at the Langelinie Harbor."

"Katie," Christy said with a finger to her lips. "You don't have to announce where we're going to the whole world."

"They don't care," Katie said, glancing around. "It's obvious we're tourists. Hey, that's the bus we're supposed to take. Come on!"

They dashed to catch the bus, and Katie asked the driver, "You are going to the harbor, right?"

"Yes, the harbor."

"Great."

Christy and Katie took two seats near the front and disembarked when the driver turned and, pointing to the large Tuborg Beer factory, said, "The harbor."

"Thanks," both of them said as they headed toward the water. They were at a huge harbor. Sea gulls swooped down to snatch treats from the large fishing boats. Katie and Christy walked and walked all around, looking for a statue in the water but with no success.

"You'd think they would have a few signs up or something," Katie said. "This is ridiculous."

A huge ferry pulled in while Katie and Christy walked back to where they had started. As they stopped to rest for a moment, the monstrous craft released a long line of cars from its underbelly. Hundreds of people stood on the deck. A group of children all wearing bright yellow T-shirts lined up at the guardrail and called down to Katie and Christy.

"Wave," Katie said. "They're being cute and friendly."

Christy didn't feel very cute or friendly, but she waved. The children got excited and waved and yelled even more enthusiastically. It was as if they had been playing a game, trying to make someone notice them, and Christy and Katie were the first to play along.

A familiar pain brushed across Christy's heart. It was the hurt she felt whenever she worked with the children at the orphanage. *So many children in this world are crying out for love and attention.* She wondered how all the little ones were doing back in Basel.

"I see a bus coming," Katie said. "Let's take it back to town. I've lost all interest in the missing mermaid."

To their surprise, the driver was the same person who had dropped them off a half hour earlier.

"We didn't see any mermaids," Katie told him, taking the seat right behind him. "I suppose she was diving under the water, and that's why we couldn't see her."

The driver turned the large steering wheel on the bus and smiled at Katie in the rearview mirror. Christy wondered if the poor man had any idea what Katie was rattling on about. He then looked at Christy in the rearview mirror. She felt obligated to try to translate for Katie.

"We were looking for the statue of the *Little Mermaid*," she said slowly.

When he didn't respond, Katie pulled out the tour book and said, in a voice that Christy thought was way too loud, "*Lille Havfrue.* We're looking for the *Lille Havfrue.*"

Christy was certain Katie's accent was wrong. But the driver somehow still understood. "Ah, *Lille Havfrue.*" He broke into a deep, jolly laugh. "*Lille Havfrue* is not at the harbor."

"So we discovered," Katie said. "Where is she?"

"I will take you," he said, still laughing. Then he added with his delightful accent, "She is not large like your Statue of Liberty."

Christy glanced at Katie.

"Well? How was I supposed to know? It says here she's at the harbor."

The driver stopped by a park and opened the door. "Here," he said. "You will find the *Lille Havfrue* here."

"Thanks." Christy smiled at him as they got off. She couldn't help but feel that as soon as the door of the bus closed, the whole busload of Danish people would burst out laughing at the crazy American girls.

"Well," Katie said, undaunted. "I guess we made his day a little brighter."

"He did seem humored," Christy said. "This place looks totally different from where we just were."

"And look! There's a sign. *'Lille Havfrue* this way.' " They followed the pathway through a garden area.

"It pays to consult the tour book and to learn the local lingo, doesn't it?" Katie asked.

Christy couldn't pass up the opportunity to tease her friend. "Oh, what's this about consulting the tour book? Does that mean we are no longer on a free-spirited adventure?"

"I know, I know. I deserved that. I'm a reformed traveler, though, remember? Don't be too hard on me. I didn't understand the power of the written word."

"It sounds as if you're talking about the Bible."

"Now, there's a good analogy for you," Katie said. "We'll have to tell that one to Todd. The Bible is like our tour book for this journey through life."

"And the part about adventures? How does that fit in?"

"In case you haven't noticed yet, Christy," Katie said, "I think adventure tends to find you and me. We don't have to go looking for it."

Christy smiled at Katie. "We always were a couple of peculiar treasures, weren't we?"

Katie tilted back her head and let loose her carefree laughter. "I haven't heard you use that term in such a long time! You're right, Chris. We are a couple of peculiar treasures. And so is this little Havfrue statue, if she actually exists."

They walked a long distance before seeing the water, which appeared as flat and shallow as a pond. Then, suddenly, there she was. The *Little Mermaid*. A bronzed statue only about two feet high. She had taken on a weathered, green tinge, and she sat gracefully on a flat, reddish-colored boulder, gazing down at the water. Her back was turned toward Katie and Christy.

"Look at that, will you? We come all this way, and she won't even turn around." Katie said.

"She's a lot smaller than I thought she would be," Christy commented.

"Now I know why the bus driver thought we were so funny," Katie said. "Can you imagine this little statue being situated somewhere in that harbor? She would be run over in an instant by all the cargo ships and ferries."

"So," Christy said flatly, "this is the famous *Little Mermaid* statue."

"Yep, that's her."

They stood for a moment, staring at the statue. Then, turning to look at each other, Christy and Katie burst into the kind of laughter that could only come from two peculiar treasures caught in the midst of an adventure.

CHAPTER 16

Christy wrote about their experience in her diary that night. She entitled her entry "In Search of the *Lille Havfrue.*" Her last paragraph read,

> *I hope I never forget the lesson I learned today. Some of the things I set out to find in life aren't as grand as I thought they would be. When those discoveries turn out to disappoint, may I always be blessed with what I had today: (1) a peculiar treasure of a friend to laugh wholeheartedly with me over the disillusionment and (2) enough money for bus fare to take me on to the next episode of the adventure.*

Christy closed her diary, turned off the flashlight she had borrowed from Katie, and fell asleep with a contented smile on her lips.

The next morning both Christy and Katie found only cold water in the shower. They had slept until seven-thirty, which, in this circle of travelers, apparently was considered sleeping in.

If everything went according to schedule, Todd was to arrive at the youth hostel at nine that morning. Christy and Katie found a bakery down the street that was packed with young international travelers who had stayed at the hostel and were on their way. Backpacks bumped into one another as the travelers stood at the counter to place their orders.

"Do you want to go someplace else?" Christy asked.

"Just tell me what you want, and I'll wait in line for both of us. Why don't you see if any tables are free outside."

Christy tried not to appear obvious that she was watching the diners like a hawk, waiting for one of them to make even the slightest movement indicating that he was ready to leave. Two guys wearing hiking boots and shorts began to stand up, and Christy slid over to their table to grab it. As soon as they walked away, she pulled out one of the three chairs and plopped down.

Almost immediately a tall, slender guy wearing a leather jacket and orange-tinted sunglasses pulled out the chair next to her and sat down. *"Godmorgen,"* he said.

From Katie's drills on the train, Christy knew that was Danish for "good morning." She wished the tour book had listed how to say, "Get lost."

With a simple nod to acknowledge his greeting, Christy turned her head to see where Katie was in the line. The guy said something else, and Christy pulled out her well-used "Ich verstehe nicht."

Unfortunately, he answered her in German, but she didn't understand what he said. She didn't want to say anything in English because then he would know she was an American, and she couldn't fake a British accent well enough to pull that off.

Before Christy could decide what to do, Katie bustled out the door with her hands full. She was about to drop one of the pastries she had balanced on top of Christy's cup of hot tea.

"Hey, grab this quick, Christy," Katie said before she reached their table. Then turning to see the guy in the orange-tinted glasses, she added a friendly, "Hi. Is it okay if we sit at your table with you? It's really crowded here this morning, isn't it? Must be a good place to eat."

Oh great, Katie! I was trying to get him to leave.

Their table host graciously pulled out a chair for Katie and in perfect English said, "So where are you guys from?"

"California," Katie said.

He looked disappointed. "Me too. Fresno."

"Really? That's cool. We're from Escondido," Katie said.

Christy was stunned that this guy had managed to convince her he was a local. She lowered her head, closed her eyes, and said a quick prayer before tearing off a corner of her pastry, which was covered with powdered sugar.

"Your German is pretty convincing," he said to Christy. "I wouldn't have guessed you were an American."

Christy lifted her head. "Thanks." She liked fitting in and not sticking out. After she had been at school in Basel for a few weeks, she had decided she didn't want everyone to know she was from the U.S. She found it easier to slip in and out of everyday life if she wasn't always known as the foreigner.

"How long have you been here?" Katie asked. "I'm Katie, by the way. This is Christy."

Christy didn't feel particularly comfortable letting this stranger know her name, even if he was from the U.S.

"I'm Jade. I've been in Europe since May. This is only my second day in Copenhagen."

"It's our second day, too," Katie said. "Christy has been in Europe since last fall. She's going to school in Switzerland."

"Oh really? Where?"

Christy didn't appreciate Katie telling Jade all the details of Christy's life. She gave him basic information about the university she attended and concentrated all her attention back on her breakfast.

"What have you seen here so far?" Katie asked.

"Seen?" Jade asked.

"Have you been to Tivoli Gardens?"

"No, I'm just hanging out."

"We went to see the *Little Mermaid* statue yesterday," Katie said. "Now, that was an adventure! Not necessarily one I would recommend, but it was an adventure."

Jade gave them a look as if to say he couldn't believe they were running around looking at points of interest. Christy guessed he had a different agenda for his travels.

"You know," he said, "a good dance club is on Nysted. The band was pretty good last night." He looked at Christy. "You want to go with me tonight?"

Christy tried not to sound too shocked. "No, thanks."

"Would you come if I found a date for your friend here?"

Christy shook her head.

"Not very friendly, are you?"

When Christy didn't look up or answer, Jade said, "Yeah, well, maybe I'll see you there." He stood up and gave Christy a light punch on the arm, as if trying to get a reaction out of her. "Take it easy."

They watched him saunter over to some other girls who sat in the shade. They were smoking and offered Jade a cigarette.

"Once again," Katie said, "I, your ever faithful friend, stand by and watch guys drool over you while I mysteriously become invisible."

"Like you were really interested in that guy, Katie." Christy tried to take a sip of her tea, but it was too hot.

"I would have gone to the dance club with him," Katie said.

"Yeah, right," Christy said.

"I think guys like that are intrigued by you because you get all shy around them. And it's not an act. I know that. You start blushing, pull back, and look away. It's all very natural for you. I think they see it as a challenge and try to get you to open up. I, on the other hand, am an open book. And obviously not a bestseller."

"Katie, you're perfect just the way you are. One day a guy will come into your life who will be so stunned that you are *you*. He'll also be glad that you didn't go to dance clubs with guys in leather jackets named after cold green rocks."

Katie smiled. "You better keep reminding me of that, Chris. The longer I wait for my handsome prince, the better those green rock-heads look to me."

Christy shook her head. "You know, it always bothered me in Basel when I would see Americans like that. It's as if they're trying to figure out who they are."

"And we're not?"

"I guess we are. It just seems different to me. Almost like they are wearing a costume. You know, the leather jacket and orange glasses. Then they come all the way to Europe to try out their costume and to see if anybody believes that's who they are."

"You sound like an old lady, Christy."

"I do not."

"I liked his glasses. I was about to ask him if I could try them on. I wanted to see if they clashed with my hair."

Christy decided to play along with Katie rather than make philosophical observations so early in the morning. She casually glanced over her shoulder. "You know, you could still ask him, Katie. He hasn't left yet."

"Maybe if I keep looking over in that direction, Jade will get the hint that I want him to come back over here," Katie said.

"Please don't. My arm still hurts from where he punched me."

"Do you miss Todd at times like this?" Katie asked.

"Yes. Although I'm really glad you and I had a chance to be together for a couple days. It's been fun."

"I know; it has. I kind of wish Todd were going to be away a few more days. I liked being the old Katie with the old Christy for a while. We haven't been *us* for a long time. I've missed that. Being around you brings out the real me."

"Do you feel it's hard to be that way when Todd is around?"

"No. Well, sometimes. But it's not because of anything you've done or haven't done. I think it's just the reality of where we are in our lives. You and Todd are getting closer, and that means there's a little less room in your life for me."

Christy was about to protest when Katie cut her off. "That's not a bad thing. It's good. Isn't this what you've wanted? I know I've put in a prayer or two over the years that you and Todd would reach this point. It's nice to see a few of my prayers answered. Even if they are prayers for my friends and not for me."

"I hadn't thought of it that way, but you're right. Todd and me still being together is a little miracle, isn't it?"

"I think the miracles have only just begun," Katie said. "And I like watching you two as you're getting more serious about each other. I'll probably be even more excited than you on the day he finally proposes to you."

Christy looked into Katie's mischievous green eyes.

"What?" Katie leaned forward and grasped Christy's hand. "What was that look? Has he already proposed, and you've kept it a secret from me? You wouldn't do that, would you?"

"No, of course not, Katie. Todd hasn't proposed. We haven't talked about it at all. I was just looking at you like that because it sounded so strange to hear you say it. I mean, I think about it sometimes, but I don't say it aloud."

"Well, then I'll say it. Todd is going to propose to you, Christy. It's only a matter of time."

Christy felt her heart pounding.

"You look so shocked!" Katie laughed. "Why would that shock you? I mean, strangers coming up and asking you to go dancing, that should shock you. But why would Todd's proposing shock you?"

"I don't know. It just does."

Katie looked behind Christy, and with a widening grin on her face, she said between clenched teeth, "Don't look now, but he's back."

Christy didn't turn around. She had thought Jade would be happy hanging out with the girls he had found at the other table. "Don't say anything to him," Christy said in a low voice, looking straight at Katie.

Katie's grin was obviously for the guy who now stood behind Christy. Katie gave the guy a chin-up gesture and said, "Go ahead and kiss her. She's been hoping you would."

"Katie!" Before Christy could reprimand her friend further, the shadow of an unshaven, not-so-great-smelling man came over her. Dry, chapped lips suddenly were being pressed against hers.

Christy pulled away, grabbed her cup of hot tea, and shot the steaming liquid into the face of her perpetrator.

Todd screamed.

Springing from her chair, Christy looked at Todd and then at Katie and yelled, "Why didn't you tell me it was Todd?"

Everyone was looking at them. Someone offered Todd a paper napkin. Both his hands were covering his face.

"Todd, I'm so sorry," Christy panted. "Are you okay? Let me see your face." She gently touched his arm, and he pulled away.

"I'm okay," he said slowly.

Christy could see big, red splotches on his forehead. He wiped his eyes with the napkin and lowered himself into the chair next to Christy's with his backpack still on.

"It's okay," Katie announced to the onlookers. "He's all right."

"Does it still burn?" Christy asked, sitting down and trying to get a good look at him. "Should we find a doctor?"

"I think some cold water might help," Todd said.

"The youth hostel is just around the corner." Christy tried to help him up.

Todd pulled his arm away from her, and she remembered more than a year ago, when he had been burned seriously. If she tried to help him do anything, he would get irritated with her. So now she reminded herself that, when he was hurt, she should do what he said, get what he wanted, and then back off.

None of them spoke as they walked quickly to the youth hostel. Todd checked in and headed for the guy's side of the dorm. Christy called out, "We'll be in our room."

Like two naughty children who had been sent to their room, Katie and Christy shuffled off in the opposite direction.

"It was my fault," Katie said firmly. "I can totally see now how you thought I was talking about Jade. You had no way of knowing it was Todd."

"I should have looked before I threw the hot tea on him. I feel so awful."

"You were just reacting," Katie said. "Don't blame yourself. I was the one who set you up. I'm really sorry, Chris."

"That's okay. I know you were just having fun. It was an accident." Christy leaned against the side of one of the wooden bunk beds. "I feel so terrible."

Katie and Christy spent the next hour quietly reading on their beds while other youth hostel guests came and went. One girl came in, collapsed on a lower bunk, and appeared to fall into a deep sleep. Christy was reading from Psalms, which is where she usually went when she needed some comfort.

The God-breathed words of Psalm 61 especially helped. *"Hear my cry, O God; listen to my prayer. From the end of the earth I call to you, I call as my heart grows faint; lead me to the rock that is higher than I."*

Christy thought of the astounding, soaring-to-the-heavens rock formations they had seen on their boat ride a few days earlier. *God, you are my rock. I rely on you. I may not have traveled to the end of the earth with Todd, but I feel as if that's where I am right now in my heart.*

The door to their dormitory room opened, and a young woman who worked at the registration desk said, "Is there a Christy in here?"

"Yes?" Christy called out.

"Someone wants to see you in the lobby."

"Thank you." Christy hopped down from her top bunk and asked Katie if she wanted to come with her.

Katie put down the tour book and said, "I think I better go with you. I want to tell him it was my fault."

They walked to the lobby close beside each other. Todd was sitting on the long, wooden bench that ran along the left wall of the lobby entrance. He grinned at them as they approached.

"I'm so sorry, Todd," Katie began. "It was my fault. Christy thought it was Jade, and believe me, she didn't want Jade to kiss her."

Todd raised his eyebrows. Christy could see a big red swollen splotch across his forehead. It looked bad but not awful.

"Jade, huh?" Todd said.

Katie quickly explained who Jade was.

Christy sat down next to Todd. She gave him a sympathetic look. "I'm sorry I reacted like that without seeing who it was."

Todd brushed a long strand of hair from her cheek. "I guess I don't have to worry about you knowing how to take care of yourself. You have quick reactions, Christy. That's good."

"Except it's not good when you get hurt."

"It'll heal. So what have you guys been doing, besides turning down invitations to dance clubs?"

Christy could tell Todd was okay. He wasn't mad, and he wasn't seriously injured. Katie must have come to the same conclusion, too, because she sat down on the other side of Todd and plunged right in with a proposed itinerary of what they should do that day, as well as a long list of all the other sights they should see.

Todd looked at Christy with surprise as Katie continued to spout her knowledge of all the hot tourist spots.

"She's been reading the book," Christy told him.

Todd laughed.

Christy felt good hearing his laugh again. And good being close to him and knowing that everything was okay.

"Before we go anywhere, I want to hear about your adventure," Christy said.

"Right," Katie agreed. "And then we'll tell you about our little adventure with the *Lille Havfrue*."

Todd leaned back, stretched out his legs, and folded his hands behind his neck. "I saw a polar bear," he said proudly.

"No!" Katie said. "Not really."

"Yep. Really. Not up close, but it was a real polar bear. Lots of reindeer. Met some cool people. It was great."

Christy had insisted that he take her camera with him since he didn't have one. She asked, "And you did get a picture of you at the marker when the train stopped and let you off at the Arctic Circle, didn't you?"

"Took two pictures," he said. "Just in case one didn't turn out."

Christy smiled at him and said, "So you're glad you went, right?"

He nodded. Then, looking in Christy's eyes, he leaned closer and whispered so only she could hear, "Except I wish you had been with me."

CHAPTER 17

The three reunited travelers spent the day playing like kids at Tivoli Gardens in the glorious sunshine. They ate ice cream that was served in cones with whipped cream, a dollop of jam on top, and a thin cookie tucked on the side. They knew they had to try one when the sign said *Amerikan Cones*. They decided nothing was especially American about them.

By evening, even though it was still light, the air felt cool and sweet. They rested on one of the many benches within the garden, having gone on all the rides and then complained that they were kiddie rides. The roller coaster was, in Katie's words, "like going over speed bumps at Kelley High School."

"I think we're spoiled by all the amusement parks in California," Christy said. "Weren't you the one reading to me about how this park was built more than one hundred and fifty years ago?"

"Yeah, but I still had higher hopes," Katie said.

"It's really a beautiful park," Christy said. "Look at these trees. Their trunks are almost black, and the leaves are minty green. What kind of trees do you suppose they are?"

"Danish trees," Katie said. "Can we go see something else?"

"Sure," Todd agreed. "What do you have marked there in the book?" He broke off a triangle wedge from a Toblerone candy bar and handed it to Christy.

"I want a piece," Katie said.

"I thought you would." Todd handed Katie a piece of the honey-sweetened chocolate bar.

"I planned to eat a candy bar in each country we went to, but I blew it in Norway," Katie said. "I think I'll have to get double the bars here in Denmark. How did we end up not buying any chocolate there?"

"It's because I took you to all the bakeries, and we bought pastries instead," Christy said.

"Those haven't been too bad," Katie admitted.

"They've been fantastic!" Christy said. "I really can't wait to take both of you to my favorite little Konditorei in Basel." She turned to Todd. "Do you remember me telling you how I go there every Saturday morning? It's where I get my sanity back."

"I remember." Todd munched on the chocolate bar. "You order a coffee with cream and sit at the back corner table. Then Margie, or whatever her name is—"

"Marguerite," Christy corrected him.

"Marguerite brings you whatever they've just pulled out of the oven. Is that right?"

"Exactly." Christy felt warm inside as she realized how much Todd paid attention to her emails and how he did take notes on what was important to her. "I want to take you there. I want you to meet Marguerite and taste the delicacies she creates."

"We can do that." Todd stretched his legs out in front of him. He offered Christy and Katie another hunk of chocolate. "We'll plan our itinerary so that we get back to Basel on Sunday before you start classes, and we'll go to your bakery."

"Then the question is," Katie said, "what do we want to see between here and Basel? I, for one, must see the Eiffel Tower."

Christy thought, *If you end up with the same feeling about the Eiffel Tower that you had about the fjords, Paris will be a really short stay.*

"Okay, we'll swing by Paris. I wouldn't mind seeing Notre Dame," Todd said.

"And the *Mona Lisa*," Christy added.

"Is she there?" Todd asked.

"Yes," Christy said. "We have to go to the Louvre. That's mandatory."

"How many more days do we have?" Todd asked.

It took the three of them a while before they could decide what day it was and how many more they had. The consensus was that this was, in fact, Thursday, and they had to be in Basel by a week from Monday. Or actually, they had to be back by Sunday so they could visit Christy's bakery.

"We have plenty of time," Todd said.

"You know what that means?" Christy asked. "Today our trip is half over. We've been traveling for eleven days, and we have ten more to go."

"Are you serious? We've only been traveling for eleven days?" Katie looked stunned. "It feels like a decade. Or at least a month. I hate it when I exaggerate so much." Shaking her head, she added, "You guys, we have to make a plan! This last week and a half is going to go by like that." She snapped her fingers for emphasis.

Todd and Christy looked at each other, and Christy burst out laughing. "That's what I've been trying to say for the past eleven days. We need a plan!"

"So I'm a slow learner. Be nice." Katie pulled out the tour book from her day pack, where she now permanently kept it. "I say we find a night train and get ourselves to Paris. No, cancel that. I wanted to try to talk you guys into going to Saint Petersburg first."

"In Russia?" Christy asked.

"I was reading about it," Katie said. "I think Moscow is too far to go. It takes something like three days by train from here. But Saint Petersburg isn't far from Helsinki, and Helsinki is only a day's train ride from here. Twenty-four hours. We could see those onion-dome churches, and they have a museum in Saint Petersburg that's supposed to be even better than the Louvre. It's the Heritage, or something like that."

"I think it's called the Hermitage," Todd said.

"Right." Katie flipped through a few tattered pages. "Here it is. The Hermitage contains 2.8 million exhibits. They built the museum out of the czar's former Winter Palace. It says, 'The staterooms in the Winter Palace, with their chandeliers and opulent marble and gold-leaf decoration, should not be missed.' See? 'Should not be missed.' " She pointed to the words in the tour book. "We should go to Saint Petersburg."

"What do you think, Todd?" Christy asked.

"Whatever you guys want is fine with me." With a grin he added, "I've been to Narvik and back. I'm happy."

Christy was glad all over that she had suggested he go to the Arctic Circle. It had been a good choice. She hoped they could come up with some more good choices now.

After an hour discussing options on the bench at Tivoli Gardens, Todd suggested they find a place to eat. He said he hadn't eaten much on his journey to the "end of the world." Today all he had eaten was an "Amerikan" ice cream and the Toblerone bar.

They went to a small restaurant off the main street at the recommendation of a distinguished gentleman Todd had stopped on the street once they were back in the main part of downtown Copenhagen. Christy ordered the special of the evening, which was listed on the menu as *"flaekesteg med rodka."* The waitress spoke perfect English, and she told Christy it was roast pork with red cabbage and browned potatoes. Katie looked as if she was having a hard time not bursting out laughing.

As soon as the waitress left, Christy gave her a what's-so-funny look. Katie laughed and said, "I'm sorry. It's just that the way you said it, Christy, the last word sounded like 'road kill'! 'I would like to order the road kill for dinner, please.' " Katie kept laughing.

Christy realized how tired and hungry she was now that they were sitting in the quiet, dimly lit restaurant. Katie's laughter was fun while they were on the rides at Tivoli Gardens, but now it sounded loud and overdone to Christy. She knew Katie became punchy when she was tired and living on sugar. But the truth in Christy's heart was that she wanted to be alone with Todd. She wanted to hear all about his adventure to Narvik. She wanted to look into his eyes and listen to him without having to divide her attention between Todd and Katie.

Dinner was scrumptious, and they all mellowed after eating. A complimentary plate of various slices of cheese followed the meal. Todd ordered a coffee, and they went back to planning the next portion of their trip.

By the time the brightness in the sky had finally begun to soften into shades of tangerine and soft rosy pinks, the three of them had come up with a plan. Stockholm and Helsinki were off the list. Since they weren't headed for Helsinki, Saint Petersburg was also struck from the list.

They decided to travel to Paris with a one-day stop in Amsterdam so they could see a Dutch windmill. The train ride from Copenhagen to Amsterdam would take more than twelve hours.

Todd had been figuring out the train schedule with a book of Eurail times. "It looks as if we can leave Copenhagen at seven tomorrow morning and get to Hamburg around noon. We get on a different train at one and that takes us to Cologne, Germany. And that's as far as we can go, by my calculations. They don't list any night trains from Cologne to Amsterdam."

"What are you saying?" Katie asked. "Do you want to skip Amsterdam and go directly to Paris?"

"No, I'd like to go to Amsterdam. I'll keep checking. A night train is probably available, but it's just not listed here. If there isn't one, we could stay in Cologne tomorrow night and take a morning train to Amsterdam. I know some people we could stay with in Amsterdam. They were in Spain when I was there."

"Sounds good to me," Katie said. With a smile to Christy, she said, "Looks like we have a plan."

As they walked back to the youth hostel, Todd held Christy's hand, and she wondered how long it would be before she and Todd had a plan. He was so good at reviewing the tour book and figuring the train schedules. *Has he begun to review his school schedule to figure out when he'll finish? He's been trying to save money this past year. Was all that for college, or was he saving up for an engagement ring?*

Christy told herself she was jumping too far ahead. She knew from previous seasons of wondering and waiting in her life that if she ran ahead and tried to predict the future, she inevitably ended up robbing herself of the joy of the present.

This is where she wanted to be. Right here. Holding hands with Todd, strolling along the streets of Copenhagen under the peach-tinted trail of the midnight sun. They could discuss their future another time, but not tonight. Tonight was for dreaming, not discussing.

About halfway through their train ride to Hamburg the next morning, the train chugged into the belly of a huge ferry like the one Katie and Christy had seen at the harbor. Christy didn't know if they had been transported by a ferry on their way to Oslo because she had slept through most of that trip and wouldn't have noticed if the train was under the stars or under the sea.

She convinced Todd to exit the train with her and find a way to the top of the ferry. She wanted to wave to the tourists on the dock the way the school children in their yellow shirts had waved at Katie and Christy.

"I can take a hint," Katie said when Christy didn't include her in the invitation. "Don't worry. I'll stay here with the luggage. You two go and have a good time. Don't worry about me. I'm sure I'll be just fine."

"We'll find a candy bar for you," Todd said as they left.

"You're my hero!" Katie called out after him.

"What's it like being a hero?" Christy teased.

Todd grinned but didn't answer. She could see that the hot-water burn she had inflicted on his forehead hadn't improved much. Still red, it looked a little swollen.

"Does your face hurt?" she asked.

Todd gave her a funny look.

"I mean, your forehead. Does the burn bother you much?"

"No, I think it will be okay." Todd led her up some stairs until they reached the top deck. He immediately spotted a snack bar and stood in line for some food and for a candy bar for Katie. So many people were waiting it took nearly all of their fifty-minute ferry ride to buy the food.

At first Christy was disappointed they had spent their alone time standing in line. But when their train pulled into Hamburg a little late and they had to run to catch their next train to Cologne, Christy was glad she had something extra to munch on. The ride from Hamburg to Cologne took five hours. The three friends played chess and read the tour book to one another.

Katie was so caught up with reading every detail of every major city and giving Todd and Christy full reports, that Christy was beginning to think she actually had been to some of the cities. Katie said she had a philosophy. If they couldn't see Helsinki, Saint Petersburg, Moscow, and Berlin, they might as well know what they missed.

The descriptions Katie read of the Netherlands and France made Christy glad they had decided on those two places for their next destinations. The only problem was that Christy really wanted to see Luxembourg and Belgium, too, after hearing about them.

"I think after Paris we should go to a small city," Christy said. "Or at least a small country. We've been hitting the major cities, which is great, but we could see a lot outside the big cities. I think that way we would know more what people are really like in those countries."

"Sounds good to me," Todd said. "Where do you want to go after Paris?"

"Germany," Christy said.

"We're in Germany now," Katie said.

"I know, but we're zooming through. A Rhine River cruise is listed in the book that I marked. Did you see it, Katie? It sounds really wonderful."

"I saw that," Todd said. "Doesn't it start in Cologne?"

"No, you don't," Katie said. "Don't start changing plans on me. We're going to Amsterdam."

Christy couldn't believe how rigid Katie had become now that she had the power of the tour book at her fingertips. "What happened to the Katie Weldon who started this trip as a free-spirited woman on an adventure?"

Katie smirked. "She got information. Knowledge is power, you know."

"Knowledge can lead to arrogance and legalism," Todd said. "Let's use the knowledge to make us a kinder bunch of grace-givers."

Christy remembered hearing Todd say those exact words at a Bible study he had taught years ago. He was referring then to the Bible and how some people can get so much information and knowledge about God that they turn into a bunch of rigid rule-makers. She knew he was talking about the tour book now with Katie, but the comparison was strong in her mind. At this point, all she could hope was that Katie would extend grace to her and agree to the Rhine River cruise.

"Oh, all right," Katie said. "I don't want to be a brat about this like I was about not going to the Arctic Circle. We have to stop in Cologne anyway, don't we? We can stay there tonight, take the river cruise in the morning, and be on our way to Amsterdam before the sun goes down. Then we'll spend one day there and go on to Paris because we're going to need at least a couple of days in Paris."

Even though Katie's plan sounded clear and easy, Christy had a feeling it wouldn't go as smoothly as all that. She was just glad that they would see more of Germany, the home of her ancestors. She hoped their boat tour would be a new highlight of the trip.

Once they arrived in Cologne, at Katie's insistence, they walked around the *Dom* before finding a place to stay. The Dom was a twin-towered cathedral close to the rail station. It dominated the area because it was so large. According to Katie, the cathedral was one of the largest Gothic structures in the world, with the foundation built in 1248.

"I'm so bummed we can't go inside," Katie said as they stared up at the massive twin gray spires that pierced the evening sky. "They closed a half hour ago. I told you, didn't I, that this cathedral has relics of the wise men who brought their gifts to baby Jesus? The tour book didn't say what the relics were specifically. I wanted to see the display."

"We could come back tomorrow," Todd suggested.

"No, let's keep going. Youth hostel first, some food, and then in the morning we'll go see Christy's castles."

It didn't settle well with Christy that the reason they were spending an entire day floating down the Rhine River was because she wanted to see more castles. She would have felt better if Todd and Katie were as interested in this tour as she was.

The next day, an hour into the cruise, Christy could tell that Todd and Katie were being nice friends and acting as if this slow boat was fun. But she knew they were miserable, and that made it hard for her to enjoy the leisurely journey.

The first time they went past a castle high on the hillside, tucked behind ancient trees and overlooking the wide Rhine River, Christy could get Todd and Katie to look up and do a little imagining with her.

They answered with clever words when Christy said, "Who do you think lived there? A handsome prince, maybe? Do you think he ever had to fight any battles to defend the castle and his princess?"

By the third castle, no one, not even Christy, wanted to play twenty questions about the imaginary past of the castle. *I think I've seen too much. I feel numb. I mean, this is beautiful and romantic and wonderful, but all I want to do is find a patch of sunshine and curl up like a cat and sleep.*

The boat ride was restful, and more than any of them, Christy felt ready to rest. She knew she hadn't recovered from the exhaustion of her recent difficult school term. Traveling was exciting and fun, but it was anything but restful.

The clouds played hide-and-seek with the sun for the next few hours. While the weather never turned cold, Christy did end up pulling a pair of jeans out of her backpack, going to the rest room, and changing from her shorts.

The stretch from *Koblenz* to *Bingen* was spectacular. A hilltop castle gazed down on them every time they looked up. Christy had a feeling that this part of their trip would be something she would remember years later, as if it had been a dream.

But she was ready for the cruise to be over when they arrived in *Mainz* a little after one in the afternoon. Getting on a modern train and figuring out a way to sleep for the rest of the afternoon appealed to her, as if the gentle Rhine, with its fairy-tale guardian castles, had lulled her into a dreamland. She was eager to go there and allow her weary mind and body to rest deeply.

Todd, however, had different plans. "You guys, the Gutenberg Museum is here. Mind if we go there before heading to the train station?"

"What's at the Gutenberg Museum?" Katie asked.

"The first printed Bible. You've heard of Gutenberg, haven't you? He invented the modern printing press. And the first book he printed, of course, was the Bible. I really want to see it."

Off they went, with their bulky backpacks, to see the first printed Bible and a short movie on Gutenberg's life. Todd was really into the exhibit. Poor Christy couldn't help it; she dozed off when the lights went down for the movie.

They bought some cheese and bread at a corner market and walked to the train station, eating as they walked. Christy was happy to let Todd and Katie do all the discussing about which train to take and when. She couldn't care less where they ended up. The food hadn't helped make her headache go away, and now her throat hurt when she swallowed.

I wish I could go home to Escondido for one day and sleep in my old bed. My mom would bring me tea with honey for my throat. I would take a long bath before sleeping a full ten hours. Then I would wake up refreshed, clean, and energetic and instantly be transported back here. I wish I could do that. Then I'd be able to finish this journey and appreciate everything I'm seeing.

The train ride to Amsterdam was a blur to Christy. She carried her pack and changed trains when Todd told her to. When the conductor asked for passports and tickets, she automatically pulled her Eurail pass from her travel pouch the way she had dozens of times before on this trip. The rest of the time, she snoozed.

When Christy finally began to come back around, she opened her eyes and peered out the window. The sun had set. The world they were rolling past was filled with shadows. Darkness covered the horizon.

"Where are we, you guys? Did we miss the stop for Amsterdam?"

She turned, expecting an answer from her travel companions. But they were gone.

CHAPTER 18

Christy told herself not to panic. *Todd and Katie must have gone for something to eat and didn't want to wake me. We've done that before with each other; this isn't unusual.*

But something didn't feel right. They should have arrived in Amsterdam before dark. Christy vaguely remembered Todd waking her when they changed trains back in Cologne, around five. He had said something about taking three hours to reach Amsterdam, that they would be there before dark, and he would call his friends when the train arrived to see about staying with them.

Christy looked up and down the long aisle for Todd and Katie. The train was slowing to a stop. All she could think to do was to grab her pack and be ready to exit if this was Amsterdam. She would figure out how to find Todd and Katie later. The worst thing would be to miss getting off at the right place the way Katie had almost done in Naples.

When Christy reached up for her pack on the overhead shelf, she noticed Todd and Katie's packs were still there. They wouldn't have left without their packs. They wouldn't have left without her. But where were they? And more important, what station was the train stopping at?

Christy tried to read the station's sign as they rolled in. The sign said *Nancy.* Christy was stunned. *How did we end up in France?*

Just then Katie came bounding up and said, "Hey, Sleeping Beauty. You decided to wake and face the real world, huh?"

What Christy was experiencing at that moment felt like anything but the real world. "Katie, what are we doing in France?"

Todd was right behind Katie. Following him was a guy wearing a baseball cap and toting a backpack. "Christy, this is Seth. What was your last name?"

"Edwards," Seth said. He looked a little older than Todd and just as scruffy, evidence that he had been traveling for a while.

"Seth Edwards," Todd repeated. "This is Christy."

Then, to Christy's surprise, Todd added with a gentle smile, "Christy Miller, my girlfriend." Todd never had described her that way. If she hadn't still been confused and shocked about being in France instead of Holland, she might have taken Todd's words deeper into her heart.

"We met Seth in the dining car, and he has lots of great tips on what to see and do in Paris," Katie said.

"Would someone mind telling me what's happening?" Christy asked as the three of them sat down. "I thought we were going to Amsterdam."

"We changed plans," Katie said brightly. "We told you on the train from Mainz to Cologne, and you said that was fine; whatever we wanted."

"I don't remember," Christy said.

Seth smiled at her. He had nice eyes. They were deep blue and matched the dark blue denim shirt he wore over a stained white T-shirt. "It catches up with you, doesn't it?"

"What catches up?"

"Travel fatigue. All the new sights and sounds and food. From what Todd and Katie told me, you guys have been going at it pretty hard and fast. I'm on a much slower pace, but it still hits me about every two weeks, and I have to stay somewhere for a few more days before I can go on."

"Seth has already been to Paris," Katie said. "He had way more information than our tour book. He's going back to meet up with some friends. He just spent the last two weeks in Venice. Can you imagine spending two weeks in one place?"

Right now that luxury sounded very nice to Christy. "Did these guys tell you that all we saw was the inside of the Venice train station for a few hours?"

"You have to go back," Seth said. "You can't come all this way and not see Venice, even if it's only for a day. However, fourteen days is better than one."

"Did you happen to notice a jewelry store called Santini?" Katie asked. "Wasn't that Marcos's last name? I have it written down somewhere. "

"Their name is Savini," Todd corrected her.

"And if you ever want a good place to stay on Capri," Katie told Seth, "go to the Villa Paradiso and tell them Carlos Savini sent you." She proceeded to tell Seth all about their free deluxe hotel room in Capri.

Seth had a story about a Swiss family he had met on the train a few months earlier and how they had invited him to stay with them. After opening his pack and pulling out a small journal with several postcards sticking out, he asked if he could write their name in Christy's tour book.

"I'm serious," Seth said, pulling off the pen's cap with his teeth. "They would love to have you guys stay with them. They live in a chalet in this small Swiss alpine village called Adelboden." Seth flipped though his journal. "I'll write it all down here. You take the train from Bern to Thun to Spiez and then to Frutigen. You have to take a bus to Adelboden. The scenery is incredible."

"How long did you stay there?" Katie asked.

"Five days, I think. I slept in the hayloft, and during the day I helped out on their small farm. It was a kick. You guys would love it. I'm serious. Just tell them Seth Edwards sent you."

For the next two hours into Paris, they swapped travel stories with Seth. Christy felt a little more awake and coherent by the time they arrived, even though she was sure it was well after midnight.

Seth knew of a reasonable hotel near the train station. The four of them crashed for the night and met up the next morning at eight after taking showers.

"I need to get going," Seth said. "Sure was great meeting all of you. I hope the rest of your trip goes well."

"Yours too," Katie said. "Thanks for all the tips about what to see."

"I stuck a paper in your tour book with a list of those restaurants I was telling you about in Venice, in case you guys make it there."

"We will," Katie said. "If I have anything to say about it, we definitely will."

After saying good-bye to Seth, Todd suggested they eat something and head for the Eiffel Tower while it was still cool. He had heard someone on the train last night say that a heat wave was expected for the next few days in Paris, which was unusual so early in the summer. They could tour the air-conditioned Louvre during the hottest part of the day.

Christy hadn't slept as deeply as she needed to shake the fuzzy-headed feeling that had come over her. Their breakfast pastry and strong coffee didn't snap her out of her fog, either. She took pictures of the Eiffel Tower and agreed with Katie that it cost too much to tour the top. Todd coaxed them onto the *metro,* which was a modern subway system under the city, and directed them where to get off for Notre Dame.

As they approached the huge, light gray, west-facing front of the cathedral, Christy asked Katie if she could see the tour book. She wanted to find out how old this church was and how it compared to the cathedral in Cologne. They resembled each other some, but instead of twin spires in the front, Notre Dame had two identical towers that looked like open bell towers.

Katie handed her the book. When Christy opened it, three postcards fell out onto the pavement. The first card was of the Austrian Alps. Another one was of the Seine River in Paris. And the third was a picture of a gondola docked against a red-and-white-striped pole. The gondolier stood on the dock, complete with a wide-brimmed straw hat with a blue ribbon hanging down the back. He leaned casually against the pole and indicated with his hand that his gondola was available for the next rider.

These must be Seth's postcards. Christy turned over the one of the gondola from Venice. It was addressed to a Franklin Madison in Glenbrooke, Oregon. None of the postcards had a stamp on it. Christy tucked them into the back of the tour book and decided she would be nice and mail the postcards for Seth. They must have ended up in her book when he was sticking the list of restaurants in it.

Turning to the section on Paris, Christy skimmed the information on Notre Dame. "Can you believe this church was built almost a hundred years before the one we saw in Cologne? It says here that people have worshiped on this spot for nearly two thousand years."

She was struck with awe, the way she had been in Norway when they saw the simple, eight-hundred-year-old church and the sharp contrast it provided to Saint Peter's Basilica in Rome. "People want to meet God, don't they?" Christy said as they stood gazing up at Notre Dame. "Deep within the human heart is the desire to meet God. I never realized that as clearly as I have while we've been traveling."

"Look at that window," Katie said. "What does it say about the window?"

Christy read aloud, " 'The great rose window contains its original medieval glass. It was the largest such window of its time, and the design is so accomplished that it shows no sign of distortion after seven hundred years.' "

"Now, that's craftsmanship for you," Todd said. "Has anyone else noticed how art used to be used to demonstrate biblical truths? Man, have we come a long way from that being art's purpose!"

The three friends took more than two hours to tour the inside of the cathedral. It was dark and solemn. They climbed the winding stairs to the top, and Katie said, "Don't you feel as if you're caught inside a snail's shell when we go up these kinds of stairs?"

"It makes me dizzy," Christy said.

"I just think about what muscular legs those monks must have hid under their robes after climbing these stairs a couple of times a day to ring the bells," Todd answered.

At the top, they noticed how hot the day had become. The view of Paris looked hazy in the rising heat. From where they stood, Christy thought the Seine River looked appealing. Any kind of water at this point, either on her or in her, would feel refreshing.

It didn't take much for Todd to persuade them to descend the stairs and find something to eat before going on to the Louvre. To save money, they bought their food from a vendor's cart. Christy's hot dog-like sausage was too spicy for her, and she could only eat half of it. The Coke was as hot as the crate it was pulled from. She downed the hot, fizzy beverage but felt only thirstier.

At least inside the Louvre was cool. Christy felt spacey in the vast palace-turned-museum. She wished they had someone like Marcos to let them in a back door and lead them right to the rooms with the exhibits of greatest interest. As it was, they paid for their admission using their International Student ID cards to receive a discount. They entered through a modern, intricately designed glass pyramid, and from then on, Christy felt disoriented.

Katie was on a mission to find the *Mona Lisa*. Her determination to locate that famous little lady was much stronger than the interest she had expressed in finding the *Little Mermaid*. Once they entered the room where the small oil painting hung on the wall, Katie edged her way to the front of the crowd to have a close look. Christy and Todd stood at the fringes and peeked over people's shoulders.

"It's a lot smaller than I thought it would be," Todd said.

Christy smiled. "Funny how that goes, isn't it?"

Katie, still in her spunky mood, turned around at the front of the crowd of *Mona Lisa* viewers and shot a picture of Todd and Christy.

"That guard is going to take your camera away," Christy said as Katie came toward them.

"Why? It says not to take flash photographs of the *Mona Lisa*. It doesn't say anything about taking pictures of people looking at the *Mona Lisa*."

"Where to next?" Todd asked.

"Home," Christy said wearily.

"You want to go back to the hotel?" Todd asked.

"No, I think I want to go back to Escondido. I officially have hit overload. I don't think I can take in another wonder of the world. My brain can't hold it."

"How about if we get out of town," Todd suggested. "We could take a train or bus out to Versailles. It's only about a half hour away."

Christy didn't much care at this point. Sitting down for a half hour was what appealed to her the most. They briefly toured the Egyptian exhibit and several other rooms in the Louvre before Todd led the way back outside into the stifling afternoon heat.

After asking four people, Todd finally decided he knew where they should go to catch a bus to Versailles. They waited twenty minutes in the heat, rode forty minutes in air-conditioned comfort, and bought large bottles of water from a vendor immediately on arriving.

Standing back and surveying the massive, yellowish-cream-colored palace, Christy felt as if what she stared at couldn't be real. It was so perfectly balanced. Every window, column, and roof line seemed to be matched perfectly with the rest of the huge structure. Instead of being one long building with a flat front, the palace was constructed with stairstep-like indentations of buildings that led in tandem to the center.

Katie, who had been reading about this seventeenth-century home of the French monarchy, said, "Just look at that place. Can you image all those peasants starving to death and Marie Antoinette sitting somewhere inside that palace?"

Christy didn't know what Katie was getting at. Katie apparently read Christy's confused expression and said, "You remember, they came to her and said the starving citizens of France had no bread; so Marie Antoinette said, 'Let them eat cake.' "

For perhaps the first time on this trip, Christy wasn't intrigued by the history lesson. She liked the idea of cake, though. Or pastry. Or even a humble cookie. The half of a hot dog she had eaten for lunch wasn't doing her stomach any favors.

Blessedly, it felt cooler inside the gigantic palace. The water Christy had gulped also helped her to cool off. She found herself settling into a strange, robotic mode. Her feet moved her from room to room. Her eyes took in the sights. Each bedroom seemed more magnificent than the last. The ballroom made her think of something out of a Cinderella movie. She saw it all and took it in, but as she had told Todd earlier, she was on overload.

"Are you okay?" he asked on the bus ride back to Paris.

"I don't know," she said. "How can you take it all in? Doesn't everything you see make you feel something? And don't you reach the point where you don't have any feelings left to invest?"

Todd didn't answer right away. He seemed to be thinking about her questions. His answer came in the form of a few more questions for Christy. "Do you think that's why the work at the orphanage has been so draining this year? Do you think you take it all in and feel something deep every day about those kids? I wonder if that's what's been happening. Then you reach the point where you can't invest any more emotionally because you've spent so much of yourself."

"Todd," Christy said, leaning her weary head against his shoulder, "I think you have just figured out the answer to what has plagued me for months."

"I know you've been struggling with it because of your emails."

"The need is so great . . ." she said.

Todd turned his chin and gently kissed the top of her head. "But, Christy, the need is not the call. You are uniquely gifted by God. The key is finding out what it is you are uniquely gifted to do, and that's what you pour out of yourself. If you're operating within your gifts, you will feel energized, not emptied."

Christy pulled up her head and looked at Todd. "Are you saying I'm not gifted to work with children?" That possibility felt like a blow. For several years she had thought that was what she was supposed to do. It had started when Katie talked her into helping in the nursery class at church. Christy liked helping out. Ever since then, she had been making decisions about what to do with her life based on what she thought was a talent of working with children.

"I don't know exactly what God has gifted you to do or called you to do. That's something between Him and you. Ask Him. He'll tell you."

Christy leaned her head back on Todd's shoulder. Until this moment, she had thought her future was nicely structured. Her plans had been set long ago. She would earn a degree in early childhood education. Then she might be a preschool teacher, which was a plan she liked because she could do that no matter where she lived or if she was single or married or had children of her own.

"All I know," Todd said, leaning his chin against her head, "is that the future is wide open to you, Christina Juliet Miller. You are gifted by God, and He has called you to serve Him in a unique way. A verse in Romans says that the gifts and the calling of God are irrevocable. No one can ever take away from you who you are. You are free to dream as big a dream as you dare to dream."

If Christy thought her mind and emotions were on overload before, all circuits shut down now. Looking up into Todd's eyes, she knew he had just given her an important truth. With that truth came the freedom to become a person she had never dreamed of becoming before.

"Hold these tears for me," she whispered. Todd put his arm around her, and Christy leaned against his chest, letting the tears flow directly over his heart.

CHAPTER 19

The next morning, Christy was hot when she woke in her room at the Paris hotel. She kicked off the sheet and lay in bed, wishing with all her heart that she could find a way to express to Todd how much she appreciated the gift of his words. Shortly after arriving in Basel and beginning her work at the orphanage, she had found herself fighting against a deep sorrow and weariness whenever she was around the children. What kept her there all those months was the knowledge that they needed her.

Deep inside, Christy had felt emptied. At first she thought something was wrong with her, because when she looked at the workers around her, they all seemed to get filled up and invigorated working with the children.

"What time is it?" Katie mumbled, kicking off her bed sheets, as well.

"It's only seven. We were going to try to sleep in today, but I can't. It's too hot."

"Let's wake up Todd and tell him we're ready for breakfast. Are you sure that window is open as far as it will go?"

"Yes. We didn't have much of a breeze last night. It's not that it's so hot; it's just that there's no air. If we had a fan it would be much better."

"I doubt they have any extra fans," Katie said. "This is a budget hotel, you know. Seth told us it was the best he knew of this close to town."

"That reminds me," Christy said. "I ended up with some of Seth's postcards. They need stamps so I was going to mail them for him today and write home to my family, too. Have you sent any postcards yet?"

"Are you kidding? When did we have time to buy postcards? Or souvenirs, for that matter. Do you realize the only thing I've bought so far is food? At least you were smart and bought that diary in Italy. I wish I had gotten one."

"We sure haven't done any shopping, have we?" Christy said.

"I wish now I had bought that sweater we saw in the shop window in Oslo. Do you remember? It was a blue-and-white hand-knit ski sweater. I think we figured out it cost about eighty-five dollars."

Christy could barely even think about a ski sweater in their present sweltering condition. "Do you have that much to spend on souvenirs? I'm impressed."

"Not really, but I could have bought it and then eaten bread and water the rest of the trip."

"I feel like all we've been eating lately has been bread and water," Christy said. "I don't even want pastry this morning, if you can believe that."

"No, I don't believe you for one second."

"I want some protein. Doesn't chicken sound good right now? Or a steak?"

"I'd settle for a Big Mac and French fries," Katie said.

"Oh, don't do that to me! Do you know how long it's been since I've had American French fries?" Christy sat up and reached for the clothes she had left hanging over the end of her bed. "Come on, let's get dressed and go find some French fries. We are in France, after all. If Todd wants to sleep, we'll let him sleep. I want to eat!"

"I'm with you."

Christy and Katie had just pulled on their shorts when a knock sounded on the door. "Just a minute," Christy called out. She shook out her last slightly clean T-shirt and pulled it over her head. "Are you decent?" she asked Katie.

"I'm never just decent. I'm always extra nice."

Christy gave her a pained expression and opened the door. Todd stood there, dressed and ready to go. He grinned when he saw Christy. "You guys couldn't sleep in, either, I take it."

"We've talked ourselves into a food frenzy, Todd." Katie quickly brushed her hair. "Join us, if you dare. But I warn you, it might not be a pretty sight. Our quest for French fries is not for the fainthearted."

"I think I'm up to the challenge. Although I've never heard of anyone actually buying French fries in France. When I was in Spain, the word was that the best French fries on the continent were in Brussels."

"How far away is that?" Katie asked.

"Three hours, I'd guess," Todd said. "It's between here and Amsterdam."

"Then, let's go," Katie said. "I'm ready to blow this town, aren't you? It's too hot. And what's left for us to see? We managed to fit in all the main sights yesterday."

"What about going to Spain?" Christy asked. "I mean, aren't we half-way there?"

"Not exactly," Todd said. "It's almost twelve hours from here to Barcelona and then seven hours from Barcelona to Madrid."

"I forgot that Paris was so far north," Christy said. "But don't you want to see your old friends?"

Todd thought a moment and then shrugged. "A lot of them have taken other posts around Europe or have gone back to the States. I can't think of anyone I was close to who's still there."

"So Brussels it is!" Katie announced, throwing clothes into her bag.

"I'll go pack." Todd headed back to his room.

Christy had noticed when she opened the door that his forehead was peeling slightly where her hot tea had burned him. At least it wasn't red anymore and looked as if it was healing.

"Do you think they have a place where we could do some laundry in Brussels?" Katie asked. "I'm on my last clean everything today."

"Me too," Christy said. "It's been a week since I washed my stuff in Oslo."

Katie stopped her frantic packing. "That means we have less than a week left."

Christy looked at the round clock on the wall. "It's eight o'clock. Exactly one week from right now I'll start summer term. And now I don't know if I even want to finish those classes."

"Why not?" Katie asked.

Christy tried to explain how Todd's words on the bus had given her freedom. She felt as if God had released her from the work at the orphanage and from the drive to earn a degree in early childhood education.

Katie stared at Christy. Perspiration from their stuffy room glistened on Katie's forehead. "What are you going to do now?"

"I have no idea," Christy said with a smile.

"And that doesn't spook you just a little?"

"I think I was a lot more frightened when I was working so hard for a degree that didn't make me feel excited about the future."

"This is big-time, Christy. I mean, you were supposed to enter Rancho Corona in September with all the credits you were going to transfer from this program in Basel. You were on a fast track to graduate."

"I know."

"If you change majors now, aren't you a little freaked out about losing all those credits? It could take you a whole lot longer to finish."

"I know."

"Don't you get it?" Katie stood with both her hands on her hips. The perspiration was now streaming down her face. "That means even longer before you and Todd can get married."

Christy gave Katie a timid shrug. The same thought had crossed Christy's mind. But she was too euphoric about the thought that she could dream new, big, freer dreams to let that complication steal her sunshine.

"Let's head out of here," Katie said. "I don't want to get any more heated up in this room. I feel like I'm going to melt."

Once they walked out of the old building, the air movement allowed them to breathe again. It was warm, but nothing like it had been in their closed-off room. They walked to the nearby train station and bought rolls and cheese and funny-shaped cartons of yogurt to eat on the train.

The three hours to Brussels, Katie was quiet. Christy knew Katie wanted to talk more about Christy's life-changing decision to switch majors. But

Katie seemed to be waiting until Todd wasn't around before she continued to give Christy the rest of her mind on the topic.

Katie got her chance about a half hour before they arrived in Brussels. Todd left them alone while he went to stretch his legs, and Katie jumped right in. "So do you think you would get married before you finish college?"

"Katie, I can't believe you're asking me that."

"I know you've thought about it. I'm just trying to get you to answer your own question."

"I don't know, Katie. All I can do is take one step at a time, as God makes that step clear. Right now all I know for sure is that I have the freedom to change my major. I don't know what I'm going to change it to. I don't know if I'm going to stay in Basel for the summer session. And I really don't know what the next step is in my relationship with Todd."

"And that doesn't frighten you?"

Christy thought a moment before shaking her head. "No, it feels right. More right than anything has felt in a long time." She remembered how distinctly changed she had felt the night she and Todd had stood under the amber streetlight on the uneven cobblestone street in Capri. All doubts had flown from her heart. She knew then that she had passed through some invisible tunnel and was no longer a teenager. She was a woman. That same sense came on her now. Christy wondered if this was what a person was supposed to feel like after yielding every area of life to the Lord and waiting for Him to move.

She tried to explain it to Katie as an awareness of the Holy Spirit's presence comforting her. Katie said she thought she understood. Todd returned then and all talk of future plans ceased.

Christy didn't mind that she and Katie were done talking about that subject for the time being. However, Christy knew she needed to have an openhearted discussion with Todd. She had some decisions to make in the next few days, and she wanted Todd's input. More important, she wanted to hear what Todd's plans were for the future.

Their train arrived in Brussels, Belgium, at exactly noon. The first thing they did was search for a French fry cart. Todd said his friends from

Spain had come back with stories of such carts on Belgium streets, just like Italy had gelato carts and New York had hot dog carts.

They didn't have to go far from the station before they spotted their first *frites* cart. As they stood and watched, large wedges of already fried potatoes were fried a second time until they were crackling hot. The vendor offered them several sauces to dip the frites in. One looked like mayonnaise. Christy passed on the sauce and tried her frites *au naturel*.

"Hot!" she said after taking the first bite.

Todd tried one of the darker-tinted sauces. "Not barbecue sauce. Not ketchup. I don't know. Shrimp cocktail, maybe."

"This is so bizarre," Katie said, trying the mayonnaise-looking dip. "I like it, so maybe I don't want to know what I'm dipping it in."

"In Switzerland the kids at the orphanage like their popcorn with sugar on it instead of salt and butter," Christy said. She realized that was the first time she had brought up anything about the orphanage this trip without feeling a tightening knot in her stomach. She was free. Really free.

Christy enjoyed her frites immensely. She surprised Todd and Katie by ordering a second helping when they were ready to walk away.

"We've had our French fries," Katie said. "What do you guys think? Do you want to stick around here awhile or jump on a train and head for Amsterdam?"

"We just got here," Christy said.

"I checked the train schedule," Todd said. "It's about three hours from here to Amsterdam. A lot of trains run during the day. We could stay here for the afternoon and then go on to Amsterdam for the night. If we decide to do that, I should call my friends to see if we can stay with them."

The next goal was to return to the train station, find a phone, check train schedules, and settle their plans for the day. A short time later Todd exited the phone booth with a piece of paper in his hand.

"They're expecting us at six-thirty tonight. Mike said he would pick us up at the station and take us to The Rock for their seven-o'clock meeting. I'm going to help out with music tonight."

"Wait a second," Katie said. "What did I miss here? What is The Rock? What music are you talking about?"

Todd explained that a couple he worked with in Spain now ran a youth hostel in Amsterdam called The Rock. Every night they offered a worship service from seven to eight. Christy could tell Todd was excited about seeing his friends and probably even more excited to have a guitar in his hands again.

The heat wave wasn't as overwhelming in Brussels, but the afternoon sun was strong enough as they walked around with their heavy packs, killing time. Christy and Katie left their packs with Todd outside a small shop so they could go in and hunt for Belgian chocolate and some souvenirs. Christy bought three beautiful, delicate lace doilies that the clerk said were handmade. Katie said she wasn't exactly a doily kind of person, but the clerk talked her into buying four lace bookmarks.

"I thought they would be good gifts for people when I get home," Katie said. "Especially because they don't weigh anything." She strapped on her pack and groaned. "Is it my imagination or do dirty clothes weigh more?"

They found a park a few blocks away and stretched out in the shade.

"Oh, I was going to buy postcards," Christy said. "And stamps."

"I'll stay here with your packs if you and Katie want to go back into town," Todd said.

"You know, this seems crazy," Christy said. "We're all kind of tired and not energetic enough to see anything around here. We don't need to wait until the late afternoon train to Amsterdam. We could go now and spend our time buying postcards and stamps in Amsterdam as easily as here."

"I agree," Katie said. "Besides, I'm hungry for some more frites. Let's go."

They stopped at the same cart where they had bought the fries before and then ate them as they walked to the station. Their timing was perfect because the next train to Amsterdam was just pulling up. Once they were settled in their seats, Katie started to laugh.

"What?" Christy asked.

"Are we getting apathetic or what? We just spent two hours in an entire country. That was Belgium. Buh-bye, Belgium," Katie said, waving like a beauty queen as the train pulled out.

"It is pretty pathetic," Christy said, "when the only souvenirs we've bought this whole trip are from a country we only stopped in so we could eat their French fries."

All three of them laughed. The train pulled out of the station, and Todd challenged Christy to a game of chess. Katie announced she was going to find something to drink. "You guys want anything?"

"No, thanks." Christy pulled out a brush from her pack. While Todd set up the pieces, she worked on her hair. Most of the trip she had worn it in a loose braid. This morning, because of the heat, she had twisted it up on the back of her head, but it had been falling out slowly over the last few hours. Now she let down her hair and brushed out the tangles.

"I like your hair long," Todd said in one of his famous short statements.

Christy felt herself blush. Todd rarely made any comments about her appearance. Years ago he had said he liked her hair long after she had chopped it off. She had been growing it out since then, partly because she knew that's how Todd liked it, but mostly because she liked doing a lot of different things with it.

Todd made the first move on the chessboard. Christy playfully turned her back to Todd and then tilted her head all the way back. The ends of her straight hair almost reached to her waist.

"There," she said, her chin tipped toward the ceiling. "Is that long enough?"

She turned to Todd. He had a smile on his face. It was the same happy, contented smile she had seen when he kissed her in Norway on their way to see the *Kon-Tiki*.

She made her move on the chessboard, then twisted her hair and was about to fasten it with a clip, when Todd took his move and then said, "No, braid it. I want to see how you do it."

Christy divided her hair into three sections. "Like this," she said, quickly passing the sections between each other and making a braid in a few seconds.

"Wait, that was too fast. Do it again."

"Why? Do you want to learn how to braid or something?"

"Sure," Todd said as if her words were the only invitation he needed. Leaning forward and taking the strands from her, he said, "Okay, which side do you start with?"

"Either one. Doesn't matter." She sat patiently while Todd asked directions and slowly braided her hair. The first braid was too loose. On his second try, he pulled too hard, and Christy let out a yelp.

"This better?" Todd asked as he more gently tugged and twisted her hair.

"That's okay. It doesn't have to be really tight. Just tighter than the first time."

"There," Todd announced. "How's that?"

Christy took the braid from him and felt up and down with her fingers. "Not bad."

"Not bad?" Todd said. "I'd say it's better than not bad. I'd say it's pretty good."

"Okay," Christy said, turning and smiling at him. "It's pretty good."

Todd smiled back. "It's my move, right?"

"Very sneaky! You know it's my turn." Christy stared at the pieces on the chessboard for a long while. She wasn't thinking about chess, though. She was thinking about the way Todd had braided her hair and the way she knew he was staring at her now.

That had to be one of the most tender, romantic gestures you've ever made toward me, Todd Spencer. You're in love with me, aren't you?

She could tell he was leaning closer. Christy pretended to concentrate on the game board, but she couldn't because she could feel Todd's warm breath on her neck. All she had to do was turn her head slightly and she would feel what she wanted to—Todd's lips brushing her cheek.

"You're beautiful," he whispered after his lips touched her cheek. "In every way, Kilikina. You're beautiful." Then his lips meet hers in a warm, tender kiss.

CHAPTER 20

Never before had Christy felt so overwhelmed emotionally, spiritually, and physically. The intensity startled her and caused her to pull away. With her heart pounding, she looked at Todd, who was now a foot away instead of an inch away. His expression was the most tender, gentle, wholehearted look of love she had ever seen.

"Todd," Christy said with a thin voice. "I . . . I . . ."

"I know." Todd rubbed the back of his neck with his hand. "I didn't mean to . . ."

"I know," Christy said.

"But I meant what I said."

Christy smiled. "Thank you."

Todd rose and moved to the seat across from Christy. He leaned forward and reached for her hand, holding loosely on to only her first three fingers. The words didn't seem to be coming to him.

Christy had words she wanted to give Todd. Her mind was clear, and her heart was full. "Todd," she said, leaning forward and speaking softly, "I thought about something while you were on your polar bear journey. I decided I like kissing you just a little too much."

Todd's surprised expression made her quickly add, "What I mean is that we've never talked about standards or limits or guidelines or anything."

Todd nodded.

"Well, this may sound idealistic, but I thought about all this a lot, and I came up with some ideas."

"Go on."

Christy tried her best to explain to Todd her idea of saving her kisses and spending them sparingly. She told him about her imaginary piggy bank filling up with expressions of affection. "So you see, I wanted to spend one of my really big kisses on you just a minute ago, but I pulled back so I could save that one in my piggy bank. Then when . . ." Christy didn't want to say, "when we get married." Instead, she paused. Feeling her cheeks reddening, she finished the thought with, " . . . then it will be saved until the time is right, and I'll be able to freely spend everything."

Todd looked at Christy with what appeared to be deep admiration. He seemed to be moved by what she had said. But a minute passed before he finally spoke. "Thank you."

"For what?"

"For caring. For thinking through that part of our relationship. I'd thought about it a long time ago and decided I was only going to kiss you on special occasions. One of my guidelines was to keep our kisses short and in public so we would have nothing to hide."

Christy hadn't realized Todd had thought through this part of their relationship. But as she contemplated it, she saw that during the past five years his expressions of affection had fallen into those guidelines.

"Things are changing for us, and I'm glad they are." He gave her fingers a squeeze. "We're getting closer to each other. I think that means we're going to have a lot more decisions to make, separately and together. You've made a really wise decision ahead of me in this area. But your choice helps me, and I appreciate that. I'll be saving kisses in my bank, as well."

Christy glanced over Todd's head and saw Katie was returning.

Todd read her expression and said, "We can talk about this some more later."

Christy gave Todd a pesky little grin. In imitation of the teenager Todd used to be, with a chin-up nod, Christy pulled her hand from his and said, "Later."

Whether Todd caught the connection, Christy didn't know. Katie plopped down next to Christy, examined the chessboard, and said, "Who's winning?"

Christy glanced at Todd. He grinned back. In unison they said, "We both are."

"Whoa!" Katie said. "Did you two practice that while I was gone?"

What we almost practiced while you were gone was our kissing technique! If you hadn't gotten me thinking about setting my own limits, Katie, I think that's exactly what you would have found us doing.

"Christy was teaching me how to come out ahead," Todd said, his eyes fixed on the chessboard.

"Christy was?"

"Yep," Todd said. "And it's my turn, right?"

"Not exactly, pal," Christy teased. "It's my turn, remember?"

"This I have to see," Katie said.

All the way to Amsterdam they played a round of "group" chess in which Katie advised each of them on their moves. Once they arrived in Amsterdam, Christy grabbed her pack, and Seth's postcards spilled out on the floor. Katie accidentally stepped on one of the cards, and Christy picked them up, trying to brush off the dirt.

"I have to mail these before I lose them," she said, immediately realizing how crazy that sounded. These weren't even her cards. Yet someone on the other side of the globe in some place called Glenbrooke, Oregon, needed to receive those postcards from Seth. She wondered if she was taking this responsibility too seriously.

The three of them filed their way through the crowded train station, and Christy thought about how she took most of her responsibilities and commitments seriously. In some instances, such as in her relationship with Todd, that was a very good thing. But did she have to be so determined and responsible with everything—like postcards?

Their time to explore Amsterdam was shorter than they thought it would be. Todd's friend from Spain, Mike, showed up at six-thirty and drove them in his small car across town to the youth hostel he and his wife ran. At first Christy thought she might have met Mike and Megan during the short week she was in Spain more than a year ago. But they had come to Amsterdam and had been running the ministry at The Rock for almost two years now.

Christy liked Megan at once and asked Megan how she could help her get ready for the evening's event. Slim, energetic, blond Megan told Christy and Katie to relax. Every night they held a casual worship and praise service. She said sometimes half a dozen people came, sometimes it was just the two of them.

Mike handed Todd his guitar. Christy could hear him plucking out some of his old favorites, like one he wrote, "The Dust of His Feet." Katie and Christy settled themselves on a beat-up old couch toward the front of the small meeting room. Todd went on to play a song Doug had written, and Katie started to sing. Christy joined her, and a few people, hearing the music, shuffled into the meeting room.

Todd closed his eyes, and tilting his head toward the heavens, he sang out the lyrics, "Sing to the One who rides across the ancient heavens, His mighty voice thundering from the sky. For God is awesome in His sanctuary.' "

This is what Todd is gifted to do, Christy thought. *He told me God has uniquely gifted each of us. I believe that. And I believe Todd is gifted to lead people in worship. He has a shepherd's heart.*

The hour-long service turned into two hours. At first, only three students who were staying at the hostel entered. More began to come. Christy counted fifteen and then twenty. The worship time was awesome. About ten people stayed around to talk to Mike. Christy, Katie, and Todd had a discussion with a guy from Argentina. At nearly eleven, Christy noticed that Mike was praying with two of the guys he had been talking with.

After everyone else left, Christy, Todd, and Katie gathered in the small kitchen with Mike and Megan. Megan had just found out that they hadn't eaten since their frites in Belgium that afternoon and was making grilled cheese sandwiches for them.

"And I'm even using white bread," Megan said with a smile. "This is my one comfort food around here. It's not exactly Velveeta and Wonder Bread like my mom used to make, but it's as close to Americana as you'll find in this part of the city."

"God really did something tonight," Mike said. "Did you see me praying with those two guys? They're from Scotland, and both of them said they wanted to give their lives to the Lord. It was incredible. God really used you, Todd."

"It wasn't me," Todd said. "It was God's timing."

"Yes, it was God's timing that you were here to play and lead worship on a night when those two guys happened to stay here. But I also think God used you, Todd, because you were available and open to Him."

Christy devoured two of Megan's sandwiches and thought about how she wanted her life to be like that—open and available to the Lord so He could use the gifts He had given her to further His kingdom.

Now, if only I could figure out exactly what those gifts are.

The next morning, in the same close kitchen, Christy and Todd sat eating bowls of oatmeal and talking with Megan and Mike. Katie was still asleep. As Christy listened, Mike asked Todd questions she had wanted to ask Todd for a long time.

"What are your plans for the future?" Mike asked.

"I'm working the rest of the summer at home to save some money. In September I'll start at Rancho Corona. I have about a year left. Maybe less."

"And then what?" Megan asked.

Todd was looking down into his oatmeal. He turned his head slightly and gave Christy a sideways glance. "Not sure yet," he said.

"Have you thought about going into missions work full time?" Mike asked. "You know, raise support and make the long-term commitment?"

"I've thought about it."

"What about coming back to Europe?"

"It's a possibility," Todd said.

"You probably have figured out what I'm getting at," Mike said. "We would love to have you here. We need help running The Rock. You are a perfect fit. Meg and I got excited last night talking about what could happen if you came on staff with us."

Todd quietly ate the last of his oatmeal without responding.

"Think about it," Mike said, pulling back. "Pray about it."

Todd nodded.

"So," Megan said, obviously trying to take the attention off Todd, "tell us about you, Christy. You said last night you're going to school in Basel. What are your plans after that?"

"Well, I'm not real sure. I've been doing some soul-searching on this trip, and I just realized a couple of days ago, as Todd and I were talking, that I'm headed in a direction I don't want to go."

"Do you mean with the orphanage and all that?" Megan asked. "You were saying last night that it really took a lot out of you to be with the kids."

Christy nodded. "I'm discovering that I don't have the gifts needed for a long-term commitment like that. I need to figure out where I'm gifted and see what I should be doing instead."

"Christy is exceptionally gifted," Todd said.

"Really?" Mike looked interested. "Do you sing, Christy?"

"No, not really."

"Do you like to teach?"

"Sort of. Little kids."

"What about counseling?" Megan asked.

Christy shook her head. She was beginning to realize that the quest to find out what she was gifted at might be a rather long journey. Nothing popped right out as her specialty. It made her feel insecure.

"Christy has a rare, pure, golden heart," Todd said. He looked at her with an open, caring expression. "She gives unconditionally and is a constant source of encouragement. She's gracious and patient and organized. She looks for the best in people and in every situation. She's willing to go the extra mile, even when it's inconvenient for her. She's flexible to change, generous, and wise beyond her years. God is going to use Christy's life in a powerful way."

When Todd finished, none of them spoke for a moment. Christy was stunned at his shower of praise.

Megan was the one who finally broke the silence. "Todd, why didn't you tell us? Christy's the one you were talking about before, isn't she?" Turning to Christy she said, "I should have figured it out. When Todd first came to Spain, we kept trying to fix him up with this woman on staff who was from Pennsylvania. Todd was nice to her. He was nice to everybody.

But when he turned down all our dating tips, I asked him what the deal was. Do you remember that conversation, Todd?"

Christy glanced at Todd. He seemed to be trying to signal Megan that their conversation had been private.

Megan pulled back and said, "So he . . . I mean, you were . . ."

"I wasn't interested in Tina. That's what you're trying to say, isn't it?"

Megan grinned sheepishly at Christy. "We thought it was so cute. You know, we were Mike and Megan, and we figured Todd and Tina should be together. But Todd said he was interested in someone else, and he was waiting on God's timing. Now I guess we know who that someone was. It was you."

"It was," Todd said, giving Christy his full attention.

"Morning all," Katie said, making a grand entrance into the kitchen. "What did I miss?"

Only one of the most tender expressions of Todd's forever kind of friendship that he's given me since the day he first put this bracelet on my wrist. I'm his girlfriend, Katie! I really am. He loves me. He's loved me for a long time.

"Nothing," Christy said.

It wasn't that she didn't want Katie involved in this conversation, but the revelation had been perfect just the way it was. She didn't want anyone to repeat the details when it wouldn't have the same effect it already had had on her.

"I suppose you three are ready to see Amsterdam," Mike said, changing the subject for Christy. "Do you want to borrow a car, Todd?"

"No, we can use our train passes. You might want to give us a few tips. And if it's okay with Katie and Christy, I think we'll stay here tonight, too."

"Definitely," Katie said. "Only one small request. Do you have a washing machine, Megan?"

"Sure. It's small. Euro-size. You guys are welcome to use it. Or better yet, give me your clothes when you head out for the day, and I'll run them through for you."

"That would be great," Christy said. "Thank you."

Mike suggested several places to visit, including some art museums, the Hiding Place, where Corrie Ten Boom had lived, and the Anne Frank museum.

"Any preferences?" Todd asked.

"I'd love to see the Hiding Place," Christy said. "And at least one art museum. We sort of ran through the Louvre a little too fast. I'm feeling like we could use one more brush with culture before we go for our yodeling lessons in the Alps."

"Is that where you're going next?" Megan asked.

"Looks like it," Todd said. "But we're flexible."

Todd displayed his flexibility that day by doing whatever Christy wanted. Katie noticed it after they bought their admission for the Van Gogh museum. "I thought you said you weren't interested in any more art, either, Todd."

"Christy wanted to see this. I think it's a good idea."

In Christy's opinion, it was a good idea. Katie got more into the exhibit when she recognized some of Vincent Van Gogh's art and realized he was the tormented artist who cut off his ear.

For a long while, Christy stood in front of Van Gogh's famous painting of sunflowers. In some places, the paint was plopped onto the canvas so thick it stood up like freshly whipped cream stiffened into peaks. Only instead of white whipped cream, the colors were bright yellow. In other places, Christy could see the original canvas where no splotches of paint had landed. Such creative expression fascinated her.

When they went on to the Hiding Place, Katie complained again that she had voted for the Anne Frank museum, but Todd had decided on Christy's choice even though it was farther out of the city. To make matters worse, the Ten Boom clock shop, where the Hiding Place was located, was closed when they arrived so they weren't able to go on a tour.

The threesome returned to The Rock at six o'clock, just in time for the homemade dinner Megan had promised them. Christy told Megan that was the best meat loaf, mashed potatoes, and green beans she had eaten since coming to Europe.

"Does it make you a little homesick?" Megan asked.

"A little."

"Are you going home with Todd and Katie, or are you going to stay and finish the course even though you're changing your major?" Megan asked.

"I haven't decided yet." As soon as Christy said it, Todd gave her a surprised look. "I need to decide pretty quickly. You know what? If I could borrow your phone tonight to make a collect call to my parents, that would really help me out."

"Oh, they're going to love that," Katie said. "If I called my parents collect from Holland, they would hang up on me."

"No, they wouldn't," Christy said.

"I'm not going to call them to find out," Katie said.

Christy phoned her parents after another incredible worship service. Even though it was late at night in Holland, it was still in the afternoon in California. Christy's mom answered and immediately asked Christy if she was all right.

"Yes, we're all fine. Everything is going great, Mom. But I'm going to change my major. I don't know what I'm going to change it to yet, but I know I can't do this kind of work with little kids for the rest of my life."

"Are you sure?" her mom asked.

"Yes, very sure. The question now is whether I should stay at school for the next term or come home. What do you think?"

Christy's mom paused before saying, "I think you have to decide that for yourself. Dad and I told you we would support your decisions from here on out. But they are your decisions, Christy."

CHAPTER 21

The next morning, as Christy and Katie ate breakfast in Mike and Megan's kitchen, Christy said, "Sometimes I don't like being an adult."

"Really hard for you to make a decision about this next term at Basel, isn't it?" Katie said.

Christy nodded. "Last night I hardly slept. I kept thinking about what Todd and I decided when I was leaving England a year and a half ago and he was trying to figure out how much longer he should stay in Spain."

"Was that the conversation you two had at that little tea shop?" Katie asked.

"Yes, how did you remember?"

"You said it was the most romantic date you had with him—just the two of you, sipping tea and eating scones in London."

Christy smiled. "I think that's why I really wanted him to come to my Konditorei in Basel. I've sat at the back table so many times all by myself this past year. Every time I was there I would imagine what it would be like to have Todd seated across from me. Don't laugh, but sometimes I carried on imaginary conversations with him."

"And did he ever answer you?"

"Sometimes."

"Okay, now I'm scared." Katie reached across the table and gave Christy's arm a squeeze. "You and Todd need to talk about this. It's a big decision."

"That's what I was going to tell you. I kept remembering what Todd and I talked about that day at the tea shop. Todd had these verses from Psalm 15 that he quoted to me."

"Sounds typical. Todd would have a verse ready for any situation."

"It was about keeping your promises, even when it hurts."

Katie flipped her short red hair behind her ears and said, "Is that what you're going to do? Keep your commitment to the orphanage and the school, even though it hurts?"

Christy looked at her friend and quietly nodded. "Yes. I think that's what I'm supposed to do."

"And what are you supposed to do about Todd? Just keep him waiting?"

"I'll be back in September."

"I know," Katie said. "It's not that long. And I do think you're doing the noble integrity-thing by sticking with your commitment. I just thought that after this trip it would be hard to say good-bye because you guys have gotten so much closer."

Christy sighed. "You have no idea how hard it's going to be. But he and I seem to have said a lot of good-byes over the years. Still, I'd feel better about everything if we could define our relationship more clearly."

"You've always wanted that," Katie said.

"I guess I have."

"What woman doesn't?"

"What woman doesn't what?" Megan asked, entering the kitchen as Katie made her last comment.

"We were just talking about guys," Katie said with a smile at Christy. "So what's on the schedule today? I thought we were going to Switzerland, but I have a feeling Todd would like to stay here another night. That was a fantastic worship service last night."

Katie was right. When Mike and Todd returned from their breakfast with one of Mike's friends, Todd asked Christy and Katie if they would mind staying another night. The two of them had spent the morning helping Megan clean all the rooms and fix lunch. Christy didn't mind staying. She loved it there. Her morning chores had energized her. She quietly told that to Todd as they ate their vegetable stew and warm rolls for lunch.

"Would you like to work at a place like this more than at the orphanage?" Todd asked.

"Yes, definitely. It's hard to compare months at the orphanage with one morning here, but I understand what you meant about feeling energized instead of drained."

"Did Todd tell you about our breakfast?" Mike asked, breaking into their private conversation. "I introduced him to the group of men I partner with in this ministry. They asked if he wanted to come on staff here."

Christy hadn't expected to feel what she did at that moment. She wanted to grab on to Todd and say, "No, you don't! We're going to college together in the fall. You're not coming back to Europe in a few months, right when I'm ready to go home to California. You can't do this!"

"What did you tell them?" Katie asked, looking at Todd and then back at Christy.

"I told them the same thing I told Christy the other day. The need is not the call. I see the need here. I just don't sense the call from God. Not right now. I think my priority is to finish school. After that, I don't know."

Christy felt her heartbeat returning to a normal pace. She felt she would burst if she and Todd didn't have a chance soon to talk through what was going on in their lives and what they were deciding for the future.

"Well," Katie volunteered, "it looks as if I'm the only one who hasn't struggled with deciding what I'm going to do after this trip. Christy decided this morning that she's going to stay at the orphanage for the next term and finish her commitment there. I wanted her to come home, but she has this thing about keeping her promises, even when it hurts."

Christy looked over at Todd. She couldn't tell if he remembered that phrase or if his heart was yelling, "No, Christy, don't stay! Come home!"

Having these life decisions announced in front of others made Christy feel awkward and even more determined that she and Todd talk sometime soon.

Their alone time didn't occur that afternoon. Megan convinced Christy and Katie to go shopping with her, and Mike asked Todd to restring one of his guitars. The only good part of the afternoon was that both Christy and Katie were able to buy a few souvenirs and to find their way around Megan's local grocery store.

Thirty-two people came to the evening worship service, which was even better than the first two nights. Christy wondered how Todd was going to be able to pull away and leave in the morning. Maybe he would want to stay behind. Would he tell Christy and Katie to go on to Switzerland without him?

Christy considered the possibility of staying the rest of the week in Amsterdam. Her imagination then prompted her to ask, what if she stayed there longer than the rest of the week? What if she stayed permanently? What if she and Todd married and returned to Europe to work there or at a place like it? The possibilities of what she and Todd could do working together seemed endless. The more she thought about it, the more she second-guessed her decision to stay in Basel.

And why do I even need to finish college? I don't need a degree to sweep the floors of a youth hostel or to shop for carrots and chop them up for a stew. I'm already as equipped as I need to be to work at a place like this for the rest of my life. I love the atmosphere. I love using my hands to serve.

Christy hoped she could talk with Todd after the worship service that night. But so many people wanted to chat with him that she would have had to wait in line. Instead, she went to bed and stared at the ceiling, dreaming about what it would be like to be married to Todd and to live there.

Neither of us would have to finish college. We could start right now. We could even get married right now. The thought thrilled her. *No more of this waiting and wondering. We could both fly home on Monday. I'm sure we could pull off a wedding by the end of August, and then we could be back here in September instead of going to Rancho.*

Christy's dreams that night exhausted her. She woke with long, invisible lists wrapped around her like a mummy's bandages.

Dressing and heading for the kitchen before Katie awoke, Christy was pretty sure Todd would say he didn't want to leave that morning. When he announced his decision, she would say that she wanted to stay, too. If Katie wanted to go on, she could. She was strong and resourceful. Katie could travel around by herself for a few days and then find her way back to the Zürich airport.

Todd met Christy in the hallway. "Morning. I thought I'd be the early one today, but you're already up."

"Katie is still asleep. I thought I'd help with breakfast."

"You love it here, don't you?" Todd asked.

"Does it show that much?"

"You're using your gifts," he said.

"And so are you," Christy said. "If you're about to ask if I'd mind staying another day, I don't mind at all. I actually think we should stay here the rest of the week. As a matter of fact, I was thinking—"

He interrupted her with a motion to his backpack leaning against the wall behind him. "I'm packed and ready to go. I told Mike we would leave today. An early train rolls out of here at 7:20."

Christy felt as if the bottom had dropped out of her elaborate dream world. "Oh. You don't want to stay?"

"Not now. I don't have any peace about backing out of all my other plans and commitments. Actually, it was a God-thing that you were struggling with your decision about Basel and the orphanage. I realized I couldn't tell you that the need isn't the call unless I practiced that concept myself."

"Oh."

Todd reached his arm around her neck and drew her close in a warm hug. "You look bummed. We can take a later train. Why don't we get ourselves some breakfast? We can find a little bakery like the one you're always telling me about. I'd like to hear what's going on with you. You've been making some big decisions, too."

Christy nodded. She was ready to slip her arm around Todd's middle and have him hold her close, but Katie entered the hallway at that moment.

"What's up, guys?"

As soon as Todd mentioned the 7:20 train, Katie was ready to go. He didn't even tell her they could take a later one because he and Christy were thinking of going out to breakfast.

Disappointed, Christy left The Rock youth hostel with Todd and Katie fifteen minutes later. Mike and Megan drove them to the train station, still issuing invitations for them to return anytime. Todd told them again that he felt certain this was a matter of God's timing, and they all parted with warm hugs.

Christy knew she should take a nap as soon as they settled on the train. She had learned on this trip that she didn't do well if she didn't get enough sleep. But her mind wouldn't slow down enough to consider sleeping. Last night her wild imagination had taken her so far in her relationship with Todd—married by August, returning to Amsterdam by September—that she had to force herself to stop and move way back.

Todd was being his easygoing self, which helped Christy to get a grip on reality. And Katie's challenging Christy to a long, well-fought game of chess helped to settle her down, too. She tried to convince herself that they were simply three friends on an adventure. She didn't need to discuss her future. She just needed the mercy that God had made new to her that morning.

By the time they arrived at the Frutigen train station twelve hours later, the sun was heading for its home in the west. A flock of fluffy, cream-colored clouds followed the sun like sheep trailing their faithful shepherd. Long shadows from the distant Alpine peaks fell across the barn-sized buildings that surrounded the humble train station.

Christy felt more peace. This was familiar. The German dialect the people beside her spoke sounded very much like the German spoken in Basel.

"I hope you really wanted to get off the beaten path," Katie said, "because this place is no metropolis."

"We take a bus from here. I called the Zimmermans last night, and they're expecting us. Seth was right. They're happy to have us stay with them."

"Of course they're happy," Katie said dryly. "We're their free farm labor."

The bus ride was longer than Christy had expected, but the scenery topped anything she had yet experienced on the trip. Her biggest regret was that the sky kept growing darker, making the looming Alps fade from view. The snow, however, acted as a light reflector. The first star of the night made a grand entrance, and Todd put his arm around her and pulled her close to the window so he could point it out.

They sat snuggled close together the rest of the journey. Christy felt she could think clearly again. They were just Todd and Christy. Forever friends. That's all they needed to be right now. Certainly by tomorrow morning, in a place like this, she and Todd could have a long talk and settle all the unfinished sentences of the past few weeks.

Mr. Zimmerman met them at the bus stop. Christy wanted to laugh gleefully when she saw the look on Katie's face. Mr. Zimmerman looked like the grandfather on a *Heidi* video Christy and Katie had watched together several times. He had a huge white beard and wore a dark green felt hat with a jaunty red feather stuck in the side. With broken English, he graciously invited them to be his guests and come to his home.

"I can't believe this," Katie muttered as they followed the "grandfather" down the cobblestone street. Katie couldn't hold her amazement in any longer when they saw where Mr. Zimmerman had led them. His mode of transportation was a horse-drawn wagon. With lots of laughter, Katie, Christy, and Todd climbed up and rode on their own private hayride to the Zimmermans' home.

In the dark Christy couldn't tell how quaint the chalet was. But from what she could see by light of the handheld lantern, they were walking into a fairy-tale music box.

Mrs. Zimmerman, a round woman with a thick braid wrapped around the top of her head, greeted them warmly and insisted they eat some soup. Everything inside the house was meticulously clean and brightly decorated. Christy was certain that the ornate wooden cabinet in the corner was an antique.

When they finished the scrumptious soup, Katie and Christy were led upstairs to a tidy, small bedroom with two child-sized beds. Todd was ushered out to the barn to sleep in the straw with several wool blankets.

As soon as the door closed, Christy and Katie grabbed each other's arms and spun around in a giddy twirl. "If this weren't so cool, I'd think it was freaky," Katie said.

"Why?"

"It's like we left reality and entered the fairy-tale zone! I'm Heidi! Tomorrow morning, Peter the goat herder will come to these windows and call out for me to join him in the high country."

Christy giggled. "Look at these beds! I think they once belonged to Hansel and Gretel."

"And they were bought at Snow White's garage sale after two of the dwarfs moved out. We're going to have to sleep curled up in little balls."

Christy curled up under the thick down comforter and slept blissfully through the night. Katie, however, complained the next morning that she hadn't slept at all and her back hurt.

"Oh, come on. You're just trying to make excuses to get out of chores this morning," Christy said. She was already up and dressed and ready to milk the cows.

When she found Todd and Mr. Zimmerman, they were in the barn. Christy stood back and watched Todd try to milk a cow. Her muffled laughter prompted Mr. Zimmerman to motion for her to come closer. Christy didn't want to get anywhere near Todd's line of fire. Sprays of milk were flying everywhere.

"Come on, Christy. Help me out here, will you?" Todd said, getting up from the milking stool. "Watch my girlfriend," he said proudly. "She was born on a farm."

Christy hadn't milked a cow in years. Maybe in almost a decade. Even when she was a child on their dairy farm in Wisconsin, the milking was all done by machines. But she did know how to milk a cow. Her father patiently had taught her what he called "the dying art" when she was five.

With shaky confidence, Christy positioned herself on the stool and leaned her shoulder and head against the side of the brown Jersey cow. "Come on, girl," she said calmly. "It's okay. Stay calm."

The first squirt went right in the metal bucket and made a lovely, familiar sound that caused Christy to smile. She continued to milk with impressive success until her hands were sore and the bucket was more than half full.

"You never cease to amaze me, Kilikina," Todd said.

"Me too," Katie said, stepping in from where she had been watching in the shadow by the door. "And milking a cow is such a useful talent these days for young women of marital age."

Christy stepped back and invited Katie to give it a try.

"No, thanks. Bungee jumping I would try. Eating raw squid I would try. This, I will not try."

Before the morning was over, Katie did try several new adventures, including churning butter and feeding the chickens. She took a liking to one of the plow horses, and Christy found Katie hand-feeding it a fistful of oats.

"Do you want to go up the ski lift with us?" Christy asked.

"Who is 'us'?"

"Todd and me. Mrs. Zimmerman packed a picnic lunch for the three of us to take to the high meadow. You might see Peter the goat herder up there."

"Sure, I'll go. Unless you were hoping that you and Todd could have the time alone."

Christy was, but she didn't want Katie to know that. "Come on. It will be fun for all of us."

As they slid onto the rickety wooden benches of the chair lift and rose above the charming village of Adelboden, Christy waved at Todd. He was in the seat in front of her. Katie was in the seat in front of him. Christy could hear Katie call out as the lift pulled them to dramatic heights, "We're finally on an adventure!"

Christy smiled. *So this is what you meant when you said you wanted an adventure. Good. I'm glad you got what you wanted, Katie. It's Friday. My final chances to talk with Todd are melting away by the second. One final weekend is all we have. You got your adventure, Katie. Now that my heart has finally settled down, will I get what I hoped for—a plan for the future?*

CHAPTER 22

At the top of the ski lift, Todd took the large, wooden lunch basket from Christy and offered her a hand. They had to walk quickly to keep up with Katie.

"She thinks she's Heidi," Christy explained to Todd as they watched Katie spin around in a field of wild flowers.

Katie burst out singing, " 'The hills are alive!' "

"Wrong country," Todd called to her. "We did that one already, remember? The fountains and the abbey?"

Christy drew in a deep breath of the cool Alpine air. Over her head hung a pure blue sky, pulled taut and held aloft by jagged, snow-covered peaks. At her feet was spread an endless carpet of green meadow sprinkled with wild flowers like colorful confetti. The beauty left her speechless.

Katie, undaunted by Todd's comment, kept dancing around and singing. Christy thought how funny it was that she had been the one who had wanted to get out into the country. Now that they were there, Katie acted as if this were her adventure.

This isn't an adventure. This is a calming rest. An adventure would be dancing at San Marcos Square in Venice or horseback riding along the beach in Spain.

Todd put down the picnic basket in the middle of the wild flowers and stretched out next to it. He leaned on his elbow and gave Christy a contented smile.

I guess my friends are happy to spend our last few days together here in the Alps. How odd that, looking back, I wish we could have done the trip differently. I wish we were going camping with Tonio. I'd be a completely different camper now. I'd go fishing with Todd and bathe in the stream every day. I'm just now ready for my vacation.

"This has to be one of the most incredible, spectacular, amazingly beautiful corners of God's green earth," Todd said. He leaned back and gazed at the sky. "It's just a breath away from heaven."

"It is amazing, isn't it?" Christy sat down next to him and reached into the picnic basket. "Are you hungry? This bread looks homemade."

Katie flitted over to them and said, "Okay, I'm a happy woman. I've danced in an Alpine meadow. Now all I need is a ride in a gondola, and my life will be complete."

"Yeah," Todd agreed. "We passed that one up, didn't we?"

"I can't believe we made it all the way to the train station and then left," Katie said. "What were we thinking? We were in such a rush to get somewhere. I don't even remember where."

Christy remembered. It was Salzburg. And their decision had been a group choice, but she felt responsible since she was the one who had pushed them to go and see and do so much at the beginning of the trip.

Katie bent over and plucked a wild flower. "Did you ever hear that Norwegian legend about the wild flowers?"

"No. Where did you hear it? In Oslo?" Christy asked.

"No, it's an old tradition my grandmother taught me when I was around eight or nine. I did it at her house when I was staying there once on Midsummer's Eve."

"That's tonight," Todd said. "Mr. Zimmerman was talking to me about it in the barn this morning. I didn't understand what he was saying, but then I figured it out when he said today is the longest day of sunlight in the year. That's Midsummer's Eve, right?"

"Yes!" Katie's excitement colored her cheeks rosy. "This is perfect! Chris, do this with me. You're supposed to pick seven wild flowers and sleep with them under your pillow."

"Seven of the same kind or seven different ones?" Christy asked.

"I don't think it matters," Katie said, quickly moving on with the rest of the legend. "If you sleep with seven wild flowers under your pillow on Midsummer's Eve, you'll dream of the one you'll marry."

"I want to try," Todd said with a teasing grin. "How many? Seven?"

"You can't play," Katie said. "This is a girls-only game."

"Katie," Christy said, "are you sure this isn't some kind of medieval incantation? I don't believe in doing any of that."

"I don't, either," Katie said. "It's just a little folklore. You don't say anything magical or throw in any bat wings. It's just a bit of tradition from my heritage. Like making a wish when you blow out candles on a birthday cake."

Christy took off with Katie to find seven wild flowers while Todd watched. When they were far enough away that he couldn't hear them, Christy asked, "How are you doing with the whole boyfriend-jealousy thing?"

Katie stopped and gave her a pained expression. "Why do you ask?"

"I'm wondering. I think it must be uncomfortable for you sometimes around us, even though you don't act like it."

"I'm doing better than I was at the beginning of the trip. I guess if Antonio or Marcos had acted at all interested in me, it wouldn't have hurt so much whenever I saw you and Todd falling in love right before my eyes."

Christy smiled. She couldn't help it. And her cheeks blushed.

"You guys are so perfect for each other," Katie said with a sigh. She bent over and plucked her first yellow wild flower. "I'm happy for you, really. Deep down, I'm thrilled. If the two of you ever broke up for good, I think a part of me would shrivel up and die. You give me hope that some God-lover guy is out there who will think I'm the sun and moon and stars and one day will look at me the way Todd looks at you."

Christy plucked a tiny white flower. "There is, Katie. I know he's out there."

"Oh, he'll probably be an 'out there' kind of guy, all right," Katie said with a laugh. "He would have to be to put up with me."

"He'll probably be shy and kind of quiet," Christy guessed. "You know how they say opposites attract. What about the baseball player at Rancho? What was his name? Number 14, wasn't it? Is he shy?"

"I don't know. Matt wasn't shy or quiet when I met him, but then, they had just won their final game. He had such a look of honesty and simpleheartedness about him. He seemed like an uncomplicated person, and I like that.

"You know," Katie said a moment later, after they each had picked three more flowers. "What I really want is to trust God more in this area of my life, and I'm learning about how to do that a little bit better. Weren't you the one who told me that God gives His best to those who leave the choice with Him?"

"I don't know. I might have said that. It sounds more like something Todd would say."

"I want to trust God more," Katie said decisively.

"That's funny because I've been saying the same thing on this trip. I keep thinking I know what's best or what the future holds, but really, I don't have a clue. Only God does."

Katie looked up with her bouquet of tiny flowers in her hand and gave Christy a grin. "Guess it doesn't matter what stage we're at in life, does it? With a boyfriend or without a boyfriend."

Christy quickly added, "With a major in college or without one."

Katie nodded. "We have to, as they say, 'let go and let God.' I'm just glad we've had each other on this journey, Christy. This journey through life, I mean, not just this journey through Europe. I'd be a mental case by now if I didn't have you and Todd and the rest of our friends as my circle of sanity."

"I like that," Christy said. "Circle of sanity. You guys are that for me, too."

"Okay, we better stop this before I burst out crying. My sobs and loud wailing would start an avalanche!"

Christy laughed and held out one of her seven wild flowers to Katie. "Here, you take one of mine, and I'll take one of yours."

They swapped, and Katie said, "This means we have to be each other's maid of honor, right?"

"Definitely. We're creating our own version of this folklore."

They laughed and linked arms as they headed back to where Todd lay stretched out on the picnic blanket. Then, carefully pressing their flowers in a cloth napkin, they secured the napkin inside the picnic basket.

"Did you ever wish on these when you were a kid?" Todd plucked a dandelion with a full, fuzzy white head. "We used to pick them in the schoolyard, make a wish, and then blow off all the dandelion fuzz. I think my friends and I single-handedly kept our schoolyard seeded with dandelions."

Christy reached over and picked one of the dandelions near her. She closed her eyes and heard herself say, "I wish we could still go to Venice."

When she opened her eyes, Todd was sitting up and looking at her with a wild, blue-eyed gaze. "Are you serious? You'd be up for that?"

"Yes, I really would. I want one more adventure before Monday."

"That means we probably won't make it to your bakery for morning pastries."

"That's okay."

Todd looked at Katie and then back at Christy. "We can do it, you know. We catch the bus back to Frutigen, and then we pick up the train out of Basel that stops at Spiez. We change trains in Milan, and we're in Venice before midnight."

Katie laughed and broke off a piece of bread. "You're scary, Todd! What did you do, memorize the whole train schedule in the hayloft last night?"

"No, I looked up how far it would be from here to Venice this morning because I had the same feeling Christy must be having. I could go for one more adventure."

"Wait a minute," Katie said. "What would be wrong with staying here another night and then tomorrow going to Christy's school in Basel and hanging out there on Sunday?"

"Are you turning down an adventure?" Christy asked. "You sound like me when we started this trip, and now I'm sounding like you."

"I like it here," Katie said.

"You'll like it in Venice, too." Todd plucked a dandelion. "I wish Katie would change her mind about Venice." Then he blew the fuzzy part right in her face.

"Okay, okay! If you're going to torture me like that, we can go." Her face brightened. "Oh yeah, and we can see Marcos again. I'm with you."

Their ride down the mountain on the rickety wooden ski lift felt charged with electricity that shot between the three of them. They called out back and forth and pointed to the magnificent scenery as they rolled toward Adelboden with their faces to the world below them. A quick explanation to the Zimmermans, an even faster packing job, and they were out the door, climbing up into the back of the "grandfather's" horse-drawn wagon.

Christy felt more charged up than she ever had before. Then she remembered. "Wait! Our wild flowers!" She jumped off the back of the wagon and ran into the house, trying to explain to Mrs. Zimmerman that she had left her flowers in a cloth napkin at the bottom of the basket.

Mrs. Zimmerman chuckled and gave her the whole napkin, flowers and all, before shooing her out the door. The wagon rambled down the narrow road to the bus stop. From their uphill view of the village's main street, Todd spotted the bus as it came winding around the corner.

"That's our bus," Todd told Mr. Zimmerman. Todd had been consulting the train schedule and now announced to all of them, "If we don't catch that bus, we won't make our connection at Spiez."

"Can this buggy go any faster?" Katie asked Mr. Zimmerman.

His reply was in German, or perhaps it was French. Whatever he said the horses understood, and they took off. Christy and Katie tumbled into each other and held on, laughing all the way.

"Hold the bus!" Todd yelled when they were still a few yards off.

The bus let out a billow of smoke, and the door closed.

"Wait!" Todd yelled.

Mr. Zimmerman seemed to enjoy the chase more than any of them. He kept the horses headed straight for the bus. As it pulled out, he put his thumb and finger in his mouth and gave a sharp whistle. The bus driver didn't seem to hear it, but the horses did. They were confused and reared back.

Two men came out of the shops along the main road. One wore a long white butcher's apron. A woman in a local *Dirndl* dress exited a shop at the end of the street with two little boys wearing leather *Lederhosen*. When everyone saw Mr. Zimmerman chasing the bus and whistling, they all joined in, waving their hands, yelling, and running after the bus, as well.

Christy couldn't stop laughing. She felt as if their fairy-tale land had turned into Busy Town, and they were now cartoon characters on a mad romp. All they needed was Sergeant Murphy and his trusty whistle.

Someone in a blue Mercedes pulled around their wagon and took off after the bus, honking until the bus pulled over just outside of town.

"Thank you, thank you," Katie said, reaching out from the wagon like a parade princess, shaking the hands of all the helpful townsfolk. She hopped down, swung her pack over her shoulder, and kept shaking hands. "Thank you. We couldn't have done it without you. You guys were awesome, really."

The jovial crowd gleamed with appreciation. Mr. Zimmerman waved and laughed as Todd, Christy, and Katie ran to the bus. The bus driver was the only one who didn't find the antics of these three backpacking students humorous. As a result, Todd led them to the back of the bus so they could finish laughing and could retell every detail without the driver's critical eye staring at them in the rearview mirror.

Not until they were safely on board the train headed for Milan did Christy begin to relax. The scenery was breathtaking, and she felt as if she were still on top of the world. She didn't want this time with her two best friends to end, ever.

———

All their connections were smooth until they hit Milan. The train station was packed on this Friday night. Todd directed them to a ticket booth where they had to wait in a long line to make reservations and upgrade their tickets to first class. Todd kept checking his watch.

"Are we going to make the next train?" Christy asked.

"We have five minutes. Unless the train has been delayed, I don't think we'll make it."

"What if we run to the train? We could stand in second class," Christy said.

"Sure," Katie agreed. "We've done it before."

With another mad dash, they found the train to Venice, but the conductor wouldn't let them on. Reservations only. The train was packed. Everyone seemed to want to travel to Venice for the weekend.

They went back to the ticket booth and stood in an even longer line than before.

"How about if Christy and I find some food and bring it back to you?" Katie asked.

"I could sure use something to eat," Todd said. "Thanks."

"Sure. We'll be right back. Just don't leave this area, and we'll be fine."

Christy stayed close to Katie. Their backpacks kept bumping into the mob of travelers. This was the busiest she had seen any of the train stations so far. She wondered if it was because school was out in the States as well as in Europe and throngs of students were just starting out on their adventures. Christy knew they had avoided some of that crowd by leaving on their trip so early in June.

"There's a pizzeria," Katie said. "Let's buy some extra in case we're stuck here all night."

After waiting in another long line, Christy and Katie bought a whole pizza and three sodas. The fragrant garlic and spices tortured Christy as she carried the pizza with both hands back to the ticket booth. Todd still hadn't reached the front of the line.

Fifteen minutes later he joined them on a bench with the news that he had miraculously secured three seats in first class. The seats apparently were the only ones available for the next twenty-four hours.

"The only thing is," Todd said after he handed them their tickets, "the train leaves at six in the morning."

"Should we look for a youth hostel here in Milan?" Christy asked.

"I have a feeling it might be full already," Katie said. "The tour book said the hostels in the major Italian cities fill up quickly, and you should check in early."

Todd looked at his watch. "I'd say let's find a hotel, but I'm getting low on money. Which reminds me, I need for you both to pay me back for these first-class tickets. I'd like to say I could cover them for you but—"

"We planned to pay for them," Christy said. "And the pizza is on us."

They found a corner of the station away from the mobs and settled their money. Then they ate their cooled pizza and drank their warm soda.

210

"Where did all these people come from?" Todd asked.

"It looks as if summer travel in Europe has officially begun," Christy said. She didn't like feeling sweaty, smelly, and sticky. Whatever they did tomorrow morning when they arrived in Venice, she hoped it included a shower.

The three of them took turns walking around the huge station. Katie bought some chocolate and a key chain souvenir. Several other American students stopped to talk to them. The travelers compared stories and gave one another advice and names of places to stay. Sometime around two in the morning, Todd ate the last slice of cold pizza. The scent of garlic in their small corner of the station overwhelmed Christy. She turned down Todd's offer for another round of chess and tried to find a way to curl up against her backpack to sleep. Their spontaneous adventure to Venice was quickly losing its glamour.

Christy closed her eyes and leaned her head against her backpack. That's when she remembered the wild flowers. "Katie, where did we put that napkin with the wild flowers?"

"Oh yeah! The night is half gone, and we haven't been sleeping with our wild flowers. I think you put the napkin in your day pack."

Rummaging around, Christy found the cloth napkin and opened it carefully. The brightly colored wild flowers were not only pressed, but they also had gotten crumpled and squished with some of the stems broken off. "Do you think it will still work?" she asked Katie. "Will we dream of our future spouses even if our flowers are mangled?"

"Hey, if we can manage to have any kind of pleasant dream in a place like this, I think we're doing okay." Katie carefully extracted her seven flowers and folded them up in a wrinkled bandana scarf.

Christy found a piece of Italian newspaper and made a crooked sort of envelope in which to place her flowers. She slid the envelope into the zippered pouch on the front of her pack and tried to settle in so that her head rested against the pouch. She wiggled to get comfortable and opened her eyes. Todd was watching her with a smile. She smiled back.

"I want a full report on who you meet in your dreams tonight," he said.

You know it will be you, Todd. It's always you. Only you.

But all she said was "Okay."

Christy didn't know how long she dozed. She didn't know whom she dreamed of or if she dreamed at all. Her sleep ended abruptly when she heard Katie scream.

"Get away from me, you creep!" Katie cried.

Through bleary eyes, Christy saw a large bald man bending over Katie, trying to talk to her. He reeked of alcohol.

As soon as Todd woke and said, "Be on your way, buddy," the man ambled off, talking to himself.

"So much for the wild flower theory!" Katie said, sitting up and adjusting her sweat shirt.

"Are you okay?" Christy asked.

"That was a living nightmare," Katie said. "There I was, dreaming of my mystery man, and then I felt someone touching my hair. I thought I was about to see the face of my true love, but when I opened my eyes, I saw *him*!"

Christy couldn't help but laugh. "Oh, Katie."

Katie pouted.

Todd chuckled. "The moral of the folklore lesson could be that some mysteries are best left in God's keeping."

"No kidding!" Katie said. "What about you, Christy? Who did you dream of? Or can we all guess?"

Christy could feel Todd looking at her, but she suddenly felt too shy to look back. She especially didn't want to say that she hadn't dreamed at all. "Some mysteries are best left in God's keeping," she answered quietly.

The rest of the uncomfortable night on the floor of the Milan train station and the three-hour, early morning train ride into Venice gave Christy plenty of time to think. The panic she had felt in Amsterdam had subsided. Now she knew how crazy it had been to even think of getting married in two months and going back to work at The Rock with Todd. The decision to finish her commitment at the orphanage and complete her course work was a good choice. She felt peace about following through on what she had begun.

What remained to be settled was her relationship with Todd. It bothered her a little that he hadn't kissed her since she had talked with him on the train ride into Amsterdam about saving her kisses. She hadn't meant for him to pull back completely. While they had still been close these last few days, they weren't snuggly the way she wanted to be. Christy wasn't sure how she felt about that. Couldn't they be a little more affectionate? Or was this Todd's way of honoring her request to save their kisses?

Christy knew it would all settle itself once she and Todd had a chance to be alone and have a long talk. *But when is that going to happen? Our time together is slipping away. It's already Saturday morning. I don't mind staying in Basel another two months, but I don't think I can wait that long to have a heart-to-heart talk with Todd.*

CHAPTER 23

When the train pulled into Venice at nine that morning, the place seemed like a different station from the quiet, nearly empty one they had stayed in two weeks earlier. It was alive with noise and throngs of travelers. Todd, Christy, and Katie found their way to the water taxi and climbed aboard with dozens of other students.

As the boat sped across the water, Christy shielded her eyes from the sun and tried to memorize the sight before her. Across the gleaming water was one of the more than one hundred islands that made up the ancient city of Venice. A tall spire stretched toward the sky. Dozens of tall, very old buildings stood close together. They reminded Christy of plump old ladies dressed in their Sunday best, sitting snugly beside one another on a church pew. Some wore hats. Some seemed to be holding large handbags on their laps. All the faces of the matronly buildings were adorned with smug grins, as if the women were listening to a sermon being proclaimed to them from the heavens, but all the while, they held in their hearts mischievous secrets of their past.

"What a place!" Christy declared as they stepped out of the water taxi. "I mean, I've seen pictures, and I've seen Venice in movies, but this place is larger than life."

"Something is in the air, isn't it?" Todd said.

Christy sniffed but didn't catch any whiffs of garlic.

"No," Todd said to her, "I mean, a sort of spirit is in the air. This city has seen it all."

214

"Yes," Christy agreed. "I was just thinking how the buildings all looked like smug old ladies sitting next to each other."

Todd grinned at her. "What should we do first? Eat or find a place to stay?"

Christy knew Todd would prefer finding some food. She would prefer a shower. Katie made the choice for them when she said, "Let's call Marcos."

"We know where his father's jewelry shop is, right?" Todd said. "Let's go there and ask for him. He's more likely to be at the shop than at home. We can't assume that we can stay with him."

"Can we stow these packs someplace?" Katie asked. "I'm sick of carrying this thing everywhere we go."

"We can find the youth hostel," Christy suggested.

A girl who had been standing nearby turned to them and with a British accent said, "They won't let you check into the youth hostel until three o'clock. It's very crowded. We found a hotel that's much closer. Would you like the address?"

"Yes, thanks," Todd said.

The hotel turned out to be a good choice except that it was more expensive than the hostel. Todd admitted he was almost out of money; the plane ride from Narvik to Copenhagen had taken a huge chunk out of his budget. Katie said she figured she had about seventy-five dollars left, and Christy had a little more than that.

"We can pool our money," Christy said. "Together we have enough to eat and pay for the hotel. What more do we want? We'll have to ride second class back to Basel, but that's no big deal. I think we'll be fine." Her optimism as well as her suggestion that they all take showers before they headed out again helped tremendously. They were starving by the time they left their hotel, but at least they were clean and didn't have to carry the heavy packs.

"Let's find a quaint, authentic place to eat," Katie suggested. "None of these tourist traps. Then we can go to Savini Jewelers and see the rest of San Marcos Square."

Following their noses, the three famished friends tromped down narrow alleys and over ornate bridges with absolutely no idea where they were going.

"I haven't seen a single restaurant," Christy said. "Don't you think we should consult the tour book?"

Katie pulled out the book, and three postcards fluttered to the pavement.

"I can't believe I haven't mailed those cards yet," Christy said, bending to pick them up.

"Isn't that a post office over there?" Todd asked, motioning toward the building two doors down from where they stood. "At least, that looks like a post office. That is a mailbox out front, isn't it?"

While Todd and Katie consulted the tour book for a good restaurant, Christy ventured into the small building. She found a short man sitting behind a desk, reading a newspaper. He wore wire-rimmed glasses that rested precariously on the end of his pointy nose. Christy handed him the postcards but didn't understand what he said to her. Trying to speak slowly in English, she handed him some change for the stamps. He licked the stamps for her and looked at her over the top of his glasses. Then he motioned with his free hand that she needed more money. Christy reached into her pocket and pulled out two more coins. The peculiar man shook his head as if it wasn't enough and then waved his hand and spoke a string of Italian words. She thought he was indicating that the amount was close enough, and she could go.

Christy walked back into the bright daylight shaking her head.

"Was it a post office?" Katie asked.

"I have no idea, but the odd little man in there put stamps on the cards and took my money, even though I don't think it was enough. If Seth's postcards ever reach Oregon, it will be a little miracle."

"Those weren't your postcards?" Katie asked.

"No, can you believe it? Remember the guy we talked to on the train to Paris? He dropped them. I've been meaning to mail them for the last week."

Todd stretched his arm around her shoulder and drew her close. "My little Good Samaritan," he teased.

Christy liked feeling him close to her, especially when he smelled fresh, like soap and shampoo. She slipped her arm around his middle and rested her head against his shoulder.

"Come on, you two snuggle bugs," Katie said. "We have to find some food. I don't care anymore if it's a tourist trap. Let's find our way to San Marcos Square."

Following the map and crossing several bridges, they were almost to San Marcos Square when Christy caught the scent of garlic in the air. "Oh, just smell that."

Katie sniffed and began to follow the scent. It led them down a narrow alley to a tiny place that looked like a pizzeria. The door was open, but no one was inside.

"Should we go in?" Christy asked.

"Hello?" Katie boldly entered. "Ciao. Do you sell any chow here?"

A short, round woman wearing a white apron over her dress greeted them. "Americanos!" she said. "Come in. You are hungry, yes?"

"Yes!" all three of them answered in unison.

"You like to make your own pizza?" the woman asked. "I am, how do you say . . . breaking now."

"You're taking a break?" Todd said. "Sure. We'd love to make our own pizza." He walked behind the counter and went to wash his hands in a small sink. Christy and Katie followed him.

"You tell us what to do, and we'll do it," Todd said. "By the way, I'm Todd. This is Katie and Christy. We're from California."

"I am Cassandra. We lived in New York for a little while. What kind of pizza do you like?"

"Any kind," Todd answered for them. "Did you hurt your foot?" He motioned to where her right leg was resting on a stool.

"Yes. I did this morning."

"Have you put ice on it?"

"No."

"Here." Todd made himself at home, looking through the small refrigerator in the back while Katie and Christy grinned self-consciously. He returned with a towel wrapped around a hunk of cold mozzarella cheese. "It's not ice-cold, but this should help."

"You are an angel," Cassandra said dramatically. "Come here. Let me kiss you."

217

Todd bent over to apply the chilled mozzarella to the ankle, and Cassandra kissed him with a big smack on both cheeks. Christy thought she saw him blushing.

"Where do you keep the pizza dough?" Todd asked, reaching for an apron he saw under the counter.

For the next two hours Christy thought she had never laughed so much in her life. While Cassandra sat with her foot up, Todd, Katie, and Christy learned the fine art of tossing pizza dough into the air and then covering it with Cassandra's special tomato sauce. Two young girls entered the pizzeria while Todd was sliding their masterpiece pizza into the oven with a wide paddle.

Cassandra said something to the girls in Italian. They giggled, took a seat, and watched Todd as the perspiration glistened on his forehead.

"I told them you would make their pizza," Cassandra said.

"One Todd Special coming right up."

This time Katie tried her hand at tossing the dough into the air. Christy was certain it would come down over her head like in a cartoon, but Katie actually was better at the task than Todd had been. At Cassandra's insistence, Christy gave it a try, but on the first toss, her fist went right through the middle. She ended up wearing the pizza crust like a huge, sagging bracelet around her wrist.

"You spread it out too thin," Cassandra said. "Try it again."

Christy's second attempt was a twirling, flying success and gained her a round of applause.

Todd served the first slice of his pizza to Cassandra with a towel over his arm, like a classy waiter. Cassandra praised him and offered him a job.

"Hmm," Todd said, playfully rubbing his chin as if seriously contemplating her offer.

"Remember," Christy said, "the need is not the call."

Todd laughed and wrapped his arm around Christy's shoulders. He turned to Cassandra and said, "Sorry, but my girlfriend says no."

"Ahh!" Cassandra said excitedly. "Your girlfriend, is she? Why didn't you tell me?" The woman worked to get to her feet, all the while saying, "Stand there. Wait."

Once she was up, she patted her apron, and a cloud of fine white flour rose up to encircle them. "I must give to you a blessing."

As Todd stood there with his arm around Christy's shoulder, she slipped her arm around his middle. Cassandra raised her hands and pressed her fingers on each of their closed lips. She spoke a melodic-sounding string of Italian words. Then she pulled her hands back to her lips, where she kissed her fingers and then pressed her fingers to their cheeks.

With a wistful look, Cassandra said, "I do not know how to say it in English. It is not the same. I wish for you all God's goodness."

"Thank you," Christy said in barely a whisper. "Grazie, Cassandra. Molte grazie."

"Molte grazie," Todd repeated, squeezing Christy's shoulder and pulling her close.

"Do you happen to have any blessings for those of us who are still available?" Katie asked.

Cassandra didn't seem to understand Katie's question.

"She wants a blessing, too," Todd explained.

"You come back here when you have a man, and I will bless you both."

Christy thought those words would break Katie's heart, but to Christy's surprise, her friend didn't make a joke or let out a forlorn moan. Katie stood tall and said, "I'll do that someday, Cassandra. You wait. I'll be back. And whoever he is, he'll be worth every word of your blessing."

Christy had never felt more proud of her friend.

It took Todd, Christy, and Katie several hours before they could pull themselves away from Cassandra's pizzeria. The next stop was Savini Jewelers.

From outside, the shop didn't look like much. But once they stepped inside, they realized they were in an exclusive and expensive jewelry store. A glittering, golden chandelier hung from an ornate, domed ceiling. Marble statues stood guard in each corner. Cushioned sofas covered in gold brocade enabled buyers to sit back in comfort as they browsed the lowered glass cases.

A large man in a black suit immediately stepped up to Todd, Christy, and Katie. He looked like a bouncer.

"Hi. How's it going? We'd like to speak with Marcos Savini, if he's here," Todd said.

"Mr. Savini is not in," the bouncer said.

"Okay, but we were wondering about his son," Katie explained. "Is Marcos here?"

"Mr. Carlos Savini is not here, and Mr. Marcos Savini is not here," the hulking man said.

"Could we leave a message for him?" Katie asked.

The bouncer pulled a business card from his pocket and opened the door for them to leave.

"Thanks." Katie took the card. As soon as they were all outside she said, "Boy, was that the opposite of Cassandra's or what? I take it they don't like poor American college students around here. I guess we're not welcome here the way we were at Antonio's."

"Should we try calling and leaving a message?" Christy asked.

"No," Katie said. "He's probably out of town anyway."

"Let's go exploring," Todd suggested. "I want to check out San Marcos Square."

The sight that impressed Christy most in the square was the pigeons. They were everywhere. People held out hands full of food that could be purchased at vendor carts, and the birds would come and sit on their hands to eat. One little boy was frozen with a mixture of terror and delight as two birds sat on his head and four more perched on his arms. A man spoke to him in German and stepped back to take the boy's picture. Christy pulled out her camera and snapped a few shots of the square. She had taken only three rolls of film the whole trip. Most of the time she had been so busy absorbing and observing that she hadn't thought to use her camera.

That afternoon she made up for it by finishing the roll of film in the camera and taking another entire roll. She took pictures of the unique church at the end of San Marcos Square and then shots of the square from the top of the church. She took several shots of the Rialto Bridge as the gondolas passed under it.

Katie didn't bring up the topic of a gondola ride, and Christy didn't, either, because she had read in the tour book that the gondolas could be very expensive. It was doubtful if they had enough money left to rent one. She wondered if Katie had figured that out, as well.

Or are the gondolas another Lille Havfrue, *an illusive mermaid we traversed the globe to find? Now that we're here, is Katie feeling it's no big deal? Why do so many things in life turn out like that? Like the fjords and the castles.*

By sunset, all three of them were exhausted. The all-nighter at the Milan train station and walking around all afternoon had caught up with them. Christy wasn't even hungry. All she wanted to do was sleep.

The next morning Katie was the first one up, and she woke Christy. "Come on, sunshine," she teased. "Venice awaits you."

"What time is it?" Christy asked.

"Almost nine. This is a new record for you, isn't it? Todd and I have been up for hours. We went for coffee, and I brought you back a pastry. Wait until you taste this one. I think this is the winner of the trip so far." Katie held out a flaky pastry shaped like a cone and filled with chocolate.

"I can see why you liked this one," Christy said, indulging in a big bite while she was still in bed. "Thanks for bringing it back for me. Sorry to keep you guys waiting."

"No problem. I've decided that today none of us is going to apologize to anyone for anything. This is our last day; it's going to be perfect."

Christy thought the delicious pastry was a pretty perfect way to start the day. She felt like a new person after so much sleep.

After she took a quick shower, Todd arranged for them to take a boat to the island of Murano to watch the glassblowers. Christy loved being out on the water and feeling the wind in her hair. She was standing by the rail snapping pictures when Todd came up behind her. He put both his hands on the rail so that Christy stood securely within the circle he had created.

"I don't want you to go," Christy said softly.

"I'm not going anywhere." Todd pressed his cheek against the side of her head.

"Yes, you are. Tomorrow at this time you'll be on a plane back to California, and I'll be in class. No, actually, my first class will be over, and I'll be at my little Konditorei, drowning my sorrows in whatever Marguerite baked."

"Our plane doesn't leave Zürich until two tomorrow afternoon," Todd said.

"Okay, so I'll be at the Konditorei, and you'll be at the airport. We'll still be apart, Todd. I don't want tomorrow to come." She turned and buried her head in his shoulder. She wanted Todd to tell her he would leap into the sky, lasso the sun, and with his bare hands hold it back from circling the globe so that this day would never end. Or if he wouldn't attempt that, she wanted him to at least kiss her.

But Todd did neither.

The aching she felt inside only grew as they toured the island of Murano. They watched a skilled craftsman demonstrate the ancient art of blowing glass through a long, hollow pipe and then quickly shaping the fiery hot liquid into vases. On the boat ride back, Todd talked with a retired track coach and his wife from Ohio, while Christy stood alone at the rail, watching the lacy ripples the boat produced in the water.

"We need to make some decisions," Todd said once the three of them had disembarked and found a shady spot to stand.

"I think we should try calling Marcos again," Katie said.

"I don't know if we'll have time to see him," Todd pointed out. "We need to check out of the hotel by one, which is in twenty minutes. I've checked the schedule, and we have a couple of times when we can catch the train. No matter which train we decide on, it takes ten hours to reach Basel."

"That long?" Katie said. "I thought we were closer. I also think we need to walk while we talk so we can get to the hotel in time to check out. If they decide to charge us an extra night, I don't know if we could pay for it."

Todd started to walk and asked Christy, "Do you think it's okay if we stay at the dorms tonight in Basel?"

"Sure. Then would you take the train to Zürich in the morning?"

"Yes. It's only an hour from Basel to Zürich."

"I know." Christy wondered if that would allow them time for a short visit to her Konditorei. If they could fit that into the schedule, somehow she felt saying good-bye wouldn't be as hard.

"We could take the two-o'clock train and be in Basel by midnight. Three other trains leave after that one. The last one would be the eight-thirty train. That one would take us into Basel at six-thirty Monday morning, which is cutting it close for Christy's class."

"That's okay." Christy wanted to be with Todd as long as she could, and she didn't mind going to class directly from the train. If she could cut that class, she would. That way she could go to Zürich with Todd and Katie and see them off for their two-o'clock flight. But the summer term was so short. If she missed even one class, her grade could be dropped as much as half a grade. Since her grades last term weren't the best, she knew she needed to do all she could to keep her scores high. Otherwise the partial scholarship she had been awarded for Rancho Corona in the fall could be affected. "We could take that last train. That would give us a few more hours here in Venice."

Katie, who was agreeing with everything that day, said she thought that was a great idea. Todd suggested they retrieve their packs, go to the train station to see about making reservations, and then, with whatever money they had left, they could fill up on pizza.

After standing in line at the train station for more than two hours, they found out all first-class seats for the eight-thirty train were booked. They would have to go in second class, which could mean standing for ten hours. Or at least for the first three hours to Milan.

They bought some pizza at the train station. Christy was down to her last bit of money. With only three more hours left in Venice, none of them knew what to do.

Christy's feet and her heart felt heavier and heavier. Todd was quiet. The thought of their trip ending was too depressing to even talk about how to spend their final hours together.

Katie was the one who kept them going with her bright, optimistic attitude. She suggested they find their last taste of Italian gelato, and she said she knew just the place. They followed Katie onto a water taxi and disembarked at San Marcos Square. Christy thought Katie would suggest they call Marcos. But she didn't.

Instead, Katie marched them right up to one of the gondola stands, pulled out the last of her money, and said to the gondolier in the straw hat, "My friends here need to go for a ride. How much do you want?"

CHAPTER 24

"Katie, that's all the money you have left," Christy protested. "You don't have to pay for this."

"Yes, I do. You two don't have any money left, so this is my treat. Now, don't spoil it for me. Just take off your backpacks; I'll watch them for you. And get in the man's boat."

The gondolier took Katie's money while Christy, still protesting, was ushered by Todd into the gondola's cushioned hull.

Then the gondolier asked Katie, "You are paying for your friends? And this is all the money you have left?"

"We're going home tomorrow," Katie explained. "I just thought they couldn't come all this way and not go for a ride in a gondola."

"And neither can you!" the gondolier said. "Come. No charge. My honor. You must have your gondola ride, too."

"Do you guys mind?" Katie asked.

"Of course not," Christy said, snuggling up close to Todd. It would have been wonderfully romantic for the two of them to be alone for one final hour, but how could she say no after Katie had been so generous?

"Come aboard," Todd said.

With a burst of glee, Katie climbed into the gondola and reached for each backpack as it was handed down to her. She joked around by resting one of the packs beside her on the seat and putting her arm around it. "Oh, Milton, you are so strong! I always did go for the strong, silent types."

Christy smiled at Todd. He put his arm around her and drew her close.

"We have many beautiful palaces here along the *Canalazzo*," the gondolier said, pushing off from the dock and pointing the gondola down the Grand Canal. "The canal is two miles long, and the water is only nine feet deep. Less, in some places. It is not recommended for swimming."

Christy could see why. A disagreeable odor rose from the water, and trash floated on top. She kept her attention directed upward, toward the magnificent mansions that lined the canal, each more splendid than the last. Katie carried on a lively conversation with the gondolier while Christy and Todd sat close. Todd turned out to be as strong and silent as Katie's backpack partner. Christy wondered again when she and Todd would have their heart-to-heart conversation. On the train? So much had happened in her heart these past few weeks. She didn't know how much she needed to tell Todd and how much he had figured out.

I don't need you to promise to hold back the sun, Todd. I just need you to promise to always hold me this close.

Their ride ended near the train station, and they clambered out with smiles and waves for their gondolier. Todd took Christy's hand in his, and they ambled into the very familiar train station. Todd suggested they walk to the platform a little early so they could try to find seats in second class. He held Christy's hand the whole time they stood waiting in the crowd for the train. She wondered if he was feeling the same sadness she felt.

The train pulled in, but unlike some of the other trains they had boarded on the trip, the conductor wanted to see each person's ticket before boarding. When they finally reached the front of the line, Christy, Todd, and Katie pulled out their Eurail passes.

"No!" the conductor yelled. He thrust Todd's train pass back at him.

"No!" he said again after looking at Katie's pass and jabbing it into her hands.

"Si!" he said to Christy, handing the pass to her nicely and pushing on her back to hurry her onto the train.

"Wait!" Christy cried out, pulling away from the crush of people. "What's wrong with their passes?" She maneuvered her way out of the crowd and moved around to where Katie and Todd stood, talking to another uniformed conductor.

"What do you mean expired?" Katie said.

"The date is stamped here," the man said. "June 5 to June 25. That was yesterday."

Christy quickly looked at her pass, which she had bought separately from Katie's and Todd's. Hers was stamped June 6 to June 26.

"We had them issued a day too early," Todd said. "We flew out of L.A. on the fifth, but we didn't arrive until the sixth." He turned to the conductor. "Can they be extended for one day? We didn't even use them the first few days."

"No. You can buy a separate ticket. This pass is no longer valid."

"We don't have any money," Katie said solemnly.

"I cannot help you," the man said. "Every day I hear the same stories. You should next time plan your trip better."

He turned to help another frantic student, who was speaking to him in French. The train now was loaded, and the grumpy conductor was giving a final boarding call.

"What do we do?" Christy asked.

"You better get on that train," Katie said. "We'll figure something out. This is our problem, not yours. You can't miss class in the morning, Christy."

Christy turned to Todd, her eyes wide with panic. He seemed to be frantically searching her face, reading every detail as if trying to memorize it. Tears began to well up in his eyes as he said, "Go, Kilikina, go."

The train began to move. Christy turned, and the conductor reached out and grabbed her arm as she leaped onto the lowest step. "Ticket," he said gruffly.

With trembling hands, Christy handed him her Eurail pass, and he motioned for her to enter the packed second-class compartment. As Christy moved down the aisle toward the back of the train, she saw Todd out the window, walking quickly alongside the train, scanning the compartments for her. She pushed her way through the first compartment and into the second. Spotting an open window at the end, she ran with her heavy pack bumping against the seats. The train was picking up speed, and Todd was running to the platform's end, waving at her.

Out of breath, Christy reached the open window. Todd was less than twenty feet away, with very little platform left. As tears streamed down her face, she planted one of her very special, saved-up kisses on the palm of her hand and threw it to Todd out the open window.

He reached into the air, closing his fist around her invisible kiss. Then, with a sharp movement, he pounded his fist against his chest, right over his heart, as if he were placing her kiss in that deep place where she already knew he held all her tears.

The train entered a tunnel, and suddenly everything went dark.

Christy spent the longest ten hours of her life on that train out of Venice. For the first hour she stood by the open window. The warm breeze dried her tears. A wild confetti of thoughts sprinkled themselves into her mind. She remembered standing on the boat's deck on the way to Capri and feeling the warm air behind her. The Lord had felt so close that she could feel His breath. Tonight, He came near again.

The verse Todd had found in 2 Timothy from Paul's time in the Mamertine Prison came back to her: *"But the Lord stood at my side and gave me strength."* Christy found strength in knowing that if she was going to stand on this train all the way to Basel, at least the Lord was standing with her.

She thought of the Alpine meadow and the wild flowers she had picked, pressed, and slept on. Those wild flowers still held dreams that she had not yet extracted. She decided she would frame those wild flowers, now buried in their Italian newspaper envelope.

Closing her eyes, Christy remembered the tingling sensation from when she bathed in the stream at the campground. She could almost taste Tonio's strong coffee and see the sheer lace curtains at his mama's house as they fluttered in the breeze the morning Marcos arrived in the taxi. She thought of the brilliant midnight sun pouring through the window of their room in Oslo, and how handsome and adorable Todd had looked right after he had shaved his scruffy face.

She touched her lips and thought of how they had tingled after his kiss in Oslo when he went off to the ends of the earth without her. Christy missed him with every part of her being. She felt as if now she was the one going to the ends of the earth without him. Only instead of being apart two days, they wouldn't see each other for two long months.

Christy managed to sleep after Milan, when a seat opened up and she could lean her head against the window. She missed Todd's navy blue sweat shirt. It had made the best pillow. She missed Katie's laugh and the faint scent of chocolate that had followed her through every country.

When the train finally pulled into the Basel train station, Christy experienced an odd sensation. This was "her" train station; the one she was most familiar with. Yet being alone made her feel as if the station was foreign and cold. She walked with weary steps uphill to her dorm room. The only thing that came close to bringing a smile to her lips was the wonderful aroma she smelled as she passed the Konditorei. Marguerite was placing a basket of bread in the window. She waved when she saw Christy and motioned for her to come in.

"I'll be back," Christy promised. "Later."

Later. Now, that's a laugh, isn't it? All those years Todd told me "later," and here we are, going our separate ways again. Will it always be "later" for us?

She made it to class in plenty of time, even after stopping at her room to shower and change. The seven other tour books were still sitting on her desk, untouched for the last three weeks. Christy laughed to herself when she realized she now probably owed a library fine on all of them.

As soon as class was out, Christy headed for the Konditorei. She had borrowed her roommate's bike to get to class faster, and now she rode the bike's brakes all the way downhill, bumping on every cobblestone she hit. The front tire wobbled on the old contraption, and Christy laughed aloud at herself when she barely managed to come to a stop in front of the Konditorei.

Securing the bike, and with a smile still on her face, Christy entered. The cheery bell over the door lifted her spirits, and she walked up to Marguerite, who stood behind the counter with a big grin on her face.

"*Guten Morgen,* Marguerite. *Wie geit's?*"

"*Gut, gut. Danke. Gut.*"

Christy thought Marguerite acted a little odd. After ordering her pastry, Christy turned toward her usual seat in the back of the café.

Someone was sitting there this morning. Blocking the person's face was a huge bouquet of white carnations.

Christy stopped breathing.

Todd moved the bouquet away from his face. With his easygoing grin brightening the place like a Norwegian sunrise, he said, "Hey, how's it going?"

Christy ran to the table and threw her arms around him. "What are you doing here?"

"Having coffee with you. Here, these are for you." He motioned to the carnations that now lay across the table.

"Did you miss your plane?"

Todd leaned back and took a sip of coffee from his mug, ignoring her question. "You're right. Marguerite makes the best pastry in the world."

"You did, didn't you? You missed your plane. Todd, what are you going to do? What about Katie?"

"Our plane doesn't go out until two." Todd smiled. "I'm going to have coffee with you, and then go back to Zürich and fly home."

"What happened? How did you guys get out of Venice?"

Todd slipped his arm around the back of the seat Christy had fallen into and playfully tugged on the ends of her hair. He acted as if sitting there chatting was the most natural thing in the world for them.

"Tell me everything," Christy said.

"Well, after your train left, we tried to call Marcos. He answered the phone, which was a God-thing because he had just gotten back from a trip to Vienna and was about to leave for a trip to Zürich."

"So you rode the train with him, and he paid your way?"

Todd shook his head. "We drove to Zürich last night in his Ferrari. Katie and Marcos are in Zürich right now. He let me borrow his car so I could come have breakfast with you."

"You drove his car here?" Christy hadn't noticed any fancy cars parked out front, but then she had arrived on a rather wobbly set of wheels and hadn't been paying much attention to anything outside her immediate path.

"I parked at the train station. Seemed safer than parking in the *verboten* zones along here."

"I can't believe this," Christy said, smiling at Marguerite as she delivered Christy's coffee, cream, and pastry to the table.

"Believe it," Todd said. "And are you ready to believe something else?"

"What?"

"Marcos became a Christian."

"You're kidding! That's awesome! When?"

"About a week ago. He said he started to read Romans because we told him that was the letter written just for Italians. God's Word is powerful. Marcos read it, he believed, he repented. You should see him; he's totally on fire and telling everyone on all his business trips about his new relationship with Jesus."

Christy shook her head. "God is so incredible."

"Yes, He is."

"And it's so incredible to see you. Todd, I hate to say this, but I don't know if I can stand saying good-bye to you again. I mean, this is exactly what I wanted—to sit with you here and talk with you from my heart, but it's only for a moment, and then you have to go again."

"I know," Todd said. "I feel the same way. But I needed to see you one more time."

Todd hesitated and Christy froze. *This is it!* a torturing voice of doubt chanted in her head. *This is when he breaks up with you for good. He's probably going to leave you and go serve the Lord on some remote island, alone, for the rest of his life.*

No, Christy told herself decisively. *No more fear. No more doubting. Take each mercy that comes every morning. Whatever happens is in God's care. He's the Master Designer of our lives. He's in control.*

Todd looked at his hands and then back at Christy. "I thought we might have had a few more times to talk on the trip than we did. Alone, I mean."

Christy nodded. "I know. I thought the same thing."

"I wanted to tell you a couple of things."

Christy nodded, waiting.

Todd swallowed and looked at her intently. "You have become a part of me. Not a day goes by that I don't think of you and pray for you. When we've been on the opposite ends of the earth, I feel you right here." He patted his chest. "I hold you, Kilikina. I hold you close in my heart. I always have. I always will."

Christy felt the tears rush to her eyes.

"But," Todd said and then seemed to draw in a deep breath as if gathering the courage to finish his sentence.

No! Christy screamed inwardly. *Don't say anything else!*

"But I honestly believe I need to tell you something I've never told you before. And I feel certain this is the best time to tell you."

Todd, don't do this! Don't break my heart. Not here. Not now.

"It's not because I think you don't already know this, because I think you do." Beads of perspiration glistened on Todd's forehead. "I want to . . . No, I need to tell you this because I think you need to hear it. You need to know . . ."

Tears were now streaming down Christy's face as she braced herself for the worst.

Todd reached up and brushed away her tears with a tender hand. "You need to know, Kilikina, that I love you."

Christy couldn't breathe. She couldn't blink. She couldn't feel her heart beating.

A shy grin inched up Todd's face. "Do you need me to say it again?" He leaned closer and whispered, "I love you."

A breath of relieved joy burst from Christy's lungs, followed by a ripple of laughter.

"You seem so surprised," Todd said.

"Oh, Todd, I wasn't expecting you to say that!"

"You don't have to respond," Todd said. "Not right away. Think about what that means. We have a couple of months to pray through what the future might hold for us."

Christy nodded and blinked back the rest of her tears. She felt her lower lip quivering. "These are going to be the longest two months of my life."

"It's only a short time, really," Todd said. "Sixty-seven days, to be exact."

"You counted?"

Todd nodded. "And you know what we'll do for those sixty-seven days, Kilikina? We'll pretend we're at the ends of the earth, where the sun never goes down. Instead of sixty-seven days, it will be one long day. And then we'll be together again."

"One extremely long Narvik day," Christy said.

"That's right."

"Then you know what I will say sixty-seven times during that extremely long Narvik day?" Christy asked.

Todd reached over and brushed back her hair with his hand. "What?"

"Sixty-seven times I will say, 'I can't wait until tomorrow.' "

Todd grinned and pulled her close. Right before his lips kissed her earlobe, he whispered, "Until tomorrow."

As You Wish

To my husband, Ross.

I made a wish, and you came true.

And to our son, Ross, and our daughter, Rachel.

We wished together, and then there was you and you.

CHAPTER 1

"Todd, you are really bad at keeping secrets, you know." Christy Miller let go of her boyfriend's hand and stopped in the middle of their trek across campus.

"And who says I'm keeping a secret?"

Todd Spencer's wide grin and dimple were sure signs to Christy. "Your face told me. All you have to do now is fill in the details. With words, preferably."

"I'll tell you over dinner." Todd motioned for her to follow him.

Christy stood steadfast, folded her arms, and asked, "Where are we going to dinner? The cafeteria isn't open until Friday."

"I know. Just come with me. I made reservations at a quiet little out-of-the-way place. Come on."

Christy raised her eyebrows skeptically. "You made reservations?"

The hot Santa Ana winds that pushed their way from the desert to the Southern California coast every September grabbed the ends of Christy's long, nutmeg-colored hair and drew the strands across her cheek like a veil. She brushed back the wisps from the corner of her mouth and noticed that Todd was looking at her "that way" again.

She had been home from Switzerland less than a week, but already Todd had looked at her "that way" at least six times. Maybe seven. His silver-blue eyes seemed lit by some inner candle, and she felt as though he was waiting for her to come closer and make a wish before the flickering light went out. Each time Christy had seen that look, she had turned away.

This time she paused. *He's waiting for me to tell him I love him.*

When no words came from Christy's lips, Todd held out his arm to her and in his easygoing manner said, "Well, actually, I sort of made reservations. Come on. You'll see."

Christy responded by slipping her arm around his middle. Todd put his arm across her shoulders and drew her close. They walked across the campus of Rancho Corona University in perfect step.

What's wrong with me? I know I love Todd. Why won't those three simple words find their way from my heart and burst out of my mouth?

They entered the open plaza at the campus's center just as the sun slipped behind a clump of rustling palm trees. Filtered beams of amber sunlight sliced through Todd's short, summer-blond hair.

"Over this way." Todd led Christy to the edge of the large fountain in the middle of the plaza. Since classes didn't begin until next week, not many students were on campus. Todd and Christy had the plaza to themselves.

"Do you want to sit here?" Todd asked. "Or over on one of the benches?"

"This is fine." Christy sat on the fountain's wide edge and crossed her long legs. "What about our dinner reservations?"

"We have some time," Todd said. Then he quickly added, "Doesn't this fountain remind you of that one we saw last summer?"

"Which fountain? One of the dozen in Salzburg that Katie liked?"

"No, I was thinking of the fountain in Rome," Todd said. "Or was it in Milan? I don't remember."

Christy smiled. "When I close my eyes, this spot reminds me of the train station in Castelldefels."

"Spain?" Todd asked. "There weren't any fountains at that rundown train station in Spain. That place was a wreck."

"I know. But close your eyes. Listen. It's the palm trees. That's what reminds me of the train station in Spain. That rustling sound."

Christy watched Todd close his eyes and tip his chin toward the sky, listening. "Reminds me of Hawaii," he said, opening his eyes and looking at Christy.

The sound always made Christy think that the trees were clapping. Now she heard the echoes of Hawaii along with Todd. "You're right. It sounds like a whole row of hula dancers swishing their grass skirts."

"Hula dancers?"

"Yes, hula dancers. Tall, slender hula dancers."

Todd laughed. "Very tall and very slender."

A gentle breeze swirled around them, spraying the evening air with a mist from the fountain. Christy tilted her head. "So are you going to tell me your big secret now? Or do I still have to wait until dinner?"

"Oh yeah, my big secret. What was it I was going to tell you?" After a thoughtful pause, Todd shrugged. "Guess I forgot."

"You did not." Christy playfully grabbed Todd by the shoulders and threatened to push him into the water. Todd responded by taking hold of her shoulders. "If I go in, you're going with me."

They laughed and play-wrestled until Todd's upper-body strength from his years of surfing enabled him to overpower Christy's best efforts. He pulled himself upright and, with his left hand, scooped a handful of water to splash her.

"Hey, don't start something you can't finish," Christy teased, lightly splashing him back.

"Oh, you think I can't finish a water fight?" Todd scooped up another handful of water. "Just watch me." He splashed her again and again, his laughter dancing around her, riding on the waterdrops.

Christy's next scoop of water was the biggest yet.

"Okay, okay," Todd spouted, laughing and coughing. "You win. Truce."

Christy blinked the beads of water from her eyelashes and brushed them off her cheek and chin.

"I got the position," Todd said out of the blue. He used his T-shirt sleeve to mop his wet face.

"What position?"

"The position at Riverview Heights Church. They hired me this afternoon as their youth director. That's my big secret."

"You're kidding! I thought you said they were going to hire someone who had graduated already."

"That's what I thought. But they had their final meeting last night and voted. I'm the guy."

"Wow," Christy said. "That's really great, Todd."

"They said they liked that I could lead music as well as teach the Bible studies." Todd stretched out his feet in front of him and added, "I told them all about you, and they asked if you would be willing to teach the junior high girls' Sunday school class."

"What did you tell them?"

"I said you would."

"You said I would?"

"Yeah. I told them you were the best teacher on our missions team to Spain a few years ago and how you helped out at an orphanage this past year in Switzerland. They can't wait to meet you."

"Todd, you told them I would teach Sunday school?"

Todd turned his full attention to Christy and seemed to try to read her expression. "You've taught Sunday school before."

"Preschoolers."

"Oh. Well, you were a counselor at summer camp a few years ago."

"Those girls weren't even in middle school yet."

"Have you ever taught junior high students before?"

"No, never."

"Well, you'll love these girls. And they'll love you."

"Todd!"

"What?"

"Why didn't you at least ask me first? I mean, what if I don't want to teach the junior high girls?"

"Why wouldn't you?"

"I'm not saying I would or I wouldn't. I'm saying you should have asked me first before agreeing that I would make a commitment like that. It sounds like they hired you because they thought they could get three employees for the price of one—a youth director, a music leader, and a girlfriend Sunday school teacher tossed in for free."

Todd straightened himself and looked confused. "You think people should get paid for teaching Sunday school? Is that it? You want to be paid?"

"No, of course not. You're not hearing what I'm saying. I just . . . it seems that . . . well . . ."

"What?"

"Todd, I think you should have let me think about it before you went ahead and made a commitment for me."

"Oh." Todd nodded slowly. "You're right. I apologize. I spoke for you instead of letting you decide. I shouldn't have done that."

Christy shifted uncomfortably. "I didn't say I absolutely wouldn't consider maybe sometimes teaching or at least helping out."

Now Todd was the one who sounded exasperated. "Are you saying you will teach or you won't?"

"I don't know. Let me have some time to think about it, okay?"

"Okay. Take all the time you need. Decision making has never been your strong point, has it." The thought wasn't spoken as a question but as a statement. Christy hated to admit it, but the remark was true. Still, it felt like a slap of cold water.

"Todd," Christy stated firmly, lining up her thoughts and preparing to defend herself. "I think that—"

Before she could finish, Todd said, "Hey, our dinner is here."

Christy looked out at the parking lot and saw a young guy walking toward them wearing a red-striped shirt and carrying a pizza box.

"Are you Todd Spencer?" he called out as he approached.

"Yeah, that's me. You're right on time. Thanks." Todd paid for the pizza and took the box.

"Have a nice night," the guy said and then jogged back to his delivery car.

"This is what you meant by having reservations?" Christy asked. "This is your quiet, out-of-the-way place?"

Todd grinned. "Cool, huh? Just the two of us. Perfect night. Great atmosphere. It's not exactly the Island of Capri, but we have hula-dancing palm trees for our dining entertainment."

Christy stared at Todd. She didn't know if she should be charmed or bummed.

"I ordered their monster combo." Todd opened the box. "Looks like they went a little heavy on the onions and bell peppers. You can take off anything you don't like and put it on my half. Do you want to pray before we eat, or should I?"

"I think you better," Christy said.

She did her best to hide her feelings, which still stung from Todd's comment about her inability to make decisions. Yet the hurt hung over her like a shadow for the rest of their time together. She only ate two pieces of pizza and silently listened as Todd filled her in on more details about his new position.

When they walked back, hand in hand, to her dorm room, Christy said, "Sorry I got so stressed about the Sunday school thing."

"Don't worry about it," Todd said. "I'll be back on campus Friday to move into my dorm room, and we can talk some more then."

"Okay," Christy said. "Call me when you get here. Katie and I can help, if you want."

He stopped at the front door of Sophia Hall and leaned over to give Christy a soft kiss. If he was upset or disappointed with her, it didn't show in his words or in his kiss. "See you Friday."

Christy found her dorm room unlocked and Katie, her red-haired best friend, standing precariously on a chair, trying to squeeze a small stereo speaker onto the top of their built-in bookshelf.

"Oh, good, you're back." Katie gave the edge of the speaker a whap with the palm of her hand and commanded it to stay in place. "Where did you and Todd go to eat?"

"He made reservations at a quiet, out-of-the-way place." Christy flopped on her bed.

Katie stopped to stare. "Are we talking about Todd Spencer? Your Todd Spencer?"

"Yes. It actually was very creative. He ordered a pizza and had it delivered to the fountain in the central plaza, if you can believe that."

"How romantic!"

"It would have been if I wasn't such a bean head."

"You? A bean head?" Katie climbed down from the chair but still was eyeing the speaker as if commanding it to stay in place.

"Yes, me. What is my problem?"

"Which one should we discuss?" Katie made herself comfortable on the foot of Christy's bed. Katie was always ready for a good evaluation session.

"Forget I asked that."

"Oh, come on. Give me a hint. Why did Todd come all the way here tonight?" Katie's perceptive green eyes examined Christy's expression. "Let me guess. He drove an hour and a half from Newport Beach because he missed you so much, right?"

"Not exactly." Christy told Katie about Todd's new position as youth director at Riverview Heights, including the parts about Christy teaching the junior high girls' class and Todd's comment concerning her inability to make decisions.

"Well, that is true, you know," Katie said. "I mean, you have gotten a lot better about making decisions and everything, but I don't think you should be upset with Todd for saying that. It was an observation, not a criticism."

"Well, I am upset. I feel like crying my eyes out."

"That's probably because of the jet lag. You were in Switzerland for a year, Christy. Your body has had only a few days to adjust to the time change. Give yourself a break. That's why we decided to move into the dorm early, remember? You were the one who said you needed a chance to adjust to all the changes."

"Arrrrgh!" Christy pulled a pillow over her head. "I hate change!"

"Now we're getting somewhere." Katie grabbed the pillow and used it for a backrest. "Remember, flexibility is a sign of good mental health."

"Oh, please!" Christy yanked at the pillow. "Give me back my pillow."

"Only if you promise you'll work on a better attitude about Todd's new job. This is what he wanted, you know. It's perfect for him."

"I know. It is."

"It's a real job." Katie handed the pillow to Christy. "A career. A ministry. Something permanent. This isn't like all his random jobs over the years."

11

Christy made herself comfortable. She knew Katie was determined to shower her with advice. Resistance was futile. And even though Christy wouldn't admit it, deep down she wanted to hear what Katie had to say.

"This is it, Chris. This is the final stretch for you guys. It's possible that both of you could graduate this year."

"Only if I can figure out what I want my major to be." Christy sighed.

"You will. When is your appointment with your counselor?"

"Friday."

"That works," Katie said. "You can sleep all day tomorrow to get over your jet lag. On Thursday you can find a job, and on Friday figure out everything with your classes and your major. By the time Todd arrives Friday afternoon, your life will be in order."

"I wish," Christy said. "It's not always that easy, Katie."

"And it's not always as complicated as you make it. I mean, can I just say that it's obvious God is doing all His God-things at the right time so you and Todd can get married and get on with your lives together?"

"Katie, you're assuming an awful lot."

"Assuming a lot? *Moi?*"

Just then someone knocked rapidly on the door. Katie hopped up and swung open the door. The visitor who came floating in wore a glowing expression. Her wild, curly blond hair cascaded over her shoulders.

"And just where have you been, Little Miss Happy Heart?" Katie asked.

Sierra Jensen, a fun-loving, free-spirited freshman, gave Katie an impulsive hug and then flitted over to Christy and gave her a hug. Sierra had been roommates with Katie and Christy two years ago when they had met on a missions trip in England. Despite Katie and Christy being older than Sierra, they were all close friends.

"I've been to the chapel." Sierra twirled dramatically. She spun around to Katie's beanbag chair and lowered herself with a poof.

"I take it you saw Paul." Katie pulled up a chair. "What happened? Did you guys have a chance to talk?"

"Yes. Everything is wonderful now." Sierra fiddled with the dangling silver earring in her left ear.

"Details, please," Katie said. "Don't leave anything out."

"Well," Sierra began, "you both know how everything was so disastrous with Paul a few hours ago."

"Slightly," Katie answered for both of them.

"Everything is perfect now. We talked and prayed together in the chapel, and it's like we're starting our relationship all over. We both have the same understanding and expectations, and it's just right. Not too fast, not too slow. Just right."

Christy smiled. *I remember a few brief seasons when I felt that way about Todd. As much as I said I didn't like it at the time, those stretches—when we knew our relationship was in a holding pattern while we figured out who we were and what we were going to do with our lives—were comforting and settling. So why am I nervous about making the next round of decisions in our relationship? I wish I could figure out why I feel this way.*

Sierra pulled Katie's beanbag chair closer to Christy's bed and wiggled herself into a comfortable position. "After a whole year of Paul's being in Scotland, now he's less than an hour away. And we're both in the same place in our understanding of our relationship. Finally! No unrealistic expectations. I can't believe how I was starting to make everything so complicated."

"Did you hear that?" Katie gave Christy a motherly look. "Why would you want to complicate things with Todd when it's all finally coming together so naturally?"

"And did you hear what Sierra just said about unrealistic expectations?" Christy countered.

Sierra's expression turned somber. "Everything is okay between you and Todd, isn't it?"

Katie answered for Christy, "She's afraid of the future."

"I am not," Christy snapped. "I'm just not ready to talk about getting married."

"Who's talking about getting married?" Sierra asked.

Katie raised her hand. "I am."

Sierra's eyes opened wide. "You, Katie? Who are you planning to marry?"

Katie laughed. "I'm not talking about *my* getting married. I was talking about Todd and Christy getting married. It was the topic *du jour* right before you knocked on the door. It's the next step for Todd and Christy, and she's afraid to make such a huge decision."

"Katie, that is not what I said, and you know it."

"Okay. What did you say?"

Christy sighed. Part of her didn't want to discuss this with Katie and Sierra right now. However, another part of her had longed for the closeness of good friends while she was in Switzerland. She had even written in her diary how much she was looking forward to settling into Rancho Corona University so she could spill her guts to Katie and be open to her best friend's advice. Having Sierra to talk to, as well, was a bonus.

"Okay, this is the whole thing. Just listen, please. Both of you. I promise I'll listen to your advice, but first let me say what I'm thinking."

Katie and Sierra leaned forward, their expressions open and warm.

"This is what I know for sure. I know I love Todd."

"But you haven't told him," Katie jumped in.

"I said let me say everything first."

"Oops." Katie covered her mouth. "Sorry. Go ahead."

"I know I love Todd, and yes, I haven't been able to tell him yet. I know he loves me. He has told me he loves me at least a dozen times since that first time in Switzerland this summer. But, you see, to me there's something really deep and final about telling him I love him. It's only a tiny step away from saying I promise to be committed to him. Forever."

"And you don't feel ready to say that to Todd?" Katie surmised.

Christy looked at her hands. The overhead light in their room caught the corner of the gold ID bracelet Todd had given her years ago when he had promised that, no matter what happened, he would always be her friend. She ran her finger over the word "Forever" engraved on the bracelet.

Sierra jumped in. "Does it feel too final to you? Are you thinking that the moment you tell Todd you love him he'll say, 'Then let's get married'?"

"Maybe. I don't know."

"He's not going to propose to you on the spot," Katie said.

"And what if he does? Why wouldn't you want to marry him?" Sierra asked. "Haven't you been thinking that was the direction your relationship was going all along?"

"Yes and no. Sometimes I think I'm ready to marry him right then and there and never look back or have any regrets. Then other times I look at him and I think, 'Who is this guy?' There's so much I don't know about him."

"So? Give yourself some time to get to know Todd better," Sierra said. "That's what Paul and I are doing. Not that we're even thinking about marriage. Neither of us is. We have plenty of time to get to know each other as friends without any pressure to make it more than that."

"Right," Katie said. "But Christy and Todd have already been through that phase for . . . what? The last five years?"

Christy nodded.

"It's time for them to make decisions, and sorry, Chris, but I have to say this. Todd is right. Decision making has never been your favorite thing."

Christy didn't feel as wounded when Katie said it. She actually found it easier to agree and slowly nodded her head. But something more lay behind her uncertainty over Todd, and she felt she was on the edge of formulating that very important thought.

Katie turned to Sierra and continued her analysis of Christy as if she weren't sitting there. "Christy likes things to be planned and in a logical order. You know, 'First comes love, then comes marriage, then comes the baby in the baby carriage.' "

Sierra chuckled. "That is the way it works best."

"If only a detailed tour book for relationships existed!" Katie spouted. "Todd and I discovered when we were traveling with Christy in Europe this summer that the best way to travel is with a plan and a tour book to guide you. You miss too much along the way otherwise."

"Oh, so are you now admitting publicly that having a plan is a good thing?" Christy said.

"I told you that in Europe." Katie raised her voice.

Sierra jumped in. "But I don't know if love can always be planned and logical."

"Right," Katie agreed. "Nobody can make guarantees about the future. We have to take what we know and act on it at the moment, trusting God for the outcome."

"I don't know if I agree with that," Christy said. "I think we're responsible for our actions all the time, including the possible results of our actions."

"Yes, but," Sierra spoke in a firm tone, "there has to be a balance because we're not in control of our own lives. God is."

"And we shouldn't be afraid of the future," Katie added.

"It's like that verse in Proverbs 31," Sierra said. "You know, the one that says, 'Strength and honour are her clothing; and she shall rejoice in time to come.' "

"I memorized that one last year," Katie said. "Only my version said, 'She can laugh at the days to come.' "

Christy pulled back and became somber. The important thought she had been formulating was rising to the surface and bringing sadness with it.

"What are you thinking right now?" Katie asked. "Your face clouded over like a thunderstorm."

"You and Sierra think of laughing and rejoicing at the future part of that verse, but I worry about the strength and honor part of it. Committing myself to Todd is a huge decision. If I marry him, we'll be together for the rest of our lives. I don't want to let him think I'm ready to make such a major commitment until I'm sure I'm ready."

"But you do know that you love him," Katie reminded her.

"I think I know that."

Katie dramatically grabbed her hair with both her hands and acted as if she were going to pull it out. "You said a few minutes ago that you knew you loved him!"

"I know. But try to understand what I'm saying—"

"I do. I get it." Sierra stepped in. "I think I get it, anyway. You're saying that you know you love Todd, but you don't know if it's the same kind of love, or a deep enough love, to be certain you're ready to commit yourself to him for the rest of your life."

"Exactly," Christy said.

Katie burrowed her head in her hands and seemed to be taking it all in.

Sierra's summary of what Christy was trying to say had somehow allowed the important thought she had been formulating to become clear. "That's it! This is what I've been trying to figure out." Christy leaned forward and paused, making sure she had Katie's full attention. "I want you both to tell me the truth. Tell me your honest opinion."

Sierra and Katie both waited.

"Do you think it's possible to finally decide that you really, truly love someone but not end up marrying him?"

The room went still for a moment while the three friends exchanged glances.

"Yes," Katie said, her expression completely serious for the first time all evening. "I think it's possible to realize you love someone as deeply as you know how to love and not end up spending the rest of your life with him."

Sierra slowly nodded. "I think so, too."

Christy felt her vision blur with uninvited tears. "So do I," she said in a whisper. "And that's what I'm afraid of."

CHAPTER 2

Christy stayed up until after two in the morning talking with Sierra and Katie. When Katie rose shortly before noon and said she was going into town to get something to eat, Christy told her to go on without her. Then she did something she didn't think she had ever done before—she slept all day and all night.

On Thursday morning Christy woke with a horrible headache. She ate a soggy breakfast burrito Katie had left for her with a note saying that Katie was shopping with Sierra. After a hot shower that did her little good, Christy went back to bed, where she fell into a deep sleep for the rest of the day.

When she woke, it was almost dusk, and she felt more coherent than she had in weeks. Maybe even in months, as if she had broken through the exhaustion barrier.

Christy had just pulled herself out of bed and was stretching, when Katie came in holding a bag from the deli in town. "Hey," Katie said, "she lives! She breathes! Does she want to eat?"

"Yes, I'm starving. Thank you so much. Thanks for leaving the burrito for me this morning, too."

"No problem. You must be feeling better."

"I do. I feel normal again. No, better than normal."

"That's good to hear. I was beginning to worry about you."

Christy reached in the bag and took out one of the turkey sandwiches. She closed her eyes and said a quick prayer of thanks before taking a bite.

"You look better," Katie said. "I think those extra weeks at the orphanage in Switzerland really did you in."

Christy knew Katie was right. Her year in Switzerland had been good in many ways, but her life had been nonstop, requiring a great deal of her physically and emotionally. She gave of herself to the children at the orphanage, often for more than thirty hours a week, as well as maintaining a full schedule of classes.

"I know," Christy agreed, settling cross-legged on her bed. "You're right about the orphanage. Those kids broke my heart every day. I really felt empty by my last few weeks there."

"Are you glad you stayed through the term?" Katie asked.

"What do you mean?"

"When Todd and I were there in June, you had that big breakthrough revelation about how you weren't suited for crisis maintenance-type work. You know, all that stuff you were talking about when we were in Amsterdam. How you were going to change your major but you still thought you should stay in Switzerland to finish the program. Are you glad you stayed?"

Christy nodded, her mouth full.

"I know you felt you needed to keep your promise to the orphanage and to the university in Basel," Katie said. "I never told you, but I admired you for making that decision."

"Thanks."

"I've been thinking about all the stuff we talked about the other night. You're good for me, Chris. You cause me to think things through rather than impulsively run ahead. Sierra and I were just saying how we both have a problem with being too spontaneous."

"That's why you're both good for me. I need you guys to tell me to lighten up sometimes. I wish I'd gone shopping with you. I haven't been to a mall in more than a year."

"I think getting some sleep was more important for you," Katie said. "You honestly look a whole lot better."

"I feel better about everything, too. It really helped to talk with you and Sierra the other night. I think the most important thing I can do right now is to take each day as it comes and resolve each decision as it comes."

"The Sunday school decision was the final phone book, wasn't it?" Katie asked.

"The final phone book? What does that mean?"

"It's my new theory. You know how I told you that one of my many fascinating summer jobs was delivering phone books door to door?"

Christy nodded.

"Well, I learned the very first day that I could only carry eight phone books at a time. If I tried to pick up one more, I ended up dropping all of them."

Christy didn't see Katie's point.

"You were already carrying a lot when Todd dropped the Sunday school question on you. Think about it. You had jet lag, you had decisions to make about your major, you were worried about finding a job, you were confused about why you didn't feel ready to rush into a lifetime commitment with Todd, and then—bam!—the Sunday school decision was the final phone book."

"Kind of like that saying about the straw that broke the camel's back," Christy said.

"Exactly. Only, the things you're carrying aren't little straws. They're all heavy like phone books. You can carry a couple of them at a time, but when you hit your limit, it feels as if you're going to drop all of them."

Christy leaned back and felt herself breathing more easily than she had for several weeks. "You just described perfectly what I was feeling."

Katie beamed like a proud sunflower. "No extra charge for the advice. I wondered if you were going to have a meltdown a couple of nights ago when we went to the store and you were about to cry because you couldn't decide which laundry soap to buy. I'm glad to hear you say that you're going to take each decision separately, one at a time."

"What about you?"

"What about me?" Katie had gotten up to turn on her stereo and pulled a stick of gum from an old Muppet Babies lunch box she kept on the corner of her desk.

"Didn't you have an appointment with the counselor today?" Christy asked. "Or did you have to reschedule it?"

"No. I went into town to get breakfast with a bunch of people, and then I met with the counselor at ten. Sierra had an appointment with financial aid, and we went shopping after that."

"Did you end up changing any classes around?"

"No, I'm sticking with botany for my major. I told the counselor my goal in life was to create herbal teas, and he came close to laughing aloud."

"Didn't you tell him about the herb garden you started on campus last semester and the experiments you did?"

"No, I'll wait to tell him about that after I complete a successful experiment."

Christy grinned. She remembered an email Katie had sent last spring with the hilarious account of her first attempt to serve herbal tea she had grown and mixed herself. The experiment resulted in two out of five students in her chemistry class breaking out in hives. The other three complained of stomach pains. Apparently Katie was the only one in the class who didn't suffer any kind of reaction.

"By the way," Katie said, "your aunt called this morning while you were dead to the world and wanted to take you to lunch. I told her you weren't available today."

"Very kind of you, Katie. And true. Thanks."

"You might not thank me when you hear this part. She said she would be here at noon tomorrow to pick you up for lunch, and if you had anything on your schedule, you needed to change it because that was the only time she was available."

"Oh. Did she say what she wanted?"

Katie laughed. "Does she ever? I mean, does she need a reason to step into your life at any moment and take over?"

"She's probably upset that I haven't called her since I got back. When I asked my mom about Bob and Marti last weekend, she said she hadn't seen them or talked to them since the Fourth of July."

"That's a little unusual, isn't it?"

Christy shrugged. "My mom and Marti aren't exactly the closest sisters that ever lived."

"They're certainly the most opposite," Katie commented.

"You know, maybe one of the good things about Switzerland was that my aunt was thousands of miles away instead of an hour-and-a-half drive."

"Do you want me to come to lunch with you tomorrow?" Katie asked.

"Yes! Would you?"

"Of course. Free food. Why wouldn't I come to offer my moral support?"

Christy thought a moment and added, "It's not because I'm intimidated by my aunt, you know."

"Oh no," Katie said with a sly grin. "Never."

"It's because your being there will take off the edge, if you know what I mean. I want you to come because then I know it will be fun."

"That's me, all fun all the time." Katie tossed the crumpled deli bag toward the trash can and missed. She got up and placed it inside. "I'm going to the baseball field. Do you want to come with me?"

"The baseball field?" Christy thought that was an odd place for Katie to want to go to. Then Christy remembered. "You still searching for number sixteen?"

"His number was fourteen, and yes, as a matter of fact, I thought it wouldn't hurt to revisit the place where we met last June."

"What was his name again?" Christy asked.

"Matt."

"Matt what?"

"That's all I know. I told you I hadn't found out his last name yet. He's Matt, number fourteen, the best baseball player Rancho Corona has ever seen."

"You know," Christy said, pulling on a pair of jeans and a T-shirt, "I'm surprised you haven't employed your extraordinary detective skills on this guy yet."

Katie shook her head, making her red hair swish in trademark Katie fashion. "No, I'm really determined to let God be in charge of my nonexistent love life. If He wants to bring somebody into my life, He's going to have to do it in His time and His way. True, I've thought about Matt an awful lot in the past 104 days since I met him."

"One hundred and four days, huh?" Christy laughed.

"Yes, but I'm not going to push to make anything happen." Katie pulled a worn baseball cap over her silky red hair and tucked the chin-length strands behind her ears.

"However," Christy teased, "you still believe it's okay to just happen to be at the right place at the right time to help God along in the sovereignty department."

"Exactly."

"I'm ready," Christy said, slipping her bare feet into her leather sandals. "Let's go be 'available' for God."

"Don't mock my methods." Katie closed the door behind them. "I'm really trying, here."

"Yes, you really are trying, aren't you?" Christy suppressed a laugh.

"I'm not talking to you anymore, Christy."

The two friends exited their upper-classmen dormitory and headed down the road toward the center of campus, both still grinning. Christy felt relieved that she and Katie were back to normal in their friendship and that the jet lag blues hadn't gotten the two of them off to a bad start this year. That was one of the things she had long appreciated about Todd's easygoing personality and Katie's bouncy personality; they both let Christy go through her loopy moods without changing their friendships.

Christy and Katie walked past several trucks that were backed up to the main walkways of each of the dorms. Dozens of arriving students energetically unpacked their meager worldly possessions. Christy was glad she had moved in early and had the days she needed to adjust and to sleep, which probably wouldn't have happened at home in Escondido.

Moving in early had been her dad's idea. He had said he could either move her in right after she returned from Basel, or she would have to wait until Saturday afternoon, which wouldn't have given her much time to settle in before classes started. She knew her parents also had hoped it would give her a chance to find a job on campus, and she felt bad that she hadn't pursued that yet. That was one of the "phone books" she had been carrying around.

"I love this weather, don't you?" Katie apparently had forgotten that two minutes ago she had said she wasn't going to talk to Christy. "I love it when it's still warm and breezy like this, even after the sun has gone down. It feels like Indian summer. Maybe I'll invent an herbal tea and call it 'Indian Summer.' What do you think?"

"I like it," Christy said. "I like this time of year, too. This dry, windy heat always makes me think of new beginnings because the weather was like this when my family moved to Escondido. That's when you and I first met, remember? It was at that sleepover the first week of our sophomore year in high school."

"I will never forget that night." Katie's laughter took off like a hoot owl headed for the moon. "Remember when we tried to TP Rick Doyle's house, and you got caught, and he chased you down the street at midnight?"

Christy had to laugh. That was still among her top ten most embarrassing moments. "I wonder what ever happened to Rick."

"Why do you say that?" Katie's laughter vanished.

"Because the last time anyone saw him was more than a year ago at Doug and Tracy's wedding. Did you talk to him then?"

"No, did you?"

"No."

"You're not having dreams about Rick waltzing back into your life or anything, are you?" Katie asked cautiously.

"No, of course not. I just think it's too bad that we're all together again, but he's just out there."

"Rick always was sort of 'out there.' "

"I know. But I kept hoping he would figure out his life and be one of the gang."

"You know what your problem is?" Katie said and then plunged ahead before Christy had a chance to answer. "Your problem is you have too much mercy. That's why being with those kids in the orphanage killed you and why out of the blue you would start wishing happiness on a guy who was a jerk to both of us. Rick deserves whatever he gets."

Christy stopped walking a few yards from the baseball field. "You're still mad at him, aren't you? You haven't forgiven him for the way he led you on at the Rose Bowl Parade on New Year's all those years ago."

Katie shrugged.

"You need to forgive him, Katie. Let it be what it was. Learn from it and move on."

"He was my first kiss, Christy. Tell me, how does a girl forget the first guy who kissed her?"

Christy let her tender, blue-green eyes scan her best friend's expression before answering. "You don't ever forget."

"Exactly." Katie took off, walking at a fast clip.

Christy caught up with her. "But you can forgive him for hurting you, Katie."

"I have. I do." Katie paused. "I will. But enough of Rick Doyle, okay? I'd like to move on to Matt, number fourteen."

Christy glanced around the baseball diamond as they approached it. The two of them were the only people in sight. "Doesn't look like anyone is practicing tonight."

"I didn't think anyone would be practicing," Katie said. "I just thought . . ." She paused and stood still for a long moment. "I don't know what I thought. Let's go to The Java Jungle. I don't know why I had us come here."

"The Java Jungle?" Christy questioned.

"That's the new name for the coffee shop on the lower level of the student center. I saw the sign today. I guess no one liked the old name, The Espresso Stop."

Katie pointed out the new sign after they had hiked across campus to the student center. The large complex housed The Java Jungle, the student mailboxes, and a large lounge area on the top level. When they entered, Christy noticed more students were in the lounge than she had seen on campus the entire week. The place was beginning to feel more like a university than a ghost town. The cafeteria, which had been dubbed The Golden Calf, would begin serving meals for the first time in the morning. That meant Christy finally could stop spending her limited funds every time she wanted to eat.

They entered the coffee shop and stood in a short line to order something to drink. "My turn to pay," Christy said.

"I have money with me," Katie protested.

"But you bought the sandwiches."

"Actually," Katie said, "I got a two-for-one coupon on the sandwiches when I filled my car at that little station at the bottom of the hill."

Rancho Corona University was built on top of a mesa, and every time the students wanted to go into town, they had to go down the hill. Christy was sure Katie knew where all the gas stations were because she was so fond of her new car, a bright yellow Volkswagen Thing. It reminded Christy of a cross between a Jeep and a dune buggy. Katie seemed to enjoy making sure the gas tank on her "Baby Hummer" was always full and the windows free of smashed insects.

"Okay, then we're even," Christy said. "Be sure to thank Baby Hummer for me."

Katie motioned to a booth that had just been vacated in the far corner. "Why don't you hold that booth for us? What do you want to drink?"

"Lemonade."

"Lemonade?"

"Yes, lemonade. I don't want anything hot to drink. A good, old-fashioned American lemonade sounds good to me."

"Okay, one lemonade." Katie headed for the end of the line as Christy slid into the booth by the side window. She looked around and realized she didn't know a single person in The Java Jungle. It felt odd starting all over again in a new school. She was more grateful than ever that Katie was there. And Sierra and Todd.

Friends make all the difference in life. She thought of her two roommates in Switzerland who were both from Germany. They were nice roommates, but Christy couldn't keep up with their social activities and had spent most of her free time alone in their room. She liked the solitude after the noise of the children at the orphanage, but now that she was back in Southern California, Christy felt ready to reinvent her college experience, spending lots of time with her closest friends.

I wonder if that's another reason I reacted so strongly when Todd said he had volunteered me to teach Sunday school. Maybe I'm afraid my free time will be devoured if I commit myself to a group of younger kids again. I'm not ready to do that. I need time with my friends.

Just then Christy noticed a tall, slender guy entering The Java Jungle. A wonderful, warm feeling came over her.

26

Matthew Kingsley! Look at you! My mom was right. You are all grown-up now, aren't you? There was no mistaking the Wisconsin farm boy she had known since childhood, the guy she had developed a huge crush on in elementary school.

Matthew's brown eyes scanned the room from under his baseball cap. Christy hadn't seen him since her grandparents' fiftieth wedding anniversary three summers ago. She watched Matthew, wondering if he would recognize her right away.

Matthew's gaze passed over her at first. Then he did a double take and grinned before charging across the room toward her. A firefly sort of fluttering started in her stomach and came out in a lighthearted giggle when Matthew greeted her with an awkward hug. His shoulder smashed her left ear in the quick embrace, and she noticed he didn't smell too fresh.

"You're here." Matthew slid into the booth next to her and grinned.

"I'm here," Christy repeated. "And so are you. How are you doing?"

"Great. Just got in. I've been driving since five this morning. It's so good to see you, Christy. Did your mom tell you I called Monday?"

"No, I've been on campus all week. I haven't talked to her. Are you hungry?" Christy realized she sounded like her mom. It was the lingo Christy had grown up with on the dairy farm in Wisconsin. Whenever one of the men came in from the field, food was offered.

"No, I ate already. I'm trying to find my roommate. He said he would be waiting in here with our keys, but I don't see him. It's the same guy I roomed with last year. Pete Santos. Do you know him?"

"No, but my roommate might. She seems to know everyone." Christy turned to see that Katie was at the front of the line, paying for their drinks.

Matthew looked out the window and leaned closer to Christy to get a clearer view. "There he is. Hey, Pete!" Matthew tapped on the glass. The guy turned and motioned for Matthew to come outside.

"I should have known he'd be talking on his cell phone," Matthew said. "He should have that thing permanently wired to his head. He's on it all the time."

Christy looked away from the window and saw that Matthew was staring at her.

"I wish I didn't have to run off," he said with an honest expression. "But I left my truck in a no-parking zone." Matthew rose and gave Christy's arm a quick squeeze. "How about if we meet for breakfast? We have a lot to catch up on."

"Sure," Christy said and then quickly corrected herself. "Oh, wait, I can't. I have an early appointment in the morning."

"Lunch?"

Christy shook her head. "My aunt Marti is coming to take me to lunch."

"Then what about dinner? Six o'clock? Meet in The Golden Calf?"

"Perfect," Christy said. "I'll meet you there."

Matthew paused a moment and said, "It's great to see you, Christy."

"You too," she said.

"Six o'clock tomorrow," Matthew repeated.

"Six o'clock."

He took off, and Christy watched him stride through the crowded café, waving to several people as he went.

Matthew Kingsley. Who would have guessed that we would end up at the same college?

Christy was still smiling softly when Katie arrived at their booth. "I just saw a guy from my hometown in Wisconsin," Christy told her. "And if you can believe this, I used to have a huge crush on him."

Katie placed the tall lemonade in front of Christy and, ignoring her comment, said, "Well, you're not going to believe what I just did. Go ahead and thank me now."

"Thanks for the lemonade," Christy said.

"No, not the lemonade. Thank me now because I just found a job for you. On campus, even."

"Where?"

"You have to thank me first."

"Thank you, Katie."

"You're welcome." Katie settled into the booth and took a slow, leisurely sip of her steaming latte.

Christy waited, her expectant expression turning to an exasperated one when Katie didn't offer details.

"Oh, you want to know where it is? It's at the bookstore," Katie said at last. "I was talking to some people in line, and one of the guys said he was planning to work in the campus bookstore like he had last semester, but he just got a job today in town that pays more. The job for the bookstore isn't posted yet. He's going in at nine o'clock tomorrow morning to tell them he won't be keeping his position. If you get there at 9:05, I bet they would hire you right then and there."

"I don't know if I'll be done with the counselor by then."

"Okay, so you show up at nine-thirty. Better yet, I'll tell him he shouldn't go to the bookstore and resign until ten. That will give you plenty of time. He even said he would recommend you by name, if you wanted."

Christy hesitated. "Okay, I guess. Who is he?"

"I don't know. He's over there in the green shirt talking to Wesley. You know Wes, don't you? He's Sierra's older brother." Katie popped up before Christy could say anything and waltzed over to the guys with her plan. As Katie turned and pointed to Christy, Christy raised her hand and waved. She thought about going over and talking to them, but she was sure someone would take their booth.

Katie returned with an air of satisfaction. "That was easy. Ten o'clock. Or rather, five after ten. All you have to do is show up at the bookstore and talk to Donna. Act like you know what you're doing, and I'm sure you'll land the job."

"You know, you didn't have to do that, Katie." Christy wasn't sure why she felt resistant to this job. It sounded like an ideal situation, but Christy never had liked it when others felt she wasn't aggressive enough to make her own decisions or to take care of herself so they stepped in to make arrangements for her.

"I think it's a God-thing," Katie said brightly. "Do you know how few jobs are still available on campus?"

"I just don't want to work too many hours," Christy said. "I want to have some time for a social life this year."

"Tell that to Donna when she interviews you. She's really nice. I wouldn't mind working for her. Besides, everyone goes to the bookstore, so part of your social life will be mixed with your work. It's perfect."

29

Christy sipped her lemonade slowly. "Are you sure you don't want to show up at five after ten tomorrow and apply for the job yourself?"

Katie grinned. "I have enough in my savings to get me through until January. Then I'll be looking for a miracle job. Until then, I'm going to enjoy the rare freedom and pursue my social life to the fullest."

"You're making me feel sorry for myself, and I don't even have the job yet."

Katie didn't seem to hear Christy's comment. Instead, Katie had fixed her attention on something outside the window. Christy looked and saw about two dozen students gathered around the patio tables outside The Java Jungle. From her side of the booth she didn't see Pete or Matthew, and she was certain she didn't know any of the others. Christy guessed they all must be returning students because they were hugging and laughing and waving to others who were heading that way.

"Wait here," Katie said. "I think my number just came up."

"Your number?"

"Yeah, number fourteen," Katie called out, rushing to join the mob of returning students on the patio.

CHAPTER 3

"Christy, are you awake?" Katie asked much later that night as Christy lay in bed.

Rolling over, Christy forced her eyes open. The soft yellow light she had left on over Katie's desk several hours earlier seemed too bright.

"I'm so sorry, Chris. I started to talk to a bunch of people, and when I went back to the booth, you were gone. I know I left you there a long time. I'm sorry."

"It's okay. I could see you were having a good time catching up with everybody. I wanted to come back to the room to call Todd before it got too late. I should have told you I was leaving."

"The time just got away," Katie said.

"Don't worry about it. We can't apologize every time stuff like that happens." Christy propped herself up on her elbow and stretched her stiff neck. "You already have a lot of friends here. I don't expect you always to wait for me or to take me with you wherever you go."

"You're right." Slipping off her shoes, Katie turned on the overhead light.

Christy flinched at the brightness.

"I'm glad you said that." Katie reached for her bucket of bathroom necessities. She cleverly had arranged her shampoo, soap, and facial scrub in a bright plastic sand bucket and had poked holes in the bottom so she could take it in the shower. "Open policy between us. Always."

"Always," Christy said, feeling more awake. "Now tell me about Matt, number fourteen. Was he happy to see you?"

"It wasn't him. Or at least by the time I got outside he wasn't there. If he was even there to begin with." Katie pulled a pair of flannel shorts and a T-shirt from her dresser drawer. "I don't know for sure if he's coming back this year. I'm going to take a quick shower. Some of the guys were goofing off, and I got shaving cream down my back. See you in a bit."

Katie whooshed out the door just as Christy said, "Could you turn off the . . ."

Forcing her feet to hit the bare floor, Christy turned off the overhead light herself. "I have to buy a rug," she muttered before crawling back into bed. She knew if she and Katie started a conversation after Katie returned from her shower, they would end up talking for hours. Christy wanted to keep up on her sleep while she could, so she coaxed herself to fall asleep before Katie returned.

The next sound Christy heard was the irritating buzz of her alarm clock. It made an obnoxious sound, but Christy found she could fall back to sleep too easily with a softer alarm or music.

"What is that?" Katie bellowed from her side of the room.

"It's just me. Go back to sleep," Christy said softly. "I'm getting an early start for my appointment."

"Humph," Katie grunted, turning toward the wall.

Christy tiptoed over to the window and raised the curtain a few inches. Another clear, sunny day. The skirt and top she had laid out last night were still a good choice for the day. It was her nicest casual outfit and seemed right for the job interview that would most likely follow the meeting with her counselor.

Quietly pulling her desk chair to the window, Christy reached for her Bible and diary and settled in. The morning light fell across the open pages on her lap. After praying, she began to read where she had left off a few days ago. Her goal had been to read through the New Testament that summer. She had only made it through the first chapter of John.

Christy's eye caught on verse twelve, and she underlined it, reading it again in a whisper. " 'Yet to all who received him, to those who believed in his name, he gave the right to become children of God.' "

She made a note in her journal.

I have been given the right to become one of God's children because I have received Him into my heart and life and I have believed in His name. It's like God has adopted me into His family.

Christy chewed on the end of her pen and thought of all the orphans she had grown to care about in Basel. They were waiting for someone to give them the right to become an adopted child. Just the thought of those young hearts and eager faces was enough to bring tears to her eyes. Christy had intended to read to the end of the chapter, but instead she prayed for each of the orphans by name. The sun pouring through the window began to warm her arm, and she knew she needed to get going. She could spend the whole morning praying in a melancholy daze.

Slipping out of the room to take a shower, Christy left all the orphans behind when she closed her Bible and told herself she had to move on.

The meeting with the counselor went well. All Christy's transcripts had arrived from Basel, and the extra courses she had taken provided her with more transferred credits than she had calculated. If she wanted a bachelor's degree in elementary education, the next step was to plan her student teaching. However, Christy told the counselor she had changed her mind and no longer wanted to go that route.

"I'm thinking of changing my major to humanities," Christy said. "Or maybe English literature."

"I see," the counselor said. He wrote something in pencil on the inside of her folder. Christy tried to see what he wrote without being obvious.

"I think I'm leaning more toward literature," she said.

"Either major would work," he said. "You have a good solid base for both of them. I was adding up the credits, and if you went with English literature, you could graduate in June. You would need to add another three units this semester and carry a full load of sixteen units next semester."

"That's okay," Christy said. Then she wished she hadn't spoken so quickly. After her intense year of study in Basel, she had hoped to take it easier this semester. Especially with a job, which she didn't exactly have yet. And a social life, which was still high on her priority list.

"Would it be okay if I looked over all this and came back the first of next week?" Christy asked.

"Sure. The sooner the better. I have an open slot at four this afternoon, if you know what you want to do by then. Take this catalog with you. I've marked the classes you still need." The counselor gave Christy a reassuring grin. "It's nice to be in the final stretch, isn't it?"

Christy nodded and left the administration building fighting the panicky feelings that taunted her. A few days ago Katie had made the same sort of comment about Christy and Todd being in the final stretch in their relationship as they readied themselves to head down the church aisle. The counselor's comment reminded Christy that she was in the final stretch to head down the graduation aisle. At this moment, she didn't feel ready to walk down any aisles.

Her visit to the bookstore at exactly ten minutes after ten was less stressful. That helped her to focus on the present.

When Christy entered the busy bookstore and asked for Donna, a beautiful woman in a buttery yellow blazer stepped out of the back room and said, "Are you Christy?"

"Yes."

"Great. Come on back here." Donna's skin had a warm, caramel tone. Her golden brown hair was pulled up in a twist and held in place with what looked like two chopsticks. On her desk sat a small blue teapot alongside a china teacup.

"Please, sit down." Donna pointed to several unopened boxes of books that were stacked beside her small desk. "It's a little crowded, I know. It will be this way until we clear out all these textbooks next week. Would you like some tea? I think this is still hot." She felt the side of the teapot.

"No, thanks. I'm fine." Christy tried to figure out a dainty way to perch on top of the highest box.

Donna sat down and smiled at Christy. They chatted a few minutes before Donna asked, "How many hours a week can you work?"

"About fifteen, I think. Or less. I just found out I have to take another class this term."

"I could use you about fifteen hours a week for the first two weeks of school. After that it would be about ten or twelve hours. Would that be okay?"

"Sure. That would be just right, I think."

"I'll need a copy of your class schedule, but I don't have any open hours on the weekends, so you would work only Monday through Friday. Is that okay?"

Christy had expected more of an interview than this. She smiled at the gentle yet direct businesswoman. "That's perfect. Thank you."

"No, thank *you*," Donna said. "Ten minutes ago I thought I'd have to spend the next week going through the hassle of job posting, but you came highly recommended."

Christy thought it funny that some guy she had never met had recommended her simply because Katie talked to him last night at The Java Jungle. That must be one of the advantages of attending a small, private Christian college; the trust factor was strong in this cozy community.

In less than twenty minutes, Christy had filled out all the paper work Donna handed her, and Christy did agree to a cup of tea when Donna offered it a second time. The peach tea was refreshing.

"I'll go over all the other details with you when you start on Monday," Donna said. "Do you have any questions?"

"I don't think so."

Donna smiled. "I'll see you Monday."

Christy left the bookstore and headed back to her dorm room amazed at how easy that had been. She had almost an hour before Aunt Marti would arrive for lunch, and Christy wanted to call her parents to let them know about her job.

As she imagined, her mom sounded relieved. "Your father will be glad to hear this, honey. He was asking me again last night, and I was wondering if anything had opened up for you."

"Did you know Aunt Marti is coming to take me to lunch?" Christy asked.

"Is she?" Mom paused. "That's nice of her."

"Do you think she's upset that I didn't call or go see them when I got back from Switzerland?"

"I don't know."

"I asked Katie to come with us just in case I need some moral support."

"How are you and Katie getting along?" Mom asked.

"We're getting along great, as always. Katie is the one who helped me get this job."

"Didn't she also help you find your job at the pet store?"

"That's right; she did. I'm glad you remembered that. I'll have to thank Katie doubly now. If it weren't for her, how would I ever find work?"

Mom chuckled. "You would manage. Any young woman who can chart her way through a year at school in Switzerland can manage just about anything."

Christy was going to tell her mom she still had to make a final decision about her major. But when her mom said all those nice things about Christy managing her own life, she decided to hold her thoughts. It would be much easier to call home again after she had the major figured out. Especially since Mom's comment made Christy feel competent and accomplished.

Katie arrived at the dorm room only a few minutes before Christy received a call from the lobby letting her know Marti had arrived.

"Are you ready, Katie?" Christy was about to suggest Katie change from her shorts and T-shirt into something nicer. But then Christy knew she would be doing to Katie what Aunt Marti had done to Christy for years. She didn't want to direct other people in what they said, did, or wore, Christy decided.

Katie apparently thought she was dressed appropriately and accompanied Christy to the lobby. Christy silently inventoried the outfit she had put on that morning—the casual yet crisp skirt and the clean, unwrinkled top. Certainly Marti couldn't find fault with Christy's appearance.

The two friends stepped into the lobby, and Christy looked around, not seeing her aunt among the four people sitting in the lounge.

Then a short woman with long, flowing, dark hair and wearing a wrinkled gauze skirt, a silk tank top, and strings of tiny colored beads rose and came to Christy. The woman kissed Christy on each cheek with sublime elegance.

"Aunt Marti?" Christy choked on the words. She couldn't stop staring at her transformed aunt. This woman, who had always dressed in the most expensive, chic, and traditional outfits, this woman who always wore her hair short and perfectly styled, this woman who never even went downstairs in her own house without wearing makeup, now stood before Christy and Katie looking as if she had dressed as Mother Earth for a costume party.

"Aunt Marti?" Katie finally said, echoing Christy's surprise in face and voice.

"What do you think, girls?" Marti turned around. "It's the new me." She held out the ends of her long hair. "Extensions. Aren't they glorious?"

"Glorious," Christy repeated mechanically. It came out sounding more like a question than an affirmation.

"I surprised you both, didn't I?" Marti said. "This is the new me. Fresh. Renewed on all levels. I finally have come into harmony with my artistic aura."

Christy and Katie exchanged quick glances. If Christy hadn't known Marti to be a strict, controlling, no-nonsense person, Christy would have thought this some elaborate joke. The voice was Marti's. So were the bony fingers that grasped Christy's elbow and pushed for them to be on their way.

"I . . . um . . . I invited Katie to go with us." Christy wiggled her elbow free from Marti's grasp.

"How generous of you," Marti said sweetly. She turned to Katie and said, "Sorry, Katie dear. Not this time. This is just for Christy and me."

"No problem." Katie looked just a little too eager to pull back.

Christy gave Katie a desperate "thanks a lot" look and in complete bewilderment followed her aunt out into the afternoon heat to Marti's silver Lexus parked in front of the dormitory. Christy numbly opened the passenger door and slid onto the leather seat. She couldn't help but feel as if she were being kidnapped. Abducted by an alien. She turned to stare once more at her transformed aunt. Something inside Christy made her want to shake this woman and scream out, "I don't know who you are or what you've done with my aunt, but give her back this instant!"

Then Christy remembered what her aunt was like before she found her "artistic aura," and for half a minute Christy didn't know which version of Marti was worse.

This is absolutely bizarre! What am I doing? What is my aunt doing? I should have made an excuse and told her I couldn't go or at least insisted we eat on campus so I'd have witnesses if she tried to make me join her in a rain dance or something!

"Marti, where are we going?" Christy asked as they sped down the hill into town.

"I was going to take you to the Colony in Palm Desert, but it's not pottery day, and I'd much rather you come on pottery day. So today is simply our time to be together. I want to hear all about Switzerland, and I'm sure you want to hear all about the changes in my life."

Christy suggested Taco Bell. It was close, and lots of students stopped there. She felt safe going to Taco Bell.

Apparently Marti's aura wasn't in the mood for Mexican food, so they ended up at a quiet Japanese restaurant. They had to take off their shoes and sit on the floor at low tables. Marti ordered for both of them and then turned to Christy and said, "Now tell me all about Switzerland."

"It was a good year," Christy began.

Just then a fly buzzed past them, and Marti swatted at it with a fierceness that surprised Christy.

"Vile creature," Marti spat. "And in a restaurant, no less. You would think the proprietors would take appropriate measures against such filth."

For the first time, the old Marti sounded as if she was back in the room with Christy. But then Aunt Marti shifted her attention back to Christy and said, "You were saying?"

"Switzerland was wonderful," Christy said. "Thanks for all you did to work it out so I could go there."

"Of course. No need to thank me."

"It was a difficult year in some ways, but definitely worth it."

"Good," Marti stated firmly, sounding like a hammer driving a nail into a board. "Now, you're probably wondering about the changes in me."

That was a quick summary of my last year!

"Christina, I never would have imagined this, but it turns out I'm somewhat of an artist. It all began when I met Cheyenne at an art show in Laguna Beach. He invited me to one of his pottery classes, and no one was more surprised than I was to discover that I have substantial talent in that area. Cheyenne sponsored me into the Colony."

"Aunt Marti, it sounds like you've been pulled into a cult of some sort."

"A cult? Why, there's nothing religious at all about the Colony. We're a group of artists. Mutual spirits who find expression in the creation of beauty. Believe me, I don't want anything to do with religion. Ever since your uncle had his born-again experience last summer, the man has been impossible to live with. He has a mistress, you know. He left me for her."

Christy couldn't hide her shock. She knew Uncle Bob's conversion to Christianity had been a radical change since he had been such an outspoken agnostic before coming to Christ. But he wouldn't turn against the Lord so quickly and have an affair, would he? How could he?

"Don't look so stunned, dear. I'm referring to the church. Bob's mistress is the church. He goes to her every chance he gets and talks about her all the time. He and I have less and less in common. These past few months he's tried to get me to give up the Colony, and I've tried to get him to give up the church. It seems we've reached an impasse."

The petite waitress in a silk kimono arrived and knelt at their table. With a bow of her head, she served them soup in white ceramic bowls. They were instructed to drink it by holding the sides of the bowl with both hands instead of using a spoon.

Christy paused and prayed, wishing she were brave enough to pray aloud in front of her aunt like she used to do. Today her words felt as if they caught in her throat. The warm broth washed the words back down into someplace deep within Christy. If this wasn't all so disturbing, she would think her aunt's dramatic performance was humorous.

"When you come on pottery day to the Colony," Marti said, "I want you to bring Todd. You can bring Katie, if you wish. And bring your friend with the curly blond hair. What's her name? Sienna?"

"Sierra."

"Ah yes, Sierra. Bring her, too. I'll show all of you the pottery I've made. It has freed my inner self, Christina. Wait until you see my creations on display. You will be so proud of me."

"Marti, I . . ." Christy tried to find the words to say she didn't need to see pottery to feel proud of her aunt. And she didn't want her aunt to dictate when she would kidnap Christy again, especially since this second kidnapping involved her friends.

"You don't need to . . . I mean, I think . . ." Christy couldn't form her thoughts.

The waitress appeared with a tray to clear the soup and present each of them with a plate of sushi, raw fish, complete with tiny bowls of sauce. Christy lost her appetite altogether. It was all she could do not to lose her soup.

Marti continued to talk as if Christy hadn't even begun to say anything. "Now, before I tell you what I'm going to tell you next, I need you to promise me you won't tell anyone. Not a soul. Not Todd, not your mother. No one."

Christy felt they had played games long enough, but she was so uncomfortable she guessed the only way to speed up this lunch would be to go along with whatever Marti said. With a slow nod, Christy acknowledged her aunt's wish.

"I need to hear you say it," Marti said. "Say you promise you won't tell anyone."

Christy hesitated. She took promises very seriously. That's why she had stayed on at the orphanage even when she knew it would be a huge strain on her. She had made a commitment to stay for a certain time, and so she had stayed. To her, a promise was a vow. And the Bible made it clear that God paid attention whenever a person made a vow. He held that person to complete whatever had been promised, whether it was a vow to God or a vow to another human.

Christy felt the soup sloshing around in her stomach. Just the smell of the sushi was enough to torture her into a quick release from this luncheon meeting. Pushing the sushi away, Christy nodded slowly. "I promise I won't tell anyone, Aunt Marti."

Satisfied with Christy's sincere response, Marti drew herself up, took a long breath through her nose, and said, "You promise, then, that you will tell no one. Especially not your uncle Bob, because he doesn't know yet."

Marti paused. It seemed to Christy that Marti was waiting for her to say, "Doesn't know what?" But Christy wouldn't give her aunt the satisfaction of seeing Christy beg that way.

"You are the first and only person I've told this to." Marti seemed to enjoy the moment as much as Christy hated it. "And that's why you must keep it a secret. You see, I've made a very important decision. Cheyenne is opening a second Colony in Santa Fe. The property becomes available in January."

Christy couldn't see why that was such big news.

Marti leaned closer. "I'm going with Cheyenne. I'm moving to Santa Fe."

CHAPTER 4

"Let me get this straight," Todd said later that night. He, Christy, and Katie were sitting at a small pizza parlor in town. Todd had arrived on campus about an hour after Marti had returned Christy to her dorm, and Katie and Christy had helped him to move his stuff into his room. Then he announced he wanted to treat them to pizza, so off they went in his VW van, Gus the Bus.

Todd leaned back in the booth and swished the ice around in his plastic cup. "You're telling me Marti showed up in a wig?"

"Hair extensions," Katie corrected him. "Long. Dark. Very strange looking on her."

"And she took you to lunch at a Japanese restaurant."

Christy nodded. "I wanted Katie to come but—"

"But my aura wasn't in harmony with the moon," Katie said. "Or something like that."

"What did you and Marti talk about?" Todd asked.

"Her life. How she's finding herself through creating art. Pottery. She makes pottery."

"I've seen some of her pottery at their house," Todd said. "It's very good."

"Is it really?" Christy asked.

Todd nodded. "Did she say anything about Bob?"

"Not exactly," Christy said. She wished with all her heart she hadn't promised to keep the big move to Santa Fe a secret. When Christy had

41

asked Marti if that meant she was leaving Uncle Bob, all Marti said was "That remains to be seen."

"I wonder what your uncle thinks of her transformation," Katie said.

Christy wished she could spill the secret about Santa Fe so the three of them could discuss everything. Yet she knew that a promise was a promise. The only acceptable reason she knew for not keeping a secret or a promise would be if the person was going to be hurt and disclosing the secret would keep that from happening. Certainly Bob was going to be hurt if Marti ended up leaving him. But if Christy broke Marti's confidence, how would that prevent any hurt from happening? It might only prompt Marti to leave sooner.

Christy felt awful. Her conscience wouldn't allow her to share the information as a prayer request. All she could do was pray on her own, and she had been doing that for hours.

"What do you think is really going on with your aunt?" Katie prodded.

Christy didn't answer.

"I've never seen anyone flip out like that. I mean, she went from one end of the pendulum to the other, didn't she?" Katie shook her head and looked at Todd. "You should have seen her. With that fake hair and no makeup, you would have never known it was Marti."

"Did she say anything about Bob's being more active at church?" Todd asked.

Christy nodded. "She doesn't like the way he's so involved with church now that he's a Christian. She called church his 'mistress' since he prefers to be at church instead of with her."

"Oh, that is low." Katie picked at the pepperoni on the final piece of pizza. "How unfair. I mean, I know the church is referred to as the 'Bride of Christ' in the Bible, but how twisted to call it a mistress. How could Marti be so blind? Christianity is the best thing that ever happened to your uncle."

"I know," Christy agreed. "Uncle Bob has become a totally new person since he came to Christ."

Katie said, "Yeah, and it sounds like your aunt is trying to become her own new person. The only problem is that's impossible without the Lord."

Christy remembered the verse she had read that morning and paraphrased it for Todd and Katie. "Only those who receive Him and believe on His name have the right to become children of God."

Todd, who usually quoted Bible verses and came up with bits of wisdom at times like this, looked at Christy with an expression of pleasant surprise.

"I read that this morning. First chapter of John."

"How did you have time to read your Bible this morning?" Katie asked. "You had an early appointment. I don't know how you did it. I slept until eleven, and don't ask me about my quiet time. It didn't happen. I know that's a terrible thing to admit when you go to a Christian college."

"Just keep being honest about it, Katie," Todd advised. "It's only bad when you fake it with God or with the rest of us."

"Did I ever tell you what my roommate did last semester?" Katie asked. "She was so funny. She made this fancy sign that said *word* and taped it to the foot of her bed. Then she went around telling everyone that she had spent six hours in the word that night."

Todd grinned. "That's not exactly what I meant by honesty."

"I don't get it," Christy said.

Katie rolled her eyes. "She was 'in the word' because she put the sign *word* on her bed."

"I know, but—"

"It's a Christian college lingo thing," Katie explained. "You'll start to hear it more and more. When people talk about their quiet time with God, they say they were 'in the Word.' You know, studying the Word of God."

"Oh."

"I guess those kinds of jokes weren't real big in Basel," Katie said.

"No," Christy said flatly. "I was amazed when I met a few other Christians, and we could actually attend church together. I can't tell you how much I looked forward to being here with you guys."

Suddenly Christy remembered the other "guy" she was supposed to meet for dinner at six. Matthew Kingsley.

"What time is it?" Christy asked.

Todd turned and read the clock on the far wall. "Seven-thirty. Do you need to get back?"

Christy sunk in her seat. "No." She decided it was too complicated to try to explain that she had made dinner plans with another guy on the same night Todd arrived on campus.

How could I have forgotten? Did I forget on purpose?

Christy didn't think she had ever mentioned Matthew to Todd. At the moment, she didn't have the energy to delve into all that now. She could call Matthew when she got back to the dorm. He would understand.

However, Matthew wasn't in his room when she called him a little after nine that night. She was too tired to stay up with Katie and some of the other girls on the floor who were watching a movie in their suite lounge in the middle of the hallway. It was a comfortable family room-den that was for the women in the upper classes and only open to visitors and guys on designated nights. That meant the girls could hang out there in their PJs most of the time.

Christy slept deeply and woke feeling refreshed, until she remembered Aunt Marti and that she needed to call Matthew to apologize for not meeting him for dinner.

She left Katie sleeping and slipped out of their dorm room. Christy's plan had been to go to the chapel at the edge of the campus for her morning quiet time. On the way, she stopped at the cafeteria, wondering if Matthew might be there for breakfast. Only a few dozen students were in the cafeteria as Christy moved her tray through the line and filled a plastic cup with foaming orange juice from the machine. Matthew Kingsley wasn't one of them. She realized that the only people who would be up at this early hour on a Saturday were probably students who had weekend jobs and were on their way to work.

Christy sat at a small corner table by herself and thought about the way she had felt warmed inside when she had seen Matthew walk into The Java Jungle.

Why did I feel that way? It's not possible that I still have a little bit of a crush on him after all these years, is it? This is college, not elementary school. How can firefly flutterings left over from the playground at George Washington Elementary School have any place in my life now?

Slowly eating her yogurt and muffin, Christy watched the door in case she saw anyone she knew. Todd probably would sleep in. The two of them hadn't made any plans for the morning. He had said last night that he wanted to go over to Riverview Heights in the afternoon and set up the classroom for Sunday. Christy had agreed to go with him. Until then, she had nowhere to go, no one to see, nothing to do. It felt strange. So opposite from the last year.

With a bittersweet sense of loss, Christy remembered all the Saturday mornings in Basel when she had made her early morning trek to her favorite *Konditorei* for coffee and a fresh pastry. Those mornings were her thinking time.

"Is anyone sitting here?" a girl asked.

"No," Christy said, moving her tray and feeling grateful for the company.

Before the girl had placed her tray on the table, someone from across the room called to her. She looked relieved and hurried to join her friends without saying anything to Christy. Christy watched as the girl greeted her buddies with a hug, and the group of four girls talked and laughed. They looked like freshmen.

Christy wondered what it would have been like to go away to college her freshman year instead of staying home and taking classes at the community college. She didn't regret the past few years. The extra classes and summer school programs had paid off, and she had plenty of credits. But she hadn't had much of a social life.

An unexpected thought floated into Christy's mind. *What would it be like to go out with Matthew Kingsley?*

The thought surprised her. *Why would I think that? I'm with Todd. I love Todd. Why would I want to go out with Matthew?*

Christy suspected the thought was linked to her musings about rushing through college, accumulating units instead of dates. Todd had been in Spain when Christy started college, and aside from a bunch of fun dates she had had with Doug during her first semester as a freshman, Christy hadn't gone out with anyone. She and Doug were close buddies, and their friendship had stayed strong even after Doug and Tracy ended up getting married.

When Todd and Christy got back together in January of her freshman year of college, Christy felt certain she and Todd would be together from then on.

But what if my family hadn't moved to California when I was fifteen? What if we had stayed in Wisconsin? Would Matt and I have become a couple?

She knew her imagination was taking her into the land of if only, and she didn't trust what she was feeling. It was thrilling to speculate about dating Matthew, and for the moment those thoughts overpowered her deep, steady love for Todd. She felt dizzy, as if she couldn't trust her own instincts.

Why am I even thinking such things?

Christy pushed herself to her feet and carried her tray to the back of the large cafeteria, where she tossed her silverware in the appropriate bins.

I need to go to the chapel and have my quiet time. That will get my heart back on track.

The walk to the chapel was along a beautiful trail leading to the edge of the mesa. Rancho Corona formerly had been a working cattle ranch. When the owner donated the land to the college, he had asked that a chapel be built with a stained-glass window depicting the ranch's original insignia. The beautiful glass window, a gold crown with a cross lying in the crown's center at a slant, was above the altar. The Spanish name of the original ranch was "Rancho de la Cruz y la Corona," which meant "Ranch of the Cross and the Crown."

Christy entered the small, silent chapel and felt a welcoming hush come over her. She walked softly to the front and sat in one of the pews, where she bowed her head to pray. As she prayed, her mind began to wander.

Why am I having thoughts about Matthew? Is there something between us that would grow if it had the chance to be explored? Would it grow stronger than what Todd and I have between us?

Convinced she wasn't going to get any serious praying done, Christy opened her Bible and readied her pen and journal. She read two chapters and jotted a few notes. Then her gaze rose to the stained-glass window. She noticed how brightly the sunlight poured through the amber gold pieces of glass that made up the crown.

I should talk to Katie about all these confusing feelings. Katie always helps me get my mind out of the fog. Even if I don't always like what she says, she gives me fresh perspective, and that's what I need right now.

Christy left the chapel and took the path that led past the baseball field instead of across the open meadow. As she approached the baseball diamond, she noticed two guys standing on the pitcher's mound. One of them was Matthew.

Christy's heart did a funny little flutter. *This is it. Time to test my feelings. If there is anything between us to explore, now is the time.*

Matthew spotted Christy and jogged over to where she had stopped beside the bleachers. "Hey, I missed—" Matthew began.

"I'm so sorry—"

They both laughed at how their greetings overlapped each other.

"I'm sorry," Christy said. "I went into town with Todd and Katie, and I didn't get back in time for dinner last night."

"I thought I was the one who missed you," Matthew said. "I ended up being about twenty minutes late, and I thought you had given up and left."

"No, sorry." Christy took inventory of her feelings. She felt surprisingly calm. The initial burst of fireflies had all flown away.

"Would you be interested in joining us in a little game?" Matthew tossed the softball in the air and grinned at Christy from under his well-worn baseball cap.

The other guy approached, and Christy recognized him as Wes, Sierra's older brother.

"Sierra and her roommate, Vicki, were supposed to meet us here," Wes said. "Matt thinks they slept in. I think Sierra forgot."

When Wes called Matthew "Matt," Christy realized she still thought of him by his full name. He had become "Matthew" in grade school because two Matthews were in their class.

"What do you say?" Matt asked. "We'll even let you bat first."

"Okay." Christy was surprised to find herself agreeing to anything athletic. "I can't guarantee my catching or pitching skills, but I can usually hit the ball if you pitch it nice and slow."

"Nice and slow," Matt echoed, returning to the pitcher's mound.

Christy gripped the bat and felt a wonderful, childhood kind of happiness come over her. This felt like a funny little dream come true. She was playing baseball with Matthew Kingsley! In fifth grade this never would have happened because she would have been too shy to enter into such a game.

The first pitch came slow and too low. Christy picked up the ball and heaved it back to the pitcher's mound. It fell about two feet short.

"Did I ever tell you that you throw like a girl, Christy Miller?"

Christy laughed. "I am a girl, Matthew Kingsley, in case you never noticed."

"Oh, I noticed," he said.

She couldn't see his face because of the shadow from his baseball cap, but from his stance, he appeared to enjoy the teasing as much as she did.

"Okay, here's my special pitch just for girls who like it nice and slow." He gave an exaggerated windup with his arm, making big, slow circles in the air.

"Very funny," Christy called out. "Now see if you can manage to get it over the plate this time!"

Wes moved in from the outfield. "Right here, Christy." He slugged his fist into his mitt. "Hit it to me. Right here."

Christy took her position. The bat made contact with the ball, and a delicious thrill coursed through her as she dropped the bat and dashed to first base. Wes caught the pop fly, tagged her leg, and offered some advice. "Next time put more muscle behind it, and you'll have a nice swing. Use your shoulders and not just your arms."

Christy didn't care about his advice. She was feeling euphoric over actually *hitting* the ball and playing with the guys.

"Hey!" Sierra's voice sounded at the edge of the field. "What's the big idea starting without us?"

Sierra wore a baseball jersey and had managed to collect her wild, curly blond hair into a ponytail and had looped it through the opening in the back of her baseball cap. She looked as if she was ready for a serious game as she strode onto the field with five other people. Christy was introduced to Vicki, Sierra's roommate, who was a gorgeous brunette with flawless skin. The others, all freshmen and friends of Sierra's, seemed to know Wes, but none of them knew Matt.

After the introductions, a serious game of softball ensued. Several other students joined in, and before the morning was over, Christy had batted four times, hitting the ball three times and striking out once. The rest of the time she spent in the outfield.

Christy smiled through the entire game. She loved everything about this morning: the feel of the warm breeze across her cheeks, the friendly banter among these friends, the way Matt smiled at her. This is what she had missed during her year in Switzerland. The European trains and the scrumptious pastries at the Konditorei had been wonderful. But this—this felt like home.

A little more than halfway through the game, Christy watched Matt on the pitcher's mound, and she inventoried her feelings again. No firefly flutterings or wishful wonderings rose to the surface.

Who knows why my mind took off for the land of if-only at breakfast. Matthew Kingsley is just Matthew Kingsley. He'll always be my first crush—nothing more and nothing less.

The last play of the game, Vicki hit a ground ball. Christy ran to scoop it up and pitched it underhanded to Wes, who tagged Vicki out at second base. With a loud cheer, Christy joined the rest of her team in celebrating the win.

The thrill of victory was short lived. Sierra loudly challenged Matthew's team to make it the best two out of three games. Wes took the challenge and said they would meet Sierra and her "bunch of losers" on the field tomorrow afternoon at four.

They all headed for The Golden Calf, talking and laughing as if they had been friends for years. Matt walked beside Christy. "You know what I realized when I saw you there in the outfield?"

"Let me guess. You realized I was serious when I said I couldn't catch."

Matthew laughed. "No, you did great. You made the winning play with Wes."

"I guess I did, didn't I?" Christy beamed.

With a sincere expression Matt said, "What I realized, Christy, is that I wished you hadn't moved to California. I wish you and I had had the chance to finish growing up together. I wonder what would have happened."

Without thinking, she said, "I've been wondering some of those same things."

"You have?"

Caught off guard by her own honesty, Christy quickly added, "I mean, I think Brightwater was a great place to grow up. It would have been fun to go through high school with the same people I started school with."

"I agree," Matt said. "It would have been nice to have you around in high school."

Unsure of what to say, Christy offered only a timid smile and a nod.

They were entering The Golden Calf, and Christy spotted Todd seated at a nearby table. With a chin-up gesture he motioned for Christy and the others to join him. The instant Christy saw him she felt a familiar certainty settle over her.

Now, that's the man I'm in love with.

As if to test her response, Christy turned and watched Matthew as he went through the food line ahead of her. There was no comparison between Todd and Matt. All the "what if" questions she had entertained earlier about Matt seemed to evaporate. She didn't know why. But at the moment, it didn't matter.

She looked across the room at Todd. He was watching her with "that look" again. Even though they were at least thirty feet away from each other in the noisy cafeteria, the moment their eyes met, Christy felt as if the rest of the world had rushed away. An invisible bubble had taken just the two of them to a magical place where her heart didn't flitter and flutter, but rather beat steadily and sure.

It's a marathon for us, isn't it, Todd? Not a quick, flittery sprint. You love me with all your heart. I can see it on your face. And I love you. I know I do.

Christy followed Matthew through the sandwich line, content that her feelings had settled themselves. If she had stayed in Wisconsin, she and Matthew might have ended up testing their relationship on a deeper level.

But I didn't stay in Wisconsin. I moved here, I met Todd, and this is the relationship I want to stay committed to. I don't think God jerks us around the way my thoughts about Matthew jerked around this morning. I don't need to waste my time daydreaming about "what if." All I need to do is keep asking God, "What next?"

Just as Christy and Matthew left the sandwich line and headed toward Todd's table, Katie bounced in front of them. With all the energy she had gained from sleeping until noon, she greeted them with an enthusiastic, "Hi! I thought that was you. Hi!"

At first Christy assumed Katie was talking to her, but Katie's focus was on Matthew. Christy began to make the introduction. "Katie, this is—"

"Matt. Yes, I know. Hi! How are you?"

Then Christy made the connection and nearly dropped her tray. "Is he Matt number fourteen?"

"Yes, Matt number fourteen!" Katie beamed. "I'm so embarrassed, Matt. I don't know your last name!"

"Kingsley," Christy and Matt answered in unison.

"I guess I'm embarrassed, too." Matt looked at Christy and then back at Katie. "Have we met before? Do I know you?"

Christy watched as her best friend's heart crashed to the floor.

"Matthew," Christy said with a hint of scold in her voice, "this is my roommate, Katie Weldon. You two met last year after a baseball game."

"Oh," Matt said slowly. An awkward pause followed, and then Matt said, "You want to sit with us, Kathy?"

Katie's green eyes turned to ice. "It's Katie, not Kathy. Katie Weldon."

Christy quickly pulled her friend to the side and said over her shoulder, "We'll join you guys in a minute."

Matt headed for the table, and Christy winced when she saw Katie's pained expression.

"Katie, I am so sorry!" Christy whispered. "I never in a million years imagined that your Matt number fourteen was the same as my Matthew Kingsley."

"*Your* Matthew Kingsley?" Katie sputtered.

"We grew up together in Wisconsin. I had a huge crush on him in elementary school."

Katie stared without saying a word.

"I told you about him. I know I did," Christy said.

"No, you didn't. I would have remembered if you told me about Matt." Katie's face turned red. "Did you see the way he looked at me? I can't believe it! I committed to memory every word from the conversation we had last June. And then I wasted my entire summer dreaming about him. What a loser!"

Christy wanted to put her arm around her friend, but Christy was still holding her cafeteria tray. "You're not a loser, Katie."

"I didn't mean me, I meant *him*! Matt number fourteen Kingsley is . . ." Katie paused. She lowered her voice and said, "He's the loser. He could have gone out with the cutest, most adorable, most fun-loving redhead on campus, but he just lost his chance." With a swish of her hair, Katie turned and marched off.

Christy stood still, watching as Katie went to the frozen yogurt machine. Apparently, she planned to drown her sorrows in an extra-large chocolate mocha swirl.

CHAPTER 5

Christy felt awful as she carried her tray to the table and sat beside Todd in the noisy cafeteria. Matt had taken the empty seat on the other side of Todd, and the two guys had introduced themselves and were talking as if they were close friends. Katie had left the cafeteria with her frozen yogurt in a plastic foam cup.

Determined to remedy what had just happened, Christy tried to think of ways to smooth things over with Matt and Katie. She thought of setting up a double date with them or taking Matt aside and explaining how much Katie liked him. None of her ideas seemed like a good one.

It wouldn't have been so bad if he hadn't called her "Kathy." He could have at least pretended he remembered her when he saw how excited she was to see him. Why are guys so clueless?

"Hey, Christy," Matt said, "do you want to go to Riverview Heights with Todd this afternoon?"

She nodded since her mouth was full. *Why is Matt asking me? I already told Todd I would go.*

Apparently Todd had invited Matt along. The three of them left the cafeteria and drove to the church in Todd's van. From the conversation that was still going at a lively pace between Matt and Todd, Christy discovered that Riverview was the church Matt had attended the last school year. He was giving Todd all kinds of information, since Matt had helped out with the youth group on a couple of outings.

"The adult couple who organized everything moved in June," Matt explained. "That's when the church leaders decided to hire someone. Not many teenagers come, but a lot of them could."

"Why don't they attend?" Christy asked.

"They haven't had anything consistent except for Sunday school, and the couple who taught didn't seem to care about the students. They lectured the whole time. There wasn't any music or any chance for relationships to develop."

Christy could tell Todd appreciated all the inside information.

"You are going to start out with music tomorrow morning, aren't you?" Christy asked.

"I was planning on it." Todd parked in the church lot, and Matt led the way to the room where the group would meet.

"Do you have anyone helping you with music?" Matt asked.

"I don't have any volunteers yet," Todd said, giving Christy a grin. "Unless either of you wants to sing with me."

Christy liked to sing, but she had never been in the front, leading a group. Her voice blended well if the person next to her sang loudly. She wasn't a soloist.

"I could help," Christy said hesitantly.

Todd's clear-eyed, grinning expression told Christy she had just won her boyfriend's undying admiration. "Thanks. I know you're still thinking about teaching, and I want you to take as long as you need to decide."

Christy didn't feel pressured to say yes to teaching, but she did feel more open to the possibility. She liked being part of the start-up process in this new season in Todd's life.

"I'd be glad to help with whatever else you need," Matt said.

"Thanks, man," Todd said. "You can see I'm at ground zero on all this."

They spent a half hour setting up the room for the next morning and taking inventory of the available resources.

"You know what?" Christy said as they were about to leave. "We should pray before we go."

"Great idea," Todd said. "What's that verse? 'Unless the Lord builds the house, its builders labor in vain.' I want this to be God's youth group."

Christy smiled. "Then we should pray about it."

Todd reached for Christy's hand, and to her surprise, Matt reached for her other hand. The three of them stood in a tight circle, and the guys stretched their arms across each other's shoulders.

Todd prayed for God's blessing on the future of the group and for God's guidance over all the planning, teaching, worshiping, and fellowshiping that would happen in that room. Christy tried to concentrate. She knew they were holding hands as a gesture of being united in what they were praying, but Christy found herself comparing the two guys. Her hand felt at home in Todd's hand. It felt familiar and safe. Matt's hand was rough with the permanent calluses of someone who had shoveled snow and pitched hay. Christy thought of how her dad's hands felt the same way.

She tried to focus back on Todd's prayer as he boldly claimed this territory and these hearts for God's kingdom. "Whatever it takes," Todd prayed, "let them see how real you are, Father."

Matt prayed, then Christy prayed. Todd closed off their time with his own version of "Amen," which was, "Let it be so."

They all looked up and released their hands as Matt said, "This is going to be good, Todd. These kids are going to be so glad to have you here."

"Why didn't you apply for the position?" Todd asked Matt.

He lowered his head slightly and with a bashful expression said, "I did. But I withdrew my application a couple of weeks ago because I wanted to stick with the full class schedule I have this fall and I wanted to play baseball in the spring. I knew I couldn't give the time that would be needed. I'm better off volunteering than being responsible for the whole program."

Todd threw his arm around Matt's shoulder, hugged him from the side, and said, "I appreciate your heart, Matt."

Christy smiled warmly at Matt. She was trying to come up with something appropriate to say when the pager on Matt's belt beeped.

He jumped slightly and said, "My roommate gave me this crazy thing so he can always get ahold of me." He pulled it off and checked the number. "I'll be right back."

Christy and Todd stood alone in the youth room, and she said, "You know what? This is where you belong. You were created for this."

Todd ran his hand across his smooth, square jaw. "You think so?"

Christy nodded. "Remember when we were at that Christian youth hostel in Amsterdam? You were in your element when you led the music and taught a Bible study."

"That was only for a few nights," Todd said.

"I know. But you were at home doing that. Didn't you think so?"

Todd seemed to ponder his answer as he and Christy walked to the door. He remained silent all the way to the car, where they stood waiting for Matt.

When Matt joined them a few minutes later, he said, "Would you mind dropping me off at Stereo World on Mesa Verde? Pete wants me to check out some speakers before he buys them."

The three of them climbed into Gus the Bus, and Todd dropped Matt off in front of Stereo World. Before he got out, Matt put his hand on Christy's shoulder and said, "Don't forget, you still owe me a dinner. We need to finish the conversation we started before lunch."

As Todd drove back to Rancho Corona, Christy remained quiet, trying to process what Matt had said and what he had meant. Todd seemed to be processing Matt's comments, as well. He pulled into the parking lot of a city park and turned off the engine. Giving Christy a confused look, he asked, "Did you meet Matt before today?"

At first Christy thought Todd was kidding. "We grew up together. In Wisconsin."

Todd's expression told her he most certainly didn't know that. "I thought he was friends with Wes and Sierra and that you just met him today in the lunch line."

Christy laughed. "No, our families have been friends since before either of us was born."

Todd looked out the window and then at Christy. "Did I know that?"

"I thought you did. Didn't I tell you that I saw him the other night when Katie and I were in The Java Jungle?"

Todd shook his head.

Christy filled Todd in on Matt being the same Matt number fourteen Katie had told them about on the train in Europe.

Now Todd looked even more surprised. "And neither you nor Katie knew that until today?"

"No, and the worst part was that Matt didn't remember Katie."

"Ouch," Todd said.

"Yeah, ouch. That's why Katie didn't join us for lunch."

"He's a great guy," Todd said. "I appreciate his servant's heart."

"He is a great guy," Christy agreed. *But not the guy for me, that's for sure.*

Todd shifted in the driver's seat and turned toward Christy. "What did he mean about you having dinner with him?"

Christy wondered if she should explain to Todd her crazy little jaunt to the land of if-only that morning and how she had let herself wonder what would have happened if she had gone out with Matt. But it all seemed like nothing to her now, so she decided not to mention it.

"Matt and I were going to meet at the cafeteria last night, but I forgot all about it. That's why I asked you what time it was when we were having pizza with Katie."

It occurred to Christy that, although her fleeting thoughts about Matt had left her, she didn't know if their long-ago, unexplored interest in each other was a closed subject for Matt. Perhaps the reason he wanted to finish their conversation was because he also had taken a jaunt to the land of if-only and was possibly still there.

Did I say or do anything to make Matt think I would be interested in going out with him? I didn't mean to. He knows Todd and I are together, doesn't he?

Christy realized that she and Todd hadn't done or said anything while they were around Matt to lead him to believe they were a couple. If Todd had thought that Matt was one of Sierra's friends whom Christy had just met at lunch, perhaps Matt thought the same about Todd.

Christy realized the parked van was becoming uncomfortably hot. Todd opened his door and asked, in what sounded more like a statement, "Do you want to walk?"

"Sure." Christy was glad to climb out of the hot van and off the uncomfortable seat. She had complained a week ago that the passenger seat was "decomposing" since the springs were poking through. Todd had fixed it by covering the seat with a piece of cardboard and then placing a folded beach towel on top of the cardboard. The whole contraption slid as she got out.

Todd reached for her hand, and they walked along a cement pathway around the park's perimeter. The playground to the left was filled with noisy children who were busy swinging, climbing, and sifting sand in the sandbox.

Christy and Todd headed away from the noise.

"I wanted to talk about something you said at the church," Todd said. "You said I was 'at home' there. I think you're right. And you know why that's so hard for me to comprehend? I don't know that I've ever been 'at home' before. Not completely. Except with you, Kilikina."

Whenever Todd called Christy by her Hawaiian name, she melted. This afternoon was no exception.

"I feel at home with you, too," Christy said. "Completely at home."

"Do you?" Todd asked.

"Yes, I really do." Christy put aside her unsettled thoughts about Matt and concentrated on Todd. If she had miscommunicated anything to Matt, she could talk to him later and clear it up. Right now, this is where she wanted to be, and Todd was the one she wanted to be with.

"The thing is, I don't know what a normal family is supposed to act like," Todd continued. "I have an idea of what I want for my future family and what I consider to be normal, but I've never had that. I have few role models. When I came to the Lord, church became really important to me. I wonder if that's why it seems I'm at home, as you said, in a youth ministry situation. Church, and particularly youth groups, are the most stable, positive model I've ever had for anything."

"Was your childhood pretty awful?" Christy asked.

"Why do you ask?"

"I've wanted to ask you lots of times before, but it didn't seem as if you liked to talk about that part of your life. I want to hear more," Christy said. "Especially about your childhood."

"You knew my parents were both on drugs when they met," Todd said.

Christy wasn't sure if that was supposed to be a joke. She waited for Todd to explain. He led her off the trail to the shade of two old trees.

Todd sat with his back against a broad tree trunk and Christy to his side, facing him.

"They really were on drugs. I never told you this, but my mom was pregnant with me when they got married."

"She was?" Christy wished she didn't sound so surprised.

"She was only seventeen."

Christy realized for the first time why Todd had cared so much about Alissa, a teenage friend of theirs who had become pregnant a number of years ago. Alissa had decided to have the baby and give it up for adoption. At the time, Christy thought it strange Todd was so involved and enthusiastic about Alissa's decision. Now it made sense. Todd had been an unplanned baby of a teenage mother.

A shiver ran up Christy's spine. *What if Todd's mother had decided he was an inconvenience to her life? What if she had believed twenty-three years ago that what she carried in her body was only a mass of tissue? What if . . .*

Christy stopped. She found herself breathing deeply and almost in tears. But she didn't want to tell Todd what she had been thinking. That morning, her thoughts of Matthew had taught her it didn't do any good to take a trip to the land of if-only and spend a lot of time there.

The reality is that Todd's mom didn't choose to end her son's life. She gave birth to him. One day I'll thank her for that. And if I never thanked you, Father God, for giving Todd life, I thank you now.

"My parents got married because I think both my mom and dad wanted to do the right thing," Todd said. "I know they both tried to straighten out their lives after I was born. My mom told me once that the day she found out she was pregnant with me, she vowed never to do drugs again, and she didn't. It took my dad a little longer to sober up. When I was little . . . I don't know, maybe three . . . my parents had a fight over something, and my dad was stoned, and he hurt my mom."

"Todd, that's awful." Christy reached for Todd's hand and gave it a squeeze. The tears she had been trying to hold back were about to trickle down her cheeks.

He looked at her cautiously. "Are you sure you want me to tell you all this?"

"Yes, of course." Christy gave him an encouraging look and blinked back her tears. "I just didn't know how bad it had been for you. I was thinking of that night when we were talking out on the jetty at Newport Beach, and you and Shawn got in that big fight because he was so stoned. Now I can see why that upset you so much."

Todd looked down at their hands and said, "I still miss Shawn, if you can believe that." He stroked Christy's Forever ID bracelet with his thumb.

"That's because you really care about your friends. Forever."

Overhead a jet streaked into the west, leaving a mark like a white chalk line across the deep blue sky.

"Are you sure you want to keep talking about all this?" Todd asked.

"Yes."

"What else would you like to know?" Todd asked.

"What happened when your dad hurt your mom?" Christy asked in a soft voice.

"That was the day she left him. I don't know if he hit her or what. She never told me. I never asked my dad. He never hit me. He's never been violent or anything. I don't know. Maybe they just had a fight. Words can hurt for a lifetime, too, you know. For whatever reason, my mom left. She took me with her, and we lived on the road for a while, sort of hiding from my dad."

"I wonder if that's where you get your interest in traveling so much," Christy said. She was trying hard to be positive.

"I don't know. Maybe. After that, I'm not sure how everything fell into place. My dad sobered up. My parents got back together for a while, but it didn't work out. They tried to patch up things, but there were so many cracks it all came crashing in. When they finally divorced, they were just taking the legal steps to put on paper what was already true in their lives. Their marriage never had much of a chance. It was all a bunch of broken pieces from the start."

"Is that when you and your dad moved to Maui?" Christy asked. "Weren't you in third grade then?"

Todd nodded. "That was an important time in my life. My dad was trying to figure out who he was, and I was doing the same. We were more like brothers with eighteen years between us than father and son."

"Your dad was only eighteen when you were born?" Christy asked. "I never knew that."

"There's a lot you never knew because it didn't seem important," Todd said. "But I think it might help you to know so you can make good decisions."

Christy felt herself prickle slightly when Todd brought up her decision-making skills. But he was saying it in such a gentle way that she asked him, "Do you mean decisions about our future together?"

"Yes. And decisions about me. I realized I was beginning to assume a lot about us and about our future when I just figured you would want to teach Sunday school. What you said about getting more information and having a chance to think and pray about teaching also applies to us. You should have more information about me and my family so you can think things through carefully."

Christy felt her heart softening even more toward this man who sat before her. And he was a man. Todd was no longer a teenager, hanging around the beach, waiting for the perfect wave, taking each day as it came. She had been there through that season of Todd's life. The man who sat a few inches away was thinking about the future. He was making it clear that he wanted her to consider the whole package before agreeing to sign on for the next phase in their relationship.

"For instance," Todd continued, "I don't really know how to do stuff like birthdays and Christmas. If you and I end up together," Todd hesitated, as if trying to decide if he should go on. "I'm not trying to assume anything here, I'm just saying you should know that all the holiday kind of stuff would be up to you, or whoever I end up with. I mean, I'd help and everything, but since I didn't grow up with any traditions, I'd be learning it all for the first time."

"There's not much to learn." Christy felt compassion welling up inside. "You've been around my family for birthdays and holidays. Those times are whatever you want them to be. Whatever you make them."

"That's exactly what I mean." Todd let go of her hand and swatted away a bug from his face. "I want so much. I want birthdays to be an event. They never were for me. And if, you know, when I end up having kids

61

someday, I'd want them to think they were the coolest kids on the planet every year on their birthdays."

"I think that's important, too."

Todd plucked a blade of grass, twirled it between his fingers, then let it fall to the ground. His voice softened. "One year when I was living with my mom, she forgot my birthday. It was the year I turned five. I remember because I was in kindergarten, and we were living in an apartment in Phoenix, I think. Or maybe that was when we were in Flagstaff. Anyway, I remember this guy from her work asked her out to dinner on my birthday."

"And she went out with him?"

Todd nodded. "My mom is a wonderful person, really. It's just that she was excited about the attention, you know. She forgot it was my birthday. She left me a peanut butter sandwich and told me to put myself to bed by eight-thirty."

"What did you do?"

Todd shrugged his shoulders nonchalantly. "I ate my sandwich and went to bed with my BB gun under the covers in case a burglar broke in while my mom was gone. I don't remember if I went to bed by eight-thirty or not."

"Todd, I can't imagine what that must have been like for you." Tears blurred Christy's vision.

Todd shifted his position uncomfortably. "It's not like I was some abused, neglected child locked in a closet and forced to eat dirt." He laughed nervously at his attempt at a joke.

"In a way you were," Christy said.

"I don't want to look at it that way," Todd said. "I knew both my parents loved me. They wanted me, you know? They could have easily gotten rid of me either before I was born or after, but they didn't. They provided everything I needed. I think they just didn't know how to love on a very deep level. They didn't know how to love each other. Or maybe they did love each other, but only as much as they could at eighteen years old. I mean, when I think about it, my mom was only twenty-three when I had my fifth birthday. I'm going to be twenty-three in a couple months,

Christy. I can't imagine what it would be like to have a son in kindergarten right now."

Christy felt funny. The warm feelings that had made her so compassionate toward Todd a few minutes ago were beginning to disappear. In their place, she sensed the same sort of tired, sad feelings that had drained her so much at the orphanage during the past year. She felt sad for Todd; yet she knew she couldn't do anything to change his childhood. It seemed as if she was being introduced to a different person from the blue-eyed surfer boy she had fallen in love with. This new man-version of Todd was more complex than she had expected him to be.

"I'm freaking you out, aren't I?" Todd asked.

"No. Well, maybe. A little. But I think it's good. I want to know this stuff about you, Todd. I want you to feel that you can talk openly with me about anything. I guess I'm a little surprised that we've known each other so long and been so close—or at least, I've thought of us as being close—yet I didn't know any of this."

Todd moved closer to Christy and put his arm around her, drawing her to his side. "We are close, Kilikina. I'm closer to you than any other person I know. And maybe that's why I never told you a lot of this. I didn't want to say anything that would cause you to pull away from me. You're such a merciful person. I didn't want to hurt you."

"You're not hurting me by telling me these things," Christy said. "I'm glad you're telling me. I want to know all this."

"But you want to fix me, and you can't go back and fix my childhood, can you?"

Christy pulled her head away from Todd's shoulder and looked up at him. "How did you know that's what I was thinking?"

Todd brushed her cheek with the back of his fingers. "I know your heart, Kilikina. That's how I knew what you were thinking. I know your heart."

"I believe you do." Then pressing her head against his chest, Christy said, "And I want to know your heart, Todd."

She came very close to adding the words, "Because I love you." But she still couldn't say it. Not yet.

CHAPTER 6

That night Christy lay awake in bed. The room was dark except for the soft yellow glow from the desk light she had left on again for Katie. Squinting her eyes to read the numbers on her alarm clock, Christy wondered when she should start to worry. It was three minutes after midnight. She had slipped into bed at ten, hoping for a good sleep before going to Riverview with Todd at eight the next morning.

Instead of good sleep, for the past two hours all Christy had experienced was an endless replay of Todd's words. He had opened himself up to her, and in every way she had expressed to him it was okay, she cared, and she was glad he had told her about his childhood. But since they had parted after dinner, Christy had been bombarded with worries and fears.

She was worried about Katie, too. Christy hadn't seen her since lunch and didn't know if Katie had drowned herself in chocolate mocha frozen yogurt or had bounced back and was out romping with some of her friends.

Christy turned on her side and tried to convince herself to go to sleep and to forget everything and everybody else. It would all work out, somehow. Then a wild thought popped into her foggy brain. *What if Todd hurts me the way his dad hurt his mom?*

Christy angrily tossed to the other side. *Where did that thought come from? Todd would never hurt me.*

A moment later she thought, *What if he left me and took our kids the way his mom left his dad and took him?*

Christy tumbled out of bed. *That's ridiculous! Why am I even thinking this?*

She reached for the water bottle she had left sitting on her desk. Next to the water bottle was the bouquet of wilting white carnations Todd had given her a week ago when she had returned from Switzerland. On the shelf above her desk sat an old, beat-up Folgers coffee can. Inside were the dried brown remains of the first dozen white carnations Todd had given her on her fifteenth birthday.

Why did he wait so long to tell me what his life was really like? If we do end up getting married, will he always wait five years before telling me something? "Oh, by the way, honey, we're bankrupt and we have to move out of the house by tomorrow."

Christy plunged back into bed, more distraught than ever. Her wildly emotional thoughts turned to Uncle Bob. How would he respond when Marti told him, "By the way, honey, I'm leaving in the morning to go to Santa Fe with Cheyenne"?

I have to talk to someone about Marti. I can't hold her secret. Not when I have all this other stuff to deal with. Why did I ever promise her I'd keep her secret? That was such a stupid thing to do.

Christy's thoughts beat her up until she fell into a deep, exhausted sleep in which nightmares came one right after the other. Crazy, tormenting laughter circled her, taunting her for being so naïve as to love Todd Spencer and so foolish as to promise her aunt anything.

At close to four in the morning, Christy woke with a start and sat up in bed. The laughter from her brutal nightmares instantly ceased. The soft desk light was turned off, and she could hear Katie's rhythmic breathing in the bed across the room.

At least Katie is okay. And the rest of that stuff wasn't real. It was a nightmare. She tried to slow down her pounding heart. *It's okay. Pray, Christy. Pray and sleep. You need to sleep.*

Slowly lowering her head to the pillow, Christy prayed silently, moving her lips and whispering a word here and there. She prayed about everything. Her heart calmed. Her mind cleared. She slept a dreamless sleep for the next two and a half hours.

When Christy's alarm went off at six-thirty, Katie rolled over and gave one of her grumpy groans. "What's going on?"

"I'm going to church with Todd," Christy said. "Are you okay?"

"Yeah, I'm fine."

"Do you want to come to church with us?" Christy didn't know if her invitation was such a good idea since Matt would be there, but she offered it anyway.

"No, I'm taking Sierra down to San Diego to Paul's church. Will you wake me at eight o'clock?"

"I'll be gone before then," Christy said. "I'll reset my alarm for eight."

With a "humph-okay," Katie went back to sleep, and Christy got ready for church.

She met Todd at seven-thirty in the cafeteria for a quick breakfast, as they had planned the night before. Matt was eating with Todd when she arrived. The guys were almost through, so Christy had to gulp down her breakfast. She thought she should do something obvious to show that she and Todd were together, but the opportunity didn't present itself.

"How did you guys sleep last night?" Todd asked as the three of them drove down the hill in Gus the Bus.

"Awful," Christy said.

"Me too," Todd said. "I felt like I was being attacked. I couldn't figure out what was going on, and then I realized I needed to pray. We're stepping out to the front lines for the Lord this morning, but the enemy doesn't want us to do this."

"It was the same for me," Christy said. "Once I prayed, I finally could sleep." She felt hushed inside at the thought of evil forces trying to keep her from serving God this morning with Todd.

"Sounds like we better pray this morning, too," Matt said.

Matt had just said the word "pray" when Gus the Bus sputtered, lurched, and came to a stop in the middle of the road.

"Do you have your emergency lights on?" Matt asked as he slid the side door open and hopped out to motion to the car behind them to go around.

"They aren't working." Todd opened his door and climbed out. "Everything shut down. Christy, slide over here to the driver's seat and steer us to that parking lot, will you?"

"You mean over there in front of the dental offices?"

Todd didn't hear her. He was already around the back of the van, yelling for Christy to put it in neutral and make sure the brake was off. Christy had only driven ol' Gus a few times before and didn't feel comfortable behind the wheel at a time like this.

She followed Todd's instructions, and the car moved forward, thanks to the brawn of Todd and Matt. Biting her lower lip the entire journey of a block and a half into the parking lot, she steered as carefully as she could right into a space. It was marked *Compact Only*, but she was certain on a Sunday morning, with no one else in the lot, it wouldn't matter that Gus wasn't exactly compact.

"Put her in first," Todd called out, coming around to the open window on the driver's side. "And set the emergency brake."

Christy followed his instructions. That's when she realized her lip was throbbing from biting it. It was beginning to swell.

"What should we do now?" Christy asked. "Should we find a phone and call a repair service or something?"

"I don't think we have time for that," Matt said.

Todd had gone around to the side of Gus and opened the door. He was pulling out his guitar and his Bible.

"We better walk," Todd said. "It's at least a mile to the church from here."

Christy grabbed her Bible and strung her bag over her shoulder. Her mind flipped through half a dozen impractical solutions like calling a cab or hitchhiking. She didn't offer any of her suggestions as the three of them silently took off at a fast pace down the street.

"Probably the alternator," Matt said as they walked.

Christy knew it could be anything, since Gus was so old and subject to random seizures.

"I'll come back with my truck after church and look at it if you want me to," Matt offered.

"Sure." Todd was walking faster than Matt and Christy. His mind seemed not on his car but on what lay ahead.

Christy had gotten used to walking in Basel, and she found it easy to pick up her pace so she could keep up with Todd. "You know what? We never did pray," she said. "Matt was about to pray, and then Gus stopped."

"You're right," Todd said, as if Christy's words had snapped him out of a daydream. Then without slowing the pace, Todd spoke aloud. "Okay, Father, look at us here. I know you hold every detail of our lives in your hands. This didn't come as a surprise to you the way it did to us. You have a plan. I trust you for whatever you're going to do. We need you to make it clear because, to be honest, I'm not getting it right now."

They came to one of the town's main intersections and had to wait for the light to turn green before they could cross. Todd shifted his heavy guitar case to his other hand, and Christy wiped the perspiration off her forehead. The day's heat was already rising. The steady desert winds that had blown the past few days were absent, and the air felt close around them.

"And, Lord," Christy added to Todd's prayer, "we stand together on your Word against the enemy's plans. I think he's trying to put roadblocks in our way today. But this is your day, and we are your children. Please make our path straight."

The light turned green. They began to hoof it across the street when one of the cars at the crosswalk honked at them.

Christy thought the driver was honking to make fun of the three strolling minstrels who obviously were on their way to church wearing their nice clothes and carrying Bibles.

"Need a ride?" the driver called from the open car window.

"It's Donna," Christy said. "My new boss at the bookstore."

Within minutes, the three of them had jammed into the backseat of Donna's van, met her husband, and arrived in the church parking lot several minutes before the service started. Donna's husband, they found out, was a professor at Rancho Corona and involved in leadership at the church. He had been out of town last week when Todd was hired and asked if he could meet with Todd after the second service. With a round of thanks, Todd, Christy, and Matt dashed to the high school room.

Matt stopped to chat with two guys who were hanging out by the door. They both looked as if this was the last place they wanted to be, but they perked up when they saw Matt. Three girls arrived together. Christy followed Matt's lead and pretended she wasn't a shy person. She introduced herself to the girls and started a conversation with them.

Todd set up his equipment. The sophisticated computer on the stand in the back of the room projected the words to the first song off a disc Todd had inserted. He invited everyone to come in.

For the next fifteen minutes, Christy, Matt, and the five students sang the worship songs as Todd played his guitar. Since so few people were there, Christy didn't stand in front with Todd, but she did sing louder and more convincingly than any of the others.

Two more girls arrived halfway through and sat in the back whispering as the others sang. That bugged Christy. She knew how wonderful a time of worship could be with friends since she had experienced that as a teenager. How could she tell those girls that this time was holy and meaningful and they should enter in?

When the singing ended, Todd asked the students to pull their chairs into a circle. None of them were too eager, but they did it anyway. He then introduced himself and asked that each person do the same and tell something about him or herself.

It didn't go so well, from Christy's opinion. She and Matt talked the most, but they ended up telling that they grew up together. The way Matt talked, it almost sounded as if he and Christy were boyfriend and girlfriend, and the two of them were there to support their buddy, Todd.

I definitely need to have a talk with Matt. The sooner the better.

Todd opened his Bible and taught a simple, straightforward lesson from John. He used the verse Christy had mentioned to him the other day about how those who believe and receive Christ are given the right to become God's children.

When the group dispersed, Christy carefully watched Todd's face. He was holding his easygoing grin steady, but she could read his eyes. His heart was breaking. This wasn't what he had hoped for, and she knew it.

"It went well," she told him quietly, giving his arm a squeeze. "It's the first week. They're trying to decide if they like you and feel safe enough to come back next week."

Todd nodded, but Christy could tell he was still heavyhearted. All during the church service she sensed he was battling with himself over how the class time went. She knew he was thinking through every angle, evaluating, restructuring, and planning.

She liked the service and the pastor and the way he presented the sermon. She told Matt afterward, "This church reminds me of our old church in Brightwater."

"That's why I got involved last year."

Two older women came up to greet Matt, and he introduced them to Christy. Todd got in on the end of the introductions, and the women made a fuss over how delighted they were that he would be working with their young people. Matt was at ease with these women, but Todd looked nervous, as if he didn't know what to do or say around elderly people.

"I'm supposed to go to lunch now with the pastor and some of the leaders," Todd said to Christy. "Do you want to go with us?"

Christy looked over his shoulder at the pastor and two other men who appeared to be waiting for Todd. "Why don't you just go this time. I'll come with you the next time."

"Okay," Todd said. "Can you guys find a ride back to school?"

"Sure, we'll be fine," Christy said.

"You sure?"

"I'm sure."

"Okay, then I'll see you later."

"Yeah, later," Christy said with a grin. She wasn't used to seeing Todd so nervous. No one else would realize his actions were expressing nervousness, but she knew. It was kind of funny.

Donna gave Christy and Matt a ride to Rancho and dropped them off in the parking lot behind the cafeteria.

"If you guys ever need a ride on Sunday, just call me," Donna said. "Anytime. And I mean that."

As soon as Christy and Matt sat down with their lunch trays, Christy plunged in. "I have to tell you something."

"Sure," Matt said. "What is it?"

"I don't know if you knew this, but Todd and I are together."

"Together together?"

"What does together together mean?" Christy asked.

"Are you two serious about each other?"

"Yes. We have been for a long time."

Matt stared at his plate of spaghetti a moment before saying, "By any chance is he the guy Paula told me about?"

"Probably," Christy said. Paula, her best friend from childhood, had been crazy about Todd the summer she had come out to California to visit Christy.

"Is Todd the guy who taught Paula how to surf?"

"Yes." Christy smiled at the memory. Paula and Christy hadn't kept their friendship going much after that summer when Christy turned sixteen. But when they were close, they had had some good times together. Paula had married while Christy was in Switzerland, but Christy didn't hear about it until a few weeks after the wedding. When they were young, Paula and Christy had promised they would be bridesmaids in each other's weddings. Christy still felt a little sad that that was one promise she hadn't been able to keep.

"If you can believe this," Christy said, "Paula and I had an agreement before we were in high school. We agreed that whoever went out on a real date first would get five dollars from the other person."

"Who won?" Matt asked.

"Me," Christy said. "And guess who my first date was with?"

Matt looked at his spaghetti again. "Must have been Todd."

"It was."

"When I met him at lunch yesterday, I didn't remember that he was the guy Paula told me about," Matt said. "I knew you had had a boyfriend for a long time, but I thought he was gone. Gone, as in spending the rest of his life in Fiji or something."

"The last time I saw you, Todd was gone. He was in Spain, actually."

"But now he's back," Matt said.

"Yes, Todd's back. And I'm back from Switzerland, and we're together. Together together."

"Well, you made a good choice, Christy," Matt said. He had such a straightforward look to him. He reminded her of her dad.

Christy remembered something her grandpa had said when she had asked her grandparents how they knew they were right for each other. He had told her, *"The real way you know he's the right person is to evaluate his background. Do you come from the same place? Then you have a much better chance of making it through the hard times."*

Her grandmother had disagreed. She had told Christy it was a choice and then repeated that annoying line, *"When it's right, you'll know."*

Christy glanced at Matt. *I don't know for sure that Todd is the right one, but I do know for sure that Matt isn't.*

Just knowing one thing for sure in her life felt really good.

"You know what?" Matt pushed his tray to the side and continued to look at Christy in a straightforward way. "I'm going to put myself out there and say something. I hope you don't mind my saying it."

Christy felt so buoyed up by the insight she had just come up with about Matt that she welcomed anything he had to say.

"I think very highly of you, Christy."

"And I think very highly of you."

"I hope you'll keep me in mind if things don't work out with Todd, but I have a feeling things will work out pretty well for you two."

"I have a feeling they will, too," Christy said.

"And you and I can still be friends?"

"Of course," Christy said. "I know Todd really appreciates all your encouragement with the youth group."

"I told him I'd help any way he wanted me to."

Christy debated whether she should say anything about Katie. She was about to suggest that the four of them go out on a double date. Then she decided it would be better not to say anything until she had a chance to talk to Katie.

Matt and Christy spent the next half hour comfortably talking. Matt filled her in on news of family and friends in Brightwater, and Christy told him about her time in Switzerland. When they left the cafeteria and were about to go their separate ways, Matt gave Christy a boyish grin and tagged her arm the way he used to on the playground at recess.

"Eenie-meenie boo-boo!" Matt called out, then took off running.

Christy laughed. She wasn't about to chase him and tag him back. Those days were long gone. She strolled to her room smiling.

That felt like a phone book lifting off me. Next phone book is for me to decide on a major. And to make sure Katie is okay. And to figure out what to do about my aunt. And . . .

She stopped herself before adding any more phone books to her stack.

One thing at a time.

When she arrived at the dorm room, Katie wasn't there. The only evidence that she had been was her khaki skirt, which she apparently had worn when she went to church that morning. The skirt was wadded up in a big ball in the room's corner.

Christy changed her clothes and wondered if she should go to the rematch softball game that was scheduled for four o'clock. She didn't feel like playing softball. They had enough players yesterday, and she didn't think she would be missed.

If Katie comes back in time, I'll send her in my place. Matt will be there, and it will give the two of them an opportunity to start over.

Christy opened the window, letting in some fresh air. She thought how convenient it would have been if Matt and Katie had discovered each other at the same time. That didn't mean it was too late for Matt to find out how terrific she was.

Staring at the clear, periwinkle sky, she wondered aloud, "Is Todd the right man for me? Is he the one I'm supposed to marry? Why can't I be certain enough to tell him I love him?"

She wished God would send her the answer in writing. He could just lower it on a long string and dangle the message in front of her window. No one else would need to notice it. Only Christy. All it had to say was *Marry Todd.* She wouldn't tell a soul. Not even Todd. He would have to propose to her and everything, but at least in her heart she would know he was the right one, and she would have no doubts.

Christy blinked. The silent sky hadn't opened up. No message on the end of a long string had come her way. She would have to figure this out the hard way. The normal way. Step by tentative step with lots of prayer.

Stretching out on her bed, Christy considered writing her thoughts in her diary. It always helped her to write from her heart and then look at the words later.

Not this time, though. She didn't want anyone coming across her diary and reading those thoughts.

Christy looked at the poster she had hung on the wall. It was a picture of a bridge near Hana, Maui. Todd had jumped off that bridge into the deep pool below. Christy had driven over that bridge in a Jeep right after she turned sixteen. It was "their" bridge. Now they were at another bridge. She knew Todd was ready to "jump." He was ready to move forward in their relationship and make a lasting commitment. She had been "driving" through this decision, which took a lot more time than getting there by jumping. Todd was being patient. But Christy was stuck.

"There are no guarantees, are there?" she said aloud to God. "There weren't any guarantees for Todd's parents. It doesn't look like there are any for Bob and Marti. So how can I possibly be certain that a marriage started at such a young age will last for the rest of our lives?"

Just then the dorm room opened. Christy stared at the red-haired woman who entered. She barely looked like the Katie Christy knew by heart. Her roommate's medium-length, swishy red hair had been cut short. It feathered across her forehead and to the nape of her neck in wispy, uneven layers. Katie looked completely different. This was a new look. A softer, more sophisticated look.

"You cut your hair!" Christy examined it from all angles. "I really like it! When did you decide to cut it?"

"This afternoon." Katie tossed a few shopping bags on her unmade bed and kicked off her shoes.

"You look completely different."

"That was the idea," Katie muttered.

"Are you okay?"

Katie flopped on her crumpled bed next to the shopping bags. She held her pillow across her middle as if she had a stomachache.

Christy moved the bags and made room for herself at the foot of the bed. "Katie, what is it? What's going on?"

Katie looked away. "I'm tired of myself."

Christy had no idea how to respond.

"I've been thinking a lot about what happened with Matt yesterday. I realized I presume too much and I assume too much. I want to change, Christy. I really do."

"Change in what way?"

"I don't know. That's why I started with my hair. I bought some new clothes, too." Katie pulled a blouse from one of the bags and held it up. "What do you think of this?"

"It's pretty."

"Good. I'm glad that's the first thing you thought when you saw it because I need something pretty. My wardrobe is all jeans and T-shirts. Do you realize I only have one skirt, but when I wore it this morning, I decided I didn't like it. I don't like khaki anymore."

Katie pulled a long, flowing skirt from the next bag, and Christy said, "Okay, now you're frightening me. That skirt is too similar to the one my aunt had on the other day."

"Don't worry. I'm not going to start checking my aura. I wanted something casual yet soft. Not khaki. You should see Sierra's wardrobe. I was in her room last night, and between Sierra and Vicki, the two of them have the best outfits of anyone I've ever seen on this campus."

Christy liked the way Sierra dressed, too. She was an individualist and wore things no one else did, and she didn't seem to care if she was in style or not. Sierra made her own style. The first time Christy had met her, Sierra was wearing a pair of her father's old cowboy boots.

"Sierra shops at thrift stores, doesn't she?" Christy asked.

Katie nodded. "She was telling me about some of the vintage clothing stores in Portland, where she lives. It made me want to go there just to shop."

"Did you buy these clothes at a thrift store?"

"No, and I spent way too much money on them. But I needed to do something. Tomorrow is the first day of class, and I need this year to be better than any other year of my whole school career. I need a fresh start."

Christy folded the new skirt and placed it on the end of the bed. "Katie, may I bring up a topic that you probably don't want to talk about?"

"Do I have a choice?"

"Not really."

"Go ahead. Let me have it. You always let me shower you with my biased opinions. I guess it's only fair for you to have a turn."

"You know how you told me the thing about carrying too many phone books and ending up dropping them all? Well, I think that over the years you haven't exactly gotten over the hurt of some of your relationships with guys. You're carrying all the hurt like a stack of phone books. That's why it hurts so deeply when a disappointment comes along like Matt's memory lapse yesterday." Christy had no idea she was going to say all this to Katie. She hadn't thought it through; it all just tumbled out.

"I think you were hurt yesterday by Matt," Christy continued, "but it reminded you of the hurt and disappointment you felt with Rick, Michael, Lance, and every other guy who has let you down."

Katie's face looked stubborn, set like a stone.

Christy cautiously proceeded. "So you don't just feel the hurt from one disappointment but also the hurt of half a dozen guys at the same time."

The room fell silent as Christy wondered why she was saying all this to her best friend.

A few minutes passed before Katie straightened herself and said with an edge to her voice, "So what do you recommend I do about it?"

Christy wanted to tell Katie that she hadn't planned to present this problem and so she certainly hadn't planned a solution, either. Instead, Christy said the only thing that came to mind. "You don't need to change anything on the outside. You need to change the inside. I think you have to forgive, Katie. You have to choose to forgive and start all over."

For a moment Katie looked as if she might throw something or yell. Instead, she muttered, "I hate it when you're right."

CHAPTER 7

Katie adjusted her position on the bed and said with a challenge in her voice, "Just what makes you so sure I haven't forgiven the guys who have hurt me?"

"Well—" Christy began.

"I'll tell you something. It would be nice if just one of those jerks would acknowledge he was rude, insensitive, or mean, or all of the above." Katie rose and kicked at her wadded-up khaki skirt. "I know that's a lot to ask, but it sure would make forgiving easier."

"But what if none of them ever apologizes?" Christy asked. "Are you going to go through your life carrying all these phone books of pain with you?"

"No." Katie paced the floor. "I'll get over the hurt once I meet Prince Charming."

"Katie!"

"What?"

Christy hesitated to say what she was thinking, but she knew she couldn't hold it in. "What will happen the first time Prince Charming lets you down? I mean, even if you marry Prince Charming, he's not going to be perfect. Somewhere along the way he'll be insensitive, mean, or rude, and then what? Instead of just carrying the hurt from that isolated incident, will you pick up all those phone books and carry them again?"

"I don't know. I don't want to talk about this, Christy. I need to get some air."

Christy glanced at the clock. It was almost four o'clock. "Do you want to play softball?"

Katie looked at Christy. "Why? Do you?"

"No. I was wondering if you would take my place on Wes's team. They're playing against Sierra's team at four o'clock."

Rummaging in a drawer, Katie pulled out a baseball cap and found her mitt in the closet. She laced up her tennis shoes and left with only a quick, "I'm outta here."

Christy sat in the empty room. *Why did I say all those things to Katie? She didn't need to hear all that today. And she certainly didn't need to hear it from me.*

Deciding she would skip dinner, Christy took a long shower, washed her hair, shaved her legs, and then called Todd. No one answered in his room, so Christy left a voice message suggesting they meet for breakfast in The Golden Calf at seven-thirty the next morning.

She took her laundry to the end of the hall, and while waiting for an open machine, she joined some other girls from her floor who had gathered in the den to watch *The Princess Bride*. The last time Christy had watched that movie was before she went to Switzerland. Katie had rented it and brought it over for their final girls' night. After watching it, Katie had declared she would never trust a guy who said "As you wish" to her every whim. She wanted a guy with gusto who would say, "Get it yourself," otherwise she knew she would sit around and get fat while he catered to her.

Christy knew when Katie had made those comments a year ago that she was just being her comical self. Now Christy wished Katie was watching the movie with her, making wisecracks, being the kind of roommate Christy had looked forward to. The other girls watching the movie were all nice, but something inside Christy made her feel as if she wasn't ready to make new friends. She was much more interested in maintaining her current friendships.

After the movie two of the girls said they were going down the hill for ice cream. They invited Christy to go with them, but she declined, saying she needed to get back to her room because she and her roommate needed to talk.

Christy returned to her room with a folded stack of clean clothes and found a note from Katie. She had written it on a 3X5 card and taped it to the corner of Christy's desk.

I'm staying with Sierra tonight. K.

Christy read the note twice, not believing it the first time. She imagined the worst.

Katie is so upset by what I said that she can't stand to be in the same room with me.

The note didn't say, "Come join us" or "Meet me for breakfast" or give any hint that Katie wasn't mad at Christy.

Katie is giving herself a makeover with her new hair and clothes. Is she trying to tell me she's doing a makeover with her best friends, too?

Tears came, and with them an aching loneliness she hadn't expected to feel at Rancho. She had felt alone many times in Switzerland since she was so far from home and close friends. But she never expected to be assaulted by these feelings when she was "home" with her closest friends.

Christy debated for a long time if she should call Sierra's room or go there to try to settle things with Katie. The decision-making process, on top of her already thin emotions, exhausted her so much that Christy finally concluded she shouldn't try anything heroic tonight. She would sleep on her dilemma, pray about it, and see if she and Katie could talk in the morning.

———

The next morning Christy was glad to see Todd waiting for her in front of the cafeteria at seven-thirty. He greeted her with a kiss on the temple and said, "I tried to call you back last night, but no one answered."

"I didn't check my voice mail," Christy said. "You probably called while I was doing my laundry and watching a movie."

They moved through the line, and Christy forced herself to put some food on her tray, even though she wasn't hungry. She knew, after skipping dinner last night, that she needed some protein.

Todd led Christy to a window table with two chairs. He turned the chairs so they could look out the window and keep their backs to the rest of the students.

"We got Gus running," Todd said after they had prayed.

"That's good."

"Yeah, thanks to Matt. He has a real talent for fixing cars. And he agreed to help me put together the mission trip to Mexico."

"What mission trip to Mexico?"

"I didn't tell you yet, did I? When I had lunch with some of the church leaders yesterday, I mentioned I'd like to take the group to Mexico, and they were all for it. I'm thinking we'll go over Thanksgiving. Do you want to come?" Todd sunk his teeth into a blueberry bagel.

"Sure."

Todd stopped chewing. With a swallow he looked at Christy and said, "That was a quick decision."

"It was, wasn't it?" Christy knew her decisiveness was prompted by her feelings of loneliness. Any invitation to go anywhere or do anything with her friends appealed to her this morning.

"I think I alienated Katie yesterday," she muttered before taking a bite of her scrambled eggs.

"What happened?"

With a dozen concise sentences, Christy explained to Todd that she had given Katie unwanted advice, and as a result, Katie had stayed in Sierra's room last night.

"We only lasted a week together in the same room. I wish I had kept my mouth shut."

Todd's expression suggested he wasn't taking her doom and gloom assessment too seriously. "Don't be so hard on yourself. It sounds as if you were speaking the truth in love. It might take a while for all that truth to sink in, but I think what you said was honest and helpful. It'll work out. You'll see."

Christy shook her head. "I don't know. At least I didn't try to set up a double date for Katie with Matt like I was thinking of doing yesterday. Katie wouldn't have appreciated that at all. I sent her to the softball game in my place so she could be around Matt, but now I don't know what happened."

"Matt didn't go to the game," Todd said. "He was with me, working on Gus."

"That's not good. That means Matt and Katie haven't connected yet. I was hoping they would make a fresh start yesterday."

Todd's grin was too obvious to ignore.

"What?" Christy asked. "What's so funny?"

"You. You're in one of your save-the-world moods."

Christy put down her fork. "What is that supposed to mean?"

Todd covered her hand with his. "Don't get upset." He was still grinning. "You're cute when you get like this."

"Cute!" Christy felt the blood rushing to her face.

Todd's expression remained jovial. "Yeah, cute. It's like you don't have enough challenges of your own to figure out so you take on the world's burdens. I always know when you're feeling responsible for the deterioration of the ozone layer. You get this squiggly wrinkle across your forehead right here." He traced his finger across her forehead and laughed.

To her surprise, Christy broke into a smile. "Am I really that bad?"

"You are really that caring," Todd said. "That's not bad, as long as you don't take it to an extreme, of course. It's one of the many qualities I admire in you."

Todd's calm words and loving attention soothed Christy. She felt her appetite returning and ate three sausages off Todd's plate before he complained.

"You can go back for seconds, you know," he said.

"No thanks," she said with an impish grin. "I'm full now."

Todd and Christy left the cafeteria holding hands. After he walked her to her first class, they stopped by the door. As the other students rushed past them, Todd ran his hand over her long tresses and said in a low voice, *"Na ka Makua-O-Kalani, e malama mai ia makou."*

Christy looked at him, waiting for an explanation. His words sounded Hawaiian, but she had never heard Todd say them before.

He seemed just as surprised at his words as Christy because all he added was, "I can't believe I remembered that."

"What did you say?"

"It's a prayer that Lani used to say every morning before I left for school." Todd seemed lost in a memory.

"I'll be at the bookstore until three," Christy said. She was uncomfortably aware that all the seats were filling fast in the classroom. "Meet me there if you can." She wanted to hear who Lani was and what the prayer meant when they had more time.

Only a few seats near the center of the large auditorium were still open when Christy entered her Old Testament introduction class. Old Testament and New Testament introduction were required for all graduates of Rancho Corona, so Christy suspected lots of freshmen were in this class.

She took a seat and noticed Sierra along with several of her friends sitting near the front. Next to Vicki was an empty seat. The instructor had already begun, so Christy didn't feel comfortable moving to join Sierra's group. Even though Todd's encouragement over breakfast had helped Christy believe everything was going to turn out okay with Katie, she didn't want to face Sierra yet—just in case Katie had spent the night telling Sierra and her friends what an insensitive roommate Christy was.

When class was over, Christy slipped out and hurried to the administration building to make an appointment with her counselor. The first opening he had was the next morning at ten. She took the appointment, determined to decide on her major and settle her class schedule before the end of the week.

Christy arrived at the bookstore just as her new boss, Donna, was about to enter the store with a box in her arms. Christy reached to open the door for her.

"Good, you're a little early, Christy. Did I show you how to log in on the computer when you start work?" Donna asked.

"No."

"I didn't think I did. Come with me, and I'll help you set up."

Christy followed Donna to the back of the bookstore, where she showed Christy how to access her time card on the computer and how it automatically logged her in when she typed in her code. Beside the computer, stacks of boxes stood open with a label gun resting on the top box. It brought back memories of her first job at the pet store in Escondido. Only, there she spent hours labeling fish food and rubber cat toys that smelled like old tires. She liked the ink and paper smell of these boxes of books much more.

"The same textbooks are in these first three boxes," Donna said. "I need you to label them on the back like this and then change the label gun and mark the books in these other four boxes at $15.95. Have you used one of these before?"

Christy nodded and told her about the pet store.

"Okay. Well, let me know when you've finished, and I'll start you on the register."

Christy was glad for the chance to begin with something simple. She liked feeling productive and able to measure her accomplishments.

"You can't be done already," Donna said when Christy joined her at the register a short time later. A long line of students was waiting to pay for textbooks.

"I think I finished all the boxes you pointed out."

"Lovely," Donna said. "You are the answer to my prayers, believe me. Why don't you watch me go through a few transactions, and then you can jump in."

The computer and credit card system were similar to what Christy had worked with at the pet store. She stepped in to try the machine after watching Donna on three transactions and went through the motions as if she had been doing it for years.

"You've got it," Donna said. "I'm going to shelve some of those books, and then I'll open this other register. Let me know if you get stuck on anything."

Christy didn't know why, but the act of serving like this, of using her hands to accomplish things, gave her a sense of well-being. The world was somehow a brighter place when she could get things done. She knew she was going to like working in the bookstore.

I wonder if having a degree in literature would be useful if I ended up working full time in a bookstore?

In the back of her mind she began to imagine in the most romantic way possible how dreamy her life would be if she and Todd married and lived in a cozy little house somewhere. They would have a vegetable garden in the backyard and a woodburning fireplace. She would bake cookies for the teens in the youth group, who would hang out at their house every Friday night. Every morning Christy would hop on a bike, like the one she had borrowed all the time in Switzerland, and she would pedal off to a charming little bookstore where, at ten o'clock, she would host a story time for toddlers. Customers would come from all over to browse in Christy's bookstore. She would serve them cookies and tea—Katie's Indian summer herbal tea, once Katie perfected the recipe.

But by two o'clock, Christy's imagination was having a difficult time glamorizing a bookstore owner's life. She hadn't eaten lunch, and her stomach was complaining loudly. The line of students hadn't diminished. The computer went down for almost half an hour, and all the credit card charges had to be done manually. As more students flocked into the store with lists of required textbooks, Christy wished she had a stool to sit on or at least a thicker rug beneath her feet.

She realized she had been daydreaming about being married to Todd. It had been a natural assumption, a logical, comfortable foundation in her daydream. Christy felt a wonderful thrill of hope.

I must love Todd enough to commit myself to him for the rest of my life if I include him in my daydreams so easily. I have to tell Katie about this.

As soon as she thought of Katie, her spirits swooped down a couple of notches.

That is, if Katie is still speaking to me.

Christy finished a transaction for a girl who wore a hearing aid. She seemed to be immensely relieved when Christy presented her with the total for all her books and it was less than she had expected. That's when Christy realized that the majority of the textbooks she was selling were the ones off the used bookshelves in the back. Christy wished she had been more organized and had shopped for her textbooks sooner, before all the used ones were gone. That was one check she wasn't looking forward to writing because she knew it would drain her savings.

At three o'clock, Christy signed off the computer, and another student took her place. Christy went to the back of the store and scanned the used-textbook shelves. She found three of the books she knew she needed. The others would have to wait until she received an updated list after she made a final decision on her major and her classes.

Christy left the bookstore with her heavy textbooks and went to the guys' dorm to see if Todd was there. She entered West Hall and asked one of the guys on the couch how to call the rooms. He pointed to the phones on the wall, and she tried to call Todd. No answer.

That was one of the things that bugged her about being at a conservative Christian college. In Switzerland she had been in a co-ed dorm, and the guys and girls were both free to come and go as they wished. That meant she didn't always have her room to herself, if one of her two roommates was already there with a boyfriend. But that had only happened once. Christy was the one who stayed in the dorm room the most; so her roommates were the ones who went to visit the guys' rooms.

And there I was again last night, alone, while my roommate went off to be with someone else.

Christy left a simple voice message for Todd, saying that she would be in her room until five, when she planned to eat an early dinner. Then she had a class from seven o'clock until nine.

Trudging across campus, she silently moaned about how far the guys' dorms were from the girls' dorms. The books she had bought felt heavier with each step. *It was much easier in Basel with all the housing in one area. It's so ridiculous for them to separate us across campus like this and put all these restrictions on us.*

Christy was hoofing it past The Java Jungle when someone came running up behind her and said, "Hey, cutie, where have you been?"

With a playful smirk, Christy turned and said, "Where have *you* been?"

Todd had a stack of books under his arm and looked red in the face, as if he had been working out. "I was hung up with the counselor. When I got to the bookstore, your manager said I just missed you."

"It looks like you're all set with your books," Christy said.

"I only need two more," Todd said. He reached for Christy's arm and pulled her toward the door of The Java Jungle. "Do you have any money on you?"

"Yes, about five dollars."

"Good. I'm broke. How about buying me something to drink?"

The booths inside the air-conditioned café were packed. Only one table remained open. They dropped their books on it and spent all but three cents of Christy's five-dollar bill on drinks and snacks.

"Did you figure out your schedule?" Christy asked.

He grinned.

"I take it that means yes."

"I can graduate in December," Todd said.

"Really?"

Todd nodded proudly. "You were so right about taking those two summer school classes after I got back from Europe. That's what made the difference."

"I don't remember telling you to take summer school classes."

"That's right, that was Katie's idea. She convinced me on the plane on the way home. Of course, she didn't take any classes like she said she was going to."

"She worked all summer," Christy said. "That's why she has time for a social life this fall and why I'm working every spare minute I have."

"How did it go your first day on the job?" Todd asked.

This time Christy was the one who answered with only a grin.

"I take it that means you liked it."

"I like it so much that I was daydreaming about owning my own bookstore someday." She decided to leave out the part about being married to Todd and snuggling with him in front of the woodburning fireplace. "And having a vegetable garden," she added.

"Now, would the vegetable garden be part of the bookstore?" Todd asked. "Were you thinking the garden would be in front of the store? Out back? Inside?"

"Sure," Christy answered in an effort to avoid giving specifics. "Any of the aforementioned is possible. Don't you think a vegetable garden sounds charming?"

Todd gave her a skeptical look.

"What about a woodburning fireplace?" Christy ventured further into her imaginary world and hoped Todd would find part of her dream appealing. "Do you like fireplaces?"

He leaned back in his chair and asked, "Now, would this fireplace be in the garden or in the bookstore?"

"Never mind." Christy felt as if she was getting nowhere. "Some daydreams are best left undiscussed, I guess."

Todd gave her hand a squeeze. "I like fireplaces. And I like you. I like hearing about your daydreams. The vegetable garden, though . . . I don't know. But I know I like you."

Christy smiled.

Go ahead. Say it. Say, "I love you, Todd." Right here in the middle of The Java Jungle with all these people. Stand up and shout it!

Christy opened her mouth, but what came out was "I like you, too."

Todd grinned. "I like you a lot."

"I like you a lot, too."

"I like you more," Todd said.

"No, I like you more."

Todd leaned forward and, with the warmest glow ever in his clear blue eyes, said, "I love you, Kilikina."

Christy froze. She couldn't make her lips part. She couldn't push out the words. A single tear was all that escaped her heart and raced down her cheek.

Todd moved his chair over so that he was right next to Christy. He kept his hand in hers. With patient, gentle words he said, "You don't have to respond, Christy. I don't want you to feel pressured. Ever. In any way. Just let me love you, okay?" He leaned over and kissed the tear where it clung to the edge of her jaw. "Just let me love you."

CHAPTER 8

Todd and Christy spent most of the rest of the day together. They dropped off their heavy books in their dorm rooms, sat together in the cafeteria, and then Todd walked Christy to her evening class. At nine, he was there to pick her up after class. As he agreed to do earlier, Todd went to the library with Christy to review her schedule with her.

Sitting close on a couch in the library's lobby, they read the classes from the catalog and Christy began her list on a note pad. She felt good as she listed everything so she could see the schedule and figure out what worked.

"That's it," Todd said after reading through the list of required classes for an English literature major. "Do you want to go through the classes for the humanities major now?"

Christy did some math on the side of the page. "No, more and more I like the idea of being a lit major. It's more focused than humanities, and literature fits me better. Like you said this morning at breakfast, I already have a save-the-world complex; a humanities major would only move me further in that direction. It would be like going back to the orphanage in Basel."

Once Christy had everything written out, she stared at the paper and realized the list of classes was all that lay between her and a BA in English literature. It was bite-size, a clear road map.

"I think literature is a good major for you, especially if you want to open that bookstore someday." Todd looked at Christy's calculations. "Is that total right? You could finish in two semesters?"

Christy nodded. "That's what the counselor told me, too. I had to see it for myself, but I could graduate next spring."

Todd looked as if he had taken a deep breath and then dove, headfirst, someplace deep. She was certain that when he surfaced, he would hold sunken treasure in his fist.

Todd emerged after two full minutes from his underwater daydream. With a deep breath he said, "Okay."

Okay? That's all you're going to tell me? Okay? Where did you just go? What did you see there, deep inside?

Christy knew that Todd wouldn't tell. And why should he? She hadn't yet given him the password that would allow him to open her heart's safe so he could store his fistful of treasures there. But she already knew what he was thinking because she was thinking the same thing.

We can get married, then, can't we, Todd? Katie wasn't pushing it as much as I first thought she was, was she? We are in the final stretch. The only thing missing is my commitment. I have to decide. I have to know for sure, and you understand that, don't you?

"Do you feel ready for your meeting with your counselor in the morning?" Todd asked.

"Yes."

"Good."

You're going to wait for me, aren't you, Todd? It doesn't matter how long I take to make up my mind, your love for me is established.

"I better get back to my room." Christy felt overwhelmed by her intense thoughts. "If Katie's there, I need to talk things through with her."

Todd walked Christy to her dorm and gave her a warm hug.

"Sweet dreams," she whispered in his ear.

"Sweet dreams to you, too."

She watched him walk away and felt as if an invisible string were attached to her heart. With each step Todd took, that string unraveled another loop. If anything or anyone ever threatened to sever that invisible string, Christy knew she would fight with every ounce of her being to keep that thread intact. She and Todd were connected. Strongly, deeply, wonderfully connected.

Opening the door to her room, Christy found Katie plopped in the beanbag chair, tears streaming down her face.

"Katie, are you okay?"

"Read this," Katie said, holding up a letter.

Christy took the handwritten, one-page letter from her roommate and immediately checked the signature.

"Rick? You got a letter from Rick Doyle?"

Katie nodded and wiped the tears from her cheeks. "He says he's sorry," Katie said before Christy had a chance to read the first line. "He got his life back together with God this summer, and he's apologizing for not . . . how does he say it? For not treating me with respect."

Christy scanned the opening paragraph. "It says, 'I ran into Doug, and he told me you and Christy were going to Rancho this year.' "

"Keep going," Katie said.

Christy read the second paragraph to herself and said, "He's asking you to forgive him for being a jerk and not treating you with the dignity and respect you deserve."

"Can you believe that?" Katie said. "I never expected anything like that to happen. Remember how just yesterday I said it would help if one of the guys who hurt me would apologize?"

Christy nodded and lowered herself to the edge of Katie's unmade bed.

"This has to be the creepiest God-thing I've ever experienced," Katie said. "I make that big declaration, and the very next day I pick up my mail and find this letter from Rick. At first I thought it might be a joke, but read that last part."

" 'This summer I finally surrendered my life completely to Christ, and He's real to me now. Very real. I just want to make things right with you, Katie. You don't have to write me back. I know God has forgiven me. I hope you can, too.' "

Christy looked up. "He sounds like he really means it."

Katie nodded. "Christy, I have to apologize to you, too. And I really mean it. I shouldn't have left in such a huff yesterday. What you were telling me was all true. I just didn't want to hear it."

Christy rushed to her friend and gave her a hug. "I'm the one who needs to apologize. I was so insensitive, Katie. I'm sorry. I should have come to Sierra's room last night so we could clear things up."

"No, I needed time to think everything through. It took me a while to realize you were right. I need to start forgiving completely. I had decided this afternoon I was going to start by forgiving Rick because I think he hurt me the most. I went to the chapel after dinner and prayed, and then this." Katie pointed to the letter Christy still held in her hand. "This blew me away. I mean, Rick Doyle is asking for my forgiveness. So what am I doing avoiding you? You and I are a team, Christy. We've waited for years to be roommates, and within the first week, I go and mess things up."

"You didn't mess anything up, Katie. We got off track, that's all. We need to talk things through whenever we get upset with each other. For whatever reason."

"You're right," Katie said. She rose and tucked the folded letter into the back flap of her Bible. "Did you check your mail today?"

"No, why?"

"Don't you wonder if Rick wrote you, too?"

"Me?"

"Yes, you. Rick didn't exactly treat you with the utmost dignity while you were dating him."

"But he and I settled it all back then," Christy said. "I don't think he has anything to apologize for. I didn't exactly handle the relationship with a lot of sensitivity to him. I tend to get pretty intense about things and only see them from my point of view."

Katie's sly grin returned. "We all are basically self-centered, when you think about it. That's why we need a Savior. Has Dr. Mitchell said that yet in Old Testament Survey? He said it all the time last year. Whenever we were studying about how all those heroes of faith had messed up so badly in the Old Testament, he would say, 'And once again we see this is why we all need a Savior.' "

Christy smiled. She was thinking of Rick and the verse from John about how those who believe and receive Christ have the right to become God's adopted children.

Rick is really, truly one of God's kids now.

"You're thinking about Rick, aren't you?" Katie asked.

"How did you know?"

"I was thinking the same thing. The original 'poser' got saved for real."

"Where did that word come from? What is a 'poser'? I heard Todd use it a couple of times with the group in Sunday school."

"You've been in the Alps too long," Katie said. "I first heard it as a surfer term. A 'poser' is someone who acts like he can surf, but he never actually gets up on a board. You know the kind—they put surfing stickers on their cars, wear shirts with surf logos, and talk about how great the waves were last week, but they don't surf. They just make you think they do."

"Do you think that was the situation with Rick? He was just a 'poser' Christian when we were in high school?"

"Who knows? It's for God to judge, not us. I'm just amazed he's got it together now and he wrote me."

"Are you going to write him back?" Christy asked.

"He didn't include a return address." Katie tilted her head. The gesture was especially charming now that her hair was short and wispy. It made her look playful rather than slightly frenzied, which is what that same gesture suggested when her hair was longer and swishy. "But Doug might know where he is. Or I could send a letter to his parents' home in Escondido."

As Christy got ready for bed, Katie cranked up her stereo and went to work composing a letter to Rick. By the time Christy had washed her face, brushed her teeth, and was snuggled under her covers, Katie the night owl was ready to talk.

"How does this sound: 'Dear Rick, I got your letter, and it made me cry. Of course I forgive you, you big baboon. Now it's my turn to ask you to forgive me. I don't think I was exactly at my best as a Christian or as a friend while we were hanging out together. I'm so excited to hear about what God has been doing in your life. Let's keep in touch, okay? Friends forever, Katie.' What do you think?"

"Big baboon?"

"I had to say something like that, or he wouldn't think it was from me."

"Then it sounds good," Christy said with a yawn. "It sounds like you, and it sounds sincere."

"You're not going to sleep now, are you?"

"Katie, it's almost midnight."

"But I'm going to write letters to all my lost loves. I want you to tell me if they sound okay."

"I'll read them in the morning."

Christy never did read Katie's letters. She thought of them on Friday, the end of their first week of classes. While they were checking their mailboxes before dinner, Christy remembered and asked Katie if she had ever mailed her letters.

"I only mailed the one to Rick." Katie and Christy stepped out of the student center and strolled toward The Golden Calf. "My mom gave me his parents' address, and I sent it there. The other letters didn't need to be mailed because they ended up turning into one long letter I wrote to God asking Him to forgive me for not forgiving those guys. I put the letter in my Bible. On the back of it I wrote out some verses that really helped me. One of them was the part where Jesus is hanging on the cross and He says, 'Father, forgive them. They don't know what they're doing.' That verse helped me the most because it made me realize that most people don't know what they're doing when they hurt us."

Christy was about to respond to Katie's insight, when Matt came running across campus toward them.

Christy smiled at him and said, "Hey, Matt, where have you been all week? This is the first I've seen you."

"Hi, Christy," Matt said quickly. His gaze was fixed on Katie. "Wes just told me you're Katie. Are you?"

A cute, flirty sort of grin lit up Katie's face. The expression wasn't typical for Katie, but it fit her new, softer, more sophisticated image. "That depends," she said. "There's probably more than one Katie on this campus. Which one are you looking for?"

Matt glanced at Christy and then at Katie and said, "I don't know her last name."

"Oh, really?" Katie played this moment for all it was worth. "What do you know about the Katie you're looking for?"

"I'm trying to find the Katie who played in the softball game last Sunday afternoon against Wes Jensen's team."

"That would be me."

"Oh, good. Well, here's the deal. Wes said you were supposed to take Christy's place at their last game, but you sided with Sierra's team and single-handedly beat our team."

Christy hadn't heard all this before.

"We're trying to set up a rematch sometime this weekend," Matt said. "Best two out of three. Sierra said you were going to stay with her team. I'm playing in the rematch, and if we could get you on our team, we'd win for sure. What can I do to convince you to join with Wes and me?"

Katie glanced at Christy. Then, with her dancing green eyes locked on Matt, Katie said, "That depends. How much money do you have?"

Christy wanted to burst out laughing when she saw the look on Matt's face.

"How much were you thinking about?" Matt asked cautiously.

Katie started to laugh. Christy knew that laugh. It was Katie's happiest laugh, the one she used when the two of them had gone searching for the statue of the *Little Mermaid* in Copenhagen last June. It was the laugh she used in Christy's car her first day on the job as a Santa's helper elf, when they tried to hide from Rick, and Katie's pointed ear kept falling off.

"I'm only kidding," Katie said to Matt. "But Todd tells me you know your way around a Volkswagen engine. If you can tell me why the dashboard lights won't turn on in Baby Hummer, I might be persuaded to join you and Wes."

"And what is a Baby Hummer?" Matt asked.

"My car. It's a VW Thing."

"The yellow one?" Matt asked. "That's yours? Hey, I'll check that Baby Hummer out any day. Where did you get it?"

"One of my brothers works at an auto body repair shop."

"Do you know how rare those cars are in Wisconsin? My friend found one on the Internet that he wanted to buy, but he would have had to go to Mexico to get it."

"She's parked out in the side lot. Do you want to meet her after dinner?"

Christy rolled her eyes and pressed her lips together to keep the laughter from bubbling over as she watched her coy friend and bumbling Matthew Kingsley. It appeared the two of them had discovered each other at last.

"I'm going on into The Golden Calf," Christy said. "The line looks like it's growing."

"We might as well wait, then," Matt said to Katie. "Wait to eat, I mean. Why don't you show me your car now?"

Katie took off with Matt. She turned her head just enough for Christy to see the gleeful expression on her face.

Christy shook her head at her wacky friend. Matt hadn't given any indication that he remembered Christy introducing him to Katie a week ago and telling him that Katie was her roommate. Of course, Katie looked different with her new haircut. She was even wearing her "soft" skirt and "pretty" blouse for the second time that week. Apparently, as far as Matt was concerned, this was the first time he had ever seen Katie.

A fresh start for my dearest friend! I love it! And no phone books of unforgiveness for her to lug around.

Christy headed for the salad bar, where she proceeded to make a huge creation out of lettuce, broccoli, cheese, shredded carrots, and raisins all drizzled with ranch dressing. She had missed the variety of fresh California vegetables in Basel.

Spotting Todd at what had become their private table by the window, she walked over to join him. The first thing she said even before she sat down was "It happened!"

"What?"

"Matt discovered Katie, and I had nothing to do with it." She gave Todd the full rundown. He appeared as humored by the story as Christy had been. Digging into his salad of lettuce and peas, he added a forkful of mashed potatoes to the mix. His next bite was one of his chicken strips smothered in honey mustard dip.

"You sure enjoy variety, don't you?" Christy asked.

"Why do you say that?"

"I've been watching you eat this week. You eat a little of everything until it's gone."

"So?"

"I never noticed that about you before." Christy smiled at him. "I'm learning new things about you. I like it. We've never been able to see each other so consistently for so long."

Todd scooped up some more mashed potatoes and dipped them in his puddle of honey mustard.

Christy contentedly ate a few more bites of salad. She wondered if Todd had been noticing this week that she tended to eat just one thing at a time before moving on to the next item.

"Does it bother you that I hopscotch all over my plate?" Todd asked.

"No, not at all. I just mentioned it because I'd never noticed that about you before."

"And it honestly doesn't bother you?"

"No." Christy couldn't read the expression on his face. "Does it bother you that I usually eat everything in order?"

Todd shook his head. Then, with a half grin, he added, "Except that one time when you insisted on eating everything in alphabetical order."

Christy swatted him with her napkin. "I've never done that."

They ate quietly for a minute before Todd said, "I have to confess something to you. I've been nervous ever since our talk in the park last Saturday."

"You? Nervous? Why?"

"I felt like, after you heard about how I grew up, you had enough reasons to turn away and run for your life."

"Todd, I didn't feel that way. I was a little surprised at some of the things you told me, but you can't do anything to change who your parents were or the decisions they made. You're not responsible for their choices."

"I know." Todd's eyes fixed on Christy. He reached over and stroked the side of her face, gazing at her like a boy who had just been told the boogeyman wasn't real. "It doesn't change anything, then? I mean, now that you know what you do, you still want to move forward in our relationship?"

"None of what you told me changes anything. Todd, you are who you are because of what God has done in your life. And you are incredible in so many ways. I love you just as you are."

Everything around Christy seemed to come to a sudden stop. *Did I just say I loved him?*

Todd's steady gaze rested on Christy, waiting for her to continue. He looked neither surprised nor relieved at her slipped-out declaration. He seemed to be waiting.

I said I loved him just as he is. That's different than saying I love him. Isn't it?

Christy felt flustered. She knew her cheeks were turning red. Looking away, she said, "You're wonderful, Todd, just the way you are." Then she took another bite of her salad and chewed the lettuce to a pulp.

The day I tell Todd I love him, it will not be in a noisy cafeteria over chicken strips and salad!

Todd didn't seem at all tortured the way Christy was. He calmly finished his dinner and waited for Christy to finish hers.

In an effort to change subjects, Christy said, "Do you have any plans to go home soon?"

"Home? Do you mean to my dad's in Newport Beach?"

His answer reminded Christy of Todd saying he felt at home with her. He had lived at his dad's beach house for several years, off and on, but that apparently didn't seem like home to him.

"I was thinking I should visit my aunt and uncle one of these weekends," Christy explained. "Let me know if you have any plans to go, and I'll go with you."

"We can go tomorrow, if you want."

Christy didn't really want to; she felt she should. If Todd came with her, Aunt Marti might tell Todd of her plans, and then Christy wouldn't be the only one concerned about her aunt.

"What time would be good for you?" Todd asked.

"I should call my aunt first to make sure they're going to be home."

Todd suggested they use the phone in the cafeteria's lobby. On their way out, they saw Matt and Katie coming in to dinner.

"Guess what?" Katie said. "Matt fixed the lights on Baby Hummer."

"Does that mean you're going to play on his team?" Christy asked.

"I guess it does," Katie said.

"When's the game?" Todd asked.

"Sunday afternoon at three," Matt said. "You want to play?"

Christy noticed that Matt seemed to direct the question to Todd and not to her. That was okay. She had had her moment on the field at the first game. Now that they were recruiting all the "professionals," Christy didn't think she would enjoy playing as much as she had before.

"No," Todd said. "I was wondering if both of you wanted to go to Newport Beach with us tomorrow."

"Sure!" Katie said.

"I've been wanting to go to the beach," Matt said. "I only went twice last spring when I was here. Both times I went by myself, so I didn't know where I was going."

Christy said, "You can't be this close to the beach and not go every chance you get. Todd, you have to take Matt surfing."

Matt's expression lit up. "You have a surfboard?"

"Yep," Todd said. "You want to go surfing tomorrow?"

———

By eight o'clock the next morning, the group was on their way to the closest beach, which was San Clemente. Christy didn't mind that they weren't going to Newport, the beach where her aunt and uncle and Todd's dad lived. She could confront her aunt another time. Today was a perfect autumn day, and she was on her way to the beach with Todd and the gang.

Five cars formed their group. Sierra, her roommate, Vicki, and two other friends rode with Katie in Baby Hummer. Matt followed Todd's van in his truck and took his roommate, Pete, and another guy with him. Todd had Christy and four guys in Gus the Bus with three surfboards strapped to the roof. Wes drove by himself because he had to leave early, and Paul, Sierra's "just good friend," as she called him, was driving up from San Diego.

Todd led the way as they drove over the Ortega Highway with all the windows open and the radio blasting out Christian music from a station Todd had told Christy he now listened to all the time. Christy was using her beach towel for extra padding on the decomposing front passenger seat. That helped to make the hour-long drive more comfortable.

They parked close together and found Paul already there, waiting for them. Christy watched carefully to see how Sierra and Paul greeted each other. She was surprised to see how casual it was, as if he was just one of the guys. But then Christy remembered how casual she had been around Todd the first few years. It was better that way. Their friendship had plenty of time to grow through the ups and downs that would come along.

The group headed to the beach with their arms full of gear. Christy marched beside Todd. "We have a few memories at this beach, don't we?"

Todd nodded. "We broke up on this beach at sunset. How many years ago was that? Three? Or was it only two? That was one of the worst days of my life."

"Mine too," Christy said. "The worst part for me was that we didn't talk to each other the entire drive back to my parents' house."

"The worst part for me was that it forced me to follow through with all my big talk. I kept saying I was going to live in some faraway country, and you made me actually do it."

Christy stopped walking. "You're saying I made you go to Spain?"

"Yes and no. I always thought I wanted to go to Papua New Guinea. I ended up in Spain. But you made me live up to all my big talk. What I really wanted was to stay right here and be with you."

Christy could hardly believe Todd. She dropped her towel and bag in the sand and put her hands on her hips. "You're telling me, after all these years, that you wouldn't have left if I hadn't told you that day we should break up?"

Todd thought a moment before saying, "Probably not. Maybe. It's hard to say."

"Todd, how could we have been so bad at communicating with each other?"

"I'm not saying it should have been any different than it was." He lowered his orange surfboard, which he affectionately had nicknamed "Naranja," into the sand.

"You're saying it's my fault you left because I said we should break up."

"Not at all!" Todd protested. "I'm glad we broke up that day."

"You're glad?"

Katie approached them cautiously. "Sorry to interrupt you guys. But if you're going to fight for a while, could I borrow your board, Todd?"

"Here," he said, practically shoving it at her.

"Sorry, but one more thing. Chris, did you bring any sunscreen?"

Christy thrust her whole beach bag at Katie.

"Thanks. I'll go ahead and take your towel, too," Katie said. "I'll put it over there by mine, and whenever you want to come on over, it'll be waiting for you."

With that, Katie slinked away, leaving Todd and Christy alone by the lifeguard stand, both of them with their hands on their hips.

CHAPTER 9

"Christy," Todd said with an edge to his voice, "you're missing the point of what I'm trying to say. I believe God directed you to break up with me, which prompted me to move forward with my dreams. I don't regret any of it. The time I spent in Spain was life-changing. Then, when God brought you all the way to Spain, and you didn't even know I was there, well, it was the confirmation I needed."

Christy still was fuming. All she could think about were the buckets of tears she had cried over Todd, the months of missing him, never knowing where he was or why he didn't write. She couldn't remember any wonderful changes for her as a result of Todd stepping out of her life.

"What confirmation?" she finally asked.

Todd looked at the waves and let out a deep breath. Then he directed his gaze at Christy. "It confirmed I wasn't supposed to be a full-time missionary to some tropical isle, like I had always thought I should be."

Christy calmed down a notch. She and Todd had talked about this once before. Todd had said then that he had learned a need didn't constitute a call. Just because an opportunity existed on the foreign mission field, that didn't mean God was calling Todd there.

"While I was in Spain I found out I was pretty good at leading a group of younger teens, leading worship, and teaching. I don't know if I would have figured that out if I had stayed here. That's what prompted me to change my major to Bible and to consider going into youth ministry."

Christy folded her arms across her stomach and looked down at her feet. The sand had filled her tennis shoes, and she wished she had taken them off or had worn a pair of sandals. During the short summers in Basel, she had kicked around in a beat-up pair of sandals but hadn't brought the shoes back with her.

"I guess I wouldn't have gone to Switzerland," Christy said slowly. "Since you went to Spain, I started to think beyond what I had expected for my life. I didn't even know if I'd go to college; yet here I am, within view of a Bachelor of Arts degree."

"You know," Todd said, relaxing his stance and moving closer to Christy. "If it were only up to you or me to determine what should happen in our lives, we would have reason to be upset about decisions we made in the past. But God is very much involved. Both you and I have surrendered our lives to Christ and given Him the controls."

"Not that I don't try to take those controls back every now and then." Christy brushed her hair off her face and looked up at Todd. His expression was tender.

"We can only go on from here. We can't change the past."

"I know," Christy agreed. "Instead of saying, 'What if,' we need to say, 'What next?' "

Todd nodded. "And let's be completely honest here. I'm the one who seems to have a pretty clear view of what I think should happen next. You still have doubts or hesitations or something."

Christy was about to protest, but Todd held up his hand as a request for her to wait and let him finish what he was saying. "I want you to know that's okay. You don't have to decide about me or our future or anything until God makes it all clear to you. I'm not going anywhere. I'm right here. And I'm staying here. I'm trusting God that He will make our paths straight. He'll show us the next step to take at the right time."

Christy felt a wonderful peace as Todd spoke. Her anxiety about having to decide if her love for Todd was the kind that could last a lifetime began to float away. Ultimately, the decision wasn't hers to make on her own. God was in control. All she had to do was trust Him and wait. Hadn't Todd said the other day that trust was the most important foundation for any relationship?

"You're right." Christy offered Todd a weak smile. "God was working in our relationship the day we stood on this beach and broke up. And He's working in our relationship now."

"He is," Todd said. "All we have to do is trust Him."

"Thanks for reminding me of that."

A slow grin warmed Todd's previously set face. He was looking at her "that way." Without hesitation he said, "I love you, Kilikina. I will always love you."

Christy leaned forward and stood on her tiptoes to kiss the lips that had showered those beautiful, giving words over her. The kiss was sweet and tender and lasted only a moment.

From their friends who had planted themselves closer to the water, there arose a chorus of cheering and applause as Todd and Christy's kiss ended.

Todd waved casually, then grinned and waved some more. "Our first big argument in public, and we practically get a standing ovation."

Christy grinned at the audience and then looked back at Todd. "I think the applause is over our decision to kiss and make up rather than break up."

"I couldn't agree more," Todd said, then looked toward heaven. "Nice going, Lord," he said. "I can't say I always understand your plan or agree with your methods, but I sure like it when you surprise us with good things."

Christy was used to Todd breaking into prayer at unusual moments. They looked at each other and smiled.

"How about it?" Todd asked. "Are you ready to go in the water?"

"Sure," Christy said.

With that, Todd scooped her up and dashed to the water.

Christy squealed, "Wait! I'll go in by myself. I don't want to get this T-shirt all wet!"

Her cries had no effect on him. Before she could squirm free, both she and Todd were in the water. That seemed to be the cue for the rest of the gang, and within a blink they were all in the salty water, splashing each other and laughing like crazy.

Christy noticed that Matt was particularly enjoying the romp and that Katie was his target for splashing. A glob of seaweed floated near Christy, and she picked it up and heaved it toward the shore. She hated slimy seaweed with its rubberlike tentacles.

"Hey, Christy Miller!" Matt yelled over the roar of the breaking wave. "You still throw like a girl."

Her only response was a big smile. At that moment she felt like a girl. The happiest girl on the face of the earth.

Surely there will be beach days in heaven. And everything will be exactly as it is right here, right now. Except maybe the water will be a little warmer!

The rest of their day was filled with sunshine, laughter, teasing, and soothing ocean breezes. All they needed, in Christy's estimation, was a bonfire at sunset and some marshmallows to roast while they sang. However, Christy and Todd were the only two who had thought to bring warm clothes to change into. They knew how cold it could get on the beach at night. Especially in the fall.

Since everyone else was cold, tired, and hungry, the group packed up and drove to Rancho Corona just in time to make it to the cafeteria for what was left of dinner.

A spirit of camaraderie continued among the beach bunch through the rest of the weekend and into their second week of classes. Todd had more volunteers for helpers with the youth group than he had teens in the group. Many of their beach buddies stopped by the bookstore to see Christy early in the week.

The only negative result of their sandy adventure was that several of them got sunburned and convinced the others that it would be unfair to hold the softball rematch under such conditions. The game was postponed until the following weekend.

Katie zipped about as energetically as ever that week. Christy smiled each time Katie flew into their room and announced she was off to another practice session with Matt at the baseball field.

When Todd walked Christy to class on Wednesday morning, he again quoted the Hawaiian prayer of blessing at the door.

"You were going to tell me what that means," Christy said.

"Meet me at the fountain before you go to work," Todd said. "I'll tell you the whole story."

When they met, so many people were gathered in the plaza that Todd and Christy had to find another place to sit. They ended up on a couch inside the lobby of Dischner Hall, the music building. From down the long corridor came the sounds of someone playing his heart out on one of the pianos in the practice room.

"I never have told you much about when we lived in Maui," Todd began.

Christy gave Todd her full attention. She had the feeling this was going to be one of those important conversations like the one they had at the park before school started.

"Did you know that we lived with my dad's girlfriend, Kapiolani?"

Christy shook her head.

"She was from the islands, and my dad was really in love with her. I called her Lani. She was an amazing woman. I was closer to her than I've ever been to my own mom. She used to make Spam and rice with teriyaki sauce for my friend Kimo and me whenever he came over. That was his favorite."

Christy made a face. "Spam and rice?"

"You should try it. The first time I had it was when Kimo and I put up a tent in the backyard and slept out there." Todd smiled at the memory. "We told each other scary stories about centipedes and the *menehunes*."

"The men of what?"

"The menehunes. They're the imaginary little people of the islands."

"Oh. Like leprechauns?"

Todd nodded and went on with his memory. "Four huge plumeria trees stood in the backyard, and Lani always wore plumerias in her long hair."

Christy smiled. Todd had given her several plumeria leis over the years. She knew he loved the sweetly fragrant white flowers. Now she knew why. She wondered why he had never talked about his dad's girlfriend before.

"You said she used to say a prayer over you before school."

"Oh yeah. Na ka Makua-O-Kalani, e malama mai ia makou.

"That sounds so beautiful," Christy said. "What does it mean?"

"I'm pretty sure it means, 'Let our heavenly Father take care of us all.' It's a sort of blessing or benediction."

"I'd like to learn it," Christy said. "Keep saying it to me every day, and I'll try to repeat it."

They practiced saying it twice before Christy asked, "What happened to Lani? She sounds like a wonderful person. Why didn't your dad marry her?"

Todd grew quiet and smoothed Christy's hair by running his hand from the crown of her head all the way down her back. He did that twice before asking, "You know my surfboard?"

Christy had no idea what his beat-up orange surfboard had to do with this conversation. "Yes, I know your surfboard."

"Lani gave it to me on my tenth birthday."

Christy now understood why it was so thrashed. Before she could add up how old Naranja was, Todd finished his thought.

"She died two months later. Ovarian cancer. We only stayed on the islands a short while after that. My dad couldn't handle it. That's when we moved to Newport Beach. He never fell in love again, at least as far as I know. And he hasn't been back to the islands since then, either."

"But you have," Christy said.

Todd gave Christy a tender smile. "Yes." He leaned closer and whispered in her ear, "I have fallen in love."

Christy felt her face warming. "I meant, you've been back to Hawaii."

"That too." Todd leaned back and rested his elbows on the back of the couch and stretched out his legs in front of him, crossing them at the ankles. "I think the way I've healed up from stuff in the past is by going back and remembering. My dad seems to deal with it by going on. That's why I never talk about any of this, I guess. It's not an open topic with my dad. And of course, I'd never talk about any of this with my mom because she doesn't know any more than that we lived on Maui for a while."

Christy slipped her hand in Todd's. "I like hearing about all this, Todd. I like knowing more about you. You can talk with me about any of this, any time you want. Especially if you want to talk about Lani." Cautiously she added, "Or any other girl."

"She's the only one," Todd said in a calm breath.

Christy smiled. She was realizing that Todd hadn't thoroughly processed his life's journey yet. She suspected that, as he told each part of his story, he could process it because he knew he was safe and at home with the listener. Christy felt honored to be that listener.

Little by little, as the next few weeks unfolded, Todd gave Christy more details of his childhood, telling her aspects of his life he had never told anyone. None of his revelations was as stunning as the first two sessions were, but each bit of information drew Todd and Christy closer together.

Every Monday, Wednesday, and Friday morning they met for breakfast, and Todd walked her to class. He repeated his Hawaiian blessing over her at the door of her classroom. By the end of the second week, Christy had it memorized.

She felt that their heavenly Father was taking care of them. Life was on a straight track now. This was the way it was supposed to be. No surprises.

Each morning Christy tried to wake up early enough to read her Bible and have some quiet time with the Lord. Most mornings she managed. Not all. Every day she diligently made it to class on time, worked her full schedule, ate well, and kept up with her homework.

Those simple, routine acts helped Christy immensely. She felt settled. And that turned out to be more important to her than she had realized it would be.

Katie turned out to be the star of the well-attended Sunday afternoon softball game. She and Matt secured a nine-to-five victory for their team over Sierra's team, and the cheering could be heard halfway across campus.

Matt and Katie seemed to be spending more time together, but Katie refused to comment on how she felt about him. All she would say when Christy asked was, "What's the big rush? Can't people be friends for a while before everyone wants to know if they're dating? Give me a break!" Christy thought the new, improved, low-key approach suited Katie. More than once Christy spotted her roommate gallivanting around campus with other guys and appearing to be enjoying every minute of it.

Todd was full of ideas about what to do with the youth group. On his third Sunday at Riverview Heights, Katie, Matt, and Christy had all accompanied him. Five more students were there than the first week. Todd decided to keep all the students together for the next few weeks instead of breaking them up into classes, since there were so few of them. That meant the pressure was off Christy to decide about teaching Sunday school. She scolded herself for making such an issue of it earlier.

Everything always works out. Why can't I remember that?

At the end of their third week of classes, Todd and Christy strolled hand in hand across campus and headed for the gym, where weekly chapel was held each Friday morning.

Their conversation centered on the youth group camping trip to the desert that Todd had been talking about since Sunday. He had decided it should be the next weekend.

"A week from today?" Christy questioned. "Are you sure you can pull it off in that short time?"

"Sure," Todd said. "What's to pull off?"

"Everything. Do you have tents? Who's going to do the food? What about permission slips? Don't the kids have to have medical release forms signed or something?"

"I'm working on all that."

They entered the gym and went to the same area in which they had sat the last two Fridays with Sierra and some of her friends. Katie was already there.

Christy sat down, thinking about last summer when she had taken off on a camping trip with Todd, Katie, and their friend Antonio in Italy. None of them had done much planning ahead of time, and although the trip wasn't a disaster, it wasn't Christy's favorite experience.

"Todd, this isn't going to be like our camping trip to Italy, is it?"

"That was an awesome trip," Katie said, jumping into the conversation. "What are we talking about? The camping trip with the youth group? Did you decide on a date?"

"Next weekend," Christy said. "And you're right, Italy was an awesome trip. All I'm saying is that it would have been a *really* awesome trip if we had thought to bring a few things with us ahead of time."

"Like what?" Todd asked.

Christy gave him an exasperated look. "Oh, I don't know," she teased. "Like maybe food and sleeping bags."

Katie laughed. "It did get pretty cold, didn't it? Remember when the rain came through the tents, and we all ended up in the van?"

"But you both liked the fresh fish, didn't you?" Todd asked.

Both girls answered him with their piercing stares.

"Okay, okay." Todd held up his hands in surrender. "By any chance, would either of you be interested in helping me work on those minor details?"

"What have you figured out so far?" Christy asked.

"Well," Todd said with a boyish glimmer in his eye, "I have the weekend selected. Next weekend. How's that for a start?"

More people started to join them. Christy knew this conversation needed to be finished later. Her mind began to sort through ideas of what kinds of food would be easy to cook on a camping trip in the desert. When they had camped in Italy, all they had to eat was the fish they caught. Christy wanted to make sure they wouldn't be dependent on the local desert game for their food. Lizard stew didn't sound appealing.

Sierra joined them and sat behind Christy. She leaned over and said, "Did you hear that Randy is going to play for chapel this morning? He started up a new band with some guys in the dorm. Isn't that great?"

Sierra reached over and gently tugged on the ends of Christy's long, straight hair. "How do you get your hair so silky? You have such gorgeous hair, Christy. Trade you."

Christy laughed. "Any day. I love your hair, Sierra. Do you know how impossible it is to get mine to curl? The longer it grows, the straighter it becomes."

"What do you use on it?" Sierra asked. "Shampoo, I mean."

"Whatever is on sale."

Sierra nodded her understanding. "I know exactly what you're saying. Believe me, I am so broke. I didn't want to have to work this first semester, but I think I have to find something. Do you know if they're hiring at the bookstore?"

"I don't think there are any openings, but I'll ask."

"Thanks," Sierra said. Leaning closer and lowering her voice she added, "By the way, I was meaning to tell you, I'm glad things worked out between Katie and you. I was worried that first week of school when she came to our room because she was so upset. She never told me what was wrong, but I guessed it was something between the two of you. I used to get that way with my older sister because we always had to share a room."

Christy was surprised. To Katie's credit, she had kept her conflict with Christy private. Christy admired her friend for that.

"You and Katie are my supreme role models," Sierra went on. "I'm sure you know that. You both are such great examples to me of WOGs."

"Wogs?" Christy asked.

"Women of God," Sierra said. "WOGS. You really care for other people. I don't know if I ever thanked you for being so nice to me when we met in England. You both treated me as an equal, even though I was younger. You made me feel like part of your group, and I've never forgotten that."

Christy smiled at Sierra. She had such an innocent, clear-hearted face. Sierra's blue-gray eyes smiled back at Christy.

Randy and his band started chapel by asking everyone to stand. They played three songs in a row as the students' voices filled the gymnasium. Christy loved it. She closed her eyes and let the voices all around her move from her ears into her heart. She loved hearing Todd's strong, deep voice blend with hers as she sang and worshiped God.

When the third song ended, the silence jolted Christy to open her eyes and sit back down. She wanted to sing some more.

"Makes you eager for heaven, doesn't it?" Todd whispered in her ear. "Can you just imagine what it's going to be like to sing with the multitudes in the courts of heaven? Man!"

Christy slid her hand into Todd's and whispered, "I know!" She looked past Todd and noticed Matt had just come in and was slipping into the open space on the other side of Katie. He looked over at Christy, smiled, and waved.

Christy smiled back.

Glancing at Katie, Christy examined her friend's profile. Katie's face was more complex than Sierra's. Her expression was open and energetic like Sierra's, but Katie had an outdoorsy sort of beauty to her. She was solid, like an oak tree, yet rounded and defined in all the right places. The new haircut framed her face like the curling petals of a rose.

Katie is a woman.

Christy's thought surprised her. This tomboy buddy of hers had blossomed. Had Matt noticed that, as well?

Katie is a WOG. She's a woman, and she's a Woman of God.

Turning her attention to the chapel speaker who now stood at the microphone, Christy thought about how much she loved being at Rancho Corona. She loved sitting beside Todd, singing together, and being surrounded by their friends. It made her think that this camping trip could be close and wonderful, as well.

That evening, in the cafeteria, Todd presented Christy with a list of what he had worked on so far for the camping trip. Two items were written down:

1. Vehicles
2. Tents

"Have you arranged for these things, or is this your list of things to do?" Christy asked.

"To do," Todd said. He showered two scoops of peas over his mound of lettuce and then pressed in the center with the bottom of the salad dressing ladle. After filling the hollow center with blue cheese dressing, he stuck a celery stick in the middle.

"You make the most bizarre salads I've ever seen," Christy said, creating her usual lettuce, broccoli, and carrot salad laced with ranch dressing and dotted with raisins.

"Beauty is in the eye of the beholder," Todd said.

"Like that beautiful tostada you created yesterday at lunch?" Christy teased. "I've never seen anyone put a layer of pickles on his refried beans and then pour peas over the whole thing."

"It was pretty good," Todd said. "I like peas."

"So I've noticed."

They made their way to a table where some of their friends were seated. "Does this mean we should put peas on this to-do list for the camping trip next weekend?" Christy asked.

"Great idea. We could buy one of those ten-pound cans. Write that down on the list. Peas and what else?"

Christy gave Todd a tucked-chin, raised-eyebrow look. "Is this your way of asking me to make up the menu and the shopping list?"

"Hey, I'll help you. We already have peas on the list. Peas go with everything. What else do you think we should put on there?"

If Todd weren't so absolutely adorable, Christy would have slugged him.

CHAPTER 10

By the time Todd and Christy had eaten their fill of Friday-night cafeteria pizza and salad, they had a complete camping menu figured out. Sierra joined them and was able to help calculate amounts because she came from a family of six children. Twelve students and volunteers would go on the trip, Todd estimated.

The equipment list took a little longer to prepare. Christy wished Matt could have been in on this conversation because he had done a lot of camping with his family and would make sure they didn't forget anything. Matt wasn't at dinner, and neither was Katie. Christy thought Katie would have told her if she had plans with Matt, but then the decision to eat together could have been spontaneous, which happened often with Katie.

After dinner, Christy and Todd drove into town to check out the prices on camping equipment at a sporting goods store.

"We could buy some of the stuff we need, like the camp stove," Todd suggested on their way. "Then it would be ours."

"Ours?" Christy asked.

"Yeah, yours, mine, ours. We could use it whenever we go camping."

"I don't have much money right now." Christy wondered, *If Todd's savings are as limited as mine, why would we buy camping gear?* A fleeting vision paraded through her imagination of her and Todd living in a lean-to shelter made of palm fronds on some deserted beach. Their framed college degrees served as a welcome mat. Christy was shooing the sea gulls away from their

112

breakfast while she cooked scrambled eggs on the only material possession she and Todd owned—a gleaming, brand-new camp stove.

"I have some money saved up," Todd said. "We could use it."

That surprised her. "Did you get your first paycheck from the church?"

"No, I've been saving and making a few investments."

Christy waited until after they left the sporting goods store and had stopped for ice cream before she asked the questions that were rolling around in her head. They were seated at a cement patio table outside the small ice cream shop near the movie theater. The evening had cooled after an especially hot afternoon, so Christy had grabbed Todd's navy blue, hooded sweat shirt from the floor of Gus and put it on before they went into the ice-cream store. She felt that if she could help herself to her boyfriend's clothes and help him shop for camping stoves, she had a right to know about his savings and investments.

Todd took a bite of his top scoop of pineapple coconut.

"I never understood how you could chew ice cream," Christy said. She had picked one scoop of caramel fudge swirl and was slowly eating it from a cup with a spoon. "That would give me a headache and a toothache at the same time."

"You still seem to find my eating habits fascinating, don't you? First the salad and now the ice cream." He didn't sound upset. He actually sounded flattered that Christy would notice all these things about him.

"No, but as long as we're talking about some of the more specific, little-known details of your life, you said you have some money saved and that you've been making some investments."

"I've been trying to keep the balance in my checking account low and put everything I can into savings."

Christy wasn't sure what Todd's answer meant. She had been thinking a few days earlier that part of her hesitancy to verbalize her commitment to Todd was because, if he knew she was ready to take the next step, that would launch them into specific conversations about their future. And if they decided to get married right after college, what would they use for money?

If Todd was planning for their future the same way he was planning for the camping trip, they were in big trouble. She could see why she subliminally had avoided taking the next step. If she opened up her heart to getting married only to discover that, to be practical, they would have to wait another five years before Todd could afford to even buy her an engagement ring, she would be frustrated to pieces.

Carefully, Christy asked, "How do you have money left over to put in savings after school bills?"

"My dad's paying for college."

Christy put down her spoon. "I didn't know that. Then why have you been working two jobs like a crazy man for the past year?"

"I've been preparing for the future."

Christy's hopes began to soar. "You have?"

"Of course."

As she let the ice cream melt on her tongue, Christy wondered if this might be one of those areas in which Todd would blow her away with his careful attention to detail. He had shocked her more than once with his perception of life's realities.

"What do you think? Should we go back to buy the camp stove?" Todd asked.

"I guess so," Christy said. "Unless the church has any equipment you could borrow."

"They don't have a camp stove. I checked around. We can use all the pots and pans from the church kitchen, as well as dishes and silverware, if we wash and return everything in perfect condition. But they don't have a camp stove."

Christy noticed a bunch of people coming their way. Apparently the movie had just ended. She expected to see some students from school in the crowd, and she guessed right. Katie and Matt were headed toward them.

"Hey, how's it going?" Todd greeted them.

"That was the worst movie I've ever seen," Katie blurted out.

Matt chuckled.

"What did you see?" Christy asked.

"Something about baseball," Matt said.

"See? We can't even remember the name of it," Katie said. "It sounded like a great idea when Wes suggested it this afternoon, but then he ditched us, and the movie turned out to be a loser."

"Want to go with us to buy a camp stove?" Todd asked.

Christy held back a smile. Todd was so excited about this big purchase. It would be their first purchase together, unless she counted the bookshelf she bought years ago at a garage sale while Todd circled the block in Gus because no parking was available.

"Are you going to Bargain Barn?" Matt asked.

"Bargain Barn?" Todd said. "Where's that?"

"It's a warehouse of all kinds of surplus stuff. They have everything from patio furniture to piñatas. You'll get a good price there, if they have any stoves."

Todd's expression lit up. "Let's go."

"I don't think they're open this late. We could go tomorrow."

"Cool," Todd said. "I wonder if we could buy some of this other stuff on our list for the camping trip." He proceeded to tell Katie and Matt about his big plans for the youth group outing.

"Hey, if you need more help, I'm available," Matt said.

"You counted me in, too, didn't you?" Katie asked. "Baby Hummer loves the desert. I take it you're going to announce all this to the group on Sunday morning."

Todd nodded.

"Kind of short notice," Katie said. "How many do you think will actually go?"

"I'm not sure."

"We planned food for twelve," Christy said.

"Better make it fourteen," Todd said. "I don't think we had Matt and Katie on the list yet."

"What list?" Christy asked.

"The list we need to start with the names of all the people who are going."

Christy looked at Katie and, with a playful oh-brother look, said, "Right now the four of us are the only names on this so-called list."

"That's okay," Todd said. "If we plan it, they will come."

Katie burst out laughing. "I'll be nice and not comment on that one, Todd. But boy, could I."

"What did I say?" Todd asked Christy.

She smiled at her charming, take-the-next-wave-as-it-comes boyfriend and calmly said, "What time should we go to Bargain Barn in the morning?"

———

By eight-thirty the next morning, the chummy foursome was on its way to Bargain Barn in Todd's van. Christy had pulled back her long hair into a braid and wore a blue bandanna she had bought in Switzerland. She took a notebook with her, ready for the role of safari assistant.

Within the first ten minutes at Bargain Barn, they found a perfectly good camp stove still in the box for half the price of the one they had looked at the night before. Christy checked it off the list, and they moved on to tarps, folding camp chairs, and ropes. Everything they needed they found, and everything was a better price than they could get anywhere else. Christy thought Todd would be ready to go after she checked the last needed item off the list.

But Todd was still shopping. He seemed to be on a treasure hunt, going through bins of closeouts and examining shelves of broken and mismatched merchandise. He could think up a use for just about anything they saw. He didn't buy any of it, but he seemed to take great delight in imagining what he would do with the stuff if he did buy it.

Christy wandered off and found a rug for her room. She picked up two and showed Katie. "Do you want one of these?"

"No, I think I've reached my limit with this stuff." Katie showed Christy her three sets of pillowcases still in plastic bags.

"Do you know how old those must be?" Christy asked.

"I know. Aren't they cool? Collectors' items. Look, Winnie the Pooh, Minnie Mouse, and my favorite, the Little Mermaid!"

Christy laughed. "She looks nothing like the statue in Copenhagen."

"She's about the same size," Katie said. "Now I can lay me down to sleep and have sweet dreams of the *Lille Havfrue* anytime I want."

"As long as you wash them first," Christy said.

"Yes, Miss Tidiness. And I'm also getting this." Katie motioned toward a goldfish bowl that Matt was holding for her. "It's only a quarter."

"What are you going to use it for?" Christy asked.

"A fish, of course. We need a pet."

Christy was about to protest, when she saw Todd starting down the plumbing aisle. "Why don't you guys wait in line? I'll grab Todd so we can get out of here." Fortunately, very few of the faucets and sink stoppers prompted creativity in Todd's imagination, and the plumbing aisle was a quick trip.

"You're really enjoying this, aren't you?" Christy asked as they stood in the checkout line.

"I haven't had so much fun in a place like this since I was a kid. When we lived on Maui, an old Salvation Army Thrift Store was between my house and Kam III, the elementary school. Almost every day Kimo and I would stop in there after school and go through all the stuff. It was the best entertainment a kid could have. We read comic books and played with a huge boxful of action figures. The guys there taught me how to fix the stereos and TVs that came in. That's where I bought my first guitar."

Christy liked the way Todd had been opening up and talking more about childhood memories, especially Maui memories.

The cashier announced their total, and Christy pulled her folded-up cash from her pocket and handed it to Todd.

"What's this for?"

"That's my contribution toward the camp stove."

Todd took the money and gave Christy a big bear hug. "We must be serious about each other if we're buying appliances."

Christy enjoyed all the planning for the camping trip that week. Her only regret was that, when it came time to shop for the food on Thursday afternoon, she had to work at the bookstore.

Katie came into the store with something behind her back and pranced up to the register, where Christy was running the afternoon totals.

"Meet Chester," Katie said, holding out a plastic bag with a nervous-looking goldfish darting about in the three inches of water.

"What happened to Rudy?" Christy asked. Katie had insisted they buy a goldfish on their way home from Bargain Barn last Saturday. She had situated the fish in his new, twenty-five-cent fishbowl and had named him Rudy. She talked to him every day and fed him way too much.

"Rudy went to fish heaven this morning," Katie said sadly. "Chester wants to live with us now."

"You better get him in the bowl pretty soon," Christy said. "He looks like he's drowning in that bag."

"Drowning, ha-ha. Very funny."

"Okay, then, he's suffocating."

"I'm on my way back to the room now. I just wanted to find out when you're going shopping for all the food. I'll drive you, if you want."

"Todd has the list," Christy said. "He's at the store right now."

"You let Todd go shopping alone?" Katie asked.

"It's a grocery store, Katie, not a thrift store. He'll do just fine without me."

Katie gave Christy a wary look. "You think so?"

"Yes."

"Love sure messes with a person's logic," Katie said, turning to go. "I'll be leaving now with Chester, and you would do well to consider your boyfriend's shopping skills before it's too late."

Christy soon found out what Katie was warning her about. Friday night the group arrived at the camping area in the Joshua Tree desert, and as they tumbled out of the cars, the entourage consisted of fifteen students; six tents; one brand-new, co-owned camp stove; boxes and boxes of food; and miscellaneous paraphernalia Christy hadn't had a chance to identify. That's when she discovered that Todd had improvised on the menu she had made up.

The air was cold, and a wind snapped at the tents as the group tried to set them up by the light of Coleman lanterns. Christy asked one of the high school girls to help her organize the food. That's when they discovered enough day-old bread and gigantic cans of peanut butter to feed an army for a week. They had eaten at a drive-through hamburger place on the way to the campground, so dinner was taken care of. But Christy had planned for s'mores around the campfire when they arrived.

After quickly surveying the boxes by flashlight, Christy went to find Todd. He was telling two young guys to stay out of the girls' tents. Matt had started a fire, and most of the teens were gathering around it. As soon as Todd sent the two guys to the fire, he gave Christy his full attention.

She tried to be as nice as possible. "Todd, I can't seem to find the marshmallows, chocolate bars, or graham crackers. Do you know where they might be?"

"I forgot to tell you. I had to adjust the menu a little because of my budget. I eliminated the chocolate, graham crackers, and marshmallows because they were too expensive. I got a great deal on turkey hot dogs instead. I thought if they wanted to roast something over the fire, they could roast the hot dogs."

Christy stared at Todd. "You're kidding, right?"

"No, the hot dogs are in the ice chest. They're probably better for these guys than all that sugar anyhow."

"Todd, I saw the hot dogs. They're still frozen."

"So they'll just take a little longer to cook, right?"

"Todd, how are these guys going to cook frozen hot dogs?"

"We have some sticks around here, don't we?"

"Todd, we're in the desert. That's why I put wire coat hangers on the shopping list."

"Oh!" Todd's expression lit up. "*That's* why you put hangers on the list. I couldn't figure out why you wanted hangers. I thought it was to hang up dish towels or something. I bought six plastic hangers. They're in a bag somewhere."

If the situation hadn't been so funny, Christy might have cried. Instead, she laughed.

"What?" Todd said.

"Katie was right. I shouldn't have let you go shopping by yourself."

"I don't think these guys are hungry anyhow. We can just skip the snack and go right to the campfire time. That's the real reason for the trip anyway, isn't it?" Todd brushed Christy's forehead with a kiss and took off with long strides toward the campfire, which was whipping about dangerously in the shrill desert wind. All the students were standing back at least five feet from the fire.

"Watch out for the sparks!" Matt motioned for the teens to step back even farther. "It's too windy to keep this going. We're going to have to put it out."

Even dousing the fire proved to be a challenge. The only water they had brought was in bottles sealed in plastic and shrink-wrapped in cardboard flats. The first three water bottles did little to calm the flames. Matt found a shovel and managed to put it out with scoops of desert dirt.

With the fire out, the night turned very dark, except for the Coleman lanterns near the tents.

"Look at the stars," one of the girls said.

Christy stood shivering, her chin tilted toward the heavens in silent awe of the thousands and thousands of glittering diamonds suspended in space.

"Hey, there's a shooting star!" someone called out.

Everyone joined in with his or her discoveries.

"Isn't that Orion's belt?"

"Can anyone see the Big Dipper?"

"What is that bright, blinking star over there?"

"That's an airplane."

"No, it's not. It's a satellite."

"Where's the moon?"

Todd quoted several verses that Christy recognized from Psalm 8. " 'When I look up into the night skies and see the work of your fingers—the moon and the stars you have made—I cannot understand how you can bother with mere puny man, to pay any attention to him! And yet you have made him only a littler lower than the angels and placed a crown of glory and honor upon his head.' "

Christy was so absorbed in the canopy of wonder that she didn't notice Matt when he slid over next to her. "What was it you told me when we were watching the fireworks back in Wisconsin that summer?" he asked her. "Something about the one who rides across the ancient heavens. Your friend was writing a song about it, wasn't he?"

"I'm surprised you remembered that," Christy said.

"Did he ever finish the song?"

"Yes, it's from Psalm 68." Christy began to sing Doug's song softly.

" 'Sing to the One
Who rides across the ancient heavens
His mighty voice thundering from the sky
For God is awesome in His sanctuary.' "

Katie joined her and so did Todd. When they finished singing, one of the girls said, "Sing it again." This time, as they sang, several of the teens joined them. It seemed like a wonderful, holy moment until Christy noticed several of the guys slipping away from the rest of the group. She tapped Matt's shoulder and pointed. He took off after them.

It turned out to be that kind of night. The group ended their impromptu song time when several of the girls declared they were too cold and made a dash for their tent. Then the girls tried to sabotage the inside of the guys' tent. Matt caught them, and Todd gave the group stern instructions about how he expected them to act. Stern for Todd, at least. It didn't turn out to be stern enough for two of the younger guys, who tried to sneak out again after everyone was supposed to be zipped up in the tents.

Todd was helping Christy cover the boxes of food with a tarp to keep out sand and desert critters, when the guys tried to escape. Todd turned his flashlight on them, and they slipped back into their tent.

Christy had a hard time falling asleep. She was warm enough because she had made sure she wore sufficient layers of clothes, and she had a decent air mattress under her sleeping bag. But she kept listening for the sound of a tent zipper and wondered if Todd was going to have to sit up all night on guard duty.

The morning sun rousted all of them as soon as it appeared because the penetrating heat immediately warmed the tents. Christy hadn't spent much time in the desert and was surprised at how far she could see when she looked out across the sand. Aside from an occasional cactus lifting its two arms, as if frozen in time like an Old West bank teller in a holdup, she could see nothing for miles in any direction.

The air warmed quickly, and Christy felt her skin drying and tightening. The wind was gone this morning. Her extra layers of clothes quickly became too hot, and she peeled down to a T-shirt and shorts.

"I'm impressed," Katie told Christy after they had fed the group and were putting away what was left of the cereal and milk.

"Impressed with what?" Christy asked.

"You. Look how happy and organized you are. This is a big improvement over our camping trip last summer."

"You said the key word," Todd said, reaching into the back of Matt's truck for his guitar. "Organized. Christy likes being prepared."

"Yeah, well, she could teach you a thing or two," Katie said. "What about that shade you promised?"

"Matt is working on it with the tarps over behind the biggest tent. We're going to sing and have our morning devotions, and then we're going to take the dune buggies out for a spin."

Christy finished cleaning up and joined the others. Her favorite part of any camping trip was the chance to sing with the group. It turned out to be a short string of songs because it was getting so hot, and only a few of the kids were singing.

As Todd taught, holding his Bible open and standing before the group, Christy glanced at the teens. A few of them really were listening. Mostly the girls.

These guys don't know what a gift Todd is to them. He really cares about them. He'll be their friend for the rest of their lives, if they'll let him. And what he's telling them right now is the truth. They do need to trust God in every area of their lives. Why aren't they soaking up his words? It could mean the difference between life and death for some of these guys!

Christy decided to pray. She had been doing that a lot lately. Ever since that first Sunday morning when Gus broke down on the way to church, she realized they were fighting a battle with invisible enemies for these teens' souls. As she felt the sun pouring over her right shoulder and burning her forearm, Christy adjusted her position so the sun was to her back and kept on praying for Todd.

"Let me leave you with this thought," Todd said in conclusion. "None of us knows when his life will come to an end, and he will stand before Almighty God. The Bible says that to be absent from the body is to be present with the Lord. Each of us will stand before God one day. Not Saint

Peter at a golden gate. Not in front of a clerk at a desk like you see on TV. We will stand before the Lord."

Christy began to look around the circle and prayed for each student, even though she didn't remember all their names.

"The Lord Jesus Christ will hold out His hands to you, and you will see the scars that are still there two thousand years after He died in your place. He will say to you, 'Come on in. I've been waiting for you, my friend. The relationship we started when you were on earth can now be made complete here in my home.' Or He will say, 'I invited you to come to me, but your whole life you pushed me away. Now it's too late. You didn't want me so now you will spend eternity separated from me.' "

Christy noticed how quiet the group had become. All eyes were on Todd.

"What's it going to take for you to come to Him? Don't wait. Nobody knows when he will die. And once it's over, it's just begun. Either you'll spend eternity with Christ in heaven or eternity without Him in the place He made for the demons, those fallen angels who turned from Him."

Todd paused a moment, then added, "What's it going to be for you? Heaven is a very real place. And so is hell."

The two troublemaking guys snickered, but everyone else sat still. Todd closed the time in prayer. Instead of saying "Let it be so" at the end, he concluded the prayer in a way Christy had never heard before. "As you wish," Todd said. The group wasn't sure the prayer was over yet.

Once they figured out that they were done, the teens took off for the recreation vehicles and spent the rest of the day doing what Katie called "frolicking." They took turns going out into the desert flatness in the various vehicles Todd had arranged for the trip.

Christy stayed at the camp, and close to noon, she talked two of the girls who were there into helping her to make peanut butter sandwiches so the food would be ready for whoever wanted them after the runs in the sand.

The dry heat dried the sandwiches so quickly that all the bread was as stiff as toast within minutes after the peanut butter and grape jelly were spread on them. Christy tried stuffing the sandwiches back into the plastic bags as soon as they were made, and that seemed to help. The good thing was that Todd had bought so much bread and so much peanut butter that even if they had to toss out the entire first batch of sandwiches, Christy knew no one in the group would go hungry this day.

Around four o'clock, when the wind was returning and the blazing heat had subsided, Todd drove into camp in one of the vehicles, saying he needed to take the can of gas out to Katie, who was stranded in Baby Hummer. "Do you want to go with me?"

"Sure," Christy said. For a moment, she was reminded of when she and Todd had taken Aunt Marti for a boat ride, and they had run out of gas. A darling girl on a Jet Ski had come to their rescue. Christy had always wished she were the girl on the Jet Ski instead of being the one who was stuck in the stalled boat with her aggravated aunt.

Christy wondered what was happening with Bob and Marti. She had mentally pushed away their situation, but as soon as she thought about it again, she felt a sickening heaviness. If she couldn't talk to anyone else about Marti's decision, then Christy needed to talk to her aunt, and the sooner the better. She decided she would call her aunt right after the camping trip. What Christy would say was another matter, but at least she would open up the subject again.

Todd fastened the gas can with bungee cords to the back of the two-seater dune buggy and told Christy to buckle up. Then with a jerk and a roar, they took off across the sand. Christy held on tight to the side of the roll bar and clenched her teeth to keep from biting her tongue. Every bone in her body felt as if it was being jolted and jarred beyond anything any of them had experienced before. She turned to Todd and smiled, her teeth still clenched.

He shifted gears and roared on.

Talking to him was impossible. It was far too noisy. Understanding him might be another impossibility.

What does he see in this? It's kind of fun, but it's mostly uncomfortable.

They arrived at the spot where Katie was waiting with two of the girls in Baby Hummer. They were laughing about something when Todd cut the engine and it became quiet enough to hear.

Katie came over and gave Christy a friendly punch in the arm. "Isn't this fun? I love it." Katie's face was red from sunburn or windburn or both.

Her long-sleeved T-shirt was streaked with dirt. Only a few flyaway wisps of her short hair had dared to peek out from under her baseball cap.

"Have you driven this thing yet?" Katie asked.

Christy shook her head.

"You want to drive Baby Hummer?"

"No, that's okay."

"You're good to go," Todd said, strapping the empty can to the back of the dune buggy.

"Great," Katie said. "Thanks for bringing the gas to us." She turned to settle back into Baby Hummer's front seat but then turned to Todd and said, "Make sure Christy drives that buggy."

"You want to drive?" Todd asked Christy.

"No, that's okay."

"You sure?" His expression was classic Todd as he stood there, eyebrows slightly raised, dimple showing on the right side of his cheek. Christy was flooded with memories of other times he had given her that look, and she always had tried whatever he was willing to teach her, from surfing on a body board to water-skiing. The only time he had given her that look and she had turned him down was when he had asked her to go "to the ends of the earth" last summer to the Arctic Circle. Todd had gone on the train alone while Christy and Katie traveled to Copenhagen. More than once she had regretted missing the experience of seeing a polar bear with Todd.

"You know what?" Christy said. "Why not? Tell me what to do." She didn't know why her heart was beating so fast. She trusted Todd enough to take this chance with him, and she felt as if she was ready for anything.

CHAPTER 11

Todd hustled around to the passenger side of the dune buggy and belted himself in while Christy settled into the driver's seat. He gave her a quick run-through of the gears and the way the clutch tended to stick. Katie had taken off in Baby Hummer, so the desert was silent when Christy turned the key to start the deep, rumbling engine. She stalled it three times. Todd patiently explained what to do, and on the fourth try, they took off, jostling their way back toward camp.

"Okay, now!" Todd yelled. "Next gear."

Christy shifted, gave it gas, and shifted again. A bubbling sense of delight started in her gut as she pressed her foot to the gas. The delight surfaced in a burst of laughter as they bounced over the ruts in the sand and plowed across the Mojave Desert. She hadn't driven with Todd beside her since the bridge in Hana.

"This is fun!" she yelled, giving the vehicle more gas and becoming braver with her steering. She glanced at Todd. His smile spread from one side of his face to the other. It looked like he was laughing, but she couldn't hear him.

With a variety of twists and turns, Christy invented her own trail back to camp. A guy from their group roared past them in a one-person vehicle, with Matt following him in another one-seater. Christy tried to wave. When she took her hand off the steering wheel, she hit a rut and stalled the engine. Suddenly silence prevailed. Christy turned to Todd, who was still grinning, and then she burst out laughing, throwing her head back and bumping it on the roll bar.

"Ouch!" she hollered, rubbing her head and trying to blink back the tears that sprang to her eyes.

"You okay?" Todd asked. He sounded so compassionate.

"I bumped my head." Christy laughed at her klutziness.

Todd reached over and rubbed the tender spot.

"Ow!"

"Do you want to keep driving?" he asked.

"Maybe you better in case I have a delayed concussion," Christy said.

Todd looked at her skeptically.

She laughed again and said, "I'm only kidding!" She grinned at him, and when she did, she met his screaming, silver-blue-eyed gaze. He was looking at her "that way" again.

In one lightning-bolt second, a life-changing thought seared into Christy's thoughts. *He's the one!*

Christy could barely breathe. *Todd, you are the one for me.*

She felt as if the whole world had stopped twirling, and she and Todd were the only two people on the face of the earth. *You are the one for me. And I'm the one for you, aren't I? This is it! My grandma was right. I know! I really, truly know!*

Todd climbed out of the vehicle to change places with her. Christy felt as if everything was in slow motion as she got out. They met at the back of the dune buggy, where Todd grabbed her by the shoulders and brushed her cheek with a kiss before dashing around to take his place in the driver's seat.

Christy stood still. She knew something strange and wonderful had happened in her heart. She never would have expected it to happen now, in a place like this. But she knew this was the mysterious "it" she had waited for. She had to tell Todd she was in love with him.

No, she needed to tell Todd that she was more than in love with him. She had to tell him that she loved him. Truly loved him. And she gladly would commit to loving him for the rest of her life. No matter where they lived, or what they did, or how their lives turned out, Christy knew—absolutely knew, without a shadow of a doubt—that she wanted to be Todd's companion, friend, wife, and the mother of his children for as long as they both shall live.

Christy felt her heart pounding up to her throat as she watched him fasten his seat belt. His back was to her, but Christy knew she couldn't wait another minute to make her declaration, her commitment known. "Todd!" she called out.

He had just turned the key in the ignition, and the rumbling engine's noise drowned out Christy's voice.

"I love you!" she yelled.

Todd couldn't hear her.

Christy smiled to herself. *This is so ironic.* She went around to the passenger's seat, settled in, and buckled her seat belt. Todd punched the engine into gear.

It's enough that I know for sure right now. I'll wait until a more romantic time and place to tell him. And when I tell him, he will hear me all the way to the very core of his heart.

With a lion-sized roar, they took off across the desert.

Christy watched for a second opportunity to make her declaration known to Todd. As she was fixing the evening meal, she let her giddy imagination examine every possible way she could communicate with him. One crazy idea was to write the words on paper towels with the mustard bottle and hang the message inside Gus from the plastic hangers. But someone else might see it, and this was just between her and Todd.

More important, Christy decided as she lay awake in her tent that night, when she told Todd she loved him, she needed to tell him with her voice. He needed to hear the words, not just to read them.

Sunday morning was cooler than Saturday because a thin layer of clouds had drawn themselves over the sky like a sheer mosquito netting gathered over a bed in the tropics. And like a weary safari assistant tucked safely under that mosquito netting, Christy didn't want to get up. She ached, was tired, and dearly wished she could stand under a warm shower to revive herself slowly.

A shower came, but it wasn't warm. Great drops of rain splashed on the group gathered for morning worship. The sprinkling lasted only a moment.

Then the sun shone through and instantly dried everything. Christy looked at her arm. It was as if the rain's objective was to turn the dirt on her skin into mud and then to send the sun to bake the mud on permanently.

None of them had to be coaxed to tear down the tents and clean up. Matt joined Christy as she tried to yank two tent poles apart.

"Let me try," he said. With a twist, he had them separated.

"Thanks," Christy said. "It's as if the dirt turned to glue when the rain hit it. Can you give that pole over there a try?"

Matt succeeded to divide that pole, as well. He came back over to Christy, looking as if he was checking to see if anyone was close enough to hear them. "Can I talk to you a minute?"

"Sure." Christy kept working on tearing down the tent.

"Over here." Matt motioned for her to follow him to the back of his truck. "I know this may sound like we're back in elementary school, but I have to ask you something." He kept his voice low. "Do you think Katie is, you know, interested in me?"

Christy felt funny talking to Matt about this. "I think you should talk to her about that," Christy answered. "I mean, I thought you and Katie were getting pretty close. You two have been together a lot." The truth was, she didn't know. But she didn't want to tell Matt that.

Matt looked hard at Christy. As he did, his eyebrows pushed inward. "Does it look like we're together? Because I didn't mean to give that impression to her or anyone else."

Christy felt sorry for her best friend. Had Matt been leading Katie on? Was Katie expecting the relationship to be more than it was?

"You and Katie just need to find a time and place to talk privately about all this." Christy lightly touched Matt's arm.

Just then one of the high school girls stepped over toward them, oblivious to the privacy of their conversation. She asked Matt if he could come help her with the tent.

Christy looked over her shoulder toward the main camping area and saw that Katie was watching them.

"Thanks for the advice." Matt placed his hand on Christy's shoulder and gave her a big smile. "I appreciate you, Christy."

That evening, after the group returned to the church and began to unpack the gear, Katie asked Christy, "So what were you and Matt talking about this afternoon?"

Christy knew anyone could easily overhear their conversation, so she said, "I'll tell you later."

————

They didn't reach their dorm room until almost eleven-thirty, and Christy was exhausted. She gathered her shampoo and soap to indulge in the long-awaited shower. But before she could leave the room, Katie said, "Oh, Chester, you poor little thing. Look, Christy, Chester went belly up, too."

"Did you feed him too much?"

"I don't think I fed him enough. Or maybe the bowl got too much direct sun from the window. The water feels pretty warm." Katie scooped up the lifeless creature and followed Christy to the rest room to conduct what she called "burial at sea."

"I'll buy two goldfish tomorrow," Katie said. "I think Chester died of loneliness since we were gone all weekend."

"Katie, you're going to end up spending so much money on goldfish. If you're buying more than two, you're better off with an aquarium instead of that small bowl."

"*Now* you tell me all this." Katie placed her hand over her heart and had a personal moment of silence before sending Chester to the "Great Goldfish Pond Beyond the Sewer."

Christy shook her head and entered the shower, where the warm water felt heavenly.

Katie stood outside the shower stall and said, "So are you going to tell me what Matt said to you this afternoon? Or do I have to figure it out for myself by trial and error, as well?"

Christy had hoped for five minutes of privacy and silence under the shower. She had dreams of Todd to tend to. However, she knew Katie wouldn't leave her in peace until Christy answered her every question.

"I think I'll take a shower while I'm here, too." Katie's voice was now coming from the shower stall next to Christy's. Katie raised her voice over the rush of water from both showers. "Let me borrow your shampoo. And do you have any soap over there?"

Christy handed Katie her soap and shampoo and finished her shower in much shorter time than she had planned. "I'm going back to the room," she said.

"Don't fall asleep," Katie warned. "I'll be right there."

Changing into her favorite pajamas, Christy brushed and dried her hair. Katie returned and got ready for bed, as well, but the dryer's noise made it impossible for them to talk. So Christy was tucked in her bed before she divulged her information to Katie.

"Matt and I talked about you," Christy said.

"Me? What did he say?"

"I told him he needed to talk to you."

"And what did he say to that?"

Christy paused. "Katie, do you like Matt a lot?"

Katie's expression became pinched. "No," she said slowly. "I know you probably can't believe this, after the way I made such a dramatic scene out of seeing him again this year. But now that I've had a chance to get to know him, I don't think there's anything between us."

"You don't?" Christy hadn't expected that response.

"I know, I know. I was so flipped out about him, but I was never so wrong about anything in my life. I think Matt is a great guy and a good friend. I just don't feel anything more for him." Katie roughed up her short hair with a bath towel and let the feathery ends fall where they may.

"I think the image of him was what I had the crush on, you know?" Katie said. "The safe, friendly boy next door who loves baseball and apple pie and eventually would decide he loved me." Katie came over and settled herself on the end of Christy's bed. "Tell me he doesn't have a big crush on me."

The words popped out of Christy's mouth. "Matthew Kingsley does not have a big crush on you."

Katie snapped to an upright position and looked hurt. "He doesn't?"

Christy wished she had been less direct. Slowly shaking her head, Christy said, "He told me he's only interested in you as a friend. I'm sorry."

"Why do you keep apologizing for stuff that isn't your fault? This is good, actually," Katie said. "I was afraid he was going to ask me to spend more time with him, and I was trying to figure out how to turn him down nicely."

"Then I guess it's a good thing," Christy said. "You two can keep being friends, and the three of us can keep helping Todd with the youth group. You and Matt can skip that whole 'Are we a couple?' phase of your friendship." Feeling as if the matter was sufficiently settled, Christy dove under her covers.

Katie wasn't about to let the subject end there. "What about you?"

"What about me?"

"What's happening with you and Todd?"

"We're in love," Christy said brightly. "My heart is completely settled. I love him. And I told him."

"You did?" Katie's eyes grew wide.

"But Todd couldn't hear me because the noise from the dune buggy was so loud." Christy chuckled at herself. "Typical, huh?"

"So Todd doesn't know," Katie surmised.

"Not yet."

"Christy, how can you do that to the poor guy? Go call him right now and let him hear you say you love him. He's been waiting long enough."

"It's the middle of the night!" Christy protested. "I don't want to tell him over the phone. I want to say it to his face so he can see I mean it."

"Hey! That's like that line from the John Donne poem." Katie sprang over to her desk and lifted the literature textbook she had been reading before they left for the camping trip. "Have you read this section yet on John Donne?"

"Yes." Christy and Katie were taking the lit class together.

"Did you read this one? Listen. This is from the poem called 'The Good Morrow.' "

> "My face in thine eye, thine in mine appears,
> And true plain hearts do in the faces rest;
> Where can we find two better hemispheres,
> Without sharp North, without declining West?"

Katie looked up from the book with a glow on her face. "Isn't that romantic?"

Christy loved poetry and usually was the one to present Katie with lyrical gems. She wasn't sure what this one meant.

"That's you and Todd," Katie said. "You are two true plain hearts. You balance each other perfectly with your differences. You round each other out."

Christy smiled. Her heart felt full. She knew all over again that she was in love. Forever-after kind of love.

"Do me a personal favor," Katie said. "If you won't call Todd tonight, call him first thing in the morning, okay?"

"I'll see him at breakfast."

"Then you better tell him at breakfast. I don't think the actual setting is going to matter to Todd when his 'face in thine eye and thine in his appears.' You don't need to wait for the perfect romantic setting with the sun shining and the birds singing and all that. You just need to tell Todd that you love him." Katie pointed to the title of the John Donne poem and with a twinkle in her eye said, "Tell him on the 'Good Morrow.'"

Monday morning Christy waited for Todd at their usual table in the cafeteria. When he didn't show, she guessed he had slept in after the exhausting weekend. She wished she didn't have an early class so she could have done the same.

Hurrying so she wouldn't be late to class, Christy settled into her seat just as Dr. Mitchell was discussing blessings. He read Deuteronomy 28:2, which Christy turned to and underlined in her Bible. "And all these blessings shall come upon you and overtake you, if you will obey the voice of the Lord your God."

I want always to obey you, Christy silently prayed. *Let me hear your voice clearly. I want to always do what you direct me to do.*

Very softly, very clearly, as soon as she finished her prayer, Christy felt compelled to find Todd and to give him her words, her heart, her blessing. But she stayed in her seat, logically evaluating that she should wait. She was paying for this class. She was here. She shouldn't leave.

I mean, really, God. It doesn't make sense that you would want me to ditch class to find Todd and tell him I love him.

Christy ignored the promptings she was feeling and stayed in her seat. The longer she sat still, the more her heart pounded. It seemed to be pounding so fiercely that Christy thought for sure the people around her could hear it. She thought of how Sierra had said a few weeks ago that love isn't always planned and logical.

Compelled by something stronger than her logic, Christy finally clutched her backpack and exited as quietly as she could. As soon as she was outside the air-conditioned building, she felt she could breathe again.

Now what? What next, Father?

Christy suddenly felt foolish. Her declaration to Todd could wait at least until that afternoon. She was missing important information in class. Besides, she had no idea where Todd was. If he wasn't asleep in his room, she could search the campus all morning and still not find him.

This is crazy!

Christy hiked all the way to West Hall, the guys' dorm, and called Todd's room. His voice mail answered, just as she had expected. He might still be asleep. Or he could be in The Golden Calf. Or in the library or a dozen other places on campus.

Trudging back toward class, Christy realized she only had twenty minutes before her next class started. Todd knew she worked in the bookstore that afternoon; he would probably come see her there. She could stand with him at the end of the row of used theology books because that part of the store smelled more "bookish" than any other spot. There she would look into his eyes and make her heart's declaration known in hushed whispers that would sink all the way to the bottom of his heart. All the way down to that place where he dove for treasure. A smile played across her lips, just imagining the romance of that moment.

Christy passed The Java Jungle and went inside, just in case Todd was there. She didn't see him, but she saw another couple sitting close and studying together in one of the booths.

Something continued to push Christy to find her beloved, but she fought against it. The reasonable thing to do would be to check her mailbox and then go to her next class.

But her heart wouldn't stop pounding. Picking up her pace, Christy dashed through the student center. She slipped into the cafeteria. He wasn't there.

She checked out all the places they usually went to talk: the couch in the music building, the library, the chapel. She now was late for her second class, but she didn't care.

As fast as she could trot, she hurried to West Hall and called his room again on the phone in the lobby. Once again she got his voice mail, but this time she left a message. "Todd, I have to see you right away. Where are you?"

Hurrying back to the student center, Christy walked through the building twice, scanning each face, begging Todd to be there. He wasn't. She finally went to the central plaza and sat on the edge of the fountain.

Where is he? Where could he be?

Kicking off her shoes and dipping her toes into the water, Christy remembered, for some reason, a portion of the Song of Solomon she had read last summer after Todd had gone back to California and she was still in Basel. Three or four times in that short book, located in the very heart of the Bible, Christy had underlined the repeated phrase, "Do not arouse or awaken love until it so desires."

That phrase had become her counsel to herself whenever she thought of Todd. They were so far apart that she knew it was useless to stir up or awaken those deep feelings within her or to dwell on them because she couldn't do anything about them. She had taken everything in stride, sending Todd emails and praying for him regularly. During this past month they had been together, Christy felt she still had done a good job of controlling her feelings and letting everything between her and Todd unfold calmly and naturally. But now it seemed love had indeed been stirred up and awakened inside her. She could barely think straight.

Did God literally have to knock me over the head to get me to release my true feelings for Todd?

Christy splashed her toes in the cool water. She felt like the woman in the Song of Solomon who ran around the town seeking her beloved but couldn't find him. She remembered something about the woman crying out to her friends, the Daughters of Jerusalem, and telling them that she was "sick with love."

I don't know if I'm sick yet, but I'm feeling something. I don't know what this feeling is.

Christy held her stomach and pulled her wet toes from the water, letting them air dry. Inside she ached. *Todd, where are you?*

Matt and several other guys she knew called out to her as they passed through the plaza.

"Matt," Christy cried out, "have you seen Todd?"

He left the others and came over to the fountain. "I haven't seen him since yesterday. I think he was going to return the tents this morning to whoever let us borrow them."

"Oh," Christy said, feeling herself calm down. "That makes sense. Thanks, Matt."

"Are you okay?" He sat beside her. "You look a little spooked."

"I've been trying to find Todd. I need to talk to him."

"Seems to be a lot of that going around," Matt said. "I thought about what you said at the camping trip yesterday, and you're right. I do need to talk to Katie before any misunderstandings start up between us."

Christy was about to say something general to Matt about how he didn't have to worry, but she noticed Katie pulling into a no-parking area in the lot and jumping out of Baby Hummer.

"It looks like you may have your chance soon enough." Christy waved to get Katie's attention.

Katie broke into a run as she came toward Matt and Christy.

"Is it my imagination," Matt said, "or does she look like she's about to strangle someone?"

Christy jumped to her feet. She had never seen Katie look like that before. "What's wrong?" Christy called out.

Katie rushed to Christy and grabbed her by the shoulders. Katie's skin was gray and perspiration poured from her face.

"What's wrong?" Matt was beside her now, too.

Katie gulped air. "Gus!" she spouted. "There's been an accident! Come on!" Katie grabbed Christy's arm, and the two of them ran to the parking lot. Matt was right behind them as they jumped into Baby Hummer.

"Katie," Matt said firmly, "what kind of accident? What did you see?"

"I saw them putting Todd in an ambulance."

CHAPTER 12

Christy and Matt pelted Katie with questions and yelled at her to slow down as they zoomed through town to the first freeway on-ramp. Katie said she didn't know much more than the half dozen words she had already offered them. She had been driving back to school from the nursery where she had gone to buy some fertilizer for her herbs. When she had moved into the slow lane to take the off-ramp to Rancho, she saw a vehicle that looked like Gus the Bus smashed up. As she drove by, she saw the paramedics wheeling someone into the ambulance.

"Was he moving?" Christy's fingers gouged into the passenger's seat.

"I couldn't tell. I just saw someone with blond hair being rolled on the gurney into the ambulance." Katie started to cry. "I'm going right to the hospital."

Christy's heart pounded fiercely as they entered the freeway. She heard herself say, "Calm down, Katie. Maybe it wasn't Todd. Maybe it was a VW bus that just looked like Gus. Maybe . . ."

But then she saw the tow truck on the other side of the freeway and the smashed wreckage. Christy knew it was Gus. "Katie!" She covered her mouth in terror. "Katie, look!"

"Try to stay calm," Matt said firmly as Katie kept the steering wheel steady. "The hospital is about five more exits down."

"That stupid, stupid, stupid van!" Christy yelled. "Why didn't Todd trash that piece of junk years ago?" She closed her eyes and tried to swallow gulps of air.

"Pray!" Katie commanded. "Pray, you guys!"

Christy grabbed the seat cushion with both hands and squeezed with all her might as Matt began to pray aloud. Some of the terror siphoned from her shaking body. By the time Katie peeled into a parking space by the hospital's emergency entrance, Christy was trembling all over. She jumped out of the car and ran with Katie and Matt to the emergency room's desk.

Katie spoke first, articulating fairly well that they were checking to see if Todd Spencer had just been admitted after an auto accident.

The attendant went to check and left Christy and Katie holding each other and trembling.

"Yes," the attendant said as she came back around to the counter. "Todd Spencer is here."

"Is he . . ." Christy couldn't finish her sentence. She felt as if she might black out.

"How is he?" Katie kept a strong-armed grip around Christy's shoulders.

"I can't say." The clerk sat down and handed Christy a clipboard. "If you'd like to sign in, I'll have a doctor speak with you as soon as possible. You'll have to wait over there."

Christy had watched emergency-room shows on television, and somehow in her frantic state, she thought she should be allowed to go in, the way the television camera went behind the closed doors and did a close-up of the patient's face. She wanted to hear the assessment immediately. She wanted to help them save his life.

"Come on," Matt said. "We'll wait over here." He directed Christy and Katie to the waiting area. The three of them sat on an empty couch in the corner. None of them spoke.

Christy felt her head throbbing as she closed her eyes and saw the sight of Gus all over again. The roof had been smashed down, the sides bashed in, and glass was everywhere.

Don't take him to heaven, God! Please, not yet! Let me at least tell him I love him. He hasn't heard me say it yet. Let me at least tell him. She dissolved into a puddle of choking tears.

Katie braced Christy with her arm and kept murmuring, "Hold on. Keep praying. Keep praying."

Both of them managed to calm down. Christy realized for the first time that other people were in the waiting room, and she felt self-conscious about them watching her. Matt had gone to the edge of the waiting room and nervously paced, watching for the doctor. Christy turned to stare out the window at the parking lot, not saying anything. Her silent prayers became more coherent. God was with her. She knew that. She could feel His peace calming her.

"We should call his dad," Christy said. She knew Todd's phone number in Newport Beach by heart. She rose to find a phone. No one followed her, and she was glad because, for some reason, she thought she would be stronger if she was by herself. As she took each step toward the phone, she felt as if Jesus was walking right beside her.

The answering machine picked up the call, and Christy tried to calmly leave the appropriate information for Todd's dad. Her hand was shaking, and her voice quivered so much that she didn't know if she said everything correctly. If nothing else, his dad knew where they were.

Christy then called her parents. Her mom answered, and as soon as Christy heard her mom's voice, she cried again.

Matt had come over to the phone area. He placed his hand on Christy's shoulder and softly said, "Would you like me to talk to her?"

Christy nodded. The tears had drowned out her voice. Matt explained to Christy's mom that they were at the hospital waiting to hear from the doctor.

Christy could hear her mom's stunned voice through the receiver when she asked Matt, "Is Todd still alive?" For the first time Christy allowed the thought of his being dead to fully enter her mind. She backed up to the wall and pressed herself flat against it.

"We don't know yet," Christy heard Matt tell her mom. Then he said, "Yes, I think it would be good if you could come." He gave the name of the hospital and then hung up the phone.

"Is there anyone else we should call?" Matt asked.

"Uncle Bob," Christy said in a small voice. "Uncle Bob would want to be here." She dialed the number for Matt and let him relay all the information.

"Do you want to go back to the waiting room?" Matt asked.

Christy didn't answer him because she saw a doctor in a white coat heading in that direction. She hurried to catch up with him and asked if he had been taking care of Todd.

The doctor asked if they were friends or relatives.

"Friends," Christy and Matt said in unison.

"We called his dad," Christy said. "He wasn't there, but we left a message for him to come to the hospital."

"I see." The doctor looked at Matt and then at Christy. "I can tell you this. It's a miracle that he's alive."

Christy reached for Matt's hand and squeezed it with all her might.

"The paramedics said they had never seen anyone come out of such an accident alive. Apparently the van rolled three times. The roof and the driver's door and the whole front end were smashed, they said."

"Yes," Christy said nervously. "I saw the van. But how is Todd?"

The doctor looked over the top of his glasses at Christy. "We've moved him upstairs to surgery. My guess is it will be several hours before we can give a thorough assessment. Until then, if you or anyone else you know can donate blood, it looks like he's going to need it. I'll let you know when we learn more."

"Thank you," Christy said. She realized how tightly she had been squeezing Matt's hand. She let it go. "We better tell Katie."

The next two and a half hours floated past Christy in a haze. She found out from the nurse that Todd had type A blood. Christy also had type A, and so did Matt. Katie phoned a bunch of students at Rancho. Sierra and Wes arrived within twenty minutes and had eight other students with them.

They all donated their blood and then sat with Christy in the waiting room. Everyone had questions and speculations. Christy was beginning to feel irritated. They didn't have enough information to come up with so many solutions. She knew everyone was trying to help, but she was glad when her parents arrived, along with her thirteen-year-old brother, David.

The three of them looked sick with worry. Christy hugged them and cried on her dad's shoulder.

Two more students from Rancho came, and Christy began to shiver from the chill of the air-conditioned building.

"Will you go outside with me?" Christy's brother asked. He had been standing quietly to the side, listening while all the others discussed the bits of information they had. Christy was glad for the chance to warm up and followed her brother into the autumn afternoon.

"Christy, I'm scared." David was five-six, only an inch shorter than Christy. He had big hands and feet and thick, reddish hair like their father. He wore glasses and was now wiping away the embarrassing tears that he had managed to keep back in the waiting room.

"I am, too," Christy said, wrapping her arms around her brother. During the year she had been away, she had communicated with David only when necessary. The wide span in their ages had kept them from ever being close. But at this moment, Christy felt more like David's sister than she ever had before.

David adored Todd. He had for the past five years. Often when Todd came to see Christy at her parents' house, Todd would end up spending just as much time with David as with Christy. Sometimes Christy thought Todd had been a better sibling to David than she had. "Do you think Todd is going to live?" David asked.

"I don't know." Christy held her brother close. "I've been praying. You heard how the doctor said it was a miracle he was alive."

"If Todd dies, he's going to heaven," David said. It was a statement, not a question. It sounded exactly the way Todd would have said it.

"Yes."

"I know because he told me. He told me lots of times that I needed to give my life to God so that, when I died, I'd go to heaven, too, and then we'd be there together. Todd said we'd build a skateboard ramp if they didn't already have one."

Christy swallowed hard and silently prayed, *Not yet, Father. Please. Don't take Todd yet. Let him build a few more skateboard ramps here first. Let him keep telling kids like my brother that they need to get their lives right with you.*

"I never did it yet." David pulled away and looked at Christy. "I never prayed and turned my life over to Jesus."

Christy had been fourteen when she had realized she wasn't a Christian simply because she had grown up going to church with her family. This was the first time it occurred to her that her brother was almost the same age.

"Are you ready to make that decision?" Christy asked.

David nodded. "I want to. I want to pray right now. Will you pray with me?"

Christy felt her throat tighten and tears rush to her eyes. "Of course," she said in a small voice.

"What do I say?"

"Just say whatever is on your heart. God knows what you're thinking, David. He knows that you're choosing to believe in Him. Now tell Him just that and receive His gift of forgiveness and eternal life."

Christy closed her eyes and bowed her head. David prayed four or five short, no-nonsense phrases stating that he believed Jesus was God's only Son and that he wanted Jesus to forgive his sins and come in and take over his life. When David ended his prayer with the words "Let it be so," Christy knew David had heard Todd pray more than once.

As she opened her eyes, Christy drew in a deep breath. "You've just been adopted into God's family." A smile came to her tense lips, despite all the trauma of the past hour. "I'm really happy for you, David. Todd will be thrilled." The tears wove their way down Christy's cheeks all over again.

David nodded. "I want to tell Todd I finally did it."

"Maybe they'll let us see him soon. Come on." Christy put her arm around her brother and walked back into the waiting room. She felt stunned and amazed at what had just happened.

"Any word?" Christy asked.

Her mom shook her head. "Your father went to give blood in case they need more."

"I want to give my blood, too," David said.

Mom looked surprised. "You're too young, honey. Even with our consent, you have to be sixteen."

David looked a little disappointed.

"I'm sure your dad could use a little moral support," Mom said. "Let's go find him."

After Christy's mom and brother left the waiting room, Christy thought about what had just happened. She turned to Katie. "My brother gave his life to the Lord when we went outside." Her voice held little emotion because she had so little left to give.

"That's incredible." Katie spoke in a monotone, as well. "How did that happen?"

"Todd has been talking to him about the Lord for a long time. I guess David wanted to finally make a firm decision. I wish I could feel as happy as I should about it."

Just then a tall, broad-shouldered man with thinning blond hair, wearing a Hawaiian-print shirt, entered the waiting room with Christy's uncle Bob. She had seen Todd's father only once or twice before, but Christy rushed to him and hugged him before she hugged Uncle Bob.

"What have you heard?" Uncle Bob asked. He lived a few blocks from Todd's dad, and apparently the two men had come together.

Christy gave them the rundown and had just finished when the doctor entered the waiting area. He spotted Christy and went to her first.

"This is Todd's dad," Christy said to the doctor.

"Bryan," Todd's father said, shaking hands with the doctor. "Bryan Spencer. How is he?"

"I'm Dr. Johannes. Todd is coming out of surgery right now. We were quite fortunate in that we were able to locate the bleeding right away. He had a perforated colon. The surgeon repaired it and went ahead and removed his appendix because it was swollen. That may or may not be a result of the accident. Everything else looks good. We put quite a few stitches in his hands, and he may need a few more after they get the rest of the glass out."

"He's going to be okay, isn't he?" Katie blurted out.

"I can't guarantee that," Dr. Johannes said. "He's lost a lot of blood, but amazingly, he didn't break any bones. We'll be able to make a better diagnosis in the morning. He'll be in the recovery room for at least another hour or two."

"Can I see him?" Todd's dad asked.

The doctor checked the chart one more time before nodding. "Yes, he's still sedated, of course, so he won't know you're there. But, yes. You can go see him. No more than two visitors, okay?"

Dr. Johannes turned to go and then came back and added in a low voice, looking over the top of his glasses at Todd's dad. "His face is pretty swollen from the impact of the crash. He has a black eye, and they haven't cleaned the blood out of his hair yet. I wanted to tell so you'd know he really is better off than he looks."

Bryan Spencer nodded. Then he turned to Christy and gave her a tentative look. "Would you like to go with me?"

Christy wasn't sure if she was being included because he was hesitant to see Todd by himself or because he knew how much it meant for her to see Todd right away. Christy instinctively linked her arm in his and walked down the hall to the hospital elevator. Bryan's arm was trembling. She knew they needed each other to be strong for what they were about to face.

The nurse on duty in the recovery room led them to where Todd lay on his back with a white sheet covering most of his body. Both arms were on top of the sheet, and several tubes were connected to his right arm. A soft, fluorescent light above the bed flickered on his face, revealing the black eye and swollen mouth as well as the ugly black stitches in his hands, just as Dr. Johannes had described them. Todd wore what looked like a paper shower cap on his head. Christy could see the dark bloodstains in his hair showing through. It took everything within her not to burst into tears at the sight.

"Hey, son," Bryan Spencer's deep voice spoke over Todd. "It's Dad." His voice quavered. He moved closer and touched Todd gently on his left shoulder. It seemed to be about the only part of Todd's body that wasn't bloodied or stitched up or connected to some tube. "The doctor says you're doing good, son. You rest, okay?"

Todd didn't respond.

"Christy's here. She wants to talk to you." He stepped back and let Christy move in next to the bed.

All she could hear were the beeping, ticking, humming sounds of the machines as Todd lay motionless beneath the dull light that kept flickering. Christy wanted to take Todd in her arms and hold him. Her sense of mercy overwhelmed her to the point she had no more tears.

Reaching for his left hand, Christy carefully lifted it. She noticed four places where a series of stitches threaded his skin together. His hand felt cool and heavy. She gently gave it a squeeze. There was no response.

"Todd," she whispered, leaning close, "I'm here with your dad." She raised her voice a little. "We've all been praying for you, Todd. The doctor says you're doing well. They said they would know more after you get some sleep. So don't worry about trying to talk to us. Just sleep, Todd."

Christy drew his heavy hand to her lips and kissed the back of it in between the black suture thread they had used to sew him up after pulling out the shards of windshield glass.

"I have a lot to tell you when you wake up, Todd, so get lots of sleep, okay?" Christy kissed his hand again. She turned to Todd's dad, who stood behind her, pressing his lips together.

"Do you think it would be okay if I stayed here with him?" Christy asked.

"I don't know the hospital rules. Would you like me to ask?"

Christy nodded. "If you need to get back home tonight, I can stay. I'd like to stay."

Mr. Spencer slipped around the other side of the sliding white curtain. Christy could hear him talking to the nurse. She was saying that they prefer not to have people wait in the recovery area, since the space is so limited and the patients often become ill when the anesthesia wears off. She said they would be better off in the waiting room, and when Todd was transferred to a room, the staff would let them know.

Christy kissed Todd tenderly on his swollen cheek and said she would see him later. Joining Todd's dad, she returned to the waiting room, where the two of them reported to the others. After hearing the news, Matt and most of the students left. They told Christy to keep them updated. Katie and Uncle Bob had gone to buy drinks for everyone. That left Christy's parents, Todd's dad, and Christy's brother, David.

"Is he unconscious?" David asked, sidling up to Christy while their parents talked with Todd's dad.

"I don't think so. The anesthesia will wear off soon, and I would guess that by morning he will be able to talk to you."

"Did you tell him? About what I did? About how we prayed?" David asked.

"Not yet. Would you like me to tell him or do you want to tell him when he's awake?"

"I heard Dad say that we're going to go now since we can't do anything. I guess you better tell Todd."

"Okay." Christy smiled at her brother. "I'll tell him. And, David?"

He stopped and let Christy put her arms around him and hug him. "I'm really happy for you." She kissed David on the cheek and said softly in his ear, "You made the most important decision of your life today, and I'm so glad I got to be with you when you did."

He looked like he was dying to wipe her kiss off his cheek but was trying hard to be mature about all this. "Thanks," he said awkwardly.

Then, because Christy felt as if she had made the biggest mistake of her life by not leaving class and running to find Todd to tell him that she loved him, she said, "I love you, David." She decided right then and there that she would never pass up the opportunity to tell the really important people in her life that she loved them.

When her parents were ready to leave, Christy said, "I love you, Mom," and kissed her on the cheek.

"I love you, Dad." Christy hugged him, and he kissed the top of her head.

"Call us in the morning," Dad said. "And if you need anything, or if there's any change, we'll come right back."

"Okay. Thanks, Dad."

"Try to sleep," Mom said.

Katie and Uncle Bob arrived with several cans of soda pop. "Where did everybody go?" Katie asked.

"Home," Christy said. "You can go, too, if you want. I'm going to stay."

"I'll stay with you," Katie offered.

"Are you staying, Bryan?" Uncle Bob asked Todd's dad.

He nodded and took one of the cans of pop that Katie had placed on the coffee table in the waiting room. "At least until he comes out of the anesthesia. If you need to go, Bob, I can make other arrangements to get home."

"Don't think twice about it," Bob said. "I'm happy to stay. I'd like to." He put his arm around Christy and gave her a sideways hug. "I don't get to see my favorite niece enough these days. I'll take any excuse I can."

Christy wrapped both her arms around her kindhearted uncle and said, "I love you, Uncle Bob. Have I ever told you that? I don't know if I ever have. I love you."

Tears welled up in Bob's eyes. "I love you, too, honey."

Christy didn't know if she imagined it, but Bob's body seemed to flinch when he looked up. Christy followed his gaze and then heard a familiar voice. Then she knew why Uncle Bob had flinched.

"But I am a relative," Christy heard the voice stating emphatically. "I don't understand why I'm not able to see Todd Spencer immediately." No one had as much of an edge to her voice as Aunt Marti did when she was pushing her agenda to the limit.

Christy took off in step with Uncle Bob, and the two of them headed for the front reception desk, leaving Katie alone with Todd's dad. But the two of them followed right behind.

Christy thought she was prepared to face her flamboyant aunt. The hair or the clothes wouldn't shock Christy. Not even Marti's lie about being Todd's relative was a surprise. Marti was a woman who got what she wanted, even if she had to rewrite the rules.

But what Christy wasn't prepared for was the huge man with the copper-colored skin and flowing white hair who towered over Marti as if he were her self-appointed guardian angel.

"Hello, Marti." Bob stood his ground less than a yard away from her.

"Robert?" She looked surprised to see him there.

"Who's that?" Katie whispered under her breath as she stepped up next to Christy.

Christy knew the answer, but she kept her lips sealed. After all, a promise was a promise. It would be up to her very startled aunt Martha to introduce Cheyenne to the rest of them.

147

CHAPTER 13

===================

"I came as soon as I heard the message on the voice mail." Marti flew to Bob's side and kissed the air next to his ear. She gave Christy the same treatment and then took her by the arms. "How is Todd? Is he going to make it? I was a wreck all the way here."

"The doctor says it looks promising," Todd's dad said. "I'm Bryan Spencer, Todd's father. I don't think we've met."

"Marti," she said, shaking hands. "And don't you look just like Todd! I'm so delighted to meet you." With her left hand Marti made a funny flipping gesture as if shooing away a troublesome gnat.

Christy watched Cheyenne. He stayed back, his expression perplexed. He didn't seem to understand why Marti was signaling for him to leave in her unsubtle way. At that moment, Marti's "aura" wasn't in harmony with anyone else's in the room.

"Hi," Katie said openly to Cheyenne. She waved at him and smiled as if he were just too shy to join them.

That was the only invitation Cheyenne needed to step forward.

"This is my pottery instructor," Marti explained quickly. "I had a class this afternoon, and I was so shaken by the news of Todd that Cheyenne graciously offered to drive me here."

Cheyenne turned to Bob, and the two of them nodded formally, as if they had met before.

"Todd is still in the recovery room," Uncle Bob said with a calm, even meter to his words. "They're going to let us know when we can see him, but it might be a while. If you'd like to go home, I'll be glad to call you with an update once we know something."

"Are all of you staying?" Marti's words were crisp.

"Yes," Bob answered, still sounding controlled.

It seemed that Christy's poor aunt didn't know what to do.

"Has everyone eaten?" Marti asked. Again the words were staccato. The familiar tactic almost made Christy smile. This was the approach to solving problems that Marti and Christy's mother both had learned back on the farm.

Christy had recognized it in herself that night in The Java Jungle when Matt said he had just arrived from Wisconsin. Her first thought was to feed him. Now she realized her aunt could play the role of sophisticated Newport Beach socialite or go completely organic—as was her current state—and play the role of Mother Earth's personal shopper. But the truth was, deep down, Marti was a farm girl from Wisconsin. For some reason, that insight doused Christy with pity for her aunt.

Katie answered for all four of them. "No, we haven't eaten. We bought some drinks out of the machine a few minutes ago, but we didn't want to be away from the waiting room too long."

"Then I'll get food for everyone," Marti announced. "Any allergies or special diets?"

When no one responded, she quickly said, "Good. I'll be back in no time." Turning on her heel, she marched out of the building. Cheyenne nodded at Christy and the others as a farewell gesture before following after Marti and her long, swishing hair.

"Someone better call the laboratory," Katie muttered after they had left the building.

"Why?" Christy asked.

"We need to tell them that their attempt to genetically clone a male calendar model has failed. The escaped mutant is chasing your aunt."

Christy kept herself from smiling at Katie's comment. After all, Marti was her aunt. And Christy's uncle was still standing next to her. She knew that once a person was treated with disrespect, it made it easy for others to jump in and do the same.

The four of them returned to the waiting area. More than an hour later Cheyenne came striding in with several plastic boxes filled with wonderful-smelling Italian food.

"Marti isn't feeling well," Cheyenne said. "I'm going to take her home."

None of them seemed surprised at the announcement.

They ate in silence. Christy had no idea what she was eating.

"I'm going to make a few calls," Bryan said.

"I need some air," Bob said after he had eaten. He left the room.

As Christy sat alone with Katie, a fearful anger began to well up inside her. For years she and Todd had driven up and down the freeways in that beat-up, old surf van. It was a miracle they hadn't both been killed. Christy never wanted to get into another old car as long as she lived.

"Does your car have air bags on both sides?" Christy snapped at Katie.

"What?" Katie asked.

"I'm not riding in Baby Hummer with you anymore," Christy said.

"What are you talking about?"

"Todd could have been killed! His van had no air bags!" The horror of the accident was sinking in, and Christy felt as if she was going to lose her dinner.

"But he wasn't killed," Katie said firmly. "Christy, think about it. God saved him. God isn't finished with him yet. God has a plan. He always has a plan. Some God-things will come from this. Don't freak out on me now. You have to stay strong!"

Katie's sharp words worked like splashes of cold water on Christy's rampant emotions. "You're right. God is here. He's in this. I know He is. He's going to do His God-things."

"Well, duh!" Katie's biting humor rubbed Christy the wrong way. "Look at what happened already. Your brother got saved."

Christy had forgotten. Still, in her pain, she didn't think that was a good enough reason for Todd to have to go through such a terrible experience.

"Chris," Katie reached over and rubbed her shoulder, "we have to keep our perspective here. We're in shock, yes. It's awful. But God isn't pacing the floors of heaven, wringing His hands, saying, 'Oh dear, oh dear, how could this have happened?' He's God. He can do whatever He wants. At this point, it appears God wants Todd to live."

Christy felt the tears on her cheeks. She couldn't believe she had any moisture left in her system.

"I'm going to get some air, too," Katie said. "Why don't you try to sleep a little bit?" Katie gave Christy a weak smile. "You know that when Todd is ready for visitors you'll want to be as calm as you can be. Try to rest."

Christy closed her eyes and leaned her head back. She drew in a deep breath. All she could smell was ammonia-scented disinfectant mixed with garlic from the marinara sauce. She pushed the food containers aside with her foot and tried to pray.

Peace came over her. She almost believed that if she opened her eyes she would see Jesus seated beside her. He wasn't wringing His hands in fear. Katie was right about that. He was in control. But Christy knew Jesus would feel her pain right along with her.

"Christy?" Uncle Bob's voice spoke into her quiet moment. "Are you okay, honey?"

She opened her eyes and nodded bravely. "I'm okay. How are you doing?"

"Okay," he said with a nod of his head. "It shouldn't be too much longer before they let us see him."

Christy looked at her uncle more closely. "How are you doing, really? I mean with Aunt Marti and everything."

"I'm sorry you had to see her that way. With . . . with him."

"I already knew about Cheyenne," Christy said. "Marti told me about the art colony and her pottery and everything when she came to see me a few weeks ago."

"Did she tell you she's planning to go with him to Santa Fe?" Bob asked.

Christy nodded solemnly. "I promised her I wouldn't say anything to anyone about it. I wish I hadn't promised her, though. I'm sorry I didn't come to you and talk about it."

"Don't apologize. You couldn't have done anything." Bob sat down and put his feet on the coffee table. "Your aunt is going her own way. You can't change her decision."

Obviously Marti's relationship with Cheyenne was no surprise to Bob. Christy wondered if Marti was making plans to leave fairly soon. Gently, Christy asked her uncle, "What are you going to do?"

"A guy I know from church directed me to a verse that relates to my situation," he said. "It's 1 Corinthians 7:15. 'But if the unbeliever leaves, let him do so. A believing man or woman is not bound in such circumstances; God has called us to live in peace.' "

Christy thought her uncle sounded like a robot as he recited the verse. She had to say something. "Are you just going to let her go?"

"I can't fight it." His voice was flat.

"Yes you can." Christy had no idea where the strength to say such words was coming from or why she was saying them. She seemed to have a different well of emotions for Uncle Bob's situation that was separate from the well she had been draining over Todd. This other well was full of opinions, and she drew from it freely. "You can still fight for her, Uncle Bob. Pray for her. Love her. You can't give up."

His eyes filled with tears. Christy didn't think she had ever seen her uncle cry.

"Uncle Bob, that may be a good, helpful verse for you right now, but a lot of other verses about marriage and love are in the Bible." Christy decided to keep talking before this well of strength gave out on her. "If I've learned one thing so far in my Bible classes at Rancho, it's that it can be dangerous to take only one verse and build your belief about a topic around that verse. We have to study everything the Bible has to say on a topic to clearly understand God's heart on the matter."

Bob looked at her quietly before saying, "You're right. I have given up on her without a fight. I was going to let her go off to that art colony, but that might not be what God wants."

Christy had to remind herself that her uncle had only been a Christian for a short time. In his enthusiasm to change everything into a peaceful reflection of Christ's understanding and love, he seemed to have forgotten that this same Jesus got mad, turned over the moneychangers' tables, and openly wept when his friend died. Jesus commanded a dead man to come out of his grave and told the wind and waves to "shut up."

All of these examples were fresh in Christy's mind because she had been getting to know Jesus better by reading the New Testament. She told her uncle about what she had read in the Gospels, and then she suggested he might want to do the same thing.

"It's the Word of God that changes us," Christy said. She had heard that in one of her classes but didn't remember which one.

Bob rubbed the back of his neck and looked up at Christy, his eyes clear. "You know what? I've never read the whole Bible."

"Not many people have."

"But you're right. How can I say I'm a follower of Christ when I haven't even read His life story?"

"He only wrote one book," Christy said. "The Bible. We just need to dig for the answers sometimes."

"You know," Uncle Bob said, "I think I've been depending too much on others to study the Scriptures for me and to pass on their wisdom to me. I don't do that with my investments. Why should I settle for that in my spiritual life?"

Uncle Bob leaned over and gave Christy a kiss on the cheek. "I've missed you, Bright Eyes. You always were my favorite niece."

Christy smiled. "And I've always been your only niece."

"Minor detail, my child. Minor detail."

Todd's dad stepped into the waiting room. "The doctor said we can go see him now. He's in room 302."

"I'll find Katie and be right up," Christy said.

Uncle Bob and Todd's dad went ahead. Christy and Katie joined them in room 302 a few minutes later. Christy could see that Todd's eyes were open, but he didn't seem to recognize her when she came in the room.

With her heart pounding, Christy forced her tears of mercy to stay back. She slipped over to the side of the bed and tenderly took Todd's hand in hers. "Hi," she said.

Todd's expression lit up only slightly, but Christy felt confident he recognized her.

"Da sove," Todd mumbled through his swollen lips.

"What?" Christy leaned closer. He looked awful. "Don't try to talk if it's too hard right now. You can tell me in the morning after you've slept."

"Ar sove," he repeated.

"Sove?" Christy repeated.

Todd nodded ever so slightly.

"Sove. Oh, do you mean stove? Our camp stove?"

Todd nodded. It looked like it hurt him to do so.

Katie stepped in and gave her interpretation. "He's trying to say that he's worried about your camp stove. It must have been in Gus."

Christy gave Todd a smile. "You're worried about our camp stove? Oh, Todd, don't worry about that. We can get another one. It's much more important that you're okay."

Todd closed his eyes.

Christy gave Katie a concerned look. It was hard to know what to do or what to say.

"We're going home for a few hours," Todd's dad said, stepping next to Christy. "I'll be back tomorrow."

Christy felt Todd grasp her hand a little tighter.

"I won't leave you," Christy said. "I'll stay right here."

Todd's grasp released, and he appeared to fall into an exhausted sleep.

"Are you sure you want to stay all night?" Uncle Bob asked.

Christy nodded. "You can go back to school, if you want, Katie. I don't mind staying alone."

"I think I'll do that," Katie said. "I'll come back tomorrow morning. Do you want me to bring you anything?"

"No. I'll call you if I think of anything."

They all hugged good-bye, and Christy was left alone beside the bed. She pulled up the chair from the corner next to the bed and tried to quietly lower the metal bed railing so she could hold Todd's hand more easily.

The first ten minutes Christy prayed. The steady ticks and muffled bleeps of the monitors became the echo of her pleas to God. As long as those ticks and bleeps stayed constant, Todd was stable. He was alive.

Christy looked at one of the tubes that entered Todd's body through his right hand. *He has my blood in him now. My blood and the blood from my family, his family, and his friends. Oh, Todd, you said the other day that you felt so isolated your whole life because you grew up without brothers or sisters. And now look! You are surrounded and supported by a whole family of brothers and sisters in Christ. Our blood runs in your veins.*

Christy gently traced her fingers along the veins on the top of Todd's left hand. She studied where the stitches had been taken, knowing that the scars from those cuts would be with him for the rest of his life.

Just like Jesus. That's what you told the youth group last weekend. When we enter heaven, Christ will hold out His hands to us, and we will see His scars.

Christy closed her eyes and imagined Jesus standing right behind her, His nail-scarred hand resting on her shoulder. She had felt this close to the Lord only a few times in her life. With the closeness came peace. She felt calmed, imagining His hand on her shoulder, her hand in Todd's.

"Can you feel how connected we are, Todd?" Christy whispered. "God is here. He is in this with us. His presence is so real right now. Katie was right. God isn't wringing His hands, asking why this happened. He's reaching out with those hands. Touching us. Drawing us to each other. Drawing us to Him."

Christy's thoughts spilled into a whispered prayer. It was a precise prayer, thanking God for His mercy in sparing Todd's life. She then surrendered to the Lord their future together. Christy ended with the words Todd had used on the camping trip, "As you wish."

Suddenly Christy opened her eyes, surprised by an insight. *I always want to control and schedule and plan everything. Ultimately, I'm not in control of my life. Not really. God is.*

Christy thought of how, when Christ was on earth, He prayed, "Not my will, but yours be done."

That's what Todd meant when he said, "As you wish." He was saying, "God, you do what you want, and I'll agree with it."

She and Todd might never know why this terrible accident had happened. But together they could say to God, "As you wish. You do what you want in our lives, and we willingly will agree with it, even if we don't understand."

Christy wished Todd were awake. She wanted so badly to share her thoughts with him. But he was sleeping. Peacefully sleeping. She couldn't rob him of that precious gift in his long journey to recovery.

For the next few hours, Christy sat, wide awake, beside her beloved, basking in the peace of Christ's presence. The night nurse came in several times to check on Todd. She offered Christy something to eat or drink, but Christy declined. She didn't need anything. Her heart and body were full.

Sometime in the middle of the night, Christy stood to stretch, and when she did, Todd seemed to know she had moved. He stirred, too.

To comfort him, Christy placed her cool hand against his swollen cheek. Todd's breathing returned to a steady pace. With her finger, Christy gently traced the outline of Todd's lips. She ran her fingers across his defined, square jawline and memorized the angle of his face.

"I love you," she whispered. The words tumbled out naturally and unrestricted. A straight path had been cleared from Christy's heart to her mouth. Along that path, those three beautiful words ran unhindered, leaping from her lips and joyfully sprinkling themselves over Todd as he slept.

Christy giggled as she spoke them aloud again and again. "I love you! I really, truly love you! I know you can't hear me, Todd. That's okay. When you wake I'll tell you again with my face in your eye, or whatever Katie's poem said. I will give you the best gift I've given you so far. I will give you evidence of my promise to you. The promise I've already made in my heart."

Drawing in a deep breath, Christy smiled and said clearly, "I love you, Todd Spencer. Forever and ever, and nothing can change that."

CHAPTER 14

Christy woke when she felt someone's hand resting heavily on her head and slowly stroking her hair. She opened her eyes, and it all came back—Todd, the accident, the hospital room.

She had fallen asleep seated in a chair with her head resting on her folded arms propped against the side of Todd's hospital bed.

"Hey, you're awake," she said, lifting her head and seeing Todd's eyes were open. She realized she had been drooling. Quickly reaching for a tissue from the end table, she wiped her mouth. "How are you doing?" she asked.

"Hi." His voice was hoarse.

Christy smiled and touched his arm. "Are you okay?"

"I hurt." Todd moved only his lips and swallowed hard.

"Would you like me to call the nurse?"

Todd didn't answer. He floated back into a fuzzy sleep induced by the pain medication, which was dripping slowly into his body.

Christy waited by his side another ten minutes, but Todd was out. So she pulled herself together, washing her face and going to the hospital cafeteria. Hot tea sounded good. She also bought an oatmeal cookie and an orange. As she peeled the orange, the fresh fruit's scent brightened the air and revived her.

Todd slept all morning, only waking three times. Katie came with Matt, Wes, two college professors, and Todd's roommate. They laid their hands on Todd and prayed for him while he slept, then they left to hurry back to class. Katie said she would let Donna know that Christy wouldn't be in to the bookstore again that day.

Uncle Bob called Todd's room twice. The second time, the ringing phone woke Todd, and he looked up just as his dad entered the room. The painful grin on Todd's face showed Christy and his dad how glad Todd was that they were there.

A bouquet of yellow roses arrived from Aunt Marti, and Todd's mom called. Christy answered the phone and then turned it over to Todd's dad. From the way the conversation went, his parents sounded as if they were friendly enough with each other. Clearly, both cared a lot for their son. Christy wished Todd had been awake so he could have talked to his mom. But he was oblivious to everything around him, including the second bouquet that arrived with a get-well balloon attached.

Dr. Johannes made his rounds at noon and gave them an update, saying the pain medication would keep Todd in this stupor for at least another day, possibly up to three days. The doctor assured them the critical stage had passed, and everything looked good. Todd was a strong, healthy young man, and his body would heal. It would just take time.

"How long do you think he'll be in the hospital?" Christy asked.

"I'd like to keep him at least a few more days," the doctor said. "You're welcome to stay with him, of course. But don't feel that you need to."

Christy had difficulty deciding if she should stay. She talked it over with his dad and decided she would go back to school. So she leaned over the bed, kissed Todd twice on the cheek, and whispered, "I love you. Sleep deeply. Sleep well. Dream of me."

Todd didn't respond. She didn't expect him to. Yet she couldn't wait until his eyes were open and clear again so she could lose herself in his gaze. Then she would tell him she loved him, and he would be able to hear her and fully understand.

"Would you like to stop for some lunch before I take you back to Rancho?" Todd's dad asked.

"Sure." Since Christy hadn't been around Todd's dad much, she welcomed the chance to know him better.

They were walking out the automatic front doors of the hospital when Christy spotted some of her and Todd's closest friends, Doug and Tracy, coming toward her, calling her name. As they greeted her with hugs, Christy began to cry again. She didn't know why.

"Everything is okay," she told them. "The doctor thinks he's going to be all right."

Doug enveloped Christy in one of his famous Doug hugs. "Katie called us this morning. I wish she had called last night. We would have been here in a flash. You know you always can call on us if you need anything." Doug pulled back and gave Christy a concerned, close-up look. "How are you doing?"

"Okay. Good, actually. I'm tired, but I'm okay." She made her tears stop, and that felt good.

Christy thought petite Tracy looked older than last time she had seen her friend. More mature. She wore small oval glasses, which complemented her heart-shaped face.

"Do you think we can see him?" Tracy asked.

"Sure," Todd's dad said. "He's been sleeping ever since the surgery last night. Don't be surprised if he doesn't wake up or acknowledge you." He went on to give Doug and Tracy an update on the surgery and what the doctor had told them.

"Were you both leaving now?" Doug asked. He was as tall as Todd's dad, but his face still held the little-boy look he always had. His short, sandy blond hair stuck straight up in front, accentuating the mischievous look.

"We were about to eat some lunch, and then I was taking Christy back to Rancho."

"We can take her," Tracy said, reaching for Christy's arm and pulling her close. "Do you mind, Christy? I'd love to spend a little time with you, if you don't have to hurry back."

Christy looked at Todd's dad. She was too tired to form an opinion on anything. "Would that be okay?"

"Of course. Here's my cell phone number. Would you call me if there's any change? I plan to come back tomorrow afternoon and stay awhile."

Christy nodded and took his business card. "Thanks."

Bryan Spencer smiled appreciatively at Christy. "No, thank you, Christy. You're an exceptional woman. Everything Todd told me about you is true." He leaned over and kissed her soundly on the cheek. "Call if you need me for anything at all."

"I will," Christy promised.

Tracy, Doug, and Christy returned to Todd's room. He was sleeping, as his dad had predicted. Tracy cried quiet tears when she saw his swollen, black-and-blue face.

Doug suggested they pray, and so they did, joining hands with Christy holding Todd's left hand and Doug resting his hand on Todd's right shoulder. When Doug said, "Amen," Christy whispered, "As you wish." She liked those words being her secret message of surrender to the Lord.

They stood close to the bed, talking softly, until the nurse came in and said she needed to take Todd's temperature and adjust his medication.

"Why don't we wait in the cafeteria?" Doug suggested. "I could use some food."

"I wish Todd at least knew we were here." Tracy looked longingly at him.

"We can come back," Christy suggested.

They found an empty table at the cafeteria and talked like the old friends they were, catching up on what had happened since they had seen one another. Christy found herself telling Doug and Tracy that she had come to some conclusions about Todd. Both Doug and Tracy leaned forward, as if they had been waiting as long as Todd to hear what Christy was going to say.

With a self-conscious little shrug, Christy said, "I love him. I love Todd. I haven't told him yet—at least, he hasn't heard me say it—but I know without a doubt I love him."

A charming giggle escaped Tracy's lips. Doug leaned back with a satisfied look on his face and nodded. "It's about time."

Christy gave him a look that said, "Well, thanks a lot!"

"It's just that Todd has been sure of his love for you for so long," Doug said. "I know he never wanted to rush you. This will be good. This will change his life."

"Change his life?" Christy asked.

Doug and Tracy glanced at each other in a way that indicated they both held a few of Todd's confidences. Apparently they were confidences Christy didn't hold yet.

"Should I ask what you two are thinking right now? You look as if you can read each other's minds."

"We can," they said in unison.

All three of them laughed.

Tracy took off her glasses and placed them on the table next to her half-finished turkey sandwich. "Christy, you probably know this already, but Todd has been in love with you for a long time."

Christy had hoped that, but her insecurities had caused her to doubt it many times.

"A long time," Doug said. "I didn't know that until after Tracy and I were married. Todd was over at our apartment one night, and we were talking about when you and I were going out while Todd was in Spain. He asked Tracy if that had been hard on her."

Christy gave her friend a sympathetic glance. Looking back, Christy wished she hadn't caused Tracy any pain by going out with Doug when Tracy was so intently interested in him.

"I told Todd that, back then, we didn't know for sure we were supposed to be together," Tracy said. "Neither Doug nor I was ready to make a commitment. I mean, I was hoping, praying, and thinking things might work out for us one day, but I didn't know for certain."

"And that's when Todd told us that he knew," Doug said. A grin grew on his boyish face. "He said he knew you were the one for him from that first day when we met on the beach. Do you remember, Christy?"

Christy buried her face in her hands. "How could I forget? I was only fourteen years old, and this wave scooped me up and tossed me at your feet all wrapped in seaweed."

Doug chuckled. "Then Todd and I taught you how to ride a body board."

Christy looked up. "You both were so nice to me. I'll never forget that day."

"Todd won't ever forget it, either," Tracy said. "He told us he knew then and there that you were the one for him. The one woman he would love for the rest of his life."

"You're kidding," Christy said. She had heard Todd make comments to that effect before, but she had thought he was teasing. She looked at Doug and then at Tracy to make sure they weren't teasing her. They both looked serious.

"I'm sorry," Christy said, "that is just weird. How could he know something like that when he was . . . how old was he? Sixteen? That's crazy."

"See?" Tracy said. "That's the same thing I said when Todd told us, but Doug got upset with me."

"I wasn't upset with you."

"You told me I shouldn't judge another person's feelings and call them crazy. You said that right in front of Todd."

"What did Todd say?" Christy asked.

"He didn't say much of anything. He didn't defend himself or act embarrassed. He just seemed real matter-of-fact about how he felt." Tracy looked at Doug again before saying, "Todd said he knew he loved you and he didn't have to do anything to prove it. To anyone."

Christy let Tracy's words sink in. She knew she had liked Todd when she had first met him. She had spent plenty of hours dreaming about him and dreaming about what it would be like to end up with him. But love? Forever, true love? No, Christy couldn't say she knew Todd was the one for her until last Saturday during their crazy dune buggy ride.

"You know what?" Tracy said. "I don't think we should have told you all this. This is really personal. It's between you and Todd."

"It's also between Todd and you two," Christy said. "I mean, he told all this to you guys, so he must have trusted you with his thoughts and feelings about me. I don't mind you telling me. It's good, actually, because it helps me to know he started out thinking I was special to him."

"Special?" Doug echoed. "Christy, you were it. You *are* it. No other girls have ever been in his life. It was always you."

"Only you," Tracy agreed.

Christy couldn't believe how quickly the tears found their familiar trail down her face. She never imagined that Todd had chosen to commit his heart to her all those years ago or that he never had wavered from that decision.

"I wish I weren't so bad at making decisions," Christy said between tears. "Why did it take me so long to open my heart to Todd? Why did I ever go out with any other guys?"

"Oh, Chris, don't feel that way," Tracy said. She placed her hand on Christy's shoulder.

"Yeah," Doug agreed. "Speaking as one of the other guys you went out with, I'd like to think you don't regret that time in your life."

Christy quickly sobered. "I don't, Doug. Your friendship and what I learned while we were spending time together were extremely valuable."

"And fun," Doug added. "Don't forget fun. We had some great times."

Tracy said, "What you went through to come to the conclusion that you really love Todd is normal. That's what I was telling Todd that night at our apartment. Maybe it's different for women. I thought I loved Doug, but I wasn't positive until we were in England. Do you remember when I asked to be taken off your team? That was because it hit me so hard that I was in love with him, I couldn't be around him. Especially when I knew he didn't feel that way about me."

"I know," Christy said. "But that's why I feel so bad. I'm thinking of how much I hurt Todd when he was sure about me, but I wasn't sure about him."

"Don't worry about Todd," Doug said. "He's tough. Tough and patient. It's good that you didn't know before, Christy. I think going to Switzerland was a great choice for you. If you and Todd had decided a year ago or even five years ago that you couldn't live without each other, you both would have missed out on so many important experiences. It's all God's timing. There can't be any regrets."

Christy knew Doug was right. It was God's timing. The verse from Song of Solomon about "not arousing nor awakening love until it so desires" was a hidden blessing in her life. Apparently, God now pleased to awaken love fully within Christy.

She composed herself and remembered something Dr. Mitchell had talked about in class on Monday when she had felt compelled to leave and find Todd. He had said something about blessings coming upon you and overtaking you because you obey the Lord's voice. Christy knew she had no reason to regret the way things had gone.

With a little smile she said, "I guess God has been working out the details between us for a long time. A deeper level of love for Todd has just awakened inside me, you know?"

Both Doug and Tracy smiled.

"We know," Tracy said.

"I feel as if God has overtaken me with something new. Something stronger and deeper than ever before. It's so real. I know Todd is the one. He is the one for me." Even as she heard herself speaking the words, Christy ached to go back to Todd's room and declare her love to him.

"You know," Doug said, "some of what you're feeling could be from the shock of the accident."

Tracy swatted her husband on the arm. "Don't try to take it away from her! Christy is in love. Let her just be in love without analyzing it." She turned to Christy and shook her head. "Men!"

"Okay, okay," Doug said. "So it's different for everybody. I'm happy for you, Christy. Todd will be thrilled. And, sweetheart," he said, turning to his pretty little wife, "are you going to finish the other half of your sandwich?"

Christy laughed for the first time in two days. "Some things never change. Doug, you still eat more than anyone I've ever met."

He chomped into the turkey sandwich and said, "And I'm getting the love handles to prove it, aren't I, Trace?"

"Hardly." Tracy shook her head. "You don't slow down long enough to let all that food find a place to stay on you."

"Have things been really busy for you guys?" Christy asked.

Tracy nodded. "Everything is going well, though. Did you hear that we ran into Rick Doyle? He is so changed, Christy; you wouldn't even recognize him. God has . . . what was the term you used earlier? Overtaken? Yes, that's what you said. God has overtaken Rick."

"It's awesome," Doug said with a bite of sandwich still in his mouth.

"Katie heard from him," Christy said. "It sounded as if he was doing great."

"Well, God was certainly tough and patient with Rick," Doug added. "I ought to know—Todd and I were roommates with him when we were in San Diego."

"I remember," Christy said.

"You don't remember half of what I remember," Doug said. "And you don't want to."

"He's definitely changed," Tracy said.

"What's that phrase you were telling me, Tracy?" Doug asked. "Something you read in a book about God pursuing us?" Doug pushed aside the empty plate.

"God is the relentless lover," Tracy said. "And we are His first love. He will never stop pursuing us because He wants us back."

"Yeah, exactly," Doug said. "That's how God is. That's how He was with Rick. I'm telling you, Christy, it's awesome. When Todd's better, we'll have to all get together and go to the beach or something."

"I would love that," Christy said.

"Are you guys ready to go back upstairs and check on Todd?" Tracy asked.

"I am," Christy said.

They returned to room 302, and Todd opened his eyes long enough to recognize Tracy and mumble a few words to Doug. Christy held Todd's hand the whole time, and when Todd fell back to sleep, Doug asked if she was ready to go back to Rancho.

Christy hesitated. "I think I'd rather stay here. I can call Katie and have her pick me up later. I just don't want to leave him yet."

"Are you sure?" Doug asked.

Tracy smiled and tugged on her husband's arm. "Trust me, Christy is making the right choice."

"Do you need some money for food?" Doug asked.

"No, I have money. Thanks. And thanks for buying lunch."

"Anytime." Doug gave her a strong hug. "I'm serious about our getting together as soon as Todd is ready. You let us know when a good time is for you guys."

"We really missed you while you were in Switzerland." Tracy gave Christy another hug good-bye. "I'm glad you're back, and I'm glad that . . ." She glanced at Todd. "I'm glad that everything is settled in your heart."

"Me too," Christy said.

Tracy whispered in Christy's ear, "And I'll pray that Todd wakes up all the way real soon so you can tell him what you told us."

About half an hour after Doug and Tracy left, Todd woke up.

"Hey, you," Christy said.

Todd's eyes were wide, staring at Christy and barely blinking.

Thrilled to have his complete attention, Christy came close and said, "Todd, I have something important to tell you."

He looked at her peacefully, waiting.

"Todd, I love you. I love you with all my heart."

When he didn't respond, Christy repeated her declaration. "I love you, Todd."

Todd moved his left hand slowly. Christy thought he was going to reach up and touch her face. Instead, he brushed his fingers across the top of the blanket. His eyes grew wider, and he flicked invisible bits of something from the blanket. His breathing became more rapid.

Christy reached over and pushed the buzzer for the nurse. "Are you okay?" Christy asked Todd.

"There are so many of them," he mumbled. "Look out! They're com- ing! So many!"

The nurse stepped into the room, and Christy said, "Something's wrong."

"Todd?" the nurse said in a loud voice. "Todd, what is it?"

He continued to flick his hand across the blanket without answering her.

"Do you see something, Todd?" the nurse asked.

"Spiders," he muttered. "So many of them. They won't leave."

Christy's heart began to pound fiercely. *Did the accident affect his brain? What's going on?*

"Okay, Todd," the nurse said firmly. "We'll take care of the spiders. You're hallucinating. We'll put you on a different pain medication right away." She checked the IV bag and detached it from the metal stand.

"The medication is making him hallucinate?" Christy surmised.

"Yes, it's common. We can put him on something else that won't affect him. Don't worry. He'll be okay."

Christy did worry. She stayed beside Todd for the rest of the afternoon. He slept soundly and didn't appear to have any more bouts with invisible spiders. By evening, Katie came to the hospital and urged Christy to return to the dorm with her to get a decent night's sleep.

"You're going to need a shower pretty soon," Katie said, "if you don't mind my saying so. You really should sleep in your own bed tonight."

Christy convinced Katie to stay a little longer. She was glad Katie did because, at about nine o'clock, Todd woke up and talked to both Katie and Christy, telling them how much better he felt. He even laughed a strange, hoarse kind of laugh. The nurse had warned Christy the new medication would make him a little high, and he wouldn't necessarily remember what he said or what they said to him.

Despite the nurse's admonition, Christy nestled in close to Todd and said, "Todd, I love you."

He grinned oddly with his swollen lips and said, "Of course you do."

Katie sympathetically pulled Christy's arm and said, "We need to go. Let him sleep. He'll be able to hear you and process your words better tomorrow. Come on, Chris."

Reluctantly, Christy left room 302 once Todd was asleep again. She followed Katie to the parking lot. When they reached Baby Hummer, Christy stopped.

Katie seemed to read her mind. "I know it doesn't have air bags. Are you nervous about driving with me now?"

"It's not driving with you, Katie, it's getting in a car—any car—and going on the freeway."

"I know. I had the same queasy feelings last night when I left here."

"You did?"

Katie nodded. "I drove extra slow, and I prayed all the way."

"Then let's do that again. You drive extra slow, and we'll both pray." Christy buckled her seat belt. "Only don't drive so slow that you become a danger to other drivers."

"Yes, Mother," Katie quipped.

Christy grinned. "Have you been keeping the room clean while I was gone?"

Katie looked at Christy as if she hoped her roommate was kidding. "Yes, of course. And by the way, Dixie and Daisy are doing just fine."

"Who?"

"Our new goldfish. I bought twins."

Christy shook her head. After working several years at a pet store she knew goldfish didn't have twins. As many as thirty goldfish could be in a tank, and they would all look alike.

"I moved the fishbowl, so they aren't getting heated up from the afternoon sun that comes in the window."

"Good," Christy said.

"Guess what Matt did today?" Katie steered Baby Hummer out of the hospital parking lot.

"I have no idea."

"He found out where they took Gus and went to salvage what he could."

"Did he really? That was so nice of him."

"Yeah, look in the backseat."

Christy turned, and there, on Baby Hummer's backseat, was Todd and Christy's camp stove, still in the box, looking unharmed.

"It was under the backseat. Apparently just about everything else was demolished."

"Todd is going to be so happy about the stove," Christy said.

"I know. That's why I brought it with me. I was going to take it into the hospital to show him, but when I got there, I forgot to grab the stove."

"I'll have to bring it with me tomorrow when I go to see him," Christy said.

"Matt pulled one other thing from Gus."

"What?"

"You'll see. It's in our room. On your bed. I even washed it."

"Can't you tell me what it is?"

"You'll see," Katie said.

As promised, Katie drove nice and slow all the way to school, and they arrived in the dorm parking lot without incident.

Christy hurried to their room, driven by curiosity as to what other item had been salvaged from Gus. As soon as she opened their door, Christy felt a surge of warm nostalgia and smiled at her roommate.

"Oh, Katie, I'm so glad Matt saved this. Thanks for washing it." Christy lifted Todd's old navy blue hooded sweat shirt and pressed her face into it.

"Yeah, I thought you two needed each other tonight," Katie said.

She was right. After Christy took a long, hot shower, she pulled on her favorite flannel boxer shorts and a T-shirt. Then, crawling into bed, she wrapped herself up in Todd's sweat shirt, pulling the hood over her head.

CHAPTER 15

For Christy, the rest of the week was filled with trips to the hospital, meals on the run, and the understanding nods of her professors and Donna whenever Christy explained why she was leaving campus again. By Friday, Todd was ready to leave the hospital. The doctor ordered two weeks of bed rest.

After exploring all the options, everyone agreed Todd would stay at Bob and Marti's, since his dad had a business trip to Canada and Todd wouldn't receive the care he needed in his dorm room.

Matt and Katie had come to the hospital together on Thursday and offered to run the youth group programs at Riverview Heights while Todd was out of commission. Sierra was going to arrange for her friend Randy to bring his band on Sunday for a miniconcert.

On Friday, Bob and Marti arrived at the hospital together to pick up Todd. That surprised Christy. Her aunt showed up with her hair plaited into a single braid down her back and wearing conservative black pants and a simple white shirt. It looked as if she wore a little makeup. Lipstick, for sure.

Christy was glad Cheyenne wasn't there. She wondered if Bob had insisted Todd stay in their home as a way of keeping Marti around and allowing the two of them to join efforts on a project.

A hospital attendant rolled Todd's wheelchair to the parking lot as Marti and Christy followed with the bouquets he had received. Earlier that morning Matt had brought some of Todd's clothes stuffed unceremoniously in a plastic grocery bag, which now rested on Todd's lap as they exited.

Bob had gone to pull the car up to the front. To Christy's surprise, Bob arrived in a blue Volvo station wagon. He got out, all smiles.

"How do you like her?" he asked Todd. Then grinning at Christy, Uncle Bob said, "She's not brand-new, but she's sturdy. Safest car on the road, they say. I got a great deal on her."

Christy couldn't imagine why her uncle would be so proud of his "soccer mom" car. It had a rack on the top and peeling surf logo stickers on the back window.

"The car is for you." Marti spelled out to Christy what she obviously hadn't understood.

"For both of you," Bob said. "I put it in both your names. You'll have to sign the papers when we get home. And you'll have to cover your own insurance after the first six months."

Christy was stunned. She didn't know what to say.

"I got a good deal," Bob said again, as if to convince Christy that she should be happy.

"I suggested he buy a Land Rover, but the insurance payments were ridiculous," Marti said. "I know this isn't the brightest and newest vehicle on the road, but when you compare it to that ridiculous death trap Todd was driving . . ."

Christy quickly jumped in. She wanted to preserve dear ol' Gus's memory as positively as she could. "It's wonderful, Uncle Bob. Thank you. You really didn't have to do this. Thank you so much."

Christy wasn't sure if Todd caught all that was going on. He had been much more alert the past two days, but Christy knew he still was on pain-killers. That was why she hadn't attempted to tell him again that she loved him. She wanted to wait until he settled into Bob and Marti's house and things calmed down some. Then he would be able to hear her and to understand.

Leaning over and making eye contact with Todd, who sat patiently in the wheelchair, Marti said, "Well? You haven't said anything, Todd. What do you think?"

"Thank you," Todd said flatly. "Thank you, Marti, Bob. You didn't have to do this. I'll pay you guys back."

"You will do no such thing," Marti said. "If you had any idea how much fun Robert had this week trying to find a car for you, you wouldn't dare rob him of his happiness. Or my happiness, either. I had a small hand in making this choice. It was either this blue one or a drab, olive green one. I said buy the blue one. Don't you think blue is much better than olive green?"

"It's perfect," Todd said. He raised his hand and gave Marti's arm a squeeze. "Thank you."

"Enough of all the thank-yous," Marti said. "Let's get you in the car. We have the den all made up for you, and the sooner you get home, the better."

Christy was amazed at her aunt's caring and efficiency as she gave directions on how to get Todd into the car as painlessly as possible and where the flowers should be situated in the back of the station wagon. She even insisted Todd sit in the front seat while she and Christy took the backseat. Christy couldn't remember a time when her aunt had given up the front seat to anyone.

The hour and a half drive to Newport Beach went by quickly as Bob told the story of how he had searched for the right car. He had researched the Internet for cars ranked highest in safety ratings. Then he checked for the best year for Volvo station wagons and hunted for one with low miles and in good condition. He was proud of his accomplishment in finding this beauty. Todd and Christy both showered him with their exclamations of appreciation.

Christy felt pretty excited about having a car. She liked this one. In high school she and her mom had shared a car. She didn't need one in Basel, and the way her savings were going, she wouldn't have been able to buy her own for a long time. She smiled as she thought about how she and Todd now shared two possessions: a camp stove and a car. All they needed was a grungy dog, and they could get married and hit the road like a modern American gypsy couple.

Marti was right about having the den all fixed up for Todd. She had moved the leather couch back and set up a rented hospital bed in front of the wide-screen TV. Stacks of videos, magazines, and snack food were arranged on the coffee table, waiting for Todd. She had purchased several new T-shirts and surf shorts and had them folded on the end of the bed with the top sheet turned down, the way a fancy hotel would prepare a bed.

Christy knew Todd wasn't himself yet because he passed by all the food and extras. Instead, he crawled right into bed and fell asleep within minutes.

"I'm going to keep his medication right here." Marti showed Christy a tray she had placed on the end table. A pitcher of water sat ready with a glass and a straw and a thermometer.

Marti, you would have made such an efficient mother. It's really too bad you never had children. Although, what am I saying? After the way Marti always tried to make me into the daughter she never had, how could I wish on her unborn children what I had forced on me for so many years?

"Come see what I've done to your room," Marti said. She led Christy upstairs in their modern beach-front house to the room Marti originally had fixed up for Christy when she came to stay with them the summer she turned fifteen. The decor had been a feminine combination of white eyelet curtains, pink ruffles, and flowers.

When Marti opened the door, Christy couldn't believe she was viewing the same room in which she had spent so many hours during her teen years. Now the motif was southwestern, complete with a stenciled desert landscape painted on the walls. The wall on the far left was covered with a blazing orange-and-pink sunset behind what looked like an actual wooden vegetable cart, complete with strings of red chilies hanging from the top. The mission-style bed was raised from the ground by adobe bricks. Dozens of tiny white twinkling lights were strung from the four wooden bedposts, and a sheer swath of ivory fabric draped the entire ensemble. In front of the window sat an antique table with a brightly painted ceramic water pitcher and washbowl.

The swirl of color and commotion overwhelmed Christy. She didn't know how anyone could be expected to actually sleep in such a room. All it needed was the piped-in sounds of a coyote howling under the moon, and it could be the prototype of an attraction at a theme park.

"What do you think?" Marti asked eagerly. Bob had joined them, and Christy caught his glance before she spoke. He seemed to be cautioning her to think carefully before she answered.

"It's really something," Christy said slowly. It was the most honest phrase she could come up with. She added, "You must have worked very hard on this."

"Yes, I did, thank you. Come see my pottery." Marti marched to the dresser near the adjoining bathroom and told Christy about each bowl, vase, and painted plate that was displayed on the dresser top as well as on hooks on the wall behind the dresser.

"They're really beautiful, Aunt Marti." Christy meant it. The colors and shapes of Marti's pottery were stunning.

"Do you really think so?" Marti asked.

"Yes. I love this small dish, and the way you did the edges in blue."

"I made that as a ring dish. You know, for when you take off your rings at night or to wash your hands. It's a nice place to put them. I'd like you to have that ring dish."

"Oh, I like it, but you don't have to give it to me. I don't want to break up your collection. Besides, I don't have any rings." Christy showed Marti her bare hands. "I mean, I don't usually wear any rings."

"Then use it for your bracelet, Christina." Marti nodded toward the gold ID bracelet Todd had given her, which Christy always wore on her right wrist. "At least until he gives you a ring to wear." Aunt Marti's grin was cunning.

"Thank you." Christy took the small blue dish her aunt had been holding. "I appreciate this very much. I also appreciate all that both of you are doing for Todd. It's really nice of you to let him stay here."

"No problem at all. You know he's like a son to us," Bob said.

Marti looked at Bob over her shoulder and seemed to be softening. She turned to Christy. "There isn't anything we wouldn't do for either of you. You know that."

Before Christy could stop herself, she blurted out, "Then don't leave, Aunt Marti. Don't go to Santa Fe. Stay here where you belong."

White-hot anger flared on Marti's face. But no words spewed from her mouth. Christy pulled back, expecting the lava to come at any moment.

"I already knew." Bob touched Marti gingerly on the shoulder.

She jerked away, as if his touch hurt her. "You told!" she hissed at Christy.

"No, I didn't tell anyone. I promised I would keep your secret, and I did."

"Cheyenne told me," Bob said.

Marti spun around. "Cheyenne? When?"

"Several weeks ago. He came by when you weren't home. I guess he thought you and I had discussed the situation, and he spoke to me about his plans for the art colony and how you were involved."

"Why didn't you tell me?" Marti spat the words at Bob.

Bob paused before answering softly, "Why didn't you tell me?"

"You know what?" Christy said. "I'm going to check on Todd. I'm sorry I said what I did." She hurried to leave the southwestern guest room and paused before closing the door behind her. "But I meant what I said, Aunt Marti. I did keep your secret. And I don't want you to go. I love you."

As soon as Christy shut the door behind her, she heard her aunt yell at her uncle. Christy felt awful as she descended the stairs.

Why did I have to open my mouth? Where did that come from? It just popped right out. I didn't mean to start this war between Bob and Marti.

Christy knew she hadn't actually started anything between her aunt and uncle. Their problems existed long before Christy opened her mouth. She just wished she hadn't said anything. She wished she and Todd weren't here right now. She wished . . .

Suddenly Christy remembered Todd's phrase, *"As you wish."* She stopped at the foot of the stairs. She could hear her aunt and uncle's muffled voices as they argued. Christy sat on the bottom step and prayed for them, concluding with, "And, Lord, I know what matters isn't what I wish would happen. I want things to turn out the way you wish. As you wish. Let it be so."

Tiptoeing into the den, Christy was glad to see Todd still was asleep and couldn't hear Bob and Marti fighting upstairs. Christy smiled when she saw the peaceful expression on Todd's face. All over again she wanted to tell him she loved him. She wanted to kiss him and hold him and tell him that she would love him forever as intensely and sweetly as she loved him at this moment.

"I love you," she said aloud, her voice low and steady. "The whole world and everyone around us might go completely mad, but that won't change my love for you, Todd."

He didn't respond.

Christy padded off into the kitchen and found some apple juice and string cheese in the well-stocked refrigerator. She saw the menu for the weekend written in Bob's handwriting and stuck on the refrigerator door by a magnet in the shape of a sailboat. He had listed lasagna for Friday night. If Christy knew her uncle and his interest in cooking, he already had made the lasagna, and it was waiting to be baked.

Her guess was right. The glass casserole dish was on the refrigerator's bottom shelf. Christy glanced at the clock. It was almost five o'clock. She decided to take the initiative, pop the lasagna into the oven, and put together a salad so dinner would be ready when everyone felt hungry.

As it turned out, Christy ate alone. Todd said he was just thirsty but thought he might eat some toast later. Lasagna didn't sound good to him.

Uncle Bob and Aunt Marti hadn't come downstairs yet, and Christy certainly didn't feel comfortable going upstairs.

Choosing to sit alone in the kitchen, Christy thought of all the meals she had eaten in this house and all the emotions she had gone through in front of her aunt and uncle. She wasn't frightened by the high-pitched level of their emotions she had seen today, as long as everything ended up settled between them.

"Please let them work things out, Father God," Christy prayed. She ate and prayed and then put away the huge quantity of leftovers. She decided to make the toast for Todd, even if he wasn't awake yet. Spreading some butter on the bread, she then drizzled it with honey, the way her mom used to make toast whenever Christy was sick.

For a fleeting moment, Christy wondered if she would make a good mom. She thought she would. She hoped she would. But first of all and above all, she hoped she would make a good wife.

With her heart full of warm thoughts, Christy carried the toast into the den and found Todd sitting up with a handful of tissues over his nose.

"Are you okay?" Christy put down the plate. She noticed blood on the sheets and reached for more tissues.

Todd nodded. "Bloody nose," he garbled. Pulling away his hand, Christy could see his nose had stopped bleeding.

"Can I get you anything?"

"No," Todd leaned back. "Man, all this medicine is messing me up."

"I'll get you a washcloth." Christy returned with a damp cloth and a hand towel.

"I keep thinking one of these times when I wake up, I'll feel normal again, but I don't," Todd said.

"You will," Christy assured him. "One of these times. I'm amazed at how much you're sleeping."

"It's the drugs," Todd said. "I'd take myself off of them if I weren't still hurting so much." He pressed his hand against his side, above his right hip, where the incision had been made for the surgery. He had mentioned before that the area was sore and that he could feel the sutures tugging any time he moved the wrong way.

"I could call the doctor." Christy glanced at the clock. "I don't know if he's still at the hospital, but he might prescribe a different medication. When you were in the hospital, they had to change your pain-killer because you were seeing spiders."

"Oh yeah," Todd said slowly. He wiped his face with the washcloth. "I think I remember that. It's all so fuzzy. They were crawling across my bed, weren't they?"

"I wouldn't know," Christy teased. "I didn't see the spiders. But you certainly did. The nurse said it was common to hallucinate like that."

"Will you call the doctor for me? Ask him if I can take something that won't knock me out or make my nose bleed."

"Okay." Christy turned to go back to the kitchen and then realized she was still holding the plate in her hand. "I brought you some toast with honey."

"Thank you, honey," he said with a teasing grin.

Christy grinned back. That was the first time Todd had called her honey. She liked it.

He called her honey again on Saturday morning when she brought him more toast and orange juice a little after nine o'clock. Todd had turned on the TV and was watching Saturday-morning cartoons. Christy returned to the kitchen, prepared herself a bowl of Cheerios, and made herself comfortable on the couch.

"How did you sleep?" Todd turned to watch Christy instead of the cartoons.

"Not great. My aunt and uncle had a big argument when we arrived last night. I didn't have the nerve to go upstairs since they never came down. So I slept on the couch in the living room." She put her bowl of Cheerios on the floor and stretched out her neck from the kink that was tightening up on the right side.

"Do you think they're okay?" Todd asked.

"I don't know. Todd, I'm worried about them; I prayed for them. Then I got mad at them. I don't know what to think anymore."

"I had a feeling a couple of weeks ago, when I saw your uncle, that things weren't going real great between Bob and Marti."

"I hope they try to work things out. Doesn't it suddenly feel as if you and I are the adults, and they are the volatile teenagers, like we used to be?"

Todd yawned and turned the sound on the cartoons to mute. "I was never volatile."

"Okay, the volatile teen I used to be." Christy went back to her bowl of Cheerios, aware that Todd was still watching her.

"You were never volatile," Todd said. "Emotional, maybe. But not volatile. You always think things through. And you feel everything intensely and honestly. Those are qualities I've long appreciated about you."

Christy paused, her spoon midway to her mouth, dripping milk into the bowl. *Tell him! Go ahead. Look at the way he's looking at you! Tell Todd you love him.*

Returning the spoon to the bowl and composing herself, Christy said, "I've long appreciated many of your qualities, too, Todd. As a matter of fact, I've been wanting to tell you that—"

Before Christy's important words could hit the air, Aunt Marti entered the den with her usual dramatic flair. "How is our precious, precious patient this morning? I am so, so sorry we left you alone last night. Were you able to manage by yourself, dear Todd?"

The sweetness dripping from Marti's words irritated Christy; yet she wondered if the attitude change reflected any changes in her aunt's heart.

"Christy took good care of me," Todd said. "She called the doctor and got a different medication, and that seems to be helping."

Marti blinked. "When did you get new medication?"

"Last night. Christy had the doctor call in the prescription to the drugstore over in the Westcliffe Shopping Center. She picked it up last night just before the pharmacy closed."

Marti looked even more surprised that Christy had managed such a feat.

Uncle Bob appeared and asked if anyone was interested in waffles for breakfast. His expression looked more peaceful than it had the night before. Christy hoped all these subtle changes indicated things were better between her aunt and uncle.

"I got some cereal already," Christy said.

"I could go for a waffle," Todd said.

"Does that mean your appetite is returning?" Bob asked. "That sounds like a good sign."

Marti noticed the blood drops on the sheets and immediately made a fuss. When Todd told her it was from a bloody nose, she insisted he go to the emergency room.

"I'm sure it was from the change in climate from the desert to the ocean air," Todd said. "Either that or from the medication. I'm on different stuff now. It's okay, really."

"If it happens again, I think we should go to the emergency room. And we will go immediately," Marti said. "Your health is too volatile right now."

Todd and Christy exchanged glances. It wasn't the last time they read and sent silent messages to each other that weekend. They seemed to know what the other person was thinking. Christy loved this silent, intimate exchange.

Marti and Bob, however, didn't seem to be experiencing as intimate an exchange as Christy had hoped. They didn't offer any information on their conversation the night before. And even though they seemed cordial to Christy and Todd and each other, Christy couldn't tell if they actually had settled anything or if they had put their difficulties aside to focus on Todd. She guessed it was the latter.

Christy spent the weekend indoors, watching movies, watching Todd sleep, and watching Bob and Marti be cordial to each other. Christy felt strange leaving Sunday evening to drive back to school in the new Volvo. She wanted to stay with Todd. That wouldn't have been a good idea since she had missed so many of her classes and work last week. It was time for life to move back to a regular schedule. But her heart wasn't regular about anything.

Christy called Bob and Marti every day and received a full report on how "Marti's patient" was doing before the phone was handed over to Todd. From the way he communicated in short sentences each time she called, Christy guessed Marti was always in the room with him.

Christy's brother called Todd later in the week to tell him he had become a Christian at the hospital when Christy had prayed with him. Christy called her aunt's house on Thursday, and Todd said, "Hey, David called me last night. Can you believe what happened with him?"

"I was supposed to tell you. I can't believe I kept forgetting. I know; it's wonderful, isn't it?"

Her next thought was, *And I need to tell you something else that's wonderful and will make you exceptionally happy. I told you so many times when you couldn't hear me, but now I need to wait until no one else is around.*

During the week, people Christy didn't know stopped her on campus and asked how Todd was doing. By the time she left work on Friday afternoon and loaded up her clothes in the back of the Volvo, she thought she would burst from anticipation.

But the drive to Newport Beach felt as if it were taking hours. The freeway was thick with weekend traffic.

"Come on, come on!" Christy sputtered at the cars in front of her when she entered the Mission Viejo area. The traffic slowed to a crawl at the La Paz exit.

Unless there's been an accident, you people better have a good excuse for slowing down like this!

Christy realized she needed to calm down and slow down before she became part of an accident herself. She breathed more slowly and let her imagination go back to her planning. It had been a week of planning. Planning quietly, when she lay awake unable to sleep at night, planning with Katie when the two of them went to the grocery store on Thursday night and bought eggs, bacon, croissants, and Todd's favorite gourmet mango–papaya jam.

A light October drizzle danced across the windshield. "Oh no you don't," Christy muttered as she switched on the windshield wipers. "You little raindrops are going to be on your way by tomorrow morning, aren't you? Because you aren't invited to breakfast on the beach. I've planned it all out. Breakfast for two. Just Todd and me. No sea gulls. No raindrops. Got it?"

The traffic came to a stop, but Christy's heart raced on ahead to the beach. *Just Todd and me. Just the two of us cuddled close by the fire when I give him those three eternal words that are burning a hole in my heart.*

CHAPTER 16

When Christy arrived at Bob and Marti's house after her aggravating trek on the crowded freeways, she was surprised to see how much Todd had improved. His face was no longer swollen, and his black eye had faded. He greeted Christy at the door with a big hug and told her she was just in time for dinner. Apparently Uncle Bob had been showing Todd how to make chicken enchiladas.

The four of them sat down to eat in the kitchen. Marti eagerly gave Christy a full report on how Todd had improved during the week under Marti's careful attention. Christy and Todd exchanged warm glances and smiles while they ate. In the back of Christy's mind, she continued to plan how her breakfast on the beach would be executed the next morning.

Just before Christy went to bed, she told Todd, "I'd like to make breakfast for us in the morning."

"Sure," he said. "I'll help. Your uncle has been showing me some of his secrets in the kitchen. I think I've learned more about cooking this week than I ever have before."

"Actually, I wanted to make our breakfast on the beach—at the fire pit we used to go to." She gave him a hopeful, expectant look. "Does that sound like a good idea to you?"

Todd's smile told her it was more than okay. His tender gaze said he loved her idea. "What time?"

"Whenever. What time have you been waking up?"

"Seven. Seven-thirty. Is that too early for you?"

"No, I'll be ready."

Christy was ready at seven-fifteen the next morning. She had packed all the food in Bob and Marti's old picnic basket. It was the same basket Uncle Bob had sent with Todd and Christy the first time they had a breakfast picnic on the beach. She had the firewood, fire starter, matches, blankets, and everything else she thought they would need for a cozy morning on the beach. The raindrops politely had complied with her wishes and hadn't returned with the morning.

The only thing missing was Todd. Her breakfast companion was sound asleep.

Christy considered going to the fire pit, setting up everything, and then waking Todd before she started to cook the eggs. She was trying to figure out how she would carry everything, when Uncle Bob stepped into the kitchen and greeted her by saying, "You sure are up early, bright eyes."

Christy told Uncle Bob her plan, and he eagerly agreed to help her by carrying the wood and necessary cooking utensils out to the fire pit. Christy followed him onto the cool sand as she lugged along the blanket and basket of food.

The morning sun hid behind a gray cover of thick clouds. Only a slight breeze ruffled across the sand.

You're just like Todd, Christy thought, looking for the absent sun. *You're nestled under the covers when you should be here, with me. Come on, I'm waiting for you.*

"Could you kids go for some coffee? I could bring a Thermos out to you," Bob said.

"That would be fine as long as . . ." She hesitated, not sure how to say the rest of her sentence politely. "As long as you just bring the coffee and then . . ."

"And then be on my way?" Bob unloaded the wood at the fire pit and gave Christy a curious grin. "You make it sound as if you two want to be alone."

Christy tried not to blush. "I hope that didn't sound rude."

"Oh no, not at all. It sounded to me like a woman in . . . a woman who is in . . . what's that word?"

Christy grinned. "In love."

"Ah yes, a woman in love."

"I am," Christy said quietly. "I really, truly am."

Uncle Bob tilted his head and, with a merry twinkle in his eyes, asked, "Is it anyone I know?"

"Yes, as a matter of fact, it is someone you know. And don't you dare say anything because . . ." Again Christy hesitated, looking for the right way to phrase her thoughts.

Her uncle seemed to know just what she was thinking. "Because, perhaps, you would like to be the one to tell him?"

Christy nodded.

"Then why don't you wait right here? Get your fire going. I'll make the coffee and roust Prince Charming for you. I don't need to bring the Thermos out here; Todd can bring it."

"Thanks, Uncle Bob. You are so good to me."

Uncle Bob brushed off her compliment and hustled back to his beach-front house. Christy made herself comfortable on the blanket by stretching out on her stomach. For several luxurious moments she gazed contentedly at the magnificent, endless Pacific Ocean. She breathed in deeply until the moist, chill air made her lungs ache, and she could feel a slight tingle of sea salt in her nostrils.

This is it, Father God. This is your day. You have aroused love and awakened it in me, haven't you? Thank you for this amazing gift of love. I know this pleases you. Keep my heart set on you and on your path.

Christy thought about how in years past she would have prayed a testing sort of prayer right about now. She would have said something like, "God, if you don't want me to tell Todd I love him and if you don't want us to end up married, then take away these feelings and make me know somehow that he's not the one."

However, Christy had come a long way in her relationship with the Lord. She knew God wasn't a "this or that" dictator. Her life was not about going "this way" and living or going "that way" and dying. Life was a series of choices and a process of choosing God and His path and then trusting Him for each step along the way. She knew that God was her heavenly Father. Her Shepherd. The Lover of her soul. He wanted what was best for her and had directed her through the years to make choices that would benefit her future and strengthen her relationship with Him.

Christy sat up and hugged her bent legs close, warming her cold nose by wedging it between her knees. She remembered something Todd had told her a long time ago when they were talking about knowing God's will. She had been trying to decide if she should go to Switzerland. Todd's advice had been *"Love God and do what you want."*

His statement had seemed flippant to her at the time. Going to school in Switzerland was a huge decision; yet all Todd had done was to tell her he would support whatever she decided.

Now Christy understood the wisdom of Todd's advice. As she had begun to fall unreservedly in love with the Lord over the years, her heart was so turned toward Him that more and more she wanted to do whatever was the most pleasing and honoring to God.

"Love God and do what you want," Christy whispered in the gentle morning quiet. She felt complete peace. No doubts. This was right. A smile pressed Christy's lips upward in what felt like a permanent expression. She felt full inside. Full of love. Full of God. Full of hope.

Rising to her feet and stretching, Christy decided she'd better start the fire. The wood caught right away, and the grill she placed across the top of the cement fire ring balanced just enough for her to settle the skillet in the center. She placed the bacon strips in the skillet and waited for them to sing their splattering tune in harmony with the melody that was sizzling in her heart.

The bacon was just beginning to smell promising when Christy looked up and saw Todd coming toward her, Thermos in one hand and two coffee mugs in the other. His steps were slow but steady. Straight. His eyes were set on Christy, and he looked as if nothing in this world could stop him from coming to her.

Christy's heart danced a waltz as she counted his deliberate steps toward her.

Step, two-three-four. Step, two-three-four. Do you have any idea how incredibly handsome you are, my beloved, my friend?

Christy playfully touched her fingers to her lips, kissed them, and tossed her kiss to Todd on the fresh morning breeze.

Since his hands were full, Todd quickly turned his head and stretched his neck, as if to catch her kiss on his cheek. His smile seemed as permanently in place as hers was.

Christy's gaze never wavered from Todd coming toward her. In her mind and her heart, Christy knew she would never forget the sight of this man walking to her in the sand. This man who had brushed up against death two weeks ago and was now very much alive and very much in love. With her.

"Smells good." Todd stopped in front of the fire.

Christy thought it funny that his opening words for this momentous occasion were so common.

"I love you," Christy blurted out. Her hand immediately flew to her mouth. She had meant to say, "It's the bacon," but she was so full of love for Todd that the declaration just tumbled out.

Todd slowly lowered himself next to her on the blanket. He put down the Thermos and mugs and looked at her as if he wasn't sure he could trust his ears. His expression invited her to repeat the words.

Lowering her hand from her mouth, Christy looked at Todd's ocean blue eyes, and taking a deep breath, she dove in all the way to his soul. "I love you," she said slowly and deliberately. "I love you, Todd."

"I thought that's what you said." His voice caught with emotion as he added, "I love you, Kilikina."

Neither of them moved.

The bacon seemed to send sputtering firecrackers into the air while the flames snapped brightly in the fire ring. Overhead, three sea gulls circled and squawked loudly, like trumpeters heralding a proclamation from the King.

Slowly, tenderly, Christy and Todd moved toward each other until their lips met in a kiss that filled Christy even more full of love. As they drew apart, the overflow brimmed in her eyes and spilled down her smiling face.

Todd wiped her tears with his steady hand. Then he did something he had done when they were in Europe. He pressed his moist hand to his chest, right over his heart. Christy knew that was his way of saying he was holding her tears in his heart.

She touched his warm lips with her fingers. Todd grasped her hand and placed a long kiss in the palm of her hand. Christy let go and pressed his kiss to her heart. In a steady, sure whisper, she said, "I love you."

Todd's grin broadened. "You know what they say about a vow being established. If a declaration is stated three times, that means it's established forever."

Christy nodded. She didn't know if Todd was trying to give her a final opportunity to change her mind, but nothing could prompt her to alter her declaration. He knew what these words meant to her, to him, to their future. Her vow before God was established.

"I love you," she stated firmly, pausing between each word. This time an unexpected giggle escaped at the end. "I had it all planned. We were going to eat, and we were going to be all snuggly and romantic, and then I was going to tell you."

Todd moved closer and took her in his arms. "How's this for snuggly and romantic?"

Christy giggled again. "I can't believe I just blurted it out like that."

"You know," Todd said, his deep voice rumbling from his chest, "I've been dreaming for the past week or more that you told me you love me."

Christy pulled back and faced him. "Those weren't dreams, Todd. I have been telling you. I told you the very first time on the camping trip, but you couldn't hear me over the dune buggy motor. I told you again and again at the hospital while you slept, and also at Bob and Marti's."

"Then I guess I wasn't dreaming." Todd brushed Christy's flyaway hair from the side of her face.

"No," Christy said. "You weren't dreaming then, and you're not dreaming now. This is real. As real as it's ever been for me."

Todd's silver-blue eyes were fixed on hers, filling her, adoring her, speaking to her all the cherished messages she knew he held in his heart for her.

Just then a daring sea gull swooped closer.

"Oh no you don't!" Christy grabbed the spatula and swatted the air. "You guys stay away from the food this time."

Todd reached for the tongs and flipped the bacon. "This is looking like it's almost ready."

"I have eggs and croissants, too," Christy said. "And I even bought mango-papaya jam."

"You are amazing," he said. "How about some coffee? It's strong, but I added cream and sugar in the Thermos, the way you like it."

Christy knew Todd didn't drink coffee very often, but when he did, he drank it black. She thought how considerate he was to remember she liked her coffee spiffed up and to be willing to drink it the way she liked it.

Side by side, heart by heart, Todd and Christy prepared their beach breakfast. The sea gulls kept their distance. The raindrops stayed to themselves on some other corner of the planet while the lazy sun stretched and peeked out from under its thick gray comforter every ten minutes or so.

Todd and Christy's long, slow, private picnic leisurely rolled through the calm October morning. They laughed, teased, kissed, prayed, and ate until they could take in no more. Christy knew she couldn't have asked for a more perfect morning. Everything was more wonderful than any dream she had ever dreamed of Todd.

Yet, as they gathered up the blanket and packed up the cooking gear, Christy felt uninvited remorse come over her. Todd hadn't proposed to her.

She knew she hadn't expected him to. Not really. But after she had opened her heart so wide and felt him responding with equal openness and joy, the next step should have been for Todd to say the life-changing sentence that naturally would follow. He needed to say, "Will you marry me?"

And he hadn't said that at their picnic. He had said lots of other wonderful things. He had told Christy how he had been waiting for her to be sure of her love and to verbalize it. He told her that, yes, Doug and Tracy were right: He had known she was the one for him from that first day on this beach when he had seen her tumble to shore, draped in seaweed. He affirmed to Christy that there had been no other girls for him. She was the only girl he had ever kissed. The only girl he had ever loved. The only one.

But he didn't say, "Marry me."

They walked slowly through the sand back to the house. Todd hadn't taken his medication before joining Christy on the beach, and he was suffering now. Christy carried the heavy picnic basket with the frying pan, dishes, utensils, and leftover jam. All Todd carried was the folded-up blanket and the empty Thermos, but those two items seemed almost too heavy for him.

By the time they entered the warm kitchen, Todd's face was pale, and he had broken out in a sweat. He placed the blanket and Thermos on the kitchen counter and immediately went to bed, where he stayed for the rest of the day.

Christy knew she had no reason to feel anything but delight over their time together. Todd had given her every ounce of energy he had. She reminded herself of that when the nagging thoughts of *Why didn't he propose?* came flying at her the rest of the weekend.

———

On Sunday morning Bob and Christy went to church together, while Todd stayed in bed and tried to regain some of his strength. Christy and her uncle both invited Marti to go with them, but she insisted Todd needed her.

As it turned out, the message that morning was on baptism, and Christy wasn't sure that was what her aunt needed to hear right now. Marti needed to come to Christ and surrender her life to Him. Christy thought of her brother as the sermon came to a close. She wondered how he was doing and realized she hadn't called home for more than a week.

Her parents would understand. Todd was her top priority right now. She knew they would be supportive of her decision to move forward in her relationship with Todd, too. Yet she felt sad that they were so removed from her life. The separation had begun when she went to Switzerland and had continued even after she settled into school at Rancho. She never had been the kind of daughter who discussed everything with her mom. Christy had grown up as someone who kept to herself and worked through life's dilemmas quietly, in her room with the door closed.

Now that she had entered this next wonderful stage with Todd, Christy regretted that her mom hadn't been the kind of mom who was a best friend and a pal. But then, Christy's mom didn't have that kind of relationship with her own sister, Marti.

"You know," Bob said on their way home, "I made a decision this morning."

Christy, thinking her uncle was ready to talk about his strained relationship with his wife, positioned herself on the leather seat of Bob's Mercedes to pay full attention. It struck her that sitting in this position in ol' Gus was a miserable experience. But in Bob's car, it felt warm and comfy. She didn't know what it felt like to sit in the front passenger seat of their new Volvo because she hadn't had that pleasure yet.

"I've been doing what you suggested, Christy. I've been reading the Bible. I started in the New Testament with those first four books: Matthew, Mark, Luke, and John."

Christy nodded.

"And what I keep reading over and over is how Christ loved people through their weaknesses. He didn't pretend their problems didn't exist. He spoke the truth in love, but He said what needed to be said."

Christy felt a little nervous. How did her uncle intend to live out his revelation?

"I'm going to speak some truth to my wife," he said firmly.

"In love," Christy added.

"In love." Then Bob paused and said, "Christy, hand me the cell phone, will you?"

Christy handed it to him as he drove. She watched Bob punch in the automatic speed dial number for his home. "Are you going to tell her now? On the phone?"

"No, I'm checking to see if she wants us to pick up some lunch on our way home."

Christy felt nervous about Bob's plan while they stopped at Betsy's Deli to pick up sandwiches and salads. She felt nervous as Bob drove down his street and pulled the car into the garage. She felt nervous when Marti entered the kitchen and asked if the deli had her favorite chicken salad.

To Christy's surprise, instead of Uncle Bob's blasting out to his wife how she needed to make some decisions and some changes in her life, he went to her, wrapped his arms around her, and said, "I love you, Marti. With all my heart, I love you." Then he kissed her soundly on her surprised lips.

Christy couldn't remember ever seeing her uncle shower such affection on her aunt. Bob always had been kind and generous with Marti. But not passionate like this.

Marti pulled back, flabbergasted.

"I haven't told you that in a long time," Bob said, undaunted. "But it's true. It will always be true. I love you, and I always will love you. I'd give my life for you, Marti. Jesus said, 'Do not let your hearts be troubled. Trust in God.' I want your heart no longer to be troubled. I want you to trust in God."

Bob paused in his message of adoration just long enough for Christy to grab two of the deli sandwiches and make her exit, saying she would check on Todd.

He was sitting in the living room by the window, reading one of the textbooks Christy had brought for him, along with a list of assignments from his professors.

"You wouldn't believe what's going on in there." Christy settled in next to Todd and handed him a sandwich.

"Are they arguing again?"

"No, the opposite. Have they been arguing a lot while you've been here?"

"I couldn't sleep the other night because they were yelling so loud about who was right and who was wrong. Bob backed down, as he often does. He apologized, but it didn't settle anything."

"Well, he's in the kitchen right now telling her he loves her and would give his life for her and quoting verses to her."

Todd grinned. "Was the sermon on the book of Ephesians this morning?"

"No, baptism. Why?"

"Ephesians 5 says husbands are called to love their wives the way Christ loved the church and gave himself for her. You know, the way He gave His life for us. It talks about the husband washing his wife with the Word to make her clean."

Christy stared at the unwrapped sandwich in her hand. "That's beautiful. And so poetic. But let me tell you, it's weird to watch."

Todd laughed. "I don't think we're supposed to watch a husband as he washes his wife."

The imagery of Todd's words stirred Christy. She felt herself blushing and turned away. They ate quietly while she processed the concept of being washed clean and made presentable to God by His Word. The thought tied in with what the pastor had said that morning about baptism.

"Todd," Christy said, "I think I should get baptized."

He didn't look surprised by her sudden declaration. But then, she had been doing a lot of declaring lately.

"I was baptized when I was a baby. Or dedicated or something," she said. "I don't remember what they called it at my church in Wisconsin. I have a certificate that says the date and everything. But I want to be baptized now, as an adult, as a way of saying I choose to identify with Christ. To publicly show that I'm His follower."

"Must have been a pretty convincing sermon this morning."

"Not really. Well, maybe. I don't know. I've thought about this before. And that whole picture of being washed and made ready like a bride, well . . ." Christy wondered if she should press forward with her thought. "I see the deeper symbolism of baptism. It's like I said, I want to publicly take a stand and show I have set my heart on following Christ."

Todd nodded. She didn't feel the need for him to say anything. And she didn't need to say anything. She and Todd were moving on to the next level of their relationship, and she had reached a point in her relationship with the Lord in which she was ready to move on to a new level with Him.

"Where would you like to be baptized?" Todd said when he was about halfway through his sandwich.

"I don't know. You were baptized in the ocean, weren't you?"

"How did you remember that?"

"You told me the night Shawn died when we were at the jetty. You said you were baptized on my birthday, July 27."

"That's right."

"I think I'd like to be baptized at Riverview Heights since that's our church now. I'm not really connected to my parents' church in Escondido anymore. This is such a strange era in our lives, isn't it? What do we call home?"

Christy thought about her comment as she drove back to Rancho Corona that night. It was already dark, and she wished she had started back earlier, but she hadn't wanted to leave Todd. She thought about how Bob and Marti's house felt almost as much like home as her parents' house in Escondido—except that she felt as if she were sleeping in a covered wagon every night when she crawled into the raised bed in the southwestern guest room. She missed the pink ruffles more than she would have imagined.

Her dorm room felt temporary the way Basel had felt temporary. What Christy looked forward to was making her own home. A home somewhere with Todd.

She thought about how the weekend had gone. Their breakfast couldn't have been more perfect. Even the way she ended up blurting her "I love you" turned out to be wonderful and thrilling because it had tumbled out.

That Todd hadn't turned around and proposed didn't bother her as much as it had when they were picking up after their breakfast. She could think of all kinds of reasons Todd hadn't taken the next step. The poor guy hadn't recovered from his accident, and the medication made him groggy so he still slept a lot. He probably needed a chance to clear his head and think things through.

Besides all that, Christy thought, as she turned onto the road that led to Rancho Corona, *what would Todd and I use for money to start this new home of ours?*

She smiled at the vision that came to her. She and Todd were cashing all their wedding gift checks and heading for the Bargain Barn. But at least they were driving there in the blue Volvo instead of falling-apart Gus.

Maybe everything will come together little by little.

CHAPTER 17

The moment Christy stepped into the dorm room, Katie told her how terrific everything had gone in the youth group that morning. Seventeen students had shown up, and Randy's band was so popular they were playing again at the church Tuesday night.

"Look," Katie said, handing Christy a large get-well card. Pictured on the front was a crowd of funny-looking lions, tigers, and panthers. Inside the card read, *We all miss you fiercely!*

"Every one of the kids signed it," Katie said. "We can mail it to Todd tomorrow. You would be amazed how some of them are getting serious about God. One of the girls stood up this morning and talked about how Todd had said on the camp-out that none of us knows when we're going to die, and then the very next day he was in the accident. One of the guys brought three of his friends to church this week, and they all said they would bring some more friends Tuesday night."

"That's amazing." Christy put the card back in the envelope and unpacked her weekend bag.

"I told you God was doing God-things." Katie turned down her stereo and made herself comfortable on Christy's bed since Katie's wasn't made.

"You'll have to call Todd tomorrow to tell him all this," Christy said. "He'll be so excited. I know he's been praying for the group every day. That is, when he isn't sleeping."

"He's still pretty out of it, huh?" Katie fluffed up Christy's pillow and leaned on her elbow.

"He's doing a lot better." Christy stuffed her dirty clothes into the bag in the back of her closet and flashed a big grin. "Yes, he's doing a lot better."

"What is that smirk on your face, girl?" Katie said. "Am I to read into your comment that Todd is doing a lot better because you finally made your grand confession?"

Christy stood up straight and, with her hands on her hips, said, "Yes, I did. Our breakfast turned out perfect, and my very incredible and wonderful boyfriend should have no doubt in his mind as to how I feel about him."

"Ah, at last you can say, 'I'm my beloved's, and he is mine,' " Katie said with poetic flair.

"Where have I heard that before? It's from the Song of Solomon, isn't it?"

"I guess."

"Have you read that book lately?" Christy went over to Katie's bed, briskly pulled up the sheets and comforter, and then tidied up Katie's pillows, one of which was stuffed in the Little Mermaid pillowcase and the other in the Minnie Mouse pillowcase.

"Nope," Katie said.

"I read Song of Solomon when I was in Basel, and it's the strangest, most exotic, lyrical book. It only has eight chapters."

"Did you read the part that says, 'Your hair is like a flock of goats'?" Katie asked. "How romantic is that? Or that other line, 'Your neck is like the tower of David.' Oh, now, that sounds real attractive! If some guy tried those lines on me, I'm sure I'd fall instantly in love with him."

Christy laughed so hard she had to sit down. "Now I know why poor Matthew Kingsley was checked off your list. He didn't use the right lines on you."

"Poor Matthew Kingsley," Katie said with a sigh. "He never learned the goat hair pickup line back in Brightwater."

Christy laughed again. "Be nice. Matthew is still my dearest friend, you know."

"Oh, I know. Don't get me wrong. I think he's a wonderful guy. He sure jumped in and ran the show Sunday. Matt's a great guy. He's just not great for me. I need someone with pizzazz!"

"Are you saying Rancho Corona is low on guys with pizzazz?"

"Yes, I would say that. But don't read anything into this, Christy. I'm content. I honestly am. My days of searching for the perfect guy are over."

"And why is that?"

"I've decided to become one of those Proverbs 31 women."

"Is that a new club on campus?"

"No, but that's not a bad idea. It could replace the 'P.O. Box Club' Sierra and I started in England."

"And what did that stand for?" Christy asked.

"Don't you remember? The *P* is for 'pals' and the *O* is for 'only.' Sierra and I were the only two members. Our motto was to be Pals Only with guys. But after hearing Sierra's latest report on how she and Paul are getting along, I'm afraid our club has dwindled to one member. Me. So I think I'll start a new club. P-31, for the Proverbs 31 woman."

"I see," Christy said, hiding a smile. "Do I want to ask what the requirements are for entry to this P-31 club?"

"Very simple. We go by the first part of verse ten in that chapter. It says, 'An excellent wife, who can find?' "

Christy raised her eyebrows questioningly as she waited for an explanation.

"Don't you see? It doesn't say, 'An excellent hubby who can find?' It says a good wife. I would say that indicates the guy is the one who should be doing the seeking."

Christy laughed and threw her pillow across the room. Katie ducked, and the pillow hit the wall.

"You think I'm kidding? Believe me, I've thought through every angle of this. From here on out, I'm completely available to God. I'll just keep going about my business, right here, in the very center of God's will for my life now. And if there's a 'beloved' out there for me, then he can start seeking me for a change. I'll be here, an excellent future wife, just waiting for him to find me."

Christy was about to speak when Katie silenced her.

"Don't you dare say anything about how you feel bad that you and Todd are so sure and so close while nobody special is on the horizon for me."

Christy lowered her eyes.

"That's what you were going to say, isn't it?"

"How did you know?" Christy asked.

"Let's just say that you and I are on about verse eighty-four of that familiar song. You know, eighty-fourth verse, same as the first, a little bit louder and a little bit worse."

Christy walked over to sit on the bed next to Katie. "We do sound pretty good together when we sing."

"Not this song." Katie handed the Little Mermaid pillow to Christy for a backrest. "Not anymore. We need to give that old tune a rest. You are about to sing a brand-new song, Chris. Now your duet will be with Todd. Let me sing a new solo now, okay? None of the old verses apply to either of us anymore."

Christy wondered if she had ever admired her dearest friend more than she did at that moment.

"You let God do His God-things in your life, and I'll invite God to do His God-things in my life, and we won't compare ourselves with each other. Okay?" Katie seemed eager for Christy to agree.

With a bow of her head Christy said, "As you wish."

Christy noticed a genuine change in Katie as the week progressed. For one thing, she borrowed Christy's nail file and worked on her fingernails Tuesday night. Christy had never seen her tomboy friend file her nails. Bite them, yes. Pick at the cuticles, yes. But never file them and then rub her hands with cocoa butter lotion.

Katie filed away cheerfully while Christy looked up information on the Internet for her report on Milton, the blind poet. Katie mentioned that she was on the brink of perfecting her latest herbal tea recipe.

By Thursday, Katie was certain she had the mixture just right. To celebrate her breakthrough, she had gone to Bargain Barn to buy a china teapot and enough mismatched cups to host a tea party in their room.

Four of Katie's girl friends came on Thursday evening at seven-thirty. Katie said she would have invited more, but she had found only six china cups at Bargain Barn. Christy had cleaned their room and arranged it so all six "testers" had places to sit. Katie brewed her special tea in a hot pot plugged into the wall. While waiting for the tea to steep, Katie passed around a plate of Oreo cookies.

Sierra was telling the other guests about how her older sister, Tawni, was getting married at Thanksgiving and how Tawni's fiancé had taken a job in Oklahoma.

Christy was interested to hear all the details, but she slipped off into the corner where Katie was straining the herbs from the tea as she poured each cup. "Katie," Christy whispered, "I want to ask you this one more time. Please don't get upset. But are you sure no one is going to break out in a rash after drinking your tea this time?"

"I'm 99.9 percent positive," Katie said. "This is a completely different combination from what I used last spring. There aren't any nettles in this one."

"You used nettles last time?"

"I didn't realize they were stinging nettles, all right?"

"Why do you grow nettles?"

"Because nettles are good for people who have a snoring problem. I just got the dried nettles mixed up with the dried hibiscus. And I only used a pinch. But not this time. This concoction is my Indian summer blend. It's apples, ginger, cinnamon, and other spices. All safe ingredients, I assure you."

Christy would have felt more assured if Katie hadn't used the term "concoction" to describe the tea. Returning to her seat, Christy smiled graciously when Katie offered her a steaming cup of the fragrant brew.

"Katie, this is delicious!" Sierra was the first guest to sip her tea. Her positive report prompted the others to venture bravely where no woman had gone before.

"It is good." Christy nonchalantly checked the skin on the inside of her arm to see if any spots were appearing. None so far.

"It's a perfect blend," Sierra raved. "I like the balance of the ginger and the spices. Is that clove I taste?"

"Yes."

"It's just right. Not too strong. You've done it, Katie! You've come up with a winner."

Christy and the other guests soon agreed.

Katie beamed. "Then I officially announce the birth of Katie's Indian Summer Tea!"

The group applauded.

After Christy had gone a full twenty-four hours without any spots showing up or experiencing any other adverse effects, she took a small bag of Katie's tea to the bookstore. Donna often drank tea, and Christy thought she might want to try Katie's new blend.

Donna liked the tea as much as Christy, Sierra, and the others had. Later, as Christy was about to leave work to make her weekend trek to Newport Beach, Donna asked if she could get some more of Katie's tea.

"I can bring some in on Monday," Christy said. "Or you could call our room and ask Katie for some more."

"I'd like to pass it on to a friend of mine," Donna said. "He recently opened a bookstore in Murietta Hot Springs with a specialty café adjacent to the store. I thought he might want to add this tea to his menu at the café."

"Wouldn't something like this have to be approved by the Food and Drug Administration before it's served to the public?" Christy asked. She didn't want to discourage such a terrific opportunity for Katie, but she could just see Katie whipping up a batch in a hurry and mistaking nettles for one of the herbs. Christy envisioned café customers doubled over from the tea, and Katie sued for damages.

"I'm sure you're right," Donna said. "The laws have gotten so strict. That's good. But it's also limiting, isn't it?"

Christy felt glad for such laws. She didn't voice her opinion, though.

"If you and Katie have a chance to visit the café, I think you really would like it. It's called The Dove's Nest. They call the bookstore The Ark. Clever, isn't it?"

Christy studied Donna for a moment. She was wearing a pumpkin-colored turtleneck under a cream cable-knit cardigan, and her hair was pulled back in a wide gold barrette. With the rows of books behind her and the empty teacup in her hand, she looked as if she could be a model in an ad for Katie's tea. Donna personified everything that was cozy, welcoming, and warm.

"It sounds like fun," Christy said. "Todd should be able to get out more in the next few weeks. Maybe we could all go together sometime."

"How is he doing?" Donna asked.

"Lots better."

"And your relationship is still strong?"

"Stronger than ever. It's all just about perfect."

Donna placed a hand on Christy's shoulder. "Then remember this time, Christy. Write about it in your diary. Write about this perfect time so you will remember what you know to be true and what you feel bubbling over in your heart. In the years to come, you might experience a season of confusion or doubt. It will help so much if you have this time recorded."

Christy appreciated Donna's words, especially since she seemed to speak from experience. That weekend, Christy made sure she wrote in her diary everything she was feeling about Todd. Part of one of her entries read,

> *Right now I can't imagine going on in my life without being partnered with Todd in whatever comes our way. It seems so natural and like such a perfect fit for us to be together.*
>
> *I know he's going to propose soon. I just know it. Maybe before this weekend is over I'll hear those words dancing from his lips. I wonder how he will ask me. I'm sure it will be creative.*
>
> *Or maybe not. Todd has a very practical side to him, as well. I wouldn't be surprised if he just turned to me over tacos and said, "So do you want to get married?"*
>
> *I don't know how he will ask me or when, but I know I'm ready . . . more than ready to say yes.*
>
> *Yes, yes, a thousand times yes. I will marry you, Todd Spencer, and I will spend the rest of my life loving you with all my heart.*
>
> *And one more thing. Donna told me to write everything down in detail, so I have one detail to add. I love being in love. I love the way I wake each morning, and as soon as I do, I think about Todd and how I'm wildly, completely in love with him, and I smile.*
>
> *I've been smiling all the time lately. Nothing gets me down. Katie said I had that mysterious glow of love in my cheeks last week. She said it looked as if my eyes were always laughing about some secret and that even my posture was improved. That made me laugh. She said Todd's love for me had made me beautiful and that my love for him was healing him.*

All I know is that love has enabled me to soar higher into the heavens and into my relationship with God than I ever have gone before. Love has given me breath as I have plunged deeper into the ocean of understanding and patience. Love has focused my eyes to the minutest details, as minor as a ladybug inching across a daisy petal. And at the same time, love has enlarged my embrace so that I can gather friends and family closer to my heart than ever before.

Love is . . . oh, how I wish I had the words. Love is God's greatest gift and His most cherished reward. It is the echo of His own heart, sounded back to Him by us, His children, so that a decaying world might see firsthand the power of resurrection and new life. Love is all I know in my world right now.

I feel like laughing at my own giddiness.

I realize that I'm such a virgin in every way. I have never tasted a sensation as intoxicating as being in love. It has me reeling. Ha! I'm emotionally drunk on God's greatest gift, love. Imagine that!

Christy reread her diary entry a week and a half after she had penned her "Ode to Love," and she still felt euphoric. Todd had returned to classes and to his position at Riverview Heights Church. A little more than a month had passed since the accident. He was still moving slowly and sleeping a lot, but he had his life back. And Christy had Todd back. Life was rosy.

The report Todd gave Christy regarding Marti and Bob was that Bob was still pouring love over his wife. Washing her with words. Marti had neither pulled away from him nor pulled closer to him. She was stuck. Todd concluded that, for now, that was probably the best place for her to be.

Christy attended the two classes the church required for a person to be baptized and was signed up for the Sunday-evening baptism the week before Thanksgiving. She bought some beautiful ivory parchment cards at the bookstore and wrote invitations to her family and friends. As she addressed each envelope in her best handwriting, she wondered how long it would be before she was addressing wedding invitations to these same people.

Todd hadn't proposed yet. She knew it was only a matter of time. They even had talked a few times, in general terms, about how Doug had gone to Tracy's dad and asked him for Tracy's hand in marriage before Doug had proposed to Tracy. Christy guessed Todd was planning to talk to her dad. But when?

They would all be together in a few weeks for her baptism. And for Thanksgiving her parents had invited Todd, his dad, Bob, and Marti to come to their home. Christy wondered if Todd would get on his knees right there, after the turkey and before the pumpkin pie, to ask Christy in front of their relatives to be his wife. That would be memorable.

Christy knew the suspense would be driving her crazy if she didn't delight in surprises. That, and knowing she was ready. Any time, any place, in any way, Todd could pop the question, and she knew her answer would be yes.

The day before her baptism, Christy was in her dorm room, trying to finish typing a paper on Katie's laptop, when her mom called. "We were a little surprised to receive your baptism announcement," Mom said.

"You guys are coming, aren't you?"

"Yes," Mom said slowly. "You do realize, don't you, that you were baptized as an infant."

"Yes," Christy said. "And I completely honor that. Please don't think I'm not agreeing with what you and Dad did in that sacred ceremony. I'm actually trying to demonstrate with my life that I agree wholeheartedly, and that's why I want to be baptized as an adult."

"Both your father and I were baptized as infants, and we didn't feel the need to be baptized again when we were adults."

"I know. And that's what was right for you guys. I feel differently. Can you and Dad honor my choice to do this, even if you don't agree completely?" Christy didn't understand why something like this should unsettle her mom. Her parents were Christians. Why wouldn't they be happy to see her take this step of faith?

Christy and her mom ended the conversation with both of them agreeing to try to see the other's point of view.

When Christy's parents arrived at Riverview Heights on Sunday evening, her mom came into the changing room, where Christy was waiting in a white baptismal gown. Her bare feet were freezing on the linoleum. She wished she hadn't gotten ready so soon. She was the only woman getting baptized that evening, and so she felt especially glad that her mom had come to be with her.

"I'm so glad you guys came," Christy said.

"We wouldn't miss this for anything." Mom gave Christy a hug. "I wanted to make sure you didn't misunderstand my phone call yesterday afternoon. Your father and I have discussed this, and we do honor your decision. We are very proud of you. We always have been. I think you kids today are more emotionally connected to your faith than we ever were. Todd helped us see that you are taking ownership of your faith by doing this. Your father and I can see why this demonstration of your beliefs is important to you."

"Thanks, Mom," Christy said, giving her another hug. In many ways, this moment was a fulfillment of Christy's wish that she and her mom could be closer and more like friends. She didn't know if her mom felt any different right now, but Christy definitely felt as if the two of them had crossed a bridge into a new place where they were both women. As women, they could view each other more as friends.

Her mom must have had some of the same feelings because she gave Christy a tender smile. "Your father and I want you to know that we support all your upcoming decisions. And we're very happy for you. For both of you."

As soon as Mom left and Christy was alone again, with her bare feet tapping on the cold linoleum floor, she wondered what the last part meant about her mom being happy for both of them.

Did you mean you're happy for Todd, too? He's not getting baptized.

Christy remembered that Todd had taken their car all day yesterday and hadn't returned in time for dinner in the cafeteria. He didn't say where he had gone, and Christy hadn't asked because she was so swamped with homework.

Mom also said that Todd helped them to understand why I'm getting baptized. Did he go to their house yesterday?

Christy's heart began to beat a little faster. *Did Todd go there to ask my parents if we could get married? Is Todd about to propose? Tonight?*

The pastor tapped on the door and said she should come to the baptismal when she heard the music. Christy put aside her dreams and concentrated on the event at hand. She had prepared something to say and knew she would be first. Sounds of a familiar hymn echoed through the closed door.

"Like a river glorious, is God's perfect peace."

Christy smiled. She loved that hymn. It was one of her childhood favorites when they sang it at her old church in Brightwater. It felt as if a part of her childhood had joined her on this important evening. After spending so many years only singing contemporary choruses for worship, Christy loved having one of the oldies there to usher her forward into the built-in baptismal.

The baptismal was a square sort of "hot tub" at the front of the sanctuary and usually was hidden by silk ficus trees. This evening the trees were gone, and Pastor John stood waist-deep in the water, giving Christy a gentle smile and welcoming her to come into the water.

"Stayed upon Jehovah, hearts are fully blessed."

Christy took a cautious step into the water and found it was warm.

"Finding as he promised, perfect peace and rest."

She waded to the center and stood facing Pastor John, not quite ready to look out at the congregation.

The hymn ended, and Pastor John spoke about how Jesus was baptized in the Jordan River. The pastor explained how Christy was responding in obedience to the command found in the book of Acts, " 'Repent and be baptized, every one of you, in the name of Jesus Christ for the forgiveness of your sins.' "

Christy hesitantly looked out and saw Todd in the front row, his face beaming at her. He was surrounded by at least twenty students from the youth group. They all seemed serious as they watched Christy.

What a crowd of witnesses! I had no idea these guys were all going to come!

Pastor John quoted from Matthew 28. " 'Therefore go and make disciples of all nations, baptizing them in the name of the Father and of the Son and of the Holy Spirit, and teaching them to obey everything I have commanded you. And surely I am with you always, to the very end of the age.' "

He turned to Christy, placed a reassuring hand on her shoulder, and said, "I've asked Christy to tell you why she has decided to be baptized today."

Christy realized for the first time that this was a decision. A good decision. And one she had made on her own.

"I surrendered my life to the Lord when I was fifteen," Christy began. She noticed Katie and Sierra sitting with Todd and the youth group. Matt was with them, as well as Sierra's brother and five other students from Rancho.

"Since that day, when I got on my knees and asked Christ to forgive my sins, come into my heart, and take over my life, I have seen Him at work in so many ways." She realized she was speaking fast and tried to calm down so she could slow her words.

"God has changed me, and I know He is always with me. All the time. And I'm learning to trust Him more for all the details." She paused a second, then added, "All the decisions of my life."

The "decisions" part hadn't been in what she originally wrote out, but it was true.

"I decided to be baptized as a way of, first of all, agreeing with my parents' direction in my life when they had me baptized as a baby." Christy made eye contact with her mom. Mom's smile gave Christy all the assurance she needed to know that this was the right decision.

She noticed Aunt Marti sitting next to her mom. Christy hadn't expected her aunt to come.

As she finished her little speech, Christy kept her gaze on Aunt Marti. "The second reason I'm getting baptized is because I see it as an act of obedience. Like those verses Pastor John just quoted. We are commanded by God to turn from living to please ourselves, to come wholeheartedly to God so that we can live the life He has designed for us."

Feeling a burst of boldness, Christy added something else that wasn't in her original notes. "It's like God is the Potter, and we are the clay. He doesn't want us to run off and try to make ourselves into something we weren't created to be. He wants us to stay on His potter's wheel even when we get dizzy sometimes, spinning around and being squeezed and reshaped. He's the One who created us. He knows how to make us into our own person. Or actually, into His own person. The person we were meant to be. He wants us to stay on the wheel so He can shape us with

His hands." Christy paused and then added with a final breath, "With His nail-scarred hands."

She realized that everything she had just said was unplanned and that her aunt probably would be upset. But Christy felt clean. Clean and ready to publicly identify with Christ's burial and resurrection by being submerged under the water and coming up new.

Pastor John quietly asked Christy to fold her hands in front of her. She did and she closed her eyes.

Pastor John's deep voice washed over her as he said the words from Scripture, "In the name of the Father, the Son, and the Holy Spirit, I now baptize you, Christina Juliet Miller."

She felt herself being lowered backward by strong hands until her entire body, hair, face, everything, was submerged. For an instant, everything was silent. Dead.

Then those same strong hands pulled her from the water. A rousing burst of applause from the congregation met her as she came back to the land of the living. As she emerged, water dripping everywhere, an unexpected giggle tickled its way from her closed lips.

"Go in peace," the pastor exhorted her. "For Christ Jesus, the Lord of your life, will be with you always."

CHAPTER 18

Aunt Marti didn't make a scene about Christy's sermon from the baptismal pool. She didn't acknowledge any of it until that Thursday when the extended family was gathered at Christy's parents' house for Thanksgiving.

Christy and Todd had arrived in Escondido Wednesday night, and both of them had helped Christy's mom make pies. The methods of the three cooks were all different, and the kitchen was small. The four-hour pie-making adventure provided constant laughter and one unauthorized fight between Todd and Christy with small handfuls of flour. But it was enough to put Christy's mom into a cleaning frenzy.

When the pies were presented at the end of Thanksgiving dinner, Todd and Christy playfully boasted about their combined efforts. Mom set the record straight by saying that Christy and Todd had gotten a little too creative with the spices in the pumpkin pie. She suggested that if anyone was interested in a milder dessert, the apple pie she had made would be a good choice.

"Christy does tend to get creative and spice things up, doesn't she?" Marti said. She had been quiet most of the dinner. When she did talk, it was to Todd's dad, who was seated on her right.

Christy took Marti's comment to mean the baptismal message.

"Who wants what?" Mom asked, ignoring her sister's comment. Christy guessed her mom had done that most of her life.

"Did you make mincemeat?" Dad asked.

207

Christy smiled. He asked that every year. Every Thanksgiving for the past twenty-some years, Mom made one mincemeat pie. And every year, Dad was the only one who ate any of that pie. Yet he still asked, as if maybe she had forgotten this year.

"Mincemeat?" Todd's dad asked. "I'll take mincemeat, if you have it."

"You take yours warmed with vanilla ice cream, Bryan?" Christy's dad asked.

"Is there any other way?" Todd's dad said with a smile.

Christy went to help Mom slice the pies. She was grinning to herself at the way her dad had just bonded with Todd's dad over mincemeat pie.

Whatever it takes!

She wondered what it would take now for Todd to ask her to become his wife. All he had to do was slip into the kitchen, come up behind her, put his arms around her, and whisper in her ear, "How would you like it if we made Thanksgiving pies together for the rest of our lives?"

Christy daydreamed how she would answer with something witty like, "As long as we always keep it spicy."

Or maybe something sweet and mushy would be better, like, "You know I'll always be your punkin."

"Christy?"

She turned to see her mom watching her with concern. Christy had frozen in her daydream with the knife halfway suspended over the first pie.

"I was just, ah, trying to decide how many pieces to cut."

"It doesn't matter. We have plenty. Would you put these two mincemeat pieces in the microwave?"

"Sure." Christy turned from her mom, feeling the blood rushing to her cheeks.

When will I become old enough to stop this crazy blushing? I could understand it when I was fifteen. Or even eighteen. But I'm twenty years old. I'm a woman about to promise herself to a man, and I still blush like a little girl.

Christy wondered if Todd struggled with feelings of shyness. Perhaps that was why he hadn't proposed yet.

After they had eaten pie, Uncle Bob insisted they all gather in the living room so he could take a group picture. He had a remote switch on his camera that allowed him to place the camera on a kitchen chair.

Mom, Marti, Dad, and Todd's dad all squashed themselves together on the couch. David plopped in the middle of the floor in front of the couch. That left openings on either side of David. Christy sat on the right, in front of her mom, and Todd sat in front of his dad on the left side.

To Christy's surprise, David, the nondemonstrative child, put his long arms around Todd's and Christy's necks and let his appendages hang there like thick gray octopus tentacles.

"Everyone say 'hey!' " Bob positioned himself on the couch's arm and leaned over next to Marti.

"I thought we were supposed to say 'cheese,' " David said. Christy noticed that his voice was changing. It sounded especially funny since she was so close to him.

"Try saying 'hey' this time," Bob said. "It makes for a more natural smile than a stiff 'cheese.' "

"A stiff cheese!" David repeated and burst out laughing.

Todd and Christy turned their faces toward each other under the mutual lock of their guffawing octopus jailer. They exchanged a look that said, "Oh, brother, tell me we weren't like that when we were his age."

Just then the camera flash went off.

"Take another one," Marti cried. "I had my eyes closed."

Christy and Todd turned back to the positioned camera.

"On the count of three," Bob said. "One, two, three!"

A merry chorus of "Hey!" rose from the couch, and the picture was snapped.

"Now just Todd and Bryan," Bob said, getting into his role of family photo historian. "Why don't you two use this chair here? Let me put you over by the window so I get better light. Bryan, why don't you sit, and, Todd, you stand behind him."

Everyone watched while the father and son took their positions. Christy noticed how much the two resembled each other, and she felt a warmth rush through her.

Wow, Todd, if you look like that twenty-five years from now, I will be a happy woman! What am I saying? I'd be happy with you twenty-five years from now no matter what. But if you turn out like your dad . . .

Christy casually glanced at her mom. She was at least three or maybe four inches shorter than Christy and had a round figure. Her face was round, her body was round. Her hair had gone almost completely gray, and she hadn't colored it or changed the short style. Christy's mom didn't use makeup. She was a simple, uncomplicated, reserved, honest woman. And Christy always admired her for that.

But I hope my looks turn out a little more like Aunt Marti's. Not with the hair extensions or any of that. I just want to keep myself looking appealing to Todd. At least I have some height from my dad's side. Hopefully I'll be able to keep my weight down.

Christy had a feeling that just trying to keep up with Todd for the next twenty-five years would be a thorough workout.

"Okay, that's good." Bob adjusted the camera. "Todd, how about if you put your hand on your dad's shoulder? Yes, like that."

Christy noticed that Todd appeared slightly self-conscious about his hands ever since the stitches had been removed. Both his hands were covered with dashes of white scar tissue where the glass had sliced his flesh. He placed his hand on his dad's shoulder but turned the top of his hand away from the camera so the scars wouldn't show.

For the first time, Christy thought how blessed Todd was that none of the glass had cut his face or throat. Uncle Bob had been severely burned on his neck and left ear several years ago. Christy had gotten so used to how he looked after he healed up that she didn't even notice it anymore. It made her wonder if Marti, who spent her life striving for perfection, found it hard to accept Bob's scars.

Your scars are beautiful to me, Todd. They always will be evidence that you could have died, but God kept you here for a reason. For me. For us. For whatever we do together to further His kingdom.

"Terrific." Bob took the third snapshot of Todd and Bryan Spencer. He proceeded to take shots of Christy's family and then five shots of Todd and Christy together.

"Hey!" Christy said, following Bob's advice for a natural smile.

"Hey yourself, pumpkin pie breath," Todd teased her.

"Are you saying the pie turned out too spicy?"

"I think we should keep the double cinnamon next year but leave out the cloves."

"As you wish," Christy whispered.

Bob snapped a final shot, and his camera began to rewind. "End of the roll," he said.

Christy glanced over and noticed that everyone was still watching her and Todd as they engaged in their snappy exchange.

Marti came closer with a knowing smirk on her face. "Those will make perfect photos for the newspaper announcement."

"What newspaper announcement?" Todd asked.

Marti raised an eyebrow slightly to Christy. Christy didn't need any hints. She knew what her aunt was getting at. The society section of Marti's local newspaper ran engagement announcements complete with the couples' photos. Christy didn't spell it out for Todd.

And Todd didn't spell out any kind of proposal to her that Thanksgiving weekend. Christy thought she was okay with that. Her dreams weren't dashed. A little postponed, perhaps.

It didn't really bother her until she was back at Rancho on Monday, and Sierra came into the bookstore to see her. Sierra was bubbling over with news about her sister's wedding that weekend. Tawni and Jeremy had gotten married at Paul's church in San Diego, where Jeremy and Paul's dad was the pastor. Sierra made an exaggeratedly gruesome face when she described the frilly, mint green bridesmaid dress she was forced to wear. The two friends made plans to meet at The Java Jungle after Christy's class that night so she could hear the rest of the details.

After Sierra left the bookstore, Christy did a little math. Doug and Tracy had been married now for a year and a half. Tawni and Jeremy had met the week that Doug and Tracy got engaged. Katie told her last night about a girl on their floor who had met a guy the first week of classes, and they had gotten married over Thanksgiving break.

Why is everyone else getting married, but Todd and I aren't even engaged? How slow is Todd going to be? He's not waiting for me to say something, is he? No, he would want to be the one to officially do the proposing. So what is he waiting for?

Christy found it easy to come up with a half dozen logical explanations. School and money were at the top of the list. She tried to put it all out of her mind and work hard to complete the class assignments that needed to be turned in before Christmas break. Her only time to study was in between work and classes. Long ago she had discovered that she wasn't a night owl like Katie. Christy reserved her evenings for taking long walks around campus with Todd or for meeting friends to laugh and talk in The Java Jungle.

Weekends inevitably were gobbled up by church and youth group activities, which Christy was beginning to love. The youth group was growing each week. On the Sunday after Thanksgiving they had twenty-four students in the morning session and sixteen of them showed up at evening service. Two of the girls told Christy they had decided to be baptized after they had seen Christy's baptism.

Todd was planning an outreach trip to Mexico the week between Christmas and New Year's since his plans for the Thanksgiving outreach had been cancelled after his accident. It looked as if they might have as many as thirty Rancho students and teens from the church going down to an orphanage in Tecate.

A week and a half before Christmas break Christy volunteered to prepare all the food on the trip, including the shopping this time. She and Todd were sitting at their usual table in the cafeteria with their usual group of friends, when she told Todd she would take care of all the food.

"I'll help you," Todd said.

Christy shook her head. "Oh no you won't!"

In response, Todd kissed her soundly and whispered, "I love you," in front of everyone. He had never been so outwardly demonstrative around their friends before. Christy knew then that if any of them had doubts about Todd and her being an established couple, they wouldn't question it now.

No one questioned anything. They all seemed comfortable being around Todd and Christy even in their new, greatly improved, truly-in-love season of life. Even Matt seemed comfortable and completely himself.

Matt announced to the gang at dinner that same night that he had decided to ask a girl from his earth science class to go out with him on the Friday before Christmas break. He turned to Christy and Katie for their advice.

"You have a week and a half," Katie stated. "That means you should at least ask her by this Friday because it's nice to have a week's notice on a first date." Then she muttered, "Not that I would know."

Christy elbowed her. Katie elbowed Christy right back.

"I'm just saying I would think a week's notice would be nice," Katie said defensively. "That's all."

"Where are you planning to go to dinner?" Sierra asked.

"I keep hearing about this new café that opened up in Murrieta Hot Springs. It's called The Dove's Nest. There's a bookstore connected to it called The Ark. On the weekends they have live music."

"Why didn't you tell me?" Randy asked. "Our band is looking for more gigs."

"I've heard about that place," Christy said. "Donna at the bookstore said that the manager of the café might want to buy some of your Indian Summer tea, Katie."

"Why didn't you tell me?" Katie mimicked Randy.

"I didn't know if you needed to have approval from the Food and Drug Administration or something."

"Bring the tea with you to Mexico," Todd said. "The people at the orphanage in Tecate would love it. And you don't need any government approvals there."

Katie gave Todd a pained expression. "Yeah, like I'm going to set up a little tea cart under an umbrella and pass out Dixie cups of herbal tea to all the people in the village."

"Do you think The Dove's Nest is too casual a place for me to ask Jenna to go on a first date?" Matt asked Christy, trying to get back on the topic.

"No, I think it sounds perfect."

"Would you mind if I went with you?" Randy asked Matt.

Matt gave him a strange look.

"I mean, I could come up with a date, if I had to. I just want to check out the place."

"What do you mean you could come up with a date if you had to?" Sierra punched her buddy on the arm.

Randy answered her with a crooked grin. "Does that mean you want to go with me?"

"No, you clueless bubble brain. Why don't you ask Vicki?"

Christy knew that Vicki, Sierra's roommate, never seemed to be at a loss for attention from guys on campus.

"Is she still speaking to me?" Randy asked.

"There's one way to find out," Sierra said. "Ask her out."

Randy tilted his head and gave Sierra a timid look. "Will you ask her for me?"

"Wimp!" Sierra spouted.

"What is with all you guys?" Katie asked. "Why are you so afraid of us women?"

"I'm not afraid," Todd said.

"You don't count anymore," Katie said with a coy glance at him.

Todd playfully clutched his chest as if her words were arrows that hit their mark.

"I'm serious, you guys," Katie said. "Why is it no men on this campus . . . no, make that no men in this world, know how to initiate a relationship with a woman?"

"What is she talking about?" Sierra asked, looking directly at Christy.

"I'll tell you what I'm talking about. I'm talking about romance and risk and men who aren't afraid to be men. I'm talking about a man who will walk boldly up to a woman and say, 'Hey, your hair is like a flock of goats. Will you go out with me?' "

Christy burst out laughing, and the others joined in. She didn't know if any of them understood Katie was referring to a quote from the Song of Solomon.

"Flowers are optional," Katie stated over the subsiding laughter.

"You know what?" Matthew said. "You're right. I'm going to go find Jenna right now, and I'm going to ask her out."

"You sure you don't want us all to go with you?" Sierra teased.

Matt's eyes lit up, and he turned to focus on Sierra. "That's a great idea. Instead of Randy and me trying to put together some kind of awkward double date, why don't you guys all come? I could tell Jenna a bunch of us are going, so it won't feel like a date."

"You're hopeless," Katie said. "Here I try to offer you useful advice, and you turn us all into a bunch of decoys to hide behind."

"You're no decoy, Katie," Matt said with an admiring expression. He leaned across the table, and even though everyone could hear what he said, he spoke the words to Katie only. "You are a one-of-a-kind woman, and I'm certain some guy out there will match your wit and your charm. I'm sure you've figured out, though, that it won't be a farm boy."

"Aw, shucks," Katie said. "I thought farm boys were the only ones who knew that flock-of-goats line."

"Not this farm boy."

"No, not you." Katie said the words so tenderly, Christy was certain Matt and Katie had firmly established their friendship.

That night, once the two of them were back in their room, Christy asked Katie, "What was all that between you and Matt and the farm-boy stuff?"

Katie was tapping away on her laptop, throwing together a three-page summary that had been due that day in one of her classes, but she had forgotten about. Katie seemed to forever be turning in papers a day late, but for some reason she charmed her teachers into not lowering her grades.

"We had a talk yesterday. No, the day before," Katie said between taps of the keys. "It was Monday. Monday afternoon we talked about you and Todd."

"You didn't tell me that."

"You were asleep when I came in the past two nights."

"What did you say about me?"

Katie looked around the corner of her desk to where Christy was snuggled under her covers. "Wouldn't you like to know?"

"Yes, I would!"

"It was nothing big. Just how happy you and Todd are and how totally in love you are and how that's what we all wish for someday."

"Awww," Christy said. "How sweet."

"Yeah, I know. Matt and I also decided that, since chances are good we two would end up in your wedding party, we better stick close so we can help each other out when it comes time to pull those prewedding pranks on Todd."

"Prewedding pranks?" Christy said. "You might be waiting awhile. We don't even have reason for you to come up with pre-*engagement* pranks."

"It's only a matter of time," Katie said. "You know that. I know that. All of us know that. You'll see. Todd is clever and creative. He'll make the moment memorable."

Christy slipped back under the covers and listened to the speedy *click-click*ing of the laptop keys. Her heart was at rest. Whenever Todd did get around to asking her to marry him, she knew she would be ready with the answer.

Katie kept typing but asked, "Are you and Todd going to The Dove's Nest with everybody?"

"I think so. Are you?"

"No, I don't think I'll go."

"Why?"

"Oh, come on, do the math, Chris. You and Todd, Matt and Jenna, Randy and Vicki, Sierra will bring Paul. I obviously would be Mambo number nine."

"But we're all friends," Christy said. "I want you to come. No one would make you feel left out. You could bring some of your tea, like Donna suggested. It's going to be fun. Come on. We'll invite Doug and Tracy. You haven't seen them in a long time."

"Oh, Doug and Tracy. Make me Mambo number eleven, then. Christy, any way you work it, I'm the leftover. I'd rather stay here."

"No, you wouldn't," Christy said. "You would be miserable here, knowing that all of us were out having a good time."

"You know what?" Katie walked to the door. "We weren't going to sing this song anymore, were we? The old chorus about poor Katie. I'm going to open this door, and that old song is going to leave. Ready?" She opened the door, made a few grand whooshing motions with her hands, and then soundly closed the door. "End of discussion. Now, if you don't mind, I have a paper to type."

CHAPTER 19

Christy didn't bring up the subject of going to The Dove's Nest with Katie again. After thinking about Katie's response to the situation, Christy decided to let it go.

Matt stopped by the bookstore late Friday morning to tell Christy that Jenna had agreed to join the outing and to say that the two of them would drive in his truck unless Todd and Christy still had room in their car.

"I think Todd offered Sierra a ride if Paul doesn't come."

"What about Katie?"

Christy tried to make her voice sound causal. "She's not going."

"Why not?"

"You would have to ask her." Christy didn't know if that was too telling an answer or if Matt would read between the lines and drop it.

Fortunately, Christy had a customer and had to cut the conversation short.

"We'll see you there, then," he said.

Christy nodded and waved. When work ended, she went to her dorm room to grab a sweater. The Dove's Nest was only ten miles from Rancho Corona, but going there as a group had become a big event for everyone.

Christy considered leaving Katie a note, urging her to grab a couple of girls from their floor, jump in Baby Hummer, and drive on down to The Dove's Nest. But Christy didn't.

Todd was waiting for her in the lobby. To her surprise, he handed her a single white carnation.

"Just because," he said.

Christy was touched but also curious about where he had bought the flower. She knew no place on campus sold flowers.

"Did you go into town this afternoon?" she asked.

"I went to church for a couple of hours."

They drove down the hill with the windows open and the heater on full blast. It had become a habit because they liked the feel of the fresh air, but it was cold outside, now that the desert climate had settled in to its winter season. The days could still be warm and bright if the sun was shining, but as soon as the sun went down, the thermometer dipped dramatically.

"Were flower vendors on the street corner like at Thanksgiving?" Christy twirled the carnation and drew in the spicy sweet fragrance.

"No." Todd looked at her with a grin. "It's killing you trying to figure out where I got that, isn't it?"

Christy hid her grin. "I'm just curious." She imagined his making a special stop at a florist and ordering a single carnation. Only the flower didn't come wrapped in florist tissue.

"I saw it at church in the Dumpster," Todd said.

"Oh." Christy laid the flower across her lap. Suddenly it didn't seem so sweet or sentimental.

"They had tossed out the flowers from a luncheon or something, and I saw that lone white carnation, and it made me think of you."

Christy knew it was the thought that counted. She knew with Todd it was always the thought that counted, and it most likely would always be that way.

"Thank you," Christy said. "I love it." Then, leaning over and giving his cheek a kiss, she said, "And I love you."

"I love you more," Todd teased.

"No, I love you more."

"I loved you first," Todd said.

Christy laughed. "Okay, you win. You loved me first. But I still love you more."

"Don't think so." Todd glanced at her as he drove. "I don't think it's possible for you ever to love me as deeply and as completely as I love you.

I don't think anyone could ever love another person on this earth as much as I love you."

Christy couldn't compete with that. She didn't want to.

"I talked to your uncle today," Todd said. "Have you talked to him lately?"

"Not since Thanksgiving."

"He said the pictures turned out great, and he's sending them to us. He also said Marti told him last night that she's not leaving."

"Really? What did he say?"

"I guess she quit her art classes and told Bob she was willing to put the effort into working on their marriage as long as he was willing, too."

"Do you think she'll go to church with him?"

"I don't know," Todd said.

"Do you think they'll go to a marriage counselor?"

"I couldn't say."

"I'm glad you told me. That's a big relief. I'm glad she decided to try to work things through. Don't you think that when you stayed with them it helped bring them back together because they had you as a mutual project to work on?"

"Possibly," Todd said.

"I think that helped a lot."

"Are you saying they should have a baby?"

Christy was surprised at Todd's suggestion. "They're too old, aren't they?"

Todd shrugged. "Don't ask me."

There was a pause before Todd said, "How many kids do you want to have?"

Christy thought a moment. "I don't know. Sometimes I liked that there were only two of us, even though David and I weren't real close. When I was younger I thought I wanted to have a huge family with six or eight kids. Then I worked at the orphanage. I think two is good. Four maybe. I think even numbers are better."

A wide grin spread across Todd's face. The afternoon sun was low in the December sky and came streaming in through the driver's window, illuminating his profile. "I want four," he said soundly. "Two boys, two girls. But I'll take whatever God grants. And if they're healthy, so much the better."

Christy was amazed they were talking so naturally about their family. Their future. Although she shouldn't be surprised. They had been having more conversations like this lately. Both of them spoke freely and openly, even though neither of them had yet used terms such as "our children" or "whatever God grants *us.*" The understanding that they were discussing their life together was there, under the surface.

Todd reached over and took her hand in his. He glanced at her with a contented smile, then looked back at the road. Christy smoothed her finger across his hand, delicately tracing each scar.

"Do these hurt anymore?" she asked.

"Not really. A few of them are tender."

"I love your hands." Christy drew his hand to her lips and kissed it before pressing it against her cheek.

"You do?"

"Yes, I do."

They both glanced at each other a little awkwardly and smiled. Christy's "I do" had prompted her, and apparently Todd, as well, to think of how those were the words they would one day say to each other at the altar.

Go ahead, say it, Todd. Say, "Will you marry me?" You know I'll say yes.

Todd didn't say anything. He pulled into the parking lot of The Dove's Nest, and Christy felt a mixture of bliss and impatience. If she had a single brazen cell in her body, she would construct a sentence that had the word "marry" in it that ended with a question mark. That would prompt Todd to speak up.

But in the secret place in her heart, Christy was at rest. She and Todd had come so far. They were so close. Everything was just about perfect. If Todd uttered his anticipated proposal to her in three minutes or in three days or in three years, she could wait.

As they walked hand in hand through the parking lot, Todd said, "Isn't that Baby Hummer?"

"Katie came?"

"That's good," he said. "I'd hoped she would."

"Did you say anything to her about it today?"

"No."

Christy was proud of her friend. She must have thought it through and realized she would be happier spending Friday night with her friends than letting the couples part of the event bother her.

When Todd and Christy entered the contemporary-looking café, Christy was drawn to the fireplace, where the dancing golden flames waved to her and bid her come closer.

"Todd, they have a fireplace," Christy said. She noticed Sierra, Paul, Randy, and Vicki all seated near the fire. They had pulled together two small, round tables and had collected a sufficient number of chairs.

"Christy!" Sierra waved to her. Paul, wearing a tweed cap, was seated next to Sierra. Christy had seen him only a few times before, but she hadn't remembered the round glasses perched on his straight nose.

"Have you seen Katie?" Christy asked after she greeted the four.

"She's in the bookstore with Matt and Jenna."

"Did anyone come with Katie?"

"I don't think so."

"Are you guys going to order something to eat?" Todd asked.

"We already did," Sierra said.

Just then a deep voice behind Christy and Todd said, "Did you say *food*?"

They turned to see Doug and Tracy.

Christy laughed as they all hugged. "I should have known you would show up when food was mentioned," she said to Doug.

"Do you know what you want?" Todd asked Christy. "I'll order for us if you do."

She hadn't seen a menu; how could she know what to order? How could she decide?

"Any kind of sandwich would be fine," Christy said. "Roast beef, if they have it. If not, then whatever."

Todd and Doug exchanged glances as if they were sharing a private insight into Christy's restaurant-ordering abilities.

"That had to be the quickest meal decision I've ever seen you make," Doug said. He punched Todd's arm. "Looks like you two are having a good effect on each other."

"Yeah," Todd said, "she even talks me into putting gas in the car before the gauge registers in the red zone."

"My point exactly," Doug said. "What a team you two make!"

Tracy looked meaningfully at Christy, who read her married friend's expression to mean, "Has he asked you yet?"

Christy closed her eyes slowly and shook her head ever so slightly.

"We'll place the order," Doug said to Tracy. "You might need to pull up another table or at least a few more chairs if all these already are spoken for."

Christy and Tracy figured out how many were in their group and arranged the chairs accordingly. Christy took the seat closest to the fire and let the warmth seep through her jeans. She loved the café's ambience. The fireplace was draped with a fragrant evergreen swag decorated with tiny Christmas ornaments and bright red berries. Glowing white Christmas lights lined the windows, and a large wreath hung on the front door.

The café reminded Christy of a coffee shop she and her friends used to go to in Basel. The amber-toned lights and dark wood tables, doors, and trim made the café feel homey. Christy liked the large windows and the deeply aromatic coffee.

What she liked most, though, was being with her friends. She noticed a bronze plaque inset on the side of the fireplace that read *Is any pleasure on earth as great as a circle of Christian friends by a fire? C. S. Lewis.*

Christy decided that when she lived in her dream house with Todd one day, they would have that quote engraved on a plaque and displayed by their fireplace.

When Katie, Matt, and Matt's date, Jenna, joined the group, Christy felt the circle was complete. And having the café decorated for Christmas made it magical.

"I'm glad you came," she quietly said to Katie.

Katie sat down in the empty seat beside Christy. "What did you say?"

"I said, I'm glad you came."

"Me too. You were right. This is where I belong."

Christy smiled.

"Is it seven o'clock yet?" Randy asked, getting up.

"It's five after seven," Tracy told him.

"I'm going to see if the manager is in yet. They said he was coming back at seven."

As Randy walked away, Tracy said, "Why does he want to see the manager? Does he know him?"

"No," Sierra explained. "He's in a band, and they want to play here sometime."

Todd arrived at the table with napkins and silverware, which he handed to Christy. He took the chair directly across from her.

"Do you want to sit next to Christy?" Katie asked.

"No, I'm happy to sit here and gaze into her killer eyes."

Christy hadn't heard anyone refer to her as having "killer eyes" since high school. And that phrase had not come from Todd.

Todd leaned over to Matt, who was seated on his left, and using his hand to cover his mouth, Todd whispered something to Matt.

"No fair telling secrets," Katie said.

"It wasn't a secret," Todd said.

Matt didn't comment. He just left the table. Christy couldn't figure out what was going on. She decided not to try to wring out of Todd the un-secret he had told Matt, even though whatever it was had made Matt leave.

Christy was facing the door; the order window was behind her. She noticed that more people were arriving, and she was glad they had claimed their seats by the fire when they did.

"I ordered you some soup," Todd said. "Beef barley."

"Oh," Christy said. "Did they have sandwiches?"

"Only turkey and ham. I figured the soup had beef in it. It comes with a roll."

"Okay." Christy should have remembered how logically challenged Todd became when he was sent shopping. Actually, the soup was perfect; better than what she had requested. It would warm her up. Todd knew. She slid her leg under the table until she found his foot, and then she rubbed her foot against his ankle.

"Katie, are you trying to play footsie with me under the table?" Todd asked.

"Why would I do that?" Katie spouted.

Christy gave Todd an exasperated look and kicked him playfully. He gave her a slight wink. Either that or he was winking at someone behind her.

A booming voice behind Katie announced, "Hey, your hair is like a flock . . ."

Katie and Christy turned around at the same time and gasped.

Katie was the first to find her voice. "Rick?"

"Katie?"

Rick's voice faltered only for a moment before finishing his line, as if someone had paid him to say it to her. A wide grin spread across his face as he stated loudly, "Your hair is like a flock of goats. Will you go out with me?"

Everyone but Katie and Christy broke into delighted laughter. That had been Katie's wish, her exact words, in fact, when she had said she wanted a stranger to ask her out using the crazy compliment. Only, the tall, broad-shouldered man with dark, wavy hair who was scanning Katie's every detail with his chocolate brown eyes was no stranger to Christy or to Katie.

Katie slowly rose, and he greeted her with a hug. "Okay," she declared wildly. "I'll go out with you since you asked so nicely."

Rick laughed. "Look at you!" He pulled away and examined Katie even more closely. "Wow, when did you grow up?"

"It's my hair. I got it cut."

"Some guy named Matt told me to come over and say your hair was like a flock of goats, but I didn't know it was you. And it's not, you know. I mean it's you, but your hair isn't goat-like at all."

Christy had never seen Rick Doyle fumble his words. He seemed more like a kid than the snobby football star he had been in high school.

Rick pulled his gaze from Katie to see who else was at the table.

"Hi, Rick," Christy said warmly.

"Christy." Rick stooped to hug her around the neck. "It's so great to see you guys. When Todd and Doug walked up to the register, I couldn't believe it. Todd told me you two are . . ." Rick looked at Todd.

Christy looked at Todd.

Todd's expression remained steady.

"Todd told me you two are closer than ever," Rick said. "I'm glad for you. I really am. That's so great."

"I think it's pretty great, too." Christy was glad to know she could sit there and talk to Rick Doyle and know that nothing awkward remained between them from the up-and-down season they had while dating in high school.

Matt returned to his seat, and Katie gave him a hard time for talking Rick into playing a joke on her when really the joke turned out to be on Rick.

"He made me do it." Matt pointed to Todd.

Todd put on his best innocent look and turned to Doug as if it had been his bright idea.

"Don't look at me," Doug said.

Christy realized at that moment that every guy she had ever cared for seriously or deeply in her life was gathered at this table. And none of them was anything like Todd. Her heart turned up another notch in its steady devotion to Todd Spencer. No guy would ever compare.

"Do you want to eat with us?" Katie asked after all the introductions had been made.

"I have to get back to my office. They told me a guy's waiting to talk to me about his band playing here."

"He's with us," Sierra said. "It's Randy."

"Your office?" Katie asked.

"I'm the manager here. Didn't Doug tell you?"

"No, Doug didn't say anything. You're the manager?"

Rick nodded. "My dad bought the place and put me to work. Come with me. I'll show you around." The invitation clearly was for Katie only.

As Katie began to follow him, Christy heard her say, "Have you ever considered serving any gourmet herbal teas here?"

Christy turned to Todd, her eyes wide. "Should I be in shock?"

"Not when God is doing God-things," Todd said smugly.

"With a little help from His friends," Tracy added.

"With a little help from His friends," Todd repeated.

Then the food arrived. The group joined hands around the table, and Doug prayed aloud. When he ended the prayer, Christy and Todd said softly in unison, "As you wish."

They both looked up. Their eyes met. To Christy it seemed as if she were gazing into a reflecting pool. The other half of her heart was gazing back at her, smiling.

Katie's food sat untouched at the empty place beside Christy while the rest of them ate. Randy returned with news about a date in February when his band would play at The Dove's Nest. The soup was good, and the fire had warmed Christy down to her toes. She was happy.

Two guys with guitars, who had been setting up by the front window, began to play. That made it harder for Christy to hear the conversation at the end of the table, where Sierra sat, but Christy was content to stick with the close conversation between Doug, Tracy, Todd, and her. They were discussing the upcoming trip to the Mexican orphanage when Katie returned to the table, her green eyes lit up like a Christmas tree.

"Can I just say I am stunned? Did you get a chance to talk to that guy? Everything is about how 'the Lord did this,' and 'God took care of that.' It's so fun to be around him now."

"It's awesome," Doug said.

"Yes," Katie agreed, "it is awesome. And you guys are awesome. Rick said you kept in contact with him over the years and sent him letters encouraging him to turn his heart to the Lord. And you know what? He finally listened. I'm just . . . well, I'm stunned and amazed and . . . ."

"A bit dazzled?" Christy ventured.

"Maybe a little."

The close group grew silent, waiting for Katie to embellish.

"Well, the guy told me my hair was like a flock of goats, all right? I mean, how can a girl not be dazzled by such poetic brilliance?"

They all laughed with her.

"And look what I found in the stock room." Katie placed a bag of candy hearts on the table. "Dessert!"

"Can you imagine how old those are?" Tracy asked. "I mean, this place is new, isn't it? They aren't selling Valentine's candy anywhere now.

It's still Christmas candy everywhere. I don't want to know where these came from."

"Bargain Barn." Todd tore open the bag and spilled the pastel hearts onto the table. "I was in Bargain Barn today, and they had a whole crate of these up front. Now's the time to buy them."

"Buy them, maybe. But eat them? I don't think so." Tracy picked up a heart and read the message. " 'Fax me.' Fax me? When did they start writing 'Fax me' on these things? I thought they said, 'Be mine' and 'Stay true' and . . ." She picked up another one. " 'Kiss me'?"

"Don't mind if I do." Doug pulled Tracy close and planted a big one on her lips.

She giggled as if that had been the first time she had ever been kissed. The sight of her two friends so in love made Christy smile. Doug had never kissed a girl until his wedding day, and when he and Tracy married, their kiss at the altar had prompted the loudest roar of applause Christy had ever heard at a wedding.

"Check this out," Katie said. " 'Page me.' "

They all looked for messages in the hearts. Doug pulled out an "e-mail me" and said, "This must be the interactive bag."

Todd placed a pink heart in front of Christy as if to prove Doug's point. It read, "Marry me."

Christy looked up. "I can't believe what they put on these now. I'm with you, Tracy. I remember when they used to say, 'Be sweet.' "

"Here you go," Katie said. " 'Sweet lips.' "

"I want that one," Tracy said.

"What are you doing, making your own sentence over there?" Katie asked.

"Sure. Try it."

"Here you go: Another 'Page me.' " Christy handed a yellow candy to Tracy.

Todd placed a second candy heart in front of Christy. It also read, "Marry me."

"I think we already have one of those." Christy moved the hearts around and looked for one that no one else had found yet.

Todd was looking, too. He picked up a heart and then came around to Christy's side of the table. He placed the third candy heart in a row with the first two he had given her. "There. Once it's spoken three times, it's established. Forever."

Christy froze. All she could see were the three candy hearts lined up in front of her. All three of them said "Marry me," "Marry me," "Marry me."

She turned as Todd went down on one knee. He covered both her hands with his. His voice washed over her like a waterfall as he stared into her eyes and said, "Kilikina, my Kilikina, will you marry me?"

"Yes," Christy whispered without a moment's hesitation. "Yes," she repeated more loudly. Then a third time, with complete confidence and a cascade of tears, she said, "Yes, Todd, my Todd. I will marry you."

For a moment the whole world stopped, and Christy and Todd remained still. Not breathing. Not blinking. Not moving. Lost in the depths of each other's souls. The only sound Christy heard was her heart beating. But she wasn't sure if it was her heart or Todd's. The two seemed to beat as one.

"What are you doing, Todd?" Katie asked. "Did you lose one of the candies on the ground over there? There are plenty more up here."

Todd didn't move. Christy smiled.

No one knows! Todd just proposed to me, and no one knows. It's our secret.

Christy and Todd's secret bubble was burst when Katie looked at Christy's lineup of hearts. Katie screamed as only Katie could. Everyone in the café stopped talking and eating, and the two guys playing guitars in the corner paused.

"Finally!" Katie shouted. She bounced up from her chair and yelled, "I have an announcement to make! My best friend just got proposed to!"

A rush of hugs and well wishes poured over Todd and Christy.

Katie looked at Christy. "And what did you say?"

Christy grinned confidently. "I said yes!"

"She said yes!" Katie burst into applause, and the rest of the people in the café joined her.

Matt wrapped his arms around Christy and gave her a home-boy kind of hug. "Your grandma is going to love him," he said. "And I won't say eenie-meenie boo-boo to you anymore because it's obvious that Todd is 'it.' "

Christy grinned and giggled. "Yes, he is."

Tracy dissolved into a puddle of tears and so did Sierra. When Sierra hugged Christy, Sierra said, "I didn't cry this much at my sister's wedding! What is it with you and Todd?"

Rick appeared and gave Christy a warm smile. He leaned over and kissed her cheek. "You held out for a hero," he said in her ear. "Good for you, killer eyes."

"Thanks, Rick."

Christy looked at Todd. He was taking in all the well-wishing with the biggest smile.

He looks like a five-year-old, and everyone just showed up for his surprise birthday party.

As Christy thought that, one of the waiters approached the table carrying a round carrot cake with one lit candle in the middle. "Compliments of Mr. Doyle," the waiter said.

"Make a wish!" Katie chanted. "Make a wish!"

"I already did." Todd wrapped his arms around his beloved. "And she came true."

"That is so sweet!" Tracy said. "Todd, I never knew you were such a romantic."

"You haven't seen anything yet," he said. Tilting Christy's chin up with the slightest touch of his finger, Todd kissed her like he had never kissed her before.

As they slowly drew apart, Christy saw the still-burning candle out of the corner of her eye. She had nothing left to wish for. And most certainly not enough breath left to blow out a candle.

"The candle," Katie said. "What about the candle?"

Christy looked into Todd's eyes. He was looking at her "that way." The warm glow seemed brighter than ever behind his screaming silver-blue eyes.

"Let it burn," Todd murmured. He held her cheek gently in his hand. "Let it burn for the rest of our lives."

Christy kissed the palm of Todd's strong, scarred hand, and in a voice so soft that only God and Todd could hear, she whispered, "As you wish."

I Promise

For all the Christys I have known.

May your promises last forever.

CHAPTER 1

Christy opened her eyes and focused on the empty bed across from her in the dimly lit dorm room. The digital alarm clock read 5:05 A.M.

Katie never came to our room all night. Where is she?

Getting up and snapping on the overhead light, Christy checked to see if Katie had left a note while Christy slept. No note.

Suddenly Christy stopped. Her fuzzy morning brain woke up. She remembered where she had been the night before and what had happened.

The Dove's Nest Café. We were all together. The whole gang.

A smile drew her lips heavenward as it all came back.

It wasn't a dream. Last night Todd asked me to marry him. And I said yes.

Opening the shades, Christy gazed outside. The streetlights that lined the campus of Rancho Corona cast a cool, bluish gray tint on the world outside her window. Rows of tall palm trees stood in a sacred hush waiting for the familiar breath of wind from the nearby desert to awaken them. Whenever the wind came, the palm trees danced, and something inside Christy compelled her to join them.

This morning she didn't need the rustling palm trees to call her heart to the dance floor. Inside, she already was twirling and spinning.

Todd and I are going to get married!

The phone rang, and Christy jumped to answer it.

"Hey, how's it going?" The deep voice on the other end was the same voice that had echoed in her sweet dreams all night.

"Hey yourself," Christy answered softly. "I was just thinking of you."

"Couldn't sleep?"

"I did a little. I woke up about ten minutes ago. Todd, did last night really happen? Did you really propose to me?"

"Yes, I did. And you said yes."

"Yes, I did."

"Yes, you did."

Christy closed her eyes and felt his voice's warmth wash over her.

"I spent the whole night playing my guitar," Todd said. "I'm working on a new song."

"How did your roommate feel about that? Or did you spend the night in the lobby?"

"I'm the only guy left in my wing. Everyone else has gone home for Christmas break."

Christy remembered her missing roommate and asked, "Did you hear Katie say anything last night about going home?"

"No."

"I thought she was staying here this weekend with me, but she never came back last night."

"Did she stay in Sierra's room?" Todd asked. "She's done that in the past, hasn't she?"

"Yes. That's probably what she did. I know I shouldn't worry about her. She's a big girl and can take care of herself. It's just that with Katie I never know what's going to happen next."

"So, what are you doing right now?" Todd asked. "Do you want to meet me down by the chapel? We can watch the sunrise."

Christy laughed at the spark of spontaneity in his voice. "Sure, I'll be there in ten minutes."

Dressing in several layers in case it was as chilly outside as it looked, Christy paused only a minute in front of the mirror. Her long, straight, nutmeg brown hair was pulled back in a clip. She let it down and shook her head before giving her tresses a quick brushing. Todd liked her hair long. She smiled. Even though she had slept only four and a half hours, her blue-green eyes were bright and full of glimmering hope. Her cheeks had a rosy glow, and the longer she gazed at herself, the wider her smile grew.

So this is what a woman in love looks like. An engaged woman in love. A bride to be.

With a quick stop in the bathroom to wash her face and brush her teeth, Christy headed across the Rancho Corona campus to the small chapel at the mesa's edge. From the trail that ran along the rim of the school's property, the Pacific Ocean was visible on exceptionally clear days.

This morning a fine winter mist hovered low to the ground as Christy crossed the meadow. When the sun rose, it would be too hazy to see much of the view that stretched between the campus and the coast. She didn't mind. She wasn't trotting at such a fast clip to see the valley. She was going to meet her beloved, and she couldn't stop smiling.

Finding the door of the chapel open, Christy stepped into the sheltered warmth of the small, hushed building and spotted Todd. He was kneeling at the altar, eyes closed, head bowed.

With her heart still racing, Christy tiptoed to the altar. She knelt beside Todd. His short, sandy blond hair was wet. From him rose the subtle scent of Lifebuoy soap. As he lifted his head, his screaming, silver-blue eyes turned toward her. Christy immediately knew she wasn't the only one who had been smiling all night. The dimple on his right cheek seemed as if it had turned into a permanent mark.

Neither of them spoke. Their eyes did all the talking. Neither words nor touch were needed as they knelt there, silent before God and each other, talking to God, talking to each other. Heart to heart. Soul to soul.

Todd was the first to speak. It was a prayer of thanks. He asked God to direct their future steps and guide them as they made plans for their wedding. When he concluded, Christy joined him in saying "As you wish," which to them meant "Amen" or "May it be according to your will."

Todd stood and offered Christy his hand. "How does some breakfast sound?"

Christy smiled at how quickly Todd could go from intensely spiritual to immensely hungry. "Sure, I have the whole day free."

"Me too."

Hand in hand they stepped into the cool morning. The light from the sun broke through the mist like thin streamers made of silver glitter. The meadow before them had become a fairy-tale world, lit by tiny drops of light.

"It's so beautiful," Christy whispered.

"Let's get married right here," Todd said, stepping into the enchanted meadow.

Christy chuckled. "Okay. Right now?"

"I'm serious," Todd said. "Let's have the ceremony right here." He let go of her hand and, with wide arm motions, described the scene as he saw it. "We'll put an arch right here. Is that what you call those things you stand under? They're rounded on top and covered with flowers."

Christy nodded. "Yes, that would be an arch. Or a trellis."

"Let's get married right here under an arch." Todd seemed to size up the field. "What do you think? We could fit enough chairs in here. You could wait over there in the chapel. When the music starts, you would walk down the aisle to here."

Todd stepped over to a spot where he stood in a direct line with the chapel. "This is where we'll put the arch. You'll come walking down the center there, wearing a white dress with some flowers in your hair, and I'll be waiting for you right here."

Christy's heart soared. "Sounds beautiful." She had assumed they would be married inside a church, but this meadow was as much a holy ground as a church, she thought. Especially this morning. Especially this very moment, with Todd's eyes lit up and the meadow sprinkled with a shimmering mist of celestial light.

"This would be a beautiful spot for an evening wedding," Christy said. "It would be too hot to sit out here in the afternoon in the summer."

Todd stopped. He turned to Christy. "Summer?"

"Don't you think it would be too hot to sit outside in the afternoon without any shade? I think August evenings are beautiful."

"August?" Todd repeated. "Are you thinking we should get married next summer?"

"Of course. We both will have graduated by then and had time to plan everything and—"

"I want to get married sooner than that," Todd said.

"Sooner? How much sooner?"

"I don't know. Next week is Christmas. Then we have the missions trip to Mexico with the youth group the week after that. What about the second weekend in January?"

Christy laughed. Todd didn't.

"Todd, we can't get married in three weeks!"

"Why not?"

"We have to plan everything! We have to find a place to live and buy rings and order invitations. I have to find a dress and—"

"You're great at planning things, Chris. That's what you do best. We have all of Christmas break to work on it."

"No, we don't. We're going to Mexico after Christmas, remember? We haven't even finished planning that trip yet."

"Okay, then how about the third week of January? Or the last week, right after I graduate?"

Christy felt panic rising inside. "Todd, how could we possibly pull off a wedding in a month? People will think we *have* to get married."

Todd's voice was calm and soothing as he reached for her hand. "You and I and everyone else know that isn't the case. Is that what you're afraid of? What other people think?"

Christy grasped Todd's hand tighter and tried to calm her rising emotions. "No, I'm not worried about what other people think. It's just that I would like our wedding to be special and well thought out. I want us to have enough time to plan everything the right way and not to feel rushed down the aisle. Does that make sense?"

Todd bent over and kissed Christy tenderly on the cheek. "Yes. That makes sense. What you're trying to tell me is that January is too soon."

"Yes, January is too soon." Christy wrapped her arms around him and rested her head on his shoulder. Her breathing returned to normal. She liked the idea of getting married here in the meadow. She could picture the two of them standing right here in the cool of the evening sometime next August.

Todd pulled away so he could look her in the face. "So, if January is too soon, what are you thinking? February?"

"No, I'm still thinking August would be best."

"August!" Todd laughed. "We don't need eight months to plan a wedding."

"Yes, we do."

"March." Todd held her at arm's length. "Easter vacation. It'll be perfect weather. You'll almost be done with school."

"Easter vacation is in April."

"Okay, then April. Not August. April. I want to marry you, Christy. I want to be with you. I want us to start our life together. This is what we've been waiting for."

"We've both been waiting, Todd. We've both been thinking and praying about it for almost six years. Eight more months is nothing. We can wait until August."

Todd looked out over the meadow. The risen sun now cast its filtered light through the mist, shining on the droplets of moisture that clung to the grass, turning them into tiny diamonds. All across the meadow it appeared as if the stars had fallen from the heavens and were scattered at their feet, creating new constellations in miniature.

Christy watched as Todd stuck out his chin and seemed to be processing all this with a firm determination. He was usually Mr. Whatever, laid back about everything. He had told her several months ago that he was inexperienced with things like birthday parties and holidays. Evidently he knew even less about planning weddings.

"Trust me, Todd," Christy said softly. "April is too soon."

"Yeah? Well, August is definitely too far away. We can fit in a wedding before this summer. I'm sure we can."

"Why fit it in? Why not wait until I graduate and have the wedding in June?" Christy asked. "The meadow will be beautiful in June."

Todd shook his head. "No, not June. It's looking like my position at the church will turn into full time on June first. I don't see how I could take a week off in June for our honeymoon."

"Maybe if you asked them now and explained—"

Todd turned his perplexed face toward Christy. "You know what? I don't want to talk about this right now. Let's get something to eat." He reached for her hand and started for the parking lot.

Christy noticed how the sun had pierced the morning clouds that previously had spread across the meadow. The glittering field of diamonds had evaporated, leaving a long stretch of dried winter grass. Nothing was enchanting about the world around them anymore.

Is this what happens when a match made in heaven tries to walk on the earth? How can the glimmering magic disappear so quickly?

Todd remained deep in his own thoughts as they drove into town in their Volvo station wagon. Christy told herself she should have been more spontaneous as they dreamed aloud about their wedding date.

I could have simply said yes to January or any other month. As soon as Todd was presented with the details, he would have changed his mind and adjusted to a more practical date. This is the time for me to be dreamy, not practical.

"It looks like that restaurant is open." Christy pointed to a café they were approaching. She hoped they could sit down and calmly discuss their wedding plans over a leisurely breakfast. This time around she would be less practical and more dreamy.

"I was thinking of a breakfast burrito," Todd said. "Do you mind if we go to Roland's Drive Thru?"

"I don't think there's a Roland's around here."

"I know one is near Doug and Tracy's house at the beach."

"That's a long drive. Are you sure you want to wait that long to eat?"

"I don't mind," Todd said. "Do you?"

Stop being so practical about everything! Just agree for once.

"Okay, Roland's is fine with me." *Even though it seems crazy to drive such a long way just to get a certain type of fast food.*

"Can we work on the Mexico trip?" Todd asked.

"What do you mean?"

"Can we start planning while we drive to Carlsbad?"

"You don't want to talk about our wedding date anymore?"

"Not now. I think a note pad is on the backseat. A pen should be in the glove compartment. It would help me a lot if we could work on the Mexico trip. Could you make a list like we did for the camping trip to the desert?"

Christy found the note pad and pen. In fat letters she wrote *MEXICO* at the top of the paper.

"We need tents," Todd said. "Could you put that on the list? And we need extra tarps, in case it rains."

As Todd continued with the list of what they needed, Christy took notes. All her letters came out thick and angry.

Why is it you can be practical about Mexico, Todd, but not practical about setting a wedding date?

The longer they talked, the longer the list became. Todd expressed surprise every time Christy thought of another necessary component of the trip, such as medical release forms for each teenager and whatever parental permission they needed to take the students across the border.

She wanted to say, "See? Every event takes careful planning. Especially something as huge as a wedding."

But she didn't. The frustration expressed itself only in the thick black printing that filled two pages on the note pad.

As soon as they exited the freeway in the beach town of Carlsbad, Todd rolled down his window. He seemed to need to fill his lungs with salty ocean air. Christy was glad for the fresh air, too. Her emotions had begun to spiral into a nose dive.

Where are all the lovey-dovey feelings I felt for Todd this morning? Why can't we spend the day dreaming about us? Did I ruin everything by not being spontaneous enough when he was in a dreamy mood?

"Hey, how's it going?" Todd said to the speaker box at the drive-through. "I'd like four breakfast burritos and two large orange juices." He turned to Christy. "What would you like?"

Christy tried to see the menu printed on the box outside Todd's window, but his arm blocked the sign. "Do they have French toast?"

"French toast?" Todd repeated as if he had never heard of such an item before.

"Never mind. I'll just have an egg and cheese breakfast sandwich and a milk."

Todd repeated her order and drove up to the window.

"Are you okay?" Todd asked.

Christy tucked her hair behind her ears and glanced at his handsome face. *How can I explain to you all the intense feelings colliding inside me for the past hour? I'm afraid that if I say anything, I'll be sorry later and hammer myself to pieces for making a big deal out of nothing.*

"I'm okay," Christy said in a low voice.

Todd paid the employee at the open window and handed the food to Christy. She was going to ask if he wanted to park the car so they could eat, but he turned left onto the main road, and she knew where he was headed. The call of the wild that always beckoned to Todd was the ocean. They were less than a mile from where the blue Pacific ran to meet the California coast. Christy knew she should have guessed that was why they had driven all this way for breakfast burritos. Todd wanted to eat their first breakfast as an engaged couple on the beach.

Only Todd didn't head for the beach. He turned toward the freeway.

"Are we going back to school?" Christy asked.

"No, I just thought we could share our breakfast."

Share our breakfast? What's he talking about?

Todd pulled the car to the side of the road under the freeway overpass and grabbed one of the large orange juices.

"Can you hand me two of those burritos?" he asked Christy. Then, leaving the engine running, Todd jumped out of the car and took the food to a homeless man huddled under a cardboard box. She hadn't noticed the guy when they had exited the freeway, but obviously Todd had.

As Christy watched Todd smile and offer the hot food to the surprised man, her heart beat a little faster. A troubling thought settled on her like an ominous shadow. *I'm going to spend the rest of my life with a man who is given to random acts of impulsiveness. I'm never going to know where we're going or what we're doing or with whom we'll be sharing our meals. Nothing will be predictable about our life together. Nothing orderly or steady or sure.*

Christy swallowed hard. Todd was jogging back to the car wearing a wide grin of contentment. She tried hard to press a welcoming smile across her face to greet him, but in her heart, all she could think was, *I don't know if I'm ready for this.*

CHAPTER 2

Todd turned the car around and drove to the beach, where they parked and carried their breakfast over to a large, smooth boulder. Christy ate slowly, her eyes fixed on the endless ocean stretched out before them. She could feel Todd's gaze on her. Because they had sat together many times at the ocean without exchanging words, the silence felt familiar and had a comforting effect on her. Folding up the uneaten half of her breakfast sandwich, she let out a deep breath.

"Does it scare you?" Todd reached over to brush his fingers across Christy's cheek.

"Does what scare me?"

"Getting married. Or more specifically, marrying me?"

Unnerved at how Todd could read her thoughts, Christy threw up a smoke screen. "Why do you think I'm afraid?"

Todd traced the rim of her ear with his finger and didn't answer. She knew he was waiting for her.

"We don't think the same way," Christy blurted out.

"No, we don't."

Christy leaned her cold cheek against his warm hand. She decided to go ahead and hook a few of her fishy feelings onto the end of the line he patiently was holding over the deep waters of her heart. "Todd, I'm afraid that being married is going to be hard."

"Mmm-hmm."

"It will be a gigantic adjustment for both of us. We're opposites in so many ways."

"Mmm-hmm."

"You approach life differently than I do. You see things differently. I don't think the way you do."

"That's okay." Todd stroked her hair. "I don't see our differences as a problem."

"Of course you don't! That's my point. What's major to me is minor to you."

"I think our differences are good," Todd said. "We balance each other out."

"I think our differences will make it harder for us."

Todd lifted a handful of her long hair and brushed the ends across his lips.

"Todd, I don't think you and I know each other as well as we think we do. We have a lot of adjustments ahead of us."

"And a whole lifetime to work on them." Todd pulled her toward him so her head rested on his shoulder. In a calm voice he said, "Learning about each other and working through the adjustments are part of what makes a relationship alive and growing. I'm looking forward to that part of our future."

"I'm not," Christy heard herself say. "I think we're going to drive each other crazy. I'm so determined to have everything organized, and you're so spontaneous and so, so . . . random!"

"Yeah, I guess I am. What was it Katie called me a couple of months ago on our camping trip?"

"You mean when you brought plastic hangers instead of metal ones because you didn't realize I wanted to use them to roast marshmallows?"

Todd nodded.

"Katie said you were 'detail impaired.' "

Todd laughed. "That's right. And Matt told her it wasn't nice to discriminate against people who have disabilities." He drew Christy's head down till it rested against his chest.

"You know what I think?" Todd asked. "I think we all have disabilities or areas where we're impaired. You help me where I'm weak, and I help you where you're weak. That's what makes us strong together."

Christy wrapped her arms around his middle and cuddled up close. With a sigh she said, "I don't know, Todd. I hope you're right. Katie says I have a 'tidiness' issue. She says I have to have everything in place all the time or I'm not happy."

Todd chuckled.

"Do you think she's right?" Christy pulled back and looked into Todd's face.

"I think God brought us together so I could learn the rewards of being spiritually disciplined from you and so you could learn the joys of walking by faith from me. We're made for each other, Kilikina."

Christy reached for Todd's hand and drew it to her lips. She kissed it three times. One kiss for each of the scars that remained after the near-fatal car accident he was in that fall.

"I hope you're right," she said.

"I am." Todd chuckled. He held her left hand and ran his rough fingers across the top of her long fingers. "Did you wish I had a ring for you when I proposed last night?"

"No."

"Are you sure? Because I asked my dad if I should buy a ring for you before I proposed. He said you probably would want to choose your own. Doug told me last night about a jeweler he likes here in Carlsbad. That's where he bought Tracy's ring. It's not far from here. I thought we could stop by this morning to see what they have."

Christy drew back and examined Todd's expression. "Is that why we came all the way to Carlsbad for breakfast burritos? You wanted to go ring shopping today?"

"Yeah." Todd grinned.

She closed her eyes and shook her head.

"What?"

"Todd, you know you can tell me these things ahead of time, don't you? I mean, it would have helped me to know that was why you wanted to drive down here."

"Okay, next time I'll tell you. See? We're learning to adjust already."

Todd helped her stand up, and they headed for the parking lot hand in hand. Christy felt herself warming up from the inside out as they drove into an older part of Carlsbad. She had fond memories of a jewelry store she and Todd had visited last summer when they were in Venice, Italy. It was owned by their friend's uncle and had to be the most elegant shop she had ever been in, complete with a uniformed guard at the door and gold chandeliers.

This Carlsbad jewelry store was located next to a bakery and a bookstore and didn't look nearly as opulent as the jewelry store in Venice. But what it lacked in golden chandeliers and uniformed guards it made up for in cozy ambience. Todd held open the door for Christy, and the fragrance of fresh-baked bread from the bakery next door swirled through the air.

Romantic visions of exchanging whisper-filled glances with Todd as she tried on engagement rings danced in Christy's head.

"Morning!" Todd greeted the gentleman at the back of the shop. "Is it okay if we look around?"

"Yes, of course. If I can answer any questions, please don't hesitate to ask. I'm Mr. Frank."

Christy felt like a princess as Todd motioned for her to take a seat at the padded bench in front of the first jewelry case. He stood behind her and, leaning over, pointed at the most noticeable ring in the center of the case. It had a large diamond in the center and three rubies on either side.

"Look at that one," Todd said.

"It's beautiful. But kind of big, don't you think? I like the smaller, simpler rings. Like that one." Christy pointed to a gold ring with a single diamond in a plain setting. "Only not that plain. I want my ring to be unique, you know?"

"Is there anything I can show you?" Mr. Frank came their way with a key in his hand.

"I'm not sure," Christy said quickly.

"Go ahead. Try it on," Todd said. "That way you'll know if you like the style or not."

Mr. Frank reached into the case for the padded velvet display box and took out the diamond solitaire. Christy slid the ring onto her left hand; it fit perfectly. The diamond was cut boldly and raised high on four prongs. She felt her hands begin to sweat. She had read the price on the attached tag when she slipped the ring on her finger and knew it must be an exceptional diamond. And she knew she could never feel comfortable wearing a ring that cost so much.

"What do you think?" Todd asked.

The phone rang, and Mr. Frank excused himself with a polite nod, leaving Christy and Todd alone for a few minutes. Todd leaned over and planted a kiss on Christy's unsuspecting lips.

With a chin-up gesture he asked again, "So, what do you think?"

Christy teasingly returned the chin-up gesture that had been Todd's trademark for years and whispered, "I think you kiss pretty good."

Todd suppressed his laughter. With a finger to his lips he whispered, "I'm serious. What do you think?"

Christy blinked her eyes innocently and said, "I was serious, too. I think you kiss pretty good."

Todd reached over and tickled her. A burst of laughter almost escaped her lips, but she kept them pressed together until they hurt.

Mr. Frank finished his phone call. As he headed back toward them, Christy turned to Todd and whispered, "This ring is way too expensive."

Todd took her hand and turned it so he could read the price. "That's okay. If you like it, we can make payments. Don't let the price hold you back."

"It's not just the price, it's the ring. The style. I've never worn a lot of rings, but I know I'd like something smaller. Flatter. Something different."

"Different?" Todd questioned.

Mr. Frank stood before them and began to quote more facts about the diamond's clarity and size. "All of these rings are original designs made right here by my son and me."

Christy took the ring off her finger and tried to keep from giggling as she felt Todd's hand on her shoulder. If his fingers slipped behind her hair and started tickling her neck, she knew she would burst out laughing.

"Do you have anything different?" Todd asked in a controlled voice. "Anything flatter? And what did you say, Christy? Smaller?"

"Ah!" Mr. Frank seemed to enjoy the challenge set before him. "Something other than the traditional diamond. Perhaps a sapphire or a blue topaz, to match your lovely blue eyes. We have some particularly nice tanzanite."

For the next fifteen minutes, Todd refrained from tickling her as Christy tried on half a dozen non-diamond rings, with Mr. Frank giving a comprehensive lesson on each of the stones. With each ring she began to see potential options. Her imagination exploded with ideas when she tried on a particularly colorful Australian blue opal ring. The deep aqua blue stone with its flashes of green and purple reminded her of an ocean wave. And that reminded her of Todd and how they first had met at Newport Beach. However, the ring was too large, and the complicated setting didn't suit her.

"Do you have anything with this same sort of stone only in a smaller setting?" Christy asked. "Or even a flat setting like those bands with the diamond chips?"

"I don't believe we do. But as I mentioned earlier, we can make anything."

Christy was ready to design her ring right then and there. However, she glanced up at Todd before asking for paper and pencil. His expression was glazed over; he appeared to have reached his limit on looking for rings and learning the history of gemology.

"You've given us a lot to think about." Christy smiled at Mr. Frank. "I appreciate all your time."

"Allow me to present you with my card. If I may be of any further assistance, please don't hesitate to call."

"Thank you," Christy said.

"Are you sure you don't want to try on any more rings?" Todd asked a little too politely.

Christy couldn't hold back her laughter any longer. She released a light giggle that floated on the air like a band of glistening soap bubbles. "I would love to, Todd, but I think I've already tried on every ring in the store."

They left with Todd's arm around her middle while he threatened to tickle her again.

"That poor man!" Christy exclaimed. "He kept looking at us like we weren't old enough to know what we were doing."

"I thought he was looking that way because he knew we didn't have enough money to buy anything but the peppermints in the dish by the register."

"Those were free," Christy said.

"They were? Hey, let's go back and get some." Todd turned around, but Christy grabbed his arm with both hands and pulled him toward the car. His comment about not having enough money sobered her.

"How are we going to pay for the rings and everything else?" she asked as soon as they were in the car.

"I have some money set aside," Todd said. He didn't start the engine but looked at her carefully. "It's not a lot, but my goal was to have enough for the ring, the tux, and the first three months of rent before I proposed. And I have that. Otherwise, I would have asked you to marry me a long time ago."

"You would have?"

Todd nodded. "I wanted us to get married before you went to Switzerland, but I knew that was an important year for you, and I didn't want to take it from you."

Christy thought a moment. "I don't think I would have been ready then. I don't even know if I'm ready now."

"Is that why you want a longer engagement?" Todd asked. "Do you need more time to be sure?"

"Oh, I'm sure I want to marry you." Christy reached for his hand and held it with both of hers. "I didn't mean that to sound the way it did. I'm sure with all my heart that I want to marry you. Only you. What I meant was I'm not sure I'm ready for all the adjustments and planning and decisions, like with the ring. I mean, you would think I would have an idea of what I want already, but I've never given it much thought. I just want it to be uniquely ours so that every time I look at it I'll think of us. Does that make sense?"

"Sure," Todd said. "You heard what he said. They can custom make anything you want. I'm sure you could have him put a stone like that blue one you liked into a different setting."

"It might take a while to do that," Christy said.

Todd flashed her a mischievous grin. "That's okay. It's not like we have to have the ring by January or anything."

Christy playfully thumped him on the arm. "Todd, seriously, do you think we could pull off a wedding in less than a month?"

Todd shrugged. "Hey, all we need is a ring and a minister, right? And before you comment on that, how do you feel about stopping by to see Doug and Tracy?"

"Okay."

"Now, I like that answer." He started the car. "Quick, clean, decisive."

Christy settled back in her seat and thought about how much sense it made to wait until August for their wedding and about designing her own ring and about how much money they needed for rent. She thought about how many decisions they would need to make and how Todd appreciated "quick, clean, decisive" answers.

As Todd drove into a residential area where cottage-style beach bungalows lined the street, Christy came to a conclusion. "You know what, Todd? That's going to be my goal over the next few months. I'm going to work at making quick, clean decisions."

"You have good instincts, Christy. You should trust yourself and go with your gut feelings more often."

She studied his profile as he pulled up in front of Doug and Tracy's house. This man of her dreams who sat beside her had grown into a strong God-lover who was also deeply in love with her. Christy felt her heart pounding until she thought it would go *zing!* and fly right out of her.

"What?" Todd glanced at her as he backed their Volvo into a space along the curb.

Christy pressed her lips together, intending to keep her zingy feelings inside. But then Todd stopped the car, looped his arm over the steering wheel, and turned to her with his silver-blue eyes peering deep into the secret place of her heart. Suddenly August seemed very far away.

"Okay," she said, following her gut instincts yet speaking in barely a whisper. "You win. January it is."

Todd leaned closer. "What did you say? I couldn't hear you."

Christy's heart raced. Her cheeks flushed. Never had she felt so overcome with the intensity of her love for Todd. Did she dare repeat the whispered words that had escaped her heart?

"What I said was . . ."

A flicker of an image came to Christy. The two of them were pulling away with a squeal from the very curb they had just parked in front of and driving one hundred miles an hour to the first drive-through wedding chapel they came to in Las Vegas.

She blinked. *No, this isn't one of those moments when I should trust my gut for a quick, clean decision. If I did, I'd end up dashing ahead of you and God and everyone else.*

"I said I love you," she whispered. "That's all."

"Oh, is that all?" Todd teased, pressing the back of his hand against her warm cheek. "Then why are you blushing?"

"Sunburn?" she ventured, raising her eyebrows and trying to look as innocent as possible.

"In December? I don't think so." Todd smiled at her. He seemed to be studying every detail of her face. His hand rose to the crown of her head. Gently, he stroked her long hair.

"Oh, Kilikina, if you only knew." He smoothed his thumb across her lips. "You have no idea what you and your love have brought to my life. You are the other half of my heart. Without you, my life would be only a shadow." He paused. "I love you, Kilikina. I love you more than you will ever know. More than you will ever ask. Nothing will ever change my love for you."

"Oh, Todd." Christy tilted her head toward him and offered him her lips.

Todd accepted her gift and kissed her slowly.

Just then a loud horn sounded in front of them, shattering their forever moment.

CHAPTER 3

Todd and Christy reluctantly drew away from each other and looked through the car's windshield. They saw Doug pulling his truck into his narrow driveway, wildly waving at them. Jumping out of his yellow truck, he came over to Todd's open window and said, "Hey, did I just catch you two making out in front of my house?"

"We weren't making out." Christy felt her face turn red all over again.

Doug laughed. His face lit up with a little-boy expression that had become familiar to Christy over the years. Doug was taller than Todd, but with his short, blond hair and mischievous grin, he could have passed for a high school freshman. "I suppose you're going to tell me Todd was checking your hair to see if it smelled like green apples."

"No, that's your line, Doug." Todd glanced at Christy with an equally charming little-boy grin and stated matter-of-factly, "We were kissing." He pressed the back of his fingers against Christy's cheeks. "This is my blushing bride. We're going to get married. Did you know that, Doug?"

Doug punched Todd in the arm. "The whole world knows it after last night. You two space cadets better come in and see everyone. Tracy will be thrilled you're here. We had a big sleepover last night. Rick is going to make omelets."

"Rick?"

"Yeah, Rick's here. It's been awesome hearing what God has done in his life. He and Katie had us laughing all night."

"Katie?"

"Yeah, Katie is here, too. So were Sierra, Paul, Vicki, and Wes." Doug opened Todd's door. "You two want to help me carry in the groceries? I had to make a run for supplies."

"That explains what happened to my roomie last night," Christy said.

Todd and Christy followed Doug to the front door, each carrying two bags of groceries. Doug and Tracy's cozy cottage was four blocks from the beach and was the only yellow house with white shutters on their street. It had one bedroom and one bathroom. The living room area opened into the kitchen, and they had a small backyard, where Tracy had worked hard to start a flower garden.

As soon as they entered, Katie leaped from the couch and met Christy with a huge hug. "Did you get my message? Why didn't you come last night? We had a great time celebrating your engagement. You should have been here. When I called you late last night the line was busy."

Katie seemed even more energetic than usual.

"I was talking to my parents," Christy said.

Taking one of the grocery bags from Christy, Katie asked, "Were they surprised about your engagement?"

"No. Todd talked to my dad earlier and asked for my parents' blessing."

"It was more like asking his permission," Todd said.

"Permission or blessing," Christy said. "My dad gave both. My parents were waiting for me to call. They're thrilled. My mom cried. Then I called my aunt and uncle."

"Did they know Todd was going to propose last night?"

"No, but they weren't surprised. They're real happy for us, too." Christy stepped into the kitchen area of Doug and Tracy's compact house and received a warm grin from Rick.

"We're all real happy for you." Rick reached in front of Katie and offered Todd a handshake. "You two have a great future ahead of you."

Christy noticed that although Rick was still his tall, dark, and handsome self, he didn't seem to wear an attitude of arrogance like a prince's crown, which is what he had done when he was in high school. Standing next to

Katie in Doug and Tracy's homey kitchen, Rick appeared average. Katie's flashing green eyes and soft, distinctive new look with her short, feathery red hair made her the first person Christy's eyes went to.

"Where's everyone else?" Doug asked, unloading the bountiful groceries.

"Tracy is in the shower; Paul had to go to work; Sierra, Wes, and Vicki had to get back to school because they're driving home to Oregon for Christmas break." Katie's expression lit up another couple of watts as she turned to Christy. "I wish you guys had come last night. We stayed up all night talking. It was awesome."

"Uh-oh." Rick gave Katie a playful tag on the arm. "You've been around Doug too long. You're starting to say 'awesome.'"

"Well, it was an awesome time for all of us last night. You guys would have loved it. We laughed so hard!" Katie began to recount the previous night's events while Christy moved to the living room and lowered herself into the chair beside the couch. Katie looked radiant as she spoke with charming animation. What an improvement over the way Katie looked twenty-four hours earlier when the gang was planning to go to The Dove's Nest. Katie had proclaimed she would rather stay alone in their dorm room since she didn't have a date. That was before Rick stepped into the center of their group.

Christy thought back on the way she had fallen for Rick in high school. Katie had a huge crush on him, too. But Christy got over Rick pretty fast; Katie never seemed to have recovered. Katie's love for Rick had turned to anger and simmered deep and low within her for years.

Then a few months ago a letter from Rick arrived. He told Katie how he had completely turned his life over to the Lord, and he asked Katie for her forgiveness for the way he had treated her in the past.

From the way she's looking at him right now, I would say Katie has forgiven Rick completely.

"Hey, Todd," Doug said after Katie concluded her entertaining summary. "I need to check on Tracy real quick, and then I need your help on something. I've been working on a song, and these guys helped me last night, but I can't get one part in the chorus right."

"Do you want us to start the omelets?" Katie called out as Doug headed for the bedroom.

"Sure," Doug said. "Go ahead."

"Do you know where they keep their cheese grater?" Rick asked.

"Try the cupboard on your right," Katie suggested.

"Anything I can do to help?" Christy asked.

"Sure," Rick said. "You can find a mixing bowl larger than this one."

"I think Tracy keeps those over here." Christy opened a cupboard as Katie's spontaneous laughter came rolling over her. Whenever Katie got going with her most joyful strain of laughter, others found it nearly impossible to keep a straight face. Her laughter carried the sound of glee at its freest, happiest, lightest moment and tickled all those who heard it.

Christy turned around and saw Katie holding up a couple of aprons she had found in a drawer. "This one is for you," Katie said to Rick. "And this one is mine."

Rick tied a frilly yellow apron trimmed with pastel flowers around his waist. It barely fit. Katie laughed again. Echoing Katie's winged laughter came the bass notes of a concert of mirth from Rick. It was a richer and more genuine laugh than Christy had ever heard spill from him.

Katie's apron was denim with stripes. Across the bib were the words *File All Complaints Here*. An arrow pointed to a tiny pocket that wouldn't hold many complaints.

"Trade you," Rick said.

"Not a chance."

Christy placed the large mixing bowl on the counter. "Anything else I can do?"

"We need plates," Rick said. "Can you find six dinner plates?"

The cupboard was empty, so Christy unloaded the clean dishes from the dishwasher while Rick and Katie went to work. Within a few moments, it appeared that they had turned the kitchen into a quirky cable cooking show. They had mushrooms cooking in a small frying pan and sausage going in a larger pan. Bowls and various cooking tools were scattered everywhere.

"We'll make an assembly line so everyone can custom-order their omelets," Rick explained. "If you want, Christy, you can grate the cheese."

Christy took her project over to the kitchen table to get out of the way. With amazement she watched the marvel of Rick and Katie, working side by side as if they had practiced the steps to this kitchen dance for years.

Todd strummed Doug's guitar as he sat on the living room couch. Christy didn't recognize the tune he was playing. She wondered if that was the song he had been working on last night.

Then, as if Todd felt her gaze on him, he looked over at her. A slow smile played on his lips. He kept strumming and then mouthed a word she didn't catch.

Christy gave him a look indicating she didn't understand him.

Todd mouthed the word again. "January."

Christy broke into a smile as bright as the sunrise. *You heard me in the car, didn't you, Todd? You heard me whisper "January" to you. Well, I know we can't pull off a wedding in January, but maybe we can pull it off by February. We could get married right after you graduate. I'd only have one more semester to go and—*

Doug stepped into the living room, blocking Christy's view of Todd.

What am I thinking? February is too soon. We can wait until this summer, can't we?

Doug began to play his new song. Christy pulled her thoughts back to the present. She felt a comforting sense of warmth come over her as Doug's familiar voice filled the cozy home where these good friends gathered.

"When the Lord brought us together
We were like those who dreamed
Our mouths were filled with laughter
Our tongues with songs of joy.
Then it was said
The Lord has done great things for them
Yes, the Lord has done great things for us
And we are filled with joy."

"Isn't that a great song?" Katie asked.

"What Scripture did you base it on?" Todd asked.

"Psalm 126," Doug said. "And this is the problem, here on this line. How do I make the transition from 'When the Lord brought us together' to 'We were like those who dreamed'? It isn't smooth."

Christy stopped grating the cheese. *Boy, that was a true statement, Doug. You don't realize it, but that's the question I've been struggling with all day. How do two dreamers make a smooth transition when the Lord brings them together?*

She wished he would play the whole song again. She wanted to hear the part about the Lord doing great things and about being filled with joy.

Just then the bathroom door opened, and petite Tracy stepped out with a huge smile on her heart-shaped face. "Hi!" she greeted Todd and Christy.

"Hey, how's it goin'?" Todd greeted her with a chin-up nod.

Christy rose and went over to give Tracy a hug. As soon as their arms went around each other, Tracy whispered in Christy's ear, "Guess what? I'm pregnant!"

"What?!" Christy squealed, pulling back and looking at Tracy's face to be sure she had heard right.

"Trace," Doug scolded, "did you tell her?"

"Tell her what?" Katie asked from the kitchen.

All eyes were on Tracy.

"We were going to wait until we sat down to eat." Doug handed Todd the guitar and went over to his wife, who was standing next to Christy and biting her lower lip.

"I'm sorry, honey! I didn't mean to say anything. It just flew right out of my mouth," Tracy confessed.

Doug put his arm around her and gave her a look of unfaltering devotion. "Go ahead, sweetheart. Tell everybody."

"You," she said.

"Oh, now you've turned shy." Doug laughed and gave his wife a big hug. "It looks like the Lord has decided to bless us with a baby."

A cheer rose from the group. They all took turns hugging and congratulating Doug and Tracy.

Todd crossed the room in four steps and slipped his arm around Christy. He kissed the side of her head, above her right ear. She knew he was thinking the same thing she was thinking. One day, Lord willing, they would be the ones making a similar announcement to their friends.

"Is something burning?" Tracy sniffed the air.

"It's the olive oil in the pan." Rick jogged back to the stove. "I'll turn it down."

"Could you open the window above the kitchen sink?" Tracy asked.

"Morning sickness," Doug explained. "She's not real steady until about two in the afternoon. She's sensitive to strong scents."

"When is the baby due?" Christy asked.

"July, according to our calculations," Tracy said. "We'll find out more after my appointment with the doctor next week."

"When did you guys find out?" Katie asked.

"Yesterday morning. It's been torture keeping it a secret from you guys, but we agreed we wanted to tell our parents first, and we weren't able to get ahold of them on the phone until this morning, right before Doug went for the groceries."

"I can't believe you didn't say anything last night," Katie said.

"Last night was Todd and Christy's night." Tracy sent Christy a gentle smile.

"Yeah, one major announcement at a time is about all this group can handle," Doug added.

"Don't worry about me!" Katie said. "I don't have any announcements or secrets this morning."

A crazy thought flitted through Christy's mind. She wondered if Katie would soon be announcing that Rick had asked her out. Christy shooed away the notion. It was far too early for that. Or maybe it was far too late, since they had already given that a try in high school.

Doug kissed his wife soundly. "We're open to suggestions on names because so far we haven't agreed on any names for boys or girls."

After a round of suggestions, none of which struck a chord with the happy couple, Doug returned to the couch with Todd to work on the song.

"Do you have a fan on this stove?" Rick asked. "I can't seem to find one."

"It's broken," Doug said.

"Is the smell still too strong for you, Tracy?" Rick said.

"No, it's okay." Tracy opened the front door to let in more air. "This will help. So, Rick, when did you become such a gourmet chef?"

Christy thought Tracy's redirection of the conversation was so typical of her. She didn't like having the attention on herself. Tracy seemed most comfortable when she was listening to her friends or offering them kind advice. Christy had a long list of questions to ask Tracy about her engagement and wedding details, but she decided to wait until the two of them could be alone.

"Cooking is one of my hidden talents," Rick replied to Tracy's question.

"I don't remember hearing about your cooking much when you and Doug and Todd shared the apartment in San Diego," Tracy said.

Rick laughed. "That's because we never had any food in our apartment!"

"You got that right," Todd said.

"Amen!" Doug agreed.

"I learned a few things at the restaurant where I worked."

"The Blue Parachute," Katie said.

Rick looked surprised. "That's right. How did you know that, Katie?"

"We went there one night after the Bible study at your apartment, remember? Christy and I came down to San Diego, and you were at the hospital when we arrived because you sprained your wrist."

"Oh yeah, that's right." Rick seemed to be having a hard time remembering that night. "You guys came down, and we went to the zoo."

Christy remembered the experience vividly because she had watched Rick kiss Katie the night of the Bible study. The next day at the zoo Rick treated Katie terribly. He acted as if nothing had happened between them the night before.

Standing only a few feet from Katie, Christy watched her expression. She saw no indication on Katie's face that the memory of Rick and the zoo was still painful.

"My mom is the real cook in our family," Rick said. "That's how my dad came up with the idea of starting The Dove's Nest Café next to the Christian bookstore."

"Why did your dad build The Dove's Nest and The Ark out in Murietta Hot Springs instead of where they live in Escondido or here at the beach?" Doug asked.

"He got a great deal on the property in Murietta. It would have cost two or three times as much here."

Katie turned to Christy. "And guess where I'm going to work starting in January?"

"Let me guess. The car wash in Temecula?"

"Nooo," Katie answered playfully. "Guess again. It starts with a 'dove' and ends with a 'nest.' "

"Wait a minute," Christy said. "I thought you said you didn't have any big announcements or secrets?"

"This isn't exactly a secret," Rick said. "We've been looking for people who can work evenings. It's entry level, but I have a feeling she'll work her way up to just about any position she wants."

Christy studied her best friend even more carefully. "And just what position do you want, Miss Katie?"

"To attend the Natural Food Faire in San Diego."

Christy hadn't expected an answer, especially such a random one.

"It's held every February. Rick says we can go and introduce my new Indian Summer herbal tea."

Christy took note of her roommate's answer. Katie had said "we." That meant Katie and Rick. The two of them were planning to go together. And the fair wasn't until February.

"Are you ready for this?" Rick asked Christy.

No, I'm not ready for Katie and you to be making plans together so naturally, Rick Doyle. Katie may have forgiven you for the way you treated her years ago, but you're going to have to prove to me you're worthy of renewing such a chummy relationship with my best friend.

Rick pointed to the frying pan and repeated his question. "Are you ready for me to make your omelet? Tell me what you want in it."

"Oh. Just some cheese."

"Is that all?"

Christy nodded.

"Don't worry," Katie said. "My omelet will allow you to showcase your culinary skills."

"That's my girl." Rick flashed Katie a big smile. He didn't say it with the manipulative edge his voice had carried in high school. His words, his tone, his expression all reflected warm genuineness.

And it gave Christy a shiver up her spine. *Katie, girl, you and I need to talk.*

CHAPTER 4

The opportunity for Christy to have a heart-to-heart discussion with Katie seemed to present itself late that night when Katie finally returned to their dorm room. Christy was busy packing her things to go home for Christmas vacation as Katie burst in, bright as a sunbeam.

"Hello, favorite of all the roomies in all the world! Is God incredible or what?" Katie twirled around and flopped on her unmade bed. "I'm telling you, Chris, life is never dull when God is doing His God-things. I'm speechless. No, I'm overly full of speech. Full of praise, actually."

Katie jumped up and dashed across the room to tackle Christy in a hug. "And speaking of miracles, I still can't believe you and Todd finally are engaged! I loved watching you two sitting close on the couch at Doug and Tracy's. It was adorable the way you were sharing bites of each other's omelets. You both looked so happy, and by the way, weren't those great omelets? Is Rick amazing or what?"

"Katie!" Christy laughed and grasped her friend firmly by the shoulders. "Take a breath! I've seen you hyper before but never this hyper. How much caffeine have you had today?"

"I don't know. Enough to keep me awake after staying up all night. And I drank a lot of homemade hot chocolate. Todd and you left before Rick made it. I had three mugsful! You should have stayed; it was so good. Did you guys go to the mall?" Katie flitted over to her dresser and began to pull out clothes and cosmetics and toss them on her bed.

"No. We were going to look at more rings, but we ended up talking for a long time, and then Todd dropped me off here so I could take a nap before we went to dinner."

"You wouldn't have needed a nap if you had had some of this hot chocolate! You know how they say that chocolate can give you the feeling of being in love?" Katie wagged her toothbrush at Christy. "Well, I never believed it before today, but after three mugs of pure chocolate, I'm definitely in love!"

"In love with chocolate?" Christy ventured.

"No, not in love with chocolate. In love, in love. You know. Really in love." Katie's green eyes sparkled as she stopped long enough to give Christy a sideways glance. "Do you think that could be possible?"

Christy wasn't sure she was following Katie's logic. "Are you asking if it's possible for you to be in love someday?"

"Yes, but not someday. Today. With Rick." Katie's face went red. "Do you suppose I'm really, truly, finally in love?"

"Katie, it would make more sense if—"

"I know, I know." Katie turned on her heel and pulled out a large gym bag from her closet. "I'm just hyper. It must be the hot chocolate high. Rick used dark chocolate. I think there's a difference." She tossed a pair of shoes into the bag and a crumpled pair of jeans. "Dark chocolate probably has more caffeine. Or more of that stuff that induces feelings of being in love."

"Maybe," Christy answered cautiously. Then in an effort to move the conversation to a neutral topic so Katie would come down a notch, Christy said, "Are you going to drive home in the morning?"

"No, I'm going home tonight. Didn't I tell you?" Katie paused and added, "Rick is taking me. He's waiting in the lobby. Oh, and I almost forgot. He said he wanted to talk to you if you were here."

"He wants to talk to me? What about?"

Katie shrugged.

"So, if Rick is driving you home, are you leaving your car here during Christmas break?" Christy asked, trying to make sense of Katie's last-minute plans.

"No. See, I drove Baby Hummer home last night after your engagement party. Rick followed me, and then he and I drove to Doug and Tracy's since their house is only twenty minutes from my parents' house."

Christy nodded.

"Then, when we left Doug and Tracy's this afternoon, we went to the movies. Then Rick drove me back here to pick up my stuff. Now we're going to Escondido." Katie casually flipped a feathery strand of hair off her forehead as if her suddenly exploding social life made complete sense.

"Katie?" Christy asked in a small voice.

Katie either didn't hear her or chose not to hear as she continued to haphazardly toss things into her bag and kept talking. "Oh, and I should tell you, Rick wants to go to Mexico with us next week, so we need to add one more to the list when we go buy the food. He said he would help us cook when we're down there. He suggested spaghetti."

"Katie . . ."

"I told him you probably had the grocery list already figured out. If you'd like, I could ask him to go shopping with us. I'm sure Rick would—"

"Katie!"

"What?" Katie turned and faced Christy, and when she did, her entire countenance fell. "Oh no you don't. I know that look." Katie set her jaw and lowered her chin.

"What look?"

"I know exactly what you're going to say to me."

Christy laughed nervously. She hadn't thought she was that transparent. Her concern for Katie obviously showed all over her face.

Katie put down the gym bag and crossed the room in three steps. "You're going to ask me if I've thought this through and if I think that spending all this time with Rick is a good idea."

"Well . . ." Christy hesitated. Katie was exactly right, but Christy didn't want to admit it.

"And you know what?" Katie planted her hands on her hips. "I won't let you ask me those questions right now because I didn't go looking for this, Christy. You know I didn't. It just happened. Rick was there at The Dove's Nest, and the guys tried to play a joke on me by having Rick come over and ask me out. But the joke is . . ." Katie's eyes brimmed with tears, and her voice quavered. "The joke is that it isn't a joke. This is the most wonderful, amazing thing that has ever happened to me, Christy Miller, and you are *not* going to analyze it away from me!"

Christy swallowed all the sisterly words of caution that had been filling her mouth. She kept her lips together, not daring to let out a single sound.

"Thank you." Katie turned with her head held high. "Thank you, my best friend. That's the nicest gift you could give me at this moment." She grabbed her bag and motioned with her head for Christy to follow her. "Come on, Rick wanted to talk to you, remember?"

Christy followed quietly, wondering if she was doing the right thing to keep her apprehensions to herself.

In the middle of the dorm hallway, Katie said, "If this is a God-thing, it will last. If not, it will dissolve. I know that because I've never been so completely open to God's leading in my life as I am right now. I think it's the same for Rick. Neither of us is trying to make this happen. It's just what it is, and it will be whatever it's going to be."

Christy nodded her agreement, and a surprising calm came over her. For some reason she thought of how her aunt had always tried to control Christy's social life and how much Christy disliked it when Aunt Marti interfered. If it had been Aunt Marti's choice, Christy would never have developed her friendship with Katie. But what did Aunt Marti know?

The last thing I want to do is to take on my aunt's controlling characteristics!

"I love you, Katie," Christy said just before they walked into the lobby.

Katie flashed Christy a smile. "I love you, too."

"Hey, Christy," Rick said as they strode toward him. "I have something I wanted to give you. I was going to mail this." He pulled an envelope from his back pocket. "But I hoped to somehow be able to hand it to you. I guess this is the opportunity I was hoping for."

"Would you like me to leave you guys alone?" Katie asked.

"No, I don't mind if you hear this, Katie. I mean, if Christy doesn't mind."

"No, it's fine."

"I guess you both know I've been trying to make things right with people I hurt in the past and . . ." Rick seemed to have run out of words. He held out the crumpled envelope to Christy.

"Rick," Christy felt as nervous as he looked at this moment, "you don't need to apologize to me for anything. You and I settled everything a long time ago. I don't—"

"We didn't exactly settle everything," Rick said. "I, uh, I did something really cruel and foolish when . . . well, you know . . ." He drew in a deep breath. "When you and I were dating, Christy, I stole your bracelet. Or rather, Todd's bracelet. Or, I mean, the bracelet Todd gave you."

Christy bit the inside of her lower lip. She knew she had forgiven Rick for that long ago, but watching him so tortured as he made his confession to her brought all the emotions back to the surface for her, as well.

"I'm very sorry, Christy. That was wrong. I know you've forgiven me. But I also know that Doug and you made payments on the bracelet to the jewelry store where I traded it in."

Christy noticed that Rick's forehead was glistening with perspiration as he continued. "I've made things right with Doug, and now I'd like to make things right with you. Christy, please accept this with my apology." Rick's deep brown eyes begged for forgiveness.

"Thank you, Rick. I already forgave you, like you said."

"But you'll keep what's in that envelope," Rick said. "Promise me you'll keep it."

"Okay, I promise. Thank you."

Rick nodded. He looked relieved.

"I, um . . ." Christy felt another wave of awkwardness come over her. She didn't want to open the envelope in front of Rick and Katie, and she didn't want to prolong the conversation. "I guess I shouldn't hold you two up. You have a long drive ahead of you."

"Yeah, I guess we should get going." Rick reached for Katie's gym bag and backpack. "Is this all you have?"

"Yep," Katie said. "I travel light these days, thanks to my best friend's influence. Christy taught me all about traveling light when we were in Europe."

"I want to hear more about your trip," Rick said. "You guys went to Italy, right?"

"Yes."

"Did you go to the island of Capri?"

"Yes." Katie seemed to anticipate his next question. "And yes, we went to the Blue Grotto that you are so crazy about."

"You did?" Rick's expression lit up.

"Yes," Katie said with a grin at Christy. "Christy and Todd loved it, but I thought it was dark and cold and highly overrated. I mean, if you think about it, it's just a dark cave with water and a bunch of men wearing straw hats and singing loudly in Italian."

Rick's mouth dropped open.

Christy laughed. *Rick, I'd say you just had a full dose of the real Katie.*

Regaining his composure, Rick said, "You know, you're right, Katie. It is just a dark cave with water and singing Italian boatmen. I guess it's who you're with in the dark cave that makes it romantic."

"Oh, you want to talk romantic," Katie said, heading for the door, "then let's talk about Venice. I loved Venice. When you were there, did you go for a ride in a gondola? Now, that's a boat ride with a view."

"You guys went for a gondola ride?" Rick followed Katie to the door.

As Katie recounted the details of their adventure, Rick turned and gave Christy a warm smile. "See you later."

"I'll give you a call tomorrow." Katie waved over her shoulder. "You're going home after church, aren't you?"

Christy nodded.

"I'll call you," Katie said.

Christy waved. "Bye, you guys. Drive safely."

Turning to go back to her room, Christy chided herself. *Drive safely? Why am I talking like their mother would?*

Once Christy was back in the solitude of her dorm room, she reached for the phone and dialed Todd's number. She could tell from the sound in his voice that she had awakened him, but she asked the obvious anyway. "Were you asleep?"

"That's okay. What's up? Are you all right?"

Christy summarized her conversations with Katie and Rick. But before she could mention Rick's envelope, Todd said, "That's how it is when God's working in our lives. We always need to save room for the unexpected."

Christy thought of how Todd's life seemed to have plenty of room for the unexpected. He even seemed to look for the unexpected, like when he took breakfast to the homeless man that morning.

"I don't do that very well," Christy said. "I don't leave room on my calendar or in my daily schedule for God to do unexpected things."

"That's okay," Todd said. "I have a pretty good idea God will keep finding ways to fit them into your life anyway."

"God sure did that tonight." Christy told Todd about the envelope Rick had given her.

"You haven't opened it yet?" Todd asked.

"No, I don't know if I want to. In a way, I just want to throw it away and let it be over."

"Didn't you say Rick asked you to promise to keep it?"

"That's right, he did."

"You don't have to open it now," Todd said. "And you don't have to tell me what's in it when you open it. But you do have to honor your promise to Rick."

"You're right," Christy said quietly. "And I will. I think the best thing for now would be if I went to bed and got some sleep."

"Good idea. I'll see you in the morning."

"Good night, my Todd."

"Good night, my Kilikina. I love you."

"And I love you."

A settled calm came over Christy and over the dorm room after she hung up. She sat in the silence and stared at the envelope in her hand. Rick had written her first name in small, cursive letters. From the wear and tear on the envelope, he had been carrying it with him for some time.

Putting aside the envelope, Christy packed her neatly folded clothes that were still sitting on her bed. Right before she pulled down the covers, she reached for Rick's envelope and tucked it into her suitcase's side pocket.

The next day after church, as she and Todd drove home to Escondido, she thought again of the envelope. She wasn't sure why she hadn't opened it the night before. She should have opened it while she was talking to Todd on the phone so the entire incident could have been concluded. She knew Todd would never ask her about it.

When I get home, I'll open the envelope, show the contents to Todd, and it will be over. Settled. We'll all be able to move forward. I don't know why I'm being so squirmy about this. It's probably a letter of apology like the one he sent Katie.

What Christy hadn't anticipated was that Aunt Marti and Uncle Bob would be at her parents' house when she and Todd arrived.

"We couldn't wait until Christmas at our house to see you two." Marti kissed Christy on both cheeks and then turned her affectionate attentions toward Todd.

Marti had gone through a lot of personal changes during the past year. In September, she had arrived at Rancho to take Christy out to lunch. But after seeing Aunt Marti, Christy and Katie had concluded Marti already was "out to lunch." Her hair extensions, minimal makeup, and long, flowing gauze skirt, along with an announcement that she was considering going to Santa Fe with her new pottery instructor, served as all the proof Christy and Katie needed.

But Marti hadn't gone to Santa Fe. She and Uncle Bob seemed to be working on their relationship. And Marti's dark hair was cut in a short crop that framed her face in a softened style. Even Marti's perfume smelled like a fragrance Christy remembered from years ago.

Uncle Bob gave Christy a hug, and she noticed his dark hair was going gray by his ears. Bob and Todd both had been burned several years ago when Bob's gas grill went haywire and exploded. The black turtleneck Bob was wearing hid the scars on his neck.

Christy smiled at her patient uncle and wondered how his scars on the inside were doing, the scars from the hurts he must have suffered while Aunt Marti was going through her mid-life crisis.

Christy hugged her mom and dad, and then Marti jumped in and said she was ready to discuss wedding plans.

"I'll be back in a minute." Christy excused herself from the clutch of family members in the living room and carried her suitcase into her bedroom at the end of the hall. Closing the door, she leaned her back against it and swallowed hard.

Marti always had delighted in a project. Could it be that Todd and Christy's wedding was her latest grand event? Why hadn't Christy seen this coming? It made her clench her teeth to think of her aunt elbowing her way into Todd and Christy's plans and trying to take over. Yet, at the same time, Christy knew that as long as Marti had a project that kept her in Newport Beach with her husband, she was less likely to run off to join her new friends at their art colony in New Mexico.

A tap on the door made Christy jump. "Who is it?"

"It's me, David. Can I come in?"

Christy opened the door to let her fifteen-year-old brother into her private enclave. "Hi. How are you?" She gave him a quick hug, since he never had been a big fan of snuggling.

"Mom said you're getting married." David had passed up Christy's five-foot-seven-inch frame some time ago, but now he was filling out across the shoulders. His hair had always had more of their father's red tones than Christy's, but now it carried a stronger hue of blond, and Christy was stunned at how much older he looked.

"Where are your glasses?" Christy asked.

"Didn't Mom tell you? I broke my glasses twice this year while skateboarding. I told Mom and Dad all I wanted for Christmas was contacts. I got them yesterday, and Mom said I could start wearing them because I wanted to get used to them during the school break."

"Look at you. David, you are so grown-up. You're cute. No, you're handsome." Christy gave her brother a big smile. "David, you are adorable!"

David cracked a slight grin. "I'm glad you aren't one of those people who judge others simply by their outward appearance."

Christy laughed. "And a sense of humor, too! David, when did you get so cool?"

"I've always been cool, Christy."

She laughed and gave him another hug even though he didn't seem comfortable with all her gushing and squeezing.

"Did Mom tell you I joined a Christian club for skaters?"

"No." Christy flopped on her bed. "Where do they meet?"

"You make it sound like we have a clubhouse or something." David leaned against the closed door. "We just hang out at the skate park. This guy from our church comes every Thursday afternoon at four-thirty, and some of us sit down with him, and he has a Bible study. I'm learning a lot."

"Do you have a good Bible?" Christy had been with David when he gave his life to the Lord while Todd was in the hospital, but she realized she hadn't done much to follow up with him. She knew he was going to church with her parents, and this skaters' Bible study was good to hear about. But since she didn't have a Christmas present for him yet, a Bible sounded like a good idea.

"No."

"Do you want one?" Christy asked.

"I guess. I mean, I have a kid's version I got when I was like eight, but it has pictures, and I don't want to take that one to the skate park."

Christy remembered when she got her first "real" Bible. Todd and Tracy gave it to her for her fifteenth birthday. At the time, she hadn't appreciated it. She decided then that she would buy David a contemporary version for Christmas, but she would buy him something else, too.

"So are you guys really getting married?" David asked again.

"Yes." Christy's grin broadened. She kicked off her shoes and folded her legs under her, settling comfortably onto her old bed.

"When?"

"We haven't decided yet."

"Mom says it probably won't be for another year."

"A year?" Christy questioned.

"But Aunt Marti says it will be in June."

"Oh, she does, does she?" Christy leaned forward. "And what does Dad say?"

"Nothing. He just listens. Mom and Aunt Marti almost got into an argument before you came. Aunt Marti says you have to have the reception at some boat club in Newport Beach, and Mom says it's going to be at the church."

Christy shook her head.

"What do Todd and you want?" David looked more sensitive and interested in her life than he ever had before.

A slow, appreciative smile grew as Christy said, "David, you might be the only one here today to ask me that question. So will you do me a favor and ask it again in front of everyone else?"

"Okay." David appeared not to see why it was a big deal. "I mean, it's your wedding, right? It's your life. You should do what you want. You guys have been waiting a long time."

"Yes, we have."

They were quiet for a few moments. Through Christy's closed bedroom door, she could hear Aunt Marti's voice rising as she shared her wedding insights with poor Todd.

"I guess I should go back out there and support my fiancé," she said.

"Todd's okay," David said. "He won't let Aunt Marti push him around."

Christy wished she had as much confidence as her brother on the subject. She stood and headed for the door. David didn't budge. Christy looked at him with questioning eyes.

David looked away shyly. "I don't know what the right word is, but whatever you're supposed to say when somebody gets engaged, I guess . . . well, I'm happy for you guys. I'm glad you're getting married."

Impulsively leaning forward, Christy kissed her brother on the cheek. "Thank you, David. I love you."

He stiffened up as his face turned pink. "Yeah, me too."

With her heart light, Christy opened her bedroom door and went forward to meet her formidable aunt. Her embarrassed baby brother lumbered down the hall behind her.

CHAPTER 5

"There you are," Marti said when Christy and David entered the living room.

Todd was wedged in the middle of the couch with Marti on one side and Christy's mom on the other. On his lap was a stack of bridal magazines. Christy would have burst out laughing if it weren't for the shocked look on Todd's face. If he was going to figure out how much detailed planning went into a wedding, it would be here and now.

"I was just telling Todd we had the photos Bob took of you two at Thanksgiving developed and then sent copies of the best one into our newspaper's society section as well as yours," Marti said. "They'll appear this weekend. Oh, and I took the liberty to write a little story about your engagement."

"That was fast," Christy said.

"It's perfect timing, really, this weekend being Christmas and all. I didn't want to miss the opportunity to get it in there in time."

Christy nodded and gave Todd an encouraging grin. "I'm getting a drink of water. Anyone else want anything?"

"Sure," Todd's voice squeaked out.

Christy had to smile again. *My poor Todd. I don't think he's ready for this. But I do know that the reality check will be good for him.*

She walked toward the kitchen, where she could hear her dad and Uncle Bob talking.

"You're not leaving us, are you, Christina?" Marti called out. "I've barely begun to go over the details here."

"I'll be right back."

"I only have one question for you to answer," her dad said as Christy reached for two glasses from the cupboard. "Have Todd and you discussed a wedding date?"

"The sooner the better." Uncle Bob raised his bottle of mineral water in a mock toast.

"Have you been talking to Todd?" Christy asked her uncle as she filled the glasses with ice.

"No, not yet. But I'll tell him the same thing I'm telling you, which is what I was just telling your dad. Don't let finances hold you back. Martha and I would love to help out on that end."

"Your mother thinks you should wait until next Christmas," Christy's dad said.

"So I heard. What do you think, Dad?"

He was a large, quiet man who tended to hold his comments until he had time to think them through. His expression told Christy he was honored she had asked his opinion.

"Well, you know how I feel about your having the privilege of getting a college education. Neither your mother nor I had that opportunity."

"I know," Christy said. "I agree. I told Todd we should wait until I graduate."

"You're so close to being finished," Bob said. "I don't see why you couldn't complete your final semester after the wedding. You could even skip this next semester, get married after Todd graduates in January, and then go back in the fall."

"Hello in there!" Marti called from the living room. "We're waiting out here. You three aren't discussing wedding plans without me, are you?"

"Yes," Christy called out brashly.

Her uncle grinned and toasted her again. "Go get 'em, bright eyes!"

Christy motioned with her head for her dad and uncle to follow her as she carried the two glasses of water back to the living room and handed one to Todd. "Come on. You two should be in on this."

"Sit over here." Marti handed Christy a thick bridal magazine and pointed to a picture of a model in a wedding dress with a full skirt. "I was glancing at this on our drive down here, and I wondered if you had considered this sort of veil. I'm assuming you'll be wearing your hair up and back to show off your face."

Christy placed the magazine on the floor. She smiled at Todd. "I'm going to wear flowers in my hair."

Todd smiled back at her. His expression of frozen panic began to melt.

"I don't see why you couldn't add some flowers to the connecting headpiece of this veil." Marti retrieved the magazine and studied the picture.

"Aunt Marti, we're not ready to talk about those kinds of details."

Marti looked up at Christy. "You're right. First things first. Todd tells me you've begun to look at rings but haven't made a decision yet. I'm sure you know that you'll be hard pressed to size the ring in time for Christmas. But it can be done, if you make your selection today. Tomorrow morning at the latest, I would imagine. I'm assuming you're going to get your ring for Christmas."

"Martha," Uncle Bob said firmly, "let the kids take it at their own pace. You said on the way here that you wanted to listen to them and let them tell you where they wanted us to help out. I think we better let them do the talking here."

Marti pulled back. She seemed to take Bob's reproof better than Christy would have guessed. "Yes. Of course. Fine. Go ahead. Tell us your plans. All we know so far is that you haven't decided on a ring. Or a date. Or any of the other essentials." Aunt Marti glanced at Christy's mom and in a lower voice added, "But she knows she's going to wear flowers in her hair."

Christy felt a familiar mixture of anger and pain rising inside. She knew she should ignore the barb. That's what the others in the room seemed to do automatically.

"Why don't we start with the date," Bob suggested. "Todd, I was telling Christy and Norm that the wedding's expense shouldn't hold the two of you back. You know that Marti and I would be honored to help out in that area."

"What about school?" Christy's mom looked concerned.

Marti jumped in. "You do know that most reservations need to be made a year ahead of time for your reception to be held at, say, the Newport Bay Yacht Club. And a custom-made dress can take at least six months, sometimes nine, depending on how many fittings you need."

Christy noticed that David had disappeared. This would have been a good time for her brother to ask his key question about what Todd and Christy wanted to do.

"We've been discussing the options," Todd said calmly. "We haven't come to a conclusion yet."

Christy wished they had. She wished they had every detail planned so that this impromptu meeting would be about their outlining a well-thought-out schedule instead of the free-for-all it was becoming.

As if by prearrangement, footsteps sounded on the front porch, followed by the voices of a couple of Christmas carolers belting out, "We wish you a merry Christmas."

"Do people still do that?" Marti asked.

Christy went to open the door. There stood Rick and Katie, grinning and singing merrily.

"Ho, ho, ho! Wouldn't you know? Your wreath fell off the doe," Katie said, holding out the evergreen circle as Christy invited them to come in.

"It didn't fall off the door. We haven't put it up yet," Christy said. "Todd and I bought it at a tree lot on the way here. I left it on the porch so the pine needles wouldn't get all over the carpet."

"Oh." Katie turned around and returned the wreath to the front porch. "Sorry about that."

"Rick?" Marti called out from the couch. "Rick Doyle? Goodness, we haven't seen you in years."

"I wondered if that was Bob and Marti's Lexus in the driveway," Katie muttered under her breath.

Christy nodded and whispered to Katie, "Your timing is perfect!"

Rick stepped into the living room, where Aunt Marti greeted him with a string of questions.

Marti glanced beyond Christy to see who had come with Rick. "Well, hello, Katie. I suppose you've heard the good news about Todd and Christy."

"No." Katie put on a straight face. "What happened with Todd and Christy? Did they win the lottery?"

"Katie knows." Christy gave Katie a hidden pinch on the arm.

"Ouch!"

"Rick and Katie were both there when I proposed," Todd said.

"Rick, you were there?" Marti's brain seemed to be working hard to put all the pieces into place. "You didn't tell me all this, Christy."

Rick explained about his position as the manager of The Dove's Nest, and Marti promised she would visit the café sometime.

"Why don't I get us something to eat?" Christy's mom rose from the couch. "You kids must be hungry. Katie, have you and Rick eaten yet?"

"Not exactly," Katie said.

"I'll make some sandwiches."

Christy thought of how some things never changed. Her aunt always would find delight in holding court, and her mother always would revert to feeding people when she didn't know what else to do.

The next hour and a half developed some twists and turns Christy never would have imagined. Todd flipped through one of Marti's bridal magazines in the kitchen while Christy and her mom made sandwiches. Dad went out front and busied himself hanging the wreath. Marti grilled Rick for details of his life since she had last seen him and actually listened respectfully as Rick described his new commitment to Christ and the way his life had changed.

Twice during the conversation Christy exchanged subtle glances with her uncle. Ever since Bob had turned his life over to the Lord, tension had existed between Marti and him since Marti didn't see eye to eye with Bob on his views of Christianity. Over the years Marti had heard it all from Christy and Todd. For some reason she seemed willing to listen to Rick. It was a mystery to Christy.

"We came by to see if you guys want to go Christmas caroling with us tonight," Katie said after they had eaten. "A group is going to meet at the church at six and go from there."

Christy looked at Todd as he rose to help Christy's mom clear the kitchen table. Moving out of the wedding-decision spotlight sounded good to Christy, and the caroling would be fun.

"It's up to you." Todd leaned over and spoke to Christy as he slid past her. "Your aunt and uncle have an hour-and-a-half-drive home. I think they would like a little more information from us before they leave."

Christy excused herself from the table and followed Todd to the kitchen sink, which was less than ten feet away from the company gathered at the table. In a low voice she said, "Are you suggesting we come up with a wedding date right now to satisfy my aunt?"

"Not necessarily."

"I think you and I need to talk about it some more," Christy said. "It needs to be our decision. Yours and mine."

"I agree," Todd said.

"So what do we tell them?"

"That depends. Do you want to go caroling with Rick and Katie?"

"Sure. Do you?"

Todd shrugged. "Whatever."

Just then Christy's mom stepped over to the sink with more dishes. "Are you two going caroling?"

"I guess so," Christy said less than wholeheartedly.

"We don't have to," Todd said quietly.

"I think we should." Christy took a step toward her goal of being more decisive in their relationship. "After all, it is Christmas. We should focus on celebrating Christ's birth, not on figuring out all our wedding plans in one afternoon."

Christy thought her statement made perfect sense. However, later that night, as she and Todd were standing side by side singing "Silent Night," she thought of how her decision—their decision—to go caroling had prompted anything but a silent night around her parents' house. Marti and Bob left with Marti in a controlled huff, and Bob saying, "When you two are ready, you let us know how we can help." David reappeared and announced he had hoped Todd would take him to a movie. Mom returned a stack of board games to the closet after she realized everyone was leaving. And Todd started coughing halfway through the caroling. He stood silently at the last two houses they went to and told Christy his throat was too scratchy to sing.

The ones who seemed to enjoy the caroling the most were Rick and Katie. They were awfully chummy while dashing from house to house, laughing all way—ho, ho, ho.

Bah humbug. I wish we had stayed home where it was warm, even if it meant dealing with my aunt for another few hours. She certainly was ruffled when she left without any answers.

Christy thought about her aunt's comment concerning how long it would take to size a ring. It would take even longer to have one custom made.

We shouldn't be here. Todd and I should be at the mall, checking out the rings at the jewelry stores. Maybe the ring I have in the back of my mind has already been designed, and it's out there somewhere.

One look at Todd told Christy she wouldn't be able to convince this guy to go ring shopping that night. Besides, all the stores probably were closed. They could go tomorrow.

It was almost ten when the caroling concluded. Rick and Katie invited anyone who wanted to join them at Rick's parents' house for his fabulous hot chocolate.

"I'm fried," Todd replied to the invitation. "If you want to go without me, Christy, that's okay."

"No, I'm pretty tired, too."

They strolled back to their car in the church parking lot while the others took off for Rick's house.

"What a night." Christy linked her arm in Todd's and gazed up at the sky. Only a few stars peeked out from behind the thin clouds that looked like lacy ribbons woven through the December sky. "It's so beautiful."

"It is beautiful. And so are you," Todd said in a deep voice. He stopped by the side of their car and drew Christy to him in a warm hug. Pressing his lips against the side of her cheek, he murmured, "So when do you want to get married?"

She could feel his warm breath circling the back of her neck, lacing invisible fingers through her hair. "I don't know. We have to figure it out."

She kissed his earlobe. "The sooner the better." She planted a string of little kisses on his neck. "When do you want to get married?"

Todd slowly, deliberately pulled away. "Red light."

"Hmmm?" Christy felt snuggly and dreamy and wanted to stay cuddled up in his warm embrace.

"This is getting a little too, ah . . . yeah. A little too close for me."

A space of several inches now separated them. The cold night air moved right in and sobered Christy.

"I think we're better off talking about this another time. Another place." Todd unlocked Christy's car door. "Until we're married, we're going to be sitting at one very long red light. I don't think it's going to do either of us any good to start revving our engines."

Christy hadn't realized that the close snuggling and her tiny kisses would have such a strong effect on him. "Okay," she agreed, getting into the car. "Red light. I agree."

That moment, as Christy's thoughts cleared in the cold car, she thought, *It's only a few months of sitting at the red light. Then the rest of our lives it will be one long green light. We can wait. We have to wait. We will wait.*

She knew that no matter how many days stretched between that night and their wedding day, what lay ahead were days that would test her heart, mind, and will more than any she had ever experienced.

They didn't talk about their strong feelings on the way home. Todd hummed a song Christy didn't recognize and tapped his fingers on the steering wheel.

Christy thought it would be nice if they could sit in the kitchen and discuss their wedding over their own homemade hot chocolate. But Todd went directly to David's room and crashed on the air mattress Christy's mom had set up for him on the floor.

The next morning Christy showered and dressed and made French toast for breakfast. Her dad had gone to work at his usual five-thirty departure time, and her mom was sleeping in. No sound could be heard from behind the closed door of David's bedroom. At 9:10, on the first Monday of Christmas vacation, Christy sat alone at the kitchen table, eating delicious French toast and reading her Bible. She didn't mind the time alone. It gave her a chance to pray and think. And plan.

She padded on stockinged feet to her bedroom, where she dug into the closet and found a journal-style notebook she never had written in. Returning to the kitchen, she made herself a cup of tea and christened the journal her wedding planner. On the cover page she wrote *Todd and Christy* in loopy letters and then playfully drew a big heart around their names. Turning to the first page, Christy listed every detail she could think of that needed to be discussed. She was three pages into the list when Mom joined her in the kitchen.

"I thought you might have slept in," Mom said. "The boys are still asleep."

"I have too much on my mind. I made lots of French toast. It's in the microwave, if you want to warm it up and have some."

"What a treat! Thank you."

Before Christy's mom could join her at the table, Christy heard the bedroom door open down the hall. A minute later she heard the shower turn on in the bathroom. Ten minutes later, Todd emerged, blowing his nose.

"Oh, sorry," he said when he noticed Christy and her mom. "I didn't realize you were there. I thought a shower might help my sinuses but . . ." He began to cough.

"Sounds like you have the flu." Mom stepped over to feel Todd's forehead. "Oh dear, you're burning up. Is your throat sore?"

Todd nodded.

"Why don't you go back to bed? I'll bring you some hot tea."

"I can get it for him, Mom." Christy hopped up. "Do you want to try eating anything?"

"No, a little juice is all I want. I should get on the road and head back to my dad's house."

"Even though you're sick?" Mom asked.

"Why would you go to your dad's?" Christy asked.

Todd leaned against the kitchen counter. "I told him I'd be home today so we could spend some time together. He has this week off work."

"I didn't know that. I thought you were planning to stay here all week." Christy looked at her long list and thought of all the items she had planned to start checking off in the next few days.

"Why don't you stay here until you're better?" Mom asked. "It won't do your dad any good to have you bring home a flu bug with you."

"I don't think it's going to do your family any good if I stay." Todd turned his head and covered his mouth as he coughed some more.

"You sound awful." Christy felt bad that she had put her to-do list ahead of her fiancé's health. "Why don't you go back to bed? At least for a few hours."

Todd nodded. "I'll lie down for an hour. I'm guessing the fever will be gone by then."

"I'll get you some juice," Christy said. A few minutes later she carried in some cranberry juice on a tray, along with a thermometer, a box of tissues, a cold washcloth, a box of cold and flu tablets, and some cough drops.

Todd didn't want any of it. Not even the juice.

"Just water," he said with his eyes closed. He had bundled himself up and was lying there with the hood of his navy blue sweat shirt pulled over his head, looking as if he was determined to sweat out every drop of flu virus.

When Christy returned with the water, he took only a sip and rolled over. David was up and dressed, so Todd had the room to himself. He stayed there in a deep hibernation, occasionally punctuated by a raspy cough, for the entire day.

At dinnertime he came out of his cave and announced he was driving home. This time he had all four members of the Miller family to argue with.

"Just sleep," Mom urged.

"Get some fluids in you," Christy pleaded.

"Take another shower," David suggested.

Christy had to agree; Todd didn't smell his freshest. He looked awful.

"Let me wash your sweat shirt," Mom said. "Do you have anything clean to put on after your shower?"

Todd looked irritated. "I'm okay. I can take it from here. Thanks for letting me sleep."

Christy realized that Todd, an only child who lived with his divorced dad since he was young, probably never had anyone to baby him when he was sick. After his car accident, he was willing to let others care for him, but that was different. In matters of the flu, Todd seemed to prefer to go it alone.

Despite another round of protests, Todd carried his stuff out to the car at a little after seven that evening. Christy followed him to the driveway. As Todd climbed into their car, he said, "I'll see you at Bob and Marti's on Christmas Eve."

Christy didn't mean to let her thoughts slip out, but before she could stop them, the words "What about getting a ring?" tumbled from her mouth. She realized how selfish and inconsiderate it sounded, but it was too late.

"I heard you say last night you were planning to go to the mall with your mom this week." Todd fastened his seat belt. "Why don't you look for rings while you're with her?"

The thought of shopping for an engagement ring with her mother didn't sit right with Christy. "I'll wait until you and I can go shopping."

"You're not shopping; you're just looking. I thought you were pretty close to figuring out what you wanted."

"Yes, but—"

"Listen." Todd covered his mouth and coughed something awful. "I want you to end up with a ring you really like. I'm guessing it's going to take you a little while to make your final decision. I don't think you need me to look at everything with you."

Christy recognized he was trying to be understanding and patient. She felt terrible for even bringing up the topic.

"Don't worry about it," Christy said. "You just work on getting better. We can talk on Christmas Eve."

"Okay. Thanks, honey. I appreciate your understanding."

Christy didn't remember him ever calling her "honey" before, and she thought it was awfully sweet. She also thought of how 1 Corinthians 13 described true love as "patient." That took on deeper meaning for her now as she realized she would have to place the ring hunt on hold. Todd had told her their future together would be full of adjustments. She didn't like having to adjust, but it seemed she had no choice.

Todd reached for her hand, but instead of kissing her good-bye, he held her hand and gave her three squeezes. With each squeeze he said, "I-love-you."

Christy gave him three squeezes back and repeated the message, "I-love-you. I'll see you Thursday. Please take care of yourself."

"I always have." Todd slowly backed out of the driveway.

Christy watched their blue Volvo cruise quietly down the street. Inside, she missed him already.

Am I going to feel this way for the rest of my life? Every time he leaves, am I going to feel like a part of me has gone with him?

"Father, please send your guardian angels to watch over my Todd as he drives to his dad's tonight. Keep him safe. And, Lord, even though he thinks he's always taken care of himself, I know that you have been the One who has really watched over him. Please take care of him tonight."

Todd stopped at the corner and honked the horn three times. Christy smiled. "Yeah, I love you, too, ya big lug."

CHAPTER 6

By Tuesday evening of Christmas vacation, Christy had a good idea of what she wanted her ring to look like. She had made a rough sketch in her wedding notebook and pasted three magazine photos of rings on the same page. She and her mom had gone to the mall that morning and looked in several jewelry stores. They also had thumbed through a book of invitations in a stationery store, discussed the color of the bridesmaids' dresses over frozen yogurt, and picked up information on the cost of tux rentals.

Christy had spent an hour on the phone with Todd before dinner telling him all the details.

"You sound good," Todd said in a raspy voice.

"You sound awful," Christy countered.

"I know. This cold is really hanging on. What I meant is that you sound happy. I'm glad you and your mom got to spend some time together and work on a few of the details."

Christy couldn't resist teasing Todd. "You're just saying that because you're happy you weren't the one being dragged through the mall today."

"Yeah, I am," Todd said.

"Are you sure you didn't fake that cold to get out of spending the week here planning with me?"

"Nothing is fake about this beast," Todd said. "I don't remember the last time I felt this awful."

"Maybe you should go to the doctor," Christy suggested. "You might have strep throat. Didn't you say your ears hurt? If the virus settles in your ears, you could have an ear infection, and you'll need antibiotics to clear it up."

"That's okay, Christy. I'm sure I'll be all right in a few days." Todd's voice carried a hint of aggravation. Christy realized she was being motherly, and that was something Todd never had responded well to.

"Sorry," she said. "I hope you feel better."

"I will. I'll be over this by the time you see me Thursday."

Todd's prediction turned out to be wishful thinking.

When Christy and her family arrived at Bob and Marti's house, Todd took Christy in his arms and held her close. "I missed you so much." His voice was little more than a gravelly whisper.

"I missed you, too."

They stood in the kitchen, holding each other, slightly swaying, neither of them willing to let go.

"I love you." She leaned close and brushed his cheek with a kiss.

"Aw, come on, you guys. Cut it out." David had stepped into the kitchen with his sleeping bag and suitcase and made an exaggerated effort to walk around them. "You guys are making a spectacle of yourselves."

"A spectacle?" Todd repeated in a hoarse whisper, followed by a horrible-sounding laugh.

Christy laughed at her brother as well as at Todd's laryngitis-affected laughter.

"I'm impressed, David. When did you start using words like 'spectacle'?" Todd asked.

"What happened to your voice?" David replied.

Todd shrugged and gave a sheepish grin, as if he had misplaced his voice and wasn't sure where he had put it.

"Are you still sick?" David asked.

"I feel a lot better," Todd said.

"Dad wants you guys to help carry in the presents," David said.

Christy slipped her hand into Todd's, and he squeezed three times. She smiled and returned the squeezes. They walked out to the driveway hand in hand, smiling.

Aunt Marti stood beside the car and viewed them skeptically. "I hope you didn't kiss her, Todd. The last thing Christy needs is to get sick. It's a wonder all of us didn't end up with the flu since we were with you on Sunday."

"If I had known I was getting sick, I wouldn't have gone over to the Millers and exposed everyone." Todd's pathetically thin voice added to the apologetic expression on his face.

Marti seemed satisfied with his response. She waited while Christy's dad loaded the two of them up with gear from the car. Then she picked up the handles of a shopping bag full of Christmas gifts and followed Todd and Christy into the kitchen.

"I have a few things to go over with you two right away."

"Like what?" Christy asked cautiously.

"Oh, just a few items we need to discuss. I thought we could sit down and go over all this now." Marti planted the handled bag on the kitchen floor and pointed to the oak table in the kitchen's corner.

Christy noticed several stacks of paper neatly stapled together and placed in front of the chairs as if in preparation for a business meeting.

"I think we should help my dad unload the car first," Christy said.

"I'll make some coffee," Marti said. "As soon as you're finished, please join me."

"Where's Uncle Bob?" Christy instinctively knew it would be a good idea to have her uncle nearby when Marti started in on the two of them.

"He went to pick up our Christmas Eve dinner. We ordered everything from D'Angelo's this year. Bob is going to prepare it for us, and we'll eat at six. That gives us a little more than an hour for our meeting. I mean, our discussion."

Christy's dad entered with his arms full, and Mom was right behind him.

"Does anything else need to come in?" Todd asked.

"No, this is the last of it," Dad said. "Would someone move this bag of gifts so I don't knock it over?"

Christy quickly scooped up the handled bag Marti had left in the middle of the floor. Carrying it into the living room, she placed each of the gifts under the tree. Bob and Marti had set up the Christmas tree in its usual spot in front of their beach-front home's huge window. Marti went all out decorating and changed her theme every year. This year the tree was a Douglas fir that touched the ceiling and filled the living room with a fresh, outdoor fragrance. Marti had chosen to decorate with just two colors, white and red. She even had changed the window treatment to white velvet swags across the top, held in place with wide red velvet bows.

Tiny white lights, looking like icicles, hung from the ceiling. More tiny lights glimmered from every branch on the tree. All the ornaments were red. Christy examined a tiny red sled that hung from one of the branches. Beside it was a red apple ornament tied to the tree with a red-and-white-plaid ribbon.

Christy was about to return to the kitchen when she noticed an envelope attached to a red-striped ribbon that looped over one of the lower branches. The envelope had David's name on it, but for some reason, the sight of it reminded her of Rick's envelope.

I never did open that envelope. I wonder where I put it?

"Christina," Marti called from the kitchen, "the coffee is ready."

Christy drew in a deep breath and headed for the kitchen. Todd, her parents, and Marti were all seated, waiting for her.

As soon as Christy slid her chair close to Todd's, Marti dived in. "I should begin by telling you I took the liberty of calling my country club this week and found that they miraculously had a cancellation the last weekend of June. Of course, I reserved it. I had to put down a substantial deposit, but as you might guess, the only other opening was at the end of November and—"

"Wait," Christy said. "Open for what? What are you talking about?"

Marti pointed to the first item of business on the printed agenda that rested on the top of the papers stacked in front of each seat. "The reservation for your wedding. I can't think of a nicer place to have your ceremony than at the Newport Country Club, can you?"

Christy shot a stunned look at her mother, who was sitting directly across from her.

Her mother said, "Your father and I were under the impression you would get married at our church in Escondido. We could hold the reception in the gym. They have lots of round tables that we could cover with—"

"A gymnasium!" Marti looked at her sister incredulously. "You can't be serious, Margaret. You wouldn't want your only daughter to have her reception in a gymnasium!"

"Our church has receptions in the gym all the time. I went to a luncheon there last spring that was lovely. They hung ferns from the basketball backboards and—"

"I won't hear of it," Marti said firmly. "Christy deserves an elegant, classy wedding. She and Todd should have the best facility available for the most memorable day of their lives. Don't you understand it was a minor miracle for me to secure the Newport Beach Country Club in June?"

Marti turned to Christy and Todd with a pleading expression. "I thought you two, of all people, would see this as a sign from God that you should get married the last Saturday in June."

A dead-air moment followed. Christy didn't know where to begin in her argument with her aunt. Her mother appeared mortally wounded, and her father was looking down into his coffee cup.

Todd leaned back and broke the tension by saying in his raspy whisper, "I'm confident the Bridegroom will show up wherever we hold the ceremony."

Marti's expression showed she didn't appreciate his comment. "Of course you will show up, Todd. That's not the point."

"I didn't mean me. I meant *the* Bridegroom. Jesus Christ. He's with us here right now. He'll show up wherever Christy and I are on the day that we promise our lives to each other. That's all that really matters."

Marti's face grew red. "Todd, I have held my tongue for a very long time, but I can't remain silent any longer." She leaned across the table and with fire in her eyes said, "I love you like a son. You know that. There is nothing I wouldn't do for you or give you. But you have failed to show me the slightest courtesy in areas that matter the most to me. I've listened to you spiritualize for the last time."

She rose to her feet and pressed white knuckles to the table. "This is not about your heavenly view of everything. This is the wedding day of my one and only niece. I am offering my time and my resources to help create an unforgettable day for the two of you. And how do you respond? By being rude, disrespectful, and inconsiderate. Well, that's it!"

Todd stood. "You're right." His voice broke, and he reverted to a loud whisper. "I haven't honored your considerable efforts. I'm sorry. Will you forgive me for being insensitive and not appreciating all you do for Christy and me?"

Marti didn't seem to know how to respond. She stood rigidly and stared at Todd as if trying to determine if he was sincere or if this was another spiritual tactic to break down her defenses.

Todd waited. His expression was open and expectant.

Marti continued to stare at him; her jaw remained firm.

"Ho! Ho! Ho!" came a jovial voice as the door to the garage opened. "It's Santa and his helper! Have we got a prime rib dinner for you! And wait until you see the cheesecake . . ." Bob stopped in his tracks and sized up the standoff at the kitchen table.

"What happened?" David asked, following Uncle Bob and carrying a large white cake box.

Marti tilted her head slightly and in a low voice said, "I suggest we start over. Let's all take a deep breath and go on from here."

"That won't erase the offense." Todd cleared his throat and tried to continue. "I hurt you, Marti. I was wrong. I apologize. Please forgive me."

With a wave of her hand and a stilted laugh, Marti said, "Don't worry about it, Todd. We're all running on heightened emotions. I suggest we take a five-minute break and then reconvene with an agreement to all communicate with a renewed level of respect."

Christy thought her aunt had turned into a robot and was spouting phrases she had heard before rather than saying what sprang from her heart. Maybe that was how issues were discussed when Marti was involved with the art colony.

"What did we miss?" David asked.

Mom shot him a look that said, "Don't ask such questions, David!"

"Are we still on for a six-o'clock dinner?" Bob asked, unloading his bags of food on the counter. "Or should we adjust that?"

"Six-thirty would be better." Marti moved over to the coffee maker and poured a fresh cup of coffee. "We're just getting started."

Uncle Bob caught Christy's eye. He held her gaze with a silent, questioning look. Christy gave a little nod and mouthed the words, "It's okay."

Bob slowly nodded.

"Would it be all right if I made some tea?" Christy asked.

"Of course," Bob said. "You know where it is. Help yourself. I bought some Christmas peppermint tea yesterday that you might like. How about you, Todd? A little something warm for your throat? Or would cold feel better? We have plenty of everything."

"Tea."

"I'll get it." Christy rubbed Todd's back as she slid past him. "Is peppermint okay?"

He nodded.

Christy had just turned on the flame under the teakettle when Marti returned to the table and announced they were ready to continue.

"Go ahead and sit down," Bob suggested to Christy. "I'll bring your tea over to you."

With fresh determination, Marti went back to her agenda, skipping the first point until later. "Let's go on to the third point. The cake. If you will look at the third and fourth pages on your handout, you will see some color copies that are examples of Cakes by Emilie. Her bakery is in great demand because she interviews the couples, finds out what is meaningful to them, and then designs a cake specifically for them. No two cakes are ever alike."

"Are those skateboards on the border of that yellow cake?" Christy's mom asked.

"Cool!" David looked over Christy's shoulder. "How did they make the little black wheels? Is that a birthday cake?"

"No, these are all wedding cakes. The groom was an architect. He met his bride when he was designing a skate park for the city of Solana Beach. I asked about that one because I thought it was unusual, too."

Christy wanted to protest the use of skateboards as an appropriate decoration on a wedding cake so Todd wouldn't get any ideas about using surfboards on theirs. But she knew it would be better not to challenge her aunt. At least not yet.

Marti seemed to have calmed down. David went into the den to watch TV, and Bob brought Christy and Todd their tea and then quietly worked in the kitchen while Marti worked her way down the list. She went on with her presentation for fifteen uninterrupted minutes. No one else said a word. No one agreed or disagreed or challenged her on any of her seven points. When she returned to the first two points, she presented her opinions with an enthusiastic tone.

"As I mentioned earlier, I went ahead and reserved the country club for June. Point number two is the wedding coordinator I've been working with to gather all this information. Her name is Elise, and I made an appointment for us to meet with her on Saturday afternoon at two o'clock. Now for discussion. Who has questions?"

No one moved or spoke up.

Christy had so many conflicting feelings she didn't dare try to say anything. Todd was the brave one again. For a man with so little voice left, he was sure set on having his say. "Thank you, Marti. You worked hard on all this. I appreciate it. This will help Christy and me as we make our decisions and put everything together."

Christy thought his choice of words was great. "Put everything together" could mean they would take all Aunt Marti's ideas, some of her ideas, or none of her ideas. The part Marti heard was the thank-you. That seemed more important than anything else.

"You're welcome. This is only the beginning, you know. We have much more planning to do. That's where Elise will help us out on Saturday."

Christy determined right then and there that she and Todd would find time in the next day and a half to talk through all their wedding plans. They would decide on their own, just the two of them, when, where, and how they would get married. If they had to stay up all night for the next two nights, they would form their own plan. If they had to go somewhere else to talk, they wouldn't come back until they had their own completed list. Even if Todd lost his voice completely and could only communicate by sign language, they *would* figure out everything before two o'clock on Saturday. And the decisions would be all theirs because, after all, this was their wedding.

CHAPTER 7

"Wait a minute," Katie said, stopping in the middle of the produce section at the grocery store. "Todd and you went ahead and met with the wedding coordinator on Saturday even though you guys don't want to get married at the yacht club?"

It was the Monday after Christmas, and Katie and Christy had returned to Rancho Corona to prepare for the Mexico outreach trip with Todd's youth group. Christy and Katie hadn't seen each other since the night they went caroling but had agreed earlier on the phone to meet in front of the grocery store down the hill from their college campus.

They stood in the parking lot talking for nearly ten minutes before Christy suggested they shop while they talked. Entering the grocery store with Katie pushing the cart, Christy continued to summarize her Christmas weekend at Bob and Marti's in a more positive tone than she felt.

"Yes, we met with the wedding coordinator," Christy said. "She's not from the club. She's independent. I liked her. She had a lot of good ideas for us."

"So when did you tell your aunt that you don't want to have the ceremony at the yacht club?"

"We haven't told her yet, but we will," Christy said. "Todd and I spent hours discussing everything even though his voice was barely above a whisper."

"And after all your discussing you didn't come up with a wedding date?"

"We have a possible date." Christy checked her shopping list and put a bag of red apples into the cart.

"As your best friend and possible maid of honor, may I ask what your possible wedding date is? Or are you keeping it a secret from everyone?"

"It's not a secret, Katie. The date is May twenty-second. But you're the only one who knows it so don't say anything until we can confirm it. And you are more than my possible maid of honor. You *are* my maid of honor. Or I should say, I'd like you to be, if you want to."

"Of course. I'm honored. Honored to be your maid of honor. But now I have to ask, how did you come up with May twenty-second as your date? I thought Todd wanted to get married sooner."

"Todd and I went over every possible weekend between now and next Christmas. Believe me, the only date that worked was May twenty-second. We wanted to have at least a week for our honeymoon, and that was the only time we could fit it in. It's nine days after I graduate and nine days before Todd starts to work full time at the church for the summer."

"Okay, that makes sense," Katie said. "But I still don't get it. Why didn't you announce you had decided on a date?"

"Because we don't know if we can have the meadow yet. We have to wait until the Rancho Corona administration people return to their offices next week."

"Wait a minute. I am so lost. What meadow?" Katie had stopped pushing the cart and looked as if she wasn't going to move until Christy explained every detail.

"The meadow at school. By the chapel. That's where we want to hold the ceremony and the reception."

"You're kidding."

"No, that's where we want to get married."

Katie tilted her head and scrutinized Christy. "How do your parents feel about that? I would think they would want you to have the ceremony at their church in Escondido."

"They do."

"But you don't."

"We want to get married in the meadow." Christy pulled the cart over toward the bread and tossed in five of the least-expensive loaves.

"Could you change one of those whole wheat loaves to white?" Katie asked. "Rick likes white bread. His mom made these incredible leftover turkey sandwiches on white bread the day after Christmas. Have you ever had a turkey sandwich with stuffing and cranberry sauce?"

Now Christy was the one tilting her head and scrutinizing Katie. "No, it sounds good."

"It's my new favorite. But it has to be on white bread. The stuffing makes it all stick together." Katie pushed the cart toward the peanut butter and jelly. "Didn't you have peanut butter on the list? I think the cheapest jelly is this big bucket of grape."

Christy told Katie to pick up three jars of peanut butter and then said, "So tell me all about your Christmas. How did everything go with Rick?"

"Great. Wonderful." Katie put the peanut butter in the cart. "But you didn't finish telling me about you and Todd. Is he going to be well enough to go to Mexico?"

"Yes, he's fine now. His voice is almost back to normal. There's not much else to tell about our plans. We didn't get to the jewelers so we don't have a ring yet. And I already told you we have to check on reserving the meadow before we can set our date."

"And break the shocking news to your aunt and everyone else."

"Exactly," Christy said. "Oh, and my uncle offered us the use of his condo on Maui for our honeymoon."

Katie grinned. "Well, at least you have one important detail taken care of."

Christy motioned for Katie to push the grocery cart down the canned-food aisle. She studied the prices on the tomato sauce cans.

"You know," Katie said, "if you get married in the meadow, you can release butterflies instead of the usual."

Christy laughed at her friend's suggestion. "Don't you dare suggest that one to my aunt! She already has a long list of creative ideas for our cake and my veil and the bouquet."

"I'm serious," Katie said. "I saw it on TV. The bride ordered these butterflies that came in individual boxes. They looked like Chinese take-out boxes. As soon as the couple said 'I do,' the guests opened the boxes. I thought it was a great idea."

"Well, we're not going to say 'I do.' "

"You're not?"

"We talked about our vows last night. Todd and I decided we're going to say 'I promise,' because that makes it clearer that we're making a vow to love, honor, and cherish and all the rest of it."

"I'm sure the butterflies would flap their little wings on cue whether you said 'I do' or 'I promise,' " Katie said sarcastically. "Or if you want to hold the butterflies until the end, you can launch butterflies at the same time you heave your bouquet."

Katie's expression created an image in Christy's mind of "launched" butterflies and "heaved" flowers all tumbling through the air in the meadow.

"Now tell me, Katie." Christy faced her friend. "Would I be making an accurate guess if I said I should plan to heave my bouquet in your direction?"

"You can heave it anywhere you want," Katie said. " 'The Lord will fulfill his purpose for me.' "

Christy raised her eyebrows, trying to interpret Katie's response.

"That's my new verse. Rick and I found it this weekend. It's in Psalm 138. Verse 8. Took us only two seconds to memorize it. 'The Lord will fulfill his purpose for me.' That's it. Isn't that incredible? I've decided to make that my life verse. How many cans of spaghetti sauce did you want?"

Christy checked her list. "Six of those large ones on the lower shelf. Get the brand on the right; it's four cents less."

"Do you want these jumbo-sized packages of spaghetti noodles?"

"Yes, three of those, and why don't you grab one more can of sauce just to be sure we have enough."

"That's right," Katie said. "Doug is coming. He eats more than anyone I know. Tracy is still planning to come, isn't she?"

"The last I heard she was."

"I hope she's not having a lot of morning sickness," Katie said. "That wouldn't be much fun in Mexico."

"Maybe she won't be able to come after all," Christy said. "I'll give her a call tonight. Do you have any gum or mints with you? My throat is really dry."

"No. Do you want me to get some gum at the checkout for you?"

"No, I'll buy some cough drops when we go down that aisle. It would be good to have some with us in Mexico. I already put together a first-aid kit, but I didn't add any cough drops."

"I wish Sierra and the rest of her gang would have come back early from Christmas break so they could join us," Katie said.

"We might make another trip in the spring. From what Todd said, this orphanage needs a lot of work."

"Rick might have to leave early. Did I tell you that? He's having a hard time with the work schedule for the end of the week. I might come back with him, unless you still need my help with the food and everything."

"It's only for four days," Christy said. "I mean, if you have to leave early, that's okay. But it's not a very long trip."

"I know. And he might be able to work it out so he can stay the whole time. The problem with being the manager of The Dove's Nest is that he's the one who's ultimately responsible, you know? They really need more help on weekdays."

"Are you still planning to work there?" Christy asked.

"Yes. I start right after New Year's. I might as well have started last week because I was in every day Rick was there. I've already pretty much learned everything I need to know to start taking orders. I have a feeling I'm really going to like working there."

Christy bit her lip. She had almost said, "Oh, and I wonder why?" But she didn't want to jeopardize her communication with Katie. Especially after the tangle they had had more than a week ago in their dorm room.

The rest of their shopping went smoothly. Unfortunately, Katie didn't open up much about her budding relationship with Rick.

After they unloaded all the groceries at the church kitchen, picked up a pizza, and returned to their dorm room, Christy was hopeful Katie would open up more. However, a minor distraction consumed their attention.

Katie unlocked their dorm room door with the pizza box in her hand and immediately froze in place.

Christy didn't have to ask what made Katie stop and stare. Christy already knew. Todd had come with her to the dorm room earlier that morning and had carried in the object Katie now was gaping at.

"It's my Christmas present from Todd," Christy said in a low voice. "He made it."

"Ohhh! Is that Naranja?" Katie slowly stepped into the room, sounding as if she were recognizing a long-lost friend.

"Yes, the backrest is Todd's old surfboard, Naranja. And that's the backseat from Gus the bus. Todd sort of welded them together and now . . . it's . . . a couch, I guess."

"What do you mean it's a couch, you guess?" Katie sat down and looked up at Christy with an expression of delight. "This is the most amazing, authentic, memory-filled *objet d'art* I've ever seen. I could just cry! And you know what? It's actually sort of comfy, too."

Christy forced a smile. It was the same smile she had forced when Todd presented her with his unique gift on Christmas. He had tied a long red string to the homemade sofa and hid it in the garage at Bob and Marti's. He looped the string all the way through the house, and Christy was full of giggles and anticipation as she followed the thread. But when she opened the garage door and saw the one-of-a-kind couch sitting there with a big red bow on it, she was speechless.

Todd, on the other hand, raspy voice and all, couldn't stop talking about his creation. He had gotten the idea while recovering from the car accident and had worked on it for several weeks at his dad's before coming up with the right combination of parts to hold the surfboard in place as the backrest to the car's bench seat. He was so proud of himself that Christy knew she had to offer some kind of praise.

After the oohing and ahhing event was over, Christy felt she should have been nominated for an Oscar in the category of best supporting actress in a romantic comedy.

"Don't you love it?" Katie adjusted her position and stretched out her legs. Then, as if in need of an appropriate prop, she reached into the carry-out box and grabbed a slice of pizza.

Christy delivered one of her well-rehearsed lines. "I appreciate Todd's hard work. It's very creative."

Katie stopped munching. "You hate it, don't you? Did you tell him that?"

Christy reached for a slice of pizza, and with a sigh she flopped on the edge of her bed. "No, of course not. It would have devastated him."

With quiet bites, Katie adjusted her position again. "Does Todd consider this actual furniture?"

Christy nodded. "We have a couch and a camp stove. Todd thinks all we need now are two sleeping bags that zip together, and we can start our life of marital bliss."

Katie cracked up. "I'm sorry. That's not funny, is it? Does Todd have any idea how clueless he is when it comes to civilization stuff? I mean, he's a great guy, but his idea of normal life is . . . well . . . you would think he had spent his life in a jungle hut."

"In some ways, I think he did," Christy said. "Not a jungle hut, of course. Although, I'm sure he would have enjoyed that. I think his growing up as an only child and living with his dad made him a minimalist. The more we discuss our plans for the future, the more obvious our differences become."

"And you are telling him what's important to you as you go along, aren't you?" Katie asked.

Christy thought hard before nodding her head. "Yes, most of the time."

Katie put down her half-eaten piece of pizza and walked over to where Christy sat on her bed. With Katie's face mere inches from Christy's, she shouted, "Hello! This is your wake-up call!"

Christy turned away. She found her friend's tactics annoying and unhelpful.

Katie returned to the surfboard sofa and resumed her pizza consumption with a critical eye fixed on Christy. "That was a little too overt, wasn't it? Sorry. But you get my point, don't you?"

"Yes, I get your point, Katie."

"I mean, you guys are marrying each other. This is getting serious. This *is* serious. Let me ask you one thing. Do you want to get married in the meadow or was that Todd's idea?"

"It was Todd's idea, but I like it."

"Are you sure?"

Christy nodded.

"Are you falling into one of those zombie modes where you don't know what you want and you don't care?"

"I care!"

"Don't get upset," Katie said. "I'm just looking at you, and you're looking kind of spacey."

"I'm fine. I'm a little tired, but that's all. Todd and I need to work on our communication skills," Christy said. "And we are. We will. Todd is going to talk to one of the pastors at church about setting up some pre-marital counseling sessions for us. I think that will help."

Katie nodded.

"It's not like we aren't communicating at all," Christy said defensively. "It's just that we both want to get better at it. All couples have to make a lot of adjustments. We'll work it out."

In a calm voice Katie said, "I know you will."

They were quiet for a minute. Christy felt her head pounding. She had been trying to ignore a growing headache since they were grocery shopping, but now it was on her with full force.

"That saying about opposites attracting must be true," Katie said. "You and Todd are opposite in a lot of ways. Maybe that indicates you'll balance each other out."

"That's what Todd says," Christy said. "He's says we're good for each other because we think differently and do things differently."

"Hmm." Katie reached for a second slice of pizza.

"What are you *hmm*ing about?"

Katie picked a slice of pepperoni off her pizza, and a long string of mozzarella cheese followed the pepperoni up to her mouth. "Do you think Rick and I are opposites?"

Christy paused only a moment before saying with a sly grin, "Oh, did you just notice that?"

"That could be a good thing, couldn't it?" Katie cast a sideways glance at Christy, as if her future might be determined by the way Christy responded to this all-important question.

"Yes, it could be a good thing," Christy said. "It could be a God-thing for all I know."

Katie nodded thoughtfully. "Yes, it could. It could be a really surprising God-thing. Hmm. Who would have guessed?"

"Not me," Christy said quietly.

Christy hoped Katie would take that as an opportunity to open up about what was going on with Rick. But Katie announced she had to get going. Grabbing another piece of pizza, she bounced up and left to meet Rick at The Dove's Nest before Christy had even finished her first slice of pizza.

Alone in her dorm room, Christy stared at the surfboard sofa. It took up the center open area of their room. "You belong in a store that sells wet suits and skateboards," she muttered to the bright orange fiberglass room centerpiece. "Not here. What was Todd thinking?"

Once again she reminded herself Todd had lovingly taken two of the only valuable items he had owned in his life and had tried to salvage them and make them into something useful. That was commendable. It was sweet of him to give it to Christy. She needed to be more appreciative.

Why can't I be spontaneous and enthusiastic about things like Katie? Why can't I let whatever comes just come?

She glanced at the alarm clock and realized it was almost time for her to pick up Todd at church. He had promised her they would go ring shopping that evening. The plan was for them to stay at her parents' house that night. In the morning they would drive back to church and start the huge task of packing up all the gear for the Mexico trip.

However, by the time Christy had gathered her things and had met Todd at church, she was feeling awful.

"Do you have a fever?" Todd asked when they were about ten minutes from her parents' house.

"I don't think so. I feel kind of cold. I have a ripping headache."

Todd reached over and felt her forehead. "You have a fever. At least it started here and not in Mexico. You'll feel better by Friday, and you'll sound better by the time classes start up again a week from today."

"What makes you so sure I have the same virus you had?"

"It's going around. If you didn't catch it from me, you probably got it from that wedding coordinator on Saturday. Do you remember how she said her throat felt scratchy? That's how it starts."

Christy swallowed. Now her throat hurt. "I can't get sick. I have to do the food in Mexico."

"I can do it. Or Doug or Rick and Katie. Tracy isn't coming because of her morning sickness."

"I might feel better in the morning," Christy said. "We don't have to go ring shopping tonight. I could head right to bed when we get to my parents' house. That will help a lot, I'm sure."

Todd wore a knowing grin as he pulled into her parents' driveway. "I'll bring in your stuff. Why don't you go on in. I'll see you in a week."

Christy shot Todd an incredulous look. "What do you mean you'll see me in a week? I'll get some good sleep and be ready to go in the morning. You'll see."

Todd broke into a full smile as he turned off the engine. "Yes, dear. Whatever you say."

CHAPTER 8

Todd was right. Christy was sick for a week.

His being right bugged her for the first three days she lay in bed feeling miserable. She was missing the Mexico trip and missing Todd and missing the latest developments with Rick and Katie.

The only thing she wasn't missing was the wastebasket. After going through two boxes of tissues, she had become an expert at tossing the tissue into the wicker wastebasket in the corner.

Christy had made an observation about another difference between Todd and her. When she was sick, she wanted lots of attention every hour on the hour. She didn't care for the caveman approach to "sweating it out" and cutting oneself off from all forms of society until the virus had run its course.

By day three, Thursday, Christy was convinced the highlight of the week had been her mother's kind attention, which came complete with daily doses of toast and herbal tea sweetened with honey. The most depressing part of her confinement had been realizing how different things were going to be once she and Todd were married. Her mother would no longer bring toast and tea and put fresh sheets on the bed while Christy soaked in the tub. She conjured up a disturbing image of herself lying in a contorted position on the surfboard sofa while trying to lean over and light the camp stove to heat water for her already used tea bag.

I have to tell him, that's all. I have to tell Todd what I want and what I need. When we're married, if he knows that I want him to bring me tea, I'm sure he'll gladly do that. I just have to tell him.

An idea occurred to Christy that afternoon. She was over the achy fever part of the flu and into the laryngitis phase. She was feeling well enough to get up, but she decided to spend one more day in bed just to be sure.

With her bedroom door closed, Christy pulled out from under her bed a shoe box she had covered with wrapping paper years ago. Inside the shoe box were fourteen letters, all sealed in individual envelopes. On the cover of each envelope she had written the same four words, *To my future husband.*

A satisfying smile started in the secret corner of Christy's heart and, like sweet-smelling perfume, wafted its way to Christy's lips. When she had started writing those letters, she didn't know whom she would marry. Many times she had hoped it would be Todd, but every time she had deposited another letter into the box, she hadn't been sure the letter would end up in Todd's hands.

Today she knew. Todd was the man she had saved herself for. He would be the one to read those letters on their wedding night. He would know even more fully that for the past five years she had prayed for him, waited for him, hoped in him.

Christy decided she had one more letter to write. Pulling a piece of stationery out of a box she had purchased in Switzerland, Christy began the letter with,

Dear Future Husband, my Todd,

It felt good to write his name in the greeting. He didn't have a middle name, which Christy thought was unfortunate. Their children would all have middle names. Noble, poetic-sounding middle names like hers, which was Juliet.

Proceeding with the letter, she wrote,

As I write this, you're in Mexico, and I'm in bed with the flu. I've had some time to think these past few days, and I want to tell you two things. No, three.

First, I'm so happy we're getting married. I can't wait to be your wife. I know we'll have a lot of adjusting to do, but we'll work on it together. I know we'll become better communicators.

And that brings me to my second thought. Whenever I'm sick, I need attention. I don't like to be left alone to sweat it out. I'd like you to check on me and bring me tea and toast. I know we're different in this area, and I thought you should know this is important to me.

I remember one time in high school when I was sick, and you came to my parents' house and sat by my bed doing your homework while I slept. Maybe you thought that once I woke up I'd spring out of bed, and we could go do something. But you were there with me. I never told you that I considered that one of the most romantic and tender memories of our early years together. I can't wait until we're married so that every morning when I wake up the first thing I'll see is your handsome face. Soon.

Now, on to my final thought before I get lost in a daydream about our future together. I want all our children to have middle names, okay?

> *With all my love, forever,*
> *Your Christina Juliet Miller*
> *(soon to be Spencer)!*

P.S. I love you.

Sealing the letter in an envelope, Christy wrote on the front, *To my Todd.*

She tucked away the letter with the others and returned the box to its hiding place under her bed. The letter reminded her of something: Rick's letter.

Where did I put Rick's letter?

A tap sounded on her bedroom door, and her mom entered. "How are you feeling?"

"I'm feeling lots better." As soon as she spoke, she started a coughing jag that made her sound anything but better.

"I thought I heard you moving around in here. Would you like me to bring you anything?"

"Did Marti leave those bridal magazines here?"

Mom nodded. "They're in the living room. Would you like me to get them?"

"Please."

For the rest of the afternoon, Christy browsed through the magazines. As darkness came over the world outside her window, she slumped into a nap in which she dreamed of a fashion show of outrageous bridal dresses punctuated by advertisements for Oneida silverware.

By one o'clock the next afternoon, Christy had cut several dozen pictures from the assortment of bridal magazines and pasted them into her wedding planner notebook. She felt as if she were playing paper dolls as she cut the bodice from one gown and matched it with the skirt from another. She found the exact dress she wanted for the bridesmaids. It was shown in an apricot color, but she wanted it in pale blue. Four different veils looked as though they might work for her, but she decided it would be difficult to know unless she tried them on.

Putting away her notebook and pulling out a pair of jeans and a sweat shirt from the stack of clean clothes her mom had washed and folded, Christy headed for the shower. She felt good. Or at least better. She had no voice, and when she coughed, her head hurt, but she was ready to join the rest of the world.

Half an hour later, fresh and clean, with her long hair still damp on the ends, Christy ventured into the living room, where her mom was taking down the Christmas decorations. The tree was gone, and all the ornaments were tucked back in their boxes.

Mom looked up from where she knelt, wrapping the figures of the nativity set in tissue and nesting them in a sturdy box. "You certainly look better."

Christy nodded.

"Still no voice?"

"It's gone," Christy whispered. "But at least it doesn't hurt to whisper like this. Would you like some help?"

"I'd love some help. Could you pull the vacuum cleaner out of the closet and try to pick up those pine needles in the corner?"

For almost an hour the two of them worked efficiently and silently. As Christy helped carry the last box out to the garage, she cleared her throat and said, "I've come up with some ideas for my wedding dress and the bridesmaids' dresses."

"I'd love to see them," Mom said. "How about if I make some soup, and you can show me what you found?"

Over chicken noodle soup, Christy showed Mom her wedding planner. "This top," she whispered in a raspy voice, "with a skirt like this. I like the wide band at the waist."

"I see," Mom said. "That would be very flattering with your small waist."

"Only I want embroidery around the bodice like this one. But with little tiny white flowers. White on white. Don't you think that would be pretty?"

"Gorgeous," Mom said. "And do you like the bodice plain like this with the ballerina-style rounded neckline and three-quarter-inch sleeves?"

Christy nodded. "I love the sleeves. Especially if they have some embroidery on them."

Her mom smiled. "I'm surprised that's what you decided on."

"Why?"

"Have you ever seen my wedding dress?"

Christy had seen pictures of her parents' wedding, but she didn't remember what her mom's wedding gown looked like. She shook her head.

"Come with me." Mom led Christy down the hallway to her bedroom, where she pulled a box from the back of the closet. It was labeled with a Wisconsin dry cleaner's advertisement.

"I remember this box," Christy said hoarsely. "I found it in your closet once when I was a little girl."

"Paula and you wanted to use it for dress-up," Mom said. "I had a fit."

"Yes, you did. I remember." Christy noticed the box had been taped shut on the right side where it had been torn. Apparently that was the side she and her childhood best friend had tried to break into.

Christy studied her mom's profile as she carefully opened the box. Christy's mom was a simple woman. Pleasantly plain in her appearance, she was shorter than Christy and rounder. Her hair had gone almost completely gray. She had never colored it. She kept it short, straight, and tucked behind her ears, which Christy thought looked better than when Mom used to wear it in what Christy called the "bubble-head hairdo" whenever they looked at old family photos.

The older Christy got, the more she admired her mom. Margaret Miller was a steady woman who always put her family first. When Christy was younger, she had longed for a peppy, outgoing mom who was more like a best friend or big sister than a mother. Her mom, however, remained the same, consistent, untrendy mom she had always been, and now Christy appreciated it. While Christy never had confided all her secrets to her mother, she had been a mom who was always available and listened with an uncritical spirit. Mom rarely offered advice. When she did, she usually had thought it through before speaking.

"Now, I want you to know," Mom began, "that this is just an idea, based on what you showed me in your pictures. I don't know if you would be interested. If you're not, please feel free to say so, because you certainly won't hurt my feelings."

Christy was beginning to feel nervous. If Mom was going to suggest Christy wear her wedding dress, Christy knew it would be a problem. Mom was shorter, for one thing. And Christy and her mom rarely shared the same taste.

"Do you see how the bodice is cut?" Mom asked, unwrapping the dress.

Christy nodded in surprise. It was the same style as the dress in the picture she had cut out. Not too scooped and slightly off the shoulders.

"These could be made into three-quarter-length sleeves," Mom said. "I know the skirt would be too short, but we could replace it with a long skirt and the wide waistband you mentioned. You could have any train length you wanted."

Christy examined the top of the dress. The scoop was just low enough to show the collarbones, and she loved the fabric. "What is this?"

"The material? I don't know. It's a blend of some sort that was very popular in my day. I don't know if my idea is any help . . ."

"May I try it on?" Christy asked.

"It will be too big on you," Mom said. "And too short."

"That's okay. I'd like to see how the top fits."

"All right."

Mom closed the bedroom door, even though they were the only ones home. Christy pulled her sweat shirt over her head and wiggled out of her jeans.

With her mom's help, Christy slid into the gown. As predicted, the dress was too big and too short, but the neckline was perfect.

"I like your idea, Mom. I would love to have your wedding gown made into my wedding gown. Are you sure you don't mind?"

Mom's face softened in a sweet smile. "Oh, Christy, I would love nothing more. Are you sure that's what you want to do?"

"Yes!" Christy pushed up the sleeves in an attempt to visualize them as three-quarter length. A cough welled up in her throat, and she turned her head and coughed for several seconds.

"It would be easy to change these into three-quarter-length sleeves," Mom said. "This will be a nice style no matter what season you finally decide on for your wedding."

Christy wondered if she should tell her mom about the potential May 22 wedding date. If she did, she would also have to explain about how she and Todd wanted the ceremony and reception in a meadow instead of a church. At this moment, she had neither the voice nor the energy to approach the complicated subject.

Fortunately, her mom went on to another topic. "I don't know if it would be hard to match the material for the skirt, but we could try. I'm sure I can buy a pattern and make the skirt. But what about the embroidered flowers? It sounded as if that was the part you liked the most about the dress you saw. I don't think I'd want to attempt embroidery. Maybe we can find someone who does that."

"I could do it," Christy said.

Mom looked surprised.

Christy cleared her throat and in a whisper said, "I never told you, but one of the things I learned in Switzerland was embroidery. I spent hours at the orphanage embroidering handkerchiefs and pillowcases with the older girls."

"You're right, I didn't know that."

"It was a skill they could use to make salable items. Some of them were really quick and good at the details. I worked on a lot of pillowcases and a couple of tablecloths. They were finished by the girls and sold, so I didn't bring anything home that I had worked on. I think I could do it. And I think that's why the wedding gown in the magazine caught my eye. The embroidery reminded me of that year of my life."

"Let's give it a try," Mom said. "I'll take the dress apart and shorten the sleeves this weekend. You can take the bodice with you and work on the embroidery at school. If you want, we could run to the fabric store now to find a pattern and the material for the skirt. I'm sure they have a book of embroidery patterns, as well. Let me get a tape measure."

Christy stood still, with her arms outstretched. Mom measured her and estimated how much fabric they would need for the skirt.

"One thing we should both keep in mind," Mom said as she wrote down the measurements. "We should have enough time before the wedding for you to change your mind. It won't hurt my feelings if we get into this and discover it's too big of a project or if it's not turning out the way you would like."

Christy nodded. She had all kinds of optimistic thoughts about the dress turning out exactly as she wanted. Then she wondered if this was her mom's way of backing out of the project gracefully.

"Mom, if you're thinking it's too big of a challenge, we can stop. I'd hate for you to tear your wedding dress into a bunch of pieces, but then we didn't end up using it."

"We will never know unless we try," Mom said in her matter-of-fact way. "I think we can do this."

Christy gave her mom a big hug and whispered in her ear, "Thank you for sacrificing your wedding gown for me."

"It's not a sacrifice, honey. It's what I have to give. All the time you were growing up I wanted to give you so much more than we had. When Marti stepped in and treated you to so much during your teen years, I thought you would grow to resent me."

"No, Mom, not at all."

"I know my sister means well, but she called again yesterday asking if you were well enough to go up there and work on wedding plans. She reminded me that she and Bob want to pay for whatever expenses Dad and I can't cover."

Christy's heart went out to her mom, whose face had taken on a melancholy expression.

"Please don't take this to mean that your father and I don't want them to help out with the wedding. It's fine with us if she and Bob help. I know it would make them happy, and it means we can make your wedding nicer than what your father and I could afford. But I wanted to have one thing to give you that was mine."

"And you're giving me your wedding gown," Christy whispered warmly.

"Such as it is."

Christy smiled. "I already know that my dress will be one of my favorite parts of the wedding."

"I hope it will be." Mom's round face had a warm glow. "Actually, sweetheart, I have a feeling the favorite part of your wedding will be your honeymoon."

For the next twenty minutes, Christy and her mom sat close together on the edge of the bed. Christy was still wearing her mom's wedding dress. She sat perfectly straight, being careful not to crumple any part of it.

It struck Christy that she wasn't a little girl playing dress-up in her mommy's wedding gown, as she had once attempted to do. This was real. Not pretend. She was a woman, listening to another woman talk in hushed tones about the beauty and sanctity of giving herself to her husband on their wedding night.

Mom's choice of words was delicate. She spoke in generalities, saying she regretted that her shyness had kept her from having such an important and intimate conversation with Christy before now. Christy said she didn't know if she would have appreciated such a conversation with her mom before.

"I know that Todd and you have made wise and mature choices," Mom said. "It shows in the way you look at each other and the way you treat each other. You'll benefit from the rewards of such deep respect."

More intensely than ever Christy understood the power of virginity. Not only for Todd and her but also for their children. She realized that one day she might sit on the edge of her marriage bed with her own daughter, having this same conversation. How powerful to look her daughter in the eye, as her mother was now looking at her, and to say without a speck of regret, "Your father and I both waited for each other, and it was worth it."

With renewed determination, Christy promised herself that no matter how many months or years she and Todd had to wait until their wedding night, she would continue to save this priceless gift that could only be given once. This gift from God that would be given to only one man, a man who had saved himself for her, as well.

By the time Christy slipped out of the wedding gown and left for the fabric store with her mom, she felt as if she had met her mother for the first time. She also knew that the closeness of their newly established friendship would last for the rest of their lives.

CHAPTER 9

Christy's favorite part of her first day back on campus after Christmas vacation was having breakfast with Todd at "their" table by the window in the cafeteria. Her flu bug was gone. Her voice was back, and she had done a lot of planning over the weekend. She and Todd had talked on the phone several times after he returned from Mexico, but this was the first time they had been together in a week.

Christy had her wedding notebook with her, and the first thing she said to Todd when she sat down was, "Are you ready to get organized?"

"Organized?" Todd asked.

"For our wedding."

"Sure. I see you have a list going."

"Yes, I do." Christy turned to the first page and dived in. "We should set a time to look at rings this week. I have my wedding dress pretty well figured out, but you don't get to know anything about it or see it, so that point doesn't include you. We need to start looking at wedding invitations and decide on the number of guests before we make a decision on the food. As soon as we have a date, we need to make airline reservations because my aunt said yesterday that some flights to Maui fill up quickly. Have you talked to the associate pastor yet about setting up our premarital counseling sessions?"

Todd leaned back and grinned broadly. "I love you."

"Don't get mushy on me." Christy pulled a pen from her backpack. "We have work to do."

Todd laughed. "Don't you think we should go to the administration office first? Then we'll know if May twenty-second is okay for us to hold the ceremony in the meadow. We can work back from there."

"Okay, but we can talk about a few things while we eat. For instance, how many attendants do you want to have? I've asked Katie to be my maid of honor, but I'm not sure who else to ask. Tracy, of course. That's assuming we get married in May. Their baby is due in July, right?"

Todd stopped eating his scrambled eggs and suspended his fork in midair. "What do you think about naming our first daughter Juliet? She could go by Julie so she wouldn't get slaughtered with Romeo jokes."

"Todd, you're getting mushy again," Christy said with half a grin. She knew Doug had discussed baby names with Todd while they were in Mexico. Todd had told her on the phone a few nights ago that Doug and he had come up with the name Daniel for the baby, if it was a boy. Christy hadn't talked to Tracy yet to find out how she felt about that name. The guys hadn't suggested a girl's name.

"I looked it up in a book Doug had," Todd continued. "Juliet means 'youthful one.' I like that. Although I've always liked Hawaiian names because of the way they sound like a little song when you say them. Maybe we could give our kids Hawaiian middle names. What do you think?"

Christy put down the pen and gave Todd a stern look. Inside, her heart was dancing. He was thinking about their children's middle names, just as she had been when she wrote him the letter last week. Maybe they weren't so opposite in their thinking after all.

With a forced expression of firm seriousness, Christy said, "Do you want to talk mushy or business? Make up your mind."

Todd laughed. "Okay, okay. Mushy later. Business now."

A grin escaped as Christy lowered her voice. "And when we do talk mushy later, you can talk as mushy as you want for as long as you want. I love it when you dream aloud."

"Dream aloud," Todd repeated. "That's what it is, isn't it? I like that, Kilikina. For so many years you and I didn't know what the future held for us so we had to keep all our dreams to ourselves. I'm glad we did that. It would have been unfair to both of us if we had started to dream aloud before we were engaged."

"I agree, Todd. You have no idea how deeply I take dreams into my heart, and how tightly I hold on to them."

"It's the same for me," Todd said. "I would have to say that we managed to do a couple of things right. Like the piggy bank. That was a good idea."

Christy knew Todd was referring to something they had discussed months ago. Because it had been difficult for them to hold back when they wanted to physically express their affection for each other, they had come up with the image of each of them having a piggy bank. Whenever they wanted to give the other a kiss, they could stop and evaluate if they truly wanted to spend that kiss at that moment or to save it in the piggy bank. They knew that if they saved most of their physical expressions and spent only a tiny portion now, they both would enter their marriage wealthy in saved-up physical expressions.

"And that night after we went caroling, and you said we were at a red light—that helped me a lot," Christy said.

"It's getting more difficult, though, isn't it?" Todd asked.

Christy had a pretty good idea she knew what he was talking about, but she felt too shy to actually say it.

Todd leaned across the small corner table where they sat by the window. "It's getting more difficult, but we have to wait another 135 days."

Christy felt little bubbles of anticipation rise in her heart. "Is that how long until May twenty-second? Only 135 more days?" She sat up straighter. "Well, then, we better get going on this list. We have a lot to do in the next 135 days."

Todd reached across the table and grasped Christy's hand before she could pick up the pen. "Come on, Kilikina, stop with the list for just a moment. Tell me, haven't you thought about it? Us becoming one? Giving ourselves to each other?"

As Christy looked into Todd's wide eyes, she was surprised she didn't feel herself blushing. This was the man she was going to marry. In 135 days, she would give herself completely to him. And they would enjoy each other for the rest of their lives. She wasn't embarrassed to think about that or to talk about it with him. It made her think of the account in Genesis that said Adam and Eve were naked and not ashamed.

Moving her chair next to Todd's, leaning close and choosing her words carefully, Christy said, "Todd, with all my heart I long to be yours. I know that I'm going to love you so completely and with so much passion that I promise you, Todd Spencer, you're going to be the happiest man who ever lived."

Todd appeared surprised and delighted with her words. Tears glistened in the corners of his eyes. He wrapped both his arms around Christy and pulled her close. Burying his face in her neck, Todd whispered into her long hair, "And I will make you the happiest woman who ever lived, my Kilikina. I promise."

As they drew apart, Christy's heart pounded so hard it seemed to reverberate in her throat and in her ears.

"You know what? I don't think we should dream aloud about that part of our future again," Todd said in a husky voice.

Christy nodded.

"Or at least not until after we stand under our trellis in the meadow 135 days from now," Todd said firmly. He pulled back and looked at his unfinished breakfast as if he had forgotten what scrambled eggs looked like.

Christy scooted her chair back to her side of the table and took a sip of her orange juice. She doodled a flower-laced trellis at the top of the list. Their wedding arch was becoming a symbol of the passing from one stage of life into another for Todd and her.

Both of them had held on to the symbolism of a certain bridge in Hawaii that had represented life passages for them. She wondered if their wedding arch could be covered with vines and tropical flowers the way the bridge at Kipahulu had been. Todd would like that.

"Hi, kids, am I interrupting anything here?" Katie pulled up a chair to their small table. "I'll leave if you two want to be alone."

"Yeah, we want to be alone more than you can guess," Todd said. "But we'll wait 135 more days for that."

"Oh-kay." Katie glanced at Christy. "I don't think I want to know what you two were just talking about, but I have a pretty good idea."

"Have you been to our room yet?" Christy asked.

"No, I just got back on campus. I have a class in twenty minutes. I told my new boss I'd come to work early, so you probably won't see me again until after eleven tonight."

"Is today your first day at The Dove's Nest?" Todd asked.

"Yep." Katie reached for half a bagel on the corner of Todd's plate. "Are you going to eat that?"

"Help yourself. You want me to get you some eggs?" Todd offered.

Katie grinned. "Would you? You are such a sweetheart, Todd. You should have seen him in Mexico, Chris. He was Mr. Servant of All."

"Rick and you were the real heroes," Todd said, rising from his chair. "We couldn't have pulled it off if it weren't for the way you two ran the kitchen."

He walked away, and Katie turned to Christy. "What he's really saying is that it took two of us to do your job, Christy. We all missed you so much. You should have heard your honey. He talked about you constantly. All the girls in the youth group wanted to know if you were going to invite them to your wedding."

Then, glancing over her shoulder as if to make sure they were alone, Katie lowered her voice. "I have to talk to you."

Christy waited.

"Not here. Not now. Do you have any time open today before I go to work?"

"I only have two classes this morning, and I don't have to be at work in the bookstore until two."

Katie twisted her mouth in a perplexed expression. "I don't think it's going to work with my schedule. I'll just talk to you when I get back to our room tonight."

Todd returned with eggs for Katie and another bagel for himself. They chatted about how great the Mexico trip was and all the people they had met at the orphanage. Christy wished she could have gone, but she was glad for the time she had with her mom and all the planning she had done.

"I gotta fly," Katie said. "See you guys later." As she stood up, she knocked Christy's wedding notebook to the floor.

Todd and I sure didn't get very far on our to-do list.

Exactly ten hours later, Todd and Christy were seated again at their table by the window in the cafeteria. Todd was about to dig into one of his favorite handcrafted salads that resembled a green volcano with an eruption of peas flowing down the side in rivers of white ranch dressing.

"Well, I called my mom," Christy announced right after they prayed.

Todd raised an eyebrow. "What did she say?"

"She thought May twenty-second was a good choice, and she was sure Dad would agree. But when I told her we could use the meadow for the ceremony and the reception, she got real quiet."

"My dad thought it sounded great," Todd said.

"You called him already?"

Todd nodded. "I couldn't wait. I called my mom, too. I had to leave a message on her cell phone."

"Did you tell her about your graduation the end of this month? I mean, she's coming for that, too, isn't she?"

"I gave her the dates for both the graduation and the wedding. I hope it works out with her schedule."

Christy caught an edge of hurt in his words. She couldn't imagine what it must have been like for him to grow up without his mom's involvement in his life. His mother had remarried years ago and had settled with her new husband and family on the East Coast. Todd had lived with them for a short time. He rarely talked about his mother, and when he did, it was briefly and with the explanation that she had been too young when she had Todd to know how to be a mother.

"I hope she can come to both your graduation and our wedding," Christy said.

"Me too." Todd quickly moved to other topics. "What about your aunt and uncle? Did you call them?"

"No, my mom said she wanted to talk to Aunt Marti about the wedding and reception being held here. I think she felt she could commiserate with her sister since they both wanted something other than what you and I decided."

"It's our wedding," Todd said.

"I know. And I really think the meadow is the right location for us."

89

"It's the right location, and May twenty-second is the right date. We have a plan." Todd grinned. "So what else do you have on that check-off list of yours?"

"Would this be a good time to show you the ideas I came up with for a ring?"

"Sure."

Christy pulled the wedding planner from her backpack and turned to the pages on which she had pasted the pictures of rings and drawn a few rough sketches.

"This is the blue opal." Christy pointed to the angled, wave-like setting in the middle of a narrow gold ring.

"And it's inset, right?"

"Yes. I'd like it to be smooth with nothing raised up. On both sides, these angled insets are three tiny diamonds with three more over here." With a sense of delight she said, "See, the blue opal is like an ocean wave. The diamonds on this side are like the sand, and these are like the stars. Whenever I look at it, I'll think of how we met at the beach and how we fell in love while counting stars and walking barefoot in the sand."

Todd stared at her sketch and didn't say anything.

"What do you think?"

He looked up. "You're amazing, Kilikina. This is beautiful."

"You like it?"

"I love it. It's exactly what I would want you to have. You've managed to fit a world of meaning into a simple band. You made it uniquely yours."

"Uniquely *ours*," Christy corrected him.

"Yes, it's uniquely ours. Should we have Mr. Frank make it for us, or do you know another jeweler you'd like to go to?"

"I think Mr. Frank would be fine. Just make sure he uses one of those deep aqua blue Australian opals with the purple and green flecks. Not the light ivory opals. I like the ones that look like the ocean."

"Got it." Todd reached for the notebook. "Mind if I take this? I can go out to Carlsbad tomorrow."

"No!" Christy grabbed the planner. "This is my brain; you can't take it from me. And you can't see the pages with my dress design on them. I'll make a copy of the ring pages and give them to you in the morning."

"Do you want to go to Carlsbad with me?" Todd asked. "You can explain your idea to Mr. Frank in person, if you want."

Christy was about to say yes because she wanted to go and she knew it would be easier for Todd if she went. But her day was already packed.

"I have to work five hours tomorrow starting at noon. I don't think I'd have time to drive to Carlsbad and be back after my eight-o'clock class. I'll write out notes for you."

"If you know what you want for your wedding band, we could have that made at the same time," Todd suggested.

"That's easy. See this picture? I cut it out of a magazine. I would like a gold band like this that's the same width as the engagement ring. What about you? What kind of wedding ring do you want?"

Todd shrugged. "I've never worn any rings. What do you think would be good?"

Christy thought a minute. She knew Todd would settle for a plain gold band and never think twice about it. But she wanted him to have something special. "How do you feel about wearing a larger version of my engagement ring?"

"Wouldn't that look kind of girly?"

"Girly?"

"Yeah, girly." Todd studied the sketches. "You know, what about having three little diamonds inset in your wedding band? Or maybe six diamonds all across the front here." He made six tiny dots with Christy's pen.

"That would be beautiful," Christy said. "But it also would be more expensive."

"That's okay."

"Would you like inset diamond chips in your band?" Christy asked.

"Nah, just a gold band would suit me."

As Christy crawled into bed that night, she thought of how easily pleased Todd was. His tastes were simple; his expectations were reasonable. He was pretty wonderful in every way. The anxiety she had experienced a few weeks ago, when she realized how poorly they communicated, seemed to be alleviated. The more time they had to sit and talk, the more helpful it was for both of them.

She glanced at the clock—11:35, and Katie wasn't back yet. Christy was more than ready to go to sleep. She had worked on embroidering her wedding gown's bodice for two hours straight before taking a shower and washing her hair. If it weren't for how eager she was to hear what Katie had to tell her, Christy would have turned out the light and crashed.

I'm sure what Katie has to tell me has something to do with Rick. Rick . . . That reminds me, Rick's letter. I never read his letter.

Climbing out of bed, Christy pulled her suitcase from the back of her closet and ran her hand through the inside pockets. She found the crumpled envelope. Instead of returning to her warm bed, she coaxed herself over to the surfboard sofa and attempted to make friends with the beast by sitting down and leaning against the cold backrest. She tucked her feet underneath her and tried to get comfortable.

Opening the envelope, Christy pulled out two folded pieces of stationery. A hundred-dollar bill floated to her lap. Her surprised eyes quickly scanned the handwritten letter.

Dear Christy,

I hope I can hand this to you in person one day because that way I'll be able to see your eyes, and I'll know if you really have forgiven me for taking your gold bracelet. I think I already know that you've forgiven me, but it will help if I see it in your eyes.

The enclosed money is to reimburse you for what you had to pay to redeem your bracelet from the jewelers. If it's more than you had to pay, then use it for something else. Just promise me that you'll accept it as restitution for my foolish actions.

As you probably know by now, God has gotten ahold of my life. I still can't believe He didn't give up on me long ago. He patiently brought me back to himself, and I'm a different person. It's all God's doing, not mine.

What you don't know is that you were there on a significant day in my life. I didn't know it at the time, but God used an object lesson to get my attention years later. I'm referring to the first Sunday you visited our church and sat with me in class. Do you remember how the teacher had Katie stand on a chair and how he dubbed me "Peter Pagan"? "Katie Christian" tried to pull me up to her with no success. Then, with one little tug, I pulled her down to my level.

Well, I never forgot that. I realized that I had gone through my life pulling others down. When I finally hit the bottom, I kept remembering how vulnerable Katie was when I pulled her off that chair. I realized I didn't have the kind of trusting relationship she had expressed with anyone. I knew I wanted to have that kind of trust in the Lord. I had sort of made a business deal with Him. You know, I told Him I'd follow the rules if He would keep me out of hell. But it doesn't work that way. I found out He wanted all of me. He wanted me to open my heart and to receive Him fully. And once I repented, that's what happened.

So please accept this restitution and know that I'm sorry for the way I treated you.

Your brother in Christ,
Rick Doyle

Before Christy had a chance to respond to the letter, the door opened, and Katie entered holding a bright bouquet of mixed flowers. Her face glowed.

"Well," Christy said, "must have been a good first day at your job."

"My boss gave these to me."

"Nice welcome present."

"Rick doesn't give flowers to every new employee." Katie was still standing by the closed door, as if she were caught in a dream and unable to move forward.

"No, I wouldn't imagine he does."

"I don't know what to do with them."

"They probably would like some water," Christy suggested.

Katie swallowed and gave Christy a shy smile.

"What?" Christy asked.

Katie drew the bouquet to her blushing face and sniffed its fragrance. With a twinkle in her shimmering green eyes, she said in a very small voice, "I really like him. I mean, really, really."

Christy said, "Oh? Really?"

"Yes, really."

CHAPTER 10

"Christy, I never expected this." Katie sat down on the surfing sofa and held the flowers in her lap. "It's only been a few weeks, but did you know that we've seen each other every day since you and Todd got engaged? Rick and I talk about everything. We had a great time together in Mexico, and Christmas was wonderful with his family. His mom loves me. His dad told me on New Year's Eve I was a gift from God to their son." Tears rolled down Katie's cheeks.

Christy was waiting for the bad news. "So, what was it you wanted to talk to me about this morning? In the cafeteria you said—"

"What's that?" Katie looked at Rick's letter that Christy had left on the sofa.

"The letter Rick gave me. Go ahead, read it."

Katie scanned the letter. She looked up at Christy with searching eyes. "What is God doing?"

Christy smiled. "My best friend, Katie, would call this a huge God-thing."

"This is beyond huge. It's mind-bending. And God is doing it, not me. I don't want to run ahead, or get freaked and pull back. I just want to take each step as it comes and to be right in line with what God has for me. For us. I want God to fulfill His purpose for me."

Christy tried not to let out a cheer for her impulsive friend, who was showing more caution and wise thinking than Christy had ever seen in her. Instead, Christy just nodded support and understanding.

"Yesterday Rick said that having me in his life has been like the song Doug was working on. Rick said that when the Lord brought us together, his life filled with joy and laughter. The flowers are a thank-you to me for being me. But I got nervous and thought maybe he was trying to tell me that our relationship was about to go to the next level, you know?"

"So what did you tell him?"

"I opened my mouth like only I can, and I told him exactly what I was thinking."

Christy knew that Katie could be pretty brutal when she decided to be honest. Wincing slightly, she waited to hear Katie's report.

"I told Rick I trusted him with our friendship. I told him I didn't want either of us to make judgments based on the past. I forgave him when his letter came, and I truly know that I did. I don't harbor anything against him in my heart. But I told him I'm not interested in a speedy relationship."

Katie looked at Christy with self-doubt all over her face. "Then I said, 'If there's anything lasting that's going to grow out of our friendship, then it will be here five months from now or a year from now or ten years from now.' "

Christy's eyes grew wide. "How did he react to that?"

"He said he felt the same way. He said he was interested in a friendship that would last forever, no matter what. He had no expectations of me and wasn't in a hurry to make any predictions about what God was doing in our lives."

"That's wonderful."

"I know. So tell me I said the right thing."

Christy sat next to Katie, putting her arm around Katie's shoulders. "Of course you did the right thing. You're an amazing, strong, incredible woman, and you handled what could have been an awkward situation with honesty and integrity."

Katie smiled slowly, followed by a rhythmic nodding of her head. "Yeah, I did, didn't I? For once in my life I did the right thing."

"You do a lot of things right."

"Not when it comes to guys. You know my long list of failures in that arena better than anyone. And if by any remote chance this guy is the one I'm going to end up spending the rest of my life with, I want to make sure

I don't go crazy and make all my decisions on impulse. I don't want to run ahead of God."

Christy gave Katie a glowing smile. "You are absolutely amazing."

"Amazing nothing! I'm exhausted! Do you know how much emotional energy I've spent in the last twenty-four hours processing my feelings, starting a new job working for him, and trying to figure out how I was going to tell you all this?"

"I hope you expected me to be supportive."

"I didn't know what you would think."

"I think God is doing His God-thing. Katie, you deserve the best, and I only want God's best for you. For both of you. That's all I've ever wanted."

"I know," Katie said quietly. She sat next to Christy and let out a deep sigh. "Chris, I have to tell you something. I know I should have told you a long time ago, but things changed in both of our lives, and I decided to let it go. However, in light of what's been happening with Rick during these past few weeks, I think I better tell you."

Christy couldn't imagine any secret Katie could have kept from her, let alone a secret she had kept for a number of years.

"Do you remember the night we went to the sleepover at Janelle's when we were sophomores?"

"Yes, of course."

"Do you remember how we all went out that night and T.P.'d Rick's house? You didn't run fast enough, and we took off in the motor home. You were left hiding in the bushes."

"Katie, of course I remember all this. Rick's dad sent him outside to clean up the toilet paper. I jumped out of the bushes, and Rick chased me down the street."

"Right. And that's when Rick became obsessed with you."

"I wouldn't say he was obsessed with me."

"Well, that's how I saw it," Katie said. "Now, this is the part that's hard for me to tell you. I thought then that if I became your friend, I could get closer to Rick, and that's pretty much what I did."

Christy let Katie's words sink in.

"I used you, Christy. I've wanted to apologize to you for years, but it got kind of complicated."

"That's okay. I never felt as if you used me."

"That's because you welcomed me into your life. I had never had a best friend before, and I ended up wanting to be your friend more than I wanted Rick to notice me. So I told myself I didn't care about Rick. The truth is," Katie said slowly, "I was being eaten alive with jealousy."

"You never showed it."

"Oh yes I did. You're being gracious, Christy. I struggled all the time, and you know it. When you dumped Rick, half of me cheered that you took a stand and let him know what a jerk he had been to you. The other half of me hoped I might finally have a chance to get him to notice me. How sick is that?"

"I don't think it's sick, Katie. I think it's honest. It's complicated, like you said. Everything was a lot more confusing in high school."

"I wish I had talked to you about all of this back then. There never seemed to be a good time. I almost said something during the spring of our junior year, when we went to visit the guys at their apartment in San Diego."

Katie paused and then leaned forward before continuing her confession. "Actually, I should go back to January of that year, when we went to the Rose Parade. Rick kissed me at midnight—you know that. It was a spontaneous Happy New Year's kiss. A big nothing for him. But it was my first kiss, and it was with Rick, and it was huge for me."

Christy hung her head. "And I gave you a hard time about it."

"Hey, this is my confession, not yours. Your heart was in the right place. You didn't want me to get hurt. But I did get hurt. And then when we stayed at Stephanie's next to the guys' apartment in San Diego, Rick walked me to the door late that night. He kissed me, and I kissed him back. I never told you."

"I knew," Christy said softly.

Katie turned with a surprised look on her face. "You knew? Why didn't you say anything?"

"It was awkward, like you said."

"Yes, it was. I gave Rick plenty of opportunities the next day at the zoo to make good on his kiss and to express interest in me. But he was a blob."

"That was pretty awful," Christy agreed.

"Do you remember what you said to me in front of the koala bears at the zoo?"

"In front of the koala bears? No, I have absolutely no idea what I said to you in front of the koala bears."

"You made me promise you something. You said, 'Promise me you won't let Rick use you.'"

"I don't remember that."

"Well, I do, because your advice cut me in half. I knew that's what I had done with you in the beginning. I had used you to get to Rick. I confessed it to God right then and got my heart right with Him, but I was too chicken to confess everything to you and ask you to forgive me. But I want to ask your forgiveness now, Chris. I'm so sorry."

"Katie, I forgive you. Please don't worry about that. It was complicated, like you said. I never held any of this against you."

"I know you didn't. But I still had to get it off my chest. You have this way about you, Christy. You open your heart, and you make people feel as if they can mosey on in, take off their shoes, and stay awhile. That's what I did back in high school and, well, here we are. Still friends."

"Best of friends," Christy echoed.

"I guess a couple of peculiar treasures like us don't come along every day, do they?"

"Definitely not." Christy paused before adding, "And a God-lover like Rick Doyle doesn't come along every day, either."

Katie stared at her hands.

"Let me pray for you. For us." Christy placed a comforting hand on Katie's shoulder and thanked God for what He had done in their lives in the past and for what He was doing now and would do in the future. She prayed for wisdom for Katie and Rick and for direction for Todd and her.

Katie prayed, as well. They hugged and both cried a little. Then Katie went to the laundry room, where she found a plastic pitcher and filled it with water for her flowers. It was almost two in the morning when Christy finally coaxed Katie to turn out the light.

In the dark stillness of their room, Katie said, "I didn't tell you one other thing."

Christy was almost asleep and didn't think she could handle any more surprise announcements or confessions.

"We haven't kissed yet," Katie said simply.

Christy opened her eyes and stared across the dark room at Katie's bed. All she saw was the silhouette of Naranja's top curve.

"Rick told me he made a promise to God that he would clean up his act in that area. He wanted me to know, as our relationship progressed, that he would be taking it really slow in physical expression. I think that's a good choice. For him. For us. It takes a lot of the pressure off, you know? Well, I just thought I'd tell you. Good night."

"Good night." Christy rolled over on her side. Now she was wide awake with not-so-pleasant memories of when she had dated Rick, before his act was cleaned up. Christy was fifteen. She was trusting and inexperienced. Rick was direct and expressive. She knew that the handful of kisses Rick had stolen had been part of what she forgave him for a long time ago. As the unsettled feelings now tried to come back and torment her, she reminded herself that it was in the past. It was forgiven. Forgotten. Erased from God's book. Buried in the deepest sea.

A saying came to mind. *"When the enemy comes knocking on a door you closed long ago, you just call out, 'Jesus, it's for you!'"*

Christy smiled. She pulled up the covers to her chin and let Jesus answer the door while she floated off to dreamland.

Three weeks later the saying came to her again. This time Todd heard the enemy knocking on a door he thought he had closed long ago.

It was the evening of Todd's graduation. Christy's parents, her brother, her aunt and uncle, and Todd's dad all had come to cheer for him when he received his diploma. Christy took a roll of film of Todd in his cap and gown and handed her camera to David to take several shots of Christy and Todd together. Katie, Rick, Sierra, and a bunch of other friends came from school. Christy made sure they all posed in a group picture with her favorite graduate.

Afterward, a group of eleven family and friends went to a steak house in town. Todd's dad treated them to a fabulous dinner in a private room. The day had been filled with cheers, laughter, and applause. Christy thought it couldn't have gone better.

Yet, as Todd drove Christy back to the dorm, she could tell he was upset or sad about something by the way his shoulders slumped. Christy reached over and gave his arm three squeezes. A slow grin of appreciation came to his face. He glanced over at Christy.

"You know," he said, turning his attention back to the road, "I thought she couldn't hurt me anymore. I thought I was over it. But when my mom called yesterday and said she wasn't coming, I found myself remembering every important event in my life she's missed. She was really never there for me. Ever."

Christy felt her heart go out to him.

"Except when I was born, of course." He lightened his tone, as if trying to make a joke. "I guess that one was mandatory."

During the past month, ever since Christy had tried on her mom's wedding dress, she and her mom had become closer than ever. They spoke on the phone almost every day and were working closely together on all the wedding details. She couldn't imagine what it would be like to have a mother who would call at the last minute to say she found it "inconvenient" to come to Christy's college graduation.

"I was thinking about that quote you told me a few weeks ago about asking the Lord to answer the door when the enemy comes knocking," Todd said. "I guess that's what I need to do in this situation. It's a door of hurt and disappointment that I shut long ago when I forgave her. It's not a door I should open again."

"It might be," Christy said cautiously.

"What do you mean?"

"You know how last week in our premarital counseling session Pastor Ross said we should feel free to discuss with him any areas of our lives that we think might be a challenge after we're married? Well, I think this might be a challenge for you, for us, for the rest of our lives. It might help to talk openly to someone about it."

"Maybe," Todd said.

"Do you think your mom will come to our wedding?"

"I don't know. In a way, I don't know if I want her there. I know this is going to sound crazy, but I'd almost rather have Bob and Marti sit in the front row where my parents normally would sit."

"I'm sure they would be honored if you asked them. I know they both feel like you're a son to them. But what about your dad?"

"I asked him to be my best man."

"You did?" It was the first Christy had heard of it. She had listed Doug as Todd's best man in the wedding planner, but then she didn't remember Todd and her ever talking specifics. She had just assumed.

"Is that allowed in the world of wedding etiquette? Can you have your dad stand up as your best man?" Todd pulled into the parking lot behind Christy's dorm and parked the Volvo.

"I don't know. We keep saying it's our wedding, so I guess we can do whatever we want."

"My dad always has been there for me. He's the first person I thought of. I want him to stand beside me."

"Okay," Christy said. "I think that's great." Her mind was busy rearranging details that had been penciled in her notebook. "You and I should set aside some time this week to work on our plans. My aunt gave me some wedding invitation samples today."

"I saw her hand them to you. Do you like any of them?"

"Not really. I'd prefer it if you and I could go to a stationery store and look at more samples together. We have to decide on the wording, and Marti said that she arranged for an artist friend of hers to address the invitations in calligraphy, but she needs six weeks to do them. The invitations need to be sent out six weeks to a month before the wedding. If it takes a month to print them, we're almost out of time already."

"You're starting to sound panicked," Todd said. "There's no need to panic. We can go sometime this week, just not on Monday. That's when I start my new job."

"What new job?"

"Painting houses."

Christy didn't try to hide the shocked expression on her face this time. "What job painting houses?"

"I didn't tell you?"

"No."

"A guy at church asked if I wanted a part-time job helping him paint houses since the position at church is only part time until June. I told him I could start as soon as I graduated. It's only thirty hours a week."

"Todd, that's a lot."

"The money is good. We need it, Christy. I can work flexible hours around my schedule at church. It won't interfere with our counseling sessions on Tuesdays, and I have weekends off. Are you sure I didn't tell you about this?"

"I think I would remember." Christy adjusted her position in the passenger's seat. "This is exactly the kind of thing I was talking about last week at counseling when Ross asked if I felt any areas needed to be addressed right away. You don't tell me things, Todd."

"I thought I told you about this job."

"I don't remember ever hearing about it until this minute." Her voice was elevating. "And this is the first time you said anything about your dad being your best man."

"I didn't think it would be a problem," Todd said. "We have plenty of time before the wedding to do all this planning."

"Not if you're going to be working sixty hours a week!"

"It's not sixty hours. It's thirty for the painting job and twenty at church."

"Todd, you work more than twenty hours a week at church. You're there for meetings and on call whenever one of the teens or a parent wants to talk to you about something. Like last week when you never showed up for dinner because you took some of the guys skateboarding and ended up talking to one of them until eleven o'clock."

"That's how youth ministry goes sometimes. He had a lot of questions about God."

"I know." Christy tried to pull herself down a notch and be more understanding. "And that's what you're good at. I just want to make sure I'm still on your list of priorities once you start working a second job."

"You're at the very top," Todd said.

"Then you give me a time when we can look at invitations this week."

Todd seemed to be flipping through an invisible calendar in his mind. "What about next Saturday. I could meet you after the men's prayer breakfast at church."

"Next Saturday is the soonest you could go with me?"

"You could go by yourself or with Katie or somebody and find what you like and then show it to me. I don't have a strong preference on the invitations."

Christy felt herself about to boil over. Usually she swallowed her frustration and went along with whatever Todd suggested. Not this time. If she was going to learn to communicate with her future husband, it would be now or never.

"No, Todd!" she spouted. "I don't want to go shopping with Katie or my mom or anyone else. This is *our* wedding, and you need to participate in the planning. It makes me so mad when you sit back and expect me to do everything!"

"Okay, okay!" Todd held up a hand, as if to hold back the force of her words. "When do you want to go shopping for invitations?"

"I don't know," Christy said sullenly. She didn't like the way she felt right now. "Saturday, I guess, if that's the soonest you're available."

"Okay," Todd said. "Saturday. Around eleven. Is that okay with you?"

"Fine."

"Okay."

"Okay." Christy drew in a deep breath and tried not to burst into tears.

Am I going to have to wrestle you to the ground on everything that's important to me for the rest of our lives, Todd? We have to communicate better. I'm still mad; you're mad. When do things get better for us instead of worse?

CHAPTER 11

The first week of February turned out to be one of the worst weeks of Christy's life but, strangely, one of the best weeks, too.

On Monday she started classes for her last semester, only to find that one of the classes she needed to graduate had been cancelled. To take the class at the only other offered time meant readjusting her work schedule at the campus bookstore. She was cut back from twelve hours a week to eight, which meant less money.

On Tuesday, Todd didn't show up for their second premarital counseling session at church. He left a message with Pastor Ross saying he couldn't break away from his painting job and to please tell Christy he was sorry, but he would be there for sure next Tuesday.

Christy was stuck at church because she had gotten a ride there with Katie and then expected Todd to take her back to school. She decided against staying with Pastor Ross and discussing anything because she was so mad at Todd, she was certain she would later regret anything she said in the counseling session. She hadn't figured out how to express her feelings without exploding in a burst of pent-up fury.

Being too upset and too proud to ask for a ride back to campus, Christy decided to walk the five miles. She had walked everywhere during her year at school in Switzerland and felt certain the trek would help her to release her anger. All it gave her were blisters and more anger toward Todd for putting his job above her.

She rehearsed all kinds of conversations she planned to have with Todd once he showed his face. None of them were pretty.

To make matters worse, Todd didn't call her Tuesday night. Since he had moved in with Rick the day before he graduated, each time Christy called, she got Rick's voice mail. Finally she gave up and went to bed early. Katie was at work, and Christy was too upset to do homework or to embroider her wedding dress bodice.

Wednesday morning the phone rang at six-thirty. Christy was certain Todd was calling with an apology. But it was her mom, and her voice was low.

"Grandpa passed away last night," she said. "He had been complaining of stomach pains, and Grandma took him to the hospital yesterday afternoon. He died while they were doing exploratory surgery."

Christy already felt drained. This news sent her into a flood of tears. She loved her grandparents and suddenly regretted that she hadn't seen them since their fiftieth wedding anniversary back in Wisconsin the summer after she graduated from high school.

Marti called an hour later and said she had plane tickets reserved for Todd and Christy to attend the funeral on Saturday.

Friday night Todd and Christy took a red-eye flight with her parents, her brother, and Bob and Marti. They landed at O'Hare airport in Chicago at five o'clock in the morning. Their connecting flight to Madison left at six. After renting a van, they drove through a light snowstorm for three hours, arriving in Christy's hometown of Brightwater, Wisconsin, only a half hour before the funeral.

Christy and Todd hadn't talked about their unresolved tension. She was still upset with him, but those feelings had been set aside to deal with the grief of her grandfather's death.

Todd was the perfect gentleman as he met Christy's relatives for the first time. She knew her grandma was taken with him, even in the midst of her grief and shock.

Marti was on a mission to stay in Wisconsin until she had grilled every doctor and hospital staff member involved in caring for her father. She was certain his death was unnecessary and the result of human error. Instead of grieving her father's death, the way Christy's mom was, Marti was fighting for justice.

"It won't bring Grandpa back," David said as they stood around in the living room at Grandma's house after the funeral.

Everyone stared at him. David wasn't the sort to speak up in a group about anything.

"It will make things right," Marti declared. "And that's important in this world."

"But Grandpa isn't in this world anymore. He's in heaven," David said. "You'll see him again if you give your life to the Lord like I did."

Christy stared at her little brother. He sounded just like Todd. She could tell David's evaluation of the situation was the last thing Marti wanted to hear. She made a swift exit. Christy wasn't surprised to see Todd follow Marti. While Todd talked to Marti, Christy prepared to leave.

The rest of her family planned to stay in Brightwater until Monday, but Christy and Todd had a flight back that night so Todd could be at church in the morning. The snow had stopped, and Christy's grandma said she was certain the main roads would be plowed so they should make it to the airport just fine.

With their brief visit almost over, Christy wanted to have a special moment with her grandma. She drew her grandmother into the hallway, took her hands, and spoke condolences softly, telling her grandma how much she loved her.

"Thank you, precious. And thank you for coming all this way."

"I wish we could stay longer."

"No," Grandma said. "There will be so much commotion here for the next few days. Todd and you will have to come another time to see me when you can stay for a nice little visit. I would like that."

"You will come to our wedding in May, won't you?"

"I wouldn't miss it for anything. You have a real gem there, Christina. I'm happy for you both."

"Thank you, Grandma." Christy gave her grandmother's cool hands a squeeze. "Do you have any advice for me? For us?"

Christy was remembering her grandparents' fiftieth wedding anniversary party when she had asked them how they had met and how they had known they were right for each other. Her grandfather had offered some advice about making sure they came from the same background. Grandma, however, had told Christy to wait until things were difficult and then to ask herself if she still wanted to spend the rest of her life with this person.

That thought had come back to Christy several times during the past week while she was mad at Todd. She knew she still wanted to spend the rest of her years with him. She just wanted to get along better with Todd.

"It goes very fast." A tear glistened in Grandma's eye before finding its way down her wrinkled cheek. "It's over so soon. Keep short lists, honey. Learn to forgive quickly and go on because one day you'll wake up and find that somehow you got old when you weren't looking. Your lists won't matter at all then."

Christy wrapped her arms around her sweet grandmother and held her close in a warm hug. She could feel her grandma shaking as she sobbed quietly into Christy's shoulder. Tears flooded Christy's eyes.

She blinked them away and noticed a photograph only a few inches away from her. The hallway in which they stood was one long family photo gallery. The photo in front of Christy was a picture of her parents' wedding. Her mom was wearing the dress that now had been dissected to create Christy's wedding dress. Her parents looked so young. Mom had rich brown hair that fell gracefully onto her shoulders, and Dad stood tall, strong, and straight. Beside her parents stood Christy's grandmother and grandfather, dressed in their finest and smiling wildly.

For the first time, it really struck her that her grandfather was gone. She drew her grandmother closer and cried her eyes out.

Several hours later, when Christy and Todd were in their seats and the airplane was taking off, Todd took Christy's hand in his. He drew it to his lips and tenderly kissed the back of her hand again and again. She leaned her head against his shoulder and cried some more.

For the first half of the flight, they didn't speak. Todd had lifted the armrest between them, and they sat as close as they could, with her head on his shoulder and his head resting on hers. She stopped counting the number of times he pressed his lips to her hair, showering her with tiny kisses like snowflakes that melted as soon as they touched her.

Christy studied Todd's hands. The wounds from his horrible car accident had healed, but the scars remained. For the rest of his life, Todd would bear the marks of the places where the shattered glass had pierced his skin.

Christy traced the scars with her fingers, as if her homework assignment were to memorize each wound.

When they finally spoke to each other, Todd's deep voice rumbled through her ear all the way to her heart. "I'm sorry," he whispered.

Christy pulled up her head so she could face him. They were only inches apart as she whispered, "We're going to get old, Todd. We're going to get old together. Lord willing, we'll have fifty years or more like my grandparents did. When it comes to things that upset me, I promise to keep a short list. I'm determined to learn how to communicate with you in a way that allows me to express my opinion, but kindly. Love is patient and kind, right? I'm also determined to learn how to forgive you quickly. I don't ever want to hold as much against you as I have this week."

Todd stroked her cheek. A funny little expression played across his eyes.

"What were you just thinking?" Christy asked.

Todd looked into her eyes. "I said I was sorry because I was thinking about your grandfather. I didn't realize you had been mad at me all week."

Christy paused before answering. This was a good time for her to practice speaking the truth in love. "I was mad that you missed our counseling session. I'm not mad anymore."

"What about the invitations?" Todd asked.

"What about them?"

"We missed our appointment to look at invitations this morning," Todd said.

"We can look next week. Or I can look and tell you what I've found. Or you can look and tell me what you found. I have to learn to be more flexible."

"And I have to learn to be more dependable."

"Okay," Christy said with a tender smile.

"Okay." Todd returned the smile. His lips traveled the tiny distance that separated them, and he met her mouth with a warm kiss.

"Excuse me," the flight attendant said, leaning toward them. "Did you want chicken or lasagna?"

Christy straightened herself and made a quick decision. "Chicken."

"I'll have the same," Todd echoed.

As they ate, they discussed their busy schedules and how they could find more time to be together. This semester was the fullest for Christy, and as she had predicted, Todd often worked more than fifty hours a week. They talked about what could be adjusted in both their schedules and ended up coming to the same conclusion. Every Saturday would be theirs. Their weekly schedules left them little time to see each other, so every Saturday between then and Saturday, May 22, would be set aside for them to do whatever they wanted or needed to do together.

"Do you realize," Todd said, "that's only thirteen Saturdays? Or is it fourteen?" He moved his fingers as he recounted.

"It's not a lot, no matter how many it is," Christy said. "Whatever I can do without you, I'll try to do. I'll make certain I tell you all the details, though."

"Are you sure that will be all right? Because I can try to adjust things if you want me to go along shopping or something."

"No, it doesn't bother me now that I have a more realistic view. I was being sentimental, thinking we should do everything together and trying to make a memory out of every wedding detail. I've watched too many movies. This is reality. You're working fifty hours a week so we'll have enough money to eat after we're married; I'm finishing my toughest semester so far and working part time. We have to make adjustments."

"Your mom and your aunt are dying to be involved and do more of the planning. Can you delegate some things to them?"

Christy handed her finished meal tray to the flight attendant and closed her tray table. Todd did the same.

"You're right," Christy said. "I'll go down the list and delegate like crazy as soon as they get back from Wisconsin."

"Good. Do we have plans already for what we're going to work on next Saturday?"

Christy wasn't sure how to answer that. It was the weekend before Todd's birthday, and she had been thinking about a party for him. Nothing had been arranged yet, but she wanted to have a big surprise party.

"I'm not sure yet," she answered.

"I thought maybe you and I could go to the beach for the day. We could cook breakfast on the beach, and I could try out the surfboard my dad gave me for Christmas."

"It's February," Christy said. "Won't it be cold?"

"Yes."

She knew that was a poor excuse if she was trying to dissuade him. He hadn't been surfing for months, and she realized he was eager to get back in the water. They had cooked their breakfast on the beach in cold weather more than once. Christy decided to come right out with it.

"It's right before your birthday, and I—"

"I know. That's why I want to go. Just you and me. Breakfast on the beach. What do you say, Kilikina? That's all I want for my birthday."

Christy decided not to mention the plans she had been formulating for his surprise party. Todd's idea of a memorable party obviously was a private affair.

"Sounds perfect," Christy said. "I'll organize the food."

"That's what I was counting on." Todd reached for her hand, stroking her Forever ID bracelet with his thumb.

They were quiet a minute while Christy readjusted details in her mind. It could work. She could stay at her aunt and uncle's, and she and Todd could have an early breakfast. That would leave them the entire afternoon to look at wedding cakes and invitations and—

"Kilikina," Todd murmured, breaking into her planning. He drew her hand to his lips and kissed her ring finger. "I just decided something."

"What?"

Todd adjusted his position and reached into the back pocket of his jeans. He pulled out a wadded-up tissue and held it in his hand.

"I was going to do this on the way home from my graduation dinner, but neither of us was in a very good mood that night. Then I thought I'd take you to a fancy restaurant this weekend, but here we are on an airplane eating chicken. If I were a patient man, I'd wait till next Saturday on the beach or come up with a special plan for Valentine's Day. But I've waited too long, and I'm too eager for you to have this."

Todd unfolded the wad of tissue, and there, in the crumpled nest in his hand, sat Christy's engagement ring.

"Marry me, Kilikina." Todd slipped the ring on Christy's finger. "Marry me and grow old with me."

At that moment, flying thirty thousand feet somewhere over Colorado, Christy knew more deeply and more profoundly than ever that she always would be in love with Todd Spencer. The intensity of her love for him at that second made it seem as if she hadn't even begun to love him until now.

"Yes," she whispered. "I will marry you."

They kissed a long, slow, promise-sealing kiss.

Christy glanced at her hand on which she now wore a glorious, one-of-a-kind engagement ring. "It's beautiful."

"Yeah, I was real happy with how it turned out. It fits you perfectly."

"Yes, it does. In every way."

Even though they had been engaged before this moment, and even though Christy never had thought she needed a ring to prove she was promised to Todd, the ring seemed to change everything for her. It reminded her that one day very soon she and Todd would become man and wife. It also was evidence to everyone who noticed it that she was taken. She was going to be given in marriage very soon. She was loved and desired and waiting for her wedding day.

Christy jotted all those thoughts in her diary on Thursday night of that week. Katie still wasn't back from work, which was typical. Things still were moving along at a steady pace with Rick and Katie, and she seemed happier than ever.

With Katie gone so often and Todd not around on campus for Christy to meet in the cafeteria for meals, she found herself spending a lot of quiet time in her dorm room doing homework, working on her embroidery, and thinking.

At ten o'clock that night, Christy put away her embroidery and crawled into bed, full of thoughts. She pulled out her diary to record what Todd had said to the group of teenagers he had taught Sunday morning. He had told them about giving Christy her ring on the plane the night before and how her face had lit up.

Then Todd made the most incredible analogy between us being engaged and the way God views us. In the Bible God describes the church as the Bride of Christ. Todd said the Holy Spirit is like the engagement ring that God gives us as evidence of His promise that He will always love us and one day will come and take us to be His bride to live with Him forever.

It was amazing the way the students responded. Todd said that weddings on earth are a reflection of the great wedding feast of the Lamb that will happen when the Lord comes to take His bride, the Church, to be with Him.

I realized more deeply what a mystery that is. I felt so different and so much more in love with Todd after he placed the ring on my finger. I find myself growing more deeply in love with Christ as I see these parallels acted out in my life. Christ wants me and is waiting for me one day to be with Him forever. Until that day, His Holy Spirit in my life is evidence to others that I am promised to Him and I am waiting for Him.

That verse in Ephesians 4:30 makes more sense to me than it ever did before. "Do not grieve the Holy Spirit of God, with whom you were sealed for the day of redemption." Todd told the class it would be like my covering my ring finger with duct tape because I didn't want anyone to know I was engaged. He said that as my fiancé, it would break his heart if I did that. Yet we do the same thing when we don't let the Holy Spirit work in our lives.

Todd's charge to the class was to boldly let the whole world know that we're spoken for, that we belong to Christ. Then he said, "But if you're really in love with the Bridegroom, people will know instantly when they look at your face. Just look at Christy."

The whole group turned to stare at me, but I didn't care. My face and my heart were so brightly lit on fire with my love for God and Todd that I didn't feel at all embarrassed. I felt as if I were floating on clouds.

Christy stopped writing for a moment and thought about how clouds figured into the future of all Christians everywhere.

That's what's going to happen when Christ comes for His bride, isn't it? He's going to meet us in the clouds.

Her thoughts reminded her of a certain magnificent early morning, when she and Todd had met in the chapel and had walked in the meadow. She had felt as if the clouds had come to earth that morning.

Reaching for her Bible, Christy looked up all the references to clouds she could find. She remembered 1 Thessalonians 4:17 was the one about being caught up in the clouds and meeting the Lord in the air. A lump grew in her throat as she read the last part of the verse and underlined it. "And so we will be with the Lord forever."

Christy grabbed her diary and wrote,

Todd was right about what he said to the teens. My brother was right about what he said to Aunt Marti after the funeral. My grandma was right, too. What we're doing here isn't about this life only. The real us, our souls, will last forever. God wants us to say yes to His Son so we can be with Him forever. It's the ultimate "I do." The eternal "I promise."

Overwhelmed by the intense insights, Christy put away her diary and turned out the light. Then quietly, she turned her face into her pillow and cried. Part of her tears were a good-bye and I'll-see-you-in-heaven to her grandfather; part were for her joyous love for Todd; part were for the mystery of God's loving her and wanting her to be with Him forever. The final batch of tears was for her aunt, who still hadn't said yes to Christ. Christy knew that according to God's Word, Aunt Marti wouldn't be with Him forever unless she surrendered her heart to Him.

The door opened, and Katie slipped in, humming. "You awake?" she whispered.

"Hmm," Christy responded. She didn't want Katie to turn on the overhead light and keep Christy up talking all night. Yet, if Katie had any big announcements to make, Christy didn't want to miss them.

"I'm leaving early in the morning for the Natural Food Fest in San Diego. Rick is picking me up at six. I just wanted you to know."

"Mmm-hmm," Christy answered.

"Are you okay?"

"Mmm-hmm."

"Good. Everything is going great with Rick. I'll see you sometime tomorrow night."

"Mmm-hmm."

Christy fell asleep to the happy sound of Katie humming her way into her pajamas.

CHAPTER 12

The calendar that hung on Christy's wall in her dorm room stared back innocently at her as she tried to find some white space to write down her scheduled trip to the dentist. She had made the appointment at work that afternoon without the benefit of consulting her crowded calendar.

"March twelve," she muttered to herself. "How did it get to be March twelve already? If I go to the dentist at four o'clock next Tuesday, that means I'll be late for our counseling appointment at church."

Christy chewed on the end of her pen and tried to decide if she should ask Todd for the car that day or for him to take off from work to drive her to the dentist. They could reschedule their counseling appointment for a little later.

Christy was trying hard to remain flexible. It was getting more and more difficult to coordinate schedules, what with Todd working so much. The past few weeks had flown by. The only fun time the two of them had managed to fit in was their Saturday breakfast on the beach. The morning had turned out to be clear, crisp, and sunny, and they had enjoyed every minute of it. Christy had bought fifteen small gifts that she had wrapped for Todd. He opened the first one at seven o'clock while the bacon was sizzling over the dancing fire. It was wax for his surfboard.

From then on, every hour on the hour, she gave Todd another little present until nine o'clock that night. The last gift was a picture of the two of them that Tracy had taken years ago on the beach. They were sitting with the rest of the gang, and the late-afternoon sun shone on their faces just right. Tracy had captured them on film at the very second Todd and Christy were exchanging glances. Their expressions were lit up with the glimmer of wonder and joy at the birth of first love.

Christy didn't remember the picture being taken, but the morning they had eaten omelets at Doug and Tracy's, Tracy had pulled it out of a photo album and given it to Christy.

She loved the picture and had made a special mat for it by gluing on dried, browned carnation petals extracted from the first bouquet Todd had given her. The flowers had been stored for more than five years in an old Folgers coffee can and smelled a little funny. In her nicest printing, Christy had written at the bottom of the mat, *I hold you in my heart. Forever, Your Kilikina.*

Todd got choked up when he opened his final gift and stared at the picture. "We were so young." Then he held Christy close and told her this was the best birthday he had ever had.

The warm memories of that special day had been Christy's only company in the midst of her overly full schedule. The only good thing was that the time was going by quickly.

Every free moment Christy had, she spent working on embroidering her wedding gown. She nearly was finished with the string of tiny white forget-me-nots that lined the neckline and was trying to decide if she wanted to put the time into adding the flowers on the sleeves or to leave them plain. The embroidery was taking a lot longer than she had thought it would.

Katie's opinion was that it didn't matter. She said no one would notice the flowers on the sleeves. Sierra, however, said the little things would matter the most to Christy on her wedding day. At least, that's how it had been for Sierra's sister when she got married.

Sierra had come to Christy's dorm room two nights ago and had arrived just in time to hear Katie's opinion on the sleeves. A freshman, Sierra was one of the most free-spirited young women Christy had ever known. Katie and Christy had met Sierra three years ago, when they had shared a room in England while on a missions trip.

Sierra's visit to the dorm room had been prompted by her need to ask if Christy could pick up Sierra from her job at the local grocery store Friday night.

The last thing Christy needed was to add anything to her brimming schedule. But she said yes to Sierra because Christy knew she would have the car since Todd was going on an overnight backpacking trip with some of the guys from the youth group. Even though the trip had been scheduled before Christy and Todd had made their agreement to spend every Saturday together, Todd had offered to cancel the trip. But Christy thought it would be better if he went. She planned to work on wedding plans with Marti and her mom on Saturday.

Marti was back from her extended stay in Wisconsin and had dropped her investigation of the hospital. Apparently, when she had interviewed the surgeon, he told her he had found an inoperable tumor in Grandpa's stomach. Apparently, it had been there for some time and must have bothered him, but he never complained. So by the time it was discovered, it was too late to do anything.

Christy's mom said that Marti had accepted the facts better than any of them had expected. She had dropped the idea of filing charges and had come home ready to dive in to plans for Todd and Christy's wedding. Todd's having asked Bob and Marti to sit on his side in the front row seemed to give Marti even more incentive to be involved.

At the appointed time Friday night, Christy showed up at the grocery store to find Sierra already waiting out front. Sierra was easy to spot because she had long, wild, curly blond hair, and she dressed in unique outfits. Tonight Sierra wore a mid-calf skirt that appeared to be made from neckties sewn together. Her feet were clad in the same pair of cowboy boots she had worn in England when Christy first met her.

"Have you been waiting long?" Christy opened the car door from the inside.

"No, only a few minutes. I finished early because I ran out of sausage."

Christy gave Sierra a strange look. "The grocery store ran out of sausage?"

"No, I did. I was demonstrating. Didn't I tell you that's what I was doing? I go to different grocery stores and hand out samples of whatever the company tells me to. Tonight it was sausages, but they told me only to use twenty packages. I didn't figure out until halfway through that they wanted me to cut the sausages into little pieces and stick toothpicks in them. I was passing out entire sausages, and people were standing there waiting, like I was working at a free hot dog stand."

Christy laughed. "Sounds like a fun job."

"It's perfect for me, except for the transportation. I hate having to bum rides off someone. I really appreciate your doing this for me, Christy."

"No problem. It worked out fine." Her plan was to zip Sierra back to campus and then drive up to her aunt's in Newport Beach since her mom was already there. That way they could start their planning early in the morning.

"Your skirt is adorable," Christy said as she headed out of the parking lot. "Did you make it?"

"My mom helped me. We worked on it over Christmas vacation. I had a short skirt made out of ties, but it got ruined a couple of summers ago. These ties were my grandpa's. Aren't they hilarious? Look at this one."

Sierra pointed to a green-and-brown-striped tie that ran down her left side. It had tiny orange curlicues and thin blue triangles on top of the stripes.

"I guess it would match about anything with all those colors in it," Christy said.

Sierra laughed. "Or not match anything because of all the colors in it. My Granna Mae had a story to tell me about every one of these ties while we were sewing them together. She has serious memory lapses and gets confused and disoriented, but she could remember every minute detail of places she and Grandpa had gone and things they had done when he was wearing these ties."

Christy told Sierra how her grandpa had passed away last month and how much it made her think about the brevity of life.

"I know what you mean," Sierra said. "I've been thinking about that this semester because I've had some big decisions to make."

"By any chance would those decisions be about relationships?" Christy asked.

"Sort of. Are you hungry?" Sierra asked.

"Hungry?"

"Well, The Golden Calf is closed by now, and I've been standing in the grocery store cooking sausages for the past three and a half hours. I could go for something substantial to eat. If you have the time, I'd love to hear your opinion on a few things."

Christy couldn't remember the last time she had hung out with a girl friend for an evening. She could readjust her plans and make the hour and a half drive to Newport Beach early in the morning. After all, she had just made a little speech about the brevity of life. This would be a good time to *carpe* the *diem*.

"Sure," Christy said. "Where should we go?"

"How about The Dove's Nest? Randy and his band are playing there tonight. That's why I couldn't bum a ride from my usual source."

"Okay, it'll be kind of refreshing to see my roommate."

"You and Katie never see each other?" Sierra surmised.

"We're both pretty busy."

"I told my sister that Katie and Rick were getting really close, and she was shocked. Did you know that Rick tried to flirt with Tawni at Doug and Tracy's wedding?"

Christy smiled as she pulled onto the freeway. "I'm not surprised."

"But Katie says he's changed a lot."

"Oh yes, Rick has changed a lot. God has been working in big ways."

"You know what?" Sierra said. "I think Katie and Rick are good for each other. I wouldn't be surprised if they ended up getting married."

"Why do you say that?" Christy asked.

"They're both so vibrant," Sierra said. "The few times I've seen them together, a sort of electricity flows between them. They spark each other. Katie is energetic all by herself, but when she's with Rick, she's brighter than ever, and so is he. Without her, he's kind of blah."

"That's an interesting way of putting it." Christy had never known anyone to describe Rick as blah. Sierra impressed Christy as someone who didn't let the outward shell of a person distract from the true self, which was hidden within.

They arrived at The Dove's Nest to find the parking lot packed.

"We might not be able to find a place to sit in there," Christy said.

"This is good for Randy and the band," Sierra observed.

"And for Rick."

They entered and spotted a bunch of people they knew from Rancho. Sierra waved at her roommate, Vicki, and Christy said, "Do you want to sit with their group?"

"I'd rather just sit with you so we can talk. Let's see if the couch is open on the bookstore side. Last time I was here people were eating on the couches by the fire."

Christy followed Sierra into the book portion of the store known as The Ark. The fireplace was open to both the café side and the bookstore side, and a couch and two cozy chairs circled around it on The Ark side. The couch was open.

"Perfect!" Christy said. "Would you like to save the couch for us while I order some food?"

Randy's band had just finished a song, and applause rose from the café. Christy was glad they weren't sitting in the noisy café. They could still hear Randy's band from The Ark but could carry on a conversation, as well.

"We could take turns," Sierra suggested. "I don't know what I want."

"Okay." Christy went first, thinking how nice it was to hear someone else say she didn't know what she wanted. That had always been one of Christy's worst problems when ordering at restaurants. She had gotten much better, though.

Tonight she knew she wanted whatever the chef's special was. Katie had been raving about the fabulous chef they recently had hired. Tonight Miguel was offering artichoke pizza with sun-dried tomatoes. It sounded a little unusual, but Christy decided to give it a try. She stepped up to the counter, and Katie noticed her for the first time.

"Chris, when did you get here?"

"Just a few minutes ago. I brought Sierra. Looks like a busy night for you guys."

"Most people are only ordering coffee drinks and desserts, so the kitchen hasn't been swamped. You should try the artichoke pizza. It's really good."

"That's exactly what I wanted. What else do you recommend?"

"I think a small Caesar salad would go nicely with that," Katie said. "Do you want to try my favorite latte?"

"Sure. We're over on the couch in The Ark."

"I'll bring it to you," Katie said. "What does Sierra want?"

"She's going to place her own order."

Rick stepped up behind Christy and greeted her with a friendly hug. "Did Katie tell you the good news?"

Christy turned to Katie with wide eyes. "No," Christy said. "What good news?"

"Her tea won an honorable mention at the food fair."

"Big whoop," Katie said. "They gave out ten honorable mentions. I'm going to perfect the blend and enter it again next year."

"I thought it was great," Rick said. "Out of thirty-seven entries, she made the top ten. Tell her that's pretty good."

"It really is, Katie," Christy said. "Congratulations."

"Thanks."

"Did Todd come with you?" Rick asked. "I thought he was backpacking this weekend."

"He is. I'm here with Sierra."

"Girls' night out, huh?" Rick turned to Katie. "Have you taken your dinner break yet?"

"No."

"Do you want to take it now?" Rick said. "Dinner is on me, for all three of you."

"Make that two pizzas, Miguel," Katie called out. "And could you put extra parmesan on mine? Thanks."

"Thanks, Rick," Christy said. "I didn't expect you to pay for us."

"My pleasure. I'd treat you more often, but you never come in."

"I know. This has been the busiest time of my life."

"Todd's too," Rick said. "We never seem to be home at the same time. Sometime the four of us will have to do something together."

"That would be fun," Christy said.

"Hey, tell Todd I was able to work out the deal with the guy my dad knows at the tux shop. It's Burton's Tuxedo Shop. They're in the shopping center down at the stoplight. Next to the video store. I went in today and got measured. All you and Todd have to do is select the style and give him the measurements for the other groomsmen."

"Okay," Christy said slowly.

Katie linked her arm in Christy's. "Come on. I only have an hour."

As they walked away, Christy asked, "Katie, is Rick going to be a groomsman in my wedding?"

"You crack me up, Christy! Of course he is. Todd asked him like three weeks ago. You must be losing it if you can't remember such details."

Christy sat down next to Sierra on the couch and tried hard to remember if Todd had said anything to her. The last Christy had heard, Todd was having his dad for his best man and Doug for his groomsman. She was having Katie as her maid of honor and Tracy for her bridesmaid. They had agreed weeks ago on only two attendants to keep things simple. The bridesmaids' dresses already were ordered.

Since when did Rick enter the picture?

Christy decided to remain calm and not to get mad at Todd—yet. If he had asked Rick to be in their wedding, he must have had a good reason. Maybe Doug had backed out. Or maybe, since Rick and Todd were sharing an apartment now, he had felt obligated to include Rick in the wedding party.

If Rick is going to be a groomsman along with Doug, then I need another bridesmaid. I wonder if I should ask Sierra now or wait until Todd gets back from his trip.

Katie, Sierra, and Christy sat by the fire and ate while Randy and the band filled the air with original songs that had a wonderfully fresh sound. Christy liked the pizza but told Katie they should have split one because she was full after the salad.

"I'll get doggie bags for us," Katie said. "It'll be just as good in the morning. Breakfast pizza! I'll be right back."

Christy leaned close to Sierra. "We haven't talked about relationships and stuff, like we started to in the car. I didn't know if you wanted to talk privately, or what. We could talk more on the way back to school."

"It's not as if I'm struggling with some huge problem. I just need some input. I'd love to hear what Katie has to say, too."

"Did I hear my name?" Katie asked, returning with a plastic box in her hand.

"I was telling Christy that I could use your advice," Sierra said.

"You came to the right place," Katie said. "It just so happens that my assistant and I are the advice queens. I think Christy is tired of hearing about my life; it'll be refreshing to hear about yours. And since you offered, why don't you start with Paul. What's happening with him?"

"Well, I can summarize that relationship with one of your famous phrases, Katie. Paul and I are 'P.O.'s.' Do you remember the little club we started in England?"

Katie laughed. "Pals Only! I forgot all about that."

"Of course you did," Sierra teased. "You dropped your honorary membership when you started going out with Rick."

"It was unintentional." Katie held up her hand in self-defense. "It was God's idea, not mine. Believe me."

"Oh, I believe you," Sierra said. "It's good to see you guys together, too. It seems natural and like the relationship is alive and growing. It helps me to remember that's how healthy relationships should be."

Christy watched Sierra's face for an indication of what that statement meant. "Did you feel it wasn't going that way for Paul and you?"

Sierra nodded. "How much do you want to hear about Paul?"

"Everything," Katie said.

"Okay," Sierra said. "But you guys asked for it."

CHAPTER 13

Sierra set her tea on the low table in front of the fire and began her story. "You guys know that Paul and I are sort of related now that my sister is married to his brother. Our families were all together at Christmas, and it just became clear to me while we were sitting on the floor watching a video that there's nothing boyfriend-girlfriend between Paul and me. I thought there was for a long time. I hoped there was. I dreamed about what it would be like if there was. And I think both of us gave it a noble effort after he came back from Scotland. But it's not electric."

"Electric?" Katie questioned.

"You know what I mean. I know you know what I mean."

Katie nodded and exchanged glances with Christy.

"Whatever it is that makes a couple realize something deeper and lasting exists between them. Well, I've come to the conclusion Paul and I don't have that . . . whatever it is. We are good, solid friends. He doesn't find me fascinating, and I think he's way too quiet and introspective."

"Have you and Paul talked about this?" Christy asked. "I mean, does he feel the same way?"

"Yes. We went for a long walk at the park the day after Christmas and talked about everything. He started out sounding like he was going to apologize for not being in love with me or something. I stopped him before he said too much and told him how I felt. I told him I was restless, for lack of a better term. I pointed out he was contemplative, which is fine, but it's not a good match for someone like me. He said he felt bad because he had thought something would happen between us, but it just didn't go anywhere. He blamed himself for insisting we take it slow in the beginning and lay a foundation of being good friends.

"I told him that was the best choice because now we are good friends, and I think we'll always be close friends. But that's all."

"You sound like you're okay with that," Christy said.

"I am. I feel free now. I didn't feel free for a long time. I kept thinking there should be something more with Paul. You guys know how much I tortured myself trying to figure out what should happen next with him. I spent months probing my heart, trying to decide how I truly felt about him. It was a long journey that only brought me back to where I started. And that's okay. It's good."

"If I've learned one thing," Katie said, sipping her latte and looking settled in her own understanding, "it's that God writes a different story for each of our lives. Sometimes you think you know what's going to happen, but then the plot takes an unexpected turn."

"And sometimes you have to end one chapter before you can start the next," Sierra said. "I have so many dreams, you guys. I want to travel. I want to be free to go wherever I want to go for the next season of my life. I've already signed up for an education extension program that Rancho offers. And guess where it's held?"

"Where?" Katie asked.

"Brazil! Doesn't that sound like a fun place to go?"

"Sounds like you're going to become a world traveler," Christy said.

"It started with that trip to England, when I met you guys. Then, Christy, you invited me to Switzerland with you and your aunt. I got the bug. I love traveling."

Christy could picture Sierra trekking around the globe in her cowboy boots. She definitely had an adventuresome spirit.

"When I started college last semester, it was strange. I had been so excited to come to Rancho. But then, there I was, sitting in classes, and all I could think about was getting out of there and traveling. I kept running into people on campus who had been to exotic places. I would tell myself I should concentrate on finishing my freshman year and getting serious about Paul. I thought I should try to arrange a normal life, like my sister and the rest of my friends have. But you know what? It didn't fit. I never felt at peace. After Paul and I had our talk at Christmas, I felt free. That's the only way I can explain it. Nothing is holding me back. It's like you said, Katie, God is writing my life story, and it's different for me than it is for anyone else."

"You're right, Sierra," Christy said. "God is going to make your path clear."

"More than that," Katie added. " 'God will fulfill his purpose for you.' That's a promise. Psalm 138. Verse 8."

Sierra sipped the last of her tea and nodded. "You know what, you guys? This is the first time I've sat down to explain my feelings as one complete thought. When I listen to myself talking to you like this, it makes sense. It doesn't sound as if I'm cutting my strings and flying off like a kite."

Christy gave Sierra a comforting smile. "And what if you are cutting your strings? If God created you to be a kite, then the only right answer for you, the only obedient response, would be to go fly—be free. It shouldn't matter if other people understand. You're the one who knows in your heart of hearts when you're obeying His direction. He's the One who will lift you up and send you soaring."

"Thank you so much, Christy. I needed to hear that." In a less-than-graceful gesture, Sierra reached over and hugged Christy around the neck. Then Sierra hugged Katie. "You two are amazing."

Christy noticed some movement out of the corner of her eye that made her hold her breath. Rick had positioned himself a few feet away. His gaze was fixed on Katie, and he seemed to be enchanted with her.

A happy, settled feeling came over Christy's heart. *Go ahead, Rick Doyle, admire Katie all you want. She's amazing, isn't she? And so are you. I have absolutely no doubt the Lord will fulfill His purpose for the two of you.*

Early the next morning, Christy stopped by the campus coffee shop for a cup of coffee to drink on the way to Aunt Marti's. She picked up her mail from her campus mailbox and found a card from her grandma. Reading as she walked back to the car, Christy checked the last few lines twice since they didn't immediately make sense to her. Her grandmother had thanked Christy and Todd for coming to the funeral. Then she wrote,

Christina, I was surprised to see how much you have grown to resemble Martha with your way of keeping on top of things. Make sure you leave room in your life for peace. I'm sure Todd will encourage you in this area.

Christy thought her grandmother must have gotten confused when she said Christy resembled Aunt Marti. *No way am I like Aunt Marti. Grandma must have meant Margaret, my mom, but she wrote "Martha." I hope Grandma isn't experiencing memory failure the way Sierra's Granna Mae is.*

It took Christy an hour and forty-five minutes to drive to Newport Beach. When she arrived, Margaret and Martha, the two sisters, were standing in the kitchen, peering at a book on the counter and having a good laugh. Christy noticed the list Marti had printed out, waiting for them on the counter.

"What's so funny?" Christy asked.

"It's more of those cakes that are designed for each couple based on how they met," Mom said, pointing to a picture on the counter. This cake was in the shape of a horse's head. The statue of the bride and groom was stuck in the icing between the horse's ears.

"Let me guess," Christy said. "They met at a horse race."

"No, a riding stable. They've been horsing around ever since!" Marti said gleefully.

Christy shook her head at her aunt's attempt at a joke. Marti's delight in her role as wedding "director" affirmed to Christy that Todd was right about delegating more details to Marti.

"I hope this isn't our only choice of bakeries." Christy turned the next few pages. "I would prefer a simple white wedding cake. And definitely without the plastic bride and groom."

Mom turned to Marti. "I told you Christy would know what she wanted. Once she's organized, she knows exactly what she wants."

"I understand that," Marti said. "That's why I said I wanted to help her get organized. I hope you brought your list so we can compare notes, Christy."

Christy nodded. *Was my grandmother right? Am I more like my aunt than I realized?*

"Where's Uncle Bob this morning?" Christy asked.

"He had a men's breakfast at church," Marti said.

Christy noticed Aunt Marti didn't sound disgusted about Bob's involvement in church the way she used to. That was a good sign that her heart was softening. At least, Christy hoped it was softening.

"You didn't want him here today to help make decisions, did you?" Marti said. "These details are beyond him. Whatever we decide, he'll be happy."

Mom smiled at Christy. "That sounds like someone else we know."

"Todd," Christy said flatly.

Todd is just like Uncle Bob. I'm like Marti. Opposites attract. But I can't be like Aunt Marti! I don't want to spend my life micromanaging everyone around me!

Christy pulled up a stool at the kitchen counter and sat down. *This is a terrible revelation. I've become my aunt!*

"I only kept these pictures to show you for fun," Marti said, placing them to the side. "Of course, I understand you want a more traditional cake. I have those pictures right here."

What was it my grandmother said about making room for peace? That's what I need to do. I have to learn to be at peace with myself and with people around me. That's what's missing from my aunt's life. She doesn't have peace.

Christy silently prayed as Marti showed her pictures of traditional wedding cakes. A peculiar peace came over Christy. It was the reaffirming sense that God had created her to be the way she was for a reason. Wasn't that what she had told Sierra last night? It was time to take her own advice and to become her own person.

No, that's not right. That's what my aunt used to say to me when I was a teenager. She said I needed to be my own person and to my own self be true. But that doesn't bring peace. The only right way to live my life is to be God's person. To fully become the woman God created me to be, tidiness issues and all. There's nothing wrong with being organized and, as my grandma said, "on top of things." As long as I don't run ahead of God and others. What matters is whether I live a life at peace with God. That's the only way I'll be at peace with myself and with others.

Christy leaned back from the kitchen counter and drew in a deep, wobbly breath.

"Are you okay?" Mom turned away from the cake pictures to look at Christy.

A smile started in the secret corner of Christy's heart and scooted all the way to her face, where it broke through with all its radiant, peace-filled implications.

"More than okay," Christy said. "I think I might be better than I've ever been. I'm not a kite like Sierra. But now I know how to go fly—be free. In here," she said, patting her heart. "I think I finally understand who I am."

CHAPTER 14

―――――――――

"Whatever are you rambling about?" Marti scrutinized Christy's big smile.

"Nothing," Christy said and then quickly corrected herself. "Actually, it's everything. It's God. He just showed me something, and I understand myself more clearly than ever."

Both Mom and Marti looked at her.

Christy giggled. "It's okay. I can tell you about it later. Go ahead, Aunt Marti. What were you saying about this cake?"

Marti cleared her throat. She seemed a bit uncomfortable that God had interrupted her presentation to have a counseling session with Christy.

It's okay, Aunt Marti. I understand your frustration more than I ever have before. Todd was right. The Bridegroom is here. And He will show up at our wedding no matter what kind of cake we have. But we can plan the cake and everything else and still live in peace. We just have to let God be in control, not us.

"I was saying, what do you think of lemon cake instead of white? They use a marvelous almond filling instead of that pasty white frosting." With that, Marti went full speed ahead with her collected information on wedding cakes. She had two cake samples for Christy and her mom to try that she had picked up while interviewing pastry chefs that week.

Christy liked the one with the raspberry filling the best. Marti questioned Christy twice before making a note of Christy's choice.

Without a moment's hesitation, Marti moved on to the flowers, presenting Christy with at least fifty pictures of possible bouquets.

"I'd like white carnations," Christy said when she looked at the first picture.

Marti ignored her and turned to a gigantic bouquet of red roses laced with baby's breath.

"I'd like white carnations," Christy said again after they had gone through half of the pictures. "White carnations with some baby's breath would be just fine."

Marti nodded and moved right on to the next stack of pictures, pointing out an exotic bouquet with miniature white roses and large white gardenias.

Christy said again, "I'd like white carnations."

"Christy, darling, white carnations are so plain."

Christy's mom stepped in. "Todd's first bouquet for her was white carnations."

"I know that," Marti snapped. "I was there. But this isn't a high school date to the prom. This is their wedding. Why not consider a variety of flowers, such as this bouquet?" She pointed to a mixture of purple, blue, and yellow flowers in a sweet, small bouquet.

Suddenly Christy had an idea. "What about this? I would really love this bouquet, but not with all the bright colors. Could you have the florist make a bouquet of all white flowers?"

"Of course," Marti said.

"I'd like it to have white carnations, baby's breath, those tiny white roses, some gardenias, and white plumeria."

"Now, that sounds like an elegant assortment." Marti reached for her pen to write it all down.

"But I don't want it to be huge like some of these. I want a small, happy, little bouquet."

"Wedding bouquets are supposed to be dramatic," Marti said. "The bouquet is used to complete the gown and veil and pull it all together in one focal point."

"My gown isn't going to be dramatic. It's simple. I think my bouquet should be simple, too."

"And what about your veil?" Marti asked.

Christy glanced at her mom. "We haven't decided on that yet. I know I want a sheer veil that hangs over my face, but I don't know what I want to use as the headpiece."

"A hat, perhaps?"

"No."

"I've got it!" Marti flipped through a stack of magazines she hadn't presented to Christy yet. "You would look adorable in one of these wreaths." She pulled out a Hawaiian magazine and pointed to the girl on the cover. "The flowers are fixed in a wreath that you wear on your head like a crown. You could place the wreath over the veil."

"I love it!" Christy exclaimed.

"You do?" Marti looked shocked that one of her ideas was received on the first pitch.

"Yes! Todd wanted me to wear flowers in my hair. That would be perfect. I'd want it to be all white flowers and narrower than the one shown here. Oh, Aunt Marti, what a perfect suggestion!"

Marti leaned against the counter and tilted her head as she examined Christy. "I believe that is the first time I've made a suggestion you've been enthusiastic about."

"That's because it's a great idea! It's perfect, don't you think, Mom?"

Mom looked a little more serious. "I'm wondering how difficult it would be to find a florist who can do something like that and make it turn out right."

"That's not a problem," Marti said. "Bob knows a florist on Maui. We'll have him make it and ship it to arrive the next day so the flowers will still be fresh and carry that irresistible island fragrance. You know, Christy, you really must use tuberose."

"Are those the little white flowers they use to make leis? The ones that smell so good?"

"Yes. And they're small. Much smaller than the plumeria. You might have trouble with the plumeria staying fresh. They turn brown when they're touched a lot, you know."

Christy felt her heart swelling with glee. Her bouquet was going to be gorgeous, and this was the perfect solution to her veil. Todd would love that she was wearing Hawaiian flowers in her hair. Christy knew she would have a hard time not telling Todd what her complete outfit was going to look like. But she knew she must keep it a secret; he would have to wait and be surprised when he saw her. She had a feeling he would be more than surprised. Todd would be amazed as only a man in love can be, a man who has waited for the day when he would see his bride dressed all in white from her heart to her toes coming down the aisle toward him.

Christy's mom continued to study the pictures on the counter. "The small white flowers in your wreath will go nicely with the flowers you're embroidering on your dress."

"What dress is she embroidering?" Marti asked.

"Her wedding dress," Mom said. "Or perhaps I should say my wedding dress."

"Our wedding dress." Christy gave her mom a warm smile. "Would you like to see it, Aunt Marti?"

"Why didn't I know about this?" Marti asked. "I was under the impression you hadn't made a decision on your gown."

"No, we have the wedding gown all figured out." Christy pulled the bodice from her overnight bag and held it up for her aunt and Mom to see. She had decided to leave the sleeves plain and was happy now with that choice because the emphasis was on the bodice's delicate flowers.

"You embroidered this?" Marti examined the careful stitches in the delicate string of forget-me-nots. "Why, Christina, it's exquisite."

"Thank you."

"This was from your dress, Margaret?"

"Yes. You did a beautiful job on this, Christy. I brought the skirt, and I'm ready to baste it to the bodice whenever you're ready for a fitting."

"I'm ready," Christy said. "Oh, and did you bring the addresses for the invitations, Mom?"

"Yes, I brought them."

"Good, because I picked up the invitations this week. They only took two weeks to print, which was sooner than they said it would be when Todd and I ordered them."

"Wonderful," Marti said. "I'll take them over to Fiona's this week, and she can start the calligraphy right away."

"What else do we need to decide on?" Christy asked.

Marti went through her list. They had an appointment with the photographer in an hour, and if they wanted to go to the bakery after that, they could taste the other cake flavors, in case Christy wanted to change her mind on the lemon cake with raspberry filling.

"No, I'm sure I want the raspberry." She knew her aunt preferred the almond filling. "Todd loves fruit, Aunt Marti. I hate nuts, so raspberry is the best choice for us."

"All right. Fine."

Christy felt at peace. This was going well.

"The last item we need to go over is the catering service for the reception." Marti had a lot of information for them to go over and suggested they wait until the afternoon.

"Okay," Christy agreed.

"I think this would be a good time for me to bring in the skirt to your dress," Mom said. She left Christy and Marti alone in the kitchen.

Christy took the opportunity to give her aunt a big hug and a kiss on the cheek.

"What was that for?"

"For being here," Christy said.

"Well, of course I'm here." Marti brushed off the comment as if she had caught Christy's deeper meaning but didn't want to acknowledge it.

Christy chose to press the point. "You could have been in Santa Fe right now making pottery at The Colony. Last fall, you told me that's what you intended to do. I'm so glad you stayed. I'm glad you kept your promise to Uncle Bob."

Marti bristled. "What promise?"

"To love, honor, and cherish him for better or worse, in sickness and in health, for richer or for poorer, until death do you part."

"I see you're practicing your wedding vows. Sounds like you have them nicely memorized." Marti straightened the pictures and lists on the counter. She wouldn't look at Christy.

"And you're practicing them, too, with your life," Christy said. "I love you, Aunt Marti. I want you to know that I appreciate your helping me by doing what you do best, lining up everything. You are the perfect wedding coordinator. More than that, I'm glad you're here for my wedding. I'm glad you're not in Santa Fe."

Marti glanced at Christy and then looked away. "It's not easy. You'll find out soon enough. Life doesn't always go the way you think it will."

"The Lord will fulfill His purpose for you, Aunt Marti." Christy hadn't expected to say that. It just tumbled out. But her heart was filled with peace, and she longed for her aunt to know that same peace.

How can I tell her in a way she'll understand? Lord, what do you want my aunt to hear?

"I know the Lord will fulfill His purpose for you," Christy repeated. "But you have to trust Him with all your heart and surrender your life to Him."

Marti drew in a deep breath without taking her eyes off the coffee mug that sat on the counter in front of her. With slow, careful words she said, "I have been considering that, Christina."

Christy's heart pounded wildly. She had waited for years to hear her aunt say she was opening her heart even just a sliver. When Marti didn't add any further comments, Christy leaned over and spoke softly, giving her aunt the image that was so clear in Christy's mind at that moment. "Can I tell you some thoughts I've been having lately about weddings?"

"Of course," Marti said. "That's what we're focusing on today, isn't it?"

"These thoughts are about heaven and how the Bible talks about Christ being the groom."

Marti turned her dark, solemn eyes toward Christy.

"I don't know if you've ever heard it explained like this, but in a way, Christ has proposed to each of us and asked us to be His bride so that we can be with Him. Forever."

Since Marti wasn't stopping her, Christy went on. "We can't come to God as we are because of our sin. He's pure and holy, and we're not. That's why God allowed His only Son to die in our place. Jesus paid the price for our disobedience. But you already know all that, Aunt Marti. You know that God wants us to be made clean so that nothing would separate us from Him."

Christy swallowed her rising emotions. "I don't know if you know this, but He wants to give you a new heart, Aunt Marti. God wants you to take His salvation like a wedding dress. It's a pure, white, immensely expensive wedding dress. It cost Him His life. He offers it to all of us to wear as we walk this long aisle of life. But we have to put on His gift."

Christy realized she was using her hands to demonstrate the act of taking off the old and putting on the new, pure, white gown offered by God. She tucked her hands behind her back and concluded her thought. "Then, when we reach the end of the long aisle of life, we will stand before Christ. He is the true Bridegroom. He loves us with all His heart and has been waiting for us to come to Him since the day we were born."

Marti didn't take her eyes off Christy. Tiny wrinkles began to crease her smooth forehead. Tears glistened in the corners of her eyes. "You believe this, don't you, Christina?"

"Yes, with all my heart."

Marti pressed her lips together as if she were commanding her words to stay locked inside.

Christy couldn't believe how clearly she had communicated the message she had wanted to give to her aunt for years. She hadn't planned the words or the imagery; it was simply there. Todd was the one who always had the great analogies.

Maybe Todd's way of seeing things is beginning to rub off on me. Or maybe the more I trust God, the more He can use me just the way I am to speak the truth in love.

Marti reached over and covered Christy's hand with hers. Christy noticed how cold and moist Marti's hand felt. In a low voice, she said, "Don't give up on me, Christina. I am very close."

Just as Christy's mom was about to enter the kitchen, Marti let go of Christy's hand.

Christy leaned closer to her aunt. "I won't give up on you, Aunt Marti. And neither will God. He is the relentless lover, and you are His first love. He won't give up because He wants you back."

Marti turned to walk away. "I need to put on some lipstick, and then we must leave for our appointment with the photographer."

"Is she okay?" Mom asked as Marti disappeared.

Christy's face was lit up with a huge smile as she nodded. "More than okay. She's great."

"Do you want to have a quick look at this?"

Mom pulled the bag off the skirt to the wedding gown, and Christy released a long "Oooh."

"I think it turned out real nice, don't you?"

"Mom, it's perfect. I love the way the folds add fullness without making it poof out." Christy held up the bodice to the skirt. "It's going to be beautiful. Thank you so much, Mom! I love it."

"Very nice," Marti concurred when she reappeared. She seemed unaffected by the intimate conversation she and Christy had just shared. "It's simple and sweet. Just like you. Have you given any thought to what undergarments would work best with that, Christy? I think we should add lingerie shopping to our list for this afternoon."

Christy had done plenty of shopping with her aunt over the years. Lingerie shopping wasn't something they had attempted yet, and Christy wasn't sure how she felt about shopping with her mom and aunt for fancy underwear.

"But first we must get to the photographer's." Marti scurried them to the door.

They met with the professional photographer, looked through dozens of albums, and selected a plan that they all seemed happy with. Christy thought the photo package was outrageously expensive, but Marti said it was one of the parts of the wedding she and Uncle Bob were covering, so Christy shouldn't worry her pretty little head about it.

"What matters is that you hire a quality professional who captures the look you want," Marti said.

Christy thought of the picture she had seen of her parents' wedding on the hallway wall at her grandmother's. She doubted if a professional who charged extravagant fees had taken the picture. Yet the photo captured the mood of the day and the delight of the parents and happy couple.

"I'd also like to have a bunch of instant cameras on all the tables at the reception," Christy said. "That way the guests can snap pictures of each other, and we'll have a lot of candid shots for our scrapbook."

"We can do that," Marti said as she drove down Pacific Coast Highway on her way to a restaurant she wanted them to try. She explained that the chef was available for catering weddings.

Christy suggested the chef at The Dove's Nest, but Marti shrugged off the idea. Then Christy reminded her aunt that the reception was being held at Rancho Corona, and it made more sense to have a caterer located close to the school. Marti said that caterers were used to traveling all over Southern California, and the location didn't matter.

Christy dropped the subject. It wasn't worth arguing over now, after they had peacefully agreed on so many other topics that day. She also felt a new sense of responsibility toward her aunt. Marti had willingly listened as Christy presented the Gospel to her that morning with the wedding analogy. Christy didn't want to invalidate any of that by being disagreeable with her aunt, who was doing so much to help with the wedding.

At the end of their full day, Christy decided to spend the night at Bob and Marti's and go to church with her uncle in the morning. She called Todd to tell him she wouldn't see him until she returned to her dorm room Sunday afternoon. She only got the voice mail again. She missed Todd. It would be so nice to feel his arms around her and to tell him about their cake having raspberry filling and the details of the photographer's wedding package.

She wouldn't tell him about the flowers or her veil. Or the beautiful assortment of lingerie Marti and her mom had bought for her that afternoon. Those would all be surprises.

Todd didn't call on Sunday after she returned to her dorm, but that didn't surprise her. He probably was exhausted after the backpacking trip and had a lot of work to do at the church sorting out the gear and putting things away.

While they had been shopping on Saturday, Marti had asked Christy if she had any idea what she would buy Todd as a wedding gift. Marti insisted the bride and groom traditionally gave each other gifts. The first thing that popped out of Christy's mouth was, "I'm giving Todd a cell phone so he won't be so hard to get ahold of." She had said it as a joke, but now it was beginning to seem like a good idea. They could get matching his-and-her phones.

Katie meandered into their dorm room at seven o'clock that evening with another bright bouquet of mixed flowers and a plastic pitcher full of water.

"He loves me," Katie said simply.

Christy smiled. "Did Rick tell you he loved you?"

"No, he just keeps showing me that he does. I was a grump all weekend because I'm so behind on schoolwork. I haven't finished my economics paper yet; so instead of playing raquetball like we had planned, Rick and I spent the afternoon at the library gathering all the info and statistics. Then he gave me these flowers and thanked me for a wonderful day."

Katie adjusted the flowers in the plastic vase. She seemed serene and dreamy in her relationship with Rick. That settledness was in sharp contrast to the way she had flown into their room on a caffeine high several months ago and asked Christy if it might be possible Katie was in love.

"You know what? I have a feeling this guy isn't going to give up on me." The tone of Katie's voice reminded Christy of her aunt when she had asked Christy not to give up on her. The comparison between a forever love relationship with God and a bride and groom making a commitment to each other seemed stronger than ever to Christy.

That's how it is with relentless lovers, Christy thought. *They don't give up, do they? In the same way Rick is wooing you, Katie, Jesus has been wooing Aunt Marti. And I don't think either of them is going to give up. Ever.*

CHAPTER 15

With her flowers perfectly arranged on her desk, Katie stretched out on what she called the surfin' sofa. "So how was your weekend, Christy? Did you make a lot of plans at Marti's?"

Christy excitedly gave Katie a rundown of all the details. She told Katie about her aunt's receptiveness as Christy talked with her about the Lord. She also told Katie about the flowers and the head wreath and how the flowers were going to come from Maui. Then she pulled two boxes out from under her bed and showed Katie her beautiful new lingerie.

"I've never owned anything like this," Christy said. "I love it. And it actually was fun shopping for it with my mom and my aunt. It made me feel like one of the girls, if that makes sense."

"What about the doctor?" Katie asked.

"What doctor?"

"Have you made an appointment yet with a gynecologist to get checked out?"

"No, I need to do that. It's on my list. I'm going to the same one my mom goes to in Escondido. She gave me the number a few weeks ago. I just haven't called yet."

"How do you feel about all that?" Katie lowered her voice. "The honeymoon, I mean. Are you ready for, you know . . . everything?"

Christy felt like shouting, "Yes! Yes! A thousand times yes!" But she nodded calmly and simply said, "Yes, I'm ready."

"Do you guys want to have kids right away?" Katie asked.

Christy realized that even though they had talked about how many children they wanted and about giving them Hawaiian middle names, they hadn't discussed the specifics of when.

"We're still talking that through," Christy said.

"Have you and Todd had any huge arguments?"

Christy wasn't sure where Katie was coming up with these random questions. "Yes, of course."

"Rick and I had a huge fight yesterday. It took us about an hour and a half to talk it through and come to an agreement. I think it was good for both of us, though. I mean, if Rick wanted to walk away after seeing me at my worst, that would have been the moment. If he was going to give up on me, it probably would have been yesterday."

"Sounds like your relationship is getting pretty real," Christy said.

"Yes, it is. It's getting real." Katie looked at Christy and then gave her short red hair a little flip. "And I think I like it that way."

On Monday afternoon Todd called Christy at the campus bookstore where she was working. "Hey, what are you doing tonight?" he asked.

She had to smile. They hadn't spoken in three days since he had left on the backpack trip. Still, he didn't start their conversation with a normal "Hi, how are you." Although Todd never had started phone conversations with "Hi, how are you." For a while it was, "Hey, how's it going?" Now it was just a leap right to the point.

Christy decided to answer him with the same forthrightness he had asked the question. "Homework."

"Homework, huh? What's that?"

"Oh, be nice!" Christy turned away from the cash register since she didn't have any customers at the moment. "Have you already forgotten what it's like for the rest of us who aren't yet college graduates?"

"Yes." Lowering his voice, he added, "I miss you, Kilikina."

"I miss you more," she countered.

"Not possible," he said. "Hey, do you think you can ignore your homework for one night and go out to dinner with me?"

"You tell me when and where, and I'll be there."

"Don't laugh," Todd said. "But I'd like to go to The Golden Calf and eat at our table by the window. I miss meeting you there."

"Okay, what time?"

"Five-fifteen if you want me in my painting clothes. Six o'clock if you want me clean."

"I'll take five-fifteen," Christy said.

Eager to make sure no one snatched their table, Christy left the bookstore immediately when she got off at five. She went directly to their table and waited only a few minutes before she spotted Todd coming toward her. It was all she could do not to jump up, dash across the cafeteria, and throw her arms around her beloved. He was wearing his grungy paint clothes and a smile on his face broad enough and bright enough to start a small forest fire.

One thing was certain. His presence lit a blazing fire in the hearth of her soul. She rose to greet him with a kiss and a tight hug.

"Good thing this paint is dry," Todd said.

Christy pulled away and checked her clothes. Todd was right. His speckled work clothes hadn't transferred any paint onto her.

"Have you already eaten?" Todd asked.

"No, I came a little early to wait for you."

"I'll get your food for you," he offered. "What would you like?"

"Anything. I'm not even hungry. I just want to talk with you."

"We have a lot to talk about, don't we. I'll be right back."

Christy watched Todd move through the line, greeting friends and getting their food. She thought again about the similarities between having a relationship with the Lord and falling in love. The parallels seemed to be everywhere, now that she was watching for them.

What would my relationship with the Lord be like if I set a time to meet with Him every day? Would I show up early just because I couldn't wait to talk with Him?

After Todd returned to the table, Christy said she wanted to pray for them before they ate. With a full heart, she thanked God for Todd and for the chance to be together during their busy week. She told Jesus she wanted to grow more in love with Him so that she would find a fire lit in the hearth of her soul every day and that she would meet with Him there with an open heart.

"Amen!" Todd said.

"As you wish," she said to conclude the prayer. Looking up, she smiled at Todd.

He smiled back.

"I wish I had understood love sooner," Christy said. "I wish I had known when I was younger what it meant to be in love like this. If I had, I think my relationship with the Lord would be so much deeper than it is now. I just didn't understand."

Todd nodded. "Hey, I talked to your uncle today, and he said Marti is really opening up to the Lord. He said you had a talk with her on Saturday that she told him about."

Christy gave Todd a summary of what had gone on all weekend. He told her about the backpacking trip. She told him about going to The Dove's Nest on Friday with Sierra and that reminded her of Rick's message about the tux shop.

"I thought I told you I was going to ask Rick to be one of the groomsmen," Todd said.

"No, I think I would have remembered if you had. It means we now have three groomsmen and only two bridesmaids."

"Four." Todd speared a piece of broccoli with his fork. "Doug, my dad, Rick, and David."

"David? My brother? When did you ask David to be a groomsman?"

"A couple of weeks ago. I know we talked about that one."

"I remember us talking about whether or not we wanted to have a candlelighter, and how David could do that."

"Right," Todd said.

"But then we decided we didn't want a candlelighter because we were getting married outside," Christy said.

"Right. So I asked David to be a groomsman. He was pretty happy about it. I think he'll feel like he's included in the wedding more, don't you?"

So that was Todd's logic. That was the way his mind worked. Deep down, he was considering the welfare of others. David would feel included. That was important to Todd.

Christy knew then that for the rest of her life, no matter how organized she would be, the unpredictable factor of Todd's logic would always come into play.

For the next ten minutes, they discussed what Christy labeled the "random factor." She knew this quality of Todd's would be with them on the long journey ahead, and she was determined to make peace with it. She gave Todd examples of when it already had affected their relationship, such as when he stopped under the freeway in Carlsbad to share his breakfast with the homeless man. Todd didn't see his pattern of thinking as anything unusual, but he said he would try to remember to run decisions past Christy before he acted on them.

"So, do you think you can live with it?" Todd asked. "Me, I mean. My logic. This 'random factor.' Will I drive you crazy?"

"Probably," Christy said with a grin. "No more than I'll drive you crazy with my tidiness issues."

"I think we're getting better at this, don't you? We're learning how to keep each other balanced." Todd returned her wide smile.

Christy noticed he had tiny flecks of beige paint across his forehead and a small piece of broccoli stuck between his front two teeth.

Okay, this is starting to get pretty real here!

Christy motioned to Todd he had something in his teeth and remembered one of their earliest dates. They had taken Uncle Bob's tandem bike to Balboa Island, and Todd had bought her an ice cream dipped in chocolate. On the bike ride back, the chocolate had somehow smeared across her face, but Todd hadn't said anything to her, even though she found out after he left that she looked ridiculous.

It wouldn't be like that now. We've come a long way in our relationship. Todd would tell me if I had chocolate on my face. Or broccoli in my teeth. We're a team. A good team. We balance each other, just like he said.

"Did I tell you about the trip to Mexico this weekend?" Todd asked.

"What trip to Mexico?"

"Several of the men from church want to go down to work on the orphanage. They plan to leave Thursday night and come back Saturday night. Do you want to go with us?"

Christy tried to remember what she had just told herself about their being a good team, but the thoughts escaped her. "Todd, I'm swamped this weekend. I have classes Friday, and I work until six. There's no way I can change things around to go to Mexico with you!"

Then, because she knew she needed to express everything she was thinking, she tried in a kind way to say, "You realize, don't you, that you're leaving for the second weekend in a row?"

"I know. That's why I hoped you could come with us. I can get out of it, I think."

"It sounds like you should go," Christy said.

"What about us? What about our wedding plans?"

"I can work on everything. We have . . . what? Seven or eight more weekends after this one."

"I'll make sure I don't schedule myself for anything during the next eight weekends," Todd said.

Christy leaned forward. "Just promise me you won't schedule anything for the weekend of May twenty-second. That weekend definitely is booked."

"Got it on my calendar."

Christy looked at him skeptically. "Do you even own a calendar?"

Todd shrugged. "No, just the one on the back of my checkbook. But I circled May twenty-second on that calendar."

Christy laughed. A few months ago she might have cried; now she laughed.

Todd watched her laugh with a settled look on his face. "Why did I think we could pull this off in January?"

Christy laughed more. "Sometimes I wish we *had* pulled it off in January. We would be married now."

"But a rushed wedding wouldn't have been as special as the one you're making for us," Todd said.

"Do you want to talk about a few of the wedding details?" Christy asked. "It would be good for us to make a couple of decisions tonight, especially since you're going to be gone this weekend."

"Sure. Like what?"

"Tuxes."

"Okay, let's go look at tuxes."

"Now?" Christy asked.

"Sure, why not?"

"Why not?" Christy echoed.

With a few more quick bites of dinner, Todd and Christy left the cafeteria, jumped into their Volvo, and drove down the hill to Burton's Tuxedo Shop. Todd hummed as he drove.

Christy reached over and gave his arm three squeezes. "Hey, you're getting pretty muscular there."

Todd raised his eyebrows. "Never underestimate the power of moving a paintbrush up and down a wall all day."

Christy grinned and gave his arm another squeeze. He flexed and she laughed, remembering how her dad used to invite Christy and David to each grab on to his arm muscles when they were little. Her dad would then flex both arm muscles like a strong man and lift them off the ground.

"You're my hero," Christy said sweetly.

Now Todd laughed. "Need any bars of steel bent? Any tall buildings you want me to leap over?"

"No," Christy said firmly. "Just stand still and let the guy measure you when we get to this tux shop."

"Got it." Todd went back to humming a song Christy didn't recognize.

"What is that? I've heard you hum it before."

"It's a song I've been working on. I'll sing it for you sometime."

"Sing it now," Christy said.

Todd flashed her a big smile. "Naw, it's better with the guitar. Just wait. I'll sing it for you one day. I promise."

They entered Burton's Tuxedo Shop hand in hand with Todd still humming. The man who stood behind the counter seemed reluctant to take them seriously. Christy guessed it was because of how Todd looked. They sat down and began to look through the book of selected styles.

On the fifth page, Todd said, "That's it. That's the one. What do you think, Christy?"

She thought she would like to look at the rest of the pages and then go back and look at them again before deciding.

"It's nice. It's basic. The classic tux," Todd said. "I think this is the one. What do you think?"

"It's nice."

"So we can go with this one?"

"Sure." Christy hadn't seen anything she particularly liked on the preceding pages, and she reminded herself Todd would be the one wearing the tux, after all. He should be the one to decide what he wanted to wear.

"Sir?" Todd called across the room. "Would you mark the Spencer-Miller party down for five of these?"

Christy covered her mouth with her hand. Having just gone through several formal meetings over the weekend with her mom and aunt, Christy thought Todd's way of handling things was atrocious. He sounded as if he were ordering five tacos to go.

"It's five, right?" Todd asked.

Christy uncovered her mouth. "Six. My dad decided to wear a tux after all. I don't know if Uncle Bob wants to wear the same style."

"Sir?" Todd hollered to the man behind the counter. "Could you make that seven?"

"Todd, why don't we just go over there and talk to him," Christy suggested.

They filled out the paper work. Todd put down a deposit. Then the store clerk asked Todd to stand in front of the mirrors so he could be measured. Todd stretched out his arms and fortunately kept his comments to a minimum.

Within ten minutes the process was complete, and they were back on the road to school. Christy wondered if some of Todd's carefree approach to life would rub off on her after they were married.

Until that happened, she still had some less-than-carefree topics to discuss with him, starting with the wedding party. They stopped at an ice-cream shop on their way back to campus and ate at a corner table.

Todd didn't seem to grasp the problem of having four groomsmen while Christy only had two attendants. "I don't think it should matter if the sides are uneven."

"It matters to me," Christy said. "I should ask two other friends to stand with me." She thought about whom she would ask. It had been so simple when it was just Katie and Tracy. Neither she nor Todd had any sisters or close cousins to include.

"I could ask Doug and Rick just to be ushers. They wouldn't have to stand with me," Todd said.

"No, I don't think the answer is to uninvite any of the men. It would be better if I chose two more women. The only problem is I don't really have any other friends I'm especially close to, or at least close enough to ask them to be in our wedding. Sierra is the only one I can think of, and I wouldn't feel right asking her now. She would know she was an afterthought."

Christy had always been a one-best-friend kind of person. Paula had been that best friend all the way through elementary and junior high. The two of them always said they would be each other's bridesmaids; however, they had grown apart when Christy moved to California. Last summer Paula got married, and Christy received an invitation but wasn't able to attend.

Then she realized how much her year in Switzerland had chopped up her relationships. She had friends in Europe, but it was unlikely any of them could come to the wedding. Her first few years of college she had lived at home and attended a community college. She hadn't developed any lasting friendships there. Her list of friends suddenly seemed very short.

"Why don't we mix the men and women on both sides?" Todd suggested. "I mean, it's our wedding, right? We can do whatever we want. We could have my dad, Doug, and Tracy on my side, and then Katie, Rick, and David on your side."

Christy contemplated Todd's suggestion. Once again, his unique way of looking at things opened a world of possibilities to her.

"What do you think?" Todd asked.

Christy had to smile, remembering when he had asked her that question as they shopped for engagement rings. With a big grin, Christy said, "What do I think? I think you kiss pretty good."

Todd seemed to appreciate her humor. He responded with one of her lines. "Do you want to talk mushy or business? I was asking about the wedding attendants."

With a playful grin Christy said, "Mushy, of course. But I'll try to refrain myself and stick to business by saying that once again your clever random factor has saved the day by coming up with an unexpected solution to a problem that had my tidiness issues and me in a panic."

Todd laughed, scooped up her empty ice-cream cup, and carried it to the trash can at the other end of the ice-cream shop.

Just then Christy noticed some students from Rancho coming in the door. Sierra was with them. Christy waved at her, and Sierra left her group to come over to talk to Christy.

Sierra sat down in Todd's empty chair. "I'm glad you're here. I wanted to ask, when is your wedding date?"

"May twenty-second."

"Good! I was hoping that was the day. I was accepted for the summer study program I told you about. My flight leaves the next Saturday. I didn't want to miss your wedding."

"Oh good. I'm glad you'll be there," Christy said.

"Me too. I've also been meaning to thank you." Sierra bent her head toward Christy.

Christy noticed Todd was talking with the students who had come in with Sierra. She gave Sierra her full attention.

"What you said to me at The Nest about being who God made me to be has really helped. Especially as I've prepared for this trip to Brazil."

"In a way, it helped me, too." Christy was thinking about how she had discovered she was a lot like her aunt but how that had turned out to be a good thing when she realized God could fulfill His purpose for her exactly the way she was.

"Well, it helped me a lot. And I started to think about what it is about you that makes me appreciate you so much."

Christy felt a little funny having Sierra shower her with such praise.

"You know what you do?" Sierra asked. "You love people. Gently, calmly, with specific, kind attention, you make people feel welcome. You put people at ease that way, Christy. It's a gift. I think God has given you the gift of hospitality as well as organization."

Christy took in Sierra's words. "I don't know about the hospitality part. I don't exactly live in a place where I can do a lot of entertaining. I never have. And being married to Todd, I have a feeling a house with lots of guest rooms isn't going to be in my future."

"Who needs a house? I'm talking about your heart. You have plenty of guest rooms there. And that's what you do. You open your heart to people. You keep lovely little rooms in there, just waiting for your friends to come visit. People feel as if they can come right in, just as they are. You don't entertain, you love. That's what lasts. That's why people like me feel as if I will always be your friend. You hold a special place for me in your heart."

Tears rolled down Christy's cheeks faster than she could blink them away. "Thank you, Sierra. Thank you."

"Don't thank me, thank God. He's the One who gifted you the way He did." Sierra flashed a bright, free-as-a-kite smile at Christy and hopped up from the chair. "It looks like those guys have already ordered. I better go. See you later."

Christy felt that a great life mystery had just been solved. She knew who she was, she knew how God had gifted her, and she felt peace coming over her like a cozy down comforter.

Wherever Todd and I end up living, however I end up using this college degree, I now know what my life is about. I can love people. I am a woman of hospitality. A woman who loves.

CHAPTER 16

As the final weeks of Christy's senior year slid past, her life seemed to fall into place. She felt her future was more defined. Sierra's words about Christy's spiritual gift being hospitality had opened up a world of understanding and possibilities to her. She liked being hospitable, and she thought being organized and detail oriented were nice companions to hospitality. It all made sense. Now she knew what her life was about, and she was eager to move forward, being true to the person God had created her to be.

The wedding plans were also coming together nicely. Their bank account was growing, thanks to Todd's painting job, and Christy was finding time to complete her class work since she rarely saw Todd.

On the Friday afternoon before Easter vacation, Christy worked extra hours in the bookstore while the other student employees left early for their vacations. Matthew Kingsley came in wearing a baseball cap over his light brown hair. He appeared to have grown an inch since she had seen him last.

"Hi," Christy said.

"Hi yourself." His warm brown eyes smiled down at her. "Where have you been hiding? I haven't seen you in weeks. I stopped by a couple of times, but you haven't been here."

"My hours changed this semester," Christy said. "I have more classes, too. I've been swamped."

"Tell me about it. They have us on a crazy schedule this baseball season."

"How are you doing?"

"Great. My mom told me about your grandfather passing away," Matt said. "I was real sorry to hear that. He was a good man."

Matt and Christy had grown up together in Brightwater. He had been her first crush at Washington Elementary School, and now they were at the same school again. Last semester Christy had seen Matt all the time. This semester they rarely ran into each other.

"Thanks, Matt," Christy said. "I agree. He was a wonderful man. I saw your sisters at the funeral. They've really grown."

"Yeah, they're both doing well. My family is coming to California this summer, so they're pretty excited."

"Are you staying here this summer?"

Matt nodded. "I got a job with the Youth Outreach Center. That's why I haven't been helping Todd with the youth group at his church. I have my own bunch of kids to work with now. They're a lot more street smart than the kids Todd works with. I like it. We have two baseball teams put together so far."

"That sounds like something you would be good at," Christy said. "How did you find that job?"

"Jenna works there. She recommended me."

"Jenna?"

"Don't you remember Jenna? I told you guys in the cafeteria one day in December that I wanted to ask her out, and you talked me into that group date event at The Dove's Nest."

"Oh yes, Jenna."

"It's okay if you don't remember much about that night. You and Todd were pretty busy getting yourselves engaged."

Christy smiled. "That was a special night. I was glad you were there."

Matt hesitated and shyly looked over his shoulder before saying, "We're still doing stuff together."

"You are? You and Jenna?"

Matt nodded.

"Good for you! She seemed like a really sweet person."

151

"She is," Matt said. "I've been wanting to tell you that because, well . . . I guess I just wanted you to know and to be happy for me. You're like the closest thing to family I have here."

"I'm glad you told me. I hope you bring her to our wedding. The invitations haven't been mailed yet, but it's on May twenty-second."

"I'll be there," Matt said. "And I'll bring Jenna with me."

"Good." Christy hoped her warm smile told Matt how happy she was for him.

"As a matter of fact, Jenna and I are going bowling tonight, in case you and Todd want to go with us."

"Bowling, huh?" Christy thought it was great Matt had found a girl who liked sports. "Thanks, but I'm not sure we can squeeze it in. As soon as I get off work, I have to drive down to my parents' house. The bridesmaids' dresses arrived, and I have to get Tracy's to her in case it needs altering."

"Oh." Matt nodded but looked as if he had no idea what she was talking about. "We can try to do something together another time."

"Sure." Christy knew it wouldn't happen. At least not in the next two months.

Maybe after we're married, Todd and I will find time to get our social life back.

On Saturday afternoon, Christy drove to Carlsbad with Tracy's bridesmaid's dress in the Volvo's backseat. She and Tracy planned to meet for lunch at the Blue Ginger Café, but Christy was a little early. That was fine with her because she was able to grab an open table outside where the fresh spring sunshine poured over her, warming her and making her eager for summer to come. She closed her menu and closed her eyes, basking in the warmth.

A few moments later, Tracy walked up, and Christy smiled to see her friend's little belly pooching out in a compact, round ball.

"I know," Tracy said, patting her tummy. "I'm definitely showing."

"You look so cute! You're adorable." Christy hugged her and patted the baby bubble gently. "You look really good, Tracy."

"Thanks, Christy. I can't say that I believe you, but thanks." Tracy pulled out a chair and sat across from Christy. "Have you ordered yet?"

"No, I was just enjoying a little sunshine break."

"It's nice today, isn't it? I hope you didn't wait long. We had an appointment with the doctor before coming here, and it lasted longer than we expected. He had some surprising news for us."

Christy took off her sunglasses to see Tracy's face more clearly. "Twins?"

"No." Tracy laughed nervously. "Thank goodness! We found out it's a boy. We want to name him Daniel."

"That's wonderful! Or were you hoping for a girl?"

"No, I'm thrilled. Doug is thrilled."

"And you like the name Daniel?"

"I love it. He can go by Danny when he's little and then use Daniel when he earns his Ph.D."

Christy grinned. "You have high aspirations for this child."

"Doesn't every parent?"

The waitress stepped up to their table, and they both ordered garden salads and sparkling mineral water.

"Are we becoming old ladies or what?" Christy asked. "Look at us, ordering salads and mineral water. That's what my aunt would order."

"I talked to your aunt this week," Tracy said.

"You did?"

"Yes. I have some more news for you. I've been planning a couple's shower for you and Todd. Doug thought we should make it a surprise, but I told him I was going to tell you today because I thought it would be easier if you knew."

"Thanks, Tracy."

"It's this Thursday, and your aunt volunteered her house because, when Doug and I started to make a list of people to invite, we realized we couldn't fit twenty or more people in our little living room."

"And my aunt agreed to this?"

"She was thrilled and honored. I told her we would do all the food, but she insisted I let her take care of everything because of my 'condition.' " Tracy settled back in her chair and rested her arm on her stomach. "I would have argued with her, but the truth is, I am pretty tired all the time."

"Todd said you were planning to quit your job after the baby . . . or should I say, after Danny gets here."

Tracy nodded and sipped the mineral water the waitress placed in front of her. "We might have to move."

"Why? You have a darling house."

"I know. But our lease is up in November, and it's so small. We only have the one bedroom. That's fine while Daniel is tiny, but he's going to need his own room eventually."

"I hadn't thought about that," Christy said. "Would you move into a two-bedroom apartment or what?"

"I don't know. It's something we've just started to talk about. Doug has this dream about buying a house, getting a dog, and having a backyard big enough for a swing set. We would have to move inland to afford that."

"I imagine you would miss the beach a lot."

"Yes," Tracy said. "But you would be surprised. We hardly ever go to the beach anymore. When we first moved there, we went all the time. I guess we need to be more responsible and frugal and live in an area that's less expensive."

Christy swished the ice and mineral water in her glass. "Who knows? We might end up in the same neighborhood."

"Are you and Todd going to live near Rancho?" Tracy asked.

"We're working on finding an apartment in the same complex where Rick lives, if you can believe that. It's only about five minutes from the church."

"I'll have to convince Doug to check out that area. He was saying last night that we should move to Oregon because he knows a guy who lives in a small town there, and we could afford to buy a house."

After the waitress arrived with their salads, Christy offered to give thanks before they ate. They chatted about everything, from the upcoming shower and Christy's wedding plans to how it felt the first time Tracy felt little Danny kicking inside her. As Christy inconspicuously picked the walnut pieces out of her salad, she thought of how this was the most relaxing, enjoyable two hours in the sunshine she had spent in months. She hoped Doug and Tracy didn't move to Oregon. She needed Tracy to be nearby after Christy was married so they could make time for more relaxing afternoons like this.

When they walked to the parking lot so Christy could give Tracy her dress, Tracy asked about Rick and Katie.

"They're doing great," Christy said. "Katie is taking it nice and slow, and Rick is treating her the way she deserves to be treated."

"Do you think they'll end up together?" Tracy asked. "I mean, do you think they'll get married?"

Christy thought a moment. "I wouldn't be surprised. Katie is determined to finish college, and I haven't talked to her about it, but I would guess she and Rick would opt for a fairly short engagement."

"Does that seem amazing to you?" Tracy asked.

"I guess, if I think about it long enough. It seems right, though. It seems evident the Lord is fulfilling His purpose for each of us."

"Yes, He is," Tracy agreed with a contented sigh.

On Thursday night Todd left work early for their couple's shower. When he arrived at the dorm to pick up Christy, he had on a freshly ironed, short-sleeved Hawaiian-print shirt and khaki shorts. He hugged Christy, and she could tell he had shaved and used a deep moss- and plum-scented cologne.

"You look great!" Christy said. "And you smell great, too."

Todd held her hand and led her to the car. "It's Rick's aftershave. What do you think?"

"It's nice."

"Rick ironed the shirt for me. He's pretty domestic."

Christy thought that was a good thing since she couldn't remember ever seeing Katie iron.

"You look really nice." Todd wrapped his arm around Christy's waist and drew her close. "I like that skirt on you. I don't know if I told you that the last time you wore it. It looks good on you."

"Thanks. Are you hungry? Do you want to stop and get something to eat before we drive to Newport Beach?"

"No, I'm fine. How about you?"

"No, I'm not hungry."

They got in the Volvo, which was parked all by itself in a nearly empty parking lot. "This hasn't been much of an Easter vacation for you, has it?" Todd asked. "Are you wishing you hadn't stayed on campus?"

155

"It was the best thing for me, really," Christy said. "I've worked twenty-two hours so far this week doing inventory in the bookstore. The income is going to help us a lot. And I'm nearly finished with my second paper. After that I only have two more to write. Finals are in three and a half weeks, and then I'm done!"

"I'm proud of you, Kilikina. Have I ever told you that? You were right about needing time to plan our wedding. I'm amazed at how much you've accomplished on top of finishing your final semester of school. If I had been at all understanding, I would have agreed to get married in August like you wanted so you wouldn't have had all this pressure on top of finishing school."

"It hasn't been too much," Christy said. "It's been a lot, but as long as I haven't tried to fit a social life in on top of everything, it's been okay."

"I know," Todd agreed as he drove onto the freeway. "We haven't been able to see each other very much, have we?"

"That will change soon enough," Christy said. "This is only a season for us. A short season. I think we're doing pretty well, don't you?"

"I do. So tell me," Todd said. "What do people do at a shower?"

"Sometimes they play games. Then we eat and open presents."

The whole concept seemed foreign to Todd. "What kind of games?"

"You know, little word-circling games on paper or dressing up the bride with toilet paper to form a wedding dress and veil."

"And this is going to be fun, right?"

Christy laughed. "You'll have a good time, Todd. At least you better. You're the guest of honor."

Todd nodded. He ran his fingers through his short hair. "By any chance, have these guys said anything about doing anything at the shower tonight?"

Christy finally understood why Todd was acting so nervous. He was expecting to be kidnapped at the shower the way he and the other guys had kidnapped Doug at his bachelor's party. They had taken Doug to the Balboa ferry, made him wear a chicken costume, and then chained him to the boat.

Suppressing a grin, Christy said, "Why do you ask?"

"Just wondering."

Christy hadn't heard any talk about the guys planning to kidnap Todd. But then, she guessed they wouldn't tell her their plans.

"I'm sure my aunt and uncle will keep this party under control."

"But it's being hosted by Doug and Tracy, right?"

"Yes, it is."

Todd looked worried. Christy tried not to giggle.

CHAPTER 17

When Todd and Christy arrived at Bob and Marti's, Christy found Tracy in the living room trying to pick up a name tag from the floor. But she seemed to find the task a challenge.

"I can get that." Christy bent effortlessly and placed the tag in the basket slung over Tracy's arm.

"Thank you. I gave up tying my shoes," Tracy said. "I had to buy these slip-on loafers yesterday because my feet are so swollen. I'm not at my best as a pregnant woman."

"You look radiant," Todd said.

Christy turned to look at her kind fiancé.

He leaned over and kissed Tracy on the cheek. "I mean that, Trace. I think you look good as a pregnant woman. You have a glow on your face. I think you're beautiful."

Tracy looked as if she might cry. "Thank you, Todd."

Oh, you sweet man! I hope you remember to say all those wonderful things to me someday when my belly swells up twice the size of a basketball!

"I didn't hear you two come in," Marti said, bustling into the living room. "Tracy, dear, shouldn't you sit down?"

"I'm okay." Tracy shot Christy a look that said, "Just wait until it's your turn to be pregnant!"

"Todd, dear, Robert would like to see you in the garage."

"What about?" Todd's question came out with an edge to it.

Marti looked offended. "He needs help with a table. I'll go with you, Todd. Come."

Todd gave Christy a "farewell forever" glance and slowly headed to the garage.

Christy whispered to Tracy, "Todd thinks the guys are going to kidnap him tonight and do something wild, the way they kidnapped Doug and chained him to the ferry."

"Would my precious husband ever do such a thing?"

"Your precious husband isn't the one I'm worried about," Christy said. "One man alone isn't a threat. It's when all these men start brainstorming that I worry—especially with Rick back in the picture."

Todd and Doug marched into the living room, each carrying the end of a banquet-sized folding table. "Marti wants the gifts set up on this table," Doug said. "She said to put it in front of the window. Could you move that rocking chair, Christy?"

They all pitched in to set up the living room the way Aunt Marti wanted it. Doug didn't seem to be scheming anything on the side. Although, who could tell with Doug? His face always had an impish grin on it.

The guests began to arrive, and Marti greeted each one. She kept Tracy by her side with the basket of name tags and made sure each guest pinned on the proper tag. The black ones cut in the shape of a groom, complete with top hat, had the guys' names written in white ink. The white paper cutouts of a bride in a full skirt had the girls' names written in black ink. Christy thought the idea was cute but kind of funny, too, since everyone at the shower knew one another. No one was going to try to crash the party only to have Marti look in the basket and say, "No, sorry. I don't see a little groom with your name on it. Go away!"

The first game Marti directed was the one Christy had expected. The girls had five minutes to dress Christy as a bride with several rolls of toilet paper while the guys watched. Sierra single-handedly made the veil, which generated the most laughs. She snagged a roll of Scotch tape and somehow managed to make the strips of the veil stick straight out every which way.

Christy saw her reflection in the living room window and said, "Sierra, I look like the Statue of Liberty!"

The living room filled with waves of laughter. Several camera flashes went off as friends captured the moment on film. Christy stood patiently, letting it all roll over her. It was fun.

Todd, however, looked as nervous as a cat when he was called up to stand beside Christy. The guys were to dress him as the groom with rolls of toilet paper. Todd shot a glance at Christy as if he expected at any moment to have a gunnysack thrown over his head, to be hauled out the front door, hoisted into a cargo plane, and flown to Aruba.

All that happened was that Todd was wrapped up like a mummy with toilet paper strapping down his arms and covering his mouth, ears, and eyes. Doug joked that this was the truth about married life and for a final twist taped a wad of T.P. to Todd's chest that looked like a boutonniere.

Christy thought Todd looked hilarious all wrapped up, but she could tell by his nervous shuffling that he didn't like being the center of attention, and he certainly didn't like being blinded from any potential gunnysacks coming his way.

A few cameras flashed as Christy stood beside Todd with her wild-woman wedding veil and her bouquet of tissue balls. Her reluctant mummy broke out of his graveclothes and pulled the tissue off his eyes and mouth.

"Is that the last game?" he muttered to Christy as he peeled his cocoon and left the remains on the floor in a heap.

"I hope so." Christy gave his muscular arm three squeezes.

It wasn't enough to calm him. They were told to sit on the love seat by the gift table and to open the gifts. Todd looked behind the couch, apparently checking to make sure no one was hiding there.

As Christy opened each gift, she warmly thanked the giver, making a point to comment on something special about each item. It was easy to praise Tracy for the gift she gave: a charming, pudgy china teapot covered with red cabbage roses.

"It's like the one we used at that teahouse in England," Tracy said. "Remember, when you and I went to tea?"

"Of course I remember. Thanks, Trace. I love it."

An image came to Christy that she knew would be humorous only to her. She saw herself heating up water on their camp stove and serving tea to Tracy from this beautiful china pot while sitting on the surfboard sofa. If she wore her wedding dress at the same time, she could have her picture taken and send it to a bridal magazine with the caption, "Outback bride at tea time."

Todd's gifts included tools, a frying pan, and toenail clippers as a joke from Rick. They received bath towels, a salad bowl, and an ice-cream scoop that played an ice-cream-truck melody when you pushed a button on the handle.

"We need one of those at The Dove's Nest," Katie told Rick.

"I don't think so." He grinned at her in response.

Christy noticed how cute they looked snuggled up next to each other. No one seemed to think their behavior unusual except for Marti. During the refreshments, she pulled Christy aside. "Just what is happening with Rick and Katie?"

Christy wanted to say, "God is fulfilling His purpose for them," but she hesitated. Marti didn't deserve a flippant answer when she was asking a genuine question.

"They are getting to know each other better," Christy said.

"How much better?" Marti raised an eyebrow.

Sierra had been standing next to them and entered into the conversation. "You know about the unwritten rule at Rancho, don't you?"

"No," Marti said, falling for Sierra's little joke.

"For every upper-class woman the guarantee is 'a ring by spring or your money back.' "

Marti didn't find that humorous. "They certainly aren't planning to get engaged any time soon, are they?"

"I don't know," Christy said. "You could ask Katie."

"No, I wouldn't ask such a thing. Really, Christina! A person's love life is a personal matter."

"Besides," Sierra said, "I've discovered that when two people are meant to be together, you can't do anything to break them up. And if they aren't meant to be together, you can't do anything to keep them together."

Both Christy and Marti looked at Sierra, who was tucking a small strawberry into her mouth. Sierra turned to talk to someone else. Her wild mane of unruly blond curls followed her.

"Honestly," Marti said, "some of your friends are such . . ."

"Individuals?" Christy offered.

"Yes, individuals and uncontrollable."

Christy smiled. "I like my friends that way. They're good for me."

Even though Marti wasn't happy at the moment, she had worn a pleased expression when Christy and Todd had opened the last gift, which was from Bob and Marti. It was two place settings of china in the pattern Christy had selected weeks ago while shopping with Marti and her mom. Todd didn't seem too appreciative, but Christy knew what the gift cost and made sure she expressed her delight to her aunt.

She thanked Aunt Marti again when Todd and Christy were about to leave. "It was a wonderful shower." Christy kissed Marti's cheek. "The food was delicious, and I love the china. Thank you so much for everything."

"You sure you kids don't want to stay the night?" Bob asked. "It's pretty late for you to be driving."

"I have to start work at seven in the morning," Todd said. "I think we'll be okay. Thanks again for everything. Thanks, too, for letting us keep all the gifts here until we get our apartment."

"No problem. Drive safely," Bob replied.

"We will."

"Bye." Christy blew them a kiss and headed down the sidewalk with Todd. She glanced above the house's roof and noticed a full moon gracing the deep night sky.

"We love you both," Marti called out.

Then Christy saw her aunt slip her arm around Uncle Bob's waist and rest her head on his shoulder as she waved to them. The grin that lit up Uncle Bob's face was as bright as the full moon winking at Christy from the heavens above.

She winked back. It was a perfect night for relentless lovers to do their wooing.

Just as Christy and Todd reached their car, a wild war cry sounded. The party guests, who supposedly had left, came rushing at Todd and Christy from behind cars and bushes.

Todd grabbed Christy and tried to protect her from whatever kind of attack was coming their way. All around them Silly String rained down. Dozens of canisters went off at the same moment as their friends circled them, and each squirted two cans over Todd and Christy. The laughing and squealing filled the night air. Christy laughed at Todd, who responded like a zealous Scottish warrior, protecting Christy with one arm and fending off the volley of Silly String with the other. Brightly colored string covered the couple; their friends were gleefully victorious.

Todd decided on the way home that if that was the worst prank to be played on him, he had gotten off easy. During the month that followed, it appeared that was the case.

The day Christy donned her cap and gown and received her college diploma, she found a glob of fluorescent green and orange Silly String in her good pair of shoes. It was also the day she started to sneeze and to experience itching eyes and a dripping nose. Her graduation ceremony and the following celebration dinner with her extended family and friends turned out to be a repeat of Todd's graduation event, with most of the same people in attendance. Only at hers, Christy sneezed like crazy.

Marti suggested Christy might have allergies since she had never lived in that area before. Different pollens existed there than the ones Christy had been acclimated to in Escondido, Marti pointed out.

Her mother commented that Christy had dark circles under her eyes and asked if she wanted to go home that night.

"I think I'll stick with the original plan," Christy said. "I'll stay in the dorm tonight and try to sleep in. Tomorrow I'll move all my things to Todd's apartment."

"Our apartment," Todd corrected her. They had secured a one-bedroom apartment in the same complex Rick lived in. Todd had moved his belongings over a few days ago, but Christy's handful of worldly possessions was still in her dorm room.

The past month had been a blur of writing papers, taking finals, working on last-minute wedding plans, interviewing for jobs, and never seeing Todd. If she had dark circles under her eyes, she knew she didn't need to blame them on an allergy. But it was over. She had made it. Now she was a college graduate. It felt good. A little too smoothly orchestrated perhaps to be as memorable as she had thought it would be, but then, she had another major event looming ahead in nine short days.

"Okay, how about this plan," Christy suggested to her mom as they left the restaurant. "I'll take some allergy medicine, get a good night's sleep in my dorm room, move my things into our apartment tomorrow morning, and then come home. You can baby me all you want."

Her plan worked fairly well. The allergy medication helped her to sleep a full ten hours, which was a rare occurrence. She didn't wake up the next morning until after eight. Within two minutes she discovered the one night's dosage of allergy pills hadn't relieved her of the sneezing. At least she felt rested.

Katie returned from her morning shower and said, "Hey, sleeping beauty, what's on your schedule?"

Christy tried to say, "Katie, I'm getting married in eight days," but her nose was so stuffed up the thought came out, "Katie, I'b gettin' barried in eight days."

"Yes, you are," Katie said with a laugh. "And aren't you going to be a lovely bride."

"I'll be better by den." Christy noticed her cap and gown hanging on the hook above her closet. It didn't seem as if she actually had graduated. The whole day had gone by so fast. She hoped her wedding day would go more slowly and remain more memorable.

Classes were still going for those who hadn't graduated, and Katie pointed out she had to take a final. "Will you be here when I get back?"

"I don't know. Todd is going to borrow Matt's truck so we can take our lovely surfin' sofa to the apartment. I'm not sure when he's coming."

"He called before I took my shower," Katie said. "He said he wasn't coming because a painting job opened up this morning. He said he talked to Matt, and Matt can take your stuff over at ten."

"That's some improvement," Christy said with a sigh before blowing her nose. "At least he calls now."

"Do you want me to go with you guys and help? I don't have to be at work until this afternoon."

"That would be wonderful."

"I'll meet you back here at ten," Katie said.

"Thanks, Katie. I'll take a hot shower and try some more allergy medication."

At 9:45 Sierra showed up. "Hi. How are you feeling?" Sierra held out a bottle of orange juice to Christy. "I saw Katie, and she said you weren't sounding very good."

"Thanks for the juice. I think it's allergies," Christy said. "Please don't tell my aunt. She enjoys it way too much when she's right. I'm feeling lots better now."

"Do you need some help moving your things?" Sierra asked.

"That would be great. Matt should be here in a little while. I have everything packed. When he comes, you can help us load his truck."

Christy opened the orange juice and took a drink. "Are you getting excited about going to Brazil?"

"I think so," Sierra said. "I still have finals to finish up. Not that you would know anything about that."

"Oh, a little."

"Is everything ready for your wedding?" Sierra asked.

"You know, amazingly enough, I think so. Everything on the list has been taken care of, thanks to my mom and my aunt. Todd and I finished our premarital counseling sessions, and they really were helpful. We got into the apartment we wanted, and everything should run like clockwork a week from tomorrow. We just have a few details about our future to work out, but we'll do that after the honeymoon."

Just then the phone rang. It was Donna, Christy's boss from the campus bookstore.

"Oh good. I'm glad I caught you," she said. "I wanted you to know that I have your final check here, in case you would like to stop by to pick it up today."

"That would be great. Thanks, Donna."

"Sure. And I have a question for you. This is a little out of the ordinary, I know, and you don't have to answer me right away. I'm resigning from the campus bookstore in two weeks."

"Oh?"

"I was offered a position as the manager of another bookstore, and I've decided to take it. I need to hire an assistant manager at my new job, and you were recommended by the owner."

"I was?" Christy had placed her résumé at several businesses around town, but she didn't think she had met any of the owners.

"My new position is at The Ark. Mrs. Doyle said you were good friends with her son. He runs the café next door."

Christy felt like laughing. "Yes, we are good friends. I put in a résumé there a month ago, but the manager said they were in transition."

"I guess I'm part of the transition," Donna said. "Think about it. Pray about it. I'd love to have you as my assistant manager."

"Okay," Christy said. "It would be perfect for me. But I couldn't start until after the first of June."

"That's fine because I start on June first," Donna said. "Let me know what you think. I'll see you at your wedding, if not before."

"Thanks, Donna."

"Sure."

Christy turned to Sierra. "It looks like I have a job after we get back from our honeymoon. I was going to tell you, before the phone rang, that one of the unsettled details was that I didn't have a job. I think God took care of that in record time."

"Hey, kids, how's it going?" Katie entered the room and tossed an apple at Christy. "This is for you, roomie. I worried about your taking allergy medicine on an empty stomach."

"Thanks."

"You guys ready to rock and roll?" Katie asked.

"Matt isn't here yet," Christy said. "But guess what? It looks like I have a job."

She told Katie the details while Katie stared at the boxes neatly stacked on Christy's side of the room.

"Don't leave me," Katie said.

Sierra laughed. "Didn't you hear Christy? She just said she's going to work in the bookstore next to you. You guys will see each other every day."

"We'll probably see each other more than we did this past semester," Christy said.

"I know," Katie said wistfully. "But at least stay in the dorm until I'm done next week, and we can move out together. This is too sad. Look at your side of the room. It's empty."

"It went fast, didn't it?" Christy said.

Katie sat on the edge of her unmade bed, the bed that had gone unmade the entire school year except for the rare occasion when Christy convinced Katie to wash the sheets.

"Do you two remember the week before school started?" Sierra asked. "The three of us were sitting in here, telling each other our woes."

"I remember," Katie said. "It's been a full year."

"It certainly has," Christy agreed.

"You know what?" Sierra said. "I think we should pray."

"Good idea," Christy said.

The three friends stood in a close circle and looped their arms over each other's shoulders. They prayed sweet, rich words of thankfulness and bold requests for God's future blessings.

When they finished, Christy said, "I love you both. You know that, don't you?"

A tentative knock sounded on their door. Katie let in Matt and in a melancholy voice said, "I guess this is it. Go ahead, Matt. Take her stuff. I always knew she loved Todd more than she loved me."

CHAPTER 18

Matt went to work clearing Christy's dorm room like the strong, steady farm boy he was. Christy, Katie, and Sierra carried Christy's boxes out to the curb while he wrestled the surfin' sofa into the back of his truck. Katie led the way to the apartment in Baby Hummer, and for the first time, Christy unlocked the front door with her very own key.

She didn't know whether to laugh or cry when she peered inside. Todd should have been there to carry her over the threshold or something. Instead, she was standing with her friends, staring into an empty apartment. Christy realized she had created a fantasy of what she thought her first home with Todd would be like. In her dreams, it was a cottage with a fireplace and flowers all in a row along the walkway.

"Where do you want this stuff?" Katie asked.

"Anywhere," Christy said. "There's plenty of room."

It took them only two trips to empty the truck. Matt adjusted the surfin' sofa in the middle of the living room and said he needed to get back to school to finish a paper.

"Thanks so much," Christy said.

"I'll see you next Saturday," he said.

"I'm going to go back with him." Sierra gave Christy a hug. "I'll email you from Brazil."

"I'll email back," Christy promised.

Matt and Sierra left, and Katie stood with her hand on her hip looking around the apartment. "This is a bit bleak, isn't it?"

"It'll cheer up once I put some pictures on the wall," Christy said.

"Or maybe add a stick or two of furniture."

A tear trickled down Christy's cheek.

"Oh, I didn't mean to hurt your feelings," Katie said. "You guys will fix it up. You'll get a bunch of wedding presents, and you'll find a real couch and a kitchen table. It'll be wonderful. You're just starting out."

Christy sniffed. "I need flowers, Katie."

"Flowers?"

"Yes, flowers in a pot by the front door. And maybe a welcome mat. That's what I need."

"Say no more. I was wondering what I could buy you for a house-warming present, and now I know. Come on, let's buy a flower and a welcome mat."

An hour later, Katie and Christy returned to the apartment all smiles with a bright, cheery potted daisy and a welcome mat. They also had a box of tissues, six homemade chocolate-chip cookies from the bakery, a bottle of liquid soap, and a bottle of lotion to put by the kitchen sink.

"Now it's home," Christy said, arranging her new treasures.

"You certainly are easy to please," Katie said.

"Todd is the minimalist. I don't require much, but the few necessities I do need are paramount."

"I wish I could stay and help you put pictures on the wall, but I have to run. Are you going to be okay?"

"Yes, I'll be fine. When Todd gets home, he's going to drive me down to my parents'."

"Did you hear what you just said?" Katie asked. "You said when Todd gets home. It worked. You do see this as your new home."

Christy reminded herself of Katie's comment as she unpacked her boxes and checked out the kitchen cupboards. She found three paper cups, one coffee mug, and a stack of paper plates. She rinsed out the coffee mug, filled it with water, heated it in the microwave, and made herself a comforting cup of tea.

Looking for the tissue to blow her nose, she found Katie had put the box in the bathroom. Christy stood there blowing her nose and noticed a big glob of toothpaste in the sink. The towel was on the floor instead of on the towel rack. Todd had been living here.

Continuing her tour into the bedroom, she was relieved to see their new bed had arrived. Todd had slept on the floor in a sleeping bag when he first had moved in. His dad offered to buy a bed as his wedding present to them, and they both gratefully accepted.

The comfy-looking bed was set up in the small bedroom, but it didn't have a headboard or any sheets on it. One rather worn wool army blanket lay at the foot of the bed. The blanket looked like a World War II relic, which was depressing. But noticing it was folded, Christy felt hopeful Todd might be a little tidier than the evidence in the bathroom suggested.

Todd had a dresser; Christy had a bookcase and a chair.

This is more pathetic than I realized. We are really poor.

Christy went to work unpacking her boxes and deciding on which empty wall she should hang her few pictures and posters. She worked quickly and had all her boxes unpacked in short order. She filled up the bookshelf, put her small rug in front of the kitchen sink, and hung the poster of the waterfall with the memorable bridge on the wall in the kitchen. The splash of color did the apartment a world of good. She dusted off the top of Todd's dresser and placed her framed pictures of the two of them next to the only item Todd had on the dresser, the picture she had given him for his birthday.

All that was left to unpack was the box with her yellow patchwork blanket, a useless set of twin sheets, two bath towels, her pillow, and a treasure she knew she wanted to keep with her always. It was her old pal Pooh, the stuffed Winnie the Pooh Todd had bought her at Disneyland. Pooh had held her secrets and wiped her tears for too many years to be left in a box in her parents' closet. She hoped Todd would understand.

Christy carried her yellow quilt into the bedroom. The bed looked so inviting. She stretched out, tucked Pooh under her arm, and pulled her blanket up over both of them. Settling in on the right side of the bed, Christy wondered if Todd preferred the right side. Or would they sleep together in the middle every night, wrapped in each other's arms?

Through her fuzzy head floated puffy, fluffy, happy dreams like summer clouds coasting through a deep blue sky. And that was the last thing she remembered.

Many hours later, Christy woke. She didn't recall where she was at first. Then it all came tumbling over her. She looked toward the bedroom doorway and gave a startled gasp when she saw Todd standing there, watching her as she slept.

He was leaning against the doorjamb, arms folded across his chest, a gentle smile on his face.

"Hey, how's it going?" That phrase, that voice, had echoed for half a decade through Christy's waking hours and in her dreams. For a moment she wasn't sure if she was awake or if this was part of her dream.

"How long have you been standing there?"

"Awhile. I took a shower. The noise didn't wake you?"

"No."

"You have no idea how beautiful you are when you're sleeping, Kilikina."

Christy wanted to hold out her arms to her beloved, inviting Todd to come to her and hold her. But she didn't move.

Todd didn't move, either. It was as if they were once again at an intersection in their lives. In the early years, the red lights had been there to give Todd and Christy a quick chance for a kiss and a memory. Today an invisible red light did the opposite. It kept them from kissing. Christy knew Todd felt what she was feeling. God was controlling the traffic lights at the intersections. He would change the light to green in eight short days. Until then, it would be foolish to run a red light.

"How are you feeling?"

"I'm okay." Christy tossed back the comforter, and Pooh tumbled to the floor. Christy didn't know if Todd noticed. "We have to be sure to thank your dad a thousand times. This is the most comfortable bed I've slept on in two years."

"The delivery guys came this morning," Todd said. "I see you brought your own blankie."

Christy folded her patchwork comforter. "My grandma made this. I've had it since elementary school."

"I never knew that," Todd said.

"I never knew you left your towel on the floor." Christy walked toward him.

"Uh-oh. Is that one of those issues they talked about in our premarital counseling? Should I hang up towels so that you feel more loved?"

"It wouldn't hurt," Christy said. "But I should confess that my last roommate never made her bed or hung up her towel, so perhaps Katie prepared me for you."

"How do those vows go, now? For better or worse? Richer or poorer?"

Christy stepped out of the bedroom. As soon as she stepped over the invisible line and stood on Todd's side, he wrapped his arms around her and hugged her close.

"I think we have the poorer part figured out," Christy said.

"Hey, I like all the Christy touches you added to our home. The flowers by the front door and the welcome mat are especially nice," Todd murmured. "Do you want to head out for your parents' house?"

"Yes, I think we better."

They both stayed at her parents' that night. Once again the allergy medication made Christy konk out. She woke in a Saturday-morning sort of daze and padded out to the kitchen in her pj's, robe, and slippers.

The house was silent. Pouring herself a bowl of cereal, she sat down at the kitchen table. A moment later Todd and David walked into the kitchen. Christy instinctively clutched the top of her robe. She knew she looked awful. Her hair was going in every direction, and she needed a shower.

"Morning, beautiful," Todd said.

"I look terrible!" Christy squeaked. She could tell by the expression on David's face he agreed with her evaluation.

If you can call me beautiful when I look like this, my soon-to-be husband, then you'll be in for a nice surprise next Saturday.

"We're going to the skate park for an hour or so," Todd said. "When I get back, you can give me the final to-do list."

"Okay." Christy tried to tuck her stringy hair behind her ears.

"See ya," David said as they marched past her.

The door to the garage closed. A moment later it opened, and Todd's face appeared around the corner, wearing a boyish grin. "Hey, you in the bathrobe and fuzzy slippers, if you're not doing anything next Saturday, what do you think? You want to get married?"

Christy grinned and held out her arms to provide Todd a full view of her frumpy robe, flannel pj's, and disheveled hair. "For better or worse," she said.

"From where I'm standing, I'm thinking it can only get better by next Saturday. At least I'm hopin'."

Christy took off one of her fuzzy slippers and heaved it at him. He shut the door just in time for the slipper to miss its target.

Christy returned to her bowl of cereal, laughing to herself. She thought back to their first date to Disneyland when she had thrown her sandal at him.

She hadn't realized her mother had stepped into the living room and was watching the scene. Mom looked surprised, as if she hadn't seen this side of her daughter before.

"Don't worry, Mom. He was laughing."

Mom shook her head. "I shouldn't wonder, dear. You really should have a look in the mirror."

One very short week later, Christy heard her mother once again say, "You really should have a look in the mirror."

Only this time, no one was laughing at how Christy looked.

She was wearing her wedding dress and was standing in the middle of the living room of a hotel suite that Marti had rented close to Rancho Corona. At Marti's insistence, Bob and she had stayed overnight close to the college and then turned over the suite as a dressing room for Christy on the morning of May 22. Marti also had insisted Christy allow Marti's favorite hair and makeup artist to come at eleven so that, after Christy showered, she could have two hours set aside for what Marti called "beautification."

It was now one-thirty. The wedding was at three o'clock. Christy was ready. In every way, she was ready.

"Your gown turned out perfect." Katie adjusted the train in the back. "I'll make sure it's smoothed out like this when you stand under the arch."

Christy inched her way to the bedroom in the suite so she could have a look in the full-length mirror on the closet. Katie followed her, adjusting the train as Christy walked.

"Wait! Don't look until we put on your veil!" Marti bustled over to the refrigerator, where they had stored the flower wreath that arrived from Maui that morning.

"Close your eyes." Tracy came up alongside Christy and took her by the hand. "It will be better if you wait and have a look once your veil is on. Then you'll see for the first time what Todd is going to see when you come down the aisle toward him."

Christy closed her eyes and felt at peace. All the extra planning had paid off. Everything was coming together perfectly. Marti's extravagant pampering had been a blessing, and Christy had told her so several times.

At the rehearsal dinner the night before, Todd had stood beside his father and praised him in a kind and generous way. Todd's mother couldn't "work out the details" to come to the wedding. Everyone knew it was a last-minute letdown and silently had sympathized with Todd, but he seemed to handle the disappointment well.

After honoring his dad, Todd had turned to Bob and Marti and thanked them for being his honorary parents. He called Marti the "mom I never had," listing how she had been there at many key moments in his life as a teenager and a young adult. He told her he loved her and always would. He kissed her, and Marti cried.

Christy let Tracy lead her into the bedroom and position her in front of the mirror. She smelled her wreath of flowers before she felt Marti place it on her head. The sweet fragrance of the island tuberose filled her with exotic memories. She knew Todd would recognize the fragrance, as well. It would circle both of them as they repeated their vows.

"Bend down, Christy, dear. You're too tall for me," Marti said. "I don't want to ruin your hair. It's perfect. Absolutely perfect. That's it. A little lower."

Christy's grandmother spoke up. "Why don't you let Margaret help you with that?"

"I've got it," Marti stated firmly.

"Don't start an argument here," Katie teased.

Behind her closed eyes, Christy thought back on the argument she and Todd had two days ago. It was one of the worst they had ever had. More than five months ago, when they had decided they were going to say "I promise" instead of "I do," Christy and Todd had agreed they would write their own vows. Christy had worked on hers off and on for months and had finalized them before their last meeting with Pastor Ross, who was performing their ceremony.

Todd, however, as of two days ago, hadn't begun to work on his. When Christy found out, she fell apart. She said some awful things, Todd said some awful things, and for one frantic moment, Christy feared the whole wedding would be called off.

But they found their heads. Cleared their hearts. Talked calmly. Then they called Pastor Ross, and he made some helpful suggestions. In the end, they decided to repeat the traditional vows so that neither of them would go blank at the last minute while under the pressure of the ceremony. Christy decided she would place her personally created vows on a beautiful piece of stationery and make it her final entry into the shoebox of letters for her future husband.

That collection of letters, complete with her written-out vows, was wrapped with a white satin ribbon and tucked into the bottom of her honeymoon luggage, directly under her white lingerie. A smile played across her lips as Christy thought about all that this very special day and night would hold for her and her beloved.

"A little more to the right," Marti said. "Katie, fix that strand of hair over on her shoulder. We want to make sure all the beautiful embroidery shows perfectly. That's it. Okay, moisten your lips, dear. Good.

Now everyone stand back. On the count of three, Christina, open your eyes."

Christy felt her heart do a little cha-cha as her eyelids fluttered, trying to remain closed.

In unison, the most precious women in her life began the countdown. "One, two . . ."

CHAPTER 19

"THREE!" the women-in-waiting cried with one voice and one heart.

Christy opened her eyes to view her reflection in the full-length mirror. The wreath of fragrant white island flowers graced her head like a crown of purity and peace. The delicate, sheer veil cascaded from the wreath and circled her shoulders like an elegant cape belonging to a fairy-tale princess who had made it from translucent firefly wings spun into the finest threads.

The wedding gown was indeed a gown and not just a dress. Christy's small waist and trim figure were accentuated by the wide band that united her mother's wedding dress with hers. The new version of both their dreams blended into one was exactly what Christy had hoped for. She knew it always would be one of her favorite parts of the wedding. The embroidery shimmered in the overhead lighting and drew attention to Christy's face.

She paused, catching her breath in amazement at her own reflection. The makeup artist had done exactly what she had asked with her hair and face. She looked natural yet with a warm glow on her cheeks and a sparkle in her blue-green eyes. Her long, nutmeg brown hair was tucked behind her ears with shimmering clips, and two long, full curls danced down her bodice, just under her veil.

"Okay, I'm going to cry now," Christy said, breaking the silence.

They all laughed except for Marti. "Don't you dare! Your eye makeup is perfect!"

"Here," Christy's grandma sidled up next to her. "I was hoping for a good time to give you this. It's the handkerchief I carried at my wedding when I married your grandfather. His mother embroidered it for me. I want you to have it."

Now Christy was certain she would cry. She blinked quickly and, lifting her veil slightly, gave her grandmother a kiss on the cheek. "Thank you, Grandma. I love you."

"I know. And I love you, too."

"Katie," Marti called, "bring Christy's lipstick over here, quick. Mom, you have a smudge right on your cheek. Oh, was that a knock on the door? It must be the photographer. Everyone stay right where you are. I'll get it."

Marti hustled to answer the hotel suite's door. Christy took in a full view of her friends in their sky-blue bridesmaids' dresses. "You two look really nice. I love those dresses on you. The little baby's breath headbands turned out nice. Do you mind wearing them? Are they going to bug you?"

"Not at all," Tracy said.

"I like it." Katie handed Christy the lipstick. "Here you go. Or am I supposed to put it on you because I'm the maid of honor?"

"I can do it. You just hold on to it for me and make sure I reapply some before the photographer takes all the pictures after the wedding."

"Why?" Katie said with a grin. "Are you planning on getting your lipstick a little smeared there at the altar?"

"I sure did." Tracy exchanged a little grin with Katie and Christy.

"All right, ladies," Marti said. "Everyone step back so that our prompt photographer here can set up for the photos. Do you want Christy in here by the mirror or out in the living room?"

The photographer didn't move. He seemed to be sizing up the situation and more. His gaze was on Christy. "I'm sorry, what did you say?" he asked Marti.

"Where would you like her to stand?"

"This is fine." He set up his tripod and looked again at Christy. "I apologize for staring. But I have to say, I see brides all the time, but you are, well . . . you are one beautiful bride."

"Thank you." Christy blushed.

"I'll make some beautiful pictures for you."

"Oh dear!" Marti squeaked. "The bouquet! Where is the bouquet? Katie, find the bouquet."

With the bouquet in her hands and her lips freshly colored, Christy posed in her gorgeous wedding dress while the loving women in her life showered her with compliments and admiration. She shifted from her right foot to her left foot in the soft-soled ballet slippers she had decided to wear. They made her feel petite and dainty.

"Todd is going to be speechless," Tracy said. "I can't wait to see the look on his face when you come down the aisle toward him."

Me too!

"Now, Katie," Marti started in as they gathered their belongings and headed down to the lobby. "Do you have Todd's ring?"

"His ring?" Katie said playfully.

"Katie!"

Katie grinned and held up her thumb to show Marti that Todd's gold wedding band was safe with her.

"This isn't a time to joke. Come on, now; the limos are waiting."

Katie slipped behind Christy and lifted the train of Christy's gown. "The limos are waiting," Katie said in a ritzy voice. Then, breaking out in song, she serenaded Christy all the way to the elevator. "Going to the chapel . . ."

Christy loved Katie's lighthearted touches and told her so once she, Katie, Tracy, and her mom were tucked into the white stretch limo's backseat. Marti and Grandma said they were going to wait for Uncle Bob, who should be arriving at any minute. "All this posh fluff is for my aunt, not me," Christy said. "She's loving this. I'm enjoying it, too, but what I'm really enjoying is having the three of you with me."

Mom beamed. She looked radiant in her two-piece, cream-colored outfit. Marti's specialist had also done Mom's makeup, and it was the first time Christy remembered seeing her mom look extra fancy. She was a beautiful woman. Inside and out.

"When we get there," Katie said, "we have strict instructions to spirit you away to the chapel so nobody sees you. Especially your groom. So be prepared in case we have to make a dash for it. The closest the limo can get us is about a hundred yards from the path that leads to the meadow. We should be the first ones there, but just in case."

Christy nodded. "By any chance did you bring extra deodorant for me along with the lipstick and hairbrush?"

"It's all in the bridal basket in the trunk." Katie leaned forward as if they were in a football huddle. "Trace, why don't you grab the bridal basket and whatever else Marti put in the trunk. Christy, you take your bouquet and loop your train over your arm. Mom, you stay with me and be ready to haul biscuits if we have to make a dash for the chapel."

Christy laughed. "Katie, I don't think we're going to need to run like we're in a football game. There won't be anyone there yet."

However, when the limo parked on the upper campus at Rancho Corona University, Christy discovered she was wrong. Dozen of cars were aready parked in the lot, and her dad and David were standing by the pathway to the meadow in their tuxes.

"Aw, Mom, look! Don't they look adorable?"

"Adorable, schmorable!" Katie said, taking over as wedding director since Marti wasn't on the scene. "Grab your train and your bouquet and be ready to hotfoot it, missy. If two tuxedos are around here, there are bound to be more."

Christy willingly followed Katie's instructions, as did her mom and Tracy. When the limo driver opened the door, they stepped out and walked to the chapel at a brisk pace. Katie held on to Christy's elbow like a bodyguard, watching every which way for paparazzi. Christy looped her train over her arm, hitched up her skirt, and picked her way along the trail in her dainty ballet slippers.

"Christy," David called out. "Wait up!"

"Sorry," Katie called. "Can't stop. I'm under strict orders from your aunt. Got to deliver this woman to the chapel immediately!"

Christy felt like an elfin fairy, prancing down the meadow trail. She laughed at the bliss of it all and followed her illustrious maid of honor. Perky, red-haired Katie seemed to be the embodiment of a guardian angel, a heroic, celestial being.

But when they were three feet from the chapel's door, Katie stopped dead in her tracks. Christy nearly rear-ended her.

"Will you look at that?" Katie drew in a deep breath. "What a fine specimen of God's best creative efforts."

Christy followed Katie's gaze. Only a few yards away, Christy and Todd's enchanted meadow was alive with color and action. Bright streamer flags on top of each canopy waved at her in the afternoon breeze. Long tables, laden with fresh flowers and blue ribbons, were adorned with a variety of food fit for a grand celebration. In the forefront stood a round table under a canopy and on the table was the wedding cake. It looked exactly the way Christy had hoped it would look.

Rows of empty chairs waited for the wedding guests. All the chairs faced "their" arch, Todd and Christy's trellis archway that would serve as the symbolic entry to their lives' next season. Fresh flowers and deep green ferns adorned the archway. It looked as if it had grown in a hidden cove on a tropical island and had been picked up that morning and transplanted here, in the meadow, for their wedding. Christy knew Todd would be thrilled.

"It's wonderful!" Christy exclaimed to Katie after taking in the grand celebration being prepared. Along the edge, dozens of tall, swishy palm trees danced in the breeze like a row of hula dancers merrily sending their aloha over the event. "It's more wonderful than I had pictured it would be."

"What are you talking about?" Katie pulled her eyes off her target and looked at Christy. "I was saying that Rick is a fine specimen of God's best creative efforts. He's standing over there talking to Todd's dad by the punch bowl. Oh no, what am I doing? You shouldn't be here! Look out, tuxedo at two o'clock."

Katie yanked open the chapel's door and practically pushed Christy inside the cool, quiet sanctuary.

"Katie, that wasn't Todd. That was Doug."

"Doesn't matter. If the best man is close, the groom won't be far away. Relax. Have a seat. Do you want some lipstick?"

"I am getting excited," Christy said, beaming.

"Nervous?"

"Not at all. Eager, yes. Bursting with anticipation, yes. This is it, Katie, girl. Todd and I are getting married today."

"So I heard," Katie said calmly. "Now, hold still. I have to fix your hair."

A knock sounded on the chapel door.

"Who goes there?" Katie boomed out.

The door opened, and Tracy timidly stepped inside with the bridal basket full of just what Katie and Christy needed to freshen up. Mom followed Tracy, and a moment later, Grandma joined them.

The door lurched open again, flooding the small chapel with light as Marti made her entrance. "The guests are beginning to arrive," she announced. "I've checked with the caterers. Everything is right on schedule. Looks as if the weather cooperated nicely. It's not too hot. Now, who needs a breath mint? Christy?"

Marti fussed with Christy's veil and her skirt for another ten minutes. The photographer came in to capture a few shots, and then Christy's dad joined them for his photos in the chapel with Christy. He looked uncomfortable in what he called his "monkey suit." But Christy thought he looked dashing and classy and so did her mom.

The photographer clicked off half a dozen shots. Christy turned to Katie and quietly asked if she could get Christy a drink of water.

"Right here," Marti said. "I had the caterers deliver a case of bottled water. It's here in the corner. Anyone else?"

They all grabbed a bottle, and for a moment the chapel was quiet. Christy looked at her mom and then at her dad. Marti looked at her watch. "Time for the mother of the bride, the grandmother of the bride, and me to exit. The ushers are out there for us. Can you think of anything else you need or want, Christina, dear?"

"No, I'm fine. I'm ready. Thank you for everything. All of you. Thanks."

"I'll see you at the end of the aisle." Mom cheerfully gave Christy a peck on the cheek.

"Check her for lipstick on that cheek," Marti instructed. "And, Katie, for goodness' sake, pull the veil over her face. Make sure it's straight all around. And Tracy? You listen for your cue now."

"I will," Tracy said.

Christy hung back as Katie adjusted her veil. She wrapped her grandmother's hankie around the stem handle of her bouquet. The handkerchief was already moist. If she actually needed to use it for tears, it might not do much to dry them. But it was helping her hands at the moment, and that was important.

A few silent minutes passed as Dad fidgeted with his collar. Katie opened the chapel's door a crack and watched to give Tracy her signal to march down the white runner. After Tracy, Katie would go. Then Christy and her dad would join the procession.

Glancing at her dad, Christy noticed he was tearing up. She only remembered seeing him like this a few times before. "Daddy, are you okay?"

"I will be." He offered her a lopsided grin. "It's not every day a man walks down the aisle with his only daughter. I guess you're not my little mouse anymore, are you?"

Christy felt a lump in her throat. He hadn't called her his little mouse in years. When she was growing up on their Wisconsin dairy farm, one of her favorite pastimes had been to follow her dad around in the barn. He was so big she could easily hide behind him. He would scoop her up in his arms, lift her over his head, and bellow for the cows to hear, "Look, I've found a little mouse! Listen to her squeak."

"I promise, Daddy," Christy said softly, "I'll always be your little mouse."

"And I'll always be as proud of you and thankful for you as I am at this very moment."

"That's my cue," Katie said over her shoulder as she exited. "Get ready now, you two."

Christy reached under her veil and dabbed the corner of each eye with her grandma's handkerchief. She linked her arm through her dad's and adjusted her bouquet.

"All right," Dad said, composing himself. "This is it."

CHAPTER 20

Right on cue, Christy stepped out of the cool chapel into the brightness of the May afternoon. The guests shifted in their seats, and she could feel their eyes on her, watching her approach the end of the white runner with her arm linked through her dad's. She couldn't see Todd yet and guessed he couldn't see her, either.

Christy and her father came to the end of the rows of chairs. At her feet, a straight white runner led directly to the arch. She knew that under the decorated arch stood her groom, dressed in a classy black tux waiting for her, just as he had promised he would be that enchanting morning in December right after she had promised she would be his bride.

Christy drew in a deep breath. She lifted her eyes under her veil and looked beyond the long white runner to the groom, her groom. And, oh, the look on his face! This patient, relentless man waiting for her at the end of the long aisle was so deeply in love with her that he didn't even attempt to wipe the tears that were coursing down his cheeks.

As Christy watched Todd, he surprised her by lifting his arms and holding out his hands, inviting her to come to him. Those familiar hands that still bore the scars of his accident were welcoming her.

Christy put one foot in front of the other and kept walking.

Doug began to strum his guitar. That's when the next unexpected "random factor" occurred. Instead of Doug's singing a familiar wedding song as he had done at the rehearsal, Todd began to sing to Christy. His rich voice swirled around her, wooing her, beckoning her.

"I have come into the garden, seeking you,
There is no one else I desire, only you
How beautiful you are, my love.
Your eyes, watching from behind your veil
As here I stand, calling for you to come
Take me into your heart. Be with me
Forever.
How long have I waited for this moment,
For this day. I will never leave you.
My heart is ever toward you.
Come into the garden, my beloved.
Come, be my bride,
Take my heart in yours,
And I will be yours
Forever."

Christy's last footstep brought her to the trellis just as Todd sang the word *forever*. Her heart pounded wildly. She recognized the tune. Todd had been humming it for months. This was the song he had been working on since the night they had become engaged; yet all these months she had only heard him hum or play the melody. She recognized the words were based on Scripture, from the Song of Solomon. When Todd had worked on the song, she had thought it was a worship song directed toward the Lord. And knowing Todd, ultimately it was.

But today, it was her song. She was his bride. He was her bridegroom. This was their forever moment. And Todd hadn't taken his eyes off her.

Pastor Ross spoke into the great chasm that separated Todd from Christy and said, "Who gives this woman to be united in holy matrimony with this man?"

Christy's father cleared his throat. All he was supposed to say was "Her mother and I." But Christy's dad apparently had a bit of the random factor at work in him, too. "Just as God, in love, gave Christina to us, now her mother and I, in love, give her to Todd."

Katie reached for Christy's bouquet, and with a squeeze, Dad placed Christy's hands into Todd's warm, strong, familiar hands. Todd ran his thumb across the gold Forever ID bracelet she had worn on her right wrist all these years.

"At last," Todd whispered.

That's when Christy started to cry. She had managed to keep the tears back all the way down the aisle. That was probably because so many surprises had kept her off guard and because Todd had been so fixed on her. But now she caught a quavering breath and felt a tear tip over the edge of her lower eyelid and trickle down her cheek. An entire flock of tears followed.

Todd's gaze remained fixed on Christy as hers was fixed on him. They barely blinked. They barely moved. The pastor spoke about the sacredness of this union. A song followed. Doug, this time. Christy barely heard. She was lost, swimming in the depths of her love for the man who stood beside her under this holy trellis and held her hands so tenderly.

The song ended, and Pastor Ross asked Christy to repeat her vows after him. Suddenly she was relieved she wasn't relying on her memory to repeat the long, elaborate vows she had written to Todd.

With a clear yet small voice, she repeated, "I, Christy, take you, Todd, to be my lawfully wedded husband. I promise to love, honor, and cherish you for better or for worse, for richer or for poorer, in sickness and in health, till death do us part."

Next came Todd's repeating of the vows. "I, Todd, take you, Christy, to be my lawfully wedded wife. I promise . . ." He squeezed her hands tighter. "To love, honor, and cherish you for better or for worse, for richer or for poorer, in sickness and in health, till death do us part."

"Now will you pray with me," Pastor Ross said.

Todd helped Christy to kneel down on the padded bench under the trellis. They bowed their heads as the pastor prayed for God's blessing on their marriage and on the children God may choose to bless them with.

"As you wish," Christy and Todd both whispered at the end of the prayer. Todd's strong grip held Christy by the elbow as they stood up.

"What token do you give as a symbol of your love for Christy?"

"A ring," Todd answered. His dad stepped forward and handed Christy's ring to Todd.

"Repeat after me," the pastor said. "As evidence of the promise we now make before God and these witnesses, with this ring, I thee wed."

Todd repeated the words and slid the wedding ring onto Christy's finger. In another surprise, he then lifted her ring finger to his lips and sealed his promise with a kiss.

"Christy," the pastor said, "what token do you give as a symbol of your love for Todd?"

"A ring," Christy said.

She turned only slightly and saw Katie's steady hand right there, holding out Todd's wedding band. Christy took the ring and repeated, "As evidence of the promise we now make before God and these witnesses, with this ring, I thee wed."

She slid the ring onto Todd's finger. Then she followed Todd's example and lifted his hand under her veil, where she sealed her promise with a kiss on his finger.

"In the name of the Father and of the Son and of the Holy Spirit, I now pronounce you man and wife. You may kiss the bride."

Christy stopped breathing. It seemed as if the whole world, including the dancing palm trees, had come to a sudden hush.

Slowly, tenderly, Todd took the ends of her delicate wedding veil and lifted it over her head. He looked on her as if he had never seen anything so wonderful, so beautiful, and so amazing in his life. Todd paused. He seemed to be drawing in the fragrance of the flowers that crowned her head. Moving closer, he slid both his hands along her jaw line until her hair was entwined in his fingers.

Christy tilted her face toward his and closed her eyes.

With all the tenderness of a patient man and all the passion of nearly six years of waiting, Todd kissed Christy. And she, with equal passion and patience, kissed him back.

As they lingered in their embrace, a gentle breeze came dancing toward them, snatching the fragrance from the flowers in Christy's hair and scattering sweetness across the meadow. The wind swirled through the palm trees. It almost sounded as if they were applauding.

In the holiness of that timeless moment, Todd whispered, "I love you, my Kilikina. Forever."

"And I love you," she whispered as silent tears raced down her cheeks. "Forever."

Then stepping from under their trellis, Christy heard a strong, steady voice behind her announcing the words that she knew would change her life forever. Until that moment, this one sentence had only echoed in the corner of her heart where she stored her most precious dreams.

Today, the words were real. All the stars of heaven were in her eyes as she gazed at the man who now stood beside her and the pastor said,

"It is my privilege to introduce to you for the very first time, Mr. and Mrs. Todd Spencer."

Looking for More Good Books to Read?

You can find out what is new and exciting with previews, descriptions, and reviews by signing up for Bethany House newsletters at

www.bethanynewsletters.com

We will send you updates for as many authors or categories as you desire so you get only the information you really want.

Sign up today!